DARK KINGDOMS

RICHARD LEE BYERS

dark kingdoms	*richard lee byers*
cover illustration	*mike danza*
jacket and book design	*john snowden*
art direction	*richard thomas*

Borealis is an imprint of White Wolf Publishing.

White Wolf Publishing
735 Park North Boulevard, Suite 128
Clarkston, GA 30021
www.white-wolf.com

First Trade Edition: November 1998

10 9 8 7 6 5 4 3 2 1

Printed in the U.S.A.

CONTENTS

The Ebon Mask

Dark Kingdoms: Volume One

Dedication

For Adrain

One

James Graham, onetime Earl and Marquess of Montrose, now Anacreon of Stygia, stood in the bow of the *Belleisle*, the galleon rising and falling beneath him, his auburn lovelocks and heavy black robe stirring in the wind. His blue eyes peered intently into the seething darkness ahead, seeking a current of water or wind that might bear his vessel along faster than the sleek cruisers pursuing her, or a warp in space through which she might escape.

All he saw were the black swell, and faint veils of blue and purple light, not unlike the earthly aurora borealis, flickering across the starless sky. He hadn't expected any better result. Though privy to many of the arcane secrets of the proscribed Harbingers' guild, he was a landlubber. Captain Pizarro possessed the same skills and had been sailing the Sea of Shadows for more than a century. Still, Montrose hadn't been able to resist the temptation to look for some means of escape the mariner had missed. It was better than loitering uselessly on the quarter-deck.

He turned, peered backward, and tensed. For the last three hours, the six enemy ships had seemed to creep closer with excruciating slowness. Now, suddenly, they appeared nearly close enough to seize their prey.

Wondering for the hundredth time just who the raiders were, Soul-Pirates, Renegades, Heretics, Spectres, or, just conceivably, the covert agents of one of his master's fellow Deathlords, Montrose hurried aft. Some of his legionnaires, newly clad in uniforms embroidered with the sigil of the Order of the Unlidded Eye, clustered anxiously him. They were veteran soldiers, but, like their commander, most had never fought at sea.

"Are we going to be all right, milord?" asked one, a bald man with the massive chest and shoulders of a Spook.

How the devil should I know? Montrose thought. He forced a reassuring smile. "Of course we are. We're Black Hawks, aren't we? We should be grateful to the captain for finding us a little sport to break up the tedium of the voyage." He clapped the fool on the shoulder, then strode on.

Captain Pizarro was a squat fellow with a drooping, grizzled mustache. At some point in his postmortem existence, a flesh sculptor had surrounded his jet-black eyes with a mosaic of iridescent multicolored scales. Glowering, he was watching some of the sailors hang scrambling nets, while others spread sand on the deck. His mouth tightened at Montrose's approach. Probably he wished the landsman would refrain from bothering him at this critical time, though he might forebear to say so outright. The other wraith was his superior officer.

"They're going to catch us, milord," Pizarro said. "We have to fight."

"I understand," Montrose replied. "What are our chances?"

The captain shrugged. "We'll come about in a moment. Then, when they're in range, we'll start shooting broadsides into their bows. If we can cripple them before they maneuver into position to return fire, we'll win. If we can't, well, they have genuine warships and we only have transports, without all that many cannons or marines. But we'll do the best we can."

Montrose nodded. "Well, you and your officers are the ones who know what you're about, so of course you're in command. My men and I are at your disposal."

"Thank you for that," said Pizarro. "Truth to tell, it's more sense and less pride than I expected from a grandee newly descended from the Onyx Tower. Since your lads don't know their way around a ship, I doubt that I'll have any complicated orders for them. Tell them to shoot when they have something to shoot at, kiss the deck if somebody tells them to duck, and keep out of the way of the crew." He looked up at the topmen laboring aloft. Two of them, blessed with a Harbinger's power of levitation, floated from spar to spar and sheet to sheet like bees flitting from one flower to the next. "Give the signal!"

A thin, crop-haired woman kneeling on the fore-top cupped her hands around her mouth and emitted a long, ululating cry. After a moment the Chanteurs on the other two vessels in the convoy wailed back. The deck heeled beneath Montrose's feet as the helmsman brought the ship around. The timbers creaked and groaned.

Montrose returned to his men on the main-deck, where two sailors, their faces tattooed with faux deathmarks, were dispensing arms from a bin. There were some firearms, but more cutlasses, pikes, bows, and crossbows, weapons which, by Skinlands standards, were as archaic as the *Belleisle* itself. But in the world of the dead, where raw materials were always scarce, and guns and machines had to be powered by a ghost's own essence or the mystical substance known as soulfire, archaic implements were more the rule than the exception.

Montrose already had a darksteel rapier sheathed at his side and a .45 automatic, a Stygian artificer's copy of a Sig Sauer Model 220, hidden under his sable Inquisitor's robe, but he took a bow and a bundle of arrows. Almost four centuries ago, at St. Andrews University, he'd won the silver arrow two years running, but he hadn't practiced his archery in almost thirty years. He hoped he could still hit a mark.

After he strung the bow, there was nothing to do but wait, wait and say what he could to hearten his soldiers. Inwardly he seethed. He didn't fear the Final Death any more than he'd feared his first, but he resented being summarily expelled from the luxuries of his master's court to face it. He'd already risked his neck sufficiently to satisfy any fair-minded overlord. And it galled him to have to fight a battle he couldn't direct; one, moreover, in which the daredevil, hit-and-run tactics which had served him so well on land had no application.

The enemy cruisers, long square-riggers flying phosphorescent scarlet pennants, heaved steadily closer. Suddenly the cannons below deck roared, shaking the planks beneath Montrose's boots, startling him. He'd expected Pizarro to shout an order to commence firing, but evidently the captain had left it to the gunner to choose his moment.

Cannonballs splashed into the dark water, and grapeshot kicked up spray as it ricocheted along the surface. But some of the salvo reached its target, cutting rigging on the nearest cruiser to pieces and punching holes in its sails.

A number of legionnaires cheered. Montrose studied the cruiser, trying to assess the extent of the damage, willing the vessel to be disabled. The raider, like its fellows, hurtled on.

The cannons thundered repeatedly, still with insufficient effect. As always at such moments, Montrose couldn't help feeling that something was missing. Firearms powered by soulfire generally didn't fill the air with smoke and a sulfurous reek like earthly guns. The cruiser turned, bringing its own ranks of cannons to bear. A sailor shouted, "Drop!"

Montrose hurled himself down, then noticed that one of his centurions, a gangly fellow whose baby-faced, adolescent features belied his centuries of existence in the Underworld, had made no move to do likewise. Perhaps fear of this unfamiliar form of combat had dazed him. Perhaps his Shadow, the perverse will to cruelty and self-destruction that dwelled inside every wraith, had momentarily seized control of his muscles. Or maybe the crash of the guns had deafened his hypersensitive ears, and he hadn't heard the sailor's warning.

Montrose knew it was too dangerous to jump back up, but some impulse, perhaps arising from his own suicidal thirst for Oblivion, made him do it anyway. As he grabbed the centurion, he saw the cruiser's cannons flash.

Frantically he flung the lad and himself to the deck. *Belleisle's* scantlings crunched and cracked as the salvo hit her. Severed lines whipped through the air. Portions of the rail dissolved into a barrage of splinters. People screamed, and sailors fell from the yards. A section of broken spar plummeted, missing Montrose by inches, crushing the skull of his companion.

Ghostly flesh rippled and bubbled sluggishly around the length of wood. Montrose rolled the spar off the centurion's head so the bloodless wound could repair itself without impediment. Since the lad hadn't been hurt by darksteel, the talons of a Spectre, or some arcane instrumentality, he should eventually recover, but not in time to influence the outcome of the battle.

Cannons thundered, steadily blowing the *Belleisle* to bits, or so it seemed to Montrose. New casualties thrashed and shrieked. He lay flat for as long as he could, but eventually he simply had to get a better idea of how the fight was proceeding. Rising to his knees, he peeked over what remained of the rail.

The attacking cruiser had come within bowshot. Wraiths armed with arbalests, muskets, and a smattering of modern guns rose from behind its rails. Sharpshooters dangled in the tops.

"Stand up!" Montrose shouted. "Attack!"

Legionnaires and sailors scrambled up, and the two forces began to shoot. Quarrels and arrows thrummed through the air, guns barked, and a few automatic weapons chattered. Meanwhile the cannons blazed on.

Some of the combatants eschewed mundane weaponry in favor of magical means of attack. The crop-haired Chanteur on the fore-top wailed and a musketeer on the cruiser went mad. Shrieking and clawing at his own eyes, he dropped his gun, lost his grip on the rigging, and fell to the deck thirty feet below. A willowy blond woman on the enemy vessel moved her hands in a complicated pattern. A Black Hawk's knees buckled. As his head thumped down on the deck, he began to snore.

Montrose loosed shaft after shaft, concentrating on the foes who seemed to be attacking most effectively, and was grimly pleased that most of his arrows found their mark. One missile, one of the few tipped with gleaming black darksteel, plunged into a burly rifleman's chest. Waves of shadow pulsed through the raider's body, and then he simply faded away, his carbine dropping straight through the dissolving substance of his fingers.

Montrose pivoted, seeking another target, and then, though it had been several seconds since the enemy ship had fired a broadside, the *Belleisle* lurched. Soldiers and sailors staggered, some yelping, some falling. Something stabbed Montrose in the back.

He clutched at the hurt and found a splinter sticking out of his shoulder. Yanking it free, he stumbled around to behold a second cruiser. The vessel had maneuvered to leeward of the *Belleisle* and had begun bombarding it from that side.

His comrades started dropping like flies. It was obvious that the *Belleisle* couldn't long endure such a cross fire. Montrose peered about, hoping to see one of the other Stygian transports coming to the rescue, but they were as hard-pressed as his own vessel.

Perhaps, he thought desperately, *we could storm one of the cruisers. The enemy wouldn't be expecting that.* But no, it wouldn't work. Only a handful of his troops shared his ability to fly, not nearly enough for the sort of headlong, frenzied charge he had in mind.

Hurdling the bodies of the maimed and unconscious, he dashed onto the quarter-deck. Though Pizarro had an arrow protruding from his shoulder he was still at his post, which was more than could be said for the majority of his subordinates. Some sprawled motionless or writhing on the deck, while others were simply gone. Montrose assumed that the Void had swallowed them.

"What can we try that we haven't tried already?" he demanded.

"Nothing," Pizarro rasped, his voice harsh with pain. "We're encircled. Half the crew are dead or disabled, and most of the guns have been dismounted. I recommend we strike."

No! Montrose thought reflexively, but he couldn't see any alternative. Further resistance would only result in additional casualties. "Very well," he said. "Do it." Pizarro gave the order and a midshipman began to haul down the colors, a magenta flag bearing a grinning golden mask, the emblem of the Smiling Lord, and a slightly smaller black one emblazoned with the red and silver Unlidded Eye. The surviving crew and legionnaires lowered their weapons.

The cannons on the cruiser to leeward roared. With a crack, the *Belleisle's* mizzenmast fell across the poop. Darksteel grapeshot tore a sailor apart, his form vanishing like a cloud of vapor dispersed by a gust of wind. Some of the Black Hawks cried out in shock.

Montrose shared their dismay. Souls were the one great resource of the Underworld, prized by nearly everyone. Thus it had never occurred to him that their attackers would decline their surrender and the attendant opportunity to take as many of them alive as possible. But perhaps it should have. The realm of the dead was full of depraved and demented spirits who delighted in carnage for its own sake, or who loathed the Hierarchy of Stygia with an unquenchable hatred.

He pivoted toward his men. "Keep fighting!" he shouted.

Each of the cruisers fired a final devastating broadside. Then the big guns fell silent, and the ships began to maneuver closer to the crippled *Belleisle*. Perhaps their cannons were finally running out of soulfire. In any case, it was obvious the raiders meant to board.

Montrose sent his remaining arrows winging at the cruiser to windward, then discarded the bow, drew his pistol, crouched behind the splintered rail, and began to fire. The luminous black crystals set just above the grip glittered with each shot.

He dispatched several raiders, but it wasn't enough. At this point, no one could do enough. With the grim inevitability of death itself, the cruiser locked yardarms with the *Belleisle*. The two hulls scraped and grated together. The attacking wraiths began to swarm onto the galleon. Montrose holstered his empty automatic, whipped out his rapier, and ran to meet them.

A Masquer ripped at him with huge, misshapen hands like the forelimbs of a mantis. Sidestepping the attack, Montrose thrust his blade into his assailant's neck. As the raider began to topple and fade, Montrose yanked the sword free, whirled just in time to parry a cutlass slash at his head, and stabbed the enemy swordsman in the chest.

He raged down the length of the ship, dealing death, knowing once again that his efforts were futile. His remaining allies were falling by the moment. No matter how hard he fought, he couldn't turn the tide.

The raiders from the leeward cruiser came aboard, accelerating the slaughter. Shortly thereafter, Montrose found himself alone by the bowsprit with a hundred hostile faces, some human, some deformed by a Masquer's art or the malice of the Void, glaring up at him.

Only one chance left, a chance that only a Harbinger could take. Montrose couldn't fly away. His foes would shoot him out of the air. But it was just possible that he could swim. He attacked the front rank of his opponents savagely, recklessly, driving them back for a moment, then threw his rapier in their faces, whirled, and dived off the bow.

He entered the cold black water cleanly. Pikes and javelins plunged down around him. Frantically, hampered by his heavy sable robe, he swam deeper, until the last of the light was gone.

TWO

Package stores, pawnshops, and tenements lined the street, and graffiti—gang names, racial insults, and obscenities—covered the grimy brick walls. Cars crept along the broken pavement as the drivers checked out the drug dealers and prostitutes loitering in the shadowy doorways. Gangsta rap pounded from an upper-story window. The air stank of exhaust and rotting garbage and left an acrid taste in Frank Bellamy's throat.

The lanky, crewcut FBI agent shook his head, wondering wryly why he so often found himself huddling with weirdoes and lowlifes in hellholes like this. Whereas whenever James Bond had a clandestine meeting, it was with a beautiful woman in an exotic resort. It was just a darn shame that the job of a real-life Fed couldn't be more like working on Her Majesty's fictional Secret Service.

Still, Bellamy had no real complaints. His work was fascinating, and it gave him a sense of purpose. He couldn't imagine doing anything else. And he was making his mark. Though he'd barely turned thirty, he'd already racked up an impressive score of arrests and convictions with the Violent Criminals Apprehension Program. And this new case was a career-maker. The agent who caught the Atheist was headed straight for the top.

That was why Bellamy had caught the red-eye up from Baton Rouge and was driving around East St. Louis in the middle of the night. He didn't intend to pass up any potential lead, even one he was ninety-nine percent certain wouldn't pan out.

At last he spotted the meeting place, a shabby concrete-block motel tucked away between a tire store and a topless joint. The dump probably made most of its money renting by the hour to hookers and johns who connected at the bar. The buzzing blue neon sign over the office window read, VAC NCY. Bullet holes pocked the door beside it.

Bellamy turned his rented Camry into the parking lot. Hoping that no one would attempt to steal or strip it, he climbed out, locked it, and started looking for Number Twenty-Five. It turned out to be the room farthest from the street. No light shone through the curtained window.

Bellamy rapped on the door. At first no one answered, though the investigator *thought* he heard stealthy movement inside. He knocked again. "Open up, Mr. Waxman. It's Agent Bellamy."

"Step back," quavered a tenor voice. "I can't see you through the peephole."

Bellamy did as he'd been told. After a moment he heard a chain rattle and a latch click. The door cracked open and a bloodshot eye peered out. The FBI agent displayed his badge and ID. Waxman had already seen them at the time of their first encounter, but you never knew what might be necessary to reassure a jittery informant. The door opened wider. "Get inside!" Waxman said.

Once again, Bellamy obeyed. Waxman was an obese kewpie doll of a man with a rosebud mouth and wispy blond hair, clad in a rumpled three-piece suit with the tie askew. His bed hadn't been slept in. Evidently he'd been sitting and drinking alone in the dark. The wan light leaking through the curtains gleamed on bottles of apricot brandy, peppermint schnapps, and mint chocolate liqueur, and as the FBI man squeezed past the other man's heaving, wheezing bulk, he caught an odor compounded of sweat, alcohol, and a cloying sweetness.

The cramped little room itself smelled faintly of mildew. Even in the gloom, Bellamy could make out the water stain on the ceiling. The accommodations, he reflected, were a considerable comedown for a guy who'd spent the last few years living in mansions and five-star hotels, which was probably why Waxman had chosen them. He hoped no one would look for him in such squalid surroundings.

His hands trembling, Waxman shut and locked the door as soon as Bellamy was inside. "Are you sure you weren't followed?" the fat man asked.

"Yes," Bellamy said.

Waxman grimaced. "No, you're not. I mean, you think you are, but you can't be."

"But nobody even knew I was coming to see you," Bellamy said reasonably. Actually, his statement wasn't quite true. Naturally he'd told Linus Hanson, his supervisor, that Waxman had phoned him. But it was close enough to the truth as to make no difference. "So it's logical to assume that no one would even try to tail me. Right?"

Waxman's face twisted as if he was struggling not to cry. "I don't know! They have ways of discovering things, ways we can't understand." He grabbed the bottle of mint chocolate liqueur, raised it to his lips, and glugged down a long drink.

"Mr. Waxman," Bellamy said, "I understand that your employer's murder came as a terrible shock, but I honestly don't think that you need to feel so afraid. So far the Atheist has always hit a site once and then moved on, usually to a different state. And he generally kills high-profile types like priests, nuns, and ministers, not people who work behind the scenes like you.

"But if you *do* have some legitimate reason to think you're in danger, if you held something back when we spoke before, then you owe it to yourself to tell me now. Once I understand the problem, I can protect you."

"But how? Eric was the only one who *ever* could. I was the watchful eye and he was the strong right arm, that's what we used to say. Maybe now the only way to be safe is to lie low. Maybe if I don't tell on them, they won't come after me."

"You mean, let the Atheist get away with cutting Reverend Weiss's heart out? From the way you talk, I thought you liked him."

Waxman's piggy eyes glared. "Of course I did! Eric Weiss was my friend! The only one who was never afraid of me, who never looked down on me for being different."

"Then help me catch his killer."

Waxman hesitated, and then finally said, "All right. I do have to do something, or I'll hate myself for the rest of my life. And maybe you *can* stop the killing. Sometimes they jump to this side of the Shroud. They have to, to hurt us, but maybe at that point you could hurt them back. And I've heard that the government has secret information. Secret weapons. Maybe your superiors will know about that end of it."

Inwardly, Bellamy sighed. Obviously, Waxman wasn't *just* drunk. He was crazy. Not that that came as any big surprise. The guy had been in and out of psych wards as a kid, and the FBI man had spotted him for a flake at their first meeting. If Bellamy hadn't already established beyond a shadow of a doubt that the Waxman had been visiting his mother in Seattle at the time of Weiss's murder, he would have wondered if the fat man might not be the serial killer himself.

But despite Waxman's manifest lunacy, Bellamy still intended to listen to his story. What the hell, he'd traveled hundreds of miles to hear it. And it was just conceivable that he might discover some legitimate information mixed in with the raving. "Shall we sit down?"

Waxman nodded. "Yes. That's a good idea." He carefully inserted his wide butt between the arms of a dilapidated chair, one within easy reach of the bottles on the table.

Bellamy perched opposite him on the sagging bed. The springs squeaked. "I want you to know I admire you for having the courage to come forward, Mr. Waxman. You won't be sorry. Now tell me what you know and how you know it."

"If it's going to be any use," Waxman replied, "you have to put aside your prejudices. I'm not stupid. I know you know about Reverend Weiss's drinking and womanizing, and the investigations for tax evasion and mail fraud. I know what you must believe. Eric was no better, no different than any other tel—" he faltered, stumbling over the word—"televangelist, milking his viewers for millions of dollars in 'love offerings.'"

"I won't deny that, based on what I've learned about him so far, I don't particularly admire him," Bellamy replied, "but I promise you, my personal opinion doesn't matter. He was the victim of a heinous crime, and I'm absolutely committed to catching his killer."

Waxman's mouth twisted. In the dimness, the expression made his round, shiny face resemble an angry, misshapen moon. "That's not the point. I—" Suddenly he stiffened, then peered wildly about. "Did you hear that? Did you *feel* it?"

"No," Bellamy said.

After a moment Waxman's shoulders slumped. "Neither do I, now." He peered at the bottle in his hand. "I shouldn't do this. It takes away the only edge I have. But I keep feeling like I'm strangling, and my heart keeps pounding and pounding in my chest. I need *something* to calm me down." He took another swig.

"You were telling me about Mr. Weiss," Bellamy said.

Waxman nodded. "Yes. He had his weaknesses. Who doesn't? But they were trivial compared to the good he did. He truly did have the power of God inside him. He healed people, and when it was necessary, he cast out devils."

And always with a camera rolling, Bellamy thought. Two days ago, trying to get a sense of the victim, he'd watched one of the "exorcisms" on tape. What with the floating objects and the shadowy figures fading in and out of view, Weiss had put on a pretty good magic act, though nothing for David Copperfield or Penn and Teller to lose any sleep over.

"And I helped him," Waxman continued. "He could hurt the demons, hurt them so badly they ran back to Hell, but most of the time, he couldn't see what they were up to. I could, because I'm a sensitive. A clairvoyant. We told the outside world I was just his secretary because we didn't want anyone getting the wrong impression. Some people might have thought that he was consorting with a witch." He peered at Bellamy as if expecting a reply.

"That's very interesting," the agent said.

"Don't patronize me!" Waxman snapped. "You don't believe. You're not even *trying* to keep an open mind."

Bellamy sighed. "I'm sorry if my skepticism bothers you, Mr. Waxman.. I don't mean any disrespect for you or your beliefs. But I'm a detective, and a detective is a kind of scientist. We operate on the basis of facts, not faith or colorful speculations. As far as I know, there isn't any hard evidence supporting the existence of demons or psychic phenomena. And I can't help asking questions like, if you do have ESP, why did you need to peek through the peephole to see who was on the other side of the door?"

"Because the power doesn't work all the time," Waxman replied. "It gives me flashes of insight. Symbols. Fragments. And it gets hazier when I'm like this." He took another long drink, his Adam's apple bobbing up and down.

Bellamy wondered how anyone could guzzle so much sweet, syrupy liqueur. He was getting queasy just watching. "Maybe so. In any case, my personal beliefs about spooks and visions don't matter either. What's important is that I'm listening. If you can give me one new fact, one lead, I'll follow it up no matter where it takes me."

"All right," sighed Waxman. "I've already put my head in the noose, just by asking you here. I suppose I might as well finish what I started. But you'd *better* follow up. You remember that I was the one who found Eric's body."

"Of course," Bellamy said.

"I told you exactly how it happened," Waxman said. "I didn't lie. But what I didn't say was that when I smelled the blood, I started having visions. I saw the black whirlpool."

"You just lost me," Bellamy said. "What does that mean?"

"You have to understand," Waxman said, "Eric and I fought the devils, but we didn't know much more about them than what we *needed* to know. Even when the spirits try to tell you things, it puts your soul in peril to listen to their lies. But over the year, I couldn't help picking up a little. And I found out that even the most dangerous demons are afraid of a terrible dark emptiness at the very bottom of Hell, a black pool that sucks down anything that comes too close. I think it might be Satan himself."

"And that's what you saw."

"Yes, Waxman said. "The whirlpool destroys anything that falls into it. Nothing can ever climb back out. But in the vision, something did, a host of shadows with the faces of animals and corpses, who walked unseen among their fellow spirits. And a voice warned me that the fiends had risen from the depths to kill and damn a million souls. Your 'Atheist' murders are only the beginning."

"Interesting," Bellamy said. "If these creatures are haunting the earth, do you know where they are right now?" It still seemed remotely possible that Waxman knew something about a real human killer, someone he'd identified with his imaginary bogeymen.

The fat man shook his head.

"Are you aware of any threats against Mr. Weiss's life, or any strange occurrences in the days leading up to the murder?" Bellamy persisted. "Something you neglected to tell me before?"

"No," Waxman said.

So much for this, then, Bellamy thought, the first twinge of a headache throbbing in his temples. *This'll teach me to be so gung-ho. I could have arranged for a local cop to waste* his *time on this fruitcake. I could be home in bed.* "Well, then, I guess we're finished. Thank you for the information. You know how to contact us if you think of anything else."

"That's it?" Waxman demanded. "What are you going to do with what I told you?"

"Report it to my superior," Bellamy said, rising from the bed, "as you suggested.

He'll decide how best to follow up."

Grunting, Waxman struggled out of his chair. Bellamy wondered if the fat man meant to physically restrain him from leaving. "I told you, don't bullshit me! Whether you believe me or not, you promised to protect me!"

Bellamy sighed. "And I would if I thought you needed it. But try to look at the situation logically. What have you actually told me? Just that a mysterious gang of spirits are committing the Atheist murders. Even if that's true, it's pretty vague, and even if the devils somehow learned that you passed along the information, I doubt they'd feel that you'd done them any real harm. If you can't get over feeling frightened, maybe you should see a doctor. He could prescribe you something for your nerves."

"I don't need medication!" Waxman snarled. "I need—" He jerked around toward the door, the liqueur bottle tumbling from his hand to thud on the linoleum. He let out a shriek and backpedaled frantically, blundering into Bellamy and nearly knocking him down.

The FBI agent flailed his arms and recovered his balance. Reflexively reaching for the Browning Hi-Power in his shoulder holster, he pivoted toward the door, only to see that it was still shut, the chain still engaged. Nothing had come through it. Evidently Waxman was hallucinating.

Bellamy scowled, annoyed at the jolt of anxiety that had sent the adrenaline buzz tingling through his hands. He shouldn't have let Waxman spook him, not when he already knew the guy was nuts.

At least Waxman was no longer blocking the way out. But Bellamy couldn't just leave the "sensitive" alone in this miserable place, not now that he'd lost it completely. He'd have to get him to a hospital. The agent moved to where the other man was cowering against the back wall, reflecting that he was lucky his informant, if that was still the proper term, hadn't decided to lock himself in the bathroom. "It's okay," he murmured.

"No!" Waxman gibbered. "No, it isn't! It came through the *wall!* It knows I *told!*"

"You have to trust me," Bellamy said. "There's nothing there."

"There is!" Waxman insisted. He clutched Bellamy's forearm, his plump fingers gripping painfully tight.

At the contact Bellamy's head swam, and his vision blurred. When the dark room swam back into focus, it looked subtly different. Puzzled, he squinted, and spotted an additional shadow looming between the window and the door. A gray-black form roughly the height and shape of a man, with pale streaks like glaring eyes and pointed fangs gleaming dully in its long, narrow head. Bellamy gasped and jerked backward. The apparition vanished.

"You see it too!" Waxman said.

No, I didn't, Bellamy insisted to himself. *I just caught a touch of your craziness for a second.* Gently but firmly, he extricated his arm from Waxman's grasp. "Maybe I did see it," he said. "And I don't want to stay locked in here with it, do you?"

Waxman shook his head.

"Then let's leave. I'll take you somewhere safe."

"But we'd have to walk right past it!"

"We're only a few feet away from it as it is," Bellamy said. "And so far, it hasn't tried to hurt us. Maybe it can't yet. Maybe it's gathering its strength. We should get away from it before it does. Come on, I'll take care of you." He took hold of Waxman's arm and tried to lead him forward.

The psychic yelped and resisted, pressing himself against the wall. *Then to heck with this*, Bellamy thought. *There's no way I'm going to manhandle a guy this big out of here against his will, not by myself. I'm calling the local cops for backup*. But then Waxman sobbed, squinched his eyes shut, and lurched forward.

Bellamy guided the other man across the room. He tried not to move hesitantly. Assuring himself repeatedly that there was nothing blocking his path, he fought the urge to pull his gun. He struggled not to imagine the phantom intruder clawing at his eyes, or flinging its long gray arms around him and burying its teeth in his throat.

When, after what seemed an eternity, his fingers closed on the cool brass security chain, the tension quivered out of his muscles. Now smiling ruefully, he thought, *I need to get more sleep. Or drink less coffee*. His psych instructors at Quantico had taught him that hysteria could be contagious; but until tonight, he'd never imagined that he himself might be susceptible.

He and Waxman stepped into the night. The nude pink neon woman on the roof of the topless bar winked at them over and over again, as if she had a tic. A convertible with a crushed fender and no muffler snarled down the street. The pollutants in the air stung Bellamy's eyes. Still, after the claustrophobic confines and imaginary terrors of the dark little room, the scene seemed almost pleasant.

"Is it following us?" Waxman whispered.

Now that his own irrational dread had subsided, Bellamy felt a surge of pity for his charge. It must be awful to feel that scared all the time. "No, it stayed inside. Everything's fine. My car's right over here." He reached into his pocket for the keys.

A low growl rumbled through the night, and then a black form rose from behind the Camry. The process seemed to take forever, as if the shape were huger, taller, than it had any right to be.

Bellamy recoiled, unconsciously letting go of Waxman, fumbling for his automatic. He knew he was staring straight at the shape's—the *creature's*—face, and yet somehow, he couldn't see it. Because it was too horrible to see.

Now Waxman was goggling at it too. He made a faint whining sound, then clutched at his chest and collapsed.

The creature bounded lightly over the car. It glided forward, arms outstretched.

Bellamy fired a single shot, then bolted. With each stride, he felt the world slipping away, his thoughts dissolving into chaos like a radio signal breaking up into static. Soon the crackle and hiss of the white noise swallowed everything.

When he became aware again, he was crouched trembling and weeping in the corner of a convenience store, between a freezer and the wall. The barrel of his pistol gleamed in the harsh fluorescent light. When a cop spoke to him, in the same kind of soft, soothing voice he'd used with Waxman, he shrieked and nearly shot him.

Three

Blind, cold, and weary, Montrose wondered grimly just how long he'd been in the water. It felt like days. He wondered if he'd ever experience light and air again.

Fearful that someone would shoot him, he'd discarded his cumbersome robe, pistol, and boots, then swum what he judged to be a good distance away from the *Belleisle* before striking for the surface, only to discover that the boundary between ocean and air didn't exist anymore. He'd kicked and stroked upward for what surely must have been hours, and the water had never grown a whit less black.

Such a prodigy was possible because the Sea of Shadows wasn't simply an ocean. Rather, it was a manifestation of the Tempest, the eternal storm that surrounded and underlay the rest of creation, an unstable, hyperdimensional labyrinth where natural law didn't exist, and any condition at all could come to be. Evidently Montrose had blundered into an area where space curved back on itself, creating the illusion of a universe completely full of water.

He ought to be able to navigate his way through. That was the fundamental purpose of the Harbinger's art. But the Arcanos wasn't infallible, and so far he hadn't had any luck.

At least the Restless didn't need air, food, or, in the general run of things, sleep. But he suspected that if he were trapped in this hellish place for too long, he'd run into a Spectre or one of the other terrors infesting the Tempest. Unarmed, sightless, and floundering in the water, he'd be easy prey. And if the monsters didn't get him, despair or madness surely would, whereupon he'd plummet into the Void.

Once again he labored to project his awareness as stooped, crotchety Adrain, his Harbinger teacher, had taught him: looking for currents and eddies, gaps and folds in the fabric of existence. And at last he sensed *something,* too distant for him to determine precisely what, below him and off to the right.

Excited, but wary as well—Spectres frequently lurked in the vicinity of Byways and gates, hoping to snare unwary travelers—Montrose swam in the indicated direction. A gray smudge of phosphorescence bloomed in the murk ahead, so faint that at first he wondered if his light-starved eyes were playing tricks on him. But then the glow grew larger and brighter, making him squint, changing from a dingy blur to a sharply defined white oval floating untethered and unsupported in the depths.

There didn't seem to be any creatures lurking around it. Eventually Montrose breaststroked near enough to determine that it was about four feet high and a yard across. And almost certainly a portal of some kind. This close, he could make out the patterns of fractured space coiling around it, like loops of iron filings defining a magnetic field. He tried to sense what lay on the other side, but to no avail. He wasn't surprised. It was relatively easy for a Harbinger to peek into the Tempest from outside, but usually impossible to spy from one section of the infinite storm to the next.

He'd have to pass through the portal without a clue as to what was waiting on the other side. But he didn't intend to go through utterly unprotected. Defying his own fatigue, he strained to invoke yet another Harbinger power. For a moment nothing happened, and then blobs of shadow oozed from his skin. The droplets expanded and flowed together, enveloping him in darkness. When the process was complete, he could still see his gray hands and forearms paddling in front of him, but while the effect lasted, no one else should be able to see him at all.

He swam into the oval. He didn't feel anything remarkable when his hands plunged through it, just more cold water on the other side. But when his face touched it, a barrage of sensations—searing heat, violent nausea, a throb of excruciating pleasure—assailed him, as sudden and disorienting as the explosion of a bomb.

He thumped down on a tile floor. Transported from water to air, he instinctively gasped a superfluous breath, then lifted his head and looked around.

He'd emerged into what appeared to be an artist's studio, full of canvases in various stages of completion, the air tinged with the sharp smells of paint and turpentine. A row of French doors stood open, admitting a gentle breeze, the twittering of birds, and yellow sunlight. There was no sign of the gate through which he'd entered.

It all looked like a scene from the world of the living, but his Harbinger senses indicated otherwise. He was still inside the Tempest and he'd better start looking for a path that would carry him on to the true Earth. He stood up, water pattering from his sopping garments to the floor.

As he slunk toward one of the French doors, a painting caught his eye. He pivoted and gaped at it, startled because it depicted a moment from his own life. Perhaps ten years old, he was jumping a favorite bay gelding over a tumble-down fence. Kincardine, his family's principal castle, rose in the background.

Disconcerted, he prowled from one easel to the next and found himself the subject of every picture. In one, he was writing a poem at his desk at St. Andrews; in a second, marrying his young bride Magdalen; in a third, leading the wild charge at Tippermuir; and in yet another, weeping over the lifeless body of his son John, slain by the rigors of a ghastly winter march. Taken together, the oils told the entire tale of his thirty-seven years of life.

And that, he reflected, wasn't good. It quite possibly meant that, his cloak of shadow notwithstanding, one of the denizens of the Tempest had noticed his presence and taken an interest in him.

All the more reason to get out of this enclosed space and begin searching for a Byway. But as he turned back toward the French doors, another door in the far wall clicked and swung open. Princess Louise of Bohemia bustled into the room.

She was exactly as Montrose remembered her, willowy, graceful, and bright-eyed, with smutches of paint on her hands and the tip of her nose, and her honey-blond tresses intent on escaping her elaborate coiffure. Clad in a faded, unfashionable gown, perhaps a hand-me-down from some more affluent friend, she moved toward one of the paintings with the brisk air of someone about to set to work.

The sight of her flooded Montrose's heart with rage and, even knowing what he now knew, a bitter yearning. Fighting for self-control, he told himself, *It isn't really her*.

And yet it was just conceivable that it was. Since his own demise, he'd encountered a couple of his earthly acquaintances among the Restless, though never before someone for whom he harbored such powerful feelings.

Suddenly he was running toward her, as helpless to stop himself as a quarrel shot from a crossbow. His veil of darkness dissolving, he grabbed her by the arm and spun her around.

Startled, she squealed and recoiled, nearly upsetting her easel. A brush fell from her hand to clink on the floor. When she looked up into his face, her expression of alarm melted into a smile. "Darling!" she gasped. "You frightened me half to death." She tried to embrace him.

Gripping her forearms, he held her slender body away from his own. "Are you truly she?" he demanded.

She cocked her head. "If you're teasing, I must be slow this morning, because I don't understand the joke."

"Are you Louise," he asked, "or just something that plucked her image out of my memory? Either way, you must be a Spectre. Otherwise, you wouldn't be here."

"Where, in The Hague? It can be tedious sometimes, but I wouldn't be so unkind as to suggest that it's only fit for the dead." She smiled another smile, then knit her brows when he didn't respond in kind. "You aren't joking with me, are you? Something's wrong."

If she *was* real—and despite himself, with every passing moment he found it more difficult to recall that she probably wasn't—was it possible that she didn't know she was dead? He'd encountered wraiths suffering from a similar state of confusion, but always in the Shadowlands, the portion of the Underworld contiguous with the world of the living, not deep in the Tempest.

"Don't you understand?" he said. "We're spirits now. It's been three hundred and fifty years since Holland."

"Don't be silly," she said. "Touch my skin. Go on, don't be shy." Hesitantly, he stroked her cheek. "Don't I feel alive?"

To his amazement, she did. Her soft flesh was warmer than the cool substance of the Restless; and when, trying not to derive any pleasure from the contact, he shifted his fingers to her throat, he felt a pulse. And then, impossibly, a similar throbbing in his own breast.

Perhaps *he* was the one who was addled. Perhaps they were *both* alive, and his long sojourn in the Underworld had merely been a kind of fever dream brought on by grief and care.

But no, surely that couldn't be. In the real 1649, Louise had painted his portrait. But she wouldn't have tried to capture his whole life on canvas, and she certainly wouldn't have used her art to prophesy his defeat and execution. Or if she had, she would have hidden the paintings away to gloat over in secret, not left them sitting out where he might see them. Roughly, he turned her toward one of the nearest oils, in which a bound and bare-headed Montrose rode the hangman's cart into Edinburgh. "If I've gone mad," he growled, "then explain this."

"I'm sorry if it disturbs you," she said. "It's just a bit of foolishness. I hoped I could paint away my fears. That it would help me be brave when you set sail for Scotland."

"Liar," Montrose said. "This scene already happened. You *made* it happen. You urged me to take that villain VanLengen with me. I trusted him to scout and he betrayed us to Strachan. Afterward, he told me that you *bade* him betray me. Why? I adored you. I meant to ask for your hand once we installed young Charles on his throne. How could you turn on me?"

Louise sighed. "At this late date, I'm not sure I even remember, and what does it matter anyway? This, my dearest James, is a magical place and time. Let's not waste it talking of hurtful things. Let's savor the warmth and the tingle of life in our veins. Let's make love the way we used to." She attempted to enfold him in her arms.

Resisting a terrible urge to respond in kind, Montrose thrust her back. "The truth matters to *me*. Tell me, or I swear I'll send you to the Final Death."

Louise grimaced. "Very well. If you must have it so. I betrayed you for money. Your enemy Argyll paid handsomely to ensure that your expedition would come to a swift and inglorious conclusion."

Montrose stared at her.

"Is it so hard to understand?" she asked, her generous mouth sneering. "My family and I were impoverished exiles, living on charity. Did you think that didn't gall me?" She laughed. "You were always such a romantic fool that you probably did. You thought I was too ethereal for such base concerns."

"Perhaps so," said Montrose heavily. Paradoxically, now that she'd admitted her guilt, his anger had suddenly lost its edge, leaving him dazed and sick. "VanLengen *said* you'd sold me for pay, but for some reason I always suspected there was a deeper explanation. I imagined that I'd dealt you some bitter hurt without even realizing, that somehow, it was my own fault—"

In the blink of an eye, Louise turned into a hunchbacked parody of her former self, with blazing, slit-pupiled green eyes, a slavering muzzle lined with jagged fangs, and tangled of writhing, hissing serpents sprouting from its shoulder blades. Even as the creature changed, it lunged, one of its huge, black-clawed hands streaking at Montrose's belly.

Miserable and befuddled as the Stygian was, the transformation caught him entirely by surprise. But he had a swordsman's reflexes, and they served to wrench him out of harm's way. The creature's claws merely shredded his shirt and grazed the skin beneath.

At once the Spectre pivoted to strike again. Instinctively drawing on what remained of his depleted strength, Montrose flew backward, knocking down easels as he went, until, his knees flexing, he touched down lightly on the other side of the room.

He'd never liked running from a fight, but it would be foolhardy to continue this without a blade, a bow, or a gun. He pivoted, seeking the nearest exit, and they all crashed shut at once. He launched himself at the nearest French door, ramming it with his shoulder, and rebounded. The panes of glass felt as strong as iron.

The Spectre charged. Glancing up, Montrose saw that the ceiling was too low to permit him to soar above the other wraith's long-armed reach. Pointless, then, to squander precious energy staying continually airborne. He snatched up an easel, dumping its picture—a depiction of a solemn Montrose signing the National Covenant—on the floor. When the creature pounded into range, he clubbed at it.

Its hands shot forward, grabbed the easel, tore it out of Montrose's grasp, and tossed it away. Without breaking stride, the Spectre hurtled on.

Montrose sidestepped, narrowly avoiding the other wraith's talons, and slammed a punch into its side. The Spectre grunted and dropped to one knee; but as it did, two of the snakes growing from its right shoulder twisted and struck, biting the Stygian on the cheek and neck.

Even as he recoiled, Montrose felt an icy burning like the kiss of Underworld fire suffusing through his substance, leaving weakness and a sensation of fluttery lightness in its wake. Like darksteel or a Spectre's ebon fangs and claws, the poison carried the taint of the Void. Another dose might dissolve him into nothingness.

The Spectre lurched up, turned, and limped toward him, its uneven gait perceptible even inside the folds of its voluminous skirt. Evidently it had landed hard on its knee. Hoping to catch the monster by surprise, Montrose gave ground, trying to look as if he were even weaker than he felt, then sprang into the air and kicked.

The bold savate attack caught the Spectre squarely between the eyes. Montrose tried to tumble over its head and fly out of its reach before it could retaliate. But his powers of flight abruptly failed and he plummeted on top of it. The two combatants collapsed in a heap together.

Montrose thrashed madly, trying to get clear, certain that he wasn't going to make it. In a second the Spectre would shred him with its talons, and the snakes would sink their fangs into his flesh. Finally, he realized that every part of the creature, including its serpentine appendages, was unconscious.

Trembling with weakness, fear, and loathing, he dragged himself to his feet and repeatedly stamp-kicked the monster, snapping its neck and smashing its skull flat, grimly aware that even those injuries wouldn't necessarily kill it. He'd need darksteel for that.

Darksteel, he realized suddenly, or the natural armament of a Spectre. Grinning, he knelt beside the creature and reached for its wrists, intent on slicing it to pieces with its own claws.

Sustained *ripping* sounds split the air, as if a giant were tearing pieces of paper. Startled, Montrose peered wildly about. Though everything still *looked* the same, his Harbinger senses revealed that the unstable substance of the Tempest was churning. This strange little world was about to come to an end, as if it had required the conscious will of its resident Spectre to maintain its existence.

Jagged black cracks snaked through the floor, the walls, the ceiling, and the air itself. Montrose extended his awareness, groping for a portal or a Byway, but found nothing. And then, with a crash and a roar, reality shattered, and water exploded through the breaches. An instant later, the light and the air were gone. He was floating in the ocean depths once more.

Grimly sure that he effort was futile, he reached out again, seeking another exit from this trap. And this time he sensed air and even a Byway above his head. Evidently he hadn't returned to the same part of the sea. He floundered painfully upward.

The black water grew gradually lighter, until even dull mortal eyes would have noticed the change. Then Montrose's head broke the surface. Paddling feebly, he swiped his long hair out of his eyes, blinked, and looked around.

The rippling curtains of phosphorescence in the starless sky were predominantly silver and violet now. The expanse of the Sea of Shadows extended as far as the eye could see in all directions, with no land anywhere.

Montrose could feel that he was indeed floating squarely in the middle of a Byway, a sea-lane leading out of the Tempest. But it didn't matter. He lacked the strength to swim or fly far enough to get to safety. Despite all his striving, he was still going to perish.

The sheer unfairness of it infuriated him. A howling tide of darkness rose inside him as, at this moment of anguish, his Shadow fought to seize control.

He wasn't sure he could muster the will to resist. What did it matter if his personal demon finally gained the upper hand? If it didn't destroy him, something else would.

And then a point of light appeared on the water.

Without meaning to, Montrose dived underwater. Frantically he fought to reassert control of his rebellious body. For several seconds, nothing happened. He couldn't even *feel* his limbs. But at last he broke the Shadow's grip. Cackling, the demon scuttled back to its hiding place in the depths of his psyche.

Montrose struggled to the surface. The light was nowhere to be seen. Perhaps the Byway had already carried it to another layer of reality.

No! It *had* to be here. It was just that his vision had gone blurry. "Help!" he cried. "Help me!" The call sounded faint and thin, more of a wheeze than a shout.

But off to his left, a soprano voice answered, "Hang on!" Turning his head, he spied the light again. Gradually it glided closer, until he could see that it shone from a lantern hanging on the ornately carved prow of a small lateener. A tall woman perched by the tiller, her face shadowed by a black cowl. She studied the man in the water for a moment, then extended an oar. Montrose clutched at it, and with no apparent effort she hauled him aboard.

Four

Montrose flopped down in the bottom of the boat. He doubted he had the strength to sit upright. It was a struggle just to roll over and look up at his rescuer. "Thank you," he gasped.

She reached into the folds of her layered cloak, brought out a tarnished silver flask, and handed it to him. "Drink," she said.

With considerable effort, Montrose managed to unscrew the cap and raise the bottle to his lips. The liquid inside it seared his throat much as liquor would burn a mortal.

At once he felt a glow of renewed strength and warmth, somewhat alleviating the chill he'd taken in the water. Simultaneously, he experienced a flare of bitter resentment directed toward his savior. It was intolerable that she should see him, an aristocrat of the Hierarchy, reduced to a helpless, shivering supplicant! And surely that was a contemptuous sneer, half hidden by the shadow of her hood!

He was able to quell the surge of anger because he understood what medicine she'd given him. Though they had no need for conventional food and drink, wraiths derived sustenance from pure emotion; and centuries ago, some forgotten genius of an artificer had fashioned flasks that could capture the essence of hatred.

Montrose would have liked to guzzle the bottle dry and recover his vitality completely, but that, he judged, would be an abuse of his rescuer's kindness. Reluctantly he replaced the cap and handed the elixir back. "Thank you," he repeated, his voice now only a little hoarse.

"Don't be too lavish with your gratitude," she replied, replacing the potion inside her cloak. Somewhere off the starboard bow, something splashed, a sound like an earthly fish jumping. She peered into the darkness for a moment, evidently making sure her craft was in no danger. "Ferrymen don't indulge in charity. We always claim a fee for our services."

"I'll pay it gladly," Montrose said. He laboriously sat up and set his back against the side of the boat. "I thought I was done for. I'm James Graham, in life Marquess of

Montrose, now an Anacreon in the service of the Smiling Lord."

"And I'm Katrina," the Ferryman said. "I know you, Lord Montrose. How did you come to find yourself in such a predicament?"

My idiot master and his idiot minister sent me on a fool's errand, Montrose thought, his resentment fanned hotter by the influence of the potion. "Raiders attacked my convoy. After they overwhelmed us, I dived into the ocean to escape."

"And what was the object of your voyage?" Katrina asked.

Montrose hesitated. Two thousand years ago the wayfarers called Ferrymen had served Charon, the now-vanished founder of Stygia, as pathfinders, psychopomps, and warriors. But they'd renounced their allegiance when he proclaimed himself emperor. Since then, they'd wandered the Underworld pursuing their own mysterious ends, never foes to the Hierarchy, but no longer allies, either. And thus, not one to whom Montrose would ordinarily confide the Smiling Lord's affairs.

"I warned you that you owe me for my help," Katrina said. "I choose to claim my due in the form of information. I pledge to hold whatever you say in confidence."

Montrose decided that in that case, it wouldn't do any grievous harm to tell her. When he reached America, his business would become public knowledge anyway. "The Smiling Lord dispatched me to lead a campaign against certain Heretics fomenting strife along the Mississippi River."

"An Inquisition," Katrina said. "That explains your current affiliation. I'd heard you belonged to the Fifth Legion."

Montrose forbore to ask how she knew he'd been transferred from the Black Hawks to the Grim Riders when he was no longer wearing the Unlidded Eye. Rumor had it that Ferrymen were masters of all the old-time guildsmen's secret arts and other, stranger sorceries as well.

Katrina trimmed the sail. "And why this particular venture?" she asked. "Why now?"

Montrose shrugged. "You'd have to inquire of my master." *And that son of a whore Demetrius.*

"Since he isn't aboard," Katrina replied dryly, "you reduce me to conjecture. Perhaps the Smiling Lord aspires to Charon's throne. People whisper that all the Deathlords do. Perhaps your master hopes a string of successful raids against Stygia's enemies will further his ambitions."

"That's an interesting hypothesis," Montrose said. Actually, as far as he'd been able to judge, it was the exact truth.

The Ferryman smiled thinly at his show of discretion. "And who better to lead the crusade that that legendary Cavalier hero, the Marquess of Montrose? All the sorrows of your life could be laid at the door of religion, couldn't they? I imagine you despise Heretics."

Montrose wondered just how much Katrina *could* tell about him, simply by looking at his face. Perhaps a wraith's entire history and personality were recorded in the invisible deathmarks graven on his countenance, if another ghost were Oracle enough to decipher them. At any rate, he didn't want to discuss his private emotions with the Ferryman. He was seldom comfortable discussing them with anyone. Perhaps he could redirect the conversation to more general topics.

"I think I'd dislike Heretics," he said, "even if I hadn't died trying to put young

Charles back on his throne. Because they're a menace. Even the few who aren't actively plotting insurrection sow the seeds of discontent with their blather about paradisical realms beyond the Underworld and higher powers than the Deathlords. And they're contemptible fools besides. While people are breathing, we invest extraordinary hope and faith in some particular religion. Frequently we even wage war on our neighbors if they want to use a different Prayer Book. And afterwards, when we die, we discover to our horror that the afterlife is nothing like what our priests and bishops taught us to expect. Our deities are nowhere to be found. At that point, rational men renounce the whole idea of gods and messiahs. But Heretics simply invent *new* religions, and commence the wretched farce all over again."

"Spoken with considerable fire," Katrina said. "A person would almost think you *wanted* to lead the expedition. And yet you didn't, did you? Had you grown too fond of your concubines, and the dreams your Sandmen wove for your amusement? Or were you afraid that some rival courtier would steal your master's favor while you were gone?"

Montrose swallowed another surge of anger. "I don't know why you're baiting me, Ferryman, but I'm too grateful for your aid to take offense. Jeer away, and I'll bear it with as good a grace as I can muster."

"I'm trying to rouse you," Katrina said. "You're treading a dangerous path."

Montrose snorted. "Really! Do you say so? And my journey thus far has been so serene and uneventful!"

"I'm not talking about the common perils, phantasms, and portents of the Tempest. Something else, something strange and powerful, is lying in wait for you. A threat you *must* confront, and not merely for your own sake."

Montrose's eyes narrowed. "And what, precisely, is that?"

Katrina sighed. "I don't know. I can't see it."

Montrose couldn't help smiling. "This is just like half the romances in the Grand Archives. The Ferryman always warns the protagonist, and the warning is always too cryptic to be of any use. It's just as annoying in real existence as I always imagined it would be."

"Now," Katrina said, "you're mocking me."

"I don't mean to. But how did you expect me to react to such a vague report? Curl up in the bottom of the boat and blubber in terror? I already know I'm headed into danger. I'm sure the Heretics pose a considerable threat. But I'll handle them."

"Perhaps," said Katrina, "and perhaps not. Your Shadow is stronger than I'd hoped, and stronger than you imagine. But it's as pointless to second-guess fate as it would be to counsel you any further." A brisker note entered her voice. "What will you give for passage to the Shadowlands?"

Montrose frowned. "If you recall, I already paid you. With information."

"That was for removing you from the water," Katrina replied, "and giving you the draught of Liquid Hate."

"You're too greedy by half," Montrose growled. His fists clenched, and he pried them open again. He didn't truly want to assault Katrina, and not just because he wouldn't have stood a chance. Grasping or not, she was his benefactor. It was the elixir seething through his system, and the seductive, malicious whisper of his Shadow, which insisted otherwise.

"If you don't want to pay," Katrina said reasonably, "you can simply disembark."

Montrose looked around. As he'd expected, there was still no land in view. And though he was in better shape than when she'd taken him aboard, he still doubted that he was strong enough to escape the Tempest under his own power.

"What do you want?" he sighed. "If I write you a note, the Smiling Lord will open his coffers for you; but you'll have to call at the Isle of Sorrows to collect your booty. All I have in my immediate possession are these sodden rags on my back."

"I rarely put in at the Weeping Bay," Katrina said, "and I don't believe your garments would flatter me. What I require is a service."

"What is it?" Montrose asked warily.

"Nothing that will harm you, or compromise your loyalty to your master." She held out her hand. Suddenly a dagger with a curved darksteel blade, a silver hilt, and a carved owl's-head pommel lay across her palm. Montrose jumped. "When you see this knife, forbear." The weapon blinked out of existence again. "Agreed?"

Bewildered, Montrose shook his head. "I don't even understand what you mean."

"You will when the time comes," Katrina said. "Do we have a bargain?"

Montrose shrugged. "You have me at a considerable disadvantage. So if it won't conflict with my duty to my master, I suppose so."

"Then hang on," the Ferryman said. She trimmed the sail, then pushed the tiller to starboard.

As the lateener came about, Montrose sensed a zone of fractured space yawning just a few yards in front of the bow. Even in his enervated condition, he didn't see how he'd missed it until now, unless Katrina had just created it by force of will.

As the boat glided through the gate, St. Elmo's fire crackled up and down the mast, filling the air with the smell of ozone. A tingling crawled over Montrose's skin, and his tangled hair did its best to stand on end.

The electrical phenomena ceased as soon as the lateener cleared the portal. Suddenly, towering walls blocked out most of the sky. Peering about, Montrose saw that Katrina had transported him from the open sea to a river hissing through a narrow canyon.

More rapidly than Montrose would have imagined possible, Katrina lowered the sail, dismounted the mast, and then leaned on the tiller. The lateener turned toward the canyon wall, space splintered, and an opening appeared in the rock. Beyond it, water roared and plunged into darkness, down an incline so steep it was nearly a waterfall.

The lateener shot over the edge and plummeted, in virtual freefall until it splashed down at the bottom of the torrent. By all rights the impact should have swamped it, or dashed it against one of the jagged rocks looming in a semicircle before it. But somehow Katrina kept it afloat and steered it through a gap.

The boat hurtled on, down a cramped subterranean channel, with boulders rarely more than a yard away. Montrose supposed he ought to be afraid. If the craft crashed into a rock or overturned, the accident might not destroy him, even in his weakened condition. But it might well cripple him, and the rapids could easily sweep him deeper into the caverns, separating him from his guide and leaving him in desperate straits again.

And yet he wasn't frightened. The precipitous, bucking flight of the fragile craft, the bellow of the rapids and the icy kiss of the spray, filled him with a joy he'd nearly forgotten, the same exhilaration that had once possessed him when he took a horse over a series of challenging jumps, or led his men to triumph at Alford and Kilsyth. Forgetting his frailty, laughing, he gripped the rail and raised himself up, the better to savor the ride.

Gradually the passage widened. The current grew gentler, its echoing roar fading to a murmur. The lateener glided into a circular grotto with a domed ceiling. Luminous crimson crystals studded the walls, providing a dim red illumination.

Montrose grinned at Katrina. "That was amazing. My teacher Adrain was a great Harbinger, but I don't know if even he could have taken a boat down that channel."

The Ferryman smiled slightly, then picked up an oar and rowed the sailboat to a dock hewn from the surrounding limestone. A flight of crude steps climbed from the platform to a cavity in the rock. "This is your stop," she said. "You'll find the Shadowlands at the top of the stairs."

Montrose wondered fleetingly how *she* was going to exit the grotto. Perhaps she meant to open another portal, though at this point, he would scarcely have put it past her to sail back *up* the rapids. "Thank you again," he said.

"Remember your promise," she answered. "And remember yourself. Remember why the Skinlanders still hold you in their hearts."

He didn't know how to respond to that, so he simply inclined his head. Then he clambered out of the boat and headed up the steps.

As he stepped through the gap, the world shifted, and he found himself standing in St. Giles's Cathedral in Edinburgh. A lovely place even though, for him, the moonlit stained-glass windows were sooty and broken, the stonework chipped and cracked, and the pews riddled with rot. A hint of decay underlay the scents of candles and frankincense, and the whispered prayers of the old woman across the chamber seemed to buzz and reverberate unpleasantly.

Montrose grimaced. He'd never quite grown accustomed to the way the Shroud, the barrier separating the living and the dead, warped a wraith's perception, encrusting his Shadowlands surroundings with a patina of ugliness and decrepitude. Another good reason to stay in Stygia!

But as always, for some reason, the white marble statue directly across from him was immune to the effect. Or at least he found it so. Another wraith, for whom it had no special significance, might have perceived it differently. Heedless of the elderly worshipper, knowing she couldn't see him, he approached the monument.

It was a carving of himself, clad in armor and lying in state. The steel sword beneath the stone hand was one he'd actually carried into battle. Above the image glowed the arms of his staunchest comrades—Gordon, Aboyne, Hay, Macdonald, Airlie, and his own cousins—rendered in stained glass. At the center of them all gleamed his own red roses and golden sea-shells, with the Montrose device—*Ne oublie*, Do not forget—underneath.

As usual, the statue filled him with a profound ambivalence. By reminding him of his victories, it made him proud. But it also struck him as a mocking tribute to a fool and a life misspent.

Because in the end, everything he'd achieved on the battlefield had been undone by schemers and traducers whispering behind closed doors. As he'd blundered through life, drunk on a bookish idealism, one trusted associate after another had betrayed him for expediency's sake. In the end, even the young King for whom he'd risked everything had sold him out. Charles had repudiated him when him he'd already set sail for Scotland, a political ploy which kept the people from rallying around him and all but guaranteed his expedition's ruin. VanLengen's treachery had merely administered the *coup de grâce*.

Fortunately, in his postmortem existence, Montrose had learned to put his own interests first, to scheme as craftily and act as ruthlessly as any foe. And thus he was faring far better as a Hierarch than he had as a champion of either the Kirk or the Scottish crown.

Every feeling the statue inspired, the nostalgia and bitterness alike, invigorated him, made him more *real*, fortifying him against the corrosive power of the Void. Wraiths generally found it easier to gain and exert strength in locations which reminded them powerfully of their mortal existences. That, perhaps, was why Katrina had delivered him here instead of taking him to the Mississippi.

The drawback was that such sites exerted a fascination that made it difficult to tear oneself away. Some wraiths found it impossible, and spent eternity lurking near their graves or wandering the corridors of their earthly abodes. Finally, two minutes after he'd resolved to take his leave, Montrose squinched his eyes shut and wrenched himself around, turning his back on the memorial.

He strode to the nearest exit, pressed his hand against the seemingly worm-eaten panel, and shoved. The door wouldn't budge.

He scowled at his own deficient memory. He'd momentarily forgotten that here in the Shadowlands, wraiths and their surroundings existed on different levels of reality. It required extraordinary measures to move any object that properly belonged to the realm of the living.

Montrose hesitated, then stepped *at* the door. He couldn't resist bracing for an impact, but of course, there wasn't one. He slipped through the panel as if it were made of air.

Outside, the night was cool. A half moon peered through shreds of cloud, and the easterly breeze carried the murmur and scent of the firth. Montrose strode down the cobbled street, wondering where the Quick kept the "airport," and how it would feel to fly inside a machine.

Five

As the chubby blond secretary ushered him into the nondescript conference room, Bellamy studied the three men who were already sitting around the Formica-topped table. Linus Hanson, his boss: a bald gnome with round, gold-rimmed glasses, his features arranged in their customary expression of grave consideration. Carlton Nolliver, one of VICAP's resident shrinks, sleepy-eyed and puffy-faced, fidgeting nervously with a Tic Tac dispenser. Rumor had it that he was constantly spritzing or sucking some kind of breath freshener to kill the telltale smell of alcohol. And Bill Dunn, the emissary from the Special Affairs Department. His shaggy black mane, russet suede jacket, and chinos made a marked contrast to the conservative suits and haircuts—pretty much the mandatory uniform for the average FBI man—of his companions. He'd also opted to defy the ban on smoking in Federal offices, a transgression Hanson would never have tolerated from one of his subordinates. An acrid blue haze hung in the air around him.

As far as Bellamy could see, none of the trio had brought a rope, but he still felt like the guest of honor at a lynching.

"Good morning," Hanson said. "Would you like some coffee?"

"No, thanks," Bellamy replied. He'd drunk too much already, parked in the waiting room. Another cup and he'd be bouncing off the walls.

"That will be all then, Betty," Hanson said. The chunky secretary departed, pulling the door shut behind her. "Have a seat, Frank."

"How bad is it?" Bellamy asked.

"Let's not lose sight of the fact," said Nolliver, "that it isn't *all* bad." He tapped the stack of manila files on the desk before him. "Your tests came back negative. You didn't have any drugs or alcohol in your system, and your EEG and CAT scan are normal."

Bellamy grimaced. "*Is* that good? If it had turned out that somebody slipped me mescaline, we'd know why I wigged out and we could get on with our lives."

"It's damn good from where I sit," Hanson said. "It means that I don't have to fire you, and you don't have a brain tumor or some other terrible disease."

"But something drove me crazy," Bellamy said heavily. "I almost shot a policeman who only wanted to calm me down."

"But you didn't," said Dunn, a puff of smoke billowing from his mouth. "You didn't hurt anybody. So don't beat yourself up over that."

"I wish we did know what happened to you," Hanson said. "The facts simply don't add up to anything much. A known mental patient—"

"Ex-mental patient," Bellamy murmured, not certain why he'd bothered to correct him.

Hanson frowned. "Since you were convinced he needed to go back to the sanitarium, I'm not sure what difference that makes, but have it your way. An *ex*-mental patient gets drunk and babbles a preposterous story. For a second you imagine you see a shadowy figure in a dark room, but when you blink, it disappears. After you take Waxman outside, you think you see another goblin rear up from behind your car. Waxman drops dead of a heart attack—according to the autopsy, he was past due—and you go into a..." He glanced at Nolliver.

"Fugue state," the psychiatrist supplied.

"Thank you," Hanson said. He looked back at Bellamy. "You see? There's nothing to go on. If you could remember *anything* else...?"

"I'm sorry," said Bellamy, feeling like a pitiful excuse for a trained observer, "I can't." He turned to Nolliver. "You could try hypnotizing me again."

The ruddy-faced psychiatrist shook his head. "Judging from our first two attempts, it wouldn't do any good. The memory is gone beyond recall. Besides, it's my professional opinion that, at least on a superficial level, you assessed your situation correctly when you worried that Waxman's delusions were contaminating your own thinking. That phenomenon's called a *folie à deux*. It's more common than you might imagine."

"In other words," Bellamy said, "I didn't *need* LSD or a brain tumor to go crazy. I just had naturally had it in me." He looked at Dunn. "Or do you think there could be another explanation?"

In the past, Bellamy, like most of his peers, had derided the whole idea of the Special Affairs Department. It had seemed ludicrous that a law enforcement agency with real, flesh-and-blood felons to catch should devote any of its resources to investigating reports of Bigfoot and little green men from outer space. Now he was glad that Hanson had requested SAD to participate in the current inquiry. But *something* weird had happened in East St. Louis, and it was just possible that Dunn could throw some light on it.

But the agent in the leather jacket shook his head. "I'm sorry, Frank. I wish I could help you out. But nothing in your story rings any bells. Of course, it's like Division Chief Hanson said. What you told us is incredibly vague. It's hard to extract any details to correlate with the information in our database. Not"—he grinned wryly—"that that would be likely to do any good anyway. I'll be straight with you. SAD has been poking around alleged haunted houses and crop circles since 1952, but it's not like we've actually learned anything. It's still an open question whether the paranormal even exists.

"I can tell you this. We keeps tab on Satanists and other potentially dangerous occultist cranks." He smiled again. "We feel honor-bound to do a *little* honest police work once in a while. As far as we've been able to determine, none of the cults and covens in our files has anything to do with the Atheist murders. And a couple years back, we checked out Eric Weiss. We concluded he was a charlatan. There was no indication of genuine wild talents. And Waxman didn't even participate in the trickery. He was just a flake who answered the phone and licked envelopes."

"Look," Bellamy said. "*I* don't believe in the 'paranormal' either. But in the course of investigating cult leaders and phony mystics, didn't you people ever discover a technique for making a man see things that aren't really there, or giving him a panic attack?"

Dunn dropped the remains of his cigarette in a Styrofoam cup, extracted a leather tobacco pouch and a package of rolling papers from a pocket inside his jacket, and dexterously began to fashion another. "Sure. Any magician will tell you there're a million ways to make people see what you want them to see and feel what you want them to feel. But every trick requires either a prepared stage, the manipulator establishing communication with the manipulatee, or both. So I don't see how anybody could have used them on you."

"Particularly since Waxman was in hiding," Hanson said. "Nobody besides you even knew where he was."

"We don't know that for sure," Bellamy said.

"I don't blame you for wanting to believe that some external agency was responsible for your experience," Nolliver said soothingly. "It's frightening to lose control. But look at it this way. You're a courageous individual. Since joining the Bureau, you've proved it time and again. No one could literally frighten you out of your mind by projecting a ghostly image on a wall, or popping up from concealment in a Halloween mask. Only a disturbance in your own psyche could upset you to that degree."

Suddenly Bellamy felt tired. He could see there was no point in arguing any further, particularly when he didn't even have a coherent perspective of his own.

"That's the verdict, then. You all think Waxman threw a scare into me, he dropped dead of natural causes, and I had a panic attack. Nothing that happened and nothing he told me had anything to do with the Atheist."

Dunn struck a match with his thumbnail. "I'm sorry, but yeah, that's about the size of it."

"But no one believes you're genuinely unstable," Nolliver said. "What you experienced was an isolated episode, and there's no reason to assume it will ever happen again. Not as long as we take the proper precautions now."

Crap, thought Bellamy. *Here it comes*.

"I've gone over your time sheets," Hanson said. "You work some very long hours."

"Everybody around here does," Bellamy said.

"Well, starting now, I want *you* to cut back to forty hours a week, and to meet with Dr. Nolliver as often as he thinks appropriate."

"To discuss whatever you'd care to talk about," the psychiatrist said.

"And finally," Hanson continued inexorably, "I'm taking you off the Atheist investigation. It's a gruesome case and it's possible you may have gotten too emotionally involved. Turn your notes over to Walter Byrd."

Under the table, Bellamy clenched his fists in frustration. He understood that Hanson was trying to give him every possible break. The older man would have been well within his rights to place him on formal probation, or suspend him pending further medical evaluation. All the same, his decision had dealt his subordinate's career a devastating blow. Once the word got out, no one in the Bureau would really trust him.

But he knew he couldn't talk Hanson out of it. If he tried, he'd just wind up looking like even more of a loose cannon. "I understand," he said, trying to keep his voice steady. "Is that everything?"

"I believe so," Hanson said.

six

As Nolliver hurried past the double doors to the morgue, he caught the stench of rotten meat, underlying the sharp antiseptic smell that pervaded the building as a whole. Once again he wondered if there was any chance at all that it was real.

When confronted, the medical examiners insisted that no one else ever complained of noxious odors leaking into the corridor. They swore Nolliver was only imagining the stink, and after some reflection, he'd decided they were probably right. But he still smelled it every time he passed!

He wished he could move his office to another area, away from the corpses, the labs, and the infirmary, but it would be a bad idea to request such a relocation. Some people already thought he was falling apart. He didn't want to give them any further cause for gossip.

The smell of death lingered in his nostrils and coated his tongue with a vile taste. He needed a drink to wash it away. His hands beginning to tremble, he fumbled his key ring out of this lab coat pocket and unlocked his office door.

Tendrils of pungent blue smoke caressed his face. "Good morning again," said Dunn.

Startled, the psychiatrist flinched. Just a twitch, really, but he could tell from the way Dunn's smile widened that the SAD agent had noticed. Nolliver scrambled into the room and locked the door behind him. "How did you get in here?" he asked.

Sprawled on the leather couch, his scuffed brown cowboy boots propped up on one of the arm rests, Dunn shrugged. "I'm a detective. I'm supposed to be able to get inside places."

"Well, you shouldn't have broken into this one," said Nolliver petulantly. He sat down behind his desk, unlocked the bottom drawer, and took out a pint of Johnnie Walker Black, noting automatically how much was left. About a fourth of the bottle, enough to see him through until he went out to lunch, at which point he could smuggle in a new one. "We shouldn't talk here."

"I don't see why not," said Dunn. "We're colleagues, aren't we? We've worked cases together. Nobody's going to think anything about it."

"You can't be sure of that." Nolliver raised the pint to his lips, tilted his head back, and took a long drink, shivering with relief as the Scotch burned its way down. "For all we know, someone could have bugged this office."

"Wrong," said Dunn. "I do know. I checked. Are you going to give me any of that booze?"

Nolliver glowered at him. "Is that why you're here? To cadge a drink?"

Dunn shook his shaggy head. "Actually, I just wanted to touch base and celebrate a job well done, but your pissy attitude is making it hard to bask in the glow."

"I can't help it," Nolliver said. "I hate this." He realized that Dunn was looking pointedly at the bottle in his hand. And he supposed it would be foolish to antagonize him. Reluctantly he stood up, circled the desk, and handed the liquor over, wincing at how much his fellow conspirator guzzled down.

Dunn sighed in satisfaction. "There's nothing like the good stuff, is there?" He held on to the Scotch for another moment, as if teasing Nolliver, and then gave it back. "I'll be damned if I know *why* you hate our little cleanup operation. You *do* remember how you got involved?"

Nolliver winced. "Of course."

"Extorting sex from teenagers in exchange for a favorable psychiatric evaluation—"

Only four times! Nolliver silently protested. *And the first time, it was the boy's idea!*

"—abusing your trust as a doctor and an officer of the court. Convincing judges to put dangerous youthful offenders back on the street. The last one even killed some people, didn't he? Just imagine what would happen if the truth came out."

"I said, I understand my situation," Nolliver said. "There's no need to threaten me."

Dunn raised his bushy eyebrows. "Who's threatening? I'm just making a point. When SAD uncovered your sordid past, our first thought was, now we can just blackmail the poor perverted bastard into doing whatever we want. But fortunately for you, we're nicer than that. You aren't *just* getting blackmailed, you're getting paid."

"For concealing the truth."

"What can I tell you? People at the top level have decided that it isn't good for anybody who lacks the proper clearance, even your average, garden-variety FBI man, to get all hot and bothered about the paranormal. Unfortunately, every year or two, some Fed stumbles over something spooky, and guys like you and me have to spring into action to put out the fire. Sometimes it feels a little slimy, but it's also our patriotic duty."

I wish I could be sure of that, Nolliver thought. It would be comforting to assume that even when deceiving people like Bellamy and Hanson, he was still serving his country. But he often had his doubts, not that it mattered. Whatever the truth, he had no option but to cooperate.

"We've wrecked that young man's career," he said somberly. He took another drink. When he lowered the bottle, he was dismayed to discover that, somehow, there was only a swig or two remaining.

"Bull," said Dunn. He blew a smoke ring. "We knocked him a rung or two down the ladder. If he's got the right stuff, he'll climb back up eventually. It's his own fault anyway. When he saw which way the wind was blowing, he should have changed his story. Claimed he got hit on the head, and screw the medical report if it said otherwise. Hanson *wanted* to let him off the hook. He would have accepted any halfway plausible explanation."

"Bellamy was too dedicated an agent to lie," Nolliver said. At that moment, he felt the agent's plight nearly as keenly as his own. "He was one of the best young investigators in VICAP. If we hadn't discredited him, if I'd actually tried to help him recover his repressed memories instead of burying them deeper, he might have caught the Atheist. The next time that monster kills someone, I'm going to feel like it's my fault *again*." His eyes throbbed as tears welled up inside them.

Dunn grimaced. "Will you get over yourself? Do you think I'd ask you to hide the truth if it meant letting a serial killer go free? I'm a cop, too, you know. I told you, SAD knows *exactly* what happened that night, and it had nothing with the Atheist. Bellamy and Waxman were just in the wrong place at the wrong time."

"How can you know that for certain?" the psychiatrist demanded.

Dunn exhaled a plume of blue smoke. "It's like our friends in the Company say, Doc. I could tell you, but then I'd have to kill you."

SEVEN

A long, cream-colored sedan turned onto the wet, gleaming street in front of the speeding taxi. The cab driver, a stocky Middle-Eastern immigrant with slicked-back pomaded hair, squawked, stamped on the brake, and wrenched the steering wheel. The taxi spun out of control, narrowly missing the white car but whirling to the left side of the highway. Luckily, there was no traffic coming the other way.

Montrose was sitting in the back seat beside the paying passenger, a thin, scholarly-looking young mortal currently frozen with terror. As the taxi came to a halt, the Stygian wryly reflected that travel was becoming *interesting* again. After a series of uneventful flights, he'd stowed away on the cab with as little difficulty as he'd boarded the airplanes. But it had soon become apparent that his chauffeur could feel his presence, though probably without comprehending precisely *what* he was sensing. He 'd started sweating, flooding the car with the stench of his perspiration, and his aura had glowed orange with anxiety. He'd kept twisting his head to peer into the back of the vehicle, and his driving had become increasingly erratic.

Montrose supposed he'd better take his leave before the Quick man wrecked the cab. Now that he'd recovered his vitality, it shouldn't be any hardship to finish his journey afoot. Indeed, he'd be virtually tireless unless something injured him, or he expended too much energy practicing the arcane arts. He slipped through the side of the cab, then watched it lurch into motion and speed away. His body tingled as the raindrops plummeted through him.

He walked on through the benighted streets, peering about, not much liking what he saw. Even allowing for the distortions of the Shroud, the Earth seemed a vile, decaying place, its gutters choked with reeking garbage, its streetlights broken, many of its shop windows covered with plywood and the rest armored by rusty steel grates. Periodically, guns cracked in the distance or sirens wailed. Nihils—cracks and holes in the surface of Shadowlands reality, breaches opening on the Tempest—seethed and glittered everywhere, a few conceivably large enough for a Spectre to wriggle through.

Edinburgh had been bad enough, and this Natchez looked even worse. Montrose wondered if the Shadowlands had been quite this unpleasant on his last visit forty years ago. He thought not. Perhaps, as some wraiths believed, the destruction of Charon had shifted the balance of power between Being and Oblivion. Perhaps the universe was crumbling away, dropping bit by bit into the Void.

He scowled and tried to shove the notion out of his head. It was Heretical, and the gloomiest, most defeatist kind of heresy at that.

Ugly or not, the stigmata of urban decay had their uses. Shadowlands wraiths tended to establish their communities in the most desolate portions of mortal cities. There, they didn't have to coexist with the Quick when they weren't in the mood. Moreover, such places frequently radiated a palpable atmosphere of misery on which the dead could feed, it being one of the ironies of their existence that joy and love didn't invest a place with the same emotional residue as fear, grief, and despair. Thus, the increasingly empty streets and the multiplying stands of condemned buildings were like signposts, pointing the way to Natchez's Necropolis.

A strain of sprightly but oddly dissonant violin music skittered through the air. Hands clapped, raggedly keeping time. Quickening his pace, Montrose rounded a corner. Before him, a narrow cobblestone street ran up a hill. A number of wraiths, many masked, their clothing a hodgepodge of styles from the last three hundred years, stood clustered here and there.

Some had gathered around the fiddler. Another group were inspecting the meager selection of goods—many no doubt forged in Stygia, the remainder cherished possessions some dying soul had managed to carry into death—laid out in an open-air market. Still other loiterers gawked as a petite blond flesh sculptor stroked a customer's features into a new configuration. Suddenly his whole head bubbled and flowed at once, the tide covering or simply annihilating his eyes, ears, nose, and mouth. The customer, a burly black man, made a muffled squealing sound, jumped up from his seat, and began to flail around. Now looking panicky, the Masquer tried to push him back down and was knocked sprawling for her pains. The spectators laughed and jeered.

At the top of the street rose a jumble of massive brick buildings that might have been an abandoned factory, a collection of warehouses, or some combination of the two. Sentries armed with crossbows prowled the rooftops. Torches ringed the entire complex as if to define a perimeter. Clearly the site was a Hierarchy Citadel, and Montrose's ultimate destination.

Smiling, he started up the street. Half a block from the top, he spotted a slender young woman, dressed like a flapper except for the gold and ivory crucifix hanging around her neck. Perched on a tenement stoop, she was haranguing several other wraiths, ranting in a shrill, excited voice about Christ, faith, and "Transcendence, our doorway out of this purgatory and into bliss."

The Stygian's smile twisted into a scowl. He took a stride toward her, intending to drag her off the stoop and take her into custody, before his better judgment reasserted itself. At the moment he was scarcely well equipped to arrest anyone, particularly when it might entail facing down a mob. Hoping that the preacher would set up shop here again, he marched on toward the top of the hill.

Since his death, Montrose had seen any number of gruesome and, by Quick standards, unnatural spectacles. He liked to believe that he'd grown blasé about such things. Even so, he didn't care for the sight of Stygian torches. The brand in front of him now was typical. A Masquer had paralyzed some poor slave, stretched his body nine feet long, melted his legs into a single rigid shaft, and fused his arms to his sides. A corona of amber barrow-flame whispered around his head, slowly, slowly burning his substance away. His mouth gaped in a silent, endless scream. Montrose shivered as he passed. He told himself it was only due to the chill radiating from the fire.

He walked on toward the two sentries flanking the nearest door into the Citadel. One could argue that it was idiotic for Shadowlands wraiths to pay any attention to doors. As Montrose had rediscovered in St. Giles's, they didn't need them, nor, in the general run of things, did they even open them. They just glided through them as they would any other barrier. But security considerations mandated that everyone enter and exit a Hierarchy stronghold through one of a few checkpoints. Any ghost who opted to do otherwise was automatically considered a thief, an assassin, or a spy.

The guard on the left leaned on a long spear and wore a Bowie knife on his belt. He'd stitched a patch with the black raptor emblem of the Fifth Legion to the breast of his khaki fatigues. A Masquer had pulled his lips into an exaggerated jack-o'-lantern grin, a common symbol of fealty to the Smiling Lord. His companion was dressed in buckskin and carried an AK-47. The question-mark brand on his cheek signaled his allegiance to the Beggar Lord. Both soldiers had a green sash emblazoned with a black hourglass, evidently the regalia of the fortress at their backs, draped over their right shoulders.

"Good evening," Montrose said.

"I don't know you," growled the sentry with the brand. "Have you got a pass?"

Montrose hadn't expected them to recognize him or show him any deference, not while he looked like a mendicant, but he was surprised by the overt hostility in the other wraith's tone. Either the fellow was having difficulty controlling his Shadow, he was subtly unhinged, or he was simply in an uncommonly foul mood. "No," the Stygian said, "but I do have legitimate business inside. I'm an Anacreon, newly arrived from the Isle of Sorrows, and I have business with your commanders."

The man with the brand sneered. "Sure you are, and I'm the Lady of Fate! Get out of here before we send you *back* to Stygia in chains."

The spearman cleared his throat. "You know, he seems harmless enough, just a little crazy. We could ask the Centurion of the Watch. Maybe he'd okay it for him to come inside."

The wraith with the brand rounded on his companion. His arms jerked as if he wanted to swing his gun up and slam the butt into the other spirit's teeth. "No!" he shouted. "Rules are rules! If he can't prove he belongs, he can't enter!"

"Okay, okay," said the spearman, shifting back a step. He looked at Montrose, the wariness in his eyes an odd contrast to the artificial hilarity of his rictus. "I'm sorry, pal. Maybe you should come back some other time."

"Oh, I will," Montrose said, half irritated and half amused. "To assign some special work details to you and most especially your friend." It was too bad, he reflected, that an army of the Restless didn't need anyone to clean latrines.

The Stygian turned and sauntered back the way he'd come, through the ring of sentient torches and on down the hill. But as soon as he judged he was out of eyeshot of the Legionnaires on the roof, he slipped into the narrow walkway between two tenements and veiled himself in darkness.

A wraith learned to take it for granted that mortals couldn't see him; but, despite the centuries Montrose had spent honing his Harbinger abilities, he sometimes found it nerve-wracking to operate on the assumption that his fellow spirits were similarly blind. As he crossed the open space around the Citadel, he kept expecting one of the Legionnaires to shout a challenge, or simply open fire. The tension prickled along his nerves and made his mouth feel dry.

But no one noticed him, and finally he reached the base of the wall. As he stepped through it, his substance resonated to the buzz of emotion lingering in the brick. Children had suffered in this place, slaving at workbenches from before dawn until after dark, breathing hot, thick air, squinting against the gloom, muscles cramping and fingers bleeding. The Stygian shuddered, invigorated and repelled at the same time.

Shaking off the sensation, he inspected the interior of the building. He was standing in a cavernous, musty-smelling chamber illuminated by the dim gray light leaking through filthy skylights. Nearby, a wraith, a budding Chanteur, was practicing her Arcanos by crooning to spiders. When she hit the right note, the small predators ran madly around their webs, or even tumbled out of them altogether.

Montrose prowled on through the complex, avoiding proximity to other ghosts when possible. Cloak of shadows or not, he saw no point in tempting fate. Where not given over to open work areas, the derelict buildings proved to be a maze of cramped rooms, snaking hallways, and blind alleys. Often compelled to backtrack, he might have saved time by slipping through walls, but he feared losing his bearings.

Finally, warmth began to prickle across his skin, warning him that his mask of darkness would soon evaporate. He supposed he had little choice but to expend the energy necessary to weave another. Then he heard a commotion up ahead.

He crept forward, reached the end of the hallway, and peered out into another open area, this one illuminated by greenish barrow-flame. A diversity of banners, emblazoned with hawks, question marks, crowns of thorns, grinning faces, begging bowls and hourglasses, hung from the rafters. Various luxuries, including a large television, one side of its mahogany cabinet a web of jagged Nihil fissures, stood here and there about the floor.

In the middle of the chamber a number of Legionnaires in the ubiquitous green sashes—officers, judging by the quality of their clothing and gear—were jammed in a circle together, crowing, cursing, and shouting encouragement. Peering, Montrose glimpsed a pair of barghests fighting in the center of the ring. The frenzied thralls were lean as greyhounds, their sculpted heads more canine than manlike, their bodies altered to enable them to stand erect or lope on all fours with equal facility. The gray iron muzzles which denied them human intelligence also prevented them from biting one another, but didn't hinder the use of their long gray claws.

A man in a gleaming steel domino, a short magenta cape, and the cuirass and helmet of a conquistador stood calmly watching the battle. As heedlessly as the other spectators jostled one another, they took care not to crowd him or obscure his view. A smirking dwarf in green and violet motley crouched at his side, a leather bag in his stubby hand. It probably contained the coins his master had wagered on the bout.

Montrose walked up behind the masked man, dissolved his veil of darkness, and tapped him on his armored shoulder. The masked man jumped and spun around.

"Hello, Manuel," the Stygian said. "It's good to see you again."

EiGHT

Manuel Gayoso de Lemos's suite occupied much of the top floor of the derelict building, where, for some reason, the echo of ancient suffering was strongest. Montrose supposed that by Shadowlands standards, his fellow Anacreon's rooms were more than comfortable. The Spaniard had even arranged for someone to sweep, dust, and scour the place clean; a task which, considering that the accumulated grime had existed on the other side of the Shroud, must have been a major undertaking. Still, to a Hierarch accustomed to the luxuries of the Onyx Tower, the place was essentially a hovel. Montrose did his best to conceal his disdain.

Gayoso ushered him into a dark office, then snapped his fingers. The three white tapers in a brass candelabrum burst into cold blue flame, their reflections of the fires gleaming on his breastplate and domino. After offering Montrose a chair, he sat down behind his desk, hesitated, and finally, as courtesy required, removed his mask, revealing pouchy eyes and a fleshy beak of a nose.

Montrose had known any number of wraiths who hated revealing their faces. Struggling to survive amid the rivalries of the Hierarchy, they didn't want anyone gleaning their private thoughts from a momentary flicker of expression. Montrose sympathized with their anxiety, but he didn't share it. He flattered himself that he was generally capable of concealing his true feelings without recourse to a tangible veil.

"Well," said Gayoso, "it's been a long time since we'd had a visitor from the Isle of Sorrows. To what do we owe the honor?"

"The Smiling Lord has ordered a war against the Heretics operating along the lower Mississippi. He appointed me to the Order of the Unlidded Eye and ordered me to direct the campaign." Montrose gave Gayoso what he hoped was an ingratiating smile. "Needless to say, I'll be relying heavily on your advice and support."

Gayoso grimaced. "I can't believe that our master would send you alone. Does he expect me to give up *my* troops and *my* resources—"

"He expects you to provide any assistance required, but in point of fact, I did set sail from Stygia with my own troops. Unfortunately, raiders attacked and overwhelmed us en route. As far as I know, only I escaped. So as it stands now, yes, I'm afraid I will have to draw on local reserves for my entire army. Surely it won't be all that much of a burden."

"Spoken like a true Stygian," Gayoso said.

Montrose lifted an eyebrow. "I fancied we were *both* Stygians, my lord Anacreon."

"I'm a Hierarch," Gayoso said. "There's a distinction. Hierarchs do the dirty work and Stygians reap the rewards. *We* struggle to keep order and enforce the Code of Charon. *You* extort levies of thralls from us to feed the Soul Forges, and keep all the newly made goods for yourselves."

"A harsh man might feel that that remark borders on treason," Montrose said. "But I don't. I understand your frustration. These are hard times. Stygia isn't receiving nearly as many souls as it used to, which means we can't ship nearly as many articles back. That's why all Legionnaires should work together to restore the empire to its former ascendancy."

"And you're going to accomplish that by destroying a few Heretics."

"It's a start," Montrose replied. "I'm amazed you haven't already set about purging them yourself. I saw one preaching in the shadow of this very Citadel. How can you command the respect of the populace if you tolerate open sedition?"

Gayoso sighed. "You don't understand the situation here. Yes, of course the Heretics are a problem, but they aren't our biggest problem. Since the emperor perished, we've had a steady string of Spectres and Maelstroms laying waste to the province. We can't afford to provoke a major confrontation with Heretics or Renegades. Particularly not right now."

"What do you mean?" Montrose asked.

Gayoso shook his head. "I wish I knew. But I governed the living folk of this settlement three hundred years ago when I was breathing, and I've dwelled here ever since. I'm attuned to this place, and I feel something new arising. Something foul."

Recalling Katrina's murky warning, Montrose felt a chill ooze up his spine. He did his best to quash the feeling. Even if Gayoso wasn't lying to excuse his reluctance to cooperate, there was always danger lurking in the Underworld. A Legionnaire who permitted that realization to cow him would never accomplish anything.

"Perhaps," Montrose said, "the Heretics are responsible for the new threat. If so, a preemptive strike could nip it in the bud."

"I don't believe that," Gayoso said. "And even if I did, there's another consideration. I don't rule here alone."

"I'm well aware of that.," Montrose said, striving not to lose his patience. During Charon's reign, a council of seven Anacreons, each representing one of the Deathlords, had governed every Citadel in the Shadowlands. In recent years, however, with manpower shortages endemic, no Legion maintained a presence in every single Necropolis. According to Montrose's information, Natchez currently belonged to the minions of the Smiling Lord, the Beggar Lord, and the Emerald Lord, a datum confirmed by the particular banners and other insignia he'd seen since his arrival. "I expect your peers to assist me also."

Gayoso snorted. "You can expect it all you like. It won't happen."

"Are you telling me that *they're* traitors, then? Every Legionnaire owes obedience to the will of every Deathlord."

"What we owe and what we pay can be two different things. With Charon gone, some people in the Shadowlands believe that propping up the Hierarchy is a lost cause. They want to establish their own kingdoms to rule as they please."

Montrose smiled. "I trust you're not speaking for yourself."

"Of course not," Gayoso said. Montrose couldn't tell if he was lying or not. "But that's what Dwight and Cramer want to do. If I turn my troops over to you, they'll seize the opportunity to depose me."

Aha, Montrose thought, *the truth at last*. Gayoso had finally revealed the primary if not the only reason he didn't want to help.

"And by ousting me," the Spaniard continued, "they'll remove Natchez from the Smiling Lord's sphere of influence. Surely he doesn't want that."

"If he didn't have faith in you," Montrose said, "you wouldn't be in charge here. I daresay he assumes you're resourceful enough to retain your position even if placed at a momentary disadvantage. By the Scythe, man, I don't mean to take every Black Hawk you've got! I'll leave you an adequate bodyguard."

"I don't understand why our master ordered this done here," Gayoso said sullenly. "Here, out of every place on Earth."

"For one thing, he has the impression that the Heretics have grown particularly impudent in this area."

Gayoso's dark eyes narrowed. "Why the devil does he think that?"

Montrose shrugged. "He's a Deathlord. One of the most powerful beings in the universe. I don't know how he comes by all the secrets he uncovers. I suspect he may also have chosen to attack the Heretics hereabouts because he *assumed* he had a loyal commander in place to help me carry out his will." He stared into the other wraith's eyes. "And you are going to help me, Manuel. Just between the two of us, I don't have any great enthusiasm for this venture, either. I went through hell just getting here. I'd far rather have been at home, savoring a Sandman chef's fantasy of roast pheasant and champagne. But we have our instructions, and that's the end of it."

Gayoso's lips twitched into a smirk so fleeting that Montrose nearly missed it. "You may have *your* orders. I don't know that I do."

"What are you talking about?" Montrose said. "I just now delivered them."

"By word of mouth," Gayoso said. "Surely such an important directive would arrive in writing with the Smiling Lord's seal attached. And by the same token, if you've joined the Grim Riders, where's your black robe? Where your lantern with the Lux Veritas shining inside it?"

"I lost everything but these clothes on my back when I fled my ship," Montrose said. "What of it? *You know me.* We met when you came to Stygia for Charon's funeral obsequies."

"Precisely," Gayoso said. "And you were a member of the Fifth Legion, not the

Order of the Unlidded Eye. A fellow Anacreon, not anyone who outranked me. In these chaotic times, with duplicity everywhere, I couldn't possibly place my command at your disposal. Not without clear instructions from higher up. I'll tell you what I'll do. I'll send a messenger to Stygia, asking for confirmation of what you've told me, just as soon as I deem it feasible. In the meantime, I invite you to enjoy the Citadel's hospitality. Fair enough?"

"Evidently it will have to be," Montrose said.

NINE

The small emergency room was full to overflowing. From what she'd overheard, the blond wraith gathered that a pickup with no brake lights had stopped suddenly in the rain, and by so doing engineered a seven-vehicle pile-up. Hearing the wail of the ambulances, a number of the Restless had hurried to the county hospital to watch the proceedings. Some were clearly soaking up the agony and terror in the air, as palpable to a ghost as the reek of blood, bodily waste, and disinfectant. They looked as if they were becoming more *real* in some indefinable way. A second contingent wagered on who would die, how soon, and whether the unfortunate in question would join the Restless. A few Reapers hovered possessively over the injured, intent on capturing any souls who did materialize in the Underworld. Those with the ability to reach into the Skinlands subtly hampered the efforts of the mortal doctors and nurses.

The blond wanderer, a slender young woman dressed in faded jeans, a baggy flannel shirt, and a silver pendant cast in the shape of an owl, climbed up onto the wheeled gurney in the corner. Beneath her insubstantial feet, the cart was no more likely to shift than a slab of granite. Next she sang, first a plaintive lament for delights and loved ones sealed away forever behind the Shroud, then a lewd, raucous satire on the Deathlords, and finally a hymn of Transcendence, of reconciliation and release. She was no Chanteur, but she had a pleasant soprano voice and did a reasonable job of accompanying herself on the mandolin. By the end of the third song, she'd lured several of her fellow spirits away from the ongoing drama of the carnage.

She took another look around the room, checking for Legionnaires, and then launched into her speech. The Sisterhood of Athena was an odd, hybrid sort of organization, Heretics or Rebels depending on how one looked at it, and her oration reflected the dichotomy. It was partly an exhortation to seek Transcendence and partly a call for revolution. But a fiery abhorrence of slavery infused every syllable. Catching the thrust of her remarks, the Reapers glared.

She kept the sermon short, partly out of concern that Legionnaires might wander in, but primarily to avoid boring her audience. As she neared the end, she searched their faces, looking for an indication that her words were hitting home. She didn't find it, though one or two of the wraiths looked genuinely thoughtful.

At least, the Sister reflected, no one had heckled her. And after she finished, some of them asked questions.

"You didn't tell us what path really *leads* to Transcendence," a stooped old man in a bow tie, suspenders, and zippered leather bondage mask said querulously. "Should we believe in the Third Coming, the Needle Dancers, the Invisible Tabernacle, or what?"

"The Increate is infinite and therefore infinitely diverse," the Sister replied. "That being the case, many creeds embody aspects of the truth. Follow the path that suits you best. Just make sure it isn't a corrupt faith, one that feeds your Shadow and grovels to the Void."

A slender woman in a red halter and a mask of peacock feathers raised a hand with a bright blue eye in the center of the palm. Wondering if the sculpted organ could actually see, the Sister gave her a nod.

"A friend of mine got depressed," the masked woman said. "Over the course of a few months, he just lost the will to go on. I was there when Oblivion took him."

"I'm sorry," the missionary said.

The masked woman scowled as if the Sister had jeered at her grief. "That isn't the point! I knew somebody else, a Holy Roller like you. She spent most of her time meditating, looking for Transcendence, and finally *she* disappeared. I was there that time, too, and you know what? It looked exactly the same!"

"Many people do believe that Transcendence is just another name for annihilation," the blond ghost conceded. "That's what the Deathlords and the Legions *want* you to believe, and I can't prove they're wrong. But I *feel* it, and I think that if you look into your hearts, you'll feel it too. There *has* to be something beyond this desolate, lonely place. Somewhere better. Something to hope for."

The masked woman sneered.

Scowling, a doctor stepped back from a motionless, gory body. The Reaper poised at the head of the bed, a rangy man wearing a latex Newt Gingrich mask and a chainmail vest, quivered with expectation, eager to snap the shackles in his hands on an Enfant's wrists. But no new wraith appeared in the Shadowlands. Finally, the Reaper abandoned the corpse and looked around. No doubt discerning that other scavengers had already laid claim to the rest of the dying, he wrapped the manacles around his waist and swaggered toward the Sister.

"I take thralls," he said curtly. "I catch them, I chain them, and I sell them."

"I can see that," the Sister replied.

"If you want to chase after Transcendence," the Reaper said, "go ahead. It's your funeral. But why do you want to screw up the world for the rest of us?"

"Whatever their differences, nearly every faith agrees that you Transcend by becoming a good person. How could I aspire to virtue, yet ignore the suffering and injustice all around me? How could I ever deserve ultimate freedom if I didn't care that others were trapped in the vilest sort of slavery?"

"That sounds real noble. But what's that mandolin made of? Or for that matter, the shirt on your back?"

The Sister frowned. "Quite possibly, they came from a Soul Forge. But—"

"You bet your ass they did! This is the Underworld. There's nothing *but* souls to make stuff out of. It's a tough break for the losers who go to the smelters, but if we let them go free, the rest of us would have *nothing!*"

Some other wraiths muttered in agreement.

"I realize it wouldn't be easy to shut down the Soul Forges," the Sister said. "I don't claim to know how we could get by without them. But I'm confident we'd find a way. After all, they're an invention. They didn't *always* exist. Freeing the thralls would change our world in a fundamental way. Perhaps we'd find it had changed us as well. Perhaps we could *all* Transcend."

The Reaper made a spitting noise, turned, and disappeared through the wall.

After his exit, the discussion lost momentum and the Sister's audience began to drift away. To her surprise, the old man in the S&M hood tossed a worn copper obolus on the gurney. She couldn't tell if she'd actually moved him or if he was merely rewarding her for a few minutes of diversion.

Either way, she thought wryly, she'd be happy to take the offering. She'd learned the value of money from childhood on, and her long mortal career as a nun and abbess had disabused her of any notion that clerics didn't need cash as much as anyone else. She hopped to the floor and picked up the coin, wincing at the ache that twinged through her fingertips. Oboli were frequently unpleasant to handle. Some wraiths believed it was because the coins still had a vestige of human consciousness suffering inside them. Unfortunately, few other Soul Forged goods emitted similar vibrations, and thus it was all too easy to overlook their gruesome origin.

As she slipped the obolus in her pocket, she took a final look around the ER, wishing the accident victims life, or, failing that, a happier destination than the Shadowlands. Then she slipped outdoors.

The pounding rain had ebbed to a drizzle, though lightning still flashed to the west, out over the wide expanse of the Mississippi. The cool air smelled clean. For once, the Shroud notwithstanding, she didn't catch even the subtlest whiff of decay; although, to her eyes, the pines at the edge of the parking lot looked twisted and blighted, with dry brown needles, and oozing chancres mottling the bark.

Skirting the large Nihil hissing and shimmering in the middle of the asphalt, her mandolin slung across her back, she headed down a narrow side street. Soon she reached one of Greenville's Haunts, an area of dilapidated, abandoned clapboard houses three blocks square. Legend had it that in the 1840s, one of the residents of the district had brutally beaten a slave, and the unfortunate woman had cursed him with her dying breath. Shortly thereafter, a terrible disease resembling a fast-acting leprosy had swept through the neighborhood. Horrified by its virulence, the city officials had taken extreme measures to contain it. Armed sentries had patrolled the perimeter of the area, shooting anyone who tried to leave. The municipal leaders had even considered burning the district down, but feared that the fire, too, might spread to the city as a whole.

The Quick had tried to demolish the old houses on any number of occasions since, but so far the local wraiths had always managed to sabotage their efforts. The miasma of grief and despair still festering in the shuttered bedrooms and moldering parlors was far too bracing to surrender without a fight.

As the Sister strolled, she looked for someone who could direct her to a market or a venue where Sandmen and genuine Chanteurs performed. At the moment, no one was in view. Perhaps the downpour had driven everyone indoors. Rain couldn't hurt a wraith or even get him wet, but some spirits disliked the tingle of the droplets falling through their bodies. No doubt what many actually disliked was any experience that served to remind them they were dead.

So many ghosts pined endlessly for the lives they'd left behind! The Sister occasionally fell prey to the same longing herself, but when she did, she fought hard to quash it. At best, it was a demoralizing distraction from the quest for Transcendence. At worst, it could lead a wraith into unspeakable crimes.

Prompted by such reflections, she began silently reciting the Pledge of Athena. *I am dead, and death is a journey. Spirit clothed in light, risen and sundered from my chrysalis of mortal clay—*

Somewhere behind her, something made a soft, brushing sound. She turned smoothly, her weight centered, the way her *sifu* had taught her, only to discover there was still no one in sight.

It was quite possible that she'd imagined the noise. Or that it had had nothing to do with her. Still, the Underworld was a dangerous place, especially for missionaries and other subversives, and it paid to be careful. She spent another moment peering about, straining her hypersensitive vision to the utmost.

She didn't see anything threatening. Somewhere to the north, a Quick baby started crying, a sweet. vital sound, and, like the scent of the rain-washed air, blessedly undistorted by the Shroud. A few feet away from the infant, a man emitted a groggy groan and clambered out of his waterbed. The mattress sloshed.

Now smiling at her own edginess, the Sister turned and walked on. Just as she completed the second paragraph of the Pledge, she heard the noise—a stealthy footfall?—again. This time it sounded a little closer.

She whirled. Stare as she might, there was still nothing to see. Just the moonlight silvering the glistening streets, and the feverish glitter of the Nihils defacing the decaying houses.

Unfortunately, just because she couldn't see anyone didn't mean there was no one there. Certain wraiths, Harbingers, for example, could become invisible. She strained her ears, listening. Lacking a heartbeat or the need to breathe, the Restless could be extraordinarily quiet when they wanted to be, but they were also preternaturally perceptive. Sometimes it balanced out.

But not this time. Down along the river, frogs chirped and the current murmured. Engines moaned, and car tires hissed over wet roads. But she still couldn't pinpoint anyone creeping along behind her.

Maybe no one was. Or perhaps he was simply good at it. In any case, now that she was concerned about the possibility, the chances of her actually enjoying the night life of Greenville, Mississippi had dropped to just about nil. She decided to head directly for her skiff and get away from land as soon as possible.

As she turned toward the river, a figure ducked behind an overgrown hedge on the other side of the street. Startled, she jumped, and soft laughter pulsed through the dark. There was something odd about the rhythm of it, though she couldn't say precisely what.

In any case, the mockery angered her. Though she generally tried to avoid violence, she was no one's helpless victim, and she would have liked to ram the laughter back down the wretch's throat. But it wasn't a practical notion, not when there were also someone skulking along behind her.

She wondered who they were. Conceivably Legionnaires, though the locals hadn't persecuted missionaries with any great zeal in the last couple years. Nor did Hierarchs generally play cat-and-mouse games. Halt-or-we'll-shoot was more their style. Most likely it was the Reaper who'd accosted her and one or more of his friends, come to enslave *her*. The notion made her muscles clench in fury.

But whoever it was, they wouldn't get her. The Sisterhood had trained her too well. She turned back toward the north and started to run, only to glimpse a flicker of motion in the darkness directly ahead.

Now truly alarmed, she lurched to a halt. Was she *completely* surrounded? If there were that many people after her, why couldn't she catch a good look at any one of them? And why didn't they just close in for the kill?

She couldn't imagine, but by hanging back, they'd given her a chance. Pivoting, she dashed across a weed-infested yard, up three steps, and through a warped door with a few flakes of yellow paint—the mark of the old-time quarantine—still clinging to the wood. In a musty foyer, she turned and ran south, plunging through the exterior wall of the house, across a strip of coarse grass, and through the side of the derelict home next door.

A wraith's power to flit through solid objects gave him an advantage when trying to evade pursuit, even when the pursuers were ghosts, too. The quarry could always dodge behind a wall, thus escaping the hunters' scrutiny, and then flee in a different direction. Intelligently employed, the tactic generally served to shake even alert and energetic adversaries off his trail.

And so, for the next few minutes, she ran, constantly changing course but trying to gradually work her way downhill toward the river, hurtling through rotting walls and filthy, broken windows, across yards where rats rustled through the underbrush and streets with weeds poking between the cobblestones. Periodically she tried to spot the hunters, but without any further success. She supposed that was all right if they'd lost sight of her as well.

Unfortunately, her strategy had one drawback: It took energy to slip through solid objects. Finally, panting just as if she still needed air, she bounded up a flight of rickety stairs and into a small bedroom, where a tiny skeleton lay in a cradle, and the stale air screamed with ancient heartbreak. A ghost in a gingham dress stood staring down at the dead baby. She slowly raised her head to regard the Sister with vacant eyes.

"I'm sorry for intruding," the missionary said, peering out the windows. No one was in sight. "I just want to rest for a moment, and then I'll go." She could already feel the grief trapped in the room revitalizing her.

The other ghost returned her gaze to the bones. Her own predicament notwithstanding, the Sister couldn't help wondering if her companion had spent the last one hundred and fifty years doing nothing but staring down at the remains of her child. It was a ghastly thought. Perhaps she could come back later and talk to the poor woman, convince her to abandon her vigil and—

She felt something rushing at her back.

Her hands snapping up into a guard position, she sidestepped and pivoted to face the newcomer. In the gloom, all she could make out was a hulking figure with something strange about its head. Agile as a panther, he hacked at her with a jagged-edged two-hand sword.

Ducking, the Sister silently called her own weapon, and the leather-wrapped hilt of the darksteel knife with its owl's-head pommel popped into existence inside her fingers. She feinted a kick at her attacker's crotch, then lunged in close, stabbing at his breast.

Her adversary twisted aside, evading the thrust. Unable to use the sword at such close quarters, he slammed his elbow against her temple, driving a spike of pain through her skull. Off balance, she stumbled toward the fungus-spotted, Nihil-riddled wall. From the corner of her eye, she glimpsed him charging after her, whirling the sword above his head for a lethal stroke.

She could see that she'd never recover her equilibrium in time to ward off the blow. Struggling to focus past the pain in her head, she willed herself completely insubstantial.

She caught a last glimpse of the wraith in the gingham dress, still staring down at the cradle as if she were all alone. Then she tumbled through the side of the house and out into the night.

When she hit the ground, she did her best to roll, her mandolin shattering beneath her. By good luck as much as facility, she managed to avoid serious injury. As she scrambled to her feet, she peered frantically about, expecting to see her attacker leaping down after her, or his accomplices charging toward her. But everything was still.

Her head and left hip aching, limping slightly, she turned and ran, trying to understand how the swordsman had tracked her, how he'd appeared so suddenly in the little nursery, and why his companions weren't already on top of her. Once he'd located her, he should have signaled them to move in. None of it made sense.

Her strategy of evasion hadn't kept her safe before, but, lacking any better plan, she held to it, working her way out of the Haunt and into a Quick public housing project, rows of identical gray concrete-block buildings with slogans like GENERATION LAST and BLOOD AND SILENCE spray-painted on the walls. Now every move through a solid barrier brought a throb of pain.

Ahead of her, six giggling teenagers, four boys and two girls, were squatting in a circle. Their auras flickered a murky violet with malice and excitement. As the Sister ran by, she saw that they were dissecting a writhing guinea pig. The animal's glistening gray viscera bulged through a long cut in its belly.

All but exhausted, the Sister peered back down the street. She didn't see any pursuers. Praying that at the moment, none of them could see her either, she tried to step into a small barbecue joint that had already closed for the night. For a second, she could feel the wall resisting her intrusion, clinging to her like flypaper, and she imagined herself getting helplessly stuck halfway through. But a final wrench of her shoulders and a last exertion of will carried her on into the interior. The shadowy diner smelled of hickory smoke and half-spoiled pork. The inky fissures in the back wall hissed.

The Sister scurried around the greasy counter and hunkered down beside it. *They can't check every room in every building*, she thought. *If they didn't see me duck in here, maybe they won't find me*. She resisted the urge to peek over the counter, for fear that one of the hunters would look through the window and see her. Instead she listened with all her might, hoping her ears would warn her if any of her enemies drew near.

For a minute she couldn't hear anything but the Quick, their breaths hissing, hearts thumping, and bowels gurgling, babbling, chewing, and grunting in the apartments all around her. Then she seemed to catch a different sound, but she couldn't make out what it was. Not a whisper and not the creak of shoe leather. Not the click of a gun being cocked, nor the metallic sigh of a blade leaving its—

Abruptly she realized that the hissing of Nihils behind her had grown infinitesimally louder. Just as her head snapped around, a long vertical crack gaped open. It still shouldn't have been wide enough to admit the swordsman, but somehow he flowed through it anyway, sweeping his jagged weapon down at the top of her head.

Kneeling, she couldn't fling herself out of the way in time. All she could do was try to deflect the blow. She whipped up her arm and the sword skated along it, gashing it, leaving a trail of momentary numbness that abruptly flared into pain.

The swordsman kicked her in the chin, flinging her back against the counter. From the sharp crack and the fresh jab of agony, she knew he'd broken her jaw. Suddenly her vision was blurry and dim. The jagged blade swung up for another blow.

Reflexively she scrambled backward, through the substance of the counter. Once again the coarse, gummy matter fought her, clutched at her, but somehow she dragged herself clear. Desperately, she struggled to her feet, certain that her assailant must already be leaping over the pitifully inadequate barrier she'd placed between them.

But he wasn't. He was still standing by the wall, watching her frantic efforts to get into a fighting stance. He laughed his disturbing syncopated laugh, and as her vision swam back into focus, she finally saw what made the sound so peculiar. It was coming from both of his wedge-shaped, jet-black reptilian heads.

The head on the right licked its upper fangs with a gray, forked tongue. Then the apparition stepped backward, and the Nihil oozed shut in front of it.

The Sister trembled. Her arm and head throbbed. Absurd though it was, she could have sworn she felt a living heart pounding with terror in her breast.

Though wraiths didn't need to breathe, her *sifu* had taught her the proper way to do so to facilitate meditation. She forced herself to take long breaths and let them out slowly. After several exhalations, her pain and fear lost some of their edge.

Her impulse was to resume running, but she resisted the temptation. Headlong flight hadn't helped her so far. Her only chance was to think, to figure out what was happening to her.

Now that she'd gotten a good look at him, and seen the singular method he used to sneak up on her, she surmised that the swordsman was a Spectre. In the Shadowlands, where wraiths of all persuasions engaged Masquers to sculpt them into gaudy monstrosities, simple freakishness was no indication that a spirit had sold himself to the Void. But most of those who took on such forms opted for the exotic allure of an angel or a sphinx, useful modifications like retractable claws or spiked knuckles, or the macabre humor of a devil's horns or a grinning skull-face. Few sane ghosts aspired to look as hideously inhuman as the two-headed bipedal crocodile.

Moreover, nearly all of them, even Harbingers, whose arcane skills had been invented to allow them to negotiate the Tempest, considered such travel a perilous enterprise. Whereas, she now suspected, the reptile man was traversing it with ease, while peeking out into the Shadowlands to keep track of her. Only one enemy had ever actually attacked her because there was only one. Exploiting the chaotic spatial distortions of the storm, he'd materialized behind her, ahead of her, and then off to the side, all in a matter of moments. Convinced she was sorely outnumbered, she'd run and so squandered her strength.

And any second now, he'd pop up behind her to finish her off! She fought to quell another surge of panic.

He'd stepped through a Nihil. Evidently he could flow through any such opening, even the smallest; but maybe he couldn't emerge where there were none at all. If she could find such a place, he might abandon the chase, and at least he wouldn't be able to leap up out of nowhere.

Her skin crawling with tension, constantly turning this way and that, she edged toward the window and peered out at the street. Then she laughed, and her eyes throbbed as if they could shed tears.

Nihils, most no bigger than hairs or grains of sand but Nihils nonetheless, pocked and creviced every surface. The walls, pavement, ground, lampposts, fire hydrant, overturned newspaper box, and parked cars all glittered with a poisonous sheen. Dear God, had there always been so many?

She supposed there had. Loath to recognize the voracity with which Oblivion was eroding the world, she'd simply avoided looking at them. At any rate, it was apparent that she couldn't possibly find some untainted corner of creation in time for it to do her any good.

Such being the case, she might as well make her stand where she was. She told herself firmly that she had a chance. She now understood the Spectre's tricks. It hadn't even seen hers. As it happened, Freda Schmidt, the founder of the Sisterhood, was an accomplished Spook, and most of her followers learned at least the basics of the rowdy guild's Arcanos. The Sister herself had often used the magic to good effect, when pain and fatigue weren't hampering her efforts.

She moved to a clear section of floor, making sure there were no Nihils immediately under her feet or in the ceiling above her head. Then she reached out with her mind, trying to *feel* the tables and chairs around her, and the metal rack, laden with bags of potato chips, Moon Pies, and other snacks, standing by the back wall.

At first she couldn't establish a connection. Then the seething sound of one of the Nihils at her back changed timbre. Desperately she reached again, and at last the power rose inside her. Suddenly it was as if she had twenty extra hands, their fingertips lightly resting on various objects scattered about the room.

She turned and saw the Spectre rushing her, his sword upraised. She scrambled backward, leading him on. When he was directly opposite the metal rack, she seized it with her invisible fists, and, grunting, jerked it into the air and lashed it at his heads.

He threw up his arms for protection. Strewing snacks across the dingy linoleum, the rack slammed into him, penetrating his form without resistance, and knocked him staggering sideways. The makeshift weapon slipped out of her psychic grip.

She didn't bother to fumble for it. Instead she picked up a round table, sending a napkin dispenser, ashtray, and salt and pepper shakers clattering to the floor, and bashed the Spectre with it. The blow hammered him to his knees.

She managed to club him twice more, and then the table simply hurtled through his body without changing his position an iota. He'd shifted himself completely out of phase with the material world, although he and his weapon—a length of wood or bone, she now observed, the edges lined with sharp black stones—would still be dangerously real to her. Both mouths snarling, baring his now-broken fangs, he started to lurch upright.

She'd wanted to batter him unconscious from a distance before he managed to neutralize her Spook magic. Now she could only hope that the punishment he'd taken had slowed him down sufficiently to give her the edge in hand-to-hand combat, her injuries and exhaustion notwithstanding. Knife leveled, she lunged at him, striving to get inside his reach before he hoisted his sword into position for a swing.

She didn't make it. The weapon streaked at her neck. Instinctively she shoved at it with her mind.

It was a risky move. She had no right to expect that she could make psychic contact with an object that small, moving that fast. But with a crack, the sword rebounded, some of the black rocks shattering, as if it had collided with a shield.

Scrambling on, the Sister buried her dagger in the Spectre's breast. The two-headed wraith reeled backward, the sword tumbling from his hands. As his knees began to buckle, waves of dark light ran through his flesh, washing his substance away. When he vanished, the knife fell out of his chest.

The Sister sank to the floor, gasping, trembling with the fear she hadn't permitted herself to experience during the battle, her arm and jaw throbbing as her body labored to repair itself. She wondered exactly what she'd done to attract the Spectre's attention. Whatever it was, she hoped she wouldn't do it again.

TEN

The shooting range, a large, low-ceilinged room in the basement of the Federal Building, popped with gunfire and smelled of burnt cordite. Bellamy loitered by the exit, waiting for Walter Byrd to finish practicing. He'd known he could catch his fellow agent here. Byrd, a fortyish man whose doughy physique belied his mental and physical toughness, showed up at the range every Monday afternoon at five, no matter how busy he was. He'd been fanatical about honing his marksmanship ever since his first shoot-out three years ago. On that occasion, he'd fired three shots at close range, missing each time, and then the perpetrator had shot him in the neck. The surgeon had told him it was a miracle he'd survived.

Scowling ferociously, Byrd emptied his Browning, then pushed the button mounted on the rail. The paper target with its black human silhouette floated across the room to him like an obedient ghost. He inspected the holes he'd put in it, then, evidently satisfied, pulled off his goggles and ear protectors, reloaded his pistol, and returned it to its shoulder holster. He stooped to collect his brass, then headed for the door. When he saw Bellamy, his mouth tightened.

So much for my winning personality, Bellamy thought. "Hi, Walt."

"Hi," Byrd replied, trying to slip past.

Bellamy turned and fell into step beside him. As they pushed through the door and out into the corridor, he asked, "So what's happening with the Atheist?"

"Nothing much," said Byrd, rubbing the scar beneath his chin.

"Oh, come on. There've been three more murders. You must have something new to chew on."

Byrd glanced up and down the hallway, obviously making sure no one else was in earshot. "You're going to get both our butts in a sling if you keep doing this. You know I'm not supposed to talk about the case to anybody outside the task force, *especially* you. Hanson's orders."

"Nolliver's, really."

"And he's your doctor. All the more reason to go along with the program."

Bellamy snorted. "Give me a break. Since when do you have any faith in shrinks? Come on, Walt, put yourself in my shoes. Imagine that you were looking for the Atheist and then got yanked off the case. Wouldn't it drive you crazy if you couldn't at least find out what was going on?"

Byrd sighed. "Probably. Here it is, then, short and sweet, and you didn't hear it from me. We've got three new victims and three new crime scenes, but it hasn't helped. We still don't have any real leads."

"Damn it, that shouldn't be. When a serial killer murders as frequently as the Atheist, it usually means he's coming unwrapped. He gets sloppy, takes more chances, and makes mistakes."

"*You* must put some stock in shrinks. Otherwise you wouldn't be quoting me that psychological profile crap."

"I used to put a lot of stock in them," Bellamy said. "Then I started therapy with Dr. Breath Mint."

They rounded a corner. Byrd quickened his pace, possibly hurrying toward the vending machines that had just come into view. "Hasn't he sorted out your Oedipus complex yet?"

"He doesn't seem to be sorting out anything, just going through the motions. It's like he just wants to support the idea that I *need* counseling."

Byrd inspected the sandwich machine. Most of the compartments were empty. "Do you believe this? Nothing but egg salad *again*. Of course, if I had any brains, I'd be on my way home for supper. Look, what are you saying, that Nolliver wants people to believe you had a breakdown when you really didn't? Why the heck would he care?" He fished in his pocket and pulled out a handful of change.

Bellamy shrugged. "I know it sounds paranoid—"

"Bingo."

"—but on the other hand, I've thought a lot about it, and whatever happened to me that night, I sure don't feel mentally disturbed now."

Byrd grinned. "The real whackos never do." He fed coins into the slot, then pressed a button. The yellow and white sandwich in its glistening cellophane wrapper slid forward, dropped, and thumped down in the bottom of the machine.

"There's something else bugging me," Bellamy said. "Dunn, the rep from SAD, decided that what happened to me had nothing to do with the paranormal. He also pointed out that since my memory has a hole in it, my story is vague. But precisely because it is, how could he rule the paranormal out? Look at what I *did* give him. A psychic who talks about evil spirits and then drops dead. Shadowy figures that appear and vanish mysteriously. An experienced field agent who inexplicably loses his mind. My god, what kind of stuff *does* SAD investigate, if Dunn isn't willing to look into all that?"

Byrd extracted his sandwich from the bin in the bottom of the machine. "So Nolliver and Dunn are in it together, working for the Atheist, who just happens to be Count Dracula. Is that about the size of it? I wonder how much he's paying them. If it's good money, maybe we should join the conspiracy ourselves."

Bellamy fought to quash a surge of irritation. "You know damn well that isn't what I think. But *something* weird is going on. Waxman worked for Weiss; he was worried that if he talked to me, he'd die, too. And right on cue, he did."

"Of a heart attack, after he'd drunk enough booze to float a boat."

"It's still too much of a coincidence."

Byrd turned to look Bellamy in the eye. "Listen to me. I don't *want* to believe you've lost it. We've been through a lot together. I keep thinking I ought to be able to kid you out of this foolishness, but it doesn't look like I can, so I'm going to talk to you straight. Nobody's out to get you. There's no such thing as the paranormal. Forget about it and the Atheist, too. Otherwise, you're going to trash your career. And you and I are not going to discuss this bullshit anymore. The next time we run into each other, we're going to talk about cars, or pussy, or football. The important things in life. *Capice?*"

Bellamy grimaced. "Okay. I know you're right."

"You bet I am. Now I should get back to work. Nothing goes better with stale egg salad than a nice juicy autopsy report. You get out of here. Go out and have a life. You can tell me what it's like."

Bellamy stood and watched Byrd walk away. *Have a life*, he thought. He supposed he'd had one, once, until his work had squeezed it out of existence. First he'd gradually stopped spending tine with any friends who weren't involved in law enforcement, and then Janice had divorced him, complaining that she never saw him anymore, and even when she did, his mind was still a million miles away.

He guessed the truly sad thing was that, deep down, he hadn't cared. His career had been too rewarding, and if he'd had to sacrifice friendships and even his marriage to keep it revving, that had been a price he was willing to pay. He'd never dreamed a day might come when he himself would feel forsaken, betrayed and abandoned by his colleagues.

He didn't *want* to stick around the building, yet he couldn't quite bring himself to leave. Perhaps it was because he had nowhere else to go. He took a slow, groaning elevator upstairs, then trudged on, moving warily past Hanson's corner office. He slipped into his own work space and quietly closed the door.

The air was stuffy. Evidently the air conditioning was getting ready to die again. Bellamy spent a moment gazing out the dirty window, hoping it would cheer him up a little. Generally speaking, the view was a depressing vista of huge, soot-stained towers, their bases scarred with graffiti and their upper stories crawling with indecipherable hieroglyphics and leering gargoyles. But at the end of North Boulevard he could just make out one end of the Old State Capitol, a quaint Gothic Revival castle with a gorgeous colored-glass skylight, and beyond that, a slice of the Mississippi, the water sparkling in the sunlight.

Sighing, he turned away and removed the top manila folder from the tall stack before him. Like the others in the heap, it was the file on an old, cold case that VICAP had never managed to close. Procedure mandated that someone periodically review such records, on the theory that he might suddenly deduce the solution like Sherlock Holmes. As far as Bellamy knew, no one had ever enjoyed this happy experience, nor did his superiors seriously expect that anybody ever would. That was why they allowed the reviews to pile up until someone needed some busywork, like an agent they no longer trusted to do anything important.

This particular record detailed VICAP's efforts to apprehend a serial killer of streetwalkers who'd terrorized Little Rock from 1986 to 1990. Bellamy made an honest effort to focus on the investigators' notes and the photos of the corpses and crime scenes. But he couldn't keep his mind off the Atheist, who was killing people *now*.

At last he decided, to hell with it. Hanson had ordered him to cut back to a forty-hour work week. That meant he was on his own time anyway. He set the file aside, switched on his computer, and logged on to the Internet.

He hadn't told Nolliver that he'd started reading the wildcat bulletin boards devoted to Wicca, crystal power, flying saucers, and a host of other crackpot subjects. The psychiatrist wouldn't have approved. He would have warned Bellamy that he was regressing into delusional thinking again.

But I'm not, the agent thought. *I* don't *believe in all this crap. But I've got to start looking for answers somewhere.*

After a moment's thought, he decided to begin with Grailnet, a board that attracted a more eclectic and peculiar mix of eccentrics than most of the others. Sliding and clicking the computer's mouse, he selected the proper address from his directory. Grailnet's opening screen, a cloaked, hooded figure beckoning mysteriously, appeared on his monitor.

Bellamy entered the first real-time conversation area—or Circle of Discourse, as Grailnet's menu called it. The screen displayed a benighted clearing, where shadowy figures with luminous eyes squatted around a pale green campfire. Lines of Gothic type, messages from other users, crawled in and out of existence beneath the illustration. "Alhazred" was raving about his pet theory that the fiction of H. P. Lovecraft was based on truth, while two other regulars ridiculed his every statement.

Bellamy thought that if the average user caught as much flak as Alhazred did, he'd flee the board forever. But the Lovecraft buff seemed to thrive on the abuse. Indeed, the FBI agent wondered if he *ever* went off-line.

In any case, Bellamy didn't want to talk to him. He'd already endured several of Alhazred's harangues about "slumbering Cthulhu," "the Lake of Hali," and all the rest of it, and if any of it had anything to do with what happened in East St. Louis, it would take a smarter man than he to make the connection. He moved on to the next Circle. The clearing became even darker, the figures subtly more misshapen. A couple seemed to have blood on their mouths and hands. At certain moments a demonic face took shape in the midst of the flames. As near as Bellamy could make out, Grailnet's progression of increasingly sinister visuals was intended to suggest that as a user explored the system, he was descending deeper and deeper into hell.

Two people had arrived before him. Bellamy knew one of them, "Astarte," whose great ambition in life was to become the "handmaiden" of some supernatural entity. He gathered that a vampire would be ideal, but any sort of phantom or uncanny beast would do. The agent imagined her as an obese, slovenly woman with a dozen cats, a bookshelf crammed with Anne Rice books and Harlequin romances, and no off-line social life whatsoever. "Vulture," the user with whom she was presently conversing, was a stranger to him.

I know they're out there, Astarte said. *They're all around us. I just have to figure out how to find them.*

They don't want to be found, Vulture replied.

They don't want to be found by the wrong people, Astarte said. *They don't want to hunted or exploited. They do want to be adored as the gods they are.*

You don't know that, Vulture said. *You don't know them. You think you do, from movies and stories and your own dreams, but they're more alien than you can possibly imagine.*

How do you know that? Astarte fired back. *Have you ever seen one?*

For a while there was no response. Bellamy guessed that Vulture had abandoned the conversation. He reached for the mouse to move on himself. Then another message appeared.

I've glimpsed things at a distance, Vulture said. *I can't be any more specific than that. Please, just believe that I know what I'm talking about. You wouldn't be the first human admirer to knock on a supernatural creature's door. Most of them wind up regretting it, even in relatively peaceful times, and the dark world hasn't been peaceful in a long while. And there are indications that it's going to get worse.*

Bellamy no longer got excited merely because someone on-line claimed to have firsthand information about the paranormal. Heck, cyberspace was swarming with people who claimed to be paranormal entities themselves. But vague as it was, Vulture's comment seemed to echo Waxman's fearful babbling. The agent quickly typed, *What kind of indications?* His keyboard clicked.

Hello, Frank, Vulture said. *I wondered if we were going to hear from you, or if you were just going to lurk in the background.*

Hi, Bellamy typed. *What kind of indications?*

To his irritation, the next message to appear was from Astarte. *If you really have seen supernatural creatures, tell me what kind, and where.*

I'm sorry, Vulture said. *There are certain facts I can only share with kindred spirits. People who already possess a certain amount of information. Otherwise I'd wind up luring defenseless people into danger.*

That's a crock, Astarte said.

Bellamy couldn't decide whether it was or not. Vulture was quite possibly striking a pose, pretending to knowledge he didn't possess. But his genuine reticence set him apart from other on-line charlatans the agent had encountered. They'd claimed they couldn't reveal their deepest, darkest occult secrets, but they'd given up any number of intriguing hints and lurid details. They'd understood they needed to say *something* specific in order to seem impressive.

If Vulture didn't *care* about looking impressive, maybe he was a different breed of cat. Even if he was a crank, perhaps he had inside information about some dangerous cult or coven. Bellamy wondered how he could get him to spill it.

Until now, the FBI man had avoided telling anyone on Grailnet who he was, or why he was interested in all their New Age mumbo jumbo. A lot of people were reluctant to talk to cops, and he didn't want somebody contacting the Bureau and reporting that one of its agents was spending hours on the boards, chatting about cattle mutilations and the Bermuda Triangle. But instinct told him it was time to take a risk. Frowning, he typed, *I understand more than you realize, Vulture. Do you know who Milo Waxman was? I was with him when he died.*

I don't know, Astarte said. To Bellamy, the white characters on the black rectangle at the base of the screen seemed to convey a plaintive whine. *Who was he?*

Once again, it took Vulture a moment to respond. *I thought Waxman died of a heart attack.*

There's more to it than that, Bellamy typed.

WHO WAS WAXMAN? Astarte demanded.

Who are you, Frank? Vulture asked.

Now it was Bellamy's turn to hesitate. *An investigator,* he answered after a moment. *And you?*

A student, Vulture said. *A watchdog sometimes. If you don't already know precisely what you're dealing with, walk away from it. Take a long vacation in another country.*

That's not an option, Bellamy typed.

It's RUDE to cut somebody out of a conversation, Astarte sulked. *You can both go to hell.*

Tell me about Waxman, Vulture said.

What's in it for me? Bellamy replied. *Will you share what you know?*

After another pause, Vulture said, *Not on-line. And not over the phone or through the mail, either. We'd have to meet.*

Bellamy tried to swallow away a sudden dryness in his mouth. *Where?*

Can you get to New Orleans?

Yes, Bellamy typed, feeling even more excited. Heck, he could drive there in a couple hours. Considering that Vulture could have been anywhere in the world, his proximity was a piece of luck. But more than that, it lent weight to the notion that the guy might actually know something about recent events in the Mississippi basin.

How will I recognize you? Vulture asked.

Bellamy described himself. *I'll wear an LSU cap,* he added.

Meet me in Jackson Square at noon on Wednesday, Vulture said. *Come alone or you won't see me.* His cartoon buzzard icon vanished from the corner of the screen, indicating he'd exited the Circle.

Bellamy did the same, wondering if he'd just taken the first step toward discovering what had happened to him, or established beyond any shadow of a doubt that he was every bit as crazy as everybody thought he was.

Eleven

Scowling, Montrose prowled the corridors of the Citadel, his new cloak swishing about his ankles. The cape was as full and black as a Grim Rider's outer garment was supposed to be, but it didn't have the Unlidded Eye affixed to it. Gayoso had promised that he'd instruct a seamstress or metalworker to fashion a proper badge for his guest, but so far, none had been forthcoming.

Happening upon a pyramidal stack of old, rusty paint cans, Montrose gave in to the impulse to kick them. His insubstantial foot couldn't shift them, making the result less than satisfying.

The Scot had studied the secrets of the Proctors as well as those of the Harbingers. If he wanted, he could project himself into the Skinlands and give the cans a proper kick. But it would hardly be an intelligent expenditure of his energies, particularly here, in what he was rapidly coming to regard as the lair of his enemies.

To hell with it. It wouldn't take *much* strength. The Shroud was even thinner here than it was in most Haunts. And more to the point, in his present humor, he didn't *care* about being prudent. He focused his power, his body throbbed, and a wraith in the distance vanished from view. He booted the cans and the stack flew apart with a satisfying clatter.

His frustration vented, he immediately began to feel sheepish for behaving so childishly. He relaxed his will and the spiritual magnetism of death instantly drew him back to his proper sphere. As he reentered the Underworld, he heard a pair of hands applauding behind him. Tiny bells chimed in time with the clapping.

Montrose turned. Gayoso's jester, whose name, he'd learned, was Valentine, stood behind him. Tonight his motley was red and green, with brass bells decorating the horns of his cap, the ragged cuffs of his gloves, and the upturned toes of his boots.

The Anacreon smiled ruefully. "You're right to mock me. That was an asinine display. When I was breathing, I rarely lost my self-control that way—"

"But now that you're a ghost, you can blame every tantrum on your mean old Shadow," the dwarf said, smirking. "Just like the rest of us. Why not, it's the perfect alibi. May a humble entertainer ask why you're so exasperated?"

Montrose hesitated. Considering that Valentine was one of Gayoso's underlings, he seemed a poor choice for a confidant. But evidently the Stygian was still feeling reckless, or too full of annoyance to contain himself, because he finally said, "I've just come from an interview with Mrs. Duquesne."

The jester nodded. "That's enough to ruin anybody's evening."

"She refused to give me any Legionnaires to fulfill my mission. Nathan Shellabarger and your master had already rejected the same request."

"None of that bunch is going to put himself in a position where he's vulnerable to the other two. So it's three strikes and you're out."

Montrose cocked his head. "I beg your pardon?"

"It's a reference to baseball. You know, the American national pastime. Ah, don't worry about it. The point is, you're out of luck. Except that the scuttlebutt around the Citadel is that you had written orders and a passel of soldiers when you left the Isle of Sorrows."

The Scot nodded. "The 'scuttlebutt' is correct."

"So why don't you just go back and get some more?"

"For one thing," said Montrose, sitting down on the grimy floor, "I daresay your governors don't want me telling a Deathlord they opted to defy his wishes. They wouldn't give me an escort, and it's dangerous to travel the Tempest alone. And even if I *did* make it home, what then? Do I go whining to the Smiling Lord with my tail between my legs? 'I'm sorry, milord, but I lost my Lantern of Truth, my ships, and my troops, and the impudent Hierarchs of Natchez refuse to heed my commands. Please, give me fresh credentials and another expedition so I can go out and try again.' I'd look pathetic. And you can rest assured that if my master ever begins to lose faith in me, I have an abundance of rivals ready to whisper slander in his ear and speed the process along." The swarthy, lantern-jawed face of Demetrius appeared before his inner eye.

Valentine chuckled. "Nice to know that the big shots in the Onyx Tower are just as kindly and honest as us little shots here on Earth. I guess you really are screwed."

Montrose scowled. "No, I'm not. There has to be a way. If I had just a *few* men—" He paused as an idea struck him.

"What is it?" Valentine asked.

Montrose jumped up. He almost dusted off the back of his cloak before he remembered that dirt from the other side of the Shroud couldn't stick to him. "How would you like to show me the sights?"

Valentine eyed him quizzically. "You mean nobody's showed you around?"

"Around the Citadel, yes. The entire Necropolis, no. I've seen how feebly your Anacreons hold the reins of power, and I'd guess there must be a quarter where the criminal element congregates. A section of Natchez which Hierarchs rarely enter, except in force."

"And that's where you want to go tonight."

"Yes. Are you game?"

Valentine grinned. "You know, I guess I am. It could be interesting."

"Can you find me a weapon?"

The jester frowned. "Hard to say. There's a shortage. Any grunt or quartermaster who loses one can be enslaved, so everyone keeps track of his gear pretty well. But if we take a look around—"

"Never mind," Montrose said. Now that he'd decided to act, he felt too eager to waste time snooping about the Citadel. "I'll take care of it." He set out for the front of the complex, and Valentine trotted along beside him.

When they slipped through the fort's front door, Montrose was pleased to see the same two sentries he'd met on his arrival. Evidently in no sunnier humor than before, the Legionnaire with the question-mark brand gave him a sneer.

"Good evening," said Montrose, smiling. "I need your rifle."

The soldier snorted. "What are you, crazy?"

"Some people have said so," Montrose said. "Even you, if memory serves. But I also truly am an Anacreon, as I believe you've been advised."

"I don't care if you're Charon risen from the Labyrinth. You're not *my* Anacreon, and nobody told me to obey y—"

Montrose kicked the other wraith in the stomach, then grabbed him by the collar of his buckskin shirt and slammed his head against the wall. The stunned sentry's knees began to buckle. The Stygian tore the AK-47 out of his hands and whirled to cover the spearman with the jack-o'-lantern grin, who was still trying to fumble his weapon into position for a thrust.

"Is there a problem?" Montrose asked.

The spearman swallowed. "No. No, sir."

"Good," the Stygian said. "Before my appointment to the Grim Riders, I was Fifth Legion myself. At heart, I still am. It would have saddened me if you'd turned out to be insubordinate, too. I'm also going to need your dagger."

The Black Hawk unclipped the Bowie knife from his belt and handed it over.

"Thank you," Montrose said. "Have a pleasant evening." He turned and sauntered toward the ring of human torches. Valentine followed.

"You know," said the dwarf as they started down the hill, "Winston—the jerk you just beat up—is going to run straight to Mrs. Duquesne."

"I don't care." Thinking that for the moment he might as well be as anonymous as possible, Montrose put on his glossy black ceramic mask. "The Smiling Lord put me in charge of these wretches. It's time I started acting like it. Besides, Mrs. Duquesne ought to thank me for disciplining the man. He needed it."

"Maybe," said Valentine, "but he wasn't the only one. We turn here." His bells jingling, he led his companion down an alley that reeked of rotting produce. A black cat, vastly more perceptive than the average Quick human, peered at them with gleaming golden eyes. Nihil cracks in the oil-stained asphalt hissed. "A lot of people have been in a nasty mood lately, inside the Citadel and in the rest of the Necropolis too. There've been a lot of fights, not the usual chickenshit but serious ones, the kind that don't end until somebody goes to the Void."

"That's interesting," Montrose said. For a moment he wondered if the phenomenon could have anything to do with the mysterious threat that Katrina had blathered on about, then pushed the witless notion out of his mind. "Do you have any idea why?"

"Nope," Valentine said, leading him around another corner. Montrose realized they were wending their way west, toward the river. The breeze carried the scent of the muddy water. "Maybe you can figure it out."

"It isn't my job to figure it out," Montrose said. Something whispered overhead. With reflexive caution, he looked up to see a bat fluttering after insects.

"But I've read some British history," said Valentine, leering, "and I know who you are. A hero."

Montrose grimaced. "You should have read through to the last chapter, where Argyll and his cronies strung me up."

"Okay, so you were a *tragic* hero."

"Rubbish," the Stygian said. "But if I was, the moral of my saga would seem to be that heroism doesn't pay. Only an ass places an ideal ahead of his own interests, or trusts his fellow man an inch farther than he has to."

"You're trusting me, a virtual stranger, to lead you through these dark streets to an unknown destination."

"That's true," Montrose said. "But since it was my idea to come, it's unlikely that you're guiding me into an ambush. I am curious, though, as to why you're helping me, when you know Gayoso wouldn't want you to."

"Reverence for the Deathlords?"

Montrose chuckled. "Somehow I find that hard to credit."

"Pretty smart on your part. Actually, I don't *like* Gayoso much. I don't like his idea of entertainment. A dwarf in cap and bells? I know he was born on another continent in another century, but give ma a break! Hell, most of my jokes aren't even funny. He just keeps me around because he thinks it's stylish for a ruler to have a retainer like me. Mainly he uses me for a gofer."

"You aren't a thrall, are you?" asked Montrose. Valentine shook his head. "If you don't want to be a clown, and Gayoso won't accept you in any other capacity, why do you stay? You could strike out on your own. Hire a Masquer to give you normal height, if that would please you."

"I've seen how you turn up your nose at the Citadel when you think nobody's looking. It seems like a dump to you, doesn't it? But the quarters Gayoso gave me are a lot more comfortable than any Haunt I could find anywhere else."

"Don't be so sure. The Hierarchy has any number of strongholds, and they all need clever, hardworking functionaries to keep them running. Perhaps you could find a comfortable berth elsewhere."

Valentine glowered up at him. "I thought you said you don't care about other people's problems."

Montrose shrugged. "I do appreciate it when someone tries to help me, and I hoped I could repay you with some advice. But of course your personal affairs are none of my business, and if my prying has offended you, I apologize."

"Let's just drop it," Valentine said. They walked on in silence until another turn brought another warren of Nihil-riddled derelict buildings into view. A wave of ancient rage, pain, and lust swept over Montrose. He closed his eyes and shuddered, exhilarated and nauseated at once. Beyond the Haunt murmured the black expanse of the river, with moonlight glistening on the ripples. Rafts, flatboats, and sailboats floated beside the ruined docks. From their generally archaic appearance, the Stygian surmised that they existed on his side of the Shroud.

"Natchez Under-the-Hill," Valentine said. "The meanest hellhole in the history of the Mississippi. The Quick shut it down a long, long time ago, but it's still going strong in the Shadowlands."

"I trust we can find a tavern, or the equivalent."

"Sure. If you were looking for an honest man, that would be tough, but a bar is no problem at all."

As they walked on, Montrose peered about, taking in the sights and sounds of the district. Behind an attic window, someone said, "Tell me where Lorenzo is, amigo. Just tell me and the pain will go away." A block farther on, the Hierarchs encountered a coffle of slaves, all shapechanged to resemble Marilyn Monroe, Sophia Loren, Mary Pickford, Clark Gable, Elvis Presley, or some other celebrity. The naked thralls trudged listlessly along, their eyes downcast and their ankle chains clinking. One of the hooded overseers suddenly jabbed Mary Pickford with a cattle prod, for no particular reason that Montrose could discern. For a moment, the Stygian felt a twinge of sympathy for the captives, but it faded almost before he noticed it.

Valentine took him all the way down to the docks. Now the water smelled foul, as if someone upriver had dumped something noxious in the current. Wavering yellow light and a jumble of voices spilled through the doorway of a tumble-down shack. Somebody with no pretensions to artistic talent had daubed a green skull-and-crossbones on the warped boards of the wall. The paint had run, as if to suggest that the bones were dripping putrescence.

"The Green Head," said Valentine. "I think I understand what you have in mind, and from one point of view, this is the place for it. But if you do go in, you'll be taking one hell of a risk."

"Why?" asked Montrose. A jovial shout and a smattering of applause sounded from inside the tavern. "Do you expect the place will turn out to be full of Heretics and Renegades?"

"No," Valentine replied. "They usually hang out in other dives. That's why I brought you to this one. Most of the guys in here don't give a rat's ass about politics or religion. But just because they don't sit around plotting the overthrow of the Deathlords, that doesn't mean they like Hierarchs. In their eyes, people like you are cops, pure and simple."

Montrose smiled. "I imagine I'll be all right. But you needn't come in if you'd rather not."

Valentine's mouth twisted. "Oh, don't worry about me. I've been inside before. They'd rather laugh at someone like me than destroy me."

"In that case, after you."

The interior of the shack was smoky and stuffy. The torches mounted on the walls burned with hot Skinlands flame. Probably a Spook or a Proctor had kindled them. Behind the bar stood a Sandman in a garish patchwork cloak, his eyes narrowed with concentration. Evidently he was maintaining the existence of the earthenware jug the wraiths before him were passing from hand to hand. Judging from their loud, slurred speech and the way they stumbled and swayed, the illusory corn liquor was quite potent. Another four ghosts, all masked, huddled whispering in a shadowy corner. One hulking man with a black handlebar mustache perched on a stool beside a large, ragged-edged Nihil in the middle of the floor, dangling a rope into the seething depths. But most of the crowd had formed a circle around an old Quick tramp in rags. The mortal reeked of sweat and urine. Tears and snot streaked his grimy, wizened face. His breath rasped in his throat, his heart pounded, and his aura flamed orange with fear. Every time he tried to edge out of the ring, the wraiths in his way would reach out and stroke his face, while others crooned, "Meat, meat, meat." Then the victim recoiled, even though it was apparent that he couldn't truly see, hear, or feel his tormentors.

As Montrose took a seat, he felt some of the other patrons looking at him, sizing him up. Though not unduly alarmed, he deemed it prudent to leave the AK-47 with its ebon soulfire crystals prominently displayed on the rickety table before him. He nodded at the old man in the circle. "Charming entertainment," he said dryly.

"Yeah," Valentine replied, "and they're breaking the Dictum Mortem, too. You should arrest them, milord Anacreon."

"That would be counterproductive," Montrose said. "I'm afraid the old fellow is on his own."

Yet the unpleasant spectacle nagged at him. Though he no longer felt any real solicitude for others, cruelty for its own sake, directed at a helpless, innocent victim, still disgusted him on a visceral level.

Besides, he had important business to attend to. He didn't want to sit idly in this wretched stew until the entertainment concluded. For all he knew, his fellow wraiths might keep baiting the tramp all night.

Abruptly he stood up.

"What are you going to do?" Valentine asked.

"What I came to do," Montrose replied. "You might watch my back if you feel so inclined." He pointed the assault rifle straight up at water-stained ceiling, then, on impulse, aimed it just over the heads of the wraiths in the circle instead. He fired a burst. Some ghosts dived to the floor, some cried out in shock, and others lurched around, fumbling for their weapons. The Shadowlands bullets disintegrated against the wall without doing any damage.

Montrose knew that when one wanted to persuade people of anything, it helped to display a bold eye, a firm jaw, and a confident smile. He doffed his mask and tossed it aside to clatter on the floor. "Good evening, ladies and gentlemen. I apologize if I startled anyone, but I wanted your attention."

"You've got it now," said the Sandman behind the bar. The phantasmal jug now lay shattered on the floor in a pool of clear, pungent liquor. Abruptly the wreckage vanished, along with all symptoms of the topers' intoxication. "And it may turn out that you didn't know when you were well off."

"I trust not." To the Stygian's right, cloth rustled. Pivoting, he spied a lanky wraith in a red leather domino easing a throwing knife from its sheath. When Montrose pointed the AK-47 at him, he quickly took his hand away from the hilt. "Allow me to introduce myself. I'm James Graham, in life Earl and Marquess of Montrose, currently Anacreon of the Order of the Unlidded Eye."

The crowd babbled and growled. "You keep getting yourself in deeper," the Sandman said. "We get a few Hierarchs in here, slumming, like your midget friend. Some of them even make it out of Under-the-Hill in one piece. But they have the good sense not to brag about kissing the Deathlords' asses."

"I understand that you aren't unduly fond of the government," Montrose said. "But how do you feel about Heretics? The Smiling Lord sent me to Natchez to make war on them. I'd like you to join me."

Some of his audience laughed. Others babbled in bewilderment. One woman shouted, "I'd rather *die* than join a stinking Legion!"

"I'm not asking you to," Montrose said. "I want you to sign on as free mercenaries. You'll serve on your own terms and quit whenever you like."

"In return for what?" demanded a bald man in dark glasses. Bandoliers crisscrossed his otherwise naked chest, and judging by the bulge in his tight gray jeans, a Masquer had enlarged his genitals to priapic proportions.

Montrose grinned. "I assumed that was obvious. Plunder, of course! After we subdue the Heretics, we'll take everything they have and sell them into slavery. Valentine told me that one or two of you are familiar with the basic modus operandi."

Several wraiths laughed. The bald man said, "Why do you need us? Why aren't you using Legionnaires?"

"That was my original intention," Montrose said, "but your illustrious local officials apparently can't spare me any troops. I've been advised that the desperadoes of Under-the-Hill are far more formidable than Hierarch soldiers anyway. I hope you deserve your reputation."

"You don't have a Lantern of Truth," said the Sandman. "How do we even know you really are a Grim Rider?"

"I suppose you'll have to take my word for it," Montrose replied. "And if that's a problem, consider this: As long as the venture turns a profit, what does it matter who I really am?"

A number of the onlookers were regarding him differently now. Their scowls and sneers had given way to more speculative expressions. The Scot didn't entirely know himself just how he'd swayed them, but he'd assumed going in that he had a reasonable chance of doing so. He'd discovered he was a natural leader three hundred and fifty years ago, when he'd held his ragtag army of unruly Highlanders together through sheer charisma.

"I'll tell you what matters," rumbled a gravely voice. Craning, Montrose saw that the speaker was the burly man, still dangling the coarse hemp rope into the Nihil.

He stood up and began to haul it in, hand over hand, neither his voice nor his movements betraying appreciable strain. "What matters is that there are *river men* here. *Real* men. What makes you think we'd follow *any* stranger, let alone a limp-wristed Stygian noble with dainty curls and a frilly velvet cape?"

The end of the line emerged from the Nihil, knotted to a heavy iron hook transfixing the torso of a semi-conscious, feebly writhing thrall. Montrose gathered that the wraith with the black mustache had been fishing for Spectres, a hazardous sport to say the least, though safer for the angler than the bait.

"You should join me because we'll win," said the Anacreon. "I know how to command an army."

The other wraith tossed the slave and hook to the floor. "Well, nobody 'commands' me. Nobody but a better man. And there aren't any better men than *Mike Fink!*" He paused dramatically, as if expecting Montrose to cower at his name.

"I'm afraid I never heard of you," the Stygian said.

Fink quivered. His dark eyes glared, while his hulking body seemed to swell like a frog's. "Well, let me educate you," he said, his voice beginning softly but building in a relentless crescendo. "My mother was a Malfean and my father was the Tempest! I can outfight, out-brag, out-sail, and out-hoodoo any spirit on the river! I eat Nephandi for breakfast, wolfmen for lunch, and bloodsuckers for supper, all with Oblivion ice-cream for dessert! I'm faster than lightning, meaner than a gator, and crazier than the Laughing Lady! I pop little pissants like you like pimples!"

To Montrose, Fink's outburst seemed more humorous than threatening, his clenched fists and outthrust jaw notwithstanding. But the Scot could tell that the audience had a different reaction. They were amused, but wary as well. They wouldn't have wanted the big man to think they were laughing *at* him. Evidently, his buffoonery notwithstanding, they held him in considerable respect.

And because they did, they'd resumed glowering and sneering at the Stygian, reasoning that if the local strongman scorned him, he couldn't be worth heeding after all. Montrose realized that if he still wanted to recruit them, there was only one way to go about it.

"What a colorful oration," he drawled, becoming the languid, condescending aristocrat Fink had accused him of being. "But let's get down to cases. A moment ago, you said that you would follow a better man. Meaning a man who can humble you in battle, I assume."

Valentine tugged urgently on his cloak, presumably to warn him he was headed for disaster.

Fink grinned. "Oh, sure, Anacreon. We'd *all* follow a superman like that."

All? That was even better than Montrose had dared to hope for. He lifted an eyebrow. "You speak for the entire room, do you?"

Fink turned, regarding his fellow outlaws. "Anybody here think he's too good to fight in the same gang with me?' Apparently no one did. Smiling crookedly, the big man pivoted back toward Montrose. "But here's the thing, Lord Jimbo. If I'm going to bet, you have to put up something, too."

Valentine yanked on Montrose's cloak even more frantically than before. The Stygian tugged it out of the small man's grip. "What did you have in mind? I don't have any cash on my person. But this is a valuable rifle, and as you pointed out, my cape is rather nice as well."

Fink made a spitting sound. Lacking bodily fluids, it was as close as the Restless could come to actual expectoration. "That's not good enough. You want a limited amount of service from all of us? Well, that equals out to an *un*limited amount of service from you. You lose, and you become my slave."

Inwardly, Montrose winced, even though it was precisely the proposal he'd been expecting. "Done. How shall we duel? Guns?" Unless Fink had a modern weapon stashed away somewhere out of view, the Stygian's assault rifle would give him a sizable advantage.

Fink grinned. "I don't think so."

"Blades, then." The Scot was more adept with a rapier or saber than a knife, but he was still confident that his swordsmanship would stand him in good stead.

Fink's leer stretched even wider. "Uh-uh. As the challenged party, I get to pick, and I say no weapons at all. Just muscles, and whatever Arcanoi either of us knows."

"Fine," Montrose said, setting the rifle back on the table. He pulled off his cape, dropped it over the back of a chair, and unclipped the scabbard from his belt. Fink stripped off his denim vest and then his homespun shirt. His physique looked even more powerful without them. Meanwhile, the other wraiths moved back, clearing a space for the fight, and the old Quick tramp finally crept unnoticed out the door.

"Run for it," Valentine whispered.

"I think not," Montrose replied. "Although I must say, if this Fink character is so dangerous, you might have mentioned it when we first entered the building."

"I didn't know he was going to take a dislike to you. *Nobody* knows what he'll do until he does it. He's crazy."

"What Arcanos has he mastered?"

"I don't know. I don't come here all *that* often. I've only seen him fight once, and that time, he only needed his hands to tear the other man apart."

Montrose smiled. "You're doing wonders for my confidence. Look after my things. Otherwise someone is likely to walk off with them."

The Stygian stepped out into the clear area. Crouching, his hands poised to grapple, Fink grinned. "Do you like fishing, Anacreon?" he asked. "I've decided to let you take Beauregard's place on the hook."

"Really," Montrose said. Fists raised, he circled, looking for an opening. "And here I thought you wanted me for your catamite. You seem like the type." He lifted his foot for a kick and the world turned red, as if he were viewing it through a pane of scarlet glass.

Startled, he hesitated. Fink bellowed and rushed him. Montrose dodged and just barely managed to avoid the larger man's clutching hands. Fink blundered past, and the room returned to its former colors.

The Scot thought he understood how Fink had affected his vision. The outlaw was a Haunter, a wraith who knew how to disrupt someone else's mind or even reality itself with a blast of primal chaos. Montrose decided it was high time he used one of his own powers. Cool shadow flowed across his skin. By the time Fink lurched back around to face him, he was invisible.

Unfortunately, he'd reckoned without the spectators, who'd watched him conjure the veil. "He's right in front of you!" shouted the Sandman. "Kill him!"

Montrose started to sidestep. Once he changed position, his adversary's cronies would no longer be able to give him away. But before he could move, his thoughts shattered into confusion. Where was he? Who were these people, and what was going on?

A powerfully built man with a black mustache lunged at him, slammed into him, knocking him to the floor, then dove on top of him. The attacker fumbled at him as if he were trying for a choke hold but having difficulty locating his neck.

The shock of being assaulted jolted Montrose's thoughts back into partial focus. He remembered he was fighting someone named Fink, and that the larger man was having difficulty grappling with him because he'd cloaked himself in shadow. But the Harbinger trick could only buy him a few seconds.

Montrose was certain he couldn't out-wrestle Fink. He had to break away before the stronger man got an unbreakable grip on him. Trapped beneath Fink's weight, he punched and thrashed as best he could, but couldn't buck him off.

Another wave of confusion swept through the Stygian's mind. Struggling to resist it, he called on his Harbinger abilities again. For an instant, nothing happened, and then he floated into the air. He'd hoped Fink would tumble off him, but the Haunter kept his grip. The audience gasped and babbled.

Now in danger of falling, Fink stopped trying for a stranglehold. Instead he wrapped his arms and legs around his opponent and started biting, plunging his teeth into Montrose's shoulder. The pain was excruciating.

Montrose rolled in midair, placing Fink beneath him, and then hurled them both at the floor. The impact hurt, particularly the way it jerked the teeth buried in his flesh. But presumably it had hurt the Haunter worse, considering that Montrose was in effect the hammer and Fink the nail.

He raised the big man up and smashed him down again. Fink's grip loosened. Simultaneously levitating and shoving the other wraith away with all his strength, Montrose broke free altogether. The Scot rocketed upward, just managing to stop before he collided with the ceiling. Meanwhile, Fink struggled to his feet.

Aching and weary, Montrose desperately craved a moment's rest. But he knew he mustn't give Fink the opportunity to recover from the pounding he'd just received. Flying around the big man like an invisible hornet, he lashed out with one kick after another, snapping the Shadowlander's head back and forth. The crowd couldn't tell precisely what was happening, but it was obvious that Fink was taking a lot of punishment. Some of the spectators groaned and winced in sympathy. Others smirked.

Another kick dumped Fink onto his back. With his flattened nose, torn lips, shattered teeth, and the raw, shiny patches on his skin—lacking blood, the Restless neither bled nor bruised—he looked incapacitated. Montrose floated back a pace and cocked his leg to administer the *coup de grâce*. Then Fink bellowed and brandished his fist.

Bolts of crackling radiance blazed across the room, turning some of the onlookers into vibrating, charring statues and flinging others off their feet. One jagged shaft of lightning blasted through Montrose's chest. He blacked out, and woke up sprawled on the floor. His ears rang, and the left side of his body was numb.

He looked around. A few tendrils of electricity still danced sizzling about the tavern, and Fink was still on his back. Apparently, Montrose had only been unconscious for a moment. He struggled to his feet and hobbled toward his opponent.

As Fink scrambled up, his body shrank, and his hair changed from black to honey-blond. In the blink of an eye, he'd become Louise.

Was it really Montrose's lost, treacherous love staring at him with terror in her eyes? He didn't know, but it didn't matter. He hated her even more than he presently hated Fink, and her image merely served to energize him with a fresh burst of rage. He blocked the roundhouse punch she threw at him—an extraordinarily powerful blow, a part of him noticed, for such a slender woman—and slammed his fist into the point of her jaw.

Louise reeled backward. By the time she hit the floor, she was Fink again. As Montrose studied the outlaw, making sure he truly was unconscious, the residual haze of bewilderment evaporated from his mind.

But his anger didn't. Fink had both sought to enslave him and caused him a considerable amount of pain, and he wanted to keep hurting the big man in return. He could stamp his body to jelly. Pick him apart with the darksteel Bowie knife. Ram the iron hook through *his* body and lower *him* into the Tempest—

No! Montrose thought. What was the matter with him? He wanted to *use* Fink, not alienate his admirers by torturing him. It was his Shadow, roused by the pain of his wounds and the fury of battle, that was filling his head with these vicious fantasies. Closing his eyes, he drew a long breath, trying to calm himself. After a moment, his lust for violence faded.

Montrose regarded the spectators, who were silently gaping at him. "So," he said. "Are you with me or not?"

"I am," said the wraith with the bandoliers. "I always said that if we all threw in together, we could own this burg."

"Me too," said someone else. The next moment they were all pushing forward to shake Montrose's hand.

When he got a chance, he turned to Valentine. "I won't be accompanying you back to the Citadel," he said. "Now that I have the resources I need, I have no intention of giving Gayoso the opportunity to stop me from putting them to use. Tell him he'll see me by and by."

Twelve

Whenever he climbed the spiral staircase to the Pinnacle of Lamentations, Howard Potter felt grateful that the Restless were virtually immune to physical fatigue. Of course, he could have flown to the top of the tower and saved himself considerable time, but to do so would have violated tradition. And so he trod slowly, striving for stately dignity, his plate armor clinking, the butt of his ceremonial halberd thumping on the basalt steps, and the train of his mantle whispering along behind him.

Occasionally a narrow window afforded him a view of the landscape outside. Like every other eye in the infinite storm of the Tempest, Stygia was a realm of eternal night, dimly lit by barrow-flame torches, Charon's lantern shining atop its obelisk, and the random flickering in the mass of thunderheads that covered the Isle of Sorrows like a dome. The metropolis of the dead was a sort of pyramid, with the Onyx Tower—actually a crazy-quilt of palaces, ramparts, reflecting pools, and faux gardens surrounding a huge central keep—at the top. Beneath the domain of the aristocrats, level after level of chambers and hallways descended to the forbidden labyrinth of caverns and crypts buried deep beneath the surface. Rumor whispered that the latter connected to the Labyrinth itself, though Potter had never believed it. The Emperor had been far too sly to link his capital to the heart of Oblivion.

On one side of the city rippled the waters of the Weeping Bay, where much of the Stygian fleet, a hodgepodge of ships from many cultures and eras, floated at anchor. Had Potter been closer to the shore, he might have seen anguished faces forming and dissolving in the waves, or heard faint, whimpering cries arising from the depths. By Charon's decree, the entire Sea of Souls was literally a liquid mass of imprisoned spirits designed to hold Oblivion at bay. Beyond it rose the seawall—another bulwark against Spectres, Maelstroms, and the terrible power they embodied—a mammoth construction of iron, steel, and less refined soul stuff. Here, too, an observer could discern the shapes of human faces and bodies protruding from the surface, although, unlike the ones in the water, these were motionless and silent. One could at least try to believe that the imprisoned thralls weren't suffering.

Mighty bridges extended from the landward side of the Isle, linking it to the sprawl of tenements, warehouses, factories, rail yards, and fortifications on the mainland. In the last eighty years, fed by an exponentially increasing mortal birthrate and the harvest of two World Wars, the city had finally outgrown its original bounds, necessitating expansion into the Iron Hills.

At last Potter reached the flat, circular roof of the Pinnacle to find that all of his fellow Deathlords had arrived before him. Masked and clad in full regalia, each stood on his appointed pedestal near their departed master's empty throne.

They looked so powerful and enigmatic, so *totemic*, that Potter had to repress a shiver of awe. He firmly reminded himself that he was the Smiling Lord. These others were his peers, not some sort of deities. "Forgive me if I'm late," he said, "but at least I arrived before the prisoner." To his surprise, he realized he didn't recall just whom they had assembled to judge. It must be either a traitor of the highest rank or a rebel of the greatest importance to merit the attention of all seven members of the council.

He headed for his own position. The Quiet Lord stepped in front of him, barring his path. Potter's colleague, traditionally the patron of wraiths who'd died of despair, wore a murky red robe dyed with the blood of suicides. He carried an empty sack—from which Potter had on occasion seen him extract a diversity of bizarre and lethal objects—and his silver mask had been cast in the form of a face without a mouth. Because Charon had taken a piece from each of his lieutenants' masks to forge his own, it had a triangular hole in the left cheek.

The Quiet Lord pressed his index finger to his invisible mouth. It looked as if he were commanding silence, but Potter knew better. The gesture helped the other Deathlord focus his power.

Potter hesitated. Was the Quiet Lord *threatening* him, here, in open council? Surely not, though it seemed nearly as unlikely that he could be making a joke. Puzzled, but not *too* alarmed, he began to edge around him.

For once eschewing her affected tremulous shuffle, the Ashen Lady moved to bar his path, her gnarled cane raised like a sword. Shadows slithered up and down the prop like serpents. Her gray robes hung loosely on her stooped, shrunken frame, and wisps of fine white hair escaped from the edges of her mask, the wrinkled, sagging, carved-wood countenance of an ancient crone, with one corner broken off to reveal the smooth, firm jaw beneath. Her flesh emitted the stale smell of senility.

Potter stared at her, trying to read her intent from her pale gray eyes. He couldn't. Cloth flapped, and, startled, he pivoted in the direction of the sound. The other four Deathlords had descended from their low daises as well, and were moving to surround him.

"What's the meaning of this?" Potter demanded. He tried to use his haughtiest tone, but his voice quavered.

"You have transgressed," said the Emerald Lord, turning his crimson dice over and over in his white-gloved hand. Somewhere above the tower, purple lightning flared, glinting on his jade crown of thorns, his verdigris-encrusted, brazen mask—an expressionless, androgynous face with its eyes closed—and the emerald-studded wheel-of-fortune amulet hanging on his breast. "You must be judged."

"What do you mean?" Potter said. "What are you accusing me of?"

The Ashen Lady tapped her mask with her withered, liver-spotted forefinger.

For a second, Potter had no idea what she was trying to convey. Then he realized he could feel a cool breeze caressing his face, and that there were no steel rings sharply defining the edges of his vision. Somehow he'd come to council without his visor!

He pressed his hands to his features, concealing them. Peering out between his fingers, he said, "Forgive me! It was an accident!"

"Perish," said the Emerald Lord. "Go to the Final Death."

The six Deathlords brandished their symbols of office, blasting Potter with bolts of arcane power. His halberd and armor shattered. Convulsed with agony, his substance shriveling, he reeled off the edge of the tower and plummeted toward the spires and rooftops below.

And then he emitted a strangled cry and jolted half out of his chair.

He was sitting alone in his scrying chamber with a clay figurine, a nude woman with fleshy thighs, stubby arms, and two smiling faces adorning her head, resting on the ornately carved teak stand before him. The statuette was an artifact, a magical object which, destroyed in the Skinlands, had begun a second existence in the Underworld. When Potter opened himself to its power, it granted him visions, often containing useful intelligence about the enemies of the state.

This time, however, it had made him an *actor* in the vision, subjecting him to an experience much like a mortal nightmare. Even now, grasping what had happened, he was still shaking. He grabbed his mask, the leering steel countenance of a savage warrior, pressed it to his face, and invoked its persona.

As always, Charon's magic took effect at once. A new parade of images flashed through Potter's head. He was Cain, striking down Abel. He was a Roman retiarius thrusting his trident into another gladiator's belly on the hot sands of the Flavian Amphitheater. An airman dropping fire bombs on Dresden. A highwayman on a moonlit road, shooting a coachman who'd rashly made a grab for his own flintlock pistol. A teenage mother, her blood aflame with crack, pounding and pounding on her baby until the tiny creature finally stopped crying.

He was War and he was Murder, the rightful lord of every soul who perished at the hands of another. Ecstatic, his nose and mouth tingling with the coppery scent of gore, he rose, took up his halberd, and began to perform a kata, turning and striking with impeccable grace and lethal precision.

With the final thrust and bellowed *kiai*, his exhilaration waned a bit. He remembered Howard Potter, the human spirit sheathed inside the ferocious archangel he'd just become. And despite the ecstasy that always overwhelmed him when he reaffirmed his mastery of his powers, he still wasn't altogether happy.

Is this what it takes for me to feel secure? he wondered. *Have I become so neurotic that I can* never *unmask, even when I'm alone?*

No. Surely not. He'd simply become upset because the vision had been inherently disturbing. Instead of wasting time on morbid introspection, he should try to figure out what the mystical dream had signified.

Unfortunately, as he recognized immediately, that train of thought led to speculations that were equally disturbing.

He realized that he no longer wished to be alone. He wanted the company of one of the handful of trusted retainers he'd occasionally permitted to glimpse the human being hidden behind his godlike facade. Montrose—

He grimaced, remembering that the Cavalier wasn't available. He'd sent him off to slaughter Heretics. Demetrius, then. He took hold of the golden bellpull and rang for a thrall.

THIRTEEN

The cramped office reeked of cigarette smoke. An overflowing ashtray sat on the desk, and a yellowish film clung to the windows. As Nolliver took a seat, he wished again that he could have handled the current situation on the phone. He *never* enjoyed meeting Dunn face to face, and when he had potentially troublesome news to report, he liked it even less.

Unfortunately, he'd become leery of conferring with the SAD agent in any other fashion. Dunn *claimed* that no one had tapped their phones, but it was quite possible that he simply didn't know. Of course, it was also possible that someone had bugged the office; but somehow, that seemed less likely, and in any case, Nolliver knew the other man would dismiss any suggestion that they needed to talk outside the building.

"You look like crap," Dunn said. "Have a drink if you need one."

Startled, the psychiatrist blinked. "Excuse me?"

"Have a drink," Dunn repeated. "I can see you aren't just stashing booze in your desk anymore. You have a flask in your coat."

"How do you know that?" Nolliver asked. God, if Dunn had noticed, then who else—

The shaggy-headed agent grinned. "Don't panic, Doc. I'm *amazingly* observant, even for a Fed. Nobody else would be able to tell. But I hope you aren't getting careless. You don't *want* to get caught, do you?"

"No, of course not," Nolliver said, feeling both defensive and vaguely ashamed. He removed the silver flask from his pocket, unscrewed the cap, and took a swallow. The whiskey kindled a warm glow in the pit of his stomach.

"Feel better?" asked Dunn. Nolliver nodded. "Then tell me what's up."

"Bellamy phoned this morning and asked Hanson for the rest of the week off. Hanson okayed it without consulting me. What concerns me is that Frank never *told* me he wanted to take a break. In fact, he seemed grimly determined to hang on here, do his job, and convince everybody that he's still competent. Of course, people do impulsively change their minds. For that matter, they catch the flu. This is probably nothing. But you said I should tell you if there was even the slightest indication that he might be inclined to make any kind of waves."

"As his kindly physician," Dunn asked, "did you call him to *see* if he's home in bed with the crud?"

"Yes," Nolliver said. "He didn't answer. But that doesn't necessarily mean anything, either."

Dunn stood up. "Let's pay a visit to his office."

"You mean, to search it?"

"No," said Dunn, "I thought we'd redecorate it. Of course, to search it."

"Do you think that's wise? What are the odds that he left something significant lying around in there? And what if someone notices us snooping?"

"Then we'll just have to kill them," answered Dunn. He looked into Nolliver's face, then grimaced, rolling his eyes. "It's a *joke*, Doc. My god, will you lighten up? You said yourself, probably nothing's wrong. But on the other hand, I at least have to go through the motions of keeping tabs on Bellamy. If anybody asks what we're doing, we'll make up a story, that's all. Now pop a Certs and let's get to it."

Nolliver could see there was no way to talk him out of it. By the time they reached the corridor outside Bellamy's office, his underarms were clammy with sweat. But no one paid them the least attention. Dunn turned the brass doorknob. It rotated slightly, then stopped.

"Locked," Nolliver whispered.

"No, it isn't," Dunn replied. He twisted it again, and this time the door swung open. Bewildered, Nolliver scrambled inside, and the SAD agent stepped in after him.

Dunn surveyed the room, a drab space decorated with a few mementos of Bellamy's career in law enforcement, but only one, a baseball covered with signatures, that reflected any extracurricular interests. "How come everybody has a bigger office than mine?" asked Dunn. "I know, our pal Bellamy has a great arrest and conviction record, but *Earl Maxwell* has a bigger office than mine, and he couldn't catch a cold."

Nolliver took a tentative step toward the beige metal file cabinet in the corner. "I could look in here."

"Just stand back," said Dunn. "Tossing a room is *my* area. If I find something you ought to look at, I'll let you know."

The SAD agent sat down behind the desk with its Rolodex, phone, PC, ceramic coffee mug, and imposing stack of manila folders. He picked up one of the files from the considerably smaller pile in the Out basket, held it near his face, and inhaled deeply. "Bellamy hated processing these," he said. "It bored and depressed him."

"How do you know that?" Nolliver asked.

"Call it instinct," said Dunn. Swiveling the chair, he picked up the phone, placed it to his ear, and set it back in the cradle. "He hasn't been burning up the wires with any exciting conversations lately, either. We should give him the number of a good 900 line." He turned again, to face the computer. Suddenly he frowned and bent forward over the gray plastic keyboard, his nostrils dilating, reminding Nolliver of a hound taking a scent.

"Is something the matter?" Nolliver asked.

"He *was* excited when he was working here," Dunn replied, straightening up. He switched on the computer, which came to life with a crackle and a tinny fanfare. "Let's see if we can find out why."

"You might need a password," the psychiatrist said.

"I told you, I'm good at getting into things."

Dunn spent the next few minutes reviewing the contents of Bellamy's hard drive. Finally he turned in the swivel chair. "There's nothing here. Maybe he's got it on a printout or a floppy." He rummaged through the desk drawers, then rose and did the same thing with the file cabinet. "No luck."

"If he did have some kind of significant information, maybe he took it home with him."

"You could be right," said Dunn, sitting back down at the desk. "On the other hand, this thing has a modem. Bellamy didn't store any funky numbers in his directory, but it's still possible that he was getting into mischief on-line." The agent picked up the phone, punched 9 for an outside line, and dialed a long distance number.

For a moment Nolliver could just hear the ringing on the other end of the line. Then Dunn said, "Pyramid." He paused. "No, it's Madonna, calling to ask if you like my new CD. Sure it's me. Is Chester there? I need a house call at 504/621-1127." The unfamiliar number puzzled the psychiatrist for a moment, and then he realized that it must be the computer's phone line. "Now would be better. There's an outside chance my problem is important. And I have company, so tell Chester to cool it with the fireworks. Right. Thanks, buddy." The agent hung up.

"Who were you talking to?" Nolliver asked.

"SAD," Dunn answered. "Who else? You and I need a hacker, and fortunately, the Department has one of the best."

Lines of text ran across Bellamy's monitor. Dunn typed a response. A few seconds later, multiple columns of words and numbers appeared.

"These are the sites Bellamy logged on to over the past week, and the dates and times," said Dunn, scanning them. "Shit."

Nolliver tensed. "What's the matter?"

"Most of these are bulletin boards for people who are into the paranormal." He gave Dunn a sour stare. "Am I confused here, Doc? Weren't you supposed to do everything in your shrinkly power to discourage Bellamy from taking any further interest in stuff like this?"

"I did my best! I swear it!"

Dunn sighed. "Yeah, I'm sure you did, and the odds are, he still doesn't pose any real problem, so calm down." He resumed typing. The keys clicked. "His last visit was to a board called Grailnet, late yesterday afternoon. I'm asking Chester to dig out what he did while he was there."

"He can do that?"

"Probably. When it comes to cyber-crap, he can do almost anything. But it may take him a couple minutes." Dunn leaned back in his chair and stretched, then slumped down so comfortably that he looked as if he might doze off. Reluctant to make the SAD agent think him any weaker or more ineffectual than he did already, Nolliver fought the impulse to take yet another drink.

At last new lines of text paraded across the screen. After skimming them, Dunn said, "Jumping Jesus on a pogo stick."

"What's wrong?" Nolliver asked.

"Bellamy is going to New Orleans to compare notes with somebody else who's interested in Waxman's death."

"Who?"

"Somebody who called himself Vulture. That's all we know. You don't have to give your real name to anybody to use Grailnet, and lots of people don't. Your patient just went by Frank. Very creative, right?"

"Whoever Vulture is," said Nolliver, "we don't know that he actually has anything to tell Bellamy. It seems more likely that he's just a crackpot."

"I know that," said Dunn. He removed his tobacco and papers from the inner pocket of his jacket and began to roll a cigarette. "But unfortunately, we can't count on it, just like we obviously can't trust Bellamy to keep his nose out of SAD business. Damn. I really thought that, working together, you and I could get the poor bastard out of trouble. Now I have to get tough."

Nolliver swallowed. "What are you saying?"

"That Bellamy and his new friend will have to drop out of sight for a while." He struck a match with his thumbnail and lit his cigarette. "Don't you worry about it. Disappearances are my area, too."

"You're going to kill them, aren't you?"

Bellamy's eyes widened with every appearance of shock. "No, of course not!"

"I don't believe you!" Nolliver said, appalled at his own sudden burst of audacity. "And I'm not going to be a party to it. Covering up the truth is one thing. Murder is different. You can't expect me to go along with it when I don't even really know what any of this is all about!"

"I know you have a problem with the idea of being implicated in anybody else's death," said Dunn, staring him in the eye. "I understand why it's hard to trust me. But even if you've decided you don't care about losing your job, your profession, or going to prison, I guarantee you, you still can't afford to give me any crap."

Nolliver felt his momentary defiance crumbling. "Why not?" he stammered.

Dunn smiled. "Because if you do, you might find yourself looking at the same sight that stopped Waxman's ticker."

FOURTEEN

Ensconced on a sunlit bench, a paper cup of café au lait warming his hand and a half-devoured oyster po-boy resting in his lap, Bellamy twisted this way and that, peering about. He supposed he'd looked like a rubber-necking tourist, drinking in the sights of Jackson Square. The bronze equestrian statue of Andrew Jackson. The Greek Revival portico of St. Louis Cathedral. The sidewalk artists' paintings and sketches, hanging on the wrought-iron fence. And the jugglers, magicians, white-faced mimes, and musicians who'd appeared to entertain the lunch crowd. A banjo player a few feet away was filling the air with a plangent bluegrass tune.

Actually, of course, Bellamy was trying to spot Vulture, most likely an exercise in futility, considering that he had no idea what the other man looked like. But he couldn't help making the attempt.

He was well aware that Vulture might not show. The guy might have been pulling his leg. Even if he did keep the rendezvous, there was every chance that he'd turn out to be a faker or a crank.

But so what? Bellamy thought, suddenly feeling, at least for a moment, relaxed and free from care. Even if Vulture himself proved to be a waste of time, a trip to New Orleans sure beat reviewing inactive files in Baton Rouge. When he was younger, he'd spent a lot of weekends and holidays in this wonderful place, but gradually he'd gotten so busy that such excursions no longer seemed practical.

He crunched down another succulent bite of his sandwich. La Madeleine's take-out was as good as he remembered. Then he felt eyes peering at him.

He turned his head, to see the same motley array of pedestrians who'd been drifting past all along. No one seemed to have been staring at him unless, perhaps, it had been a pale, long-legged girl dressed in ragged jeans and a leather jacket. She was eighteen or nineteen at the oldest, and might have looked pretty had it not been for her punkish, magenta-striped haircut, the steel rings in her right eyebrow, left nostril, and lower lip, her black lipstick, and her sullen sneer. If she *had* been looking him over, she seemed to have lost interest. She was turning away in the banjo player's direction.

Behind her, a plump, flushed little man in a sweat-stained powder-blue sports coat, a narrow-brimmed straw hat tilted far back on his head, and a wide, bright red tie came bustling through the crowd. He grinned and mouthed the name "Frank." Bellamy nodded. The chubby man hurried over and plopped down on the bench. Up close, he smelled rather pungently of Old Spice.

"Obviously, I'm Vulture," he said, wiping his hand on his slacks and then extending it. "I'm delighted you could make it."

Bellamy shook hands with him. "Nice to meet you. Do I have to keep calling you Vulture in real life?"

Vulture smiled. "Ah, that is the question, isn't it? One we merely postponed confronting when we'd decided to meet face to face. Dare we trust one another? Does either of us have enough information to offer to make it worth the other one's while?"

"I guess one of us has to take the plunge first," Bellamy said, "and just hope the other will reciprocate." Inwardly, he resolved that if he spilled his guts and then Vulture tried to walk away without doing the same, he'd lean on him hard. "My full name is Frank Bellamy. I'm an FBI agent."

Vulture cocked his head. "From Special Affairs?"

"No," Bellamy said, mildly impressed that his companion had even heard of SAD, "VICAP. Violent Criminals Apprehension Program. I work out of the district office in Baton Rouge, so as you might guess, until recently I was trying to catch the Atheist."

"You aren't now?"

"Not officially." Once again, Bellamy felt the weight of an onlooker's scrutiny. He looked casually around, but still didn't catch anyone staring. The sensation was beginning to remind him unpleasantly of his experience with Waxman, but he supposed it was just his imagination. Even if something supernatural *had* occurred that night, it was preposterous to imagine it happening again in the middle of a crowd on a bright spring day. Besides, nobody had known that he was coming here, and never mind that that was what he'd said the last time.

As succinctly as possible, he told Vulture about his encounter with Waxman. Usually, doing so made him feel like an idiot, but this time, the other man's expression of grave interest somewhat alleviated his embarrassment.

When he finished, Vulture said, "And your friend from SAD didn't take anything in your story seriously?"

"No," Bellamy said.

Vulture shook his head. "Extraordinary. They must be even more ignorant than we supposed."

"'We'?"

Vulture smiled. "Ah, yes. It's my turn to confide in you, isn't it? Either that or terminate the conversation, which is what some of my colleagues would recommend." Bellamy tensed. "After all, your story isn't all that illuminating. But it *is* information, and I *am* an activist in my small way. I believe that when it's feasible, somebody should stop the atrocities, and perhaps if we combine my esoteric knowledge with your police powers, we can. My name is Roscoe Jefferson Keene—R. J. to my friends—and I belong to an organization called the Arcanum."

"What kind of organization is it?" Bellamy asked.

"A lodge," said Keene. "A one hundred year-old brotherhood of scholars united to study the occult. Sort of a civilian counterpart to your Agent Dunn's organization, except that where SAD presumably exists to defend America from paranormal menaces, the Arcanum supposedly exists to further the cause of pure research."

"You say, 'supposedly.'"

"Many members pursue other agendas. We 'Templars.' for example, aspire to protect mankind from supernatural predators." He smiled wryly. "It could be argued that the vast majority of paranormal creatures fall into that category, so we have our work cut out for us."

Yet again, Bellamy's skin crawled with the near certainty that he was being watched. The fine hairs on the back of his neck stood on end. Unable to ignore his intuition any longer, he asked, "Do you mind if we walk as we talk? It'll help settle my lunch."

"By all means," said Keene. Grunting, he stood up.

The two men began to stroll around the square. Bellamy kept stopping and changing direction, seemingly to gawk at the shop windows, or to take a better look at a painting or a performer. In reality, he was putting his hunch to the test. If someone was following them, that person would stop and start and pivot with them, unless he was adept at the craft of shadowing others.

"What do you know about Weiss and Waxman?" Bellamy asked.

"That for all their greed and chicanery, they actually did cast out devils on occasion."

Bellamy paused to watch a prestidigitator in a red silk top hat pluck a white paper rose from the air. "That's not what SAD thinks."

"SAD also thinks you're insane, do they not? Do you share their opinion on that point?"

"Only when I'm having a bad moment," Bellamy said, pretending to inspect a painting of a horse-drawn carriage on a benighted street. "Were Weiss and Waxman members of the Arcanum?"

Keene snorted. "Lord, no! Weiss had a rather narrow perspective, metaphysically speaking. He would have regarded us as practitioners of black magic, or pawns of Lucifer at the very least."

By now, Bellamy was all but certain that someone *was* tailing them. He *felt* a person behind him, that other's movements mirroring his own, as if the two of them were dancing. It would be awkward to accost the shadow in the middle of a crowd, but perhaps he could lead him into a more private place. Resisting the impulse to look back again and so risk spooking his quarry, he headed for the facade of St. Louis Cathedral, framed between the Cabildo and the Presbytère.

"But you know something about the murders," Bellamy said. He felt torn between the urge to plunge into the heart of the matter and the wary reflection that it might be better to stall until he'd dealt with the spy at his back, even though the shadow quite possibly already knew more than either he or Keene did anyway.

"Perhaps," Keene replied, sidestepping to avoid a giggling, staggering Japanese couple with cameras hanging around their necks and half-empty Hurricane glasses in their hands. "Right from the start, I've made it a point to read the newspaper accounts of the Atheist murders, because it was conceivable that a supernatural being might slaughter ministers and Sunday school teachers for ritual purposes. But until recently, I didn't pay all *that* much attention, because I was pursuing other studies, and it actually seemed more likely that the killer was just a cunning maniac with a grudge against the clergy."

"Let's step in here for a second," said Bellamy, leading Keene onto the covered ambulatory of the basilica. "It'll be cooler. I gather that something eventually convinced you that the murderer probably *is* connected to the paranormal."

"First off, Weiss's death," said Keene, removing his hat and pulling open the church door. Bellamy pulled off his LSU Bengals cap and stuffed it in his pocket. "If you *were* a supernatural creature committing the crimes, you'd want to eliminate one of the few religious figures who might actually pose a threat to you, would you not?"

It *was* cool inside the church. The air smelled of stone and incense, and after the brilliant sunlight outside, the interior of the building seemed shadowy and dim. Two old women sat motionless as waxworks in the pews. Bellamy moved past the font and a wrought-iron rack of votive candles toward a small chapel built into the right-hand wall. Once he and Keene were inside, they'd be out of sight of the worshippers in the nave.

After a moment, the door whispered open and shut behind them, and a shoe scuffed faintly on the gleaming marble floor. The shadow was still skulking along behind them.

"But you don't need an occult killer to explain Weiss's death," Bellamy said. "If the murderer craved notoriety, he could guarantee himself a lot of press by knocking off a televangelist. And even if he didn't, well, he's killing preachers, and Weiss was one. It could just be the luck of the draw."

"You're playing devil's advocate," said Keene, fanning his flushed, sweaty face with his hat. "Good for you. Hardheaded critical thinking is crucial to the success of any investigation. But the rebuttal to your argument is that the Atheist killed Waxman, another individual with psychic abilities, immediately afterward, even though Waxman was neither a member of the clergy nor a figure in the public eye. Indeed, by killing one of his previous victim's close associates, he broke his pattern to do so."

"My colleagues in the Bureau would point out that Waxman wasn't murdered," Bellamy said. "He died of a heart attack."

"I think we can assume the Atheist *would* have killed him, if he hadn't saved him the trouble by dropping dead of terror. The puzzling thing is, why didn't he murder you as well?"

The two men stepped under a basket-handle arch into the chapel, a small space dominated by a marble life-size statue of the Virgin standing, arms open, smiling sadly, in a niche in the back wall. As Bellamy had hoped, no one was praying here.

"I've wondered the same thing," the FBI agent send. "All I can figure is, he was afraid of my gun. But look, R. J., so far, all you've given me is conjecture. Intelligent conjecture, assuming a person accepts the existence of the paranormal, but only speculation even so. Haven't you got any facts?"

"A few," Keene said, "although I don't know if you'll regard them as such. My friends and I do our best to keep the various supernatural beings in New Orleans under surveillance."

"Do you know who they are?" asked Bellamy. He strained his ears, listening to the background noise in the church. He could *feel* the eavesdropper, lurking outside the chapel, but he couldn't pinpoint the shadow's location.

Keene sighed. "Not really, but we have intimations. We've devised techniques, mostly indirect measures, which allow us to monitor or at least infer their activities. We're fairly certain that the city has a large population of spirits."

"You mean ghosts?"

"That's what I believe, although others favor different hypotheses. I also think they have two rival kings or masters. There are indications that around the time of the first Atheist murder, open hostilities broke out between the factions."

Abruptly, though he hadn't consciously registered a telltale sound, Bellamy felt certain that he knew precisely where the eavesdropper was standing. Just to the left of the arch. "What makes you think there's a connection?" he asked. Then, holding up his hand to caution his companion, he tiptoed toward the opening.

Fortunately, Keene reacted to the signal appropriately. He didn't say or do anything that would have given Bellamy away. He simply pursued the thread of the conversation. "Just a hunch, I must admit, prompted by the knowledge that the Atheist has done some of his bloodiest work at this end of the Mississippi. Be that as it may, other odd things are happening hereabouts. There's a, well, call it a clan of peculiar people living over in Lafayette. The Arcanum doesn't know if they're diabolists, the descendants of people who interbred with something inhuman, or what, but we're virtually certain they're involved in the high rate of unexplained disappearances over there. Until recently, they rarely came into New Orleans, but now—"

Bellamy lunged around the pier of the arch, grabbed the eavesdropper by the arm, and whirled the shadow inside, all in a single instant, moving so rapidly that he didn't really register that his captive was the girl with the magenta hair and the piercings until he'd already completed the maneuver.

"My goodness," Keene exclaimed.

Bellamy pressed the girl back against the wall. "Who are you?"

For a moment, she looked flustered, and then her black-painted lips grimaced. "Nice," she said. "Go ahead, FBI man, rough me up. Rodney King me. I'll scream my head off. I'll put your ass in prison."

Bellamy realized that whoever she was, she wasn't the towering figure that had risen from behind his rental car in East St. Louis, nor did she appear to pose a threat. Technically speaking, he probably hadn't had the right to put his hands on her. Reflecting that he could always grab her again should she try to run, he released his grip on her fragrant black leather jacket. "I don't want to hurt you," he said "But I *am* here pursuing an official investigation—"

"Bullshit. I've been listening to you, remember? I know there's nothing official about this."

"Trust me," said Bellamy, giving her his best intimidating stare, "I can make it as official as it needs to be."

Keene stepped forward. "Miss, as you've evidently heard, we're trying to stop a series of murders. If you have information that could help us, simple human decency demands that you disclose it."

The girl sighed. "You're barking up the wrong tree. I didn't even have any idea who Waxman was until a few minutes ago. I asked two nights ago, but you jerks ignored me."

Bellamy gaped at her. Though he knew he shouldn't feel so astonished, considering that he hadn't anything to base it on, but he could help marveling that his mental picture had been so far off the mark. "Astarte?" he asked.

"Of course," she said. "Who else was in the Circle of Discourse when you arranged your little party? I hitchhiked all the way from Ohio to crash it."

Bellamy's shoulders slumped as the tension flowed out of his muscles. "You're lucky I didn't bounce you around a lot harder than I did. For all I knew, you were somebody who came here to kill us."

"But why *are* you here?" asked Keene.

"So you could tell her where to go to meet Count Dracula," said Bellamy. He looked back at the girl. "Isn't that about the size of it?"

"Basically," she replied. "And so far, you're a big disappointment to me, Vulture. I hope you've got more to say."

"Me, too," said Bellamy. "But you're not going to be around to hear it. Take a hike."

"Screw you," she replied.

"Believe me," said Keene, "I understand your fascination with the paranormal. But we're not obligated to help you pursue it."

Astarte scowled at Bellamy. "What if I phone the FBI and tell them what you've been up to? They'll kick you out. They might even lock you in a rubber room."

Bellamy's instincts assured him that the chances of Astarte following through on her threat were minute. She wasn't the kind of kid who'd rat out anybody to heavy-duty authority figures like the Feds. "Do what you want. We're still not going to talk to you anymore."

Astarte's large blue eyes, rather pretty ones despite rings of eye shadow so heavy and black they made her resemble a raccoon, glared at him. "Then I'll go to Lafayette and ask questions there!"

"I wish you wouldn't," said Keene. "But tens of thousands of people live their whole lives there without ever running up against the paranormal. I doubt that you could ferret it out in the course of the next few days."

"You are two of the—" Astarte began. Then her eyes widened, her mouth fell open, and her body jerked in surprise. A faint rasping sound whispered through the chapel.

Keene and Bellamy spun around. At first the FBI agent didn't see anything strange. Then he realized that the statue of Mary was very slowly twisting its head, apparently in order to aim its blank white eyes directly at them. Crunching and popping, tiny cracks appeared in the marble.

Bellamy felt dizzy and sick to his stomach. A terrible fear gripped him. Not so much of the statue itself—though he *was* afraid of it—as of the possibility that his mind was about to shut down again. He struggled to get past the shock, to *hang on*, and after a moment, his head cleared somewhat. He reached for his Browning.

"Everyone take it easy," said Keene, a slight quaver in his voice. "Whatever it is, it may not means us any harm."

Crackling, the statue's lips tore apart, creating a space where none had existed before. Bits of broken stone fell from the opening to rattle on its pedestal, as if it were vomiting. Evidently it was clearing an area inside itself, manufacturing a mouth and throat where none had existed before.

When the cascade of pebbles stopped, the statue's lips worked stiffly. The motion reminded Bellamy of a stroke victim straining to speak. And a sort of grinding whisper did emerge from the figure's mouth, but too faintly for him to make out any words. Evidently realizing that the humans hadn't understood, the statue beckoned for them to come closer.

And Astarte did.

Keene shouted, "No!" He lunged after her, an action that carried him within the statue's reach as well.

Keene grabbed Astarte and started to pull her back. Suddenly moving as fast as a human being, fresh cracks zigzagging through its arms, the statue struck him a backhanded blow. The occultist reeled into the wall. The figure pivoted toward Astarte, raising one hand high as if for a karate chop.

Gripping his gun in both hands, feet spread wide in one of the marksman stances the Bureau had taught him, Bellamy began to shoot. The bullets hammered pockmarks in the statue's beatific face and the graceful folds of its mantle.

Astarte scrambled backward, but too slowly, The marble hand whipped down, striking her shoulder and dropping her to the floor. Then the figure's feet separated from their base, and a vertical fissure split the skirt of its robe. With a rumble, chunks of stone fell away from it, sculpting the lower half of its body into two crudely formed legs. It sprang off its pedestal and charged at Bellamy.

The FBI agent got off two more shots before the statue plowed into him. As he stumbled backward, his assailant hit him in the head, a jolt of raw sensation that he knew would turn to a blast of pain in a moment. But before it could, he blacked out.

The bark of a gun recalled him to his senses. Dazed, his head aching, sprawled on his side, he pried his eyes open. Every inch of its pale white form now webbed with cracks, the statue stood over Keene with Bellamy's smoking Browning in its hand. The occultist had a splash of red in the center of his chest.

Still pointing the automatic, the stone figure turned toward Bellamy. The FBI man lurched up off the floor and threw himself at it.

It sidestepped, and he only struck it a glancing blow. It stumbled backward, but stayed on its feet and kept its grip on the automatic. His own balance equally impaired, the agent fell back onto the floor, certain that he'd only succeeded in winning himself one more moment of life.

Then Astarte rushed at the statue, still tottering from Bellamy's assault, and shoved it with all her might. The image's feet flew out from under it. When it crashed to the floor, its overstressed stonework body shattered into a hundred pieces.

Panting and trembling, Bellamy struggled to his feet. "Are you all right?" he asked.

"I don't *think* it broke my shoulder," Astarte said. "How's your head?"

Bellamy gingerly touched the sore spot on his scalp. His fingers came away tacky with blood. "I don't think I've got a concussion. We were both lucky."

She abruptly pivoted toward the man on the floor, as if she'd just remembered him. Quite possibly she had. Violence could jumble anyone's thoughts. "We have to help Vulture!"

Bellamy looked at Keene. The hole in his chest was directly above the heart, and the fecal stench of death mingled with smells of gore, gun smoke, and marble dust hanging in the air. Nevertheless, kneeling beside the occultist, the agent held his hand in front of the other man's nose and mouth, hoping to discover a whisper of exhalation, and pressed his fingertips against his carotid artery, checking for a pulse. He didn't find either. "I'm afraid it's too late to help him," he said. "Let's find a phone. We have to call the police."

Something clinked and scraped across the floor.

Bellamy whirled. The pieces of the broken statue were beginning to roll and scoot together in an apparent effort to reconstitute the whole. Already bits of finger and hand had locked together to grip the pistol anew. The remade hand flopped and rocked, struggling to turn itself around to point the weapon at the humans.

Crying out in rage and disgust, Bellamy stamped on the hand as if it were a cockroach. The bits of stone flew apart again. He snatched up the gun and thrust it back in its holster. Then, driven by a common terror, he and Astarte bolted. The two old women, now huddled in the far corner of the nave, goggled at them as they scrambled for the exit.

FIFTEEN

Bellamy surveyed the green fields of Woldenberg Riverfront Park. Camelias, azaleas, and irises were blooming. Smiling, chattering tourists strolled in the sunlight, admiring the plant life, making for the entrance to the Aquarium of the Americas, or heading for the *Cajun Queen*. The white paddlewheeler currently sat moored at its dock, plumes of white vapor rising from its twin smokestacks, waiting to embark on its afternoon cruise.

It all looked so pleasant. So normal. So *real*. For a moment Bellamy couldn't help wondering if the horror he'd experienced in St. Louis Cathedral had been real as well.

Impatiently, he thrust the treacherous thought away. *Yeah*, he told himself, *it did happen. Keene was right. The paranormal exists, and it's out to get me. I have to accept that, no matter how much it scares me, or I won't have a snowball's chance in hell of dealing with it.*

"Can we stop and rest?" Astarte asked, rubbing her shoulder. Desperate to put some distance between themselves and the church, they'd fled the French Quarter, not quite running—instinct had warned Bellamy not to make himself that conspicuous—but striding along rapidly enough to tire anyone who'd just been through the stress and exertion of a fight.

"Sure," Bellamy said. He knew he *needed* to stop fleeing. He needed to pull himself together and think.

"You could call the cops in there," Astarte said, pointing at the aquarium.

"I could," Bellamy said. A twinge of residual fright prompted him to look around and make sure nothing was creeping up on him, although, God knew, his experience with the statue suggested that he might not recognize a source of danger even if he saw it. "But it might not be a good idea."

"You still don't think your buddies in the FBI would believe you, do you?" said Astarte. For the first time, Bellamy glimpsed the steel stud embedded in the tip of her tongue. Despite his focus on genuine, indeed overwhelming problems, he winced. How many piercings did she have? How could people *do* that to themselves?

"What's the matter?" she demanded.

"Nothing."

"You made a face."

"Really, we're okay. To answer your question, yeah, I am worried that my colleagues wouldn't believe me. I doubt that the pieces of the statue are still moving around back there. Any ordinary homicide detective would zero in one fact: Keene was shot with my gun. Heck, that's why the statue bothered to pick it up, instead of just beating our brains out with its hands. It wanted to make it look like I killed you and Keene and then turned the gun on myself."

"You've got me to back up your story," Astarte said.

Bellamy smiled ruefully. "I'm not saying this to put you down, but you're not the kind of person that cops consider a reliable witness."

To his surprise, rather than losing her temper, she grinned back at him. "Isn't that the truth. And when they found out I have a jones for ghoulies, ghosties, long-leggety beasties, and things that go bump in the night, that wouldn't help, would it?"

"I'm afraid not," Bellamy said. They started to saunter on toward the water. A pigeon wheeled overhead as if checking to see if they were likely to drop any food, then soared away.

"If we're worried about being accused of the crime, should we be worried about being identified by the old ladies in the church?"

"I hope not. I doubt they noticed us at all when we came in, and with luck, they only caught a glimpse of us from across the nave when we ran out."

"Good," said Astarte, turning her head to watch an Irish setter chase a Frisbee. The dog's coat glowed red in the sun. "So what are you going to do next?"

"Catch the Atheist," Bellamy said. When he said it out loud, it sounded so absurdly macho—heck, just so absurd—that he had to smile. "Why not? I've got plenty of time. I took the whole rest of the week off."

Astarte stared at him. He couldn't read her expression. "You mean it, don't you?" she said at last. "Even after what we just went through. Who do you think you are, John Constantine?"

Bellamy didn't know the reference, but he understood what she meant. "No, but I am a guy who catches murderers. I like it, and I'm pretty good at it. And I suppose that because I am, and swore an oath when I joined the FBI, I even feel that I have a *duty* to do it." He looked at his companion, expecting her to jeer at what he assumed she would consider a corny sentiment.

But she merely said, "Especially if you think that nobody else is going to do it."

"Yeah. There may be someone else involved in the investigation who could relate to the idea that paranormal forces are involved, but if so, it's because he's on the Atheist's side."

"Do you think somebody is?"

"I wish I knew. I told Hanson where I was meeting Waxman. Anybody else in the office could conceivably have found out from him, and then tipped off the killer. Of course, I *didn't* tell anybody where I was meeting Keene, but if somebody was keeping tabs on me..." He shrugged. "The only thing I'm certain of is that I'm on my own."

"I'm not saying you *should*," Astarte said, "but you could pretend today never happened. Go home and do what the FBI tells you to. Eventually your boss would probably decide you're still trustworthy. Then you could chase a bunch of other murderers."

"If I was still alive," Bellamy said. "Remember, somebody or something just tried to kill *me*. For all we know, it'll keep trying until it succeeds or I take it down. And even if my life weren't on the line, this would still be personal. The Atheist has killed two informants right under my nose. He's ruined my reputation with my colleagues. He's made me doubt my own nerve and even my own sanity. I won't lie to you, this supernatural stuff scares me, but I *have* to keep after him. Otherwise I'll lose my self-respect."

He faltered, surprised at himself. He rarely disclosed so much of his feelings, even to trusted friends like Walter Byrd. He guessed the ordeal in the cathedral had loosened his tongue.

"Do you have any idea how to catch him?" Astarte asked.

"Keene suggested a couple possibilities. I'll pick one and run with it."

"Well, *I* think we should go to Lafayette," Astarte said. The *Cajun Queen* blew a blast on its whistle.

Bellamy stared at his companion in amazement. "Don't be ridiculous. You're not going to be involved in this any further. You're a civilian."

"So deputize me or something."

"Not even if I could. I'm stuck in this mess. You're not. The Atheist only knows you as Astarte You can go back home and be safe."

"You don't know that."

The cut in his scalp, where the statue had hit him, began to throb. "It's a reasonable assumption."

"Maybe," she said, "but I'm still not leaving."

"Look," he said, "I realize that your great goal in life is to find a vampire and"—to his surprise, the first image that popped into his mind was too pornographic to express; he paused for a beat to think of another—"uh, get its autograph. But this isn't a game. It's deadly serious."

"Well, that would explain the corpse," she replied sarcastically. "I *know* it's serious. That's why you need my help."

"Oh, and you've been a huge help so far," Bellamy said. "Keene might have told me a lot more if our conversation hadn't been cut short. But he got killed trying to pull you out of danger."

Astarte stared at him for a moment, and then her face twisted. She jerked around, turning her back to him. He suspected that it was to keep him from seeing her cry.

Bellamy had merely told the truth as he saw it, but still, he suddenly felt a pang of guilt for making her miserable. He stepped closer to her, catching the sharp scent of her body—evidently she hadn't bathed since leaving home—mingled with the scent of leather and now the moist odor of tears and mucus. Awkwardly, he tried to lay his hand on her shoulder, but she wrenched herself away from his touch.

"I'm sorry," he said. "That came out harsher that I meant it to. I'm as much to blame as you are. *I'm* supposed to be a professional, but I froze. If I'd started shooting a second sooner, Keene might still be alive. And ultimately, neither of us is responsible. The person or power that made the statue move is.

"All I was trying to say is, you haven't been trained—"

She rounded on him. "Didn't you think I knew Mr. Keene is dead because of me? I was trying not to think about it, but I did. That's part of the reason I want to help you, to make up for it. And I did as well against the statue as you did. *I'm* the one who finally knocked it down."

"And I'm grateful," Bellamy said. "But you have to admit, it was a lucky shot."

"Maybe so," she said, wiping her nose with the back of her hand. He noticed that she'd bitten her black-enameled nails to the quick. "But think about this. I've read a ton of books about the occult. Maybe I don't know as much as Vulture did, but he's gone. I'm the closest thing to an expert you've got left. *Please* let me stay."

"I can buy my own books—"

"If you won't let me stick with you, I swear, I'm going to poke around on my own. Vulture didn't think I could find anything, but I will!"

The hell of it was, she just might, and get herself killed in the process. Certain people had a genius for blundering into trouble, and Bellamy suspected she was one of them.

Maybe he *should* keep her with him for the time being. There was an outside chance she could be useful. And once he learned her real name and address, maybe he could arrange for her family to come and drag her back to Ohio.

"All right," he said, "provided you agree that I'm in charge."

She twisted her black lips back into their customary half sneer. "*Jawohl, mein Fuhrer*," she said.

SIXTEEN

Montrose's tiny fleet, a motley collection of pirogues, broadhorns, keelboats, and skiffs, glided with the black current. The murmuring water smelled of silt and acidic industrial waste. Gradually, the lights of Natchez faded away astern, leaving only the stars to alleviate the darkness.

Standing with Fink on the bow of the latter's keelboat, Montrose remembered what had happened the last time he took an army onto the water. He hoped his luck had changed.

In an effort to distract himself from his misgivings, he mused on the paradox his miniature armada represented. Generally speaking, Underworld objects weren't solid in relation to matter existing in the Skinlands. Yet the boats at least appeared to sit *in* the water. Their sails bellied with the breeze, and their rudders, poles, and sweeps served to maneuver them, even though they never raised a splash. It was one of the countless enigmas of Shadowlands physics. Montrose had watched newly deceased scientists and logicians go half-mad trying to puzzle such mysteries out.

Fink pointed at the shore ahead. "There," he whispered. His crew began to steer the flatboat into the shallows.

Peering, Montrose could just make out the vague shapes of what might be a cluster of houses, and then a vague flicker of movement in their midst. "And you're absolutely certain that this is a Circle of Heretics," he said.

"I'm certain the bastards'll look good in chains," said Fink, and then he grinned. "Yeah, yeah, I'm sure. I told you, nobody knows more about what goes on along the banks of the Mississip than I do."

Montrose nodded to the Chanteur, a small man protectively cradling a cello case. In the Shadowlands, where material goods of all sorts were scarce and theft consequently endemic, many wraiths carried their prized possessions everywhere, even into situations where they were likely to prove cumbersome. The Chanteur set his instrument carefully on the deck, clambered atop the low cabin in the center of the boat, cupped his hands around his mouth, and whistled a bird call. The sound seemed so faint as to be nearly inaudible, but Montrose was confident that everyone in the raiding party would hear it. And sure enough, in a moment the other boats began to turn in toward shore.

The guerrillas beached their vessels, and then Montrose led them southward. As the raiders glided through a stand of mossy, resiny-smelling pines, their commander felt a thrill of anticipation. He'd tried not to relish warfare when he was breathing. It had scarcely seemed Christian to do so. Yet he hadn't been able to deny that a part of him delighted in the challenge and the risk, and evidently, despite his expectations to the contrary, his years at his master's court hadn't rendered him too jaded and sophisticated to experience the same excitement now.

A cluster of two- and three-story houses emerged from the gloom ahead. Like many Haunts, the structures were ruinous, riddled with Nihils, and seemingly abandoned by the Quick. They filled the air with the smells of mildew and wood rot. Peering between the derelict buildings, Montrose realized that they formed several concentric circles with an open space in the center. When the breeze gusted, the long, coarse grass in the clearing stirred, revealing crumbling gray tombstones and precariously leaning granite crosses. Scattered among the monuments, vague silhouettes swayed back and forth as if the wind were tossing them as well. A wordless chant like a whimper of pain murmured through the air.

Montrose wondered fleetingly just what sort of Quick village had been morbid enough to focus its communal life on the town graveyard, and then shoved the reflection aside. His business was with the current inhabitants of the hamlet, who had apparently assembled at its center for some sort of Heretical rite, like lambs obligingly congregating for the slaughter.

The Scot peered at the shadowy doorways, windows, and porches of the nearer houses, checking for sentries. Seeing none, he pointed right with the AK-47 and left with his empty hand. His force split up, three wraiths remaining with him but most, Fink included, skulking away in the directions indicated. The guerrillas would converge on the cemetery from every side, surrounding it, making sure none of their prey escaped.

Montrose waited a minute, giving his men time to encircle the Haunt, and then crept into the outermost ring of houses. His companions slunk after him. Rage, agony, and terror, the echo of an ancient massacre, still sang through the soil beneath his boots. A sickening exhilaration juddered up his legs and spine.

Still no sign of any guards. He noticed a Tudor-style door hanging by a single corroded hinge. Long ago, someone had carved lines of text into the top panels. Despite the worm holes and the mushiness of decay, Montrose could still read them. *I am a child of the Wasteland. Dust is my drink and stones are my bread.*

The Stygian raised his hand. His three companions halted. He glided forward to peek around the corner of a collapsed porch. As he'd hoped, he now had a clear view of the graveyard.

Standing in a ring, a dozen wraiths swayed and crooned there, their faces slack with mindless ecstasy. In the middle of the circle, and the very center of the village, for that matter, was a bare patch of earth occupied by a single gargoyle-encrusted mausoleum. The tomb's doorway was a glittering Nihil, and what at first glance appeared to be an androgynous angel hovered ten feet above the roof, its iridescent wings beating in slow motion.

On further inspection, Montrose could see subtle signs of the creature's true nature, notably the hungry blackness, a match for the restless dark in the opening to the Tempest, seething in the center of its eyes. Whatever its worshippers imagined it to be, it was actually a Spectre, no doubt risen from the portal beneath its flawless alabaster feet.

Montrose's stomach clenched in loathing and disgust. It was just as he'd told Katrina. Wittingly or otherwise, Heretics were the lackeys of Oblivion. He opened his mouth to shout a demand for surrender, and then a ragged volley of shots rang out. A wraith behind him made a choking sound.

The Stygian spun around. One of his companions, a woman in a parti-colored red and white mask, collapsed to her knees, fumbling at the crossbow bolt protruding from her neck. Waves of darkness pulsed from the wound, and then she faded away. Behind her, at the edge of town, figures were advancing. Guns flashed and barked, bows twanged, and a Chanteur wailed.

Another missile—Montrose didn't see whether it was an arrow or a bullet—ripped through the back of his inquisitor's mantle, passing between his torso and his arm. He turned again. The Heretics in the graveyard had hunkered down behind tombstones, snatched up weapons which had apparently lain hidden in the tall grass, and begun shooting also. Still floating serenely above the mausoleum, the Spectral angel looked at him and smiled.

Evidently the community of Heretics had grown considerably larger than Fink had imagined, large enough to outnumber the little band of raiders by a considerable margin. And just as obviously, they'd somehow detected the Montrose's approach and set a trap for him, an ambush he'd rendered even more effective by dispersing his force through the Haunt. Now he and his men were the ones who were truly surrounded, and caught in a crossfire to boot.

Unless he could rally his troops and rally them quickly, the expedition was doomed. Throwing off his cape, he turned to his companions. "We have to charge and take the graveyard."

"That's crazy!" replied a squat little Spook with a ruby embedded in the center of his brow. "The Spectre's there, and they've got us outnumbered besides!"

"If we don't pull our force back together," Montrose said, "we're all going to die. And the cemetery is the only place to rally. It's the only area that everyone on our side can see. Now come on!" He ran through the rubble of the collapsed porch, across a strip of weeds, and through the side of a house which listed drunkenly to one side, not bothering to glance back to see if his companions were following him. Either they were or they weren't, and if not, he didn't have time to coax them. He resisted the urge to cloak himself in shadow. If the men *were* charging after him, they might well falter if he vanished.

Racing through the interiors of houses, he covered part of the distance to the clearing without coming under additional fire. But the moment loomed when he'd have to break from cover. Exerting his will, not allowing himself to break stride, he hurtled through another wall, a broken porch railing, and bounded down onto the grass. Still running, he began to shoot.

He cut down two of the Heretics before any of them spotted him. Then all the survivors pivoted in his direction.

He fired another burst, blasting an ancient-looking, gray-haired woman's head apart. Her body imploded like a broken balloon. He turned, seeking his next target, and then someone with Chanteur powers wailed.

The screech penetrated his head and reverberated on and on inside. Fighting the pain and the sheer distraction of it, his vision blurring, he tried to pivot toward the source of the noise, but his movements were halting and spastic.

A bullet slammed into his thigh, staggering him. Even with the Chanteur's scream scrambling his senses, he could tell that he hadn't sustained a serious wound. He didn't feel the numbing caress of Oblivion scraping away his substance from within. But no doubt the next bullet or arrowhead, or the missile after that, would be both better aimed and made of darksteel.

Guns barked and rattled behind him. The screech stopped abruptly, releasing him from his partial paralysis. He realized that his companions *had* followed him, and just now saved his life.

He shot a Heretic kneeling behind a broken tombstone. The man flew backward and lay thrashing in the grass. Montrose spun toward another target and saw that this one, a thin man with enlarged, pointed ears and protruding canines, was goggling at the space above his would-be attacker's head.

Montrose threw himself to the ground. Something swooshed through the air above him. He frantically rolled onto his back and glimpsed the Spectre flashing past. No longer content simply to hover above the graveyard, the creature had changed its form—its arms had elongated and its fists had enlarged into knobs studded with black spikes—and joined the fray. It wheeled for another pass.

Scrambling to his feet, Montrose tried to fire at the Spectre. His gun only clicked. It was out of ammunition, and he didn't have time to reload. The bogus angel was already plunging down at him. He dropped the assault rifle and whipped out his new rapier.

He waited an instant, and then, when the Spectre was nearly on top of him, hurtled up to meet it, hoping that the creature hadn't realized he could fly. And perhaps it hadn't; in any case, the sudden, all-out attack seemed to catch it by surprise. Montrose's blade rammed into its breast. Cancerous black light began to lick away its flesh.

Wrenching his sword free, Montrose grinned savagely, and then a new pain stabbed him in the shoulder. Someone had shot him from the ground.

He could tell it wasn't a mortal wound, but it startled him and broke the focus necessary to use his Arcanos. He fell and crashed to the ground. The arrow in his shoulder snapped beneath him.

Gasping reflexively, dazed, he struggled to gather his strength. It began to return, but it would take a few seconds. He managed to lift his head and looked around.

Fink stood over him, leering and pointing a Mag-10 Roadblocker shotgun at his nominal commander's chest. Certain that the burly Haunter meant to avenge his humiliation in the Green Head, Montrose gave him a level stare. He hadn't lost his composure on the scaffold in Edinburgh and he wouldn't now, either.

But Fink merely mouthed the word, "Boom," and then roughly hauled Montrose to his feet. "How are you?" he asked.

"I'll make it," Montrose said, peering about. The only remaining Heretics in the graveyard were incapacitated. So was the Spook with the red jewel in his forehead, who lay motionless beside a headstone with several white, glistening slashes in his throat and chest. Montrose's other companion had vanished and had probably been destroyed. Judging by appearances, Fink and three other raiders had charged up to complete the task of taking the area.

The Stygian gingerly tested his legs. The wounded one throbbed, but they could support his weight. Extricating himself from Fink's grasp, he picked up his AK-47 and sword and swung the latter over his head. "Everybody, come to me!" he bellowed.

"Use the houses for cover!" Any soldier worthy of the name should have sense enough to take advantage of any available cover without being told, but one never knew what even seasoned troops would forget in the heat of battle, particularly when they were losing.

Alone or in pairs, their faces white and their eyes rolling with incipient panic, the raiders limped into the cemetery. About a third of the initial force failed to appear. Behind the survivors, guns banged and a Chanteur wailed as their pursuers harried them.

"What are we going to do?" cried the Sandman from the tavern, his rainbow-colored mantle now hanging in tatters. "We're outnumbered and surrounded!"

"We're going to charge," Montrose said. "Through the open this time, so we can keep together. The Heretics are spread out in a ring. *We'll* outnumber the ones comprising any given section of the circle. If we hit hard and fast, we can break out of this crossfire. Are you game?"

"It sounds like a plan to me," said Fink.

Some of the raiders cheered. Others grimly nodded their agreement.

"Then let's go," said Montrose, striding toward the edge of the cemetery. By the time he left its confines, he was running. His soldiers thundered after him.

In the darkness ahead, guns flashed, but this time, no one hit him. Montrose held his own fire, waiting till he got close enough to have a reasonable chance of hitting someone himself. After a few seconds, bullets and arrows began to whiz at the column's flanks. Witnessing the raiders' sudden maneuver, Heretics fighting elsewhere around the ring scrambled into new positions in order to continue shooting. But they didn't produce enough fire to break the momentum of the charge. Too few of them had moved up quickly enough.

The faces of the Heretics in front of the guerrillas swam out of the murk. As they shot and shot and their opponents kept coming, their eyes began to widen in dismay. Eventually one threw down his longbow, wheeled, and fled toward the edge of the village. A moment later, a second rebel bolted.

Montrose judged that he was close enough to start firing. He squeezed the trigger and the AK-47 rattled and shook in his hands. A Heretic in bib overalls, armed with a slingshot, of all things, flew off his feet.

The Stygian's column smashed into the Heretics. He shot someone, then sensed an attacker lunging at him from the side. He pivoted, ramming the butt of his rifle into the other wraith's face. Bone, or what passed for it in a ghost's anatomy, crunched. The Heretic collapsed, a tomahawk slipping form his fingers.

Montrose looked around, but failed to find another opponent. The only figures standing in the immediate area were his own troops. Evidently recognizing that they'd succeeded in breaking free, one of them threw back his head and let out a war whoop.

The Scot supposed that since they were tired, in some cases wounded, and still outnumbered, the prudent thing would be to disengage and run for the boats. But if he led them away without a victory, without loot, they'd never follow him again. Heedless of the risk of attracting enemy fire, he levitated over the outlaws' heads so everyone could see him.

"We just took away the enemy's advantage," he said. "If you're as tough as you're supposed to be, we can beat them now. We can form into squads, sweep through this rat's next, and drive the bastards before us. We can avenge our fallen comrades and capture a fortune in thralls!"

The freebooters shouted their assent, a sound like a pack of wild dogs snarling. They divided into groups of five or six, and then began to spread out.

At the head of one such party, Montrose led it from lane to lane, yard to yard, and house to house. The battle became a game of cat and mouse, blasting away at the shadowy figures that pounced out of nowhere, chasing the ones that fled, proceeding swiftly but warily in case the Heretics were leading them into a trap.

It was dangerous work. One of his men perished, decapitated by a blow from an ax. Another was temporarily crippled when a blast from an assault rifle all but tore his leg off. But the Heretics fared worse than their enemies. Montrose didn't know if they'd been demoralized by the destruction of their Spectral patron or if, indeed, they simply couldn't match the prowess of his own band of ruffians. In any case, it soon became apparent that they didn't stand a chance.

With victory all but certain, the excitement Montrose had been experiencing, a kind of wild abandon seasoned with fear, gave way to a feverish ecstasy. Without his quite realizing it, the grim satisfaction of driving home a telling blow, of staying on one's feet while the other man went down, warped into a gloating enjoyment of the terror and agony in his victim's face.

Christ, he hated Heretics! Or at least he supposed he did. At certain moments, as he slipped deeper into his delirium, he imagined that he was striking down not a rabble of deluded Shadowlanders, but Argyll, Hamilton, the two Charleses, VanLengen, and Louise. Finally wreaking vengeance on all the traitors.

Until at last he and his companions prowled through two more houses without finding anyone else to maim. Despite the haze of cruelty clouding his mind, he realized he no longer heard shooting anywhere in the Haunt. Evidently the battle was over. Suddenly feeling dazed and empty, he simply stopped and stood in the center of a ruinous parlor, like a clockwork toy running down.

After a moment, a raider in a green hood said, "Anacreon?"

Montrose jerked as if someone had startled him awake. He felt his Shadow writhing inside him. He supposed that the events of the last few minutes had nourished it in some way, though he wasn't entirely sure how. He'd just been defending himself, hadn't he, doing what needed to be done.

In any case, he didn't have time to think about it now. He looked at the outlaw. "What is it?"

"I was thinking you could fly up over the town and get a bird's-eye view of what's going on."

"Good idea," Montrose said. He floated through the ceiling, a bedroom, and finally the attic, flitting through a mass of filthy cobwebs filled with the husks of flies, roaches, and termites in the process. His passage didn't disturb a single strand, but sensing him, the spiders skittered madly about.

He soared through a warped expanse of roof that had shed half its shingles, up another twenty feet, then stopped and looked around. Below him, his men herded staggering, whimpering prisoners toward the edge of the village. Though some of the surviving Heretics had no doubt fled into the countryside, the raiders had rounded up an excellent haul.

A number of outlaws were cuffing, shoving, kicking, or obscenely fondling their prisoners. The spectacle made Montrose feel obscurely ashamed. Throughout his Scottish campaigns, he'd forbidden his soldiers to engage in gratuitous cruelty, and made the edict stick. Shouldn't he do the same thing now?

He scowled, disgusted by his own momentary squeamishness. No, of course not. The Quick Montrose had been a fool to fret about securing gentle treatment for his own enemies. And the Heretics were pawns of the Void itself, condemned to slavery and an eternity of rough treatment by his own decree. Besides, an attempt to alleviate their distress might cost him the respect of his band of thugs.

He spotted Fink marching along between two houses with his arms full of rifles and shotguns, booty as valuable as the newly made thralls themselves. He flew down and landed in front of him.

Something had singed the left side of Fink's face, charring shiny white patches and grooves on his skin and burning away an eyebrow, much of his hair, and a section of his mustache. But if he was in pain, he didn't show it. His eyes were as full of devilish mirth as ever. "I thought the Marquess of Montrose was supposed to be some kind of hotshot Cavalier general," he said.

Montrose raised an eyebrow. It was the first time Fink had indicated that he'd ever heard of his new leader's mortal career. "We won, didn't we?"

"Yeah, but not very *elegantly*," said Fink. "First we sneak into town, then we run back to the edge of town, then we sweep into town again. Kind of a Chinese fire drill, in my opinion."

"Well, if my worthy lieutenant had provided adequate intelligence...."

Fink's burnt cheek rippled, repairing itself. He shrugged. "You wouldn't even have found the Heretics if it hadn't been for me. I said I knew more about the river than anybody else. I didn't say I knew *everything* about it. Nobody does."

Montrose could well believe that. The vast expanse of the Mississippi seemed more akin to the open sea than any of the rivers he'd known in Europe. In many respects, it was as awesome as the River of Death itself, the colossal waterway twisting through much of the Tempest.

"I'm willing to stipulate that we both did an adequate job," the Stygian said. "But we did take heavy losses. I hope the rest of the men will continue to follow us."

Fink snorted. "Don't worry about that. They're too afraid of me to quit on you unless I do. Besides, you know how it is with sons of bitches like us. We think nobody could possibly kill *us*, even though a lot of us became wraiths because somebody *did*. If we didn't believe we're indestructible, we'd find less dangerous pastimes to get us through the centuries.

"Trust me. Manpower is no problem. When word gets out about the plunder we took tonight, you'll get all the volunteers you need. Every cutthroat and lowlife from Cairo to the Gulf of Mexico will beat a path to your door."

Montrose smiled crookedly. "Now there's something to look forward to," he said.

SEVENTEEN

Potter prowled restlessly about the enormous, high-ceilinged chamber, where Hittite chariots and Sherman tanks cast blurred reflections in the gleaming gray marble floor, Stealth bombers and Fokkers, supported only by an artificer's magic, hung above his head, and glass cases full of polearms, machine guns, and grenades lined the walls. The air smelled sharply of oil, and the dripping tick of a water clock echoed through the gloom.

Sometimes it soothed the Deathlord to wander the museum, or one of the twenty like it scattered through his allotted portion of the Onyx Tower. The surroundings evoked the godlike spirit inside his mask. But tonight they failed to silence the fretful human soul hiding at the core of the transcendent entity he'd become.

The door clicked. Potter turned, reflexively holding his halberd across his body as the images of the Smiling Lord in all the paintings and statuary did, standing straight and still. By the time the door swung open, he'd become a figure that might easily have been mistaken for some enigmatic idol.

Tall, thin, and saturnine, the folds of his toga draped as elegantly as ever, Demetrius stepped into the chamber. He'd tucked his carved sardonyx helmet of a mask under one arm, his naked face a token of submission and respect. Bowing deeply, he said, "My lord."

Potter relaxed a little. He didn't feel the need to maintain absolute formality with the advisor, though the question of just how much of the inner man he ought to reveal to anyone was often troublesome in its own right. "Good evening," he said. "I hope I didn't summon you away from anything you were reluctant to set aside."

"Dispatches from our Citadels in South America," Demetrius replied, advancing. His sandals made a scuffing sound on the floor. "They'll keep. Is something troubling you?"

"Another vision," Potter admitted. "In this one, this section of the castle collapsed in around me and crushed me, while everyone else's quarters remained untouched."

"I rue the day I ever brought that miserable statuette to your attention," Demetrius. "We don't even know who made it, or how it found its way into that storeroom. And I think there's a malignancy about it, some subtle taint of Oblivion, even if we can't detect it directly. Let's cast it into a Forge and be done with it."

"No," Potter said. "You don't kill the messenger for bringing bad news. You do your best to comprehend what he has to tell you."

"That assumes your dreams truly are portents of things to come."

"Since I haven't slumbered since you gave me the image," Potter said, "they can't be simple nightmares. I'd rather consider them warnings than signs of impending insanity." Feeling restless again, he turned and walked toward a trebuchet, using his halberd as a staff. The butt of the weapon clopped rhythmically on the stone.

Demetrius fell into step beside him. "I assume that was a joke."

"You shouldn't," Potter said. "It wasn't particularly easy to be a Deathlord even when Charon was in power, and it's far more difficult now. How would *you* like to have final responsibility for preserving the Hierarchy?"

"I'm sure I'd snap like a twig," Demetrius said. "But I'm not Charon's anointed lieutenant. As Hierarchs, we know there's no God, but by all accounts, our late master came close. He wouldn't have chosen you if you weren't equal to the challenge."

"No one understood Charon," Potter replied. "Not unless it was the Lady of Fate, and she's not talking. No one knew why he did the things he did. Perhaps he made me his deputy precisely because I was strong enough to assist him, but no stronger. Not nearly strong enough to cast him down and fill his place."

"Come now," Demetrius said, "naturally the Emperor's disappearance left turmoil in its wake. But Stygia has weathered times of trouble before. Your Council of Seven will hold the realm together."

As they veered around the catapult, Potter resisted a childish impulse to pull the triggering lever and send the stones in the basket crashing against the wall. "Perhaps," he said, "but will it still *be* a Council of Seven when things finally settle down? I'm absolutely certain that some of my peers are scheming to expand their power at the expense of others."

"Schemes that will likely come to nothing," said Demetrius. "But I'm confident that whatever happens, *you'll* still be securely ensconced in your place, if not more influential than before. The Master of War and Murder is too formidable a personage to assail. And your campaign against the Heretics can only serve to enhance your prestige."

"Naturally you think that," said Potter, drifting toward a mannequin in a doughboy's uniform equipped with a gas mask, carbine, and bayonet. "It was your idea."

"You miss Montrose, don't you? I don't blame you. He has a keen mind, when he can be induced to put it to use."

"Do you like him, then? I imagined otherwise."

"I appreciate his virtues. I can't afford to like him just at present. He seems to think that his own place at court won't be secure until he drives a wedge between you and any other courtier in whom you've chosen to repose any trust. Which is to say, he's fallen victim to a case of the same envy and ambition that you believe afflicts your fellow Deathlords."

"Perhaps I'm doing them an injustice," Potter said. "But it's hard to trust people when you don't even know their names and have never even seen their faces. I often wonder why the Emperor forbade us to reveal our human identities even to one another." He grimaced. "He probably figured that if we never became intimate, we'd never dare to conspire against him."

Demetrius uttered a noncommittal grunt.

"I often imagine that some of the others *have* broken the prohibition," Potter continued moodily. "I can see them, faces bare, whispering in some secret crypt. Sometimes I picture all six of them there, plotting the destruction of the only person they've elected to leave on the outside."

Demetrius frowned. "Forgive me for saying so, my lord, but that *is* paranoid."

"Probably so," Potter sighed. "Why don't you prophesy for me? With luck, your findings will reassure me. And then you can quell my Shadow. Perhaps it's responsible for my more troublesome fancies."

As always, he felt somewhat sheepish making such a request. A quasi-divine entity like a Deathlord was supposed to be a supreme master of every conceivable Arcanos. He shouldn't require the talents of some other Oracle to interpret the weave of destiny for him, nor should he need the services of a Pardoner at all. But in Potter's experience, the old notion that a seer couldn't foretell his own future was absolutely valid. And while Charon had granted him reserves of willpower and spiritual strength that lesser wraiths could scarcely imagine, the ugly realities of governing the Hierarchy, the daily trafficking in war, execution, and slavery, nourished the dark parasite lurking inside him to an astonishing degree.

Demetrius's long, thin-lipped mouth tightened. "As I've warned you before, my lord, that isn't a good idea."

The advisor did indeed raise the same objections every time. An Oracle denied the opportunity to read the deathmarks graven in a supplicant's countenance stood a fair chance of misinterpreting that individual's karma, while a Pardoner ignorant of his client's history might conceivably strengthen his Shadow instead of weakening it.

Potter felt a sudden, reckless urge to go ahead and fling his visor away. Establish a genuine intimacy with *someone*. What kind of bizarre joke had Charon played on him anyway, granting him the power of a god but isolating him from every other person in the universe?

But he knew he *wouldn't* unmask, nor should he need to. Demetrius was one of the most gifted Oracles *or* Pardoners he'd ever encountered. That was one reason the Deathlord had welcomed him into his inner circle of lieutenants so rapidly, much to the chagrin of Montrose and certain others.

"Please," said Potter. "You've always done an adequate job so far."

Demetrius grimaced. "'So far' is the proper way of putting it. Still, if my lord commands it..."

Potter inclined his head.

"Then I suppose we might as well sit over there." The two Hierarchs walked to an alcove occupied by a low, round table and three chairs. Demetrius extracted a pack of cards from the folds of his toga, sat down opposite his master, and handed the pasteboards to him. "You know what to do. Shuffle and then cut the deck twice with your left hand."

"The hand closer to the heart," said Potter wryly, removing his steel gauntlets. The cards whirred as he riffled them. "Even though the Restless don't *have* hearts. And most people would say that Deathlords are even more heartless than most."

"You aren't heartless," the Oracle said. "And in any case, the symbolism is still valid."

Potter set the deck down Leaning forward, Demetrius turned the first card over and laid it face up on the table. The illustration depicted a high stone wall with a door set midway up. A figure standing on the ground, out of reach, gazed up at the portal in seeming frustration or perplexity.

"The Rampart," Demetrius said. "You feel cut off. Friendless and alone. Vulnerable."

Potter sighed. "I didn't need you to tell me that."

Demetrius turned a second card. The new one depicted a man crouched over an open coffin in a mausoleum. Knife in hand, he was violating the corpse of a lovely young woman, cutting off her fingers to steal her rings. The Oracle stiffened.

"What is it?" Potter asked.

"The Tomb Robber," Demetrius said. "Sometimes called the Archaeologist or the Resurrection Man."

"I know that," said Potter impatiently. "Tell me what it means."

"There are a number of possible interpretations..."

"Stop stalling and tell me what you see in it *now*."

Demetrius grimaced. "Betrayal, my lord. Someone, perhaps several someones, will try to do you grievous harm."

Potter glared at him. "Why were you unwilling to warn me of that?"

"Because I'm not at all certain I'm right, and I wouldn't want to alarm you needlessly, or turn you against some innocent person."

"But this agrees with the visions from the statuette. It confirms what I feel every time I see the other Deathlords in council. How many validations do you need?"

Demetrius shook his head. "Perhaps I simply don't want to believe such a thing. The Hierarchy can survive a lot of political maneuvering, but if you Deathlords start trying to assassinate one another—"

"I need to know who my enemies are, and precisely what they're planning," Potter said. "Turn the final card."

Demetrius obeyed, revealing a picture of an ebony mask covered with upraised runes. Darkness seemed to shimmer in the left eye hole, almost as if it were a Nihil. The pasteboard emerged from the deck upside down.

"The Visor reversed," the Oracle said. "All three cards are Greater Trumps. Your current situation is of the greatest possible consequence."

"In other words, I'm in the greatest possible danger."

Demetrius hesitated, then said, "That's certainly conceivable."

"What more does the Visor tell you?"

"Nothing," Demetrius said.

Potter glared at him. "How can that be? I've seen you spend half an hour interpreting a three-card spread like this."

"The Visor masks the countenance of fate. I can't see any more."

Potter felt a surge of fury, which energized the godlike persona resident in his mask. Springing up, he seized his halberd, whirled it over his head, and, despite the close quarters, effortlessly poised the gleaming black blade for a thrust at his minister's head.

"How dare you try my patience with lies and evasions?" the Deathlord thundered. "I can tell that you *do* see *something* more. What is it?"

Demetrius quivered. "Forgive me, my lord. What I saw is simply what I warned you of already. It's your *own* mask, your own secrecy, which prevents me from helping you any further."

Potter's anger and feeling of near omnipotence ebbed, giving way to a bitter sense of frustration. Once again, he had to resist the temptation to bare his face and tell the Oracle his name. "We'll just have to keep trying," he said glumly, even though he suspected the effort would prove useless.

Abruptly he felt his Shadow stirring inside him. The sensation wasn't truly physical, but it still conveyed a sense of frenetic activity, as if the dark side of his nature was dancing with glee. He could almost hear it taunting him with a kind of singsong chant. *We're going to* di—ie, *we're going to* di—ie, *we're going to* di—ie—

He tried to block the Shadow from his awareness, but it was impossible. The spiritual parasite had waxed too powerful, battening on his distress. He sat back down. "Thank you for the divination," he said to Demetrius. "Now give me your Pardon. And I'd appreciate it if you'd hurry."

EIGHTEEN

After he finished his third drink, Nolliver zapped the TV off, hauled himself up off the couch, and trudged toward his study. He left the liter of Johnnie Walker Black sitting on the coffee table. He always needed alcohol to fortify himself for the ordeal ahead, but he couldn't drink while it was actually occurring. It would have felt like a kind of sacrilege to do so.

Stacks of professional journals sat atop his carved maple desk, while a shelf crammed with psychiatric texts ran along the wall above it. As he sat down, a little unsteadily, in his leather swivel chair, he thought, *I don't have to put myself through this*. But that wasn't true. There were evenings when he *did* have to look, and this was one of them.

He fumbled his key ring out of his pocket, unlocked the bottom left-hand drawer, pulled it open, and removed the fat yellow folder lying atop the .38 Special, a weapon he'd purchased one drunken weekend when his suicidal impulses were particularly compelling. Leaning back, he began to review the file.

Everything was there. The arrest and court documents, his interview notes, affidavits from social workers, teachers, and probation officers, and the Minnesota Multiphasic Personality Inventory profiles the psychologist had provided. His own recommendations that four vicious young criminals be released back into the community. And, of course, the newspaper accounts of the murders that Billy Cantrell had subsequently committed. Two men, a woman, and a little girl gunned down in the course of a carjacking.

Nolliver's eyes ached, brimming with tears. Even after all these years, he wondered how it had all gone so wrong. The four offenders he'd lied for had only been *boys!* They'd *deserved* another chance, hadn't they, no matter how much trouble they'd caused in school, or how elevated their scores on the Psychopathy scale of the MMPI. What had been the alternative? Try them as adults and send them to prison? Surely that would have ended any hope of their *ever* adjusting to society. And in many ways, Billy had seemed the least malevolent in the lot. There'd been an underlying vulnerability—

Nolliver grimaced, disgusted with himself. How pathetic that he could romanticize the little monster even after everything that had happened. Billy had been a sadistic, amoral punk with subnormal intelligence. Unfortunately, he'd also possessed an angelic face and body beautiful enough to seduce a shy, lonely pedophile into imagining hidden virtues where none existed.

After the murders, Nolliver had waited, half in dread and half with a masochistic eagerness, for somebody to discover that he'd traded favorable evaluations for sex, or at least to question his competence. But no one ever had. The truth of the matter was that predicting criminal recidivism was such an inexact science that people rarely found it remarkable when a shrink or a caseworker made a bad call.

Though Nolliver hadn't endured prosecution or professional disgrace, he hadn't escaped punishment either. He'd simply punished himself, with impotence and alcohol. Desperate to ameliorate his guilt, he'd joined the Bureau and VICAP. He'd spend the remainder of his career helping to take murderers *off* the streets.

And for a while, it had helped. He hadn't felt cleansed. He'd known he never would. But sometimes he'd managed simply to do his work and live his life for hours at a time without his guilt and self-loathing coming to the forefront of his mind.

That had changed when Dunn came to him, revealed that, somehow, he knew the psychiatrist's sordid secret, and demanded cooperation in return for his silence. Nolliver had tried to tell himself that the arrangement was nothing he couldn't live with. He'd surmised—accurately, as it turned out—that the SAD agent would call on him only rarely. And then Nolliver would merely use his professional powers of persuasion to convince investigators that they hadn't really experienced any paranormal phenomena after all. How much harm could that do?

Yet as soon as he capitulated to Dunn's blackmail, he'd sensed his life spinning out of control again, hurtling toward a second disaster. And sure enough, in due time, the catastrophe arrived. Once again he'd borne false witness, to discredit Bellamy, and now his every instinct warned him that as a result, another innocent person was going to die.

Unless Nolliver prevented it.

He could. Dunn had contacted him earlier today to say that his "people" had failed to apprehend Bellamy in Jackson Square, and that Nolliver should try to set up a rendezvous if the younger man contacted him. By escaping, Bellamy had given the psychiatrist another chance to reveal the truth to Hanson, who could then mobilize the resources necessary to locate his subordinate and keep him safe.

The catch, of course, was that Nolliver couldn't inform on Dunn without informing on himself as well. Then his life as he knew it would come to an end. Not that he truly *enjoyed* his existence, but still, to have his secret shame exposed to the world! To stand revealed as a liar, a pederast, and, in effect, an accomplice to murder! He didn't know if he could bear it.

He looked down at the papers rattling faintly in his tremulous hands. A black-and-white newspaper photo of a car with four shrouded bodies laid out on the ground beside it was on top of the sheaf.

How will you feel knowing that Bellamy's dead, too? he asked himself. *Will that be any better that losing this shabby little pretense of a life you have now, posing as a decent human being and drinking yourself to death?*

Abruptly he knew that it wouldn't. Eager to act quickly, before he lost his nerve, he made a grab for the phone on the desk.

Clumsy with intoxication, he only managed to knock the receiver off the cradle. The dial tone whined. And then the smell of tobacco that clings to a smoker's hair and clothing suffused the air.

Nolliver froze. *It's like the stench of the bodies from the morgue,* he told himself frantically. *It's all in my mind. Dunn couldn't just appear in my house out of nowhere.*

A large, rather hairy hand with slightly yellow fingertips reached from Nolliver and hung up the phone. "Hello, Doc," said Dunn. "I hope you don't mind me dropping by. You keep saying that it would be better if we talk away from the office."

Nolliver jerked his chair around. "How did you get in here?" he demanded, his voice breaking in the middle of the question.

Dunn smiled. "You've got pretty good home security, but nothing a real pro can't handle. Who were you about to call?"

"I was going to have some supper delivered."

Dunn gestured at the papers in Nolliver's hands. "Does reliving all this give you an appetite? Of course, I'm no psychiatrist, but that's hard to understand."

Nolliver realized that he didn't like looking up at the other man. It made him feel vulnerable and subservient. But at the same time, he was afraid to stand up. "I have to eat," he said. "No matter how much I regret the past, life has to go on."

"Not necessarily," said Dunn.

Nolliver trembled. "What do you mean?"

"That you might as well cut the crap. I know you were calling Hanson. I could smell it on you, even through the stink of the whiskey."

"That isn't true!" Nolliver said.

"It's a shame," Dunn continued, as if psychiatrist hadn't even spoken. "Hanson couldn't help Bellamy anyway. No one could. In the unlikely event that my friends in New Orleans can't throw a net over him, I'll go down there and catch him myself. But that's tomorrow's little problem. Right now we're focusing on you."

"I'm telling you, I'm loyal!" Nolliver said.

"I wish that was true," Dunn replied. "But you know, even if it was, you've been falling apart for months. Changing from an asset to a liability. A loose end I need to tie off."

Nolliver's bladder felt swollen. For a moment he thought he was going to wet his pants. He realized that, despite his guilt, he wanted to live, if only to undo the harm he'd done to Bellamy. And ironically, his .38 seemed to represent his only hope of surviving the next few minutes. He dangled his arm beside his chair and stealthily began to move his hand toward the drawer containing the gun.

Simultaneously, hoping that conversation would keep Dunn from noticing what he was doing, he said, "You haven't really been carrying out orders from SAD, have you? You're a rogue agent."

"Sure," said the man in the suede jacket. "Deep down, you've known that for a long time. Although the term 'infiltrator' might be more accurate, since I was never truly on the Bureau's side to begin with. My real job has always been to keep SAD or any other part of the government from finding out anything much about the paranormal."

Nolliver's groping fingers brushed the cold metal handle of the drawer. Now, he realized, he'd have to pull it open, grab the .38, lift it, and shoot, all before the lithe, powerful Dunn could jump him. And a minute ago, he hadn't even been able to pick up a phone!

Was there any chance at all that he could talk his way out of danger instead? "If you kill me, the Bureau will find out about you. I left sealed letters with a number of people, to be opened in the event of my death."

Dunn smiled like a parent dismissing a child's transparent lie. "No, you haven't."

Nolliver's fingers closed around the drawer handle. But he found he couldn't make himself open it, for fear of provoking Dunn into killing him *now*, as opposed to one or two precious minutes from now.

"I beg you," the psychiatrist said, "let me live. I swear I'll cooperate. Think about it—if you murder me, there's a good chance that the Bureau will figure out who did it. Your work inside SAD will be over. Even if you manage to avoid immediate capture, you'll be on the run for the rest of your life."

"That's an interesting perspective," said Dunn, "but I'm afraid I can't buy into it. It would require me to trust you, which I don't anymore. Besides, I'm not worried about exposure. I can make it look like poor, troubled Dr. Nolliver committed suicide. Everybody in the Bureau will believe it, especially when the truth about Billy Cantrell comes out.

"In other words, you can't talk me out of this. If I were you, I'd go ahead and make a try for that gun in your desk. It's your only chance."

Nolliver gaped at Dunn, stunned to learn that the rogue had known about the revolver all along. Then he jerked around in his chair, tore open the drawer, and fumbled madly for the weapon.

To his surprise, he was actually quick enough to snatch it up. But the instant he did, a hand gripped the back of his neck and jerked him into the air. Thrashing, he blindly pointed the .38 over his shoulder. Before he could squeeze the trigger, Dunn tore the firearm out of his grasp, painfully wrenching his fingers in the process.

Dunn tossed the .38 back into the drawer. The gun landed with a thud. Taking the psychiatrist in both hands, the SAD agent turned him around with no more difficulty than Nolliver would have had shifting a squirming kitten.

The psychiatrist tried to kick Dunn in the groin. The agent twisted, and the blow merely glanced off his hip. He began to shake Nolliver, jolting him back and forth, not quite hard enough to injure him but forcefully enough to demonstrate his vastly superior strength. Much as he suddenly wanted to live, Nolliver realized it would be pointless to struggle any further. He went limp in the other man's grip.

Dunn stopped bouncing him around. "It's good that you tried to fight," he said. "A man shouldn't die like a sheep."

"Who are you really?" Nolliver asked. "*What* are you?"

Dunn shook his head. "I remember I said I'd show you if you crossed me, but it's better you never know. You finally found some courage, here at the end. I wouldn't want to take it away from you again. Now, where's your john? We'll do the dirty deed in the bathtub and give the cleanup crew a break."

NINETEEN

Astarte looked at the line of French doors that made up the facade of the Old Absinthe House. A number of them stood open, leaking bright swirls of Dixieland jazz into Bourbon Street. "I think I've heard of this place," she said.

"Probably," Bellamy replied, "it's reasonably famous." A trio of sight-seers, as drunk as nearly everyone else in the Vieux Carré seemed to be tonight, stumbled off the sidewalk to detour around him.

"Let's go in. I'm starved."

"I'll get you some take-out next time we pass a stand." He had discovered during the course of their first afternoon together four days ago that she had no credit cards, no checkbook, and only a few dollars in cash.

She grimaced. "You're a real sport. I *can* probably pay for myself, at least if I order something cheap."

"The money isn't the point," Bellamy said, although heaven knew he couldn't see any reason why he should be expected to pay for her food and motel room, even though that was the way it was working out. It wasn't as if she was his date. "I'd rather not take the time."

"What's an hour going to matter?"

"You never know. It could save someone's life. Maybe even ours."

"If a person carried that attitude to the extreme—and I bet you do—he could *never* have any fun. No wonder your wife dumped you."

Bellamy clenched his jaw, holding in an angry retort. He wished he hadn't told Astarte anything about his personal life, but it had been a ploy to induce her to open up about her own. And it seemed to have worked, at least to some degree. She'd told him her real name was Emily Dodds—but *nobody*, she'd added with a scowl of warning, called her that—she was eighteen, and she worked part-time in an alternative boutique. Her father was dead and her mother received disability benefits for crippling migraines, chronic fatigue syndrome, and a bad back. Judging from her daughter's description, the woman would lack both the motivation and the moral authority to compel Astarte to go back to Ohio even if Bellamy could get in touch with her.

"You have no idea why my wife divorced me," he said, "and I have no intention of telling you. Now, maybe *you* aren't in any rush to get to the bottom of our situation. Maybe you've forgotten what happened to Keene. Maybe you feel safe. But—"

"All right!" Astarte said. "I get the point. Which way is it?"

"This one," Bellamy said. He led her northwest on Bienville Street. As they moved away from the press of giddy tourists and the raucous bars and souvenir shops on Bourbon Street into a more residential section of the Quarter, the night grew quieter, darker, and more desolate. The narrow streets were nearly empty, and most of the streetlights were broken. Wooden gates leaned drunkenly, and cryptic graffiti—GENERATION LAST, ADORE THE PALE QUEEN—blemished the walls. One of the ubiquitous balconies overhanging the sidewalk groaned ominously as Bellamy and Astarte stepped beneath it. A shadowy figure rooting through a reeking trash can scuttled away at their approach.

The gloom and general atmosphere of decay reminded Bellamy of the area in which he'd found Waxman. Grimacing, he tried to push the comparison out of his mind.

Finally a point of blue light appeared in the darkness ahead. "Bingo," he said.

"Amazing," Astarte replied. "I thought you were lost."

"You shouldn't have," he said. "I know the Quarter about as well as a non-resident can, or at least I used to."

As they moved forward, quickening their pace, the smudge of blue radiance became a tinted bulb burning beside a dilapidated, iron-bound gate. Somewhere beyond it, someone was playing the piano, the music a schizophrenic medley of schmaltzy passages from fifty year-old Broadway and Hollywood show tunes which shattered into crashing dissonance after the first few bars.

Bellamy knocked five times, just as a furtive clerk in a dusty little rare-book shop on Royal Street had told him to do. After a few seconds a brown eye appeared behind one of the cracks in the gate. "Step back," said a bass voice. "I can't see you."

Bellamy did as he'd been told. "She can come in," said the doorman brusquely. "I think you'd fit in better someplace else."

Bellamy held up his FBI credentials. The gate clicked and swung open, the hinges creaking. The agent noticed that the doorman, a handsome young black man with mocha-colored skin, a shaven head, a bodybuilder's physique, and a pink triangle tattooed on his left biceps, had to hoist the barrier up slightly so it wouldn't drag along the cobblestones.

"Did I see that right?" he asked, his tone considerably less truculent. "Was that an FBI badge?"

"Yes, but it's all right," Bellamy said. "No one's in any trouble. I just need to talk to Marilyn Sebastian. A friend of hers told me I might that I might find her here."

"Come in," said the doorman, stepping aside. "I just came on duty, but I'll find out if she's around.

The black man conducted them down a short, dark passage into a courtyard which had been converted into an open-air bar illuminated by strings of blue and yellow paper lanterns. At first glance it appeared that about half the customers were men and half, women. On closer inspection, however, it became apparent that most of the latter were transsexuals or males in drag, though in some cases the illusion of femininity was nearly perfect, marred only the breadth of their shoulders or the prominence of their Adam's apples. Same-sex couples embraced in shadowy corners, moaning and gasping, their clothing in disarray. The odor of marijuana hung in the air.

Just as Bellamy smelled it, the doorman winced as if he'd just noticed it too, and expected the Federal agent to make an impromptu drug bust on the spot. "Can I get you anything?" he asked. "On the house, of course."

"Nothing," Bellamy said.

Astarte shot him a glare, and he belatedly remembered he'd promised to feed her. "I could *really* use something to eat," she said to the doorman. "And a beer."

"We've got some good jambalaya," he said. "I'll get you some." He hurried over to the bar, and Bellamy and Astarte sat down at small round table with a Cinzano umbrella rising from its center. When the FBI agent rested his forearm on it, it rocked precariously.

"Sorry," he said. "I forgot you were hungry."

"No harm done," she said, smirking a superior little smirk. "You're probably lucky you remember what we even came here for. I'll bet this place really weirds you out."

He smiled back at her. "Sorry to disappoint you, but no, not much."

The doorman brought two mugs of beer and two paper plates heaped high with a steaming mixture of rice, shrimp, and sausage. When he smelled the spicy aroma, Bellamy realized that he was hungry, too.

"Now I'll find Marilyn," the doorman said. He turned and vanished through a door in the far wall, into what had probably been an apartment house at one time.

Astarte eyed Bellamy skeptically. "I figured a straight-arrow FBI agent would disapprove of stuff like this."

"Don't believe every stereotype you see on TV," Bellamy said, wondering fleetingly why he was explaining himself to her. "I got into police work to keep violent people from hurting innocent ones, not because I'm some kind of moral fascist. I admit, I don't go to places like this for fun, but I also don't care about what consenting adults do for sexual gratification, or if somebody smokes pot. I don't think their private lives are any of my business. Mind you, if I had to chase marijuana dealers for a while to have a career in law enforcement, well, I guess I'd do it. But I'm very glad to be part of VICAP instead." He picked up his plastic fork and scooped up some jambalaya. It tasted as good as it smelled.

"If you say so," she said, clearly not entirely convinced.

"It's true," he insisted. "I've lost count of how many times I've come to New Orleans for Mardi Gras. Do you know what it's like in the Quarter on Fat Tuesday? Thousands—well, lots—of drag queens wandering the streets in sequin gowns and feathery headdresses. People exposing themselves and groping each other everywhere you look. If I had a problem with things like that, I couldn't enjoy the party, but I do."

"I've always wanted to go to Mardi Gras," Astarte said wistfully. "Is it still as good as it used to be? Somebody told me it's getting too commercialized and touristy."

"I don't think that's true," said Bellamy, not remembering until he spoke that he'd missed the celebration for four years running, and thus was scarcely in any position to judge.

Astarte took a long drink of beer. "Okay," she said, giving Bellamy a challenging stare, "if you don't have a problem with gays, drag queens, or pot heads, why don't you like me?"

"I like you all right," he said. "But you aren't trained to handle dangerous situations. You shouldn't be here."

She shook her head. "I'm not talking about that stuff. There's something personal going on."

Well, if she really wanted to know… "Don't you think you're a little sarcastic and a little hostile?"

She peered at him as if she was honestly surprised. "I guess maybe," she said at last. "But it's just my style. It doesn't mean anything. I'm glad we stuck together. I mean, considering what happened to Mr. Keene."

"Your piercings bother me, too," he admitted. "Don't get me wrong, I know that what you choose to do with your body is none of my business, either. But it's just something that's always creeped me out. It's like self-mutilation."

She gave him a wicked smile. "Don't knock it until you've tried it. It's supposed to be great for sex. It increases sensitivity and creates new sensations for your and your partner both."

He imagined how it might feel to kiss her, the contrast between her warm, soft flesh and the hard steel in her lower lip and tongue. He tried to push the phantom sensation out of his mind.

The doorman emerged from the table and strode back over to their table. "Marilyn is here," he said. "If you'll come with me, she'll see you now."

Abandoning his half-eaten meal with a pang of regret, Bellamy wiped his mouth with a paper napkin and stood up. Astarte opted to carry her plate and mug with her, a decision which annoyed him. An investigator shouldn't arrive to interview an informant with food and drink in hand, and neither should the detective's unofficial assistant. It was unprofessional.

The doorman led them through the door, up two shadowy flights of stairs, and along a narrow hallway lit by two dimly glowing cut-glass fixtures designed to resemble gaslights. Judging from the ornate molding and the peeling, faded flock wallpaper, the onetime apartment building had been pretty posh in its day, but the current owner had allowed it to fall into decline. There were rat holes in the baseboards, rat droppings on the threadbare runner, and a stale, musty smell hanging in the air.

Sighs and moans whispered through the gloom. Evidently people were making love in various spots throughout the building, though some of the soft cries seemed less expressive of rapture than despair.

Bellamy's guide opened a door and said, "This is them."

"Come in," said a breathy contralto voice. "That is to say, 'Enter freely and of your own will.'" The speaker giggled.

Bellamy stepped across the threshold. The room beyond displayed the same kind of rotting elegance as the other parts of the tenement he'd seen. A grimy, flaking painting of fleshy nymphs and cherubs occupied the center of the ceiling, and a veil of cobwebs shrouded the softly glowing blue and red Tiffany floor lamp. Someone had chalked a line of cryptic blue symbols or hieroglyphics around all four walls, just above the floor. Glancing backward, the agent saw that the characters ran across the inside of the door as well, completing the circle, creating an indecipherable text with no apparent beginning or end.

On the brass bed in the center of the room lounged another drag transsexual, an angular figure in a lacy black negligée and a long platinum wig. From the wrinkles at the corners of "her" eyes and mouth, lines which heavy makeup couldn't quite disguise, she was probably in her forties. Propped up a mound of red satin pillows, she held the mouthpiece of a hookah in one of her large, powerful-looking, red-nailed hands. The scents of hashish and sex hovered around her, and she had needle marks on the insides of her forearms.

"Marilyn Sebastian?" asked Bellamy, displaying his credentials.

"Yes," she replied. "Go on, Tony, it's all right." She waved her fingers in a languid shooing gesture. The doorman frowned as if he didn't want to leave, but then retreated down the hall.

Marilyn nodded toward a vanity, its surface covered by a jumble of cosmetics, stained tissues, paddles, vibrators, and handcuffs, and the straight-backed chair in front of it. "One of you can sit down, anyway," she said. Astarte took the seat and balanced her plate in her lap. The voice of the piano sounded through the open window, still alternately crooning and snarling as if the instrument were afflicted with Tourette's syndrome.

Bellamy told her his name. "And this is Emily Dodds."

"Astarte," his companion corrected through a mouthful of jambalaya.

Bellamy tried not to grimace. "She's *not* in the FBI—"

"*Really,*" said Marilyn, as if she could scarcely believe it.

Bellamy felt his face grow warm. "—but she is helping me with my current investigation."

"I'll bet she is," said Marilyn with a trace of a leer. "And what might that investigation be? What brings an upright young detective and his—" she hesitated, evidently searching for the proper turn of phrase—"plucky girl Friday into this den of sin?"

Astarte shot him a glance which seemed to say, *See? It isn't just me that thinks you look like a homophobe.*

"I spoke to a book dealer named Oscar Grace today," Bellamy said. "He told me you're one of his best customers for rare volumes pertaining to the supernatural, and that he suspects you belong to a secret society called the Arcanum."

Marilyn lifted a thin, arched, painted eyebrow. "I'm very disappointed to learn he's so talkative."

"We threatened to sic the IRS on him," Astarte explained. "He's keeping two sets of books."

"How did you know that?" Marilyn asked.

"Instinct," Bellamy said, and he really couldn't explain it much better than that. Once in a great while, he met someone and just *sensed* what crime the stranger had committed. Of course, it helped if the guy was as jumpy as Grace had been, and kept sneaking guilty glances at the ledger sitting beside the cash register. "Was Grace right? *Do* you belong to the Arcanum?"

Marilyn tittered. Bellamy wondered just how stoned she was. "My goodness, darling, if it's a *secret* society, I wouldn't be very likely to admit it if I was, would I?"

"If you are a member," Bellamy said, "you probably knew a man named R. J. Keene. Someone killed him earlier this week, evidently because he was trying to help me solve a series of murders. If you want to see the killer brought to justice, you should cooperate with me."

Astarte set her paper plate on the vanity, knelt beside the bed, and took one of Marilyn's hands in both of hers. "Please," she said. "I've been searching for something like the Arcanum my whole life. If it's real, you've got to let me in." Marilyn looked her in the eye, then sighed and shook her head. "You poor kid," she said, her voice dropping half an octave, "what do you think the Arcanum is?"

"A doorway," Astarte said. "The path into something wonderful."

Bellamy wondered how she could possibly say it with such conviction, with such a gleam in here eyes, after what she'd experienced in the cathedral.

"That's what I used to think, but it isn't like that," Marilyn said. "Human beings shouldn't try to shine a light into the darkness. You never like what you see."

"Then you are in the lodge," said Bellamy, just to nail it down once and for all.

Marilyn smiled. "Do I look like your image of an intrepid ghost breaker?"

"I don't care about your personal life," Bellamy said.

"I don't blame you," Marilyn said. "Some evenings, I have trouble staying interested in it myself. Lying here with one cruel young man after another, knowing that, if I had to rely on my rather faded charms, every one of them would choose to spend the hour with someone else. But they think I can work magic to help them accomplish their hopes and dreams. Some of them even think my kiss can make them immune to AIDS."

Astarte stared at her. "Can it?"

Marilyn laughed, a sound like glass breaking. "My goodness, child, where are you from? Of course not."

"Then how can you play such a terrible trick on them?" Astarte asked.

"Easily," Marilyn said. She paused to take a long drag on the mouthpiece of the hookah, held the smoke in her lungs for about ten seconds, and then coughed it out. "Once upon a time, my sordid little trysts would have repulsed me. I wanted one true love to last my whole life through. But that was before I looked into the heart of the night. Now I need something more intense than romance to help me forget what I saw. When I'm lucky, my adventures in this bed do the trick, and so I'll do anything necessary to keep the cruel young men coming back.

"Besides, I'm not really hurting anyone. The whole world already has AIDS, haven't you noticed? It's rotting away, right on schedule, just like St. John the Divine warned us it would."

"Maybe not," Astarte said. "All through history, people have thought the world was about to end. They believed the prophecies in Revelation referred to events happening in their time. But so far, they've always been wrong, and you could be wrong, too."

Marilyn cocked her head. "Touché, little Phoenician. Perhaps you're not a credulous New Age idiot. But if one puts any stock in the occult tradition at all—and I take it you do—then one does have to accept that something rather like St. John's gibberish is going to come to pass eventually. And I see a great many signs that chaos is about to clench its mighty fist and crush us in its grip."

"This is all very interesting," Bellamy said, "but we didn't come here to talk about the Apocalypse." He smiled wryly. "Our problem isn't quite *that* big."

"Let's hope not," Marilyn murmured.

"I'm investigating the Atheist murders," Bellamy continued doggedly. "I believe the paranormal is involved, and apparently Keene did, too. But before he could tell me why, a statue came to life, attacked us, and killed him." Despite Marilyn's avowed belief in the supernatural, the agent still winced to hear himself utter such a seemingly preposterous statement. "I'm hoping that another member of the Arcanum—you—can tell me what he wanted me to know."

"And perhaps a member could," said Marilyn. "But I'm not one, not anymore. I resigned two years ago. I beat a hasty retreat from paranormal investigation after one memorable night in an old house on Conti Street."

Astarte frowned. "But you still buy occult books."

Marilyn shrugged. "Old habits—old interests—die hard."

"And you must still remember the secrets you learned," said Bellamy.

"I never discovered any real secrets," Marilyn said. "I just learned to be afraid."

Bellamy scowled. "Keene made it pretty clear that every member of the Arcanum knows *something*. Look, I just want to pick your brain. I'm not asking you to go back into the field. Why are you so reluctant to help me?"

"Keene tried, and he's dead. The dark powers don't like being gossiped about, and they have ways of finding out who's been meddling in their business."

"If you don't want to be involved," said Astarte, "we understand." Bellamy could see from her eyes that for her part, the statement was a lie. She *couldn't* imagine how anyone could discover a path into the supernatural and then decline to follow wherever it led. "Give us the name of somebody who still is a member of the Arcanum and we won't bother you anymore."

Marilyn grimaced. "Just because I left the lodge, that doesn't mean I don't care about my oath. I swore I wouldn't reveal the identities of my fellow members under any circumstances, on pain of bringing a terrible curse on my head." She smiled ironically, as if to deride the notion that the Arcanum could actually muster the magical power to lay a hex on anyone.

"That's it," Bellamy said. "I've been trying to be patient with you, but enough is enough. The Atheist kills victims two and sometimes three times a week. If you can't see that that's more important than any pledge, you've got a problem. Since I'm not your friend, your pastor, or your shrink, I don't intend to try to fine tune your sense of right and wrong. Instead I'll warn you that the Federal government can be just as obnoxious as any goblin you ever saw. We've got any number of perfectly legal ways to make your life miserable until you give us what we want. With your lifestyle, you're practically begging for it."

Marilyn glanced at Astarte. "I'm not *just* trying to keep my word. I'm also trying to protect this young lady from the consequences of her own folly." The girl bristled.

"I can appreciate that," said Bellamy, "but it isn't the most important consideration, and it wouldn't work anyway. If we can't find any answers in New Orleans, she'll just go looking in Lafayette." Marilyn winced. Evidently she, like Keene, regarded the town as dangerous.

"If I steer you on to the true Arcanum," said Marilyn, "to people far more knowledgeable than I, will you really leave me in peace?"

"Yes," Bellamy said.

"Well, maybe I can help you without violating the letter of my oath." A moth flew in the window and flitted around Marilyn's face. She brushed it away. "Did you notice the"—she tittered—"pardon the cliché, the writing on the walls?"

"Is it written in the Witches' Alphabet?" Astarte asked. Bellamy gathered that she was referring to some sort of occultist's cipher.

"Very good," said Marilyn, like a teacher complimenting a clever student. "Yes, it is, more or less. I wrote it shortly after I realized I intended to spend most of my evenings in this room. It serves multiple purposes. Theoretically, it affords me a tiny measure of protection. I suspect that, like the sex and drugs, it provides a measure of therapy. And if you examine it closely and oh so cleverly, you may find the information you need, without my having to speak it aloud."

"I can't actually read the runes," Astarte admitted. "Not without a translation chart."

"And I didn't even know what they were," Bellamy said. "Let's not play games. Just say what you know."

"Please," said Marilyn. "Try for at least a few seconds. Give me one opportunity to feel that I haven't *entirely* betrayed my brothers."

Bellamy sighed. "All right. Where does it start?"

"Everywhere," Marilyn replied enigmatically. "Begin wherever you like."

Bellamy moved to the center of the room, the spot from which he could most easily see the entire ring of symbols. Astarte came and stood beside him.

"This is kind of cool," she whispered. Annoyed by her frivolous attitude, he scowled.

He began staring at the runes, looking for the shapes of ordinary letters hidden inside them, or in the spaces between them. He couldn't imagine what else there might be to discover. At first he turned, shuffling slowly, to examine the characters on every wall.

And then, to his surprise, the characters on one particular section of crumbling plaster seemed to change. Although he still couldn't read them, the curved and angular shapes seemed charged with meaning, like a distant billboard that was just about to come into focus. Fascinated, he peered even more intently than before.

The sense of imminent comprehension increased. He turned once more and his eyes locked on a string of six symbols Suddenly, irrationally certain that they spelled out a single word, which he was on the brink of comprehending, he fixed his attention on them.

He heard Astarte gasp, though the sound seemed muffled, as if it had come from a long way off. He guessed that the symbols had changed for her as well. He considered asking her what she saw, but the impulse faded quickly. Speaking would only distract him from his own gazing.

The six runes seemed to squirm like flies in a spider's web, their tails and serifs writhing like limbs. He blinked and the characters froze once more, but only for a moment. Then they crawled to the left, like stock quotations on an electronic sign, though somehow without ever really changing their location. For a second he felt as if he were hanging above them, about to fall.

Bellamy's excitement gave way to nausea and a dazed sense of dread. Eventually, it occurred to him that perhaps he ought to look away. He was still mulling the possibility over when the six runes began to give up their secrets.

To his surprise, it wasn't like reading. A word or phrase didn't pop into his mind. Instead, he hallucinated a scene so intensely it was as if he were really there. He stood on a desolate shore, a cold, howling wind knifing into his flesh, peering across a channel at an island city not unlike a fantastic stone wedding cake, level after level of chambers, corridors, and balconies capped by an immense castle with a black tower rising from the center. After contemplating the forbidding vista for several seconds, he suddenly noticed that, imposing as the cyclopean city was, it was far from the largest thing in view. The flickering thunderheads massed above it weren't actually clouds at all, or at least, not *merely* clouds. They were the heads and shoulders of mammoth demons, one with two draconic faces on a single head, one with no flesh on his skull, and some with forms so alien that it was only through intuition that Bellamy realized he was looking at sentient entities at all. Each glared down at the world below with a tangible malevolence.

The sheer *vastness* of the creatures was intolerable to contemplate. Nothing, not even God, should appear so huge. And though common sense told Bellamy that a single human being was beneath their notice, that their loathing and loathsome gaze was actually focused on the island city, he couldn't shake the feeling they were looking directly at him. He heard himself whimper.

It's only an illusion! he insisted to himself. *You aren't really in this place. Close your eyes or turn your head. Break eye contact with the symbols on the wall and the vision will go away!* But he couldn't. Something, either a power in the runes or his terror of the devilish things looming over him, froze him the way the stare of a serpent paralyzed its prey.

He hated himself for that. It was just like the night of Waxman's death. Once again the supernatural was stripping him of his courage and sense of self. But even his outrage couldn't energize him sufficiently to break the bonds that held him.

Faintly, through the wail of the phantasmal wind, he heard the voice of the piano, the soothing strains of "Moon River" disintegrating into cacophony. Then bed springs squeaked. Marilyn must have gotten up.

He realized that she was the true threat, not the giants in the vision. Yet the latter were so awesome, so much more compelling even in their unreality, that he still couldn't tear his eyes away from them.

A floorboard squeaked as Marilyn approached, even though the surface beneath Bellamy's feet seemed uneven, studded with pebbles he felt through the soles of his shoes. Finally remembering his Browning, he strained to draw it from its holster. His arm merely trembled, the same power that kept his gaze locked on the runes afflicting it as well.

Astarte sobbed. Bellamy realized that whatever Marilyn meant to do to them, she was doing it to his companion first.

The ghastly but hypnotic vision faded and blurred a bit, and as a result, the spectacle of the colossal demons became a little less overwhelming. From the corner of his eye, he glimpsed the murky figures of Astarte and Marilyn, overlaid on the desolate landscape of the hallucination like images in a double exposure.

Exerting every bit of willpower he possessed, Bellamy wrenched himself around to face them. The giants, the island, and the beach vanished like a bursting bubble.

At the same instant, Astarte fell, sprawling against his legs and knocking him backward. He was still trying to recover his balance when Marilyn grabbed him and rammed a hypodermic needle into his neck.

TWENTY

Standing beside the Green Head and the moon-dappled river, Montrose surveyed the spectacle before him—his troops, their ranks swollen by scores of new volunteers, the hastily fashioned banners emblazoned with emblems of the Smiling Lord and the Unlidded Eye, the slave coffles, and the wagons loaded with less animate loot, drawn by still other Heretic prisoners locked in the traces—and realized that he was of two minds about it. Montrose the Anacreon rejoiced in his triumphs and the humiliation of his enemies. But another James Graham who occasionally stirred in his memory, a young man who'd written poetry and taken up arms only when his principles demanded it, regarded the spectacle as barbarous and shameful.

The Stygian grimaced. The new Montrose was a victor. The old one had perished on the gallows. It was obvious whose perspective had more merit. He tried to thrust his qualms out of his mind.

"Something wrong?" asked Fink.

"No," Montrose replied. "I was just thinking."

The black-haired wraith grinned. "Better you than me. Too much thinking's bad for your liver."

Montrose smiled back. "The Restless don't have livers, but still, I believe you have a point. Everything seems to be in order. Let's be on our way." He turned, put his foot in his stirrup, and swung himself onto his mount, a magnificent white stallion with shining crimson eyes.

The creature was a Phantasy, a spiritual being analogous to a Skinlands horse, although, according to the more highly respected Stygian metaphysicians, not actually the ghost of an Earthly animal. Such valuable rarities were occasionally found and captured in the Tempest. Montrose's ragtag army had seized this one in their last raid.

The horse—which he'd named Alexander, after the conqueror whose exploits had inspired him as a boy—was the one piece of loot he'd insisted on keeping for himself. A Grim Rider should have a steed, shouldn't he? Besides, he *liked* to ride.

He brandished his rapier. Chanteurs shouted commands or blew flourishes on their instruments, whips cracked, and harness creaked. Kicking Alexander into motion, Montrose began to lead the procession on a winding route through Under-the-Hill and other ruinous sections of the city.

The Chanteurs provided martial music, effortlessly drowning out other ruffians who, bereft of musical ability but caught up in the jubilant spirit of the moment, elected to sing along. Sandmen conjured fireworks and showers of fragrant rose petals.

Whenever the parade passed a Haunt the inhabitants watched it, often peeking warily from their lairs until Montrose's men lured them outdoors by tossing handfuls of oboli onto the sidewalks, whereupon the guerrillas pressed plundered garments, jewelry, books, boom boxes, bound thralls, and even guns into their eager hands. Afterwards, many wraiths elected to march along behind the army, either in the hope of collecting further bounty or simply for the fun of it.

Periodically it was necessary to traverse a section of Natchez still belonging primarily to the Quick. Despite the thickness of the Shroud, a number of mortals sensed that something uncanny was in their midst. Some peered nervously about, some quickened their paces, and a prostitute in red leather miniskirt and a coppery wig fainted outright. Instantly a teenager in a baseball cap scrambled out of a recessed doorway, snatched up the unconscious woman's purse, ripped the gold chains off her neck, and sprinted away down an alley.

Eventually the procession entered the principal street leading to the Hierarchy Citadel. As the raiders climbed it, they continued dispensing gifts, and their demeanor still bespoke swaggering pride and exhilaration. But, glancing backward, Montrose noticed some of them checking their weapons. He'd warned them they might meet with a hostile reception at the top of the hill.

The sprawling Citadel complex came into view. Legionnaires were hastily scrambling through the walls and trying to arrange themselves in formation in front of the entrance. As Montrose rode through the ring of frigid human torches, his Sandmen produced the most dazzling display of fireworks yet. Simultaneously the Chanteurs' song culminated in an earth-shaking fanfare. The Stygian halted Alexander on the last note. His troops stumbled to a ragged stop behind him, slightly marring the pageantry of their entrance. But it didn't bother him. His Highlanders, of whom they increasingly reminded him, hadn't known or cared how to stand at attention, or march in step either.

The echoes of the fanfare died away. A final blaze of gold and crimson light flickered out, and the shadows deepened again. Montrose regarded the soldiers massed in front of the door, and they peered nervously back at him.

Finally he said, "Good evening, fellow Hierarchs. I've come to confer with your commanders."

A small figure squirmed through the front rank of Legionnaires. His face shadowed by the dangling horns of his pink and orange jester's cap, Valentine gave Montrose an enigmatic smile. "My master instructed me to invite you inside for that very purpose."

Fink, who'd marched through the city by Montrose's stirrup, looked up at him. "I wouldn't go in alone," he murmured, so softly that no eavesdropper, not even a wraith, was likely to overhear. "Make them come out here, or at least insist on taking a few bodyguards with you."

"I'd prefer to," Montrose whispered back. "But we marched up here the way we did to conjure the image of a dauntless conqueror, a hero so formidable that only a madman would defy him. If I do anything to appear fearful, I risk cracking the facade." He looked at Valentine, raised his voice, and said, "That will be fine." He swung himself down off Alexander.

"You're the boss," Fink said dubiously. "How long should we wait for you before assuming the worst?"

"An hour should tell the tale one way or the other," Montrose said. He handed his lieutenant Alexander's reins. "Keep an eye on our flanks and rear. Don't let any Legionnaires sneak down the hill and surround us."

He walked forward into the empty space between the two groups of soldiers, his new spurs jingling and his long cloak swishing around his boots. It seemed to take a long time to cover the distance. Despite himself, he couldn't help imagining the assembled Hierarchs suddenly leveling their guns and opening fire. But they didn't, and finally Valentine walked out to meet him.

"This way, my lord," said the dwarf. He waved his hand, the bells attached to his glove jingling, and the Legionnaires shifted, opening a path to the entrance. Four Legionnaires with shotguns fell into step behind them.

As they slipped through the door into the derelict building, Montrose thrilled to the echo of ancient anguish still jangling through thc air. "We've been hearing stories about you," Valentine said.

Montrose tried to shake off the disorienting, vaguely nauseating shock of empowerment. "I thought you would," he replied, "if only because so much of our plunder has already reached the marketplace. You should have stuck with me that first night. Joined the crusade. My men are getting rich."

"Rich or killed," Valentine said. "I told you, I've got a good thing going here."

Montrose shrugged. "Whatever you say."

Valentine led him past two sentries, up a rusty wrought-iron staircase which looked as if it might collapse under the heavy tread of the living, and down a hallway toward Mrs. Duquesne's office. Beside the door stood yet another guard holding a pale, gaunt barghest on a leash. The creature's growled as the Stygian and the dwarf approached. Its nostrils flared inside its gray iron muzzle.

Ignoring the bloodhound, Valentine gripped the brass doorknob and twisted it. The door swung open. As Montrose had discovered on his previous visit, the portal existed on the deathly side of the Shroud. No artificer himself, the Scot could only imagine what sort of Arcanos magic was required to hang a Shadowlands door in a Skinlands frame.

Inside the room, sheets of Stygian iron mesh overlay the floor and walls and even covered the ceiling, a guarantee that no ghostly assassin could flit in or out by the usual method. When Montrose and Valentine entered, the guard pulled the door shut. A key clicked in the lock.

The three governors of Natchez regarded their visitor. Beneath his steel domino,

Gayoso's mouth was drawn so tight he was nearly snarling. Nathan Shellabarger, the Emerald Lord's nominal lieutenant, a small man whose features were completely concealed beneath a green hood, seemed nearly as tense. He had at least managed to sit down, but his right hand kept opening and closing, clutching and plucking at the gray fabric covering his thigh. Only Mrs. Duquesne, the Beggar Lord's vicar, a thin schoolmarm of a woman with round, steel-rimmed glasses and gray hair pulled back in a severe bun, seemed completely unruffled. Ensconced behind her massive ebony desk—its surface empty except for a large black hourglass, a glazed white mask of Tragedy, and a wooden bowl containing several coins—she studied Montrose with the slightest hint of an ironic smile.

"Hello, Anacreon," she said.

"Hello," Montrose replied. "It's nice that at least two of us are courteous, don't you think? Perhaps good manners haven't vanished from the world entirely."

"We've already shown you more courtesy than you deserve," Gayoso said. "We should have ordered our troops to whip you away from our door."

"You unmasked when I came to you as something little better than a mendicant," Montrose said. He shot Mrs. Duquesne a grin. "No offense to your master intended." He switched his gaze back to Gayoso. "It seems reckless if not perverse to refuse to do as much now that I'm addressing you from a position of strength."

"For heaven's sake, both of you, show your faces," Mrs. Duquesne said testily. "This is no time for posturing. We have business to discuss."

Gayoso hesitated, then grimaced and removed his domino. Shellabarger pulled off his hood, revealing bulging faceted eyes like huge emeralds embedded in an otherwise nondescript face. Crouching in the corner nearest the door, Valentine smirked to see the two Anacreons pressured into doing something against their will.

Montrose inclined his head to them. "And good evening to *you*, gentlemen. Once again, I've come to discuss the mission which our august master the Smiling Lord entrusted to me, or rather, to all of us."

"Come with a band of cutthroats at your back," Shellabarger growled.

Montrose raised an eyebrow. "Pardon me, my lord Anacreon, but 'cutthroats' is a harsh term for valiant members of the Order of the Unlidded Eye, even if they are irregulars."

"Are you mad?" Gayoso demanded. "Do you seriously claim that those rabble are Legionnaires? I recognize some of them. You've got the worst scum from Under-the-Hill out there, Mike Fink and twenty others nearly as bad. Condemned criminals!"

"Not anymore," said Montrose. "I pardoned them."

"You can't do that!" Gayoso said. "You can't just abrogate our edicts and policies—"

"You're mistaken," Montrose said. "With the authority of the Smiling Lord behind me, I can do anything necessary to fulfill my responsibilities. Now, let's talk frankly. I asked you to help me crush the Heretics operating in your bailiwick. You knew it was a legitimate request, but for your own reasons, you seized on every pretext to deny me. Evidently you assumed I'd spend the next few centuries sitting idle hoping you'd relent, or slink back to Stygia with my tail between my legs, and that either way that would be the end of the matter.

"But it wasn't. Denied the use of your troops, I found soldiers where I could and commenced the campaign without you. In just a few days, I've destroyed several

Heretic Circles and enriched the economy of Natchez by filling the markets and barracoons with new merchandise. I've made you look timid and weak by reminding the loyal Hierarchs of the province how an Anacreon is *supposed* to behave. It's conceivable that I could convince them to rise against you and install me in your place, and even more likely that I could prevail upon the Deathlords to depose you, now that I'm in a position to get a message to them.

"But I don't want to. Despite our rocky start, I don't bear you any ill will, nor do I have any desire to be an Earthly governor. I just want to finish my appointed task and go home to the Isle of Sorrows. And you can still help me. As effective as my mercenaries are, they'd be far more effective fighting in tandem with regular Legionnaires. And knowledgeable as my man Fink has proven to be, I have no doubt that you three have access to intelligence beyond his ken.

"So I'll ask you one last time. Will you put your resources at my disposal as our masters bade you, or rebuff me again and suffer the consequences?"

"By the Scythe," said Gayoso, "how dare you threaten us?"

"Is it a threat to delineate the reality of your situation?" Montrose asked. "Some might regard it as a kindness."

"Let's talk about the reality of *your* situation," Shellabarger said. Montrose noticed that the man's hand had slipped inside his hip pocket, probably to grasp a small pistol, or, conceivably, some more arcane weapon. "You rashly walked into this room alone. What makes you think we'll let you walk out again?"

Montrose sighed. "Now who's dealing in vulgar threats? I came here without bodyguards, but scarcely unarmed." He opened the front of his mantle, exposing his rapier and pistol. "And at the risk of sounding immodest, I imagine I'm a better fighter than any native of this Citadel, and that my Arcanoi are at least as formidable as any of yours. I'm reasonably confident that I can cut my way out of your clutches if I need to."

Gayoso sneered. "And I'm just as confident you're wrong."

"All right, for purposes of argument, let's say I am," the Scot replied. "My army is at the gate. If I don't emerge from this parley within forty-five minutes, they'll assume the worst and react accordingly."

"A band of criminals," said Mrs. Duquesne crisply, "driven by avarice. I question whether such men are capable of loyalty, and, therefore, that they'd risk their necks on your behalf. I imagine they'd be just as happy to continue their plundering without you. If you don't return to them, they'll merely slink away."

Montrose suspected that was a shrewd guess, but he wasn't about to say so. "You might be surprised. I'm making them rich. That can inspire a measure of affection even in the most depraved. Moreover, they hate you people for putting prices on their heads, and they know the Citadel holds an abundance of treasure. They just might storm the place."

"Let them try," said Shellabarger, his insectile eyes glinting. "They're just muggers and gangsters. No match for real soldiers. Our men could defeat them anywhere. Crushing them on our home ground will be child's play."

"Once again," Montrose said, "you might be surprised. My fellows are the creme de la creme of the muggers and gangsters, as my lord Gayoso pointed out himself. Besides, you could encounter difficulties even if you win. Let's suppose that in the battle, the force controlled by one governor sustains heavy casualties, while the troops of another escape relatively unscathed. Wouldn't that upset the balance of power among the three of you? Are any of you inclined to risk it?"

"You make a convincing case," said Mrs. Duquesne, fingering the base of the hourglass. "Not that I needed convincing. As a loyal vassal of the Deathlords, I always meant to place my soldiers at your disposal, just as soon as I could work out the administrative details."

Montrose bowed. "Thank you, my lady. I humbly apologize for misconstruing your intentions."

"We don't have to do this," Gayoso said to her. "Natchez is *our* territory. We don't have to cede control of it to anyo—"

Mrs. Duquesne picked up the hourglass, inverted it, and set it down with a thump. Sand, barely visible through the dusky glass, began to trickle from the top chamber into the lower. Though they tried not to show it, both Gayoso and Shellabarger quailed. Montrose surmised that the hourglass was some sort of magical weapon, and that the woman in the spectacles had just cocked it.

"I'm throwing in with our guest," said Mrs. Duquesne. "I advise the two of you to do the same. Otherwise, I suppose we'll have to consider our détente at an end."

Scowling, Shellabarger took his hand out of his pocket, stood up, and extended ii to Montrose. "I'm with you, my lord Anacreon."

"And I," said Gayoso through clenched teeth.

TWENTY-ONE

As the Sister climbed the path to the ruinous church on the bluff, doing her best to tolerate the choking stench of the paper mill in the nearby town, she realized something was wrong. She didn't hear any voices, merely the cries of birds, the sighing of the wind, and the churning of the muddy river below her. *No!* she thought. *Please don't let it have happened again.*

She often sojourned with Heretic Circles as she traveled up and down the river. Since the Sisterhood of Athena didn't proselytize on behalf of one particular faith, many of her fellow religionists didn't regard her with the same loathing they felt for missionaries of rival sects. And over the course of the last few days, working her way south toward Natchez and the Louisiana border, she'd stopped at two Heretic Haunts, only to find them silent and empty.

When the Restless fought, they didn't leave behind the same kind of mess as the Quick. The slain dissolved, their bodies devoured by the Void. No stench of blood or gunsmoke hung in the air, and ghostly missiles and explosives couldn't mark the walls of a Skinlands structure. And with raw material at a premium, someone often scavenged every broken arrow and spent cartridge.

Thus the Sister hadn't found any concrete evidence that the strongholds had fallen to violence, but she couldn't think of any other explanation. Perhaps there were more of the same type of Spectre that had nearly destroyed her in Greenville, attacking Heretics up and down the river.

She wondered if there might be some still lurking in the derelict church above her.

If so, they were likely to spot her as soon as she reached the top of the rise. Since the building sat alone on the bluff, well removed from the shanties of Grand Gulf, she couldn't see any way to sneak up on it, certainly not in broad daylight.

She hesitated, weighing caution against her desire to examine the site for some clue as to what was actually going on, and then a wail of anguish sounded overhead.

If some of the Heretics were still here and in trouble, it was her sworn duty to help them. Thrusting her trepidation aside, she broke into a run. Her owl pendant bounced against her breasts.

Fleetingly grateful that wraiths didn't get winded, she scrambled onto the top of the bluff, she heard other noises: A rapid shuffling of feet. Pieces of wood swooshing through the air and clacking together. A whack and a gasp of pain when one of the sticks slammed against flesh. Evidently, two people were fighting with clubs.

The Sister ran on past a pair of sharp-smelling pine trees. Sensing her presence, a circle of bobwhites exploded up from the tall yellow grass. As she plunged through the crumbling brick wall, between two arched windows now covered with plywood, she pulled off her sunglasses. The tinted lenses, invaluable for protecting sensitive wraith eyes against the sunlight, would only hinder her inside the building.

Indeed, the musty nave, illuminated only by the light diffusing through a few tiny holes in the rotting walls and ceiling, was so gloomy that a mortal would have experienced difficulty navigating it at all. As worshippers of Odin, Thor, and the rest of the ancient Viking gods, the resident Heretics capable of exerting power across the Shroud had painstakingly erased every bit of Christian iconography, replacing crucifixes and saints with hammers, Valkyries, miniature longships, and representations of the world tree Yggdrasil.

In front of the altar, which was carved with scenes that owed more to Jack Kirby than thousand year-old Norse art, one lanky young man stood over another, hammering his victim with a baseball bat. The fellow on the floor had curled into a ball in an effort to shield his head and the more sensitive areas of his body. His own broken cudgel, another bat, lay a few feet away from him.

The Sister knew them both, and since each was a member of the Valhalla Circle, she couldn't imagine what had brought them to this pass. "Stop it!" she cried. "He's had enough!"

Philip, the wraith on his feet, kept on swinging as if he hadn't even heard. The body of Warren, the man on the floor, began to ripple and steam. Even though the bat wasn't made of darksteel, he'd taken so much punishment that he was about to vanish from the Shadowlands into the depths of the Tempest, a transit so perilous few survived it.

The Sister sprinted forward. Unwilling to take the time to circumvent the pews, she simply ran *through* them, simultaneously marshaling her Arcanos. As soon as she felt the power rise within her, she reached out with it, grunting with effort, snatched up the spear on the altar, and whirled it at Philip, seeking not to drive the darksteel point into him but to bash him with the shaft.

The length of wood cracked him across the back of his head, staggering him, sparing Warren another blow. Plunging through one of the benches in the first row, the Sister grabbed Philip by the arm.

The contact stung her hand so badly that she nearly yanked it away again. She could *feel* the rage and self-loathing boiling through Philip's substance like a swarm of angry hornets.

"Your Shadow has taken control of you!" she told him. "You have to push it back down!"

Snarling, the pupils of his gray eyes seething, he tried to break her grip. She strained to keep him helplessly off balance. He didn't manage to tear himself free, but despite her *sifu*'s assurances that the grapple she was employing would neutralize any opponent, no matter how big and strong, he managed to shift the bat into his free hand and lash it at her skull.

She jerked up her arm to block. Pain stabbed through her wrist. She thrust her face so close to Philip's that an onlooker might have imagined she meant to bite him. "Fight it!" she said. "Ask Tyr to help you!" If she recalled correctly, the one-handed god was his particular patron.

He pulled back the bat for another blow, and then the shimmering darkness vanished from his eyes. His weapon tumbled from his hand and clattered on the floor. His knees buckled as if he meant to follow it down. Awkwardly, her battered arm throbbing, she caught hold of him anew, and he slumped against her.

She hoped he wasn't going to faint. Some wraiths did when such an episode ended. "You're all right now," she said. "It's gone."

To her relief, he drew himself up, supporting his own weight, and looked wildly about. "Warren! My god! Is Warren—"

She turned Philip around until he was looking at the motionless form on the floor. "There. See, he's out cold, but he's not fading. He'll be all right, too. What unleashed your Shadow? And where is everybody else?"

Philip began to sob.

"Please," said the Sister, "tell me. If I don't understand the problem, I can't help."

The Heretic shook his head. Strands of his long, mousy brown hair slipped down his high, bony forehead. "You couldn't anyway. No one could."

"You don't know that," the missionary said. She guided him to a pew and sat him down. "Just pull yourself together, start at the beginning, and tell me the story."

He shrugged miserably. "All right. Why not? Have you heard about the priests and the Pardoners disappearing?"

She cocked her head. "No, not unless you're talking about what the Quick are calling the Atheist murders. A string of serial killings."

He irritably waved his hand. "I don't know anything about that. I'm talking about something that concerns us wraiths. I heard a rumor that over the past few weeks, in various Necropoli along the river, a few Heretic teachers and Pardoners—"

"The two sorts of counselor to whom a wraith might turn for spiritual guidance," the Sister murmured thoughtfully.

"—have vanished. Personally, I didn't think much of it. The Restless disappear for all kinds of reasons all the time. Slavers or Spectres catch you. Oblivion grabs you and you become a doomshade yourself or fall into the Void. Or maybe you just get sick of where you are and move on, either to somewhere else in the Shadowlands or into the Tempest to look for your version of Paradise. So I wasn't particularly worried that anything would happen to our own priest and priestess, and certainly not to our entire Circle.

"But last night, Warren and I went down into Grand Gulf to watch a couple movies and then hang around the Necropolis. About two in the morning, we heard shooting and screams coming from the temple here. When we looked in this direction, we saw the muzzle flashes of the guns. We ran back as quickly as we could." He averted his face. "But we didn't charge right back into the thick of things. We stopped a ways back and tried to scope out what was going on."

The Sister didn't understand why he was ashamed. Resting her hand lightly on his forearm, she said, "I would have done the same thing."

"What we saw," Philip said, "was that the temple was under attack by a whole bunch of people. A lot of them looked more like bandits or river pirates than any Legionnaires I ever saw, but they had banners with emblems of the Smiling Lord, the Beggar Lord, the Emerald Lord, and the Unlidded Eye on them, so I guess they must have been Hierarchs even so. The leader, a guy with long, wavy red hair, had a black cape and a fancy sword, like some kind of Stygian honcho."

A swordsman with a mane of auburn hair. Old joys and sorrows stirred in the Sister's breast. But of course Philip couldn't be referring to the same person she'd known. Surely such a splendid soul had never found himself mired in the purgatory of the Underworld in the first place. Annoyed at her own sentimentality, she tried to push aside her memories and focus on the present situation.

"Warren and I could see right away that our people were losing," Philip continued. "The Hierarchs had us outnumbered and they were better armed. And so—" He faltered, then took a deep breath. "And so we just hid and watched while the Stygians took everyone else prisoner, chained them up, marched them down to the river, and carried them away on their boats. I saw what happened to Barbara. My girl friend. They took her clothes off and put their hands all over her. There was so much fear in her eyes!"

"Do you think you actually could have helped her?" the Sister asked. "Or would you merely have gotten killed or captured yourself? I'm sure she wouldn't have wanted that."

"You don't understand," he said. "When I joined the Circle, I swore to Tyr that I'd never back down. That I'd make myself a warrior fit to stand against Oblivion at Ragnarok. I promised myself that from then on, I was going to be a different person. But when the crunch came, I chickened out *again*, just like I always did when I was alive!"

"Courage doesn't mean throwing your existence or your freedom away uselessly," the Sister replied. "Moreover, people *do* change. I believe that's why we become wraiths in the first place, to refine our natures until we're worthy to Transcend. Even if you froze yesterday, you can be brave tomorrow. Simply resolve to do better. When you do, perhaps you can even free Barbara and the others."

He blinked. "Do you really think so?"

"I don't know," she admitted. "The Underworld is a bleak, cruel place, and the Hierarchy is one of the cruelest things in it. Your friends could already be on their way to Stygia. But until we know that for a fact, we mustn't abandon hope. Please, finish your story."

"There isn't much left to tell," Philip said. "After the raiders sailed away down river, Warren and I just hung around here. I guess we were too dazed to do anything else. And gradually I started to blame him for my cowardice. I told myself that if *he* hadn't stopped, I wouldn't have either. I would have run right out and attacked the Hierarchs. And maybe I could have taken out the redheaded guy, and that would have turned the tide. In the end I hated Warren so much that I just had to tear into him."

"Did any of the Legionnaires have two reptilian heads?" the Sister asked.

Clearly puzzled, Philip frowned. "Not that I noticed. They all looked pretty human. The usual sprinkling of horns, cloven hooves, and that stuff. Why do you ask?"

As briefly as possible, she told him about the assassin who had stalked her through Greenville.

"Do you think there's a connection?" he asked.

She grimaced. "I wish I knew. We have too many unanswered questions. Has someone truly been systematically destroying missionaries like me, Heretic leaders, and Pardoners? If so, one would logically suspect Spectres, since wraiths of every other stripe value Pardoners, given that we all need to quell our Shadows on occasion. But now that we know the Hierarchy is raiding Heretic communities, logic *also* suggests that it's responsible for the disappearance of the priests as well. Otherwise the synchrony of the two campaigns is too much of a coincidence."

"But why would you even bother to assassinate individual Heretic masters if you intended to destroy entire Circles at once?" Philip asked.

"It doesn't appear to make any sense, does it? Perhaps you were right, and there's nothing to the gossip you heard. Maybe it was just the luck of the draw that made the double-headed spirit decide to hunt me. In any case, we should be glad we aren't *entirely* in the dark. We do understand the nature of the greatest threat facing us. For some reason, the local Hierarchs have grown militant again. It's imperative that we Heretics strike back hard enough to convince them to leave us alone. Otherwise they'll pick off our enclaves one by one."

"But what can we do?" Philip asked. "Does the Sisterhood of Athena have an army?"

"A small one," the blond woman said, "but it won't come east of the Rockies. It has too many commitments on the West Coast."

"Then we're beaten," Philip said. "There were too many Hierarchs, and they fought too well. No Heretic Circle in the area is a match for them."

"Possibly not individually. If they unite, it could be a different story."

"It won't happen," Philip said. "They all hate each other as much or more than they hate Stygia."

"But they all want to survive," the Sister said. "And some of them don't hate me." She smiled wryly. "That's the advantage of preaching wishy-washy, nondenominational fluff. No one worries that I might lure his parishioners away. I might be able to bring a selection of the local Renegades into the coalition, too. Some of them are shrewd enough to grasp that once the Hierarchy finishes crushing Heretics, it's likely to come after them."

"But do you really think we can defeat Legionnaires?" Philip asked.

She had no idea. Perhaps no one would listen to her, or everyone who did would perish uselessly on the battlefield. But with the ease of long practice, before death and after, she concealed her doubts behind a smile. "With the Aesir's help, why not?"

TWENTY-TWO

Bewildered, Bellamy paced the frigid walkways and galleries of the dark stone city, past grotesque statuary and small, iron-bound doors sunk in odd corners of immense carved tableaux, almost as if the architect had been trying to hide the entrances amid the details of the sculptures. Occasionally the FBI agent's wandering took him across a narrow iron bridge, where, looking over the side, he saw level after level of chambers and corridors, sporadically lit by some of the ghastly anthropomorphic torches, falling away into darkness beneath his feet. Sometimes he blundered onto a terrace, where huge towers with crenellated ramparts loomed above him.

Whenever that happened, he scurried back inside as quickly as possible. Because for some reason he couldn't—or didn't want to—remember, the black, starless sky with its flickering thunderheads disturbed him even more than the obsession with suffering and death manifest in many of the carvings, the soft moans whispering from the gulfs below him, or even his own inability to remember how he'd come to this place.

After what seemed like hours, he climbed a staircase and found himself on a balcony connected by an arcing span of gray metal to a similar platform jutting from the rococo facade of the adjacent tower. On the other side of the bridge stood a slender, feminine figure in a voluminous scarlet robe. A red wooden mask concealed her features, but not the magenta streaks in her spiky hair.

"Astarte?" he asked.

She stretched out her hands as if she could neither speak nor run to him, but was beseeching him to come to her.

Even though it meant stepping out under the open sky, he was eager to do precisely that. She was the first familiar thing he'd seen since his arrival, indeed, the first *person*. With a pang of trepidation, and forbidding himself to look either up or down, he strode onto the unrailed bridge. The metal surface clinked beneath his tread.

The world blazed white, and a deafening crash split the air. Dazzled, he sensed rather than saw the length of bridge in front of him shattering like glass. He reflexively dropped onto his belly and wrapped his arms around the span of metal beneath him.

From the way it was shuddering, he doubted that he'd actually done himself any good. He wasn't sure if lightning had struck the bridge itself or merely something nearby, but in any case it felt as if the entire structure was about to tear away from its moorings and fall into the manmade canyon below.

But if didn't, and when the vibrations subsided, he cautiously raised his head. Now separated from him by the gap in the bridge, Astarte sunk to her knees in a pantomime of despair.

He felt an urge to run and jump to her. But even had he been sure he could leap far enough, either of the remaining sections of bridge might collapse at any moment, particularly if subjected to stress. As he wormed his way backwards, he said, "Don't worry! I'll still get to you. There has to be another way across."

As if to make a liar out of him, lighting flared and thunder boomed again, violently shaking his perch. This time, he saw a forked bolt of glare strike the cornice of the building on the other side of the drop. The wall disintegrated, the rumble echoing the growl of the thunder. An avalanche of stone fell down the side of the structure, and Astarte and her balcony fell with it.

"No!" Bellamy screamed, and then her tiny form vanished into the gulf.

He sobbed, though, strangely, his eyes remained dry. Then he realized the rumbling sound was still grinding on and on. In fact, it was growing louder, with a steady, rhythmic beat which suggested laughter. His section of broken bridge began to shudder.

After a moment he realized that it wasn't *just* his perch. All of the towers around him were swaying, also. Evidently the lightning strikes had triggered an earthquake.

One by one, the mighty buildings collapsed, the rubble streaming into the darkness below. Bellamy expected the broken bridge to fall at any moment. But for some reason it, and the edifice to which it was attached, endured while other structures crumbled, as if God wanted him to witness the devastation.

Still trying to inch backward to a safer position, ludicrous as such a concept now seemed, he *did* watch. And at first he wasn't particularly afraid. The spectacle unfolding before him was so huge and strange that it inspired wonder instead of dread.

But as the city dissolved, he began to glimpse what lay below it. The shards of stone weren't just tumbling to the ground, or even into some gigantic crevice that had opened in the earth. They were falling into a well of darkness that glittered and spun like a whirlpool. As soon as Bellamy caught sight of it, he sensed that it was the pure essence of annihilation and simultaneously the primal fountainhead of cruelty and madness.

The overwhelming probability that *he* was doomed to drop into the vortex filled him with terror. He tried to creep backward faster, while the bridge began to creak, squeal, and shake more violently. His groping foot brushed the edge of the balcony, and then something snapped. He and his perch lurched forward—

—and he thrashed, his arms immobilized, metal clattering. After a moment, panting, his heart hammering, he realized he'd just awakened from a nightmare.

In reality, he lay on a bed in a small room, his hands shackled, quite possibly with his own handcuffs, to a post in the carved oak headboard. A figure stood over him. He had to peer for a moment to be certain it was Marilyn. Her lean body clad in a nondescript suit and narrow knit tie, her face scrubbed clean of makeup and her wig discarded, she might almost have been mistaken for a heterosexual male. Only her plucked eyebrows, crimson nail polish, and the modest bulge of her breast implants betrayed her transsexuality.

"Did you have a bad dream?" she asked mildly.

He certainly had. Something about the dark city the mystic symbols had shown him. And a black whirlpool...Waxman had claimed to have seen something similar in his visions! Maybe the dream had actually *meant* something.

Or maybe it hadn't. Bellamy was no psychic. He'd probably dreamed about the vortex simply because Waxman *had* told him about it. And, in any case, he had more immediate problems. He tried to speak and discovered that his mouth was painfully dry.

Marilyn picked up a crystal tumbler of water from the night stand and held it to his lips. The cold liquid soothed his throat wonderfully. He was tempted to guzzle it all, but he knew too much could make him sick.

His captor took the glass away. "Where's Astarte?" Bellamy asked.

"She's safe," said Marilyn. "She's resting comfortably in another bedroom."

"Good," Bellamy said. "Who are you really?"

"The Chancellor of the New Orleans Chapter House of the Arcanum," Marilyn said with a hint of pride.

Bellamy shook his head, trying to understand, his mind still fuzzy from the drug she'd given him. "Then the place we found you in, the story you fed us..."

"Some of what I said was true. I do frequent that establishment, and I do partake of what you might consider rather sordid pleasures there. When a person carries as much responsibility as I do, it can be an exquisite relief to feel helpless and weak. But more importantly, the bondage and humiliation are a means to an end. To perform the Great Work, an alchemist has to explore every facet of his character, psyche and shadow, animus and anima, master and slave. That's why I haven't had my final surgery yet, even though my body is ready. I think it benefits me to be hermaphroditic."

"Are you telling me you let people tie you up and spank you so you can learn magic? If so, I think you can stop now. Your Witches' Alphabet hexed the heck out of me."

Marilyn shrugged. "I can create one or two minor effects, sometimes, with hours of preparation. So could you, if you undertook the proper course of study and meditation. But my tricks are nothing compared to genuine sorcery. I once spied on a true mage through a pair of binoculars. The miracles he created, one after another, as easily as you or I could snap our fingers!"

"Maybe you should have asked him to give you a lesson."

"A number of Arcanists have tried. Some have been turned away. Some have been cursed for their presumption. And a few have disappeared, perhaps because the mage accepted them, perhaps because he killed them. Suffice it to say, even if I were given a chance to make the same request, I don't like the odds. I'd rather try to discover the wizards' techniques of empowerment independently, through study and experimentation."

"I see your point," Bellamy said, flexing his shackled arms to ease a cramp. "What I don't get is why, if you are one of Keene's colleagues, you witched me, doped me, and handcuffed me. I showed you my credentials."

"Identification can be forged. And even if you were a genuine FBI agent, what does *that* mean? What master do the Federal police actually serve?"

Bellamy grimaced. "I think you've been watching too many Oliver Stone movies."

"You may be right," Marilyn said. "On the other hand, it may be that all of us, the ordinary people, the uninitiated, are simply cattle, and our laws, institutions, and the dogma we've been raised to believe are the fences our owners use to keep us in our place.

"Be that as it may, I had good reason to be wary of you in particular. It seemed unlikely that a legitimate investigator would conduct his business with someone like Astarte in tow."

"I admit, I'm poking around without Bureau authorization," Bellamy said. "That's because my boss doesn't believe in the paranormal. And I just sort of wound up saddled with Astarte."

"You also told me that R. J. was killed by a statue that came to life. I believe in such occurrences, though I've never had the good fortune to witness one. They're well documented. But the news media said he was killed with a gun." The transsexual picked up Bellamy's Browning from a small parquet table. "If I gave this particular pistol to the police for a ballistics test, I wonder what the results would show."

"That it fired the shot that killed your friend," Bellamy said. He could feel a cold sweat breaking out under his arms. "Because the statue picked it up and used it. I didn't tell you every detail of my story. I didn't see any reason to. But I can if you want."

"You already have. Shortly after you arrived, we gave you a second shot, of truth serum, and interrogated you extensively." Marilyn smiled thinly. "We Arcanists are more than a society of bookworms and theoreticians. We train ourselves to handle desperate situations as competently as Federal agents do."

Bellamy felt mingled resentment and relief. "If you questioned me under truth serum, then you know I'm on the up and up. Stop playing mind games and take off the handcuffs."

"It isn't quite that simple," Marilyn said. "I now find myself in the awkward position of having assaulted and kidnapped you."

"I'm not going to arrest you," Bellamy said. "God knows, I should, but if Astarte really is okay, and you help me catch the Atheist, I'll let you off the hook."

"But you'll know about the Arcanum. You'll know I'm a member. And you're an FBI agent. Aren't you duty-bound to report your discoveries to your superiors?"

"I know how to protect an informant," Bellamy said, "even from my bosses when I have to. Don't you want to help me nail whoever—or whatever—killed Keene?"

"I liked R. J. But he was a liability. He held the shortsighted attitude that we ought to run around protecting people and righting wrongs as if we were the police ourselves, bringing the wrath of the supernaturals down on our heads before we were remotely prepared to cope with it. You see where it got him."

"In other words, he deserved to die. And so do the rest of the Atheist's victims."

Marilyn scowled as she set the Browning back on the table. "No, of course not. You're deliberately distorting my point of view. Which is that the Arcanum has to walk softly until it can acquire enough information to make a difference for the entire human race, not just a few isolated individuals."

"If the individuals don't matter, then the whole human race doesn't either. And maybe to you, it doesn't. Maybe all you *really* care about is scoring some magic for yourself."

Marilyn's eyes narrowed. "You can't provoke me with insults."

"What about with logic? If you don't help me, or even let me go, what's the alternative? Are you going to hold Astarte and me prisoner forever? Or murder us? Are you that unscrupulous, and that stupid?"

"I hope it won't come to that," the Arcanist said. "We know how to use drugs for brainwashing as well as interrogation. We can expunge your memory of the Arcanum so thoroughly that no trace of it will remain, and then release you unharmed."

A ghastly picture popped into Bellamy's mind. He imagined a cop loading him into the back of a squad car *again*, dazed and disoriented, with a second hole in his memory. Such a fiasco would unquestionably cost him both his career and any hope of ever catching the Atheist. At that moment, even death seemed preferable.

He struggled to think of another argument, to find a way to convince Marilyn to help him, when a scream reverberated through the building. The transsexual frowned, wheeled, and ran out the door, leaving her captive alone.

TWENTY-THREE

A man shouted, "My god!" Then something crashed. Bellamy wondered what was happening.

Whatever it was, he knew he didn't want to stay handcuffed to the bed if the disturbance was going to spill into the room, or, come to think of it, even if it wasn't. He inspected the carved post that Marilyn had looped the handcuff chain around, and then he smiled.

The Arcanist might *think* she knew as much about security and restraint as any Fed, but she was kidding herself. The headboard looked reasonably substantial, but a strong man might be able to break it.

Bellamy rolled off the mattress. The motion brought a surge of dizziness and nausea. Silently cursing Marilyn and her drugs, he knelt on the gleaming hardwood floor with his body pressed against the side of the bed, anchoring himself as best he could. Then he gripped the post and pulled.

The wood cut into his fingers. It flexed and squeaked, but didn't break. Elsewhere in the house, something thumped. It sounded like a body falling to the floor. A pistol with a silencer coughed twice.

Bellamy tried to make his muscles loose and relaxed and then, shouting, wrenched at the wood again, attempting to exert every iota of his strength in one explosive burst the way his unarmed-combat instructor had taught him.

The post snapped at the top. He hastily fumbled the handcuff chain free, scrambled up, and swayed with another surge of vertigo. Ignoring it as best he could, he snatched a handcuff key off the little table and unlocked his restraints. He grabbed his Browning, made sure it was still loaded, jacked a round into the chamber, pivoted toward the door, and hesitated.

What was waiting beyond the threshold? A ghastly marvel like the living statue or something even worse, something so awful the mere sight of it would drive him out of his mind?

Grimacing, he told himself it didn't matter. Whatever it was, he had to deal with it before it murdered *another* potential informant, or wandered into Astarte's room and found her lying helpless.

Moving warily through the door, he found himself at the end of a gloomy hall, beside an upper-story window. Beyond the glass were the night sky, towering oaks, cobblestone sidewalks, and elegant houses with colonnaded facades and cornstalk fences. Evidently the Chapter House was in the Garden District.

He noticed that the palm of his left hand was bleeding. He must have cut it on a splinter when the headboard broke. He wiped it on his pants leg, then stalked on down the corridor.

The hallway led him to a curving staircase. He surmised that the noises he'd heard had echoed up from the ground floor, but everything was quiet now.

Trying to be silent himself, he crept down the steps, past a series of small Impressionist landscapes that looked familiar, as if he might have seen them, or other works by the same hand, in the Art Appreciation course he'd taken in college. His mouth felt as dry as desert sand again.

As he neared the foot of the stairs, he caught the smells of blood and gun smoke. At first glance, the ground floor of the house seemed to be furnished with the sort of antiques one would expect in an antebellum mansion, but also with shelf after shelf of books and an assortment of strange curios. The freakishly misshapen skull of either a man or some other primate. A desiccated coffin lying on trestles. An alabaster statue of a kneeling witch kissing a goat-headed Satan on the rump.

Alighting in the foyer, Bellamy saw an Asian woman sprawled motionless just inside a doorway to his right. She had a bloody dent in her scalp and a spike of broken bone protruding from her twisted arm, and she wasn't breathing. Resisting the temptation to flee through the front door while he had the chance, he stepped over her and skulked on.

Hideous faces leered from the shadows. His heart jolting, he kept pivoting and pointing his gun before he realized that he'd merely glimpsed another macabre piece of art. In the course of the next two minutes he found two more Arcanists, one unconscious, his left eye gouged from its socket, and the other dead. Then he heard a contralto voice chanting in Latin.

Following the sound, he peeked through a doorway. On the other side was a spacious room furnished with desks and leather armchairs, evidently the heart of the library which had spilled out into the rest of the house. Row after row of books covered the walls from floor to ceiling, suffusing the air with the musty scents of old paper and crumbling leather.

Marilyn stood at the far end of the chamber, brandishing a crucifix with the coils of a snake rather than the body of Jesus draped around the cross. She was the one doing the chanting. A stocky, gray-haired man in the center of the room was doing his best to approach her. From the hunch of his shoulders and his laborious, lurching movements, Bellamy understood that he was having to force his way forward, as if the air around him had thickened to the consistency of mud. Presumably the artifact in Marilyn's grip was responsible.

Despite the uncanny aspects of the situation, Bellamy felt a pang of relief, that Marilyn's assailant was a human being. Obviously a formidable one, but not some horror that would freeze him in his tracks. He was going to be all right.

Suddenly the crucifix shattered, and Marilyn reeled backward. Released from his invisible bonds, her attacker scrambled after her. Bellamy lunged through the doorway, leveled his automatic, and shouted, "Stop or I'll shoot!"

The gray-haired man spun around, and Bellamy gasped. Judging from the bloody holes, someone had *already* shot the intruder, once in the center of the chest and once in the forehead, and it didn't appear to have slowed him down at all. *There should have been exit wounds*, the agent thought uselessly. *That would have given me a little warning*.

The stranger charged. *Shoot!* Bellamy told himself. For a moment, he didn't think he'd be able to, that shock had severed the link between his will and his body, but finally his finger started squeezing the trigger.

The bullets staggered the gray-haired man, but he wouldn't fall down. Snarling, hands outstretched, he made a grab for Bellamy's throat.

Bellamy sidestepped and swept his arm in a block, but he wasn't quite fast or strong enough. His attacker missed his neck, but managed to grasp his shoulder and bull him backward.

Bellamy's spine slammed against the door frame. The gun nearly tumbled from his hand. Clutching frantically, he managed to keep his grip on it.

Using only his right hand, the gray-haired man grabbed him by the throat and jerked him into the air, a jolt that nearly snapped his spine. His assailant began to strangle him.

Bellamy tried to swing the Browning into position for another shot. With his free hand, the gray-haired man struggled to immobilize the gun. Bellamy supposed that was encouraging in its way, in that it implied the murderer *was* susceptible to gunfire. It was just that no one had shot him *enough* yet.

A roaring filled Bellamy's ears, and dark spots swam at the corners of his vision. He realized he was only seconds from blacking out. Straining, he managed to force the pistol another inch toward the gray-haired man's torso. He couldn't tell if it was actually in line to hit the target, but he knew it was as close as it was going to get. He fired three shots and then the magazine was empty.

The gray-headed man's mouth fell open. Then, to Bellamy's surprise, the slack-jawed expression of astonishment gave way, not to a grimace of anguish or another snarl of rage, but to a smile. The agent had the feeling that he was looking into the face of a completely different person, someone who was *grateful* he'd been shot.

The gray-haired man collapsed, dragging Bellamy to the floor with him. Still choking, Bellamy scrabbled at the fingers constricting his throat. Finally he managed to tear them away. He slumped on the floor, shivering and gasping.

Rapid footsteps pattered across the floor. Bellamy jerked his head up. Marilyn was running toward him with a knotted blue cord in her red-nailed hands.

It took Bellamy a moment to remember that she was a potential threat as well. And he was still too winded to wrestle with her. Hoping she didn't realize it was empty, he raised the Browning. His hand trembled as if he were ninety years old.

Marilyn skidded to a halt. "It's all right. I want to bind *him*. This particular rope should hold him."

"He's dead," Bellamy croaked. He realized that he'd never killed anyone before, not unless you counted the statue. He wondered if he'd feel terrible once he'd had a chance to think about it. "Where were you when I needed you?"

"When the Cross of Hermes broke, there was a sort of backlash," Marilyn said defensively. "It stunned me. I came running as soon as I recovered my senses. Now please, let me tie him. You can't be certain he's dead, or that death will stop him if he is."

Bellamy supposed she had a point. He shifted himself away from what at least seemed to be a lifeless corpse. Marilyn knelt, rolled it on its stomach, and hog-tied it.

The agent wished that his heart would stop hammering, and that he could catch his breath. "At least one of the people who got attacked is hurt but still alive. He needs help right away."

"We have a doctor on retainer," said Marilyn. She reached inside her jacket and brought out a cellular phone.

"I think you should get an ambulance."

The transsexual shook her head. "The Arcanum is a secret fellowship. We can't afford to let the authorities know about this mess. Besides which, at the moment you're more or less operating outside the law yourself. Do *you* want to talk to the police?"

Not without a pang of guilt, Bellamy silently conceded she had a point.

"Our man is very good," Marilyn continued. She dialed, spoke tersely to the physician, and hung up. "He'll be right over. I just hope the neighbors didn't hear the shooting. You wouldn't think it to look at the old place, but we paid a contractor to install state-of-the-art soundproofing."

Bellamy dragged himself to his feet. "I know first aid," he said, his voice still a rasp and his throat still aching. "I'll try to help your friend until the doctor gets here. *If* I can trust you not to jump me while I work."

"You can," Marilyn said. "They began to retrace their steps through the enormous house. Lightheaded, Bellamy could have sworn that a sphinx in a painting winked at him.

"What happened here?" the agent asked.

Marilyn shrugged. "I didn't see the start of it, either. I was upstairs with you. But apparently our attacker somehow broke into the house and started attacking everyone he encountered."

"How could he get hurt as badly as he was and keep coming for us? What *was* he?"

A dead body appeared in the gloom ahead. Marilyn flinched. Perhaps she cared more deeply about her fellow Arcanists than Bellamy would have suspected. "He was supernatural," she said, her cool tone betraying nothing of her dismay. "Otherwise, the Cross of Hermes wouldn't have affected him. I can't be sure of any more than that, but I do have a theory. When statues and similar objects come to life, it's supposedly because a spirit has decided to inhabit them. It's also possible for a discarnate entity to possess a living human or animal body, and such beings can remain active in the face of damage that would incapacitate a wholly natural creature. That's because they don't feel the pain to the same degree that you or I would."

"I wonder if he was the Atheist." Bellamy scowled. "No. No, I don't. Maybe he committed *some* of the murders, but even if he did, my instincts tell me that he was only one small part of whatever it is that's going on."

"So do mine," Marilyn said.

They stepped into the next room and the body of the Arcanist with the missing eye came into view. Bellamy crouched and pressed his fingertips lightly against the side of the occultist's neck. The injured man's skin was clammy and his pulse was fluttery, but at least he still had one. "Get something to cover him up, and something we can use to prop his feet up."

Marilyn pulled an afghan off a sofa and draped it over her unconscious colleague. "This is my fault," she said. "I should never have brought you here. Paranormal creatures have arcane means of locating people they want to find. I should have anticipated that your enemies might track you."

"Maybe they did," Bellamy said. He noticed that the wounded man had a blue handkerchief in his breast pocket. He removed it and packed one end in the Arcanist's ravaged eye socket in an effort to stop the bleeding. Despite his training and experience, the operation made him feel queasy. "On the other hand, they might not even have realized I was here. Maybe they decided to hit you for the same reason they apparently decided to kill Waxman, just to make absolutely sure the Arcanum wouldn't interfere in their plans."

Marilyn hoisted the injured man's feet onto an ottoman. "But except for R. J., none of us *intended* to meddle in their business."

"They may not have understood that," Bellamy said. "Or they may have figured that you guys were some of the very few people who might eventually catch on to what they're up to, and that if you did, you *would* feel obliged to get involved. Anyway, considering what's happened, you have to assume you're targets, which means you'd better clear out of this place for the duration."

Marilyn grimaced. "Yes. I thought we had the house sealed with magical wards, but evidently they don't work. But dear Lord! All the artifacts and books, unprotected! They could set the building on fire!"

"If they do, it'll be better if it burns without you inside it."

The transsexual sighed. "I can't argue with that. I suppose everyone should leave his home as well. Given that the Atheist located our headquarters, it's conceivable that he knows the identity of every member of the Chapter. Damn it!"

"Are you going to help me now?" Bellamy asked.

"What choice do we have?" Marilyn replied bitterly. "But we could still erase Astarte's memory and send her on her way."

Bellamy hesitated. The brainwashing would probably serve to remove the girl from danger. But, as he knew all too well, it was horrible to have something punch a hole in your mind. Much as she sometimes annoyed him, he could never subject her to such a violation.

"No," he said. "Now that she's come this far, maybe she's earned the right to go the distance."

TWENTY-FOUR

Kevin Bolan awoke hot and sweaty, his nerves jangling with tension, the residue, he assumed, of some forgotten nightmare, and the bedclothes tangled. Beside him, his plump, curly-headed wife Dora slept on oblivious, a soft snore buzzing from her open mouth.

Bolan looked at the glowing face of the digital clock radio on the night stand. It was almost seven. Time to rise and shine, and even though he felt as if he'd barely slept at all, he did his best to feel cheerful about it. A minister ought to be happy to get up Sunday morning.

Trying not to wake Dora, he stood and shuffled into the bathroom. After urinating, he stepped in front of the sink. He was reaching to open the medicine cabinet when the image in the mirror caught his eye.

At first it was just a peculiar shape, as though his brain refused to interpret it.

Then it snapped into focus. A misshapen head with two reptilian faces leering side by side, each with a fanged, scaly set of jaws, a pale forked tongue, and a pair of luminous amber eyes.

He squealed and stumbled backward into the doorway. His heel caught on the edge of the bedroom carpet and he tumbled onto his butt.

Dora bolted upright in bed. "What's wrong?" she cried.

"The mirror—" Bolan began, and then rapid footsteps pounded up the stairs. The minister yelped again before he realized that he must be hearing his bodyguard, rushing to his aid.

Clad in camouflage fatigues and combat boots, a CAR 15 assault rifle leveled, the red-faced, barrel-chested form of Glen McGinty burst through the door. "What is it?" he asked.

Bolan belatedly realized that he couldn't *really* have seen what he'd thought he'd seen. Though his heart was still racing, his fear began to give way to embarrassment. "I'm sorry," he said. "I looked in the mirror, and I thought the face looking back wasn't mine. I guess I was still half asleep. Still dreaming."

"Good grief," Dora said, grimacing. She grabbed a handful of covers and pulled them up to her chin, shielding her heavy breasts with their prominent nipples, inadequately concealed by her thin cotton nightgown, from McGinty's gaze.

Even though Bolan approved of her modesty, he thought that in this instance, she almost needn't have bothered. McGinty was too caught up in his role of protector to cast a lustful eye in her direction. Stepping over the minister's legs, he stalked into the lavatory as if the Atheist actually might be lurking in the mirror. He peered suspiciously this way and that, whisked the shower curtain open, and finally, almost grudgingly announced, "All clear."

"Thank you," said Bolan, clambering to his feet. "I really *am* sorry to have made you race up here."

"All part of the job," said McGinty in his manliest tones. "I'll be downstairs if you need me." He ambled out the door and closed it behind him.

"How much longer are you going to keep those people around?" Dora asked.

"Until the Atheist is arrested," Bolan said. "I'm sure the police will get him soon." He felt a twinge of guilt, because the second statement was a lie. Since he'd begun to fret about the murders, he'd read up on the subject of serial killers. Some of them operated for years without getting caught. Some were *never* apprehended.

"What do you think the odds are of the Atheist actually coming after *you?*" Dora asked.

"Probably slim," Bolan said, pulling off his striped pajama shirt. As always, he felt a pang of disgust at the ring of flab around his middle. "But for some reason, I can't stop thinking about the possibility. Call me timid, but that's the way it is. If Glen and the other members of the militia want to guard me, and that makes me feel safer, what's the harm?"

"The harm is that we don't have any privacy," Dora said. "I hope you understand that I am *not* going to have relations with you as long as there's a chance someone might overhear. Besides, you've said yourself that the Tennessee Patriots' League are a bunch of gun-crazy yahoos. Have you talked to any of them about the Atheist? They think he's a secret agent working for the Trilateral Commission and the

International Masonic Conspiracy."

"They may be eccentric," Bolan said, "but they're still my parishioners, and they're giving up their free time to help me. Please, can't you put up with them for at least a few more days?"

"Can't you try putting your trust in the Lord?" she replied, but then her expression softened. "Oh, all right. If it makes you feel better. *Do* you feel all right now? Did you hurt yourself when you fell?"

"I'm fine," he said. "Thanks for being so understanding."

She got out of bed and pulled on her quilted housecoat and fuzzy Chip 'n' Dale slippers, souvenir of a Disney World vacation two years ago. Then, to his surprise, she came to him, put her arms around him, and gave him a long kiss. "You really don't need bodyguards," she murmured. "*I* love you too much to let anything happen to you."

He felt a surge of desire and slid his hand onto her bottom, but she squirmed out of his embrace.

"I told you, no," she said, a hint of mischief in her dark brown eyes. "Not until we're completely alone. Besides, we don't have time. Get ready for work and I'll go start breakfast." She turned and exited the room.

Bolan sighed and reentered the bathroom, flinching reflexively as he glimpsed the mirror. But nothing peered back at him, nothing but his own round face, its pale blue eyes slightly bloodshot and its chin gray with stubble.

He brushed his teeth, shaved, and showered. The drumming water refreshed him and gave him hope that he might actually enjoy the rest of the day. As he dressed, the sizzle and aroma of frying bacon wafted up the stairs. His stomach growled.

He looked at his rickety tie rack, a gift from a parishioner with a distinctly limited aptitude for woodwork, and decided on the teal silk one. But as he reached for it, he faltered.

Or rather, his arm did. Nothing had distracted Bolan himself from his intent, but the limb simply froze in mid-extension, as if it had a will of its own. Numbness flowed from his fingertips down to his elbow.

Bewildered, he tried again to lift the tie off its peg. Instead of obeying, his hand closed, opened, made a tight fist, and opened once more. After that it snapped its fingers. Then, when the minister had forgotten all about the tie, it finally picked it up.

Bolan imagined his hand flipping the neckwear around uncanny dexterity, tying it into a noose, then tossing it over his head and choking him. He grabbed its wrist with his left hand, the still-obedient one, and at that instant the numbness tingled away. His right arm shuddered, and the blue tie fell to the floor.

The minister gingerly flexed the fingers of his rebellious hand. The organ felt like *his* flesh once again, as much a part of his body as ever.

I'm too tired, Bolan thought. *Dora's right, I've got to get over this morbid fear of the Atheist before I have a breakdown. I don't know why I'm so paranoid. I've never had these kinds of problems before.*

He started to pick up the fallen tie, then, with a quiver of aversion, left it on the floor. He selected a red one instead, and headed downstairs.

He found McGinty and Dora in the kitchen. The self-styled militiaman was seated at the table spreading orange marmalade on a piece of toast, and she was scrambling eggs at the stove. "Perfect timing," she said. "Everything will be ready in a second."

"Great," he said, trying to shake off the rest of his anxiety. He sat down, reached for some toast, and his arm went numb and locked up on him again.

This isn't happening, he told himself. *It's all in your head.* Exerting every iota of his willpower, he strained to grasp the bread. His hand wouldn't budge. He made a tiny whimpering sound.

McGinty gave him a questioning look. Dora turned around. "What is it?" she asked.

Bolan wanted to say, *I think I'm sick. I need to go to the hospital.* But as he opened his mouth to speak, the numbness shot all the way up his arm and into his head. To his horror, he heard himself say, "I'm all right. I just grunted because my elbow gave me a twinge. I guess I bumped it when I fell."

He tried to shout, *No, no, that's not what I meant to say!* But the words wouldn't come out. He felt as if he were a puppet and the numbness, the hand of the puppeteer, controlling his mouth.

The dead feeling tingled through his entire body, and as his sense of touch faded, another mode of perception seemed to sharpen in compensation. Suddenly he *felt* the presence of another consciousness clinging to his own, like a lamprey feeding on a fish.

This is demonic possession, Bolan thought, awestricken. He realized that even though its existence was an article of faith in his fundamentalist sect, he'd never truly believed in it until now.

The spirit squirmed Bolan's shoulders as if his hijacked body were a garment in which it was trying to get comfortable. Then it began to peer about the kitchen.

Bolan discovered that he could catch an echo of its thoughts. The forks and butter knives were too puny to bother with, and McGinty's rifle was leaning in the opposite corner, out of reach. But there must be some suitable weapon at hand.

No! Bolan thought. *I won't let you hurt them!*

To his surprise, the demon answered him. Though it was speaking silently, in thought alone, as he was, somehow its words still seemed cold and sibilant. *You can't stop me, mortal. I'm the presence you've been sensing. I spent weeks Skinriding you, preparing for this moment. Now it's your turn to go where I lead.*

Bolan strained to close his hands into fists. To regain control. His fingers didn't even twitch. *Jesus, please help me!* he prayed.

Nothing can help you, the devil replied. *Stop fighting me and enjoy the bloodshed. You can if you try.*

Bolan felt the demon's attention fix on the silvery coffee pot. Two reptilian faces sneered from the curved reflective surface. The spirit took hold of the handle, hefted the pot experimentally, and then stood up.

McGinty looked up at his pastor, or the creature he still believed to be his pastor, with an expression of mild curiosity on his square, weather-beaten face. The demon smiled, swung the pot over Bolan's head, flinging coffee behind him, and then smashed the container down on the bodyguard's skull.

Bone crunched. The shock of impact jolted Bolan's arm, and hot coffee sloshed from the pot to burn his hand. He could feel the pain even through the numbness, but the devil didn't seem to mind it.

McGinty made a choking sound and fell out of his chair. The demon stamped thrice on his skull, mashing it out of shape, and then turned toward Dora.

She was still standing beside the stove. Her face was gray, her eyes so wide that Bolan could see white all the way around the irises, and her mouth hung open. *Don't just stare!* the minister begged her. *Run!* But of course she couldn't hear him, and she didn't move.

"All right, now we're alone," the spirit said. "Are you happy?"

Dora's mouth worked, but no sound came out.

"There's no pleasing some people," the demon said. The coffee pot upraised, he started toward her. Once again, Bolan struggled desperately to reassert mastery of his body, without hindering the spirit in the slightest.

For a moment it looked as if Dora still wouldn't move. Then she snatched up the cast-iron frying pan in both hands and swung it at her attacker's head, spattering eggs and hot grease.

Perhaps her sudden move caught the devil by surprise, because it didn't quite manage to block. The black skillet bonged against Bolan's temple, bringing another jab of pain. Everything went dark. Vaguely he felt his knees buckling, and the coffee pot slipping from his fingers. *Yes!* he rejoiced. *Pass out, you horrible thing!*

But then the world swam back into visibility. The demon lurched upright, wrenched the pan out of Dora's hand, and grabbed her by the throat. It shoved her down on top of the stove and began to choke her.

She thrashed madly, clawing at its hands and forearms, but she couldn't break its grip. Flames licked along her torso as the burner set her housecoat ablaze. Before long the fire reached her throat and head, but the searing heat didn't make the spirit let go of her, either. A stink of burning hair and meat filled the air.

Finally Dora stopped struggling. The devil slapped out the flames on Bolan's sleeves and then flexed his black and red hands, evidently making sure they were still functional. Tears flowed down the minister's face, and the demon wiped them away. *Don't whine*, it said. *You know very well that there were times when you wanted to kill her. I've fulfilled one of your fantasies.*

Why? Bolan wailed. *Why are you doing this?* He had the mad feeling that if he could convince the devil it had made a mistake, then Dora would be alive again.

To settle an old score, the spirit answered. *This morning's sacrifice is just one tiny part of a scheme that encompasses the Atheist murders and much more. We should both feel proud to be part of something so grand.* The creature retrieved the CAR 15 and then opened the back door. Outside, the dewy grass, the slender white steeple of the Third Baptist Church of Memphis and the red roof of the Youth Fellowship building shone in the early morning sunlight.

Please, God, Bolan prayed, *let this end. Destroy this monster, even if it means killing me with it.*

Do you think we should begin with the church or the Sunday school? the spirit asked, examining the gun. *I think, the children.*

TWENTY-FIVE

His rapier in one hand and a pistol in the other, Montrose prowled the muddy alley at the head of a ten-man patrol, looking for any Heretics who'd escaped the battlefield. Elsewhere in the Friar's Point Haunt, other irregulars and Legionnaires crowed whenever they ferreted a fugitive out of hiding, momentarily drowning out the hiss of the Nihils riddling the row of crumbling shanties on the Stygian's left.

Abruptly Montrose heard something shift in the shadows under the eaves of a nearby hovel. He peered, but saw nothing that might have made the noise. Perhaps one of the religionists was a Harbinger, with a Harbinger's ability to veil himself in shadow. Invoking his powers of flight, the Scot hurtled toward the shack. As he landed, he aimed his blade at the spot he judged the Heretic to be.

The form of a small man with a gaping white cut in his forehead shimmered into view. He cringed against the wall. Montrose waited until he saw hope dawn in the other wraith's face, hope that the Stygian didn't mean to destroy him on the spot. Then, lunging, he thrust his blade into the Heretic's breast.

Pulsations of darkness swept through the religionist's body. He toppled, but vanished before his body hit the ground.

Grinning, Montrose pivoted back toward his men. Murderous ruffians though they were, they seemed to be eyeing him askance, and their wariness took the edge off his glee.

"What's wrong?" he asked.

The men looked at one another as if silently agreeing upon a spokesman. Eventually a Masquer, her translucent body shining with a golden inner glow, said, "I thought the idea was to take them alive when we can. Otherwise, there's nothing to sell."

Montrose blinked. "Yes. You're right, of course. I guess that in the heat of battle, we can all become overexcited."

"Do you want to go back to the command post? We can handle the mopping up."

Montrose scowled. "No, of course not. I'm fine. Come on." He stalked on down the alley and the guerrillas fell in behind him.

For a few paces, he wondered if something might actually be wrong with him. The Soulshaper was correct; they were supposed to be taking captives, and it was unsettling that he'd forgotten it. And though he'd worked hard to become as ruthless as the intrigues of the Stygian court required, he didn't ordinarily revel in needless slaughter.

But gradually his exhilaration seeped back and washed his misgivings away. The fugitive had been a Heretic, hadn't he? An enemy to all creation. As foul a thing as his own treacherous Louise. How could anyone feel remorse over slaying an abomination like that? It was remarkable that Montrose and his army managed to contain their loathing sufficiently to drag *any* of the bastards to the barracoons.

A hulking cutthroat in a bottle-green top hat and cutaway coat stuck his head through the side of a shanty, checking the interior. When he pulled it out again, he said, "I don't see anything. But I *feel* them. Somebody's in there somewhere."

"Then I suppose we'd better search it," Montrose said. He glided through the wall, and the rest of the patrol followed. It only took a moment to find the trapdoor set in the rotting floorboards.

Montrose knelt and thrust his face through the hatch. The earthen cellar below it was dimly lit by the greenish glow shining up a set of plank stairs. The cool air smelled of vegetables gone rotten.

It would be tricky to slip one's body through the substance of the trapdoor, yet avoid plummeting through the steps as well. Grunting, Montrose shifted himself across the Shroud, gripped the edges of the door with his fingertips, and pulled. For a moment the warped, swollen wood resisted him, but then it jerked upward. The Scot surrendered to the pull of the Shadowlands, and his soldiers reappeared around him.

"Let's go," Montrose said. He charged down the steps with the guerrillas behind him.

The root cellar was lined with crudely built shelves. The sickly light of a single barrow-flame candle gleamed on row after row of dusty mason jars. In the corner stood four children, three boys and a girl, with a small, dark-haired woman behind them.

Startled, Montrose froze. Because even though he knew better, for an instant, in the dim light, the young wraiths resembled John, James, Robert, and Jean, his long-lost children; the ghost behind them, their mother Magdalen, whom he'd loved deeply until his penchant for dangerous politics had driven them apart.

The tallest boy pointed a pepperbox pistol at Montrose's chest. His mother, if that was who she was, grabbed his arm and jerked the gun out of line. "No, Davy!" she cried. "There are too many of them. We can't fight them."

"Bind them," said Montrose to his troops. They hurried forward to obey.

The ruffians seemed to delight in handling both the woman and the children as roughly as possible. They slapped them, fondled them, and snarled threats and obscene endearments in their ears. The boys struggled frantically, while the little girl began to sob.

Montrose watched the proceedings with growing distaste. He searched for the delicious cruelty he'd enjoyed only moments before, but for the time being, it seemed to have abandoned him.

He reminded himself that the prisoners weren't *his* children. Indeed, judging from their homespun clothing, they were probably more than a hundred years old, not youngsters at all in any rational sense.

Yet with their piping voices and coltish frames, with the girl's terrified weeping and the boys' desperate defiance, they certainly *seemed* like children. And in point of fact, Montrose had noticed that many wraiths who died before reaching adulthood retained childlike personalities forever after, no matter how many decades or even centuries of existence they experienced.

He wished he could turn away, but he knew he shouldn't. He mustn't look weak in front of the men.

The black-haired woman stared at him beseechingly. "We haven't hurt anyone," she said. "Why are you doing this?"

Because my master ordered me to, Montrose thought. *For sport. For revenge.* All three answers made him uncomfortable. "Because you're Heretics," he said aloud. "The agents of Oblivion."

"No!" the woman said. "Perhaps some Heretics do worship the devil, but we hate him as much as you Stygians do! Our beliefs are in the Bible, and that book over there!" With her hands already bound, she couldn't point, but she jerked her head at a dilapidated workbench in the corner, and the slim volume, bound in white leather, lying atop it.

"Thank you for calling it to my attention," said Montrose. "I wouldn't want to leave subversive literature lying around to corrupt the innocent. Perhaps the artificers can melt it down and make something useful." He shifted his gaze to two of the irregulars. "Take them to the stockade and then rejoin the search."

"You got it," said the taller of the pair. He shoved the woman and the younger boy toward the steps.

The little girl wailed. The woman cried, "I beg you! Do anything you want to me, but let the children go!" She kept pleading all the way up the stairs.

Montrose supposed that he really should confiscate the book. He walked to the workbench. When he saw the gold letters embossed on the cover, he faltered, and then, his hands trembling ever so slightly, picked up the volume and started leafing through it.

It was the old Prayer Book of the Scottish Kirk, in defense of which he and his fellow Calvinists had formed the Covenant and defied the Crown. This text had set him on the twisting path which eventually led him to fight *for* the murdered King and his faithless son, and finally put Montrose himself on the gallows.

He didn't know what to feel. Or rather, he felt too many things at the same time, contradictory emotions which ground together inside him. He hated the Prayer Book. How could he not, when it had prompted him to waste his life? Yet simultaneously, he remembered the reverence with which he'd once regarded it, and the knowledge that he was persecuting women and children for embracing its teachings sickened him.

The Masquer with the luminous flesh cleared her throat. "Are you okay?" she asked diffidently.

"Yes," Montrose said, "but you know, you were right. You don't need me for this, and there are matters I ought to take up with Fink. I'm going back to camp. You report to me when you finish."

"Will do," the Masquer said. Montrose got the distinct impression that she and her companions would be glad to be rid of him.

The Stygian headed back toward the edge of the Haunt. Soon he heard the sounds of his temporary headquarters, the drone of dozens of conversations, the clink of manacles, and the cracking of whips. Fink stood loitering at the edge of the weedy vacant lot into which the men were herding the captured Heretics.

"Hello again," boomed the former pirate. "Considering the haul we made tonight, you don't look very chipper."

Uncertain that he actually wanted to confide in Fink, Montrose hesitated, but then the words started slipping out. "I suppose I'm in an odd mood. I'm wondering if there's a point to what we're doing."

Fink grinned. "If you don't see the point of getting rich, then Stygians are even odder than people say."

"I do see it," Montrose said. "I must, mustn't I, since I fought so hard to win a place at the Smiling Lord's right hand. But a philosopher once told me that the wealthiest, most powerful wraith is poorer than the neediest mortal pauper, and sometimes I think he was right. No matter how many trinkets we amass, there's a cold, barren quality to our existences that can never be dispelled. That's obvious here in the Shadowlands, where the Shroud makes the whole world ugly, but one can feel the bleakness even amid the splendors of the Onyx Tower."

Fink snorted. "You're right, you *are* in a sour mood. If you've lost interest in money and power, can't you still be happy that you're making yourself useful? How many times have I heard you say that by persecuting the Heretics, we're protecting all creation from Oblivion?"

"And I suppose I still believe that. But what if I'm mistaken? What if that notion is just an excuse to justify our brutality?"

"Who cares?" Fink replied, casually loosening his pistol in its holster. "Your problem is that you think you *need* an excuse."

Montrose cocked his head. "I beg your pardon?"

"The way I see it," said Fink, "nothing means anything. Love, morals, patriotism, religion, the crusade to hold back the Spectres—it's all a crock, or at least nobody can prove it isn't. We only know one thing for certain. Ghosts who hang on to their emotions survive, and the ones who lose them fade away. So you do whatever it takes to make you feel like you're still alive."

"Even if it means hurting people who don't deserve it."

"Isn't that how you got to be an Anacreon?"

Montrose smiled wryly. "One could certainly make a case that most of the rivals I stabbed in the back *did* deserve their comeuppance. One could also argue that they didn't deserve it any more than I did. Don't worry, Mike, I'm not turning milksop on you. But if we stop caring about right and wrong *at all*, aren't we virtually surrendering to our Shadows?"

"I don't believe in Shadows," Fink replied, "or anyway, I don't believe in mine. As far as I'm concerned, Shadow is just a word people use for the part of themselves they're afraid of. I'm not afraid of anything. But if you are, maybe you should do something about it."

"What do you mean?" Montrose asked.

"It seems like the more Heretics we hunt down, the more you enjoy making them suffer." Fink leered. "You're turning mean, like me. Which would be fine if you *were* me, or one of the other cutthroats in our happy crew, but it doesn't look natural on you. It could be that your Shadow's getting too much of a hold on you."

"You're suggesting I consult a Pardoner. I have to admit, it might not be a bad idea."

"The Three Stooges must have one or two confessors hanging around the Citadel."

"I'm not going to bare my soul to a man who might turn around and repeat what I said to Gayoso," Montrose said. "I'll go to someone in Under-the-Hill."

Fink nodded. "I suppose you can."

Montrose raised an eyebrow. "Is there any doubt?"

"There don't seem to be as many around as there used to be. I guess they moved on to other Necropoli."

Valentine had said the wraiths of Natchez were turning surly and violent. Perhaps the shortage of Pardoners was to blame. For a moment Montrose felt a pang of disquiet, as if he'd glimpsed one aspect of some grand and sinister design, perhaps even the menace Katrina the Ferryman had warned him of.

Then, grimacing, he thrust his misgivings aside. No doubt, as Fink had suggested, it was simply Natchez's bad luck that most of the local pardoners had decided to relocate at approximately the same time. And even if it weren't, the spiritual health of the province wasn't Montrose's problem. He just wanted to finish crushing the Heretics and go home.

"I'm sure I can find someone suitable," he said.

TWENTY-SIX

Gayoso closed his office door, snapped his fingers to light the three stubby tapers in the candelabrum, and whispered the word that activated the invisible wards set about the walls. Supposedly the magical glyphs would keep out any intruder. Scowling, the Anacreon wished they could block the cheering and martial music which echoed through the Citadel as well. Evidently Montrose had won another victory and was parading another coffle of captives through the streets, thus reaffirming his status as the hero of the hour. As far as Gayoso could tell, most of his own subjects didn't even resent the fact that the Stygian had begun to withhold a portion of his loot, animate and otherwise, from the local markets for shipment to the Isle of Sorrows.

Unmasking, Gayoso sat down behind his desk. Mustering his courage—or setting aside his better judgment, he wasn't sure which—he reached through the front panel of the bottom drawer and brought out a tarnished silver hand mirror. He hesitated, and then looked into the glass.

At first he merely saw his own reflection. But gradually the image changed, though he would have been hard pressed to say exactly how, until finally it grinned when he had not. The mirror turned icy cold in his hand. "Hello," the reflection said. "It's been a while." The voice was Gayoso's own, but slightly tinny, as if passing through the glass distorted it.

Since acquiring the mirror nearly a decade ago, Gayoso had had ample opportunity to grow accustomed to the sight of his image coming to independent life, yet he still had to repress a shiver. Because he was fairly certain that the entity inside the glass was actually his Shadow.

Most of his fellow Hierarchs would have deemed him mad for trafficking with the creature commonly regarded as the most insidious, relentless enemy a wraith could ever have. But the being in the mirror had often helped Gayoso when he needed help the most. He was convinced that if he hadn't had the benefit of its advice, Shellabarger or Mrs. Duquesne would have murdered him long ago. He could only assume that the magic of the looking glass *compelled* his dark side to aid him, or else that the creature didn't merely aspire to destroy him but to turn him into a Spectre, a goal which necessitated keeping him alive.

"I need your assistance," Gayoso said.

"I'm yours to command," said the Shadow, smirking.

Gayoso wondered if his own features ever looked quite that unpleasant. "Do you know what's been going on?"

"How could I, when you haven't informed me?" the reflection said. "I don't even exist except when you choose to give me form and purpose."

Gayoso scowled. "Don't play games with me. I understand what you are, and I imagine you know everything that I do."

The Shadow smiled. "In point of fact, I know things you *don't,* or at least I have instincts and intuitions you lack. That's what makes me useful. All right, I won't play the ignoramus. You're worried about Montrose." Another skirl of brassy music penetrated the wall.

"Yes," said Gayoso. "Damn the man! I should have either helped him wholeheartedly or killed him when he first arrived."

"You certainly should have," the Shadow agreed. "If you'd asked me, I would have told you as much, but alas, you kept me locked away in my musty little drawer."

"I don't run to you every time I have to make a decision," Gayoso said. He suspected that if he didn't use the mirror sparingly, he might corrupt his soul beyond any hope of redemption. "But I need to know what's going to happen next. What are Montrose's intentions?"

The Shadow nodded thoughtfully. "That's an interesting question. In his place, would you hold a grudge? Would you want to deliver the impudent provincial who hampered your mission to the justice of the Smiling Lord?"

Gayoso scowled. "That's what I'm asking you. Does he mean to arrest me?"

"Perhaps he wants to usurp your office. At this point, your subjects might well support him. So might Shellabarger and Mrs. Duquesne. And the Marquess would scarcely be the first Hierarch to decide that it's better to reign over a Shadowlands kingdom than to kiss Deathlord ass in Stygia."

"Don't give me 'perhaps.' I don't dare move against him unless I'm certain."

"Even I don't know everything, dear brother. I can't foresee every twist and turn of the future, or spy into the depths of every soul we encounter. But I can tell you this: Montrose served a purpose, but he's on the brink of becoming a liability. I recommend we dispose of him before he does."

"How? An assassination?"

"No," the Shadow said. "Even if the attempt succeeded, everyone would suspect you. Your fellow governors could conceivably bring a charge of treason against you. It would be better if Heretics slew Montrose on the battlefield."

"Obviously," Gayoso said impatiently, "but he keeps winning. And every time he does, more outlaws slink out of their lairs to enlist in his army. No Heretic Circle in the region can stand against him, not anymore."

"No *one* Heretic Circle," the Shadow said. "But a missionary, a Sister of Athena, is putting together an *alliance* of Circles in Grand Gulf."

"How do you know that?" the Anacreon asked.

The creature in the glass ignored the question. "She just might be able to destroy Montrose, given the proper assistance."

"What kind of assistance?"

"Supply our Stygian friend with faulty intelligence. Tell him where the lady's followers are assembling, but grossly underestimate their numbers. With luck, when he goes to dispose of them, he'll leave some of his own force behind to tend to other business. Arrange matters in such a way that it's primarily *your* soldiers, not Shellabarger's or Mrs. Duquesne's, who are supposed to fight alongside his ruffians, and then make sure your men don't show up for the engagement."

Gayoso nodded thoughtfully. "Inaccurate reports. Troops arriving late for a rendezvous. It happens all the time. If I'm careful, no one will be able to accuse me of a thing."

"You'll also want to warn the Sister that Montrose is coming," the Shadow said, "so she can set a trap. But your emissary mustn't refer to him by name."

"Whyever not?"

"I don't know," the Shadow said. Gayoso had the unsettling feeling that on this one point, it was lying. "But I sense it's important. And I see that if you follow the plan in every detail, Montrose *will* fall." The reflection smiled. "One way or another."

TWENTY-SEVEN

On his way from the Citadel to Under-the-Hill, Montrose noticed a newspaper box, its sides covered with spray-painted gang markings and the coin compartment levered open. Although he'd long ago lost much of his interest in the affairs of the Quick, the size of the big black headline framed in the window caught his eye. Wondering if the United States had gone to war or experienced some spectacular disaster, he reined in Alexander and dismounted for a better look.

Stooping, he skimmed the first few lines of the story, and then, intrigued, shifted himself into the Skinlands to peruse the entire thing. His luminous white stallion and the webwork of Nihils in the sidewalk vanished. With the sizzling sound of the tiny cracks cut off, the dark, deserted street seemed almost unnaturally silent.

Wondering idly if someone might look down from one of the tenement windows, and what he would make of the masked, cloaked figure below him if he did, Montrose kicked the newspaper box. The window shattered. The Scot removed a paper and continued to read.

In the past three centuries, he'd seen more than his share of marvels and mysteries, but even by his standards, the newspaper story was odd. Ten ministers, four priests, two rabbis, and an imam had all gone homicidally berserk on the same Sunday morning. The police had had to kill the majority of them to halt their rampages. The remainder had committed suicide rather than be captured. The reporter who'd written the account seemed to be hinting that the phenomenon might have something to do with the serial killer called the Atheist, but apparently didn't have any real evidence to support such a speculation.

Montrose reflected that it was almost as if he had an opposite number on the other side of the Shroud, someone attacking the religious institutions of the living as ferociously as the Stygian was waging war on the Heretical sects of the dead. Once again, he had the uneasy feeling that some sinister design was unfolding around him. That it might even be using him as a pawn.

Scowling, he thrust the disquieting notion out of his mind. He knew very well why he was campaigning in the Shadowlands. To enhance his master's status among his peers. Moreover, he couldn't imagine what anyone could hope to gain by instigating both a crusade against the Heretics and a terrorist campaign against a few Quick preachers, or even how such an effort might have been accomplished.

Surely, Montrose reasoned, he only suspected a connection because his Shadow was trying to vex him with irrational anxieties, just as it had earlier filled him with self-doubt and delirious cruelty. All the more reason, then, to get himself to a Pardoner without further delay. He tossed the newspaper into a trash can and then allowed himself to slip back across the Shroud. His scarlet eyes glowing, Alexander whickered as if he'd been waiting impatiently.

"I know," Montrose said, patting the Phantasy's neck. "I have a morbid imagination, and I'm wasting your precious time. My humble apologies." He swung himself into the saddle and kicked the horse into a canter.

The ambiance of Under-the-Hill had changed since his arrival in Natchez. Many of the residents had seen fit to abandon their criminal activities and assist the campaign against the Heretics in one capacity or another. Consequently the dark streets no longer felt quite so perilous. Yet paradoxically, with an abundance of newly enslaved Heretics available for gladiatorial combat, rape, and any number of other vicious amusements, the invigorating, nauseating miasma of sadism, terror, and pain had grown even thicker than before.

Montrose rode past a crowd of his irregulars who were watching a Masquer forcibly sculpt a bound, shrieking male slave into the semblance of a beautiful woman. The troops hailed their commander jovially. Concealing a pang of disgust at their notion of entertainment, Montrose gave them a nod, but didn't stop to talk.

He turned Alexander into the mouth of a crooked alley. A large Nihil seethed in the pavement just before him, and the crumbling buildings pressing close on either side reeked of vermin and decay. Even allowing for the distortions of the Shroud, the scene was *so* ruinous that Montrose found it difficult to imagine anyone taking up residence in this particular block. And yet, as an informant had promised, a dimly glowing iron lantern, the emblem of a Pardoner, hung above a recessed doorway a few yards ahead.

Giving the Nihil a wide berth, Montrose rode to the lamp, which radiated the chill of barrow-flame. He dismounted, stepped to the door, and called, "Hello!"

"Come in," replied a reedy voice. "Anyone seeking absolution is welcome."

Montrose slipped through the substance of the door. The interior of the shack was as deteriorated as the exterior, with a sagging floor, a few sticks of marred and broken furniture, and great masses of filthy cobweb festooning the corners. To his surprise, the dusty strands shed a faint green light. He assumed the Pardoner had used an Arcanos trick to make them glow.

The man in question sat at a rickety table in the exact center of the room. He was slight and stooped, and had chosen to conceal his features under a gray hood. Black stains, the stigmata of his craft, mottled his twisted, arthritic-looking hands. A miscellany of objects—brass finger cymbals, a fuming incense burner, long black needles with ebony heads, a jeweler's loupe—rested on the scarred wooden surface before him.

"Your custom honors me, my lord Anacreon," he said.

Montrose removed his glossy ceramic mask. "It would have honored you sooner, but you weren't easy to find."

"Salvation never is," replied the Pardoner, a hint of humor in his tone. "I refer to salvation in the most secular, non-Heretical sense, of course."

The Scot approached the table. The bitter scent of the incense stung his nose. "My Shadow has been restless lately. I'd like you to quell it. How much do you charge?"

"Whatever the client sees fit to give."

Montrose reached inside his mantle, brought out a bulging leather bag, and set it on the table. The oboli inside it clinked.

"My lord is most generous," the Pardoner said. "Please be seated."

The Stygian perched on a fragile-looking stool. Had he and it existed on the same side of the Shroud, he had little doubt it would have disintegrated under his weight. He set his mask on the tabletop. "I've been slipping into a sort of fever," he said. "A fever of anger. It makes me enjoy my task—the fighting and slave-taking—more than I should."

"Of course you enjoy it," said the man in the hood. "You aren't just shooting and stabbing rebels. You're getting even with the ogres of your past. People who betrayed you."

Montrose sighed. "I probably am. You have good eyes."

"It's all a matter of knowing how and where to look," the Pardoner said. "I also see that one treachery in particular left lasting scars. A woman you encountered in the last few months of your mortal existence, after you'd laid your wife to rest and imagined you were done with love forever. You thought the girl was an angel, but she sent you to your death."

Montrose's eyes ached as if they were still capable of shedding tears. "It's pathetic, isn't it? Louise sold me out three hundred years ago, and it isn't as if I haven't done anything since. I've won a place in the aristocracy of an empire that puts Scotland or any other mortal realm to shame. I've dallied with beauties who really *do* resemble angels, in a way coarse Earthly bodies never can. Why can't I simply forget her?"

"That isn't how we're made," the Pardoner said. "My master in the craft taught me that every ghost is inherently a creature of rage and regret. Were we not, we never would have entered the Underworld in the first place. The only way to rid yourself of your burden of passion is to confront and resolve it."

"And I missed my chance at that," Montrose said bitterly. "When I died, a Reaper seized me and sold me to the Black Hawks to fight in the ranks. I wasn't a thrall, but I was the next thing to it. A few days later, our commander marched us off into the Tempest to patrol the roads. It was decades before I made it back to the Shadowlands. By that time, I was a Proctor. I could have attacked Louise, Argyll, VanLengen, and all the rest of my enemies. But every one of them had already gone to his grave."

"Thus denying you your catharsis," the Pardoner said. "It must have felt like a final injury and an ultimate injustice. And it left an open wound in your psyche, a flaw for your Shadow to exploit."

"But, I would assume, not anymore," said Montrose, "not anytime soon. Because you're going to put the genie back in its bottle."

"Let's hope so," said the Pardoner. "Take off your gauntlets and spread your hands on the table, palms down."

Montrose did as he'd been instructed. The man in the hood picked up one of the black needles, set the point against the middle finger of his client's right hand, just below the nail, and suddenly thrust it in. Somehow the thin shaft of metal pinned Montrose's digit to the surface beneath it as if it had actually plunged into the wood.

The pain was intense. Montrose felt waves of dissolution licking at the substance of his finger: Evidently the needle was made of darksteel. "Sweet Jesus," he gasped, fighting the impulse to pull the offending object out.

"It's necessary for your treatment," the hooded man said blandly, which actually sounded plausible enough. Many Pardoners employed scourging or other forms of physical chastisement to break a Shadow's power. "And it'll only be for a little while." He picked up a second needle.

When all ten of Montrose's fingers had been impaled, the Pardoner attached the small brazen cymbals to his own thumb and forefinger. He rose and began to circle the table in a sort of slow-motion dance. Repeatedly pausing in mid-motion, he struck poses in a way that reminded the Scot of the Deathlords and their totemistic stances. The cymbals chimed. Each note seemed to echo for longer than it should.

Sick with pain, Montrose didn't realize the Pardoner had stopped circling until the hooded man rested his gnarled hands on his shoulders. Startled, the Stygian jumped. The motion jerked his immobilized arms and produced a fresh burst of agony.

The Pardoner bent down and whispered in Montrose's ear. "Whom do you hate?"

"Argyll. Hamilton. VanLengen. King Charles and the Crown Prince." With each name, he felt a flare of overwhelming rage, as if the pain in his hands was intensifying his anger. And then something writhed in the depths of his mind. His Shadow was stirring. Alarmed, he tried to twist his head around to look the Pardoner in the face. He couldn't quite turn it far enough.

The hooded man massaged the clenched muscles in Montrose's shoulders. "It's all right," the confessor said. "This time, give in. Let the venom flow, so I can neutralize it. Whom do you hate?"

"Heretics. Demetrius." The pain and fury sang on inside him.

"Whom do you hate?" the Pardoner asked.

"John," Montrose said. He was appalled at himself, but, with the rage wailing even louder, he couldn't deny that on some level his declaration must be true.

"Your son?" the Pardoner asked. "Why?"

"I took him to war and he died. He broke my heart."

"Whom do you hate?" the Pardoner asked.

"Magdalen. She refused to understand why I *had* to support the Crown, no matter what the cost. She stopped loving me. And finally she died, too."

"Whom do you hate?" asked the hooded man.

Montrose shuddered, stabbing fresh pain through his injured hands. The anger inside him was sickeningly intense. It felt as if it were shredding his spirit, and he wanted it to stop. "You know," he said. "We already talked about her."

"Say the name," the Pardoner insisted.

"Louise!" Montrose cried. "Louise!"

"What would you like to do to her?"

Images of torture and mutilation cascaded through the Stygian's mind. He felt his penis stiffen. "Tear her eyes out. Rape her. Cut off her hands and feet. Hang her a thousand times, the way they hung me."

"Whom do you hate?" the Pardoner asked.

"That's everyone," Montrose said.

"Whom do you hate?"

"No one else, damn you! Finish this! I don't want to feel this way any longer!"

"Whom do you hate?"

Montrose sensed his Shadow surging to the forefront of his mind, mingling itself with his psyche so thoroughly that he lost any sense of a separate entity coexisting with him inside his head. In a strange, odious way, it reminded him of how it had felt to be mortal. At the same time, his anger seemed to change, from a white-hot blaze to something cold and heavy.

"Myself," he said. "I hate myself."

"Why?" the Pardoner asked.

Montrose sneered in self-loathing. "So many reasons. I led my men off to die in a lost cause. I killed my own boy that way. I ruined my life for the sake of principles scoundrels like Argyll and Hamilton disdained, and it turned out they were right and I was wrong."

"Why else?" the Pardoner murmured.

"For trusting my betrayers. And for failing to win and hold their love. What was wrong with me? What ugliness did they perceive inside me, that made them feel it was permissible to forsake me?"

"Just a little more," the Pardoner urged. "Tell me the rest and the healing can begin."

"I hate the man I used to be," Montrose groaned. "But at the same time, I hate myself for casting his ideals aside. I don't know what to do or who to be!"

"You will," the Pardoner whispered, "because I'm about to tell you a secret, the greatest secret in all the universe. Once you leave this place, you may not remember it consciously, but even so, it will guide and inspire you for the rest of your days. Would you like to hear it?"

"Yes," Montrose said. He couldn't imagine what the hooded man was babbling about—it sounded like Heretical mumbo jumbo—but anything to end the pain in his fingers and the even more agonizing emotions festering in his mind.

"Here it is then. You deserve it."

"Deserve what?"

"Your own contempt. You're a monstrous, crippled thing who richly deserves every pain and humiliation existence has ever seen fit to give you."

"That's mad," Montrose said, and it certainly didn't resemble the pronouncement of any Pardoner he'd ever consulted before. Yet the truth was, it didn't seem insane at all. It simply seemed like a summary of his own confessions.

"Don't resist," the Pardoner said. "Once you know the *whole* truth, your personal piece of it needn't trouble you anymore."

"What is the whole truth?" Montrose asked desperately. He felt so *vile*, so full of despair, that it was a wonder Oblivion hadn't already claimed him. And if the Pardoner couldn't help him, he *wanted* it to.

"That no one else is any better than you," said the man in the hood. "Your own mournful history proves it. We *all* deserve to suffer. So forget your qualms and scruples, my lord Anacreon. Pursue your ambitions with a vengeance. When you look down on the underlings and thralls, you'll know that no matter how foul and worthless a creature you may actually be, at least you're better than they are. And whenever you destroy someone, you'll know you've cleansed creation of a bit of filth, and perhaps even justified your own existence in the process."

Montrose struggled to evaluate what he was hearing. It sounded demented. Wrong.

Yet it sounded *right*, also, as if it were the only possible remedy for his physical and spiritual pain.

As he began to succumb to the Pardoner's logic, he felt portions of his memory withering. He didn't forget his children or the friends who'd stayed faithful to the end, but a kind of significance drained out of his recollections. Soon he'd be able to think of them dispassionately, the way he might reflect on characters in a rather tedious play.

At the same time, the quality of his anger and self-contempt changed once again. At the core of the pain he discovered a kind of masochistic release. A promise that if he simply embraced his own inner putrescence, his shame would turn to joy.

Perhaps, he thought, the Pardoner still crooning blandishments in his ear, he *should* let go. Perhaps it was the only sensible course of action; and in any case, it certainly seemed the easiest. Then he noticed a flicker of movement from the corner of his eye. He turned his head to peer directly at it, only to find there was nothing there.

Confused and feverish as he felt, he still believed he knew what had just happened. As a Harbinger, he possessed the ability to peer into the Tempest, and occasionally he caught a momentary glimpse inside the eternal storm even when he wasn't trying to. Invoking his Arcanos, he looked again.

To behold a trio of Spectres, gaunt, gray creatures seemingly made of tatters of darkness and lengths of twisted bone. In the bewildering hyperdimensional manner of the Tempest, the creatures were still standing at the fringe of their own chaotic realm yet simultaneously clustered around the table in this very room, watching Montrose and the Pardoner with avid interest.

The Scot suddenly realized that what the monsters really hoped to see was his Shadow, essentially a Spectre in embryo, taking control of him. And they very well might. Because the Pardoner was feeding the parasite strength!

"Get away from me," Montrose mumbled, the words so slurred that it seemed impossible the Pardoner would understand them.

But evidently he did, because he said, "Don't struggle, my lord Anacreon. It's too late. And I promise, you'll be happier when it's over."

Montrose's memories continued to petrify, becoming gray and brittle. He felt the link between his mind and flesh attenuating. His sight began to dim.

Then from somewhere deep inside him came a surge of defiance, a thunderbolt of pure outrage altogether different from the cold, malicious self-loathing eroding his will. Bellowing, he leaped up off his stool, knocking the Pardoner backward, and ripped his hands upward with all his remaining strength.

His fingers tore free, but the resultant burst of pain was indescribable. Blacking out, he collapsed to the floor. When he came to a moment later, his hands were dissolving into nothingness. The black pins fell tinkling to the grimy floor.

"I was too ambitious," said the Pardoner from behind him.

Montrose was in too much pain to move, but with an enemy present, he couldn't just lie helpless where he was. Somehow he managed to clamber to his feet. The floor tilted and the glowing spider webs dimmed, as if he was in danger of losing consciousness again. He stumbled around to face the man who'd hurt him.

"I should have made your Shadow a little stronger and let it go at that," the

Pardoner continued. "That's the usual practice, and you wouldn't have noticed a thing. But you're such a wonderful prize that I got greedy. Now I'll simply have to kill you." Edging forward, he reached inside his coat and brought out a knife. It looked as if it was made of chipped black stone.

Trembling, Montrose tried to veil himself in darkness. Nothing happened. He was too spent to use an Arcanos. He attempted to retreat. His Shadow contested his intent, and his feet wouldn't move. Straining, the Scot pitted every iota of his will against the parasite's, and finally broke its grip. The sudden release of tension made him stagger.

By the time he recovered what currently passed for his balance, the Pardoner was nearly within striking distance. Montrose snatched for his pistol before remembering that he no longer had any fingers to grasp it. The hooded man laughed.

"It is rather comical," Montrose rasped. "Although I might not see the humor if I hadn't been to France." With a silent prayer, though he couldn't have said to who or what, he lashed out with a kick.

The savate attack caught the Pardoner under the chin and snapped his head back. Montrose kept kicking him, in the groin and then the knee. The knife tumbled from the hooded man's hand, and he fell to the floor.

The Stygian stamped on him, pulping flesh and snapping bones. By catching the Pardoner by surprise, he'd gained the advantage, but he was still half-crippled with pain. He didn't dare give his adversary a chance to counterattack. Besides, he *wanted* to keep hurting him. He wanted to mash his body into paste.

And eventually he did, more or less. Waves of darkness swept through the smaller wraith's flesh. His clothing slumped in on itself as the mass inside it dissolved. In another moment, the garments were all that remained.

Gasping and shuddering, cradling the stumps of his hands against his chest, Montrose dropped to his knees. Then he remembered the three Spectres. Terrified that they'd slithered through the Nihil outside and were about to attack him, he looked frantically about, but didn't see any sign of them. Evidently, in the unpredictable manner of such horrors, they'd decided to leave him alone, even though he was currently easy prey.

His Shadow squirmed inside him, quiescent for the moment but swollen with newfound power. Since he would now be leery of asking *any* Shadowlands Pardoner for assistance, he guessed he'd simply have to control it through vigilance and willpower for the time being.

At any rate, he now had excellent reason to suspect that the honest Pardoners of the region weren't simply drifting off to other provinces. Someone was eliminating them to enable *false* Pardoners, practitioners of a corrupt version of the same Arcanos, to take their places and *strengthen* the Shadow of every wraith who called on them for aid.

But *why?* What did it all mean?

Montrose decided he'd better find out. He couldn't neglect the campaign against the Heretics, but with luck, he could manage some inquiries on the side. He just wished he could shake the feeling that he'd waited too long to begin examining the overall picture. That whatever threat was advancing through the darkness, nothing could stop it now.

TWENTY-EIGHT

Looking feminine in her platinum wig and a lacy gray blouse, Marilyn nodded at the dark, recessed doorway across Ursulines Avenue. "That's it," she said. "At least, we think it is. But I still advise against this. Rumor has it that other people have gone into that house and never come out." Astarte grimaced impatiently.

Bellamy shrugged. "What are our options? I don't mean to knock the Arcanum. I never would have gotten this far without you and your friends. But the truth of the matter is, you don't seem to have any information that relates to the Atheist murders. Maybe the people inside that building do."

"If they *are* people," Marilyn said glumly, and indeed, the Arcanum's intelligence about the dilapidated Vieux Carré townhouse, like so much of its data, was maddeningly vague. The fraternity had circumstantial evidence that a group with occult connections had owned the structure since the early 1800s, but few real details except for the fact that the occupants generally convened at night. "God knows, I want to solve our problem as much as you do, but still, we should be patient. We might turn up the very facts we need tomorrow."

Bellamy shook his head. "There's no time for patience. People are getting hurt. The Atheist is still killing clergymen. It could be that he made all those ministers go berserk, too. And when I phoned my boss to get an extension of my leave, I found out Nolliver's dead."

"But you said his death was determined to be a suicide," Marilyn replied, "and that everyone knew he was a troubled individual."

"I'm not taking anything for granted," Bellamy said. "The point is that despite your help, the investigation's stalled. We haven't even been able to learn the identity of the possessed guy who attacked your house. I'm willing to run a risk to get things moving again."

"And I want to see whatever's inside there," said Astarte, her eyes shining in the moonlight. "You and R. J. gave me my first break, Marilyn. You showed me that the paranormal is real. Now I have to take the next step."

Marilyn frowned. "Suit yourselves, then. At least I warned you. If you don't come out by dawn, I'll phone the police anonymously, though I'm virtually certain they won't be able to help you."

"Thanks," said Bellamy. He and Astarte started across the deserted street.

"It's so sad," Astarte murmured.

"What's that?" Bellamy replied, studying the shuttered windows. It was impossible to tell if anyone was peeking out through the spaces between the slats.

"Marilyn wants to become a part of the supernatural so badly. Yet she's known for almost a year that this place is here, and she's never done what we're about to do. Deep down, she's chicken, and that will keep her from ever getting her wish."

"At least she'll be alive," said Bellamy. "You could use a dose of her caution herself."

Astarte stuck her tongue out at him.

They climbed up onto the stoop. No sound whispered through the door, and no light shone through the cracks around it. With its paint peeling away in long strips, the house seemed abandoned, as, perhaps, it actually was.

A pair of screw holes at eye level revealed where a knocker had hung, but it was gone now. Bellamy couldn't find a doorbell, either, so he rapped on the panel with his knuckles. In the quiet, the pounding seemed unpleasantly loud. He imagined *things* stirring in the shadows up and down the street, peering to see what all the racket was about.

No one came to the door. He knocked harder, until the bottom of his fist began to ache. Still, no one replied. He turned the tarnished knob, but the door was locked.

"I guess we'll have to break in," Astarte said.

Bellamy scowled at the notion of doing so without a warrant or probable cause. He was used to upholding the law, not flouting it. But he was operating without the sanction of the Bureau anyway, in a situation where the old rules and procedures seemed absurd. "I guess we will," he replied, fishing in his pocket for his Swiss Army knife and lock pick.

Astarte looked disappointed when he brought them out. He guessed she'd been expecting some exotic gadget from a James Bond movie, or at least an impressive array of burglar's tools. But Bellamy wasn't called upon to pick locks nearly often enough to carry such a collection of hardware around, nor should he should need it to get past what appeared to be a simple, old-fashioned mechanism.

He inserted the pick in the keyhole, then used the knife's screwdriver as a tension tool. As he exerted pressure, he felt the pins shiver, and then they clicked into the opening position.

He expected a momentary glow of satisfaction. That was what he usually felt when he finished such a task. Instead a chill oozed up his spine, and he had to swallow away a dryness in his throat. Because he'd just made it possible to go inside, and, as he suddenly realized, he didn't want to.

"Nice work," said Astarte. "Now open the damn thing."

"Okay," he said, closing the knife. "But, remember, let me go first, and do everything I tell you."

Astarte rolled her eyes. "Yes *sir*, J. Edgar."

Bellamy eased the door open. The foyer beyond it surprised him. The chandelier was glowing, if only faintly, and dim illumination from other sources spilled through the arches in either wall. Evidently someone had taken pains to ensure that not even a hint of light would leak outdoors. Fresh white roses in a crystal vase, along with a general absence of dust and cobwebs, suggested that the interior of the house was being well maintained. Yet paradoxically, a faint but noxious odor, reminiscent of both rotting meat and rats, hung in the cool air.

"Hello!" Bellamy called. His voice echoed through the building. "Is anybody here?"

No one replied.

"Let's look around," said Astarte. To his surprise, she took his hand and tugged him toward the doorway on the left. He considered extricating his fingers from her grip, but then thought better of it. Perhaps, for all her bravado, she needed the reassurance of the contact, and at least she wasn't restraining his shooting hand.

Beyond the arch was a parlor full of antique furniture dominated by a towering sculpture in the center of the floor. The construct was a twisted mass of junk: crushed fenders, bent, rusty nails, razor blades, flatware, and unidentifiable scraps of metal welded into a double helix. The component parts gleamed dully in the wan gray light.

Ordinarily, Bellamy didn't much care for abstract art. Surrounded by Victorian tallboys and ottomans, this piece was so out of place that it ought to seem particularly unappealing. Yet for some reason, it fascinated him. It seemed bigger, *deeper*, that it had any right to be, with faint fluctuations of shadow and phosphorescence rippling inexplicably at its core.

He stared at it for at least a minute, trying to puzzle out its true shape, before he realized that, even though the style was utterly different, for some reason it reminded him of the immense carvings in his dimly remembered nightmares. Obscurely alarmed, he wrenched his gaze away from it.

Astarte kept staring at it. He gripped her shoulder and gave her a gentle shake. "Are you okay?" he asked.

Blinking, she turned to face him. "I guess," she said hesitantly. "I wasn't asleep, but I feel like you just woke me up. Was it hypnotizing us, like Marilyn's runes?"

"It just *interested* you," said a silky baritone voice.

His heart jolting, Bellamy spun around. Astarte did the same. In the doorway to the foyer stood a small bald man. Despite the dim illumination, he wore heavy sunglasses, and despite the chill in the air, he smelled of sweat. Evidently he'd crept up behind the intruders while the sculpture held them in its spell.

"Their art is *very* interesting," the bald man continued. "It speaks to the part of us that's the same as they are." He giggled.

There was nothing overtly monstrous or even threatening in the bald man's appearance, but something about him made Bellamy's skin crawl. Maybe it was simply because he was on edge. "I'm sorry we forced our way in here," he said. "But I'm an FBI agent, and we're on urgent business." He displayed for his credentials.

The bald man pressed his dark glasses back onto the bridge of his nose. "What can I do for you?" he asked.

"For starters, you can tell us who you are," Bellamy said.

The bald man smirked. "Charles Tamblyn. Which is to say, no one at all. I just work for Mr. Daimler and Miss Paris. They're the ones who can help you if anyone can." He sniggered as if the idea of his employers assisting anyone was comical in the extreme. "Come with me." He limped toward the opening in the far wall. Bellamy noticed that one of Tamblyn's shoes was taller than the other, with a built-up sole and heel.

Astarte shot the FBI agent a questioning glance. He gathered that she found Tamblyn unsettling also. Bellamy gave her a nod and then they followed the bald man on through the house.

The servant, if that was the proper term for him, led them through several more gloomy but elegant rooms and finally into a study, where golden flames crackled in the fireplace and an abstract oil, rendered predominantly in shades of blue and green, hung above the marble hearth. The painting had the same disturbing yet eye-catching quality as the huge metal sculpture, and as soon as Bellamy realized it, he hastily looked away.

The most handsome man he'd ever seen stood beside the fireplace in an exquisitely tailored three-piece suit, a goblet of red wine cradled in his hand. His hair was pale gold, his skin alabaster, and his eyes sapphire blue. Across the room, a slim woman in a long dress lounged on a leather couch. White gauze bandages concealed every inch of what would otherwise have been exposed flesh, from her scalp with its waves of chestnut hair down to her fingertips.

Astarte gasped.

"What have we here?" asked the handsome man.

"My name is Frank Bellamy," the agent said, displaying his badge and ID. "I'm with the FBI. This is Emily Dodds, my assistant. I assume you're Miss Paris and Mr. Daimler?"

The bandaged woman inclined her head. The firelight flowed over her hair.

"We're sorry to disturb you," Bellamy continued.

Daimler chuckled. "You ought to be sorry to break into a private residence."

"We knocked," Bellamy said. "No one answered. And we're trying to stop a series of murderers. I assume you've heard of the Atheist."

"Yes," Daimler said, "but all I know about him is what I read in the papers. I can't imagine why you'd think otherwise."

"We believe the Atheist is involved in the occult," Bellamy replied. "We have reason to think that you are, too."

Daimler smiled. "I'm a suspect, then?"

Bellamy shook his head. "To tell you the truth, I'd never even heard of you until we broke in here. But a reliable informant told me that *everyone* who frequents this house has some connection to the occult. I came on a fishing expedition, hoping you have some pertinent information."

Miss Paris rose and sauntered toward the intruders, her long skirt swishing faintly. Head cocked, she circled them, looking them over. The faint, foul stink intensified. Evidently it was wafting from her bandaged flesh. Astarte quivered.

Daimler shook his head. A lock of golden hair slipped down his ivory forehead. "I must say, you seem to be grasping at straws."

"Tell me about it," Bellamy said. He could feel that Miss Paris had paused directly behind him. He tried to ignore her. "But sometimes an investigation is like that, and this one is worse than most."

"In point of fact," Daimler said, "I don't even live in New Orleans, or anywhere in what seems to be the Atheist's hunting range. An associate owns this house. He lends it to me when I visit."

"If you don't know anything about the Atheist," Bellamy said, "maybe he does. What's his name, and how can we get in touch with him?"

Daimler smiled. "I didn't say I didn't know *anything* that might be helpful. Miss Paris and I collect information on all sorts of esoteric topics. But why should we share it with you?"

"How about human decency? You could help me save some lives."

Daimler grinned. "Aha. That clinches it. You truly don't have any idea what we are."

Astarte stepped toward him. "I do. I've been looking for you all my life."

"Do you think so," Daimler said.

"I know so," Astarte answered. She stuck her finger into the red liquid in his goblet, then touched it to her lips. "And here's the proof. This isn't wine."

Bellamy stared in amazement. Did she mean that the drink was blood, and Daimler was a vampire? The idea seemed crazy, but no more crazy than statues coming to life, or killers who were almost bulletproof.

He almost reached for his Browning, but he didn't *know* that Daimler was a vampire; and, in any case, so far the blond man hadn't made any threatening moves. Possibly sensing Bellamy's confusion, Tamblyn giggled.

"If you think my choice of beverage proves me undead," said Daimler to Astarte, "then you underestimate your own species's propensity for cannibalism. But just for fun, let's say you're correct. What then?"

"Then maybe I'll give myself to you," Astarte said.

"What?" Bellamy cried.

Astarte glared at him. "Fuck off! It's my body and my choice!" She turned back to Daimler. "Here's the deal. You give Frank all the help you can, and I'll be your slave. I'll do anything you want."

Unpleasantly conscious of Tamblyn and Miss Paris, still standing behind him, Bellamy eased his hand toward his pistol. "Don't listen to her," he said to Daimler. "She doesn't know what she's saying."

"No," said Daimler, "she most certainly doesn't. Would you actually like to be one of my mortal servants, Miss Dodds? Mr. Tamblyn is, and some people would say it's had a deleterious effect on both his social presence and his mental health."

Tamblyn snickered.

"I'll risk it," Astarte said.

Daimler stroked her lips with his fingertip, pausing for a moment to toy with the steel ring. Bellamy's muscles clenched with anger. "Because you think I'd become infatuated with you," the alleged vampire said, "and crave your blood. But what if I drank it all without giving you immortality in return? What if I simply killed you?"

Bellamy's fingers closed around the butt of his pistol.

"I'll take that chance," Astarte said. "I knew I was risking death when Frank and I broke in here."

Daimler nodded. "I admire your nerve, if not your judgment. Perhaps I *should* grant your wish. Burn away all that beauty. Compel you to spend eternity in a body like mine."

Daimler seemed to crouch, but then Bellamy saw that he hadn't exactly *moved*. Instead, the blond man's body had changed form. Now it was bent and hunchbacked, with scab-like moles mottling its twisted hands. His face had altered as well, the straight nose becoming a wrinkled pig's snout, the perfect white teeth rows of stained, jagged tusks, and the sapphire eyes a single bloodshot orb set off-center in his forehead. Astarte's mouth fell open, and her body quaked. She looked as if she were screaming, but she didn't make a sound. Seizing her, Daimler pressed his thin black lips against her throat.

Bellamy froze for a split second, then began to snatch out his pistol. Two pairs of hands grabbed him from behind.

The FBI agent snapped his arm backward in an elbow strike. The blow connected, and one set of hands slipped away. He glimpsed Tamblyn stumbling backward, clutching at his solar plexus. The servant's sunglasses fell off his face, revealing a ring of pustular sores around each eye.

Miss Paris clutched at Bellamy with terrible strength, trying to immobilize his shooting arm with one bandaged hand and throttle him with the other. As they struggled, the putrid stench of her flesh became fouler and fouler. Tiny insects emerged from between her wrappings, jumped on the agent's body, and bit him.

He stamped on Miss Paris's foot. Bone snapped, and her grip loosened. Wrenching himself free, he spun around and slammed the Browning against her temple. She staggered back against the wall, sending a still-life in a gilt frame crashing to the floor.

Bellamy shot her in the chest. He had no confidence that he'd actually incapacitated her, but with Astarte in Daimler's grasp he couldn't waste any more time on her. Gripping the Browning in both hands, he whirled.

To his surprise, Daimler hadn't actually bitten Astarte. Rather, he was simply holding the thrashing girl in his arms, and now he pushed her away. "My compliments to your karate instructor," the cyclops said. "I didn't think you could actually get your gun out. Miss Paris will be sore for a while."

"Get away from him," rasped Bellamy to Astarte. She stumbled to his side. He glared at Daimler. "Get your hands up."

Instead of obeying, Daimler shook his head as if Bellamy had disappointed him. "I had plenty of time to bite her if I'd really wanted to, but she isn't Nosferatu material. Too innocent, though considering her punk regalia, I imagine she's annoyed to hear me say so." He gave Astarte a hideous leer. "I was only trying to teach her a little wisdom. Quixotic of me, considering the likelihood that neither of you will leave this house alive, but we all have our impulses."

"I'm the one pointing the gun at you," Bellamy said.

"Do you really think that matters?" Daimler asked. The FBI agent heard a floorboard creak behind him. He suspected Miss Paris was drawing herself to her feet. "I can just about guarantee you that it doesn't. However, there is a chance that we can avoid any more unpleasantness."

Bellamy edged around the room until he had his back against a wall and could see Daimler, Tamblyn, and Miss Paris all at once. The stain on the bandaged woman's breast looked black in the firelight. From the location of the wound, the agent figured he'd hit the aorta. Were she human, her blood would be spurting. Instead, it was seeping out in a steady flow.

"What do you have in mind?" said Bellamy to Daimler.

"My people have a law," Daimler said. "It requires us to kill any mortal who learns of our existence. But I've never been a stickler for rules, at least not when I can profit by ignoring them."

"Are you asking us to bribe you?" Bellamy asked.

Daimler chuckled. "Not with money. I have more than I'll ever need. Not with Miss Dodds's sweet blood and ripe young body, either. I'm not thirsty, and I'm no longer capable of sexual arousal. With information. I told you I collect it, as do most of my breed. Tell me everything you know about your friend the Atheist. If I find your tale significant, or at least intriguing, I'll let you off the hook. I might even help you, with the understanding that you'll share the rest of the story when you can."

"What if I bore you?" Bellamy asked.

"Then we finish our altercation," the cyclops said.

Suddenly Bellamy's eyes were drawn to Miss Paris. He had the peculiar feeling she was talking, even though she was standing silent and still.

Daimler responded to her as if she had spoken. "You're right," he said. "But I like them. And it won't be the first time we've played fast and loose with the Traditions." He turned back to Bellamy and Astarte. "Miss Paris says that if we're even to consider setting you free, you'll also have to promise never to try to learn any more about us or this house, or reveal to anyone that our race truly does exist."

Bellamy hesitated. He didn't like the idea of holding out on the Arcanum. But on the other hand, Marilyn *had* kidnapped him; anyway, stopping the Atheist, to say nothing of escaping this place alive, was a more important consideration. "It's a deal," the agent said.

"Excellent," Daimler said. He waved his blemished hand at a sofa and two armchairs clustered to form a conversation pit. "Then let's make ourselves comfortable. Charles, you can bring our guests some coffee." Tamblyn recovered his sunglasses, then hobbled from the room.

Bellamy hesitated. These creatures were hideous monsters. If Daimler was willing to show *his* true features, God only knew what sort of deformities Miss Paris was hiding inside her bandages. Bellamy had just shot the woman, and might well wind up fighting the two of them again. It would seem surreal to sit down and chat with them as if they were all old friends.

Yet things had taken much the same course with Marilyn. She'd seemed to go from enemy to ally in the blink of an eye, and given the proper circumstances, he could easily imagine her turning against him again. It was as if violence was so much a part of the world of the paranormal that all the inhabitants took it in stride.

Scratching at one of the invisible bugs still stinging his wrist, hoping they didn't carry some ghastly disease, he sat down on the sofa with the Browning in his lap. Daimler and Miss Paris settled across from him, and Astarte plopped down beside him.

Bellamy noticed her staring at the monsters. Though she was trying to hide it, there was loathing in her eyes, but now that the first shock of Daimler's transformation had passed, fascination as well. "You talked about your 'race,'" she said, a little hesitantly. "What *is* it?"

"Oh, we're vampires," Daimler said. "You were right about that much. It's just that we belong to what's generally considered one of the less desirable bloodlines. Now please, Agent Bellamy, tell us about your adventures."

Bellamy did his best, striving to be not merely clear but entertaining. As he began to describe his encounter with Keene, Tamblyn brought the coffee service on a silver tray. It smelled good, but Bellamy was far too tense to drink any. It annoyed him when Astarte poured herself a cup, dumped liberal quantities of cream and sugar into it, and began to sip it.

When he finally finished his account, Daimler said, "I'll have to let my host know that your Arcanum busybodies have discovered the existence of this residence. He may want to stop using it for a few decades, or even dispose of it altogether."

"Whatever," Bellamy said. "What I want to know is, how do things stand between you and us?"

Daimler turned to Miss Paris. Once again, Bellamy *felt* that she was speaking, even though she didn't make a sound.

The cyclops pivoted back toward his guests. "You can put the pistol away," he said. Some of the tension quivered out of Bellamy's body. "We are intrigued, and on an abstract level, we'll even agree that this Atheist person—or cabal—should probably be stopped. We'll help you to the extent we can without inconveniencing ourselves."

"Good," Bellamy said. "What do you know?"

"Nothing relevant," Daimler said, "not yet. But I may be able to find something out. If I do, I'll contact you."

"You may not realize the significance of information you already have," Bellamy said. "Let me ask you some questions—"

"No," Daimler said. "I'm sorry, but I won't give you a single fact until I'm convinced you absolutely have to have it. Powerful as we are, my people only survive through secrecy."

Bellamy grimaced. "All right. We sleep in a different place every night, to keep the Atheist from catching up with us again. When you have something, mail it to me at New Orleans General Delivery."

"Very well," Daimler said, and then he hesitated.

"What is it?" Astarte asked.

"I'm reluctant to mention this," said the vampire, "because I don't really know what it means, and I don't want to alarm you unnecessarily. But from some of my reading, I suspect that the vision of the island city you both beheld was a glimpse of the Kingdom of the Dead. It seems an ill omen that you, Agent Bellamy, have been dreaming of the same place ever since. Let's hope it isn't calling you home."

TWENTY-NINE

Potter crept through the artificial jungle with his halberd leveled, mostly to keep from catching it on the low-hanging branches and lianas. As always, he was impressed by how well the artificers who'd built this environment had done their work. The yielding mass beneath his boots felt and smelled like decaying vegetable matter. The plant and tree sculptures were indistinguishable from living Earthly verdure. The sounds of nocturnal birds and insects whispered through the humid air. Only an occasional glimpse of one of the structures outside the park, the spindly white minarets of the Skeletal Lord's palace or the colossal black cylinder of the Onyx Tower proper, marred the illusion of a genuine tropical forest.

Despite Demetrius's ministrations, Potter had found himself growing edgier and more apprehensive by the day, and his Shadow increasingly restive. Evidently even the most skillful Pardoner couldn't entirely quell a person's masochistic side, not when the petitioner sensed terrible danger looming over his head.

And so the Deathlord had ordered his animal handlers to release a Phantasy into the forest. With luck, a hunt would wake the magic of his mask almost as effectively as violence against a fellow human being. It would submerge his own flawed essence in the indomitable persona of the Smiling Lord, and in so doing, finally soothe his jangled nerves.

Up ahead, something made a coughing sound.

Potter crept forward, pulled a leafy branch aside, and saw his quarry for the first time. The menagerie keeper had chosen a truly magnificent animal, a cat striped like a Bengal tiger, twelve feet long from the tip of its nose to the root of its twitching tail. A pair of huge ivory fangs curved like scimitars from its upper jaw.

Perhaps because he was downwind of it, the sabertooth hadn't yet detected Potter. But he didn't want to take it by surprise; nor did he wish to kill it with a long, heavy weapon like the halberd. Either tactic might end the confrontation too quickly, denying him the catharsis he craved. He laid the lance on the ground and drew his dagger from its scabbard, then stepped into the open.

Instantly, the sabertooth whirled to face him. Its green eyes blazed.

"Come to me," said Potter, advancing. Already he felt more like an archangel, less like a man. He unfastened his voluminous mantle and it slipped from his shoulders.

The tiger snarled.

"No," said Potter, smiling. "You can't frighten me off and you can't avoid me, either, not for long. I'm going to kill you unless you kill me first."

As if it had understood him, the Phantasy charged.

Potter hadn't expected anything so big to move quite so fast. Even though he'd been awaiting its attack, he only barely managed to dodge out of the way. As it was, the cat's shoulder brushed him and knocked him reeling into a tree. His armor clanged.

As he recovered his balance, the sabertooth whirled and pounced at him. Sidestepping, he thrust at its neck with his darksteel blade.

The dagger punched into the tiger's flesh just above the shoulder. It was a serious wound, as the ripples of darkness proved, but it didn't finish the creature. Spinning, the sabertooth swiped at Potter with its paw, catching him on the hip. The blow hurled him to the ground, and the animal leaped on top of him.

He clutched at its throat, struggling to keep it from plunging its elongated fangs into his chest. Simultaneously he stabbed the beast, over and over again, while it raked his lower body with its hind legs. Its claws shredded his armor and the flesh beneath.

Yet he scarcely felt the pain, and for the first time in days he wasn't even a little bit afraid. A pure and joyful savagery possessed him.

He dragged the dagger down the sabertooth's chest, cutting a gaping gray incision. For a moment the cat fought even more frantically than before. Thrusting its head down, it finally rammed one of its immense teeth all the way through Potter's shoulder. But then the beast began to shudder. It collapsed on top of him, nearly crushing him, and then its carcass melted away.

As he inspected his wounds, watching them begin to close, Potter reflected that it was a shame he couldn't hold on to the tiger's head and hide for trophies. Of course, the artificers could duplicate them, but that wouldn't be the same.

And then, abruptly, even though he'd ordered the jungle cleared, he sensed someone watching him.

Since he still felt godlike, the realization didn't trouble him. Heedless of the pain it caused him, he surged to his feet. Bits of his broken mail fell clinking to the ground. He summoned his halberd and cloak. The former streaked into his hand and the latter floated upward, spread itself like a pair of wings, swooped through the air, and draped itself around his shoulders. Holding the polearm across his body, he assumed one of the Smiling Lord's ritual stances.

"Come forward," he commanded.

No one answered.

"I know you're there," said Potter in his most magisterial tones, "just as I'm sure you know it's treason to spy on a Deathlord. Nevertheless, if you show yourself *now*, I'll be lenient."

Still, no one replied.

With the joy of slaughter still singing through his soul, Potter wasn't inclined to be patient. He'd hunt down the intruder, wring an explanation from the wretch, and then punish him as his temerity deserved. He opened his senses, looking, listening, feeling for vibrations in the earth, and sifting the myriad tastes and odors floating on the breeze.

He couldn't locate the spy. And that was peculiar. Even before his ascension to his present office, he'd rarely met a ghost with perceptions as acute as his own, and Charon's grace had heightened them still further. Ordinarily, even Harbingers veiled in shadow couldn't hide from him. And yet he didn't doubt the veracity of the sensations, the small hairs standing up on the back of his neck and the chill oozing up his spine, that warned him something was amiss.

A pang of human disquiet disturbed the Smiling Lord's divine equanimity. Potter did his best to quash it. So what if he hadn't pinpointed the intruder yet? He'd simply have to move around until he did, in the same way he'd located the sabertooth. It wasn't as if he'd be in any real danger in the meantime. No lurking assassin could pose a threat to the Lord of War and Murder.

Scarlet lighting flickered and thunder rumbled in the eternal storm clouds overhead. His torn legs throbbing, Potter advanced on a stand of brush thick enough to conceal a human form. No longer meshing properly, two pieces of his battered armor scraped together.

A light prickling jittered across patches of Potter's skin. Over the course of several seconds the sensation intensified to a hot, stabbing pain. Certain he was under attack, he pivoted back and forth, trying to find his assailant. He still couldn't.

Another flare of agony wrung a grunt out of him. He decided he needed to see what was happening to his body, even though a part of him cringed at the prospect. He fumbled off one of his steel gauntlets.

His hand was changing, the fingers twisting, the knuckles enlarging, brown spots appearing on the coarsening skin. It looked as if it was withering into an old man's hand.

A wraith couldn't perish of senescence. That was an affliction of matter, not spirit. But Potter's could feel his entire body altering, shrinking, becoming stooped and frail, and a numbing trickle of Oblivion oozing through the core of his chest.

If this wasn't old age, it was a counterfeit, a weapon, just as lethal, and he suspected he had only a few seconds to find the enemy who was casting the curse against him. Any longer than that would be too late.

Dropping his gauntlet, he turned this way and that, peering about, the weight of his armor, unnoticed only a minute before, now pressing cruelly on his shoulders. He wheezed, unable to shake the panicky feeling that couldn't catch his breath even though he knew he didn't need to. He seemed to feel a heart twinging and stuttering in his breast.

And worst of all, his vision blurred, and the sounds around him—the recorded jungle noises and the clinking of his damaged mail—grew muffled. If he hadn't been able to find his enemy before, the very notion seemed risible now.

Potter's knees buckled. He toppled forward.

No! he thought. With what little remained of his strength, he jammed the butt of his halberd against the ground and clung to the shaft as tightly as he could. The polearm held him precariously upright as if he were a drunkard leaning on a crutch. *I am the Smiling Lord. Charon's anointed lieutenant. I will not end like this.*

As if it had been waiting for this declaration of defiance, his mask invigorated him with a surge of strength. The arcane energy didn't halt his deterioration, but it might allow him to function for a little longer despite it. The world swam back into partial focus. Squinting, he peered about.

And at last he seemed to glimpse a shadow shifting between two tree trunks, though his sight was still so murky he couldn't be sure. He lifted the halberd and threw it like a spear.

The darksteel head of the weapon slammed into the center of the shadow's chest. Clutching at the shaft, the assassin dropped to his knees. But despite the deadly enchantments which Charon and Nhudri, the emperor's chief artificer, had laid on the halberd, the fellow's body didn't dissolve, nor did his wounding halt the progress of Potter's destruction.

The writhing thread of Oblivion in the Deathlord's torso grew like a fungus, extending tendrils into his head and limbs. He realized he only had time for one more attack.

Concentrating with all his fading might, he struggled to conjure one of the greatest magics of the ancient Harbingers' guild, a trick so difficult that most modern students of their Arcanos never mastered it. For a moment nothing happened, but then he felt the power rise within him.

Suddenly the darkness around the assassin grew blacker, and then clutched at him with inky tentacles. He only had time for a startled yelp before the thrashing mass of shadow imploded around him, vanishing and taking him with it. Only the halberd remained, softly thumping to the ground.

Potter hadn't actually destroyed his attacker. He'd thrust him into the Tempest. But at least he was gone, and with his departure, his magic lost its bite. The Deathlord felt the seething mass of Oblivion inside him contracting. The gnarled fingers of his naked hand began to straighten.

Unfortunately, the fierce serenity he'd derived from the hunt was gone, too. Pain and terror had wiped it away. Feeling entirely human again—human, in horrible jeopardy, and utterly out of his depth—he slumped down on the ground.

Thirty

The Pentium's monitor displayed a black step pyramid. The tiny figure at the top made a stabbing motion and then held up an crimson lump of flesh. Cheering blared from the speakers, and streams of blood ran down the sides of the monument. That image dissolved into a picture of a huge stone city on an island, a bewildering complex of towers, castles, and bridges. The water around it turned inky black and began to spin, shaking the buildings apart, grinding the bedrock to shards, sucking everything down.

Chester was making his presence known.

Dunn grimaced. The cartoonish display was a waste of his time. And he always felt silly speaking out loud to a computer, even though when Chester was inhabiting the machine, he could hear him and even use the built-in sound system to answer back. The SAD agent wished that somebody else with a little authority, someone made of flesh and blood and consequently able to carry on a normal telephone conversation, had been available for a conference.

"Hi," said Dunn. "When you get done jerking off, you can let me know what's going on down there. Have you found Bellamy and the girl?"

The face of a middle-aged black man, a long, narrow countenance with wire-rimmed glasses and graying hair, appeared on the screen. Dunn assumed that Chester had looked like that when he was alive. He'd never been interested enough to actually inquire.

"No," said the ghost, his artificial voice a little tinny. "Or rather, our agent did find Bellamy at the headquarters of the Arcanum. But she didn't manage to kill him or all the Arcanists either. She only nailed a couple, and then Bellamy stunned her by neutralizing her host body. By the time she came to, everybody had cleared out of the house, and we haven't found any trace of them since."

"Nice work," said Dunn sarcastically. He reached into his jacket for his tobacco pouch.

"We'll get them," Chester said. The monitor showed Bellamy lying bloody and mangled in an alley.

"I don't know about that," said Dunn, sprinkling a line of tobacco onto a rolling paper. "Bellamy knows how to find people, which means he knows how to keep from being found. And no offense, but your crowd has certain disadvantages when it comes to a manhunt. I'm sure it's helpful to be invisible and walk through walls, but on the other hand you can't question live people. Most of you can't even flip the pages of a motel register or rummage through a wastebasket, especially if the what-do-you-call-it, the Shroud, is thick in that particular location."

"You're forgetting the Puppeteers," Chester said. The screen showed leering shadows riding piggyback on a line of stooped, naked, blank-faced human beings.

Dunn lit his cigarette and took a long drag, savoring the heat and flavor of the smoke. "I'm not forgetting anything," he said. "Most of the Skinriders are slated for other jobs. If you send them after Bellamy, you risk derailing the whole terrorism thing. I'll tell you what we'll do. I'll come down there and catch him for you. It's what I should have done in the first place."

Chester's face reappeared on the screen. "Can you get permission to come?" he asked.

Dunn shrugged. "Probably. If not, I'll go AWOL. I wasn't planning to stay on at the Bureau much longer anyway. After the big day, we won't need a mole in SAD."

"But until now, it's best if we have one," Chester said. "Don't do anything reckless. Let's stick to the plan."

"You have your priorities ass-backwards," said Dunn. "SAD doesn't have a clue. With the damage I've done to their database, it'll be years before they *get* a clue. The Arcanists have never been players, not really, and Weiss and Waxman were a joke. But you worry about them and not a guy like Bellamy."

"Because they know something about our world and he doesn't."

"You mean, he *didn't*. By now, the Arcanists have filled him in. And that means he actually could pose a problem. I admit it isn't likely, but given his skills and personality, it's possible."

Chester frowned. "And you're certain *you* could find him and take him down."

"Hell, yes. Because I'm an even better manhunter than he is. And as we already know, all I have to do is show him my other face to drive him out of his mind."

"You have a point, but I don't want to say yes or no, not right now. Let me talk to the others—"

"Hey," Dunn growled, "time for a reality check. My people and I don't take orders from you guys or even the honchos on the pyramid. We're your partners, not your flunkies. I wasn't asking your permission, I was telling you. I'm coming."

"Now you listen—" Chester shrilled.

Dunn laid his hand on the computer and discharged a crackling burst of electricity into the works. The device went dead, as did the light fixture overhead. The SAD agent heard the other FBI staffers in the surrounding offices exclaiming in surprise and irritation.

Since Dunn didn't know much about ghosts, he had no idea whether the zap had actually hurt or even inconvenienced Chester in the slightest. But it had seemed worth a shot.

THIRTY-ONE

Montrose reached the bluff south of Grand Gulf shortly after sunset. He couldn't see or hear anyone moving around the derelict church, and by the time he and his irregulars secured their flotilla and started up the trail, he was reasonably certain that they'd arrived in advance of Gayoso's Legionnaires, who were coming overland to check out reports of Spectre activity in Union Church.

As he clambered upward—it hadn't seemed especially practical to bring Alexander on a lengthy river journey—he felt his Shadow stir, a sensation like a heavy weight shifting in the depths of his mind. He'd been aware of the bloated mass of the parasite every minute since his visit to the false Pardoner. The nerve-wracking feeling made the stink of the local paper mill even harder to bear.

Yet swollen with strength as his dark side was, as far as he could tell it hadn't actually tried to *do* anything to him. He wondered what it was waiting on, and hoped it wouldn't attempt to paralyze him in the midst of the battle soon to come.

"You're solemn this evening," said Fink, marching along beside him. Once again, Montrose was impressed by the other wraith's ability to gauge his mood despite his mask. "Aren't you worried about undermining my morale?" He leered at the notion that anyone or anything could actually dampen his fighting spirit.

"I was just thinking," Montrose replied.

"Still craving a Pardoner is more like it," the big man replied with flawless insight. Montrose had told him about his near-disastrous experience in Under-the-Hill. "You know, if you're worried about your Shadow getting even stronger, you can keep yourself out of the actual fighting."

"And wouldn't that do wonders for *everyone's* morale," the Stygian answered.

"For all their virtues, our fellows are jumped-up bandits, not regular soldiers. They follow me because they imagine I'm braver and tougher than they are. If I tried to lead from the rear, they'd forsake me at the first setback."

"You have a point," the river man conceded. "It doesn't help their confidence when you look like you're going crazy, either; but on the other hand, maybe it doesn't hurt it an awful lot. They'll follow a lunatic if he's a cunning, vicious lunatic." He grinned. "Otherwise I'd never be able to find a crew."

Montrose smiled. "Over the past few weeks, I've learned a secret about you, Mike. You aren't quite as mad as you let on."

"You repeat that and you'll have to fight me all over again. How are you doing with the *big* secrets? Do you have *any* idea what these phony Pardoners are all about?"

The Stygian sighed. "Not yet. I still haven't found time to conduct anything but the most cursory investigation. But when we get back to Natchez, I'm going to *make* time." And hope he wasn't starting too late in the game for it to make any difference.

They reached the top of the bluff, which was as vacant as Montrose had anticipated. The dilapidated church, former sanctuary of the Valhalla Circle, creaked faintly in the breeze, its crumbling spire a notched black blade in the gloom. Down in the mortal settlement, electric lights were winking on.

"What now?" asked Fink.

"Wait, I suppose," Montrose replied. "You choose some pickets and scouts while I take a first look around." He soared into the air and alit atop the steeple.

Clinging there, he removed a small but powerful pair of binoculars—a treasure he'd recently discovered in the markets of Natchez—from one of his cloak pockets, raised them to his eyes, and began to peer about. The gathering darkness made observation difficult, even for wraith eyes, but he glimpsed a flicker of movement at the edge of town, in a dark, decaying block of buildings that looked like a prime location for a Haunt.

Adjusting the focus, he looked a second time. What he saw made his muscles clench in rage.

Descending so fast he was nearly in free fall, his mantle billowing around him, he flew back down to the ground, where Fink stood giving orders to half a dozen irregulars. "Never mind what I told you before," Montrose said. "I spotted the Heretics, and it looks as if they're getting ready to make a run for it. If we don't go catch them immediately, they'll slip away."

Fink frowned. "Then they know we're here. I wonder how."

"Probably a sentry watching the river," Montrose said impatiently. "Or an Oracle sensed our presence. Either way, it doesn't matter. I want the rest of the men on top of the bluff in two minutes, and then we'll move out."

A lanky wraith in a faded denim jacket, one of the guerrillas to whom Fink had been giving orders, said, "We aren't going to wait for the Legionnaires?"

Montrose had to suppress an impulse to knock the fellow down. For a second he had the uneasy feeling that his irritation was excessive, conceivably symptomatic of some sort of problem, but on further reflection, he couldn't see why. No commander liked having his orders questioned. "Absolutely not," he said. "According to our intelligence, there are only a few Heretics down there, and that's the way it looked to me. Considering that we already cleaned out Grand Gulf once, how many *could* there be? Besides, when have we ever truly needed Gayoso's clowns to help us fight?"

The other wraith smiled. "Never. So why cut them in the loot?"

"No reason I can think of," said Montrose. "You men get ready. Rejoin your squads."

It actually took several minutes for the remainder of Montrose's troops to finish scrambling up the trail. He paced restlessly until the last of them reached the top. He forced himself to give the officers a few more seconds to assemble their units, then brandished his sword and shouted, "Let's go!" He set off running toward the town, and the irregulars pounded after him.

As he'd told Fink, the unruly guerrillas weren't cut form the same cloth as conventional soldiers. The force never maneuvered with any great precision. But they nearly always managed more order than this. At the moment they seemed less an army than a mob or a wolf pack coursing through the dark.

In other circumstances, that might have troubled Montrose, but in a raid like this it shouldn't pose a problem. Speed was what mattered, striking quickly enough to keep the miserable Heretics from slipping through his fingers.

The derelict buildings he'd seen from atop the spire loomed out of the darkness ahead. About twenty-five wraiths, many carrying suitcases, backpacks, or bundles, were milling around in the open area between two crumbling tenements.

The Heretical grand alliance, thought Montrose with a sneer. Evidently the Sister of Athena who was supposedly putting the conspiracy together had been even less than successful in convincing the various sects to join forces. He studied the scene before him, looking for a woman who might be organizing the evacuation, but he couldn't see one.

Someone shouted. Evidently a lookout had spotted Montrose's raiders surging out of the night. The irregulars on the flanks of the advance began to fan out, the better to envelop their prey.

Then blinding glare and a deafening screech blasted the night apart.

Thirty-Two

Montrose staggered, squinting against the dazzling glare, fighting the impulse to throw his AK-47 away and use his hands to seal his ears. Around him, his men stumbled back and forth. Some screamed and others fired their guns, apparently at random, the cries and the shooting barely audible above the endless shriek. After a moment other firearms barked in response, and the guerrillas began to drop.

Shielding his eyes, pivoting back and forth, Montrose tried to make out the source of the enemy fire. To his dismay, when he did manage to catch a glimpse of the terrain beyond the light, he discovered that it seemed to change from one second to the next. Formations of riflemen and hordes of hideous Spectres flickered in and out of existence. The contours of the ground flowed as if made of jelly. At one point the whole world inverted itself, and he felt as if he were about to plummet into the endless abyss of the sky.

At the same time, terror yammered through his mind. The screaming, the glare, and the disorienting transformations of the environment were simply too much. He wanted to rip the eyes from his head, ram a stiletto into his own ears, put his rifle in his mouth and pull the trigger, just to make the torment stop.

What prevented him was that he knew what was going on, or at least he hoped he did. A group of Sandmen were creating the glare and spinning disorienting illusions, while a choir of Chanteurs were singing to fill the Hierarchs with terror. Montrose had never realized that the practitioners of either Arcanoi could work together to such devastating effect, but evidently, with practice, preparation, and, no doubt, a team leader possessing extraordinary knowledge of the mystic arts, it was possible.

Bolstered by his comprehension, the Scot fought his incipient panic, insisting to himself that it wasn't *his* fear, not really. The Heretic bastards were putting it inside his head. And finally it loosened its grip.

He peered about. Guns rattled and arrows arced through the air. Many of his men were already wounded or gone entirely, devoured by the Void. Others, though uninjured, wept and shuddered on the ground. Some were still trying to shoot blindly back at their assailants. A few men tried to flee in what momentarily appeared to be the direction of the old church and the river. An instant later, they staggered and fell. Apparently they hadn't truly been running away from the Heretics but directly at one contingent of them.

A big man knelt on the ground a few feet away, pumping off rounds from a shotgun. It looked like Fink, though Montrose couldn't be sure in the glare. He scrambled toward him.

The world spun like a carousel, nearly throwing him off his feet. Something in the air, probably a tactile and olfactory illusion woven by the enemy Sandmen, burned his nose and eyes. An arrow, its force nearly spent, glanced off his mask. At last he reached the man with the shotgun.

It was Fink. Grinning ferociously, he shouted, "Here's that setback you mentioned." Montrose could barely hear him over the wailing.

"Sandmen and Chanteurs," the Scot bellowed back, "working together. Sandmen hid most of the enemy behind illusions until we got to the piece of ground where they wanted us."

"Figured that out," answered Fink. "Don't know what to do about it, though, not when I can't tell where any damn thing is."

"I can." Montrose hoped that his memory and instincts weren't playing him false. "We're in a depression in the ground. The enemy has us surrounded on three sides. The town is that way." He pointed. "The Chanteurs and Sandmen are on one of the rooftops directly in front of us."

Fink eyed his dubiously. "Are you sure?"

"Yes," Montrose lied. "I'm a Harbinger and a general. Nothing can ruin my sense of direction, and I know where to position troops for optimum effect. If I were commanding the other side, I'd put the Sandmen and Chanteurs someplace they could stand together to coordinate their magic, overlook the entire battlefield, and enjoy a measure of protection. And if we're going to turn this fight around, we have to get up there *now* and stop the bombardment."

"How?" Fink asked. "It's one thing to know where they are. But to charge it blind, with the ground spinning under your feet and rows of gunmen in the way—"

"We can do it," Montrose said. "Grab a man or two, anybody who looks as if he can still fight."

Fink rose, pulled a mewling wraith with stubby jeweled horns off the ground, and shook him. Montrose grasped the shoulder of a youthful-looking wraith with a smoking revolver in either hand. "This way!" the Stygian shouted.

Over the course of the next few seconds, Montrose collected two frightened men, and Fink three. Not enough, but the Stygian doubted there was time to gather any more. Doing his best to block out the excruciating distractions of the glare and the shrieking, the fear still gnawing at his nerves, he focused his will and invoked his Harbinger powers.

A glittering circular hole opened in the ground before him. "In!" he bellowed. "Jump in!"

Grinning, Fink did so instantly, and the other men scrambled after him. Ordinarily any wraith would hesitate to leap into a Nihil. But conditions on the killing ground were so painful, so terrifying, that even the perils of the Tempest seemed preferable. Hoping that he hadn't sent his companions tumbling into the jaws of a Spectre, Montrose jumped after them.

He landed on a barren plain littered with huge gray boulders. A freezing wind, its ferocious howl faint in comparison with the screeching of the Chanteur choir, ripped at his hair and cloak, and blue lightning flickered in the churning clouds overhead. The Nihil he'd opened, a disk of shadow floating unsupported in the air, made a sizzling sound and vanished.

Fink looked this way and that. "What next?" he asked.

Montrose extended his arcane perceptions, studying the patterns of twisted and fractured space around him, and then said, "We go this way. Quickly, but warily, also. The Tempest is every bit as dangerous as you've heard."

Weapons ready, scanning the darkness for flickers of motion, the seven men skulked forward. "I think I get the idea," Fink murmured to Montrose. "We're going to pop back into the Shadowlands behind the guys who were shooting at us. It's a good trick. Why don't we use it all the time?"

"Because it's too easy for it to go awry," the Scot replied. Sensing a kink in the dimensional fabric off to the left, he led his troops in that direction. "The metaphysical structure of the Tempest is so complicated, so contrary, that often even the greatest Harbinger can't bend it to its will. I may not be able to create another doorway that will take us anywhere close to where we want to go. We may not get back for hours, even if it only feels like a few minutes to us. A gang of Spectres may jump us—"

Behind them, one of the men screamed.

Montrose and Fink whirled. "You and your big mouth," the latter said.

A few yards back, a patch of the hard, cracked ground had inexplicably turned to mush and was sucking down the last two wraiths in the procession. Already the shrieking, thrashing irregulars had vanished up to their knees. At first Montrose thought the men were merely sinking of their own weight, but then he noticed the long, thin tentacles twining around them and dragging them down.

The comrades of the unfortunate soldiers hovered helplessly about the newly formed quicksand pit. They couldn't shoot the tentacles, not without hitting the prey in their clutches as well, and the pool was too wide for them to grab their friends and drag them to safety. If they tried, they'd only topple in themselves.

Montrose levitated and hurtled to the center of the pit. He tore at the tentacles gripping the man who'd sunk the deepest, but he couldn't rip them away. Grasping the wraith by the arms, he struggled to fly straight upward, only to find he didn't have enough lift to overcome the strength of the hidden monster. Its victim continued to slide from view. The Scot had to let him go to avoid being pulled down himself. Gibbering curses and pleas for help until the muck slopped into his mouth, the guerrilla went under with a ghastly slurping sound.

Turning, Montrose saw that the second irregular was almost as gone as well. Only his hairless head and naked shoulders with their reflective brass-like skin remained above the surface. Snarling, the Stygian whipped out his rapier and began thrusting it into the slime.

The blade didn't contact anything solid. After a moment, additional tentacles shot out of the quicksand and tried to whip around him.

"Get away!" shouted one of the irregulars.

Doing his best to fend off the tentacles with his empty hand, Montrose kept stabbing. The unseen monster's arms lashed around his legs and yanked him downward, plunging his boots into the gelid quicksand. Then the point of the rapier finally punched into something solid.

The tentacles thrashed, loosening their hold. Montrose frantically flew upward, freeing himself from the tangle, and then looked down. The wraith with the brazen skin was nearly gone. Only his yellow hands remained above the surface.

Swooping downward, Montrose gripped them and then, straining, rising again, heaved the man out of the quicksand and set him on solid ground. Deep, steaming gashes spiraled around the soldier's body where the tentacles had burned their way into his flesh.

The Scot flew back over the pit. Hovering just above the surface, he plunged his arm repeatedly into the icy slime, groping for the other irregular. He couldn't find him.

After a few seconds, Montrose grimaced in frustration. For all he knew, the soldier was still alive, and mired within reach. But with scores of men in jeopardy back in the Shadowlands, there was no more time to fish for him. The Stygian flew to the fellow he had rescued. "Can you walk?" he asked.

The brazen-skinned wraith gave him a shaky nod. "I think so."

Montrose turned to another of the irregulars. "You keep an eye on him, and help him if he needs it. Let's move."

Montrose resumed his place at the head of the column, and they hurried on. "That was pretty smart work," said Fink.

Montrose scowled, disgusted with himself. "Nonsense. I should have sensed the creature's presence before it attacked. Failing that, I should have saved both of our lads." As the two wraiths neared another towering boulder, the Scot perceived a crumple in the fabric of space. "This is the place."

Fink pivoted toward the four wraiths behind them. "Look alive, boys. We're going back to the fight."

Montrose invoked his Harbinger Arcanos. For a moment the dimensional fabric resisted him, but then a round black hole opened in the side of the rock. He checked his AK-47, making sure it was ready to fire, and then sprang through the portal.

To his relief, he emerged into the Shadowlands precisely where—— and when—he'd intended, between a line of Heretic gunmen in dark glasses, all facing in the opposite direction, and a crumbling brick tenement, on the roof of which the choir of Chanteurs was keening. Fortunately, now that he was out of the target area, their song failed to rattle him anew. Presumably the Sandmen were atop the building also, though from his vantage point, he couldn't actually see them.

Fink and the other irregulars scrambled out of the rift. Montrose pressed his finger to his lips, commanding stealth, and pointed at the rooftop.

Fink nodded, turned, and led the other raiders toward the tenement's front door. Montrose levitated. Though his blood was up, he didn't relish the idea of assaulting the rooftop in advance of his companions. But his helpless men in the field of glare were dying by the second. He couldn't put off attacking until his allies appeared for fear they'd arrive too late.

He started shooting the instant he rose above the parapet, sweeping the assault rifle in an arc, cutting down Sandmen in gaudy clothing and Chanteurs clutching a miscellany of musical instruments. The deafening chorus of wailing ended abruptly.

As Montrose had hoped, he'd caught the Heretics by surprise. Alighting on the rooftop, he shot another pair of Sandmen, and then the rebels who were still on their feet struck back.

Some snatched pistols from holsters and started to shoot. Others used their Arcanoi. Ghastly shrieks jolted Montrose, or even seared away patches of his skin. Bursts of glare dazzled him, and intangible fingers fumbled at his mind, trying to make him fall asleep.

Snarling, nearly berserk with hatred, he spun this way and that, striving to keep any of his opponents from getting a fix on him, hoping their own numbers would hinder them. The assault rifle blazed and vibrated in his grip.

Three more Heretics went down, their bodies dissolving in ripples of shadow. Grinning crazily, Montrose decided this kamikaze strike was actually going to work. He didn't even need the reinforcements presumably charging madly up the stairs. He was going to clear the rooftop all by himself.

Then a Chanteur wailed and blasted Montrose's legs out from under him. But as the Stygian fell, he glimpsed Fink and the other irregulars bursting through the walls of the enclosure that presumably capped the stairwell.

Fink bellowed and brandished his shotgun over his head. Crackling strands of electricity blazed across the rooftop, filling the air with the smell of ozone. Heretics, caught in the discharge, shuddered and burned. The other intruders opened fire with their rifles.

The diversion gave Montrose the moment he needed to scramble back to his feet. He tried to shoot a Chanteur, a little man with a guitar strung across his back, discovered the AK-47 was empty, and clubbed the Heretic with the stock instead. Even as the musician dropped, the Scot reached inside his mantle for another clip.

From the corner of his eye, he glimpsed something flashing at him. As he pivoted, a tattered canvas lawn chair, hurled with considerable force, slammed against his shoulder. The Skinlands object sailed on straight through his body to vanish over the parapet. The impact didn't alter the course of its flight an iota. But it staggered Montrose.

He tried to regain his balance, and a second folding chair whizzed through his legs. He fell back down. A slender blond woman, no doubt the Spook who'd thrown the furniture, charged him, a katana in her upraised hands and a silver owl pendant, the emblem of the Sisterhood of Athena, bouncing on her breast.

And Montrose froze. Because the rebel leader was Louise.

For a moment he simply felt empty, as if his astonishment had smothered every other emotion, even the desire to survive. Then a wave of rage and hate crashed through him. Lurching to one knee, he jerked his rifle over his head. The Japanese sword clanged against the barrel.

He slammed the AK-47 into Louise's knee. Bone cracked, and she reeled backward. Dropping the rifle, he scrambled up, drew his rapier, and went after her.

Hobbling now, she started to cut at his head, then faltered, her blue eyes widening. He realized that, thanks to his mask, she hadn't recognized him until now. The enemy commander with the auburn lovelocks might have *reminded* her of the man she'd once betrayed, but if so, she'd dismissed it as a chance resemblance.

The discovery that she hadn't even known him infuriated Montrose still further. Screaming, he thrust the rapier through her forearm. Black light rippled from the wound. The katana tumbled from her grasp. Dropping his own weapon, he pounced on her, intent on ripping her apart with his hands.

They grappled, and he bore her backwards. A dagger with a silver owl's head pommel and a curved darksteel blade popped into existence in her hand.

Once again, it was Montrose's turn to be startled. Because even delirious with fury, he realized that Louise's weapon was the knife Katrina had showed him.

Louise started to thrust it at his breast. Then something smashed down on top of her head, bone crunched, and she slumped in his arms.

Montrose raised his eyes, to discover that Fink had come up behind her and clubbed her with the butt of his shotgun. Though he was leering as savagely as ever, the hulking, black-haired wraith looked somehow less real, almost translucent, as if he'd been drawing on his Haunter's Arcanos so heavily that even his prodigious strength was nearly spent.

For a second Montrose wanted to strike his lieutenant for daring to intrude on what should have been an intimate moment. But ultimately, that resentment was a puny, ephemeral emotion. It couldn't divert him from the utter loathing he felt for Louise. And even though she wasn't conscious at the moment, it would still be delightful to mutilate her. After all, as long as he was careful not to do *too* much damage, she'd heal, and he could hurt her all over again when she woke up. He threw her down, straddled her, and began to tear open her garments.

"What are you doing?" Fink demanded.

"It's all right," said Montrose. "Leave me alone."

Fink grabbed his shoulder, yanked him to his feet, and slapped him. "Snap out of it," the river man growled.

Montrose thrashed, struggling to break the other wraith's grip. "You don't understand! It's *her!*"

"I don't give a watery shit who it is," Fink replied. "There's still a fight going on. By wiping out the sons of bitches up here, we've given our boys an outside chance of winning it, but only if their leader rallies them."

Montrose's frenzy lost some of its edge. Of course, the battle. He'd forgotten all about. He gave his head a shake, trying to clear it. "I'm sorry. It's just that this woman—"

"Whoever she is, she'll keep!" Fink picked up the rapier and stuck the hilt in Montrose's hand. "Are you ready?"

The Stygian nodded. "Let's do it."

Thirty-Three

Montrose strolled from one group of irregulars to the next, inquiring about their welfare, joking with them, and listening to them boast about their valor in the battle. Most of the ruffians seemed to feel they'd won the victory over the Heretics more or less single-handedly, and never mind the jibes of their comrades, who heckled the storytellers with accusations of poltroonery, martial ineptitude, or both.

Ordinarily the Stygian could have performed this duty gladly, taking satisfaction in the sight of every survivor, grateful that a visit from their commander could distract the men from the loss of fallen friends and the pain of their wounds. But tonight, with hatred, frustration, and indecision grinding together inside him, it took a Herculean effort just to smile, pay attention to what the guerrillas were saying, and offer an appreciative response.

But at last the chore drew to a close. The final casualty was an amputee in a blue leather mask who was using a long spear for a crutch. The wispy shape of a new lower leg and foot, not solid enough to support his weight as yet, depended from his stump. Montrose kidded the fellow, a former highwayman, about his predilection for chubby women, clapped him on the shoulder, and bade him good night. Then he trudged over to one of the dilapidated tenements and slumped down with his back against the cracked brick wall.

After a minute he wished he'd gone farther away from what remained of his army. From where he was resting, he could hear the whimpering and weeping of the captured Heretics, whom his men, enraged by their near defeat, had brutalized even more thoroughly than usual. The moans reminded him of the one prisoner whom he was holding separately, on the roof where they'd tried to murder one another.

A hulking form lumbered out of the gloom. "I made the count," said Fink. "We lost half our men."

Montrose nodded. "That was about what I estimated."

"Percentage-wise, it's even heavier losses than on our first raid." Fink shrugged and sat down. "But it's war, right? People are going to die. What matters is that we won."

The Stygian sighed. "I suppose."

Fink cocked his head. "What's troubling you now, Anacreon? The Sister of Athena? What's the story on her, anyway?"

After a moment's hesitation, Montrose said, "I knew her when I was alive. Her name is Louise, and she was my lover. She also betrayed me to my death."

Fink grinned. "Ouch. No wonder you were so eager to torture her. So what are you moping around down here for? Go pay her a call."

"I want to," Montrose said. "You can't imagine how badly I want it. But I'm afraid that if I do, my Shadow will grow even stronger."

"Mask and Scythe, man, are you going to let a little thing like that stand in the way of sweet revenge? Judging from past experience, if your Shadow *does* slip its reins, all it's likely to do is make you hurt Heretics, and that's what you want to do anyway."

"You have a point," Montrose said. "This is one of those occasions when my dark side and the rest of me are in accord. But there's another problem." He described his encounter with Katrina.

"'Forbear,'" said Fink at the end of the story. "In other words, show mercy."

"Yes."

"Are you sure it was the same knife?"

"Absolutely," Montrose said. "Before Katrina picked me up, I met a Spectre wearing Louise's form. Evidently the creature was telepathic, and plucked her image from my mind. Katrina as much as told me the encounter was a portent—the Tempest is like that—meaning, no doubt, that I was destined to find the real Louise later on, but I was too thick to understand her."

Fink grimaced. "Your Ferryman was too cryptic by half. If she knew you were going to run into our friend on the rooftop, she should have told you flat out."

"She may not have known," Montrose said. "I'm no Oracle, but I'm told their insights are often jumbled and incomplete."

"Well, I think she scammed you, because she realized you hated Louise too much to pledge to spare her. And I say the trickery releases you from your promise, particularly since it was given under duress."

Montrose smiled ruefully. "I've been telling myself the same thing, but I'm not convinced."

"Well, who gives a piss anyway," said Fink. "Just break the damn promise. It wouldn't be the first time, would it?"

"No," Montrose said. "But you know, I've always *tried* to keep my word. Even when I was back-stabbing my way up the ranks of the Hierarchy, if I actually made someone a pledge, I did my best to keep it. Considering the sins I *did* commit, it was probably absurd to cleave to that one scruple, but nonetheless, I did."

Somewhere in the gloom, an irregulars began to sing a love song about a lady named Michelle. The fellow was no Chanteur, but he had a pleasant baritone voice. The gentle strains of the ballad made a stark contrast to the anger seething in Montrose's breast.

"I wonder," said Fink, "why the Ferryman even cared. What's so special about this one Heretic?"

"I have no idea. Katrina implied, in the vaguest manner possible, that the business with the knife was linked to some mysterious challenge I have to face. It sounded like gibberish at the time, but now that we've stumbled onto the business with the false Pardoners, I wonder."

"Has it occurred to you," said Fink, "that you *have* to punish the bitch? She's a dangerous rebel. She killed half your soldiers. Even if our boys would sit still for it, it would be treason to let her off the hook."

"I know," said Montrose. "As a matter of fact, I even told Katrina I wouldn't keep the promise if it meant neglecting my duty. But I *can* exercise some restraint. I don't actually have to tear Louise apart with my own hands."

Fink leered. "But you'll regret it if you don't."

Montrose nodded. "I will indeed." He stood up. "I need to make up my mind, and I'm not getting it done down here. Perhaps if I see her again, I'll be able to decide."

"Sounds sensible," said Fink. "Give her a welt or two for me."

Montrose entered the tenement and climbed the stairs. As he neared the roof, he faltered. *I don't have to do this*, he thought, surprising himself. *I never have to look at her again if I don't want to*.

But even as he framed the thought, he realized it was a lie. He *did* need to see her, even if a part of him cringed at the prospect. He stepped through the substance of a door with flaking paint and out into the moonlight.

Louise lay near one edge of the tar paper roof, her slender body wrapped in an extraordinary quantity of chains. Either Montrose's men had wanted to make certain she wouldn't slip her restraints with her Spook Arcanos, or else they'd simply decided to make her as uncomfortable as possible. A red rubber ball gag with a black leather strap filled her mouth, distending her cheeks, and a blindfold covered her eyes. A bored-looking guard with a crossbow sat on the parapet beside her.

Montrose hesitated again, then urged himself forward. "I want to be alone with her for a bit," he said to the sentry. "Wait on the stairs." Louise's head jerked around at the sound of his voice. The guard rose and sauntered to the stairs.

As Montrose knelt beside the captive, sorrow and a kind of bitter nostalgia rose inside him, not replacing his hatred but coexisting with it. *Dear God*, he thought, *what we shared together made me so happy, even in the midst of a desperate time. How did we ever come to this?* Discovering that he wanted to see her eyes, he slipped the blindfold off. They were the same clear blue that he remembered.

"Yes," he said, "it's truly me. Who would have thought we'd meet again, on another continent, after all these centuries? It's a strange world, isn't it?"

She gazed up at him beseechingly. It made him grateful for his mask. He suspected his face was contorted with hatred or anguish, but he was in control of his voice. His tone was light, conveying the message that she was a miserable creature scarcely worthy of his notice. That he valued her as little as she had him.

"I find myself in a ludicrous situation," Montrose continued. "I'd like to spend the next few months torturing you, and send you to the Void when that grew tiresome. I'm sure you aren't expecting anything less. But before I knew who you were, I promised a benefactor I'd show you mercy. What would you do in my place?"

The strap securing the gag snapped, and the rubber ball popped out of Louise's mouth. Montrose reflexively lifted his hands to defend himself, but she didn't try to strike him with the object. It simply dropped to the rooftop.

"I'm sorry, James," she gasped. "I'm so sorry. I didn't know you were leading the purge. If I had, I never would have tried to destroy you. I would have arranged to meet with you. I would have found another way."

"As you did three hundred and fifty years ago?"

She gaped at him in horror. "You...you know about that?"

"Oh, yes," Montrose said. "Your fellow Judas VanLengen was kind enough to enlighten me."

"I swear, I never *wanted* to betray you," said Louise. "I *loved* you—"

For some reason, that blatantly false claim disturbed the precarious balance of passions in Montrose's mind. "Liar!" he exploded, battering her with his fists. "Liar! Liar!"

She made a choking sound and went limp. Her head rolled sideways. Perhaps she hadn't yet fully recovered from the clubbing Fink had given her, and Montrose's blows had aggravated the injury anew. At any rate, he'd beaten her back into unconsciousness.

He hit her six more times before he was able to stop. Shuddering, he curled his fingers into hooks and reached for her eyes.

And then, somehow, he seemed to see himself from the outside, as an observer might. He beheld a gloating sadist about to inflict atrocities on a helpless women, and though the prospect thrilled him, it sickened him as well. He had a vague intuition that if he allowed himself to become such a vile, perverted creature, even for one brief interlude, he might never recover his true self again. He leaped to his feet and scrambled back several paces, like a mortal recoiling from a poisonous snake.

Still his body quivered with the lust to maim her. He turned his back on her, and the compulsion eased slightly.

"I won't hurt you anymore myself," he said to the unconscious woman. "I won't even have you destroyed, not completely. But you *will* pay. I'm shipping you to Stygia, tonight, with instructions that you go to the Masquers, or the soul-forges." He pictured her twisted into the shape of a hideous barghest, the magic in her iron muzzle warping her mind into that of a beast. Or sculpted into a torch, silently screaming as her crown of freezing barrow-flame devoured her. Or shattered into a handful of oboli, each coin retaining a splinter of sentience, just enough to suffer for eternity.

He smirked at the thought of her agony, then winced at another surge of shame and self-disgust.

"I'm sorry," he muttered, just as if Katrina were present to hear him. "I believe you were trying to help me when you extorted my pledge, and I wish I could keep it. But this is as close as I come."

He hurried to the stairwell before he could change his mind. Ss he descended, he sensed his restive Shadow stirring, swelling, invading his conscious mind. He frantically struggled to muster the will to repress it, until, suddenly, the world seemed dim and far away. He felt as if he were drifting off to sleep.

Thirty-Four

Chiarmonte, an Anacreon of the Order of the Avenging Flame and the Smiling Lord's spymaster, was a small, gray man who generally carried himself with the diffidence of a mild-mannered clerk. He'd once told Potter he attributed much of his success as a confidential agent of the commune of eleventh-century Venice to his unassuming demeanor. Now, however, he stood at parade rest with his iron mask cradled in his right hand. Potter, ensconced on a golden throne with red velvet cushions and eagle-claw feet, had the unpleasant feeling that he knew the reason for the other wraith's stiff martial posture.

"You've come up empty, haven't you?" the Deathlord said.

Chiarmonte flicked his eyes at Demetrius, who was standing in the corner of the smallish audience chamber, the bluish light of the nearest barrow-flame lamp glinting on the sardonyx helmet tucked casually under his arm. It was a subtle gesture, but Potter had no difficulty interpreting it.

"You can speak freely in front of Demetrius," he said impatiently, exasperated that, even with his life in jeopardy, his lieutenants still insisted on playing their courtiers' games, angling for his favor by subtly casting aspersions on their fellows. "Your report, please."

Chiarmonte inclined his head. "Of course, my liege. I regret that I have 'come up empty,' thus far. The Legionnaires assigned to guard the park on the night of the attack appear to be loyal. None of them deviated significantly from his story—"

"'Significantly?'" Demetrius interjected.

Chiarmonte's thin-lipped mouth tightened at the interruption. "When you torture a man and his loved ones," he explained, "and refuse to accept his story, he's likely to offer a second one eventually, even if the original version was true. But none of those alternate stories checked out. Which is to say, in my professional opinion, the men kept faithful watch over the perimeter of the park, but failed to see the assassin slip inside. As far as our agents have been able to discover, so did everyone else who happened to be in the general vicinity."

"Perhaps it isn't all that important to identify the specific man," Demetrius said. "He used a distinctive weapon, the ravages of old age. Which suggests he was working for the Ashen Lady."

"I wouldn't leap to any conclusions," Chiarmonte said. "It's conceivable that some other enemy devised that means of attack precisely because it would divert suspicion to the Seat of Shadows." He gazed into Potter's eyes. "Frankly, Dread Lord, I think it would be rash to assume that *any* of your peers instigated the attack. Our informants in their households don't know anything about such an a scheme. And you have a plethora of *known* enemies. Heretics, Renegades, Spectres, the Dark Kingdom of Jade—"

Potter shook his head. "None of them has access to the highest levels of the city."

"They certainly aren't supposed to," Chiarmonte conceded. "However, any defensive system can be breached."

"Perhaps," Potter said, "but I have other information indicating that someone on the Council is plotting against me."

Chiarmonte lifted an eyebrow. "Since I'm your chief of intelligence," he said a bit ironically, "perhaps it would be appropriate for you to share it with me."

Potter supposed he deserved the rebuke. The Venetian probably did have a right to know. But the Deathlord was reluctant to confide his troubling visions to anyone but Demetrius. They were too personal. It would make him look too human, and too vulnerable. "It's intimations derived from a mystical source. You don't need to know the specifics. There aren't any, really."

Chiarmonte sketched a shallow bow. "As you wish, Dread Lord," he said, his tone now entirely neutral. "Undoubtedly, you know best."

Wonderful, Potter thought sourly, *people are trying to murder* me, *and* he *has injured feelings*. "You're entirely right about one thing," he said, hoping to mollify the man, "it doesn't have to be the Ashen Lady who sent the assassin. Even if it was, we don't know how many other Deathlords were in on the plot. And until we do, we can't retaliate."

"I'll continue to investigate," Chiarmonte said. "I'll also confer with the captain of the household guard about tightening up security."

"Good," said Potter. "Carry on." Chiarmonte bowed and exited the chamber. "Idiot."

Demetrius cocked his head. "I've always thought him competent, if unimaginative."

"If he were competent, I wouldn't be in this predicament." Potter sighed. "Or perhaps that isn't fair. I don't know what to believe. I feel as if I'm not thinking straight. And that I might even be losing my bond with my mask. The power inside it seems sluggish and far away. If I could tap it as easily as I used to, I would have crushed the assassin the instant I sensed his presence. I keep wondering if someone has laid a curse on me."

"If so," Demetrius replied, moving closer to the throne, "it's such a subtle malediction that none of your servants, with all our various Arcanoi, can detect it. I think you're simply under stress, and feeling the effects."

"Then see if you can ease my apprehension," Potter said. "Scry for me."

The Greek frowned, but to Potter's relief, for once he didn't need to be coaxed. "Very well, my lord. As it happens, I stumbled on a new technique while perusing a volume I found in one of your libraries. I suspect someone salvaged the tome from the ruins of the old-time Oracles' guild hall."

"Do you think it will serve us better than the cards, or studying the patterns in the clouds and lightning?"

Demetrius smiled. "We'll find out."

The Greek set his mask on the dais supporting the throne, then opened the leather satchel hanging at his side. A wavering glow shone forth, staining his swarthy hand and the folds of his toga. He reached into the bag and brought out a ball of luminous, opalescent jelly. Soul stuff, smelted but not yet transformed into wood, metal, or some other less disquieting material.

Demetrius said, "Please remove your gauntlets." Potter complied, and the Oracle handed him the glowing mass. It was cool to the touch, and oozed and squirmed feebly in his grasp.

"Knead it," Demetrius said. "Roll it around. Handle it until it feels right to you." Feeling a bit like a child playing in mud or making snowballs, Potter manipulated the material for about fifteen seconds, then handed it back.

Demetrius backed two paces away from the throne, down the scarlet runner that ran from the dais to the door. Frowning with concentration, murmuring incantations, he began to draw long curling tendrils from the central mass. Occasional ripples of darkness, symptomatic of the Oblivion gnawing at the heart of all things, pulsed through the strands of light. Crude faces formed and dissolved, some blank and mindless, a few contorted in anguish, and one grinning and mugging with demented glee.

Before long the mass became a structure rather like a shrub, with multiple stems rising from a common base. The Oracle slowly, carefully released his creation, and it floated unsupported in the air. Then, murmuring once more, he moved to one of the lamps, removed the fluted chimney, and put the fingers of his left hand in the flame.

The residue of soul plasm clinging to his skin kindled instantly. Potter winced, but Demetrius didn't appear to be in any pain. He touched his hands together, setting the right one ablaze, and then returned to his creation. He began to caress the various tendrils, reminding Potter of a harpist plucking the strings of his instrument.

For several seconds his ministrations had no obvious effect. Then, suddenly, one section of the ectoplasmic sculpture caught fire. The embryonic faces screamed, a faint piping barely audible above the crackle of the blaze, and an odor not unlike the stench of burning flesh suffused the air.

Three strands quickly burned away to nothing, leaving the rest of the structure unscathed. And as the cold flames finished consuming them, a circular window opened in the air.

Beyond it was a street of derelict bungalows, their crumbling facades and verandahs fissured with Nihils. A crescent moon shone among the tatters of cloud overhead. A pair of grievously wounded Legionnaires lay amid a litter of arrows, notched and broken swords, spent cartridges, and a fallen standard emblazoned with a fountain of liquid fire, one of the thirty-odd emblems of the Smiling Lord.

Potter leaned forward, trying to see more, but the window vanished.

"Is it working?" Demetrius asked. His normally mellifluous voice was a little rough, betraying a discomfort or strain his calm expression and easy movements denied.

"Yes," Potter said. "I saw a Haunt somewhere in the Shadowlands. There'd been a battle, and my troops lost it. Show me more."

"I'll try," Demetrius stroked the phosphorescent tendrils. Another piece of the construct exploded into flame, and a second window opened.

This time Potter beheld the Isle of Sorrows as if he were soaring high above it. From such an altitude, with only ochre lightning to illuminate the scene, it was hard to make anything out. The City of Dark Echoes was an intricate, bewildering mass of vague protrusions and myriad points of light. But after a moment he realized that one light looked peculiar. It was too large.

When he focused his attention on it, the window zoomed in like a camera until he seemed to be hovering fifty feet above it. He saw that it was a great mass of barrow-fire, consuming his allotted section of the palace.

He cried out, and the window closed.

"What did you see this time?" Demetrius panted.

Potter gestured impatiently, brushing the question aside. They could talk later. "Show me more."

"As my lord commands." Demetrius ran his burning fingers along the remaining strands of glow. More of them flared and vanished.

This time Potter saw himself, stumbling through the corridors of his fortress, his halberd clutched in his hands. Or rather, what was left of his halberd. Something had snapped the enchanted weapon midway down the shaft. What was even more horrifying was that some force had cleft the Smiling Lord's *mask* as well. One half of the steel visor still clung to the left side of his face, but his right profile was exposed.

The figure in the vision stopped, sucked in a deep breath, and bellowed. Potter couldn't hear him, but he could read his lips. "Guards! Guards!"

After a moment, the beleaguered Deathlord's mouth twisted in despair. *Because he doesn't hear anyone rushing to his aid,* Potter thought. *Impossible as it seems, there* isn't *anyone to come. Somehow, he's been betrayed.*

The Potter in the vision hobbled on, until a ring of shadowy figures abruptly materialized around him. Snarling, their quarry whirled his broken weapon over his head, but never got a chance to use it. His enemies swarmed over him like wolves pulling down a fawn. Darksteel daggers flashed in their black-gloved hands.

The window snapped shut. "No!" Potter yelped. He glared at Demetrius. "More!"

"I'm sorry," Demetrius croaked, trembling. "There isn't any more." He motioned toward the luminous construct, and Potter saw that the last burst of barrow-fire had devoured all but a few wisps of it, and these were shriveling by the moment.

"There's a bit of plasm left," the Deathlord said. "Enough for one more effort." Demetrius hesitated. "Do it!"

"Very well." Looking as if he were struggling not to flinch, the Greek told hold of the last crumbling vestiges of his creation.

The final explosion was far more intense than those which had preceded it. The burst of terrible cold slammed Potter backward as if someone had clubbed him in the face. This time, no window opened. Instead, Demetrius fell down thrashing, his arms aflame from fingertips to elbows.

Potter leaped up and scrambled toward him. At the same time, clearly making a supreme effort, Demetrius rasped out another invocation. Despite the agony grating in his voice, the words of power seemed to resonate like the beats of a gong. The fires consuming his flesh winked out abruptly. So did the ones in the lamps along the walls, plunging the chamber into darkness. The Greek lay motionless.

Potter flung himself down beside his lieutenant, peering frantically, terrified that the man was about to melt away. At that moment, he felt that if Demetrius perished, his demise would leave him utterly friendless and alone.

But to his relief, there were no ripples of shadow eroding Demetrius's substance, not even within his charred and withered arms. After a moment, the Greek looked up at his master. "I think I see why that particular technique was abandoned," he whispered.

"I'm sorry," Potter said. "I shouldn't have goaded you onward when you knew it was time to stop."

"Please," said Demetrius, his voice a shade stronger, "don't say such things. I'm your servant. My only purpose is to obey you. It's for me to apologize, for bungling my task." A long, pale worm of ectoplasm wriggled down his forearm as his shriveled limbs began to heal. "If you could please move back, I'd like to try to get up. Marble floors are decorative, but they're also cold and hard."

"Of course." Potter helped Demetrius to his feet, put his arm around him, more or less carried him to the dais, and sat him down. "Is this better?"

"Yes," gasped Demetrius. Clearly, motion had aggravated the pain of his burns. "Thank you, my liege. May I ask what the divination showed you?"

"Nothing too alarming," Potter said sardonically. "Merely defeat, betrayal, and my own murder. But it was just like all the other visions. Incomplete. I still don't know which of the other Deathlords are plotting against me."

"Perhaps none of them is," Demetrius said. "Sometimes the shape of the future expresses itself *symbolically*—"

Potter gave him a withering stare.

"Forgive me," said the Greek. "I'm talking nonsense. The pain is making me lightheaded. Of course, when you see variations on the same horrible theme, time after time, when someone has already tried to slay you…."

"It was the same problem this time, wasn't it? You couldn't show me everything I need to know because you haven't seen my deathmarks. Because you don't really know who I am."

"Yes," said Demetrius. A shiny white burn on the back of his wrist rippled and turned into dark, unblemished skin. "It's a technical problem. I'll keep searching for the solution."

"But what if you don't find it before the crisis comes?"

"I hope matters won't fall out that way. But even if they do, you still have Chiarmonte to gather intelligence by other methods."

"To the devil with Chiarmonte. He just admitted his spies can't discover anything." Potter took a deep breath, steadying himself. "I'm going to do it. I'm going to reveal myself to you."

Demetrius's dark eyes widened. "I'm honored, Dread Lord, but are you certain? I'm merely one of countless functionaries. Why should I be entrusted with your greatest secret?"

"You just risked your life and got burned trying to help me," Potter said. "If I can't trust you, whom can I trust?" He lifted his hands to his visor, and then faltered.

Charon forbade this, he thought. *He called it treason. And it will leave me vulnerable in a way that no Deathlord should ever be.*

But the Emperor was gone. Why should his laws outlast him if they were no longer useful? And Potter was *already* vulnerable in the way that mattered most. Every hour of every day, he sensed his unknown enemies closing in for the kill.

Quickly, before he could change his mind, he yanked the mask away from the rest of his helmet. A bolt of panic ripped through his mind, and he shuddered. His naked skin tingled in the cool air.

After a moment, his terror loosened his grip. Ridiculously enough, he now felt shy, flustered, as he had the first time he'd taken off his clothes in front of a woman. He looked at Demetrius. The Greek was trembling also, and had lowered his eyes.

For some reason, the other wraith's manifest anxiety made Potter feel calmer. "You have to look at me," he said wryly. "That's the whole point. I promise that no one is going to burst in and execute you for it. You probably won't even turn to stone."

Demetrius nodded and slowly lifted his head.

Potter envisioned the features his lieutenant was beholding. Straw-colored hair and pale blue eyes. Apple cheeks, a snub nose, and a rather weak chin. He smiled ruefully. "It's not nearly as impressive as it ought to be, is it?"

"You died younger than I would have expected," Demetrius said, a hint of compassion in his tone.

"I was fresh out of Eton, just beginning what was supposed to be a long and glorious career in Her Majesty's army," Potter said. "But I don't much regret dying young, not anymore. My true misfortune is that I died so *recently*. I was killed in the

Sepoy Mutiny of 1857. Charon made me the Smiling Lord ten years later, even though I was only a Centurion in his service at the time. I don't know what happened to the old Smiling Lord, or why the Emperor chose me as a replacement. He wouldn't say.

"At first, it was terribly strange. I conducted myself as my mask prompted me, held myself aloof and mysterious, and even clever fellows like Montrose and Chiarmonte didn't notice the changeover. They treated me as if I were my predecessor, a demigod from the dawn of time, when in reality they'd inhabited the Underworld for centuries longer than I had."

"Even so, you were the Emperor's choice," Demetrius said, "and you've manage to carry out the duties of your office. Does the date of your ascension truly matter?"

"What matters is that I'm virtually certain that most if not all of the other Deathlords *have* been around since the beginning. They helped Charon build the city and expel the Fishers. They've had millennia to amass knowledge and arcane power. I've always thought that if they ever realized how recently I joined their company, they'd regard me as a contemptible upstart."

Potter grimaced. "Such reflections didn't trouble me too much as long as Charon was running the show and I was merely his deputy. But now I feel completely out of my depth!"

Demetrius climbed unsteadily to his feet and laid his burn-spotted hand on Potter's shoulder. "Don't despair, my lord. You've started down a new road tonight, and I promise that from now on, your existence is going to change."

Thirty-Five

Quivering with anger, Gayoso thrust his hand through the front of the desk drawer, grabbed the silver hand mirror, and snatched it out. Raising it to his face, he glared into it.

His own middle-aged countenance with its baggy eyes and curved, fleshy nose scowled back at him. His own features, and nothing more.

After a while, his angry expression wilted into one of puzzlement and dismay. Had the looking glass lost its magic?

Then, without warning, the handle of the mirror turned ice cold. His arm jerked at the chill. The reflection crossed its eyes and wiggled its ears. "Peek-a-boo," it said.

"Where have you been?" Gayoso demanded.

"You don't exactly look like a satisfied customer," the Shadow said. "I thought things might be pleasanter if I avoided you until your temper cooled down. Alas, it seems that I don't have the option. The djinn has to appear when you rub the lamp."

"If you were a djinn," Gayoso said bitterly, "you would have managed to grant your master's wish."

The Shadow lifted an eyebrow. "Do you mean that Montrose survived the surprise party we arranged for him?"

"You know damn well he did."

The Shadow sighed. "My dear twin. You don't comprehend my nature nearly as well as you suppose, so please don't make assumptions about what I know or don't know. Just answer my questions. It will make everything easier."

"Fine," Gayoso growled, "we'll do it your way. Yes, Montrose escaped along with half his men. He even won the battle, and he just returned to the Citadel."

"Did the Sister of Athena inform the gallant Marquess that you tried to help her destroy him?"

"Apparently not," Gayoso said grudgingly. "And it seems that for some reason he shipped the woman to Stygia immediately after the battle, so she's no longer available for questioning. Thank heaven for small favors."

"That particular benefaction isn't small at all," the reflection said. "It leaves you in the clear."

"Temporarily, yes. But Montrose will want to know why the intelligence I supplied him was faulty, why my troops failed to keep their rendezvous with his, and why the Heretics were so well-prepared for his arrival."

"As you yourself observed when we were hatching this scheme, the answer to the first two questions is simple bad luck and human error. And as for the third, well, how should you know?" The Shadow grinned. "Ah, those diabolical Heretics! Who can fathom their cunning ways?"

"I did cover my trail," Gayoso conceded. "I don't think Montrose can prove anything against me. But I'm certain he'll *suspect*. And if he was tempted to dispose of me before, he'll be an implacable enemy henceforth, while Shellabarger and Mrs. Duquesne will be only too happy to help him bring me down."

The Shadow nodded somberly. "I can't find any fault with your analysis. I suppose we should have let sleeping dogs lie."

Gayoso stared at the mirror in disbelief. "'Let sleeping dogs lie?' Is that all you have to say?"

"We rolled the dice and lost. Such is the nature of existence." The Shadow smirked. "Let me know when I hit on a cliché you find comforting, and I'll expand on it."

"I don't want to hear you philosophize. I want you to help me dispose of the Stygian as you were supposed to do in the first place."

"Remember, it isn't wise to ask for my help too often," said the Shadow with a mockery of concern. "You wouldn't want to stain that pristine nature of yours."

"Damn your impudence!" Gayoso barked. "I *order* you to help me!"

"My goodness," said the creature in the mirror, "you're truly frightened of Montrose, aren't you? I can't say I blame you. Any man who could forge the scum of Under-the-Hill into an army, destroy many of the local Heretic Circles in a matter of weeks, and escape the trap we set for him is a force to be reckoned with it. Which makes this the ideal time for me to renegotiate my contract."

Gayoso felt a chill, one that had nothing to do with the length of frigid metal in his fingers. "What are you talking about?"

"Up until now, I've helped you out of the goodness of my heart. It's time I received a token of your appreciation."

"I don't have to pay you," Gayoso said. "The magic of the mirror *compels* you to aid me."

"Did you ever *really* believe that?" asked the Shadow. "How quaint of you. Actually, it's simply a means of communication. A glorified telephone."

Gayoso tried to tell himself the creature was bluffing. He couldn't make himself believe it. "What do you want?" he asked.

"Hmm." The Shadow narrowed its eyes as if it were just now considering the point. "Good question. How about this? Jehovah asked Abraham to sacrifice his son, and what was good enough for the Creator should be good enough for us. Of course, you haven't seen your biological offspring in hundreds of years, but you do have some youthful wraiths among your subjects. Your children in a symbolic-cum-political sense. One of them will do."

"That's insane," Gayoso said. "I can't offer up one of my own people to the powers of darkness. The province would rise against me."

The Shadow rolled its eyes. "I'm not asking you do it in front of the whole Necropolis. A private ceremony will suffice. I'll teach you where to cut and what to chant, the prayers to the Void and all that."

I won't do it, Gayoso thought. *It would be a monstrous crime.*

But would it really? In his years as a governor, he'd condemned any number of wraiths to suffering and death, sometimes simply because it was expedient. That was the nature of politics. Would this occasion truly be any different, merely because the victim had a childlike appearance, and Gayoso recited the praises of the Malfeans?

No! the Anacreon thought. *What's wrong with me, that I can even consider such an act? I don't have to resort to this. I can solve my problems by myself.*

Yet could he? When he looked inside himself, he discovered that he doubted it. For years he'd turned to the mirror whenever he felt himself to be in dire jeopardy, and now he realized that in one sense, the Shadow had already exacted a fee for its services. It had deprived him of his confidence in his own judgment and ingenuity.

Averting his gaze from the mirror, loathing the creature inside the glass and himself as well, he whispered, "One child. My selection." If he looked, he ought to be able to find one with an adult personality, perhaps even a rebel or a criminal.

"Agreed," said the reflection. "A single sacrifice will do nicely, this time."

Gayoso glared at it. "There won't be a next time. Once I'm rid of Montrose, I'm going to smash this mirror."

The Shadow sighed. "That would be wasteful to say the least, but it's your decision. Shall we discuss how you're going to bring about Montrose's downfall?"

Gayoso blinked. "Don't you want me to perform the sacrifice first?"

"Oh, I trust you. I think you understand that when someone makes a pact with an entity like me, the universe takes note and exacts a heavy penalty if the fellow tries to welsh on his end of the bargain."

The Hierarch swallowed. "Yes," he said, "I do understand that." He struggled to thrust his guilt and self-contempt out of his mind, and focus on the benefits of the covenant. "All right, how *do* I get rid of the Stygian?"

"For a long while now, Montrose's Shadow has been waxing stronger."

"How do you know that?" Gayoso asked.

"Creatures such as myself have means of communication and other sources of intelligence which a steadfast Hierarch like you"—the Shadow leered—"couldn't understand. It's one of the many reasons we're going to win. But let's not get off on that. Let's concentrate on the issue at hand. When Montrose came face to face with Louise, the Sister of Athena, he learned she was the long-lost love who betrayed him to his mortal death. The person he hates more than anyone else in the world."

"And you knew that all along," said Gayoso, scowling. "That's why you didn't want the emissary to allude to Montrose by name. You thought that if the woman knew who was coming to fight her, she'd lose her nerve and run away. Why didn't you share this with me before?"

"If she'd destroyed Montrose on the battlefield, it wouldn't have mattered," the Shadow answered glibly. "To continue: When Montrose saw Louise, he fell prey to a terrible rage. He wanted to torture and ultimately destroy the lady with his own hands. Had he done so, his Shadow might have annihilated his psyche. He could have become a Spectre on the spot.

"But for some reason, he held back. Contenting himself with a less intimate revenge, he condemned her to torment at the hands of others. But even that expression of his hatred was enough to permit his Shadow to possess him temporarily. It knew from past experience that it couldn't compel him to commit suicide, or attack his own soldiers. Had it tried, he would have snapped out of his altered state of consciousness. But it was able to prompt him to a subtler means of self-destruction."

"And what was that?" Gayoso asked eagerly.

"Somewhere in his belongings," the reflection said, "you'll find a journal written in his hand, with his characteristic phrasing; although actually, of course, his Shadow penned it. You have to retrieve it quickly, before he stumbles across it himself."

"That could be difficult," said Gayoso, frowning. "He has his cutthroats guarding his section of the Citadel." Then he smiled. "But he likes Valentine, and his people know it. They'll let the little toad wander anywhere he pleases."

"Can you trust Valentine?" the Shadow asked.

"Yes. I know he helped Montrose at one point, but only because I hadn't ordered him not to. He's capable of small impudences like that, but ultimately he doesn't have the nerve to sell me out. His position here is the only remotely pleasant existence he's ever known, and he's terrified of losing it."

"Good. Then he can steal the papers. When he passes them to you, have a first-rate Harbinger and a detachment of Legionnaires carry them to the Smiling Lord as quickly as possible. Your problem will sort itself out in nothing flat."

Thirty-Six

When he'd first seen it, by the light of day, Bellamy had thought the motel lobby—a rectangular room paneled in oak, with a host of glassy-eyed bluefish, channel bass, cobia, and pompano mounted on the walls—looked rather comical. But at one o'clock in the morning, with no one else in view and most of the lights extinguished, some of the trophies floating in the shadows appeared less like fish with dopey expressions than hideous reptiles escaped from an ocean in hell, glaring balefully at any warm-blooded life that wandered into view.

No, they don't, Bellamy told himself firmly. *Turn off your imagination, or you never will get any sleep.* He took a drink from his can of Coca Cola, savoring the sweetness, and the pleasant burn as it went down. Then he strolled across the room and flopped down on a sofa in front of one of the bay windows.

Beyond the glass, the branches of the pines stirred restlessly. The sailboats and cruisers tied up at the docks bobbed and lurched back and forth as if trying to break their moorings. Gray clouds like fists clenched above the black expanse of Lake Pontchartrain, occluding most of the stars. The causeway was a vague streak in the distance, fading away into the night as if it some disaster had obliterated the middle section.

Bellamy grimaced. The thunderheads, the boats, and the bridge reminded him of the island city in his nightmares. He wondered if *every* sight he encountered from now on, no matter how mundane, was going to convey intimations of mystery and terror to him for the rest of his life.

Something touched him lightly on the shoulder. He jumped, squawked, and grabbed convulsively for his gun.

"Chill!" said Astarte. "Don't shoot, Officer, I surrender."

Bellamy took a deep breath, trying to slow his pounding heart. "I didn't hear you walk up."

"Apparently not," Astarte said. Her mocking grin gave way to a gentler smile. "I guess you couldn't sleep, either. Bad dreams?"

Bellamy shrugged. "That and anticipation, I guess."

She sat down beside him. The rings in her eyebrow, nostril, and lip gleamed dully in the faint illumination. Still, without her black lipstick and eye shadow, she didn't look as self-consciously pugnacious as usual. "Try not to let the dreams bother you," she said. "You don't know that you're seeing the City of Death, and even if you are, it doesn't have to *mean* anything. Marilyn says that different people see different things when they stare at the magic writing, and she's never been able to find any kind of pattern to it."

Bellamy smiled crookedly. "You mean there's something about the paranormal, about her own dirty little magic tricks, that Marilyn doesn't understand? Hey, there's a shocker."

Astarte grinned. "What a snotty comment. Just because she pumped you full of drugs, kidnapped you, and was going to brainwash you, that doesn't mean you shouldn't try to be friends with her."

"That's what's sad," Bellamy said. "I *don't* hold it against her. Life has gotten so crazy that what she did doesn't seem all that outrageous or even particularly important. If I'd had any idea what I was getting myself into, I don't think I'd be here."

"Yeah, you would."

"Don't count on it. Every time something spooky happens, I freeze up for a second or two."

"Like the rest of us don't?"

"I guess you do, but I also feel my mind *squirm*. I think it's trying to crawl inside itself, the way it did on the night Waxman died."

Astarte made a fist and punched him on the forearm.

"Ow!" he exclaimed.

"You aren't going to choke again, no matter what we run into," she said. "I know you're not, so just get over it and give me a sip of your soda."

"Okay," Bellamy said, handing her the red and white can. She threw back her head and glugged down considerably more than a sip. He was surprised and discomfited to catch himself staring at the rhythmic pulsing of the muscles in her long, white neck.

She dragged the back of her black-nailed hand across her mouth and handed the

Coke back. He could feel from the lightness of the can that there was hardly any soda left. "I'm the one who ought to feel like a chicken," she murmured.

Puzzled, Bellamy cocked his head. "Why do you say that?"

"Daimler and Miss Paris were the answer to my prayers. But when he changed, *I* choked. And even afterward, when the shock wore off, I couldn't bring myself to offer myself again."

"I had you pegged the first time I ever read your posts on Grailnet," Bellamy said. "You really are out of your mind."

"Daimler showed us two faces," Astarte said. "How do we know which one was real, and which an illusion? Maybe he was testing my courage, the strength of my commitment, and I flunked."

"I think your mom read "Beauty and the Beast" to you one too many times when you were a kid. Miss Paris had her bandages on when you first walked in, before you ever announced that you'd figured out that she and Daimler were undead." He marveled in passing at how easily he now used the corny, ridiculous term, a word he couldn't recall ever speaking before in his life. "And there was nothing illusory about the stink of her flesh, or those nits crawling around in it. She really was deformed, and I'm sure Daimler was, too."

"I suppose," Astarte said. "Still, 'beauty is in the eye of the beholder,' right? Maybe they didn't seem ugly to each other, or to themselves. Maybe if they'd changed me, I would have felt like a goddess, not a cripple or a freak."

Bellamy shook his head. "What is it with you? Why are you so hot to become a part of the paranormal anyway, especially after the gruesome things we've seen? You've never really told me."

She shrugged. "I don't know if I can explain it. Except that lots of the time, life sucks. I don't mean the parts that make you mad, or break your heart. I mean when it's plastic and ordinary. You look at somebody you're supposed to love, or hate, and you don't feel *anything,* any more than you would if you were looking at a machine. Or you find yourself slumped in front of the TV, staring at some rerun that was shitty the first time, but you can't find the energy to get up and go do something else."

Bellamy smiled. "I don't think that happens to you very often."

"It happens to everybody," Astarte said somberly. "Everywhere you look, you see people just switching off, wasting time, like they were going to be around forever.

"On the other hand, sometimes you take a bite out of a peach, or hear a great song on the radio, or look at a robin redbreast outside your window, and your whole mind and body just lights up. And you think, this is it. This feeling of delight. This is the whole point of being alive. I've got to hold on to it. But you never can. It always slips away."

"And you think that for paranormal creatures, it doesn't. Life is an endless series of highs without any lows."

Astarte shrugged. "I figure that's why we call them supernatural. I'm not saying they don't ever feel grief or pain or fear. But at least they always feel *something.*"

"And that's seems so wonderful to you that you'd want to be one, even if it meant becoming evil?"

"What's evil? Who are we to judge them when we don't know what they know, or understand what they understand?"

"In a weird kind of way, you have a point," Bellamy began.

Astarte grinned. "Hey, that's the first time you've ever admitted I might be right about anything. I feel all warm and squishy."

Bellamy chuckled. "I didn't mean you were right, just that I understand how you feel. Since I got involved in this mess, I haven't known what to believe about *anything*. For instance, maybe I should forget about the Atheist and try to destroy Daimler and Miss Paris. They might represent a bigger threat to human life than he does. There's no way to know. I'm flying blind.

"But I think we have to *try* to do the right thing, even when we're ignorant and confused. If we don't, we really won't be any better than robots." He smiled at her. "Whether you realize it or not, you care about right and wrong, too. If you didn't, you wouldn't have jeopardized your dream to help me. You would have offered yourself to Daimler with no strings attached."

She shrugged. "I never said I was consistent. You know what else is strange to think about? By this time tomorrow, we may *have* our answers."

He nodded. When he'd checked with the New Orleans Post Office yesterday afternoon, he'd received a letter from Daimler. The message, written in an elegant Spencerian hand, had provided an address where the mysterious men from Lafayette supposedly stayed when they visited the city. "It's possible. You know, I still think it would be better if you didn't come with me."

"Don't even try. I'm in, and that's that. Even if I didn't *want* to go, you need *somebody* to watch your back, and I'll be more use than any of the Arcanists, not that you could convince one of them to tag along anyway."

He had to admit, she had a point. In the final analysis, all the surviving occultists, even Marilyn, had the temperament of scientists or scholars, not daredevils or cops. On occasion, they did willingly place themselves in harm's way, but only when they believed they understood the nature of the danger and had taken appropriate precautions to protect themselves. They were more than reluctant to break into a strange building knowing only that it was occupied by people—or quasi-people—with ties to the paranormal, who were apparently to blame for scores of disappearances.

Bellamy didn't blame the Arcanists for their caution. He suspected that if he had had as much experience with the supernatural as they had, he wouldn't be so reckless, either.

"Okay," he said. "I just had to try to talk you out of it one more time."

"I know you did," she said. "It's nice, in a condescending, MCP kind of way. And it was nice when you tried to save me from Daimler." She put her arms around him and kissed him. The contrast between her warm, soft flesh and the cold, hard metal transfixing it was as arresting as he'd imagined.

At first he kissed her in return, his tongue dancing with hers, his hands slipping inside her leather jacket to caress her body. He couldn't help himself. But gradually his sense of propriety reasserted itself. Extricating himself from her embrace, he shifted sideways on the sofa cushion, putting distance between them.

"You want to go to one of our rooms?" she panted. "Mine's closer."

Breathing heavily himself, he swallowed and said, "I'm sorry. I can't do this."

She frowned. "Why not? You told me you were divorced. And I *know* you like me."

"Yes," he said, wondering how she'd known it when he hadn't ever quite admitted it to himself.

"It can't be the difference in our ages," she said. "I'm legal, and you're only a few years older than me. Is it my look? The piercings, and all that?"

"No," he said. "The problem is that it wouldn't be professional."

"You're kidding."

"No," Bellamy said. "An FBI agent shouldn't get romantically involved with a fellow investigator, or anybody he meets in the context of a case."

"Are you crazy?" she asked. "You aren't here as an official FBI guy, remember? You're poking around on your own. You're already breaking the rules, and anyway, I'm not going to rat you out to your bosses."

"You have to understand," he said, "there's a *point* to this particular rule. It helps you stay sharp and objective."

She sighed. "And you can't see your way clear to just relax and let go, even for a few minutes."

"It wouldn't be for just a few minutes. If we went to bed, things would be different afterwards. The feelings I have for you would be stronger than they are already."

"God, let's hope so."

"Look, I've always tried to be the very best cop I could be. I've always given one hundred percent, without letting *anything* distract me. And that discipline has worked for me. It's helped me catch a lot of criminals. And because it has, I'm not willing to put it aside, especially in a situation where *your* life is on the line. I care about you way too much for that."

She smiled crookedly. "I guess I have some options here. I could rip off my clothes or grab your crotch, and see if I could convince you not to be such a jerk. I could deck you. Or I could ask if there's a rule against you dating me after the case is over."

"No," Bellamy said. "I don't remember reading that one anywhere in the G-man handbook."

"Well, don't let it get your hopes up. I was just wondering. You had your chance." She leaned over and kissed him on the cheek. "Don't sit up all night," she said in a softer tone. "Try to get some rest."

She stood up and headed out of the lobby. Her hips seemed to sway more than usual, as if she was exaggerating the motion to tease him. As he watched her blend with the shadows, he did indeed feel like the biggest jerk on earth.

Thirty-Seven

A rhythmic vibration shook the floor, so softly no mortal would have noticed. But Montrose perceived it without difficulty and even divined the source. A sizable company of wraiths was marching in step through the Necropolis.

Puzzled, the Scot frowned. He made a point of keeping track of the agendas of his fellow Anacreons' Legionnaires. To the best of his knowledge, no large detachment of soldiers should have been heading out of or into the Citadel this evening. He decided to find out what was going on.

Rising, he picked up his mask and pressed it to his face, strapped on his pistol and rapier, and wrapped himself in his voluminous mantle. As he fastened the silver collar clasp, he heard familiar footsteps pattering down the corridor outside.

"Come in," he called. Valentine stuck his head, crowned with a green and yellow floppy-horned cap, through the office door. "Hello."

"Good evening, Anacreon," said the dwarf. "Gayoso told me to tell you that a column of soldiers, from Stygia by the look of them, is coming toward the Citadel. He suggested that all four of you Anacreons gather at the front entrance to greet the commanding officer."

"That sounds reasonable," Montrose replied. "Which Legion is arriving?"

Valentine hesitated, and then said, "If Gayoso knows, he didn't tell me."

"Well, I suppose everyone will know soon enough," Montrose said. "But I think I'll indulge my curiosity and find out now. If I fly up above the Citadel, I should be able to read their standards and banners. It's a pleasant night. Would you care to ascend with me? I promise not to drop you."

"No," said the dwarf, almost too quickly. "I have to get back to Gayoso. But..."

Montrose cocked his head. "What's troubling you?"

"Nothing! I'm just...nervous this evening. You be careful." He scuttled backward, pulling his head and shoulders back through the door. His running feet clattered back down the corridor.

I always am careful, Montrose thought. *But tonight, I shouldn't really have to be. Gayoso isn't likely to attempt to assassinate me in front of a group of newly arrived Stygian witnesses.* Shaking his head over Valentine's jitters, wondering if Gayoso had been abusing the small man, the Scot blew out the barrow-flame lamp, invoked his Harbinger Arcanos, and then strode through the cobwebs and grimy glass in one of the window frames.

He allowed himself to drop for an instant, enjoying the thrill of free fall, and then soared upward into the cool air. The ugliness of the decaying city, blemished and distorted by the Shroud, gave way to the unstained beauty of the moon and stars. He felt a pang of joy, and a mad desire to soar up and up forever.

Quashing the impulse, he peered across the Necropolis. Despite a lack of music or any particular attempt at ostentation, the Stygians were easy to spot. The column was climbing toward the Citadel from the south. The Hierarchs were wearing the same insignia and carrying the same black and scarlet flags as Montrose's original force, indicating that they were affiliated with both the Smiling Lord and the Order of the Unlidded Eye.

In different circumstances, Montrose might have worried that his master had dispatched a new force under a new general because he was dissatisfied with his original agent's progress. But the Scot had scored such an impressive series of victories that he couldn't credit such a notion. Perhaps the Smiling Lord was *so* pleased that he'd sent additional troops to enable Montrose to extend the scope of the campaign. Or maybe he'd provided fresh men and a new commander so that his valiant deputy could return home and be rewarded for his efforts.

To his surprise, Montrose realized that he couldn't quite anticipate how he'd react if it turned out that the Smiling Lord had recalled him. He still yearned for the splendors and luxuries of the Onyx Tower, and chafed at the thought of rival courtiers scheming to usurp his place in his absence. But he also had the obscure feeling that his recent adventures had stimulated dormant aspects of his personality, a valuable dimension of himself that had been in danger of withering away. If he left, he'd miss some of the people he'd met, Fink, Valentine, and others. And to some degree it would irk him to abandon the mystery of the false Pardoners—and the Atheist murders, if they were part of the same puzzle—for a successor to unravel.

Ultimately, of course, it didn't matter how he felt. He'd go if the Smiling Lord had ordered him to go, or stay if he wanted him to stay. He was just glad that he'd emerged from his fugue state before his fellow Stygians arrived.

Montrose's blackout had lasted nearly forty-eight hours. He'd awakened feeling more nearly himself than he had in weeks, his Shadow apparently having exhausted its strength maintaining the possession. At first, realizing what had happened to him, the Scot had been terrified, certain that the parasite must have run amok, reveling in perversions and atrocities.

But if it had, it had covered its tracks flawlessly, which seemed unlikely. It would want Montrose to discover its handiwork, to shame and sicken him. In point of fact, as far as he'd been able to determine, none of his associates had noticed anything even a little strange about his behavior. He could only assume that his psyche had managed to hold his malignant side in check, in a contest of wills inaccessible to memory.

He swooped toward the ground and alit in front of the Citadel's primary entrance. His fellow Anacreons, Valentine, and Fink had arrived before him. A smattering of Shellabarger and Mrs. Duquesne's soldiers were also present, as were a few of Montrose's irregulars, but only Gayoso, no doubt in an effort to make himself seem a better commander than his colleagues, had managed to turn out a full company of his men in all their somewhat tawdry martial finery. The wavering bluish light from the ring of torches gleamed on their weapons and on the black hourglass in Mrs. Duquesne's shriveled hands.

"Good evening," said Montrose.

"Yes," said Gayoso, a smug note in his voice, "isn't it."

Leather creaked, metal clinked, and cloth rustled. The newcomers had nearly reached the crest of the hill. A moment later their commander strode from the gloom, a lanky man with long brown hair whose outer garments were much like Montrose's, except that his mask was made of riveted crimson metal. The soldiers at his back were marching four abreast.

Montrose smiled, because he recognized the commander despite his visor. The inquisitor was Karl Reinhardt, a valued agent of the Smiling Lord these past two hundred years. Reinhardt had never seemed to aspire to a permanent position in his master's household, and thus had never posed a threat of Montrose's ambitions. As a result, though they weren't friends—the Scot made it a policy to avoid true friendship with men of equivalent rank—they shared a bond of respect, forged in a hard-fought campaign against a horde of Spectres in 1832. It would be pleasant to talk to him.

A Centurion bellowed a command, and the column halted. Reinhardt continued forward. "Good evening," he said in his German accent. "I bring the governors of Natchez greetings and instructions from the Seat of Burning Waters." He reached inside his cloak, produced a scroll bearing the Smiling Lord's personal seal, and handed it to Gayoso, who unrolled it without haste. Compromising their dignity a bit, Shellabarger and Mrs. Duquesne pressed in close to him to read the message also.

"Hello, Karl," said Montrose. "It's good to see you."

"I'm afraid you won't think so in a moment," the Grim Rider replied. "James Graham, Earl and Marquess of Montrose, Anacreon of my own Order, I have a warrant for your arrest."

"What?" Montrose exclaimed. "On what charge?"

"According to this," said Gayoso, brandishing the scroll, "treason." The gloating note in his voice was now unmistakable.

"That's absurd!" said Montrose. He'd worried that in his absence, his rivals would try to undermine his master's trust in him; but in light of his successes in the field, how could anyone have actually convinced the Smiling Lord he was a traitor? It didn't make sense.

"It's no use protesting," Reinhardt said. "I've seen the evidence against you, and even if I hadn't, I have my orders."

"What evidence?" Montrose asked.

"A journal in your handwriting. In its pages, you reveal your intention to conquer your own kingdom here along the Mississippi."

"I never wrote any such thing." Montrose turned to the three governors. "Gayoso sent the papers to Stygia, didn't he? Well, he forged them, too!"

"As I mentioned," Reinhardt said, "the document is in your own hand. Chiarmonte did the comparisons himself, and said there isn't any doubt. Even so, the Smiling Lord was reluctant to accept your guilt. He had Demetrius examine the journal through some esoteric application of his Arcanos, and he, too, is certain that you wrote it."

Montrose felt as if he were trapped in a nightmare. The more Reinhardt explained, the stranger the situation seemed. Chiarmonte was a rival, but he couldn't quite imagine the Venetian falsifying the results of a graphological analysis, if only because of the pride he took in his professional expertise. Nor could he imagine the man conspiring with Demetrius to frame him. Chiarmonte wasn't unduly fond of Montrose, but, like most of the courtiers who'd attended the Smiling Lord for a century or longer, he loathed the upstart Oracle.

Then, suddenly, Montrose's intuition told him what had happened. In effect, his *Shadow* had framed him, writing the journal during the period when it was dominant. Now that he realized the truth, he sensed the parasite laughing in the depths of his unconscious.

And why shouldn't it? Montrose couldn't *prove* he'd been possessed, and he suspected the Deathlords, whose justice was often leavened with a generous measure of expediency, wouldn't regard it as an adequate defense anyway. If his Shadow had mastered him once, perhaps it would do so again, and put its treasonous schemes into effect. It would be safer to execute him and avoid the possibility. He struggled to suppress a surge of panic.

"Surrender your weapons," Reinhardt said.

"I give you my word," said Montrose, "I'm innocent."

"It doesn't matter," Reinhardt replied doggedly. "I have orders to take you into custody, and that's what I'm going to do. Unless you compel me to destroy you instead."

Montrose looked at Shellabarger and Mrs. Duquesne. "I've helped you people. I've rid your territory of subversives. I've brought prosperity."

"You also disrupted a reasonably comfortable status quo," said Shellabarger. Montrose could just barely make out the form of the governor's bulging, faceted eyes, glinting behind the openings in his hood. "You pretty much forced us to obey your orders. To be honest, I think I can cope with the pain of your departure."

"I'm a loyal Hierarch," said Mrs. Duquesne. "I wouldn't think of disobeying a command from any of the Deathlords." She glanced at Gayoso's troops and the ranks of Stygians. "Even if it were practical."

"Listen to me," said Montrose, "there are things happening along the river I haven't told you about. A new danger, from an unknown source. You need me to help you get to the bottom of it. I understand you have no choice but to return me to Stygia, but you could intercede for me. Assure the Smiling Lord that no matter what the evidence seems to indicate, you've observed me closely over the past few weeks, and you're certain I'm loyal."

Inside the lugubrious frown of her white-glazed mask, Mrs. Duquesne's lips quirked in an ironic smile. "Tie my own fate inextricably to your own. An intriguing concept. But unfortunately, I never take it for granted that *anyone's* loyal. That's what makes me a successful politician."

Gayoso sneered at Montrose. "Did you really expect anyone to believe such a blatantly self-serving lie?"

"It's not a lie," Montrose said.

"Well," said Gayoso, "in the unlikely event that there *is* some mysterious menace lurking about, I'll deal with it. These soldiers didn't all come just to drag you back to the Isle of Sorrows, my lord Anacreon. Your military reputation isn't *that* fearsome. Most of them will remain in Natchez under my command, to continue the suppression of the rebels." He smiled coldly at his fellow governors, proclaiming without words that the balance of power had shifted, and that, henceforth, they'd better stay on his good side.

"Give me your sword and pistol," Reinhardt said.

Montrose looked at Fink. The river man grinned and shrugged. The Scot had the feeling that if the odds hadn't been quite so overwhelming, his lieutenant might actually have tried to rescue him from his would-be captors, if only for the savage, reckless fun of it. But whatever bond of friendship had sprung up between the two wraiths, it wasn't enough to prompt the former outlaw to throw his existence away. And if he didn't make a move, none of the other irregulars would, either.

The Scot was tempted to try to veil himself in darkness, open a Nihil and leap through, or project himself onto the other side of the Shroud. But his Arcanos didn't work instantaneously, and as soon as he began to generate an effect, the Legionnaires would shoot him. If he truly wanted to escape both immediate destruction and the terrible justice of the Smiling Lord, the only hope was to surrender now and try to get away later. A chance so slim it was barely worth contemplating; but still, the only one he had.

As he unclipped his scabbard from his belt, he saw Valentine's homely features twist in anguish, and suspected the dwarf had played some part in his downfall. Betrayed by yet another friend. He supposed he should have been expecting it.

THIRTY-EIGHT

As Bellamy surveyed the rows of crumbling, whitewashed mausoleums, floating like islands in a sea of tangled brush and pearly ground mist, he felt his pulse ticking in his throat. Speaking lightly in an effort to alleviate his anxiety, he whispered, "Well, this figures, doesn't it?"

"What?" Astarte replied.

"That we'd wind up in a cemetery before this mess was over."

She smiled wryly, the moonlight gleaming on the steel rings in her piercings. "I don't mind as long as it isn't a permanent stay." She pointed. "That way?"

He nodded. "Stay alert." They slunk forward, down one of the lanes defined by parallel rows of dilapidated tombs. There didn't seem to be any copings, a fact which didn't surprise him. In New Orleans, with its high water table, it was easier to lay the dead to rest aboveground that to bury them.

Try as he might, he couldn't move altogether silently, any more than Astarte could. The weeds and long grass swished and rustled around their feet. He hoped it wouldn't matter.

Astarte took hold of his forearm, halting his forward progress.

"What is it?" he asked.

"No one's keeping this place up."

He repressed a sarcastic observation about her keen grasp of the obvious. "I noticed."

"So where are the signs that other trespassers have jumped the wall? Where are the condoms and beer cans?"

He frowned. "I don't know. I did see some graffiti on some of the tombs."

"All of it funny symbols. Hieroglyphics. Nothing in English."

"In other words, the cemetery has such a nasty reputation that people are afraid to trespass. Or when they do, the men from Lafayette kill them."

Astarte nodded. "That's what I'm thinking."

After a moment's hesitation, Bellamy said, "We already knew we were headed into danger. I'm not going to turn back. But if you want to—"

Astarte grimaced. "Will you get over that sexist crap? I just thought you ought to know we were already in the danger zone. Now come on." She crept forward, and he followed her.

Five minutes later they reached the eight-foot wall, itself a tomb riddled with vaults, on the far side of the cemetery. Bellamy hoisted himself up until he could peek over the top.

The house on the other side was a massive brick edifice that reminded him of a prison. Indeed, with its few narrow windows sealed behind burglar bars, it was an eyesore ugly and ominous to stand out even in one of the city's most miserable slums. As far as he could see, no lights were burning. With luck, that meant no one was inside, though he was by no means certain of that. The mysterious people from west Louisiana might be thoroughly at home in the dark.

Bellamy hauled himself to the top of the wall, and Astarte scrambled up beside him. They dropped to the other side and sneaked on, through a yard as overgrown as the cemetery. Bearded with long gray streamers of Spanish moss, the branches of a huge cypress blocked out the stars, making the night even blacker than before.

The intruders reached the back door without anything leaping out at them or anyone shouting to announce their presence. Bellamy switched on his pencil flashlight, examined the entry, and found no evidence of an alarm system. Holding the light in his teeth, he took out his knife and pick.

After a moment's work, the lock clicked open. He cracked the door open and a faint but foul stench like the smell of rotting meat wafted out. He peered through the opening.

He was looking into a spacious kitchen. Flicking the flashlight beam this way and that, he sensed there was something odd about the room, and after a moment, he realized what. There were no pots and pans hanging from the hooks on the walls. He stepped inside and opened some drawers and cabinets. There was no cutlery, plates, or canned goods, either, and when he checked the faintly humming refrigerator, he only found wine, soda, and beer. Evidently, the rotting smell was coming from another part of the house. No one prepared any food in here.

He listened intently but didn't hear anyone moving around in the darkness ahead, just a nearly inaudible buzzing. Drawing his Browning from its holster, he led Astarte through the next doorway. The foul smell grew stronger.

The next chamber was a dining room, though it appeared as if it had been a while since anyone had used it as such. Many of the chairs lay shattered on the floor, and someone had carved sets of parallel grooves in the table. It looked as though a gigantic cat had sharpened its claws on the wood. Crudely painted on one wall was a black spiral like the design on a hypnotist's spinning wheel. Pointing to it, Bellamy gave Astarte an inquiring look. She shrugged.

Bellamy listened once again, and still didn't hear anyone. He and Astarte crept through the next arch. The stink burned in his nose and throat, half choking him. He swung the light around, and flinched at what he saw. Nausea squirmed in his stomach.

The large room was littered with human corpses and body parts. Most were little more than gnawed bone, pocked with tooth marks, but a few scraps of decaying meat remained. Enough to account for the stench and nourish swarms of flies, their wings the source of the ambient drone.

Bellamy told himself that he'd seen the handiwork of serial killers and even cannibals before, though it hadn't been on this scale. He had to get past his horror and function like a professional.

Astarte made a gagging sound. He took her in his arms and she hugged him tightly.

"I'm sorry," he whispered. "I know it's bad. But we have to cope with it."

"I know," she said. "It's just that it's worse than seeing Vulture die. Worse than feeling Mr. Daimler's teeth pressing into my neck. Worse than anything so far. But I'll be all right." She clung to him for a moment longer, then released him.

Bellamy played his light back and forth, trying to ignore the ghastly remains of the murderers' victims and see what else was in the room. The beam slid across a few pieces of dilapidated furniture and a collection of trophies and curios, many nearly as ghastly as the corpses and nearly all of them strange in one way or another.

Mobiles made of wire, sticks, and human bones hung from the ceiling, and someone had thumbtacked pairs of snapshots to the faded, floral-print wallpaper.

The first picture in each set was a candid shot of a man, woman, or child. The second was a view of the body of the same individual, torn to shreds.

On the marble mantel reposed a long ivory tusk, so flamboyantly curved that Bellamy was certain it couldn't have come from any breed of elephant alive today. It reminded him of artists' conceptions of the hairy pachyderms that had walked the earth during the last ice age. And when he approached it, he discovered that it was carved with crude representations of gigantic sloths, cave bears, and other prehistoric beasts.

The skulls of two huge canines rested on a table. Each had been painted with the black spiral and a selection of other symbols. At first glance, Bellamy assumed that they were fossils, too. But on closer inspection, they looked too fresh, almost as fresh as some of the human bones littering the bloodstained floor.

An assortment of jewelry—bracelets, rings, pendants, and earrings, most of it rather large and primitive-looking—lay on the tiers of a bookshelf, along with a straight-edged dagger the size of a Bowie knife. The color of the blade seemed a little off. Bellamy wondered if it might be made of silver rather than steel.

Once again, he looked at Astarte, asking her to interpret the significance of the various relics. Once again, she shrugged. So much for her claim to be an occult expert, he thought sardonically.

Denied any esoteric insights, he decided that, for the time being, he'd better ignore what he couldn't comprehend—the meaning of the tusk, the canine skulls, and similar enigmas—and focus on what he could. Which was that he was virtually wading through evidence of multiple murder. For a moment, he felt a swell of satisfaction, and then it withered. He scowled.

Brushing a fly away from her face, Astarte asked, "What is it?"

"We've got all the evidence any cop could ask for to prove that certain people have been killed. But—"

"We still don't know who the men from Lafayette *are*," she said. "We don't know how they figure into the Atheist conspiracy, or even *that* they do."

"Right," Bellamy said. "When you think about it, it's even worse than that. We don't even know who owns this place. I mean, we got a name and a post-office box address out of the city records, but I've got a hunch they're just a blind. I'm sure you want to get out of here. So do I. But to get to the bottom of this craziness, I need to look around some more."

Her face pale, Astarte gave him a jerky nod. "It's okay. I can handle it. Hell, here's where they kill and eat, right? The other rooms *can't* be as bad as this one."

"I hope not." He listened once again. Except for the thrum of the flies, the house remained silent. "Let's go this way. Keep an eye out for any kind of papers. File folders. An address book. A wallet with ID in it. Whatever."

They crept on through the twisting passages of the house. As they got farther away from the room containing the corpses, the stink of decay gave way to another unpleasant smell, like that of rats, though he didn't see any droppings or any holes gnawed in the baseboards. He wondered if it could be the body odor of the men from Lafayette themselves.

Occasionally he and Astarte came upon a shredded, severed human limb, or the black spiral or some other cryptic symbol daubed on a door or wall. Once he somehow missed seeing one of the grisly mobiles, and walked right into the dangling lattice of cold, clinking bones. Squawking, he recoiled, and lifted his gun to shoot. But Astarte clutched his arm and said, "It's okay, it's okay!" Her intervention brought him back to his senses.

But despite a sprinkling of such artifacts, most of the ground floor was sparsely furnished and seemed little-used. When they'd searched it all, the two intruders climbed a broad, curving staircase. A soft hum whispered down to meet them.

Astarte gave Bellamy an interrogatory look. Now it was his turn to shrug. His mouth dry, he crept on up until, suddenly, he glimpsed a point of green light. Startled, he almost fired at it before he realized it was electric illumination, not the chatoyant eye of some lurking monster.

To be precise, it was an indicator light on the base of a computer monitor, shining through a doorway. And the faint whine was the sound of the PC's cooling fan. His shoulders slumping with relief, he motioned for Astarte to join him.

Compared to the filth, carnage, desolation, and bizarre decorations elsewhere in the house, the computer room, with its desk, file cabinet, and bookshelves, seemed relatively normal, like an office that any ordinary person might set up in his home. Only a handful of clay and carved stone statues—a naked woman with two faces, a squat, warlike figure in a feather headdress—suggested a connection with the occult.

"This stuff is different than what we saw downstairs," Bellamy whispered. "The jewelry looked like something the Vikings might have made, but these—"

"Look Aztec or Mayan or Incan," Astarte said. "Do you think it means something?"

"I have no idea. I was hoping you would."

"All I know is that it makes me nervous that that"—she nodded at the computer—"is turned on."

"Some people leave their PCs on all the time. But even so, I'm not too thrilled about it either. We need to search this place, but keep listening for voices and footsteps. If somebody is around, it would be better to know about it *before* he steps into the room."

Something popped. Startled, Bellamy whirled, to see that the blank monitor had lit up. The PC's hard drive clattered softly.

A little hesitantly, he and Astarte edged closer, to see what the screen would display. Arcs of red and purple swirled inward like water vanishing down a drain, reminding him unpleasantly of the black spirals downstairs. Then the vortex gave way to a step pyramid.

"That looks Aztec, too," Astarte said, her pale face shining in the monitor's sickly glow.

"Yeah," Bellamy said, "except that the ones in Mexico aren't jet black."

A shadowy figure atop the pyramid made an exaggerated, unmistakable hacking motion, and then held up a bulb of crimson flesh. Unseen multitudes cheered. Cascades of blood poured down the sides of the edifice.

The monitor zoomed in on the top of the monument for a close-up view. The priest conducting the sacrifice wasn't human. He was a creature with two scaly ophidian faces mounted on a single head.

"What does this mean?" Astarte asked. "Why is it showing this now? Does somebody know we're here?"

"I don't know," Bellamy replied.

The picture on the screen changed. Astarte gasped and the FBI agent stiffened, because they were now looking at the island city from their shared vision. The water around it began to revolve, accelerating rapidly. With a grinding, crashing sound, the dark towers and even the bedrock beneath them began to break apart, until the whirlpool devoured it all.

After which, the swirling red and violet pattern reappeared.

Surmising that the entire animated sequence was about to repeat itself, Bellamy sat down at the computer. "You start checking the books and papers," he told Astarte. "Fast. I'll see what I can pull off the hard disk."

Typing rapidly, the keyboard clicking, he tried to enter commands. But no matter what he did, the PC wouldn't respond. It just kept showing the same scenes of bloodshed and annihilation. Finally he gave up and checked the desk drawers. He didn't find anything interesting. To his surprise, there weren't even any floppy disks.

With a growing sense of desperation, he stood up and began to help Astarte ransack the bookshelves. A small spiral notebook, almost invisible between a massive dictionary and a textbook on the principles of accounting, caught his eye. He pulled it out and flipped it open. The pages were full of row after row of tiny symbols, neatly inscribed in ink.

He showed it to Astarte. "More Witches' Alphabet?" he asked.

She shook her head. "I don't recognize it."

"Well, it looks promising," Bellamy said. He stuffed it in his jacket pocket, and then a long howl reverberated through the house.

Thirty-Nine

Astarte yelped. Bellamy involuntarily backpedaled across the office until his shoulders were pressed against the wall. His heart pounded, and his bowels felt as if they'd turned to water.

Beside him, someone laughed. He lurched around, and saw that the face of a thin, intelligent-looking black man had appeared on the computer screen. Its eyes bright with malice, it was doing the laughing. The image dissolved into the close-up view of the apex of the pyramid. Now Bellamy was the naked corpse on the altar, his gory chest hacked open, a raw cavity gaping where his heart should have been.

Bellamy felt his mind breaking up, his consciousness turning inside out. He put his knuckle between his teeth and bit down hard. The pain cleared his head to a degree.

Astarte stood wide-eyed and trembling in the center of the room. When Bellamy touched her, she jumped. "It's just a yell," he said, "just noise. It's creepy, maybe there's even something magic about it, but we can't let it get to us."

She swallowed. "All right."

"I'd just as soon not meet what's doing the yelling," he said, "so we're leaving. Get out the gun Marilyn gave you." She fumbled the little automatic out of her jacket. "Do you remember what I taught you about how to use it?" She nodded. "Good. We'll move fast, but quietly, and we'll go down those back stairs we saw. I think it's less likely that anything will be waiting at the bottom. Got it?"

"Yes," she said, grimacing, a flicker of the old Astarte breaking through her dread. "I'm not stupid."

"Says who?" he said, forcing a smile. "You're here, aren't you? Come on, let's move."

Bellamy switched off his flashlight. The monitor went black at the same instant, plunging the room into almost total darkness. Astarte gasped, and his heart jolted in his chest. Peering warily this way and that, the intruders slipped into the hall.

They turned left, away from the main staircase, and a second howl split the silence. Astarte whimpered. Shuddering violently, Bellamy struggled to keep panic from overwhelming him. The unearthly wailing was invested with some supernatural power, without a doubt. What sort of creature possessed such a cry? He had a ghastly feeling that a part of him already knew. That he'd encountered such a beast on the night Waxman died.

Though the unseen creature howled again and again, it was impossible to tell from which direction the sound was coming. Each shriek slammed into Bellamy's mind like a hammer. He peered desperately into the shadows ahead, searching for the narrow flight of stairs he'd noticed before. He didn't see them. He wondered if, addled with terror, he'd led Astarte in the wrong direction.

His companion gasped and spun around, nearly clubbing him with her gun. He pivoted. But whatever she'd thought she'd heard, there was nothing behind them.

They crept on around another corner, and finally spied the steps. Bellamy paused, listening, and heard nothing. He started down, placing his feet near the wall, wincing when, despite his care, one of the risers creaked.

He and Astarte reached the ground floor unmolested. *Just a few more steps*, he told himself, *just a few more steps and we'll be out of this place*.

Their path led them back into the room with the corpses. Bellamy hesitated for a heartbeat, deciding between the front and rear doors, then turned toward the foyer.

"Bad choice," said a pleasant bass voice behind him.

Bellamy spun around. A shadow stood in the darkness a few feet away. It struck a match with its thumbnail, and when it lifted the flame to light its hand-rolled cigarette, he saw that it was Bill Dunn.

"This is a rough neighborhood," the SAD agent continued. "You go out on the street, you might get mugged. Whereas the cemetery is usually peaceful this time of night."

Settling into a marksman's stance, Bellamy aimed his Browning at Dunn's face. The other man didn't look as if he was wearing a Kevlar vest, but in the gloom, it was impossible to be sure. "You're in on it, aren't you? Part of the Atheist conspiracy."

Dunn grinned. "Well, duh, Sherlock. Of course I am. I pressured Nolliver to discredit you. I whacked him when he got squeamish. I even took time off from the Bureau to hunt you down. So much for that Windjammer cruise vacation I was planning."

"You're under arrest," Bellamy said.

"How did I *know* you were going to say that?" Dunn replied, exhaling a plume of smoke. Bellamy caught a whiff of the acrid vapor even through the stench of the rotting bodies. "The sad thing is that catching you was so easy that, so far, it hasn't been any fun. I'm impressed that you found our little home away from home here. I'd be interested to know how you did it. But when Chester phoned me to say you'd broken in, there went *my* chance to shine as a detective. By the way, did you meet

Chester? Black guy, dead, runs around inside computers, thinks he's Steven Spielberg?"

"Put your hands up," Bellamy said.

Dunn ignored the command. "And then when I was following you around the house, I could have killed you any time. Even with fear sharpening your senses, you didn't see me. So I decided to reveal myself in this guise to give you a sporting chance. To make our final meeting at least a little bit interesting. Don't disappoint me."

"Is he crazy?" Astarte whispered. "Or on drugs?"

"I hope so," Bellamy murmured. Better that than the alternative, which was that Dunn was like Daimler, possessed of powers so formidable that he had no reason to be afraid of a gun. He raised his voice. "Listen to me, Bill. You can't hurt us. It's the other way around. We're leaving, and we're taking you with us. If anyone or anything tries to stop us, I'll shoot you. Do you understand?"

"Sure," said Dunn, staring at them. Even in the darkness, his eyes seemed to glow. Bellamy felt the beginnings of a tremor in his arms, and struggled to hold the Browning steady. "Fact of the matter is, you shot me before, though I know you don't remember it. Am amazingly lucky shot, too, right in the eye and round and round my brain until it just about cut my spinal cord in two. Anything less wouldn't have bothered me much, and I would have left your body beside Waxman's."

"What are you?" Astarte breathed.

"Something pretty cool," said Dunn, his gaze still boring into Bellamy's skull. Bellamy felt frightened and lightheaded at the same time, as if he were about to faint. A part of him was screaming for him to shoot, shoot *now*, but some force kept him from translating the impulse into action. "Something you monkeys are afraid of all the way down into your DNA. I gather you're a big fan of the occult, sweetheart, so why don't I give you a demonstration."

Dunn's body swelled, his shoulders broadening, limbs lengthening, the front of his face extending into a foaming muzzle, stretching his smile into a fanged grin like the leer of the Big Bad Wolf. He lifted his enlarging hands, now gloved in black fur and sporting long, curved claws, and ripped his clothing apart to accommodate his growth.

Bellamy recoiled and fired at the same time. As near as he could tell, the shots flew wild. He felt his awareness contracting, caving in on itself, and for a second he was grateful. Then he glimpsed Astarte from the corner of his eye.

Tears streaming down her face, her pistol hanging forgotten at her side, she stood paralyzed, like a rabbit hypnotized by the stare of a snake. Bellamy wasn't the only one whose mind was shutting down.

Except that he mustn't let it happen, not if it meant abandoning her to die. He bellowed wordlessly, a primal roar that expelled the panic from his mind. He was still terribly afraid, but the dread had lost its ability to cripple him. In fact, he sensed that no matter what terrible thing happened, he'd never freeze or lose himself again; and for one instant, in the reeking darkness, surrounded by the dead with a demon looming over him, he experienced a crazy flash of joy.

He grabbed Astarte and screamed in her ear. "Run!" He shoved her toward the front door and she began to stumble along under her own power, gaining speed with every step. He pivoted and, his hands now steady, resumed firing, emptying the clip.

By now Dunn was so tall that his head nearly brushed the ceiling, a stooped, gaunt, but horribly powerful-looking apparition with pointed, bat-like ears and lambent eyes, his flesh exuding the bestial fetor that Bellamy had smelled elsewhere in the house. The hail of bullets slammed into his face and the cigarette fell from his jaws, showering orange sparks on its long descent to the floor. Clutching at his wounds, Dunn staggered and dropped to one knee. And then laboriously started to get up again.

Bellamy suspected that, gun or no, it would be tantamount to suicide to keep fighting Dunn at close range. Whereas outside, sniping from a distance, he might conceivably have a chance, might at least prolong the encounter long enough for Astarte to get away. As he wheeled to run, he caught a glimpse of the dagger.

If Dunn was the werewolf he more or less appeared to be, a silver blade might hurt him in a way lead bullets couldn't. Unfortunately, Bellamy figured that the odds of him getting past the monster's talons and inhumanly long reach to deliver a mortal blow were pretty close to zero. Still, he detoured and grabbed the knife on his way out, then sprinted on through the dining room and kitchen. Behind him, Dunn roared.

When Bellamy opened the door, his eyes widened in surprise. The world was veiled in sheets and tatters of white. He could barely see the trunk of the cypress just a few feet away. While he and Astarte had been inside, the fog had risen and thickened.

So much for shooting Dunn at long range. On the other hand, maybe the mist would allow him to evade the creature altogether. He ran on across the overgrown yard. As he reached the wall, he heard the monster chasing him, the claws on Dunn's feet clicking on the kitchen floor.

Bellamy scrambled over the wall, dashed a few feet to the left, and then hunkered down behind a tomb to reload the Browning. An instant later, he heard a soft thud. It sounded as if Dunn hadn't had to climb over the barrier. He'd simply hurdled it.

Bellamy listened intently, but except for the muted rumble and clatter of a freight train rolling down the rails a block away, he didn't hear another sound. Finally he peeked around the side of the mausoleum. All he saw was the vague forms of the other vaults and coils of gray-white mist.

Apparently Dunn had moved off in another direction. Bellamy wished he could be certain it was because he'd shaken the monster off his trail, but he couldn't shake the nasty suspicion that the creature was merely toying with him.

Still, Bellamy was alone for the moment, and he meant to make good use of the time. The dilapidated tomb in front of him had a long crack running down the front. On impulse, he removed the notebook from his pocket and stuffed it into the fissure. If he survived, he could retrieve it later. If not, there might be one chance in a million—well, maybe a billion—that someone would find and decipher it, and, in any case, its disappearance might cause the Atheists some worry. Then he reloaded the Browning, wincing at the small clicks and snapping sounds the operation entailed.

He wondered if he should double back. Clamber back over the wall, go around the house, and into the shabby, nearly deserted streets beyond. Dunn might not be expecting that. But after a moment's consideration, he decided against the idea. Chester the unfriendly ghost was probably still keeping watch in the house as he had before. It would be better to exit the cemetery in another direction.

Bellamy thought that the east wall was a little closer than the west. Crouching, gun in one hand and dagger in the other, he headed for it. Tendrils of cool, wet mist caressed his face. Broken statues—a headless Madonna, her hands folded in prayer, an angel with chipped wings and a crumbling, leprous face—loomed out of the murk.

Then he heard a sniffing sound, and intuited instantly what it was. Dunn was near, and searching for his scent like a bloodhound.

Bellamy threw himself down behind the cover of another tomb, then looked frantically about. He didn't see Dunn.

The snuffling grew louder. Bellamy still didn't see the werewolf. His heart pounded, and his mouth was dry as sand. *Damn it!* he thought. *Dunn's ten feet tall. Even in the fog and the dark, I should be able to see him when he's obviously right on top of me.*

A vague shadow, almost invisible in the murk, fell on the ground before him. He smelled a faint, foul odor, monster mingled with tobacco smoke. He reflexively hurled himself forward, not consciously comprehending until a split second later what had spurred him into motion. Dunn had silently climbed up on the tomb Bellamy had counted on to protect his back and was reaching down to maul him.

Claws snagged the right side of Bellamy's face, ripping gashes in his flesh as his momentum carried him free. Blood gushed. He sensed that Dunn had more or less torn his ear off, but there was no real pain, not yet, not with the adrenaline flooding his system, only pure sensation. He was just glad the talons had missed his eye.

He whirled, pointing the Browning. At the same instant, Dunn bounded over the tomb and struck a backhand blow at his quarry's shooting arm. The impact snapped bone and flung Bellamy's hand to the side. The pistol flew from his grasp.

Dunn snarled and lunged, jagged, yellow fangs bared and huge hands clawing. Spinning to the side, Bellamy narrowly blocked the monster's first slashing blow, and just as Dunn's striding foot was about to contact the ground, he hooked it with his own and jerked it.

Thrown off balance, the werewolf stumbled. Bellamy rammed the silver knife into the creature's solar plexus.

Dunn went down, but even as he did, his hands shot out, sunk their nails into Bellamy's flesh, and wrenched him down on top of his adversary. Locked in a clinch, the human couldn't pull the knife out of Dunn's body for another thrust. So he jerked it back and forth, trying to enlarge the wound. Meanwhile the werewolf bit him, clawed at him, tearing and flaying the flesh from his bones.

Until, to Bellamy's amazement, Dunn's attacks began to slow and weaken, to diminish into a spastic scrabbling. The human wondered if he'd gotten lucky yet again. If by some miracle he was actually going to win.

Then Dunn gripped him by the shoulders. Even though the werewolf's musky stink, Bellamy smelled ozone, and his hair stood on end. An instant later, something crackled, and every muscle in his body convulsed.

He thought he could feel, even smell, his flesh burning, although it could have been his imagination. At any rate, he understood what was happening: Dunn was frying him like an electric eel. Another paranormal danger he hadn't had any way to anticipate. Had he still been capable of vocalization, he might have screamed at the unfairness of it.

His awareness began to collapse, not into protective embrace of madness, not this time, but into the deeper oblivion of death. He thought of Astarte, wished that he'd made love to her, and then the world went black.

THE ONYX TOWER

DARK KINGDOMS: VOLUME TWO

DEDICATION

FOR THE FENCERS OF SALLE DURAN

ONE

The world was white and cold. To Frank Bellamy, the fog seemed even thicker than it had a little while ago, when—

When what? He realized he couldn't remember. Perhaps he was sick, or injured. Perhaps he'd been drugged.

If so, he'd better find himself some help. Unable to spot any useful landmarks, he picked a direction at random and started walking. He noticed that he didn't move like a sick man. His stride was quick and easy, easier than he had any right to expect, considering—

His memory locked up on him again. Grimacing, he marched on, until a tall figure in a hooded cloak loomed out of the mist.

He recoiled and grabbed for his gun. Both the Browning and its shoulder holster were gone, but now he saw that he didn't really need it. The figure was only a pollution-stained statue of the Virgin Mary, its features blurred by weather and time.

The discovery was less reassuring than it should have been. If he wasn't mistaken, he'd recently had a terrifying experience involving just such a statue, but once again, he couldn't recall the details.

Shaking his head, he lifted his hand to rub his forehead. His fingers encountered a sheet of something cool and slimy, almost gelatinous, clinging to his face.

Maybe the fog wasn't quite as thick as he'd thought. Maybe the layer of foreign matter was obscuring his vision, and in any case, it felt disgusting. He dug his fingers into it to tear it off his skin, then hesitated.

Because some instinct warned him than when the veil was gone, it would be gone forever. Which would mean he'd completed his transformation. The transition he didn't *want* to make.

He didn't understand what that thought meant. But since he could see well enough to navigate, maybe it would be better to let a doctor remove the goo. He hurried on, catching glimpses of more crumbling statuary, most of it overtly religious in nature, and row after row of dilapidated tombs. Apparently he was wandering through a cemetery, an old one no one was keeping up, judging from the look of the weeds and brush.

With the realization came a flash of memory. Not long ago, he'd crouched behind one particular mausoleum and stuffed a spiral notebook into a crack in its facade. He'd hoped the notebook would prove to contain evidence pertinent to his current investigation, whatever that case was. He paused, wondering if he should retrace his steps and retrieve it, and a feminine voice softly called his name.

He pivoted. A slender young woman in a black leather jacket and ragged jeans stood before him. Her short hair was spiky, with magenta highlights, and steel rings gleamed in her right eyebrow, left nostril, and lower lip.

Bellamy was delighted to see her. He dimly remembered that when they'd parted, she'd been in danger. Evidently she'd escaped. "Astarte!" he cried.

Astarte gave him a smile, turned, and stepped behind a mausoleum. He hurried after her. When he rounded the corner of the tomb, he froze in surprise. Astarte—with whom, he abruptly recalled, he'd been falling in love—was in the arms of another man. Except not quite, because the interloper looked exactly like himself.

But only for a second. Then the other Bellamy's shoulders broadened, and his hair turned curly and a little shaggy. His gray suit coat melted into a russet suede jacket. Now he was Bill Dunn, the mole inside the FBI's Special Affairs Department, the traitor who'd turned out to be a man-eating monster in human disguise. Oblivious to his metamorphosis, Astarte kept on kissing him.

Bellamy tried to shout a warning, only to find he couldn't make a sound. He attempted to dash forward, but he couldn't move. Meanwhile, Dunn changed again, growing taller until his clothing split apart, and Astarte dangled in his huge, clawed hands like a doll. Black fur sprouted on his skin, his face extended into a lupine muzzle, and his ears grew large and pointed as a bat's. He opened his jaws, snapped them shut on Astarte's neck, and decapitated her with a single wrenching motion. Blood sprayed, its smell filling the air. Her head thumped to the ground and rolled, coming to rest against the base of a statue of Jesus cradling a lamb in His arms.

Released from his paralysis, Bellamy screamed and scrambled forward, intent on attacking the werewolf, if that was what Dunn truly was, with his bare hands. A part of him realized he was committing suicide, but he was too full of anguish to care.

He stepped in a depression in the ground and tripped. As he pitched forward, he felt a subtle sensation he'd never felt before. For an instant, he thought the soil had turned as insubstantial as air. Then he realized that it was his foot and ankle which had, in some sense, lost their solidity. Now they were *inside* the ground, occupying the same space as a volume of dirt.

Frightened that he wouldn't be able to pull himself free, he thrashed. His foot popped back above the surface, immediately becoming more tangible again. He remembered the atrocity he'd just witnessed, and felt a fresh burst of rage. He turned, ready to hurl himself at Dunn again, then faltered.

Astarte's body had vanished. Even the smell of her blood had disappeared. The black-furred monster was gone as well. In their place stood a man who was Bellamy's twin, watching him with a crooked smile.

"Relax," said the double. "Astarte and Dunn were never here. It was an illusion. Shock therapy. Do you remember now?"

"It's coming back," said Bellamy warily. "How did you know I was having trouble with my memory? What's going on? Who are you, and why are you impersonating me?"

"We'll do better if you answer my questions first," said the double. "Tell me exactly what you recall."

Bellamy scowled. Since he'd embarked on his investigation, he'd grown heartily sick of mysterious people who withheld information, almost as sick as he was of developing partial amnesia. But maybe talking would help to clear up his confusion, or perhaps his twin would fill in the remaining holes in his memory.

"I'm with the FBI's Violent Criminals Apprehension Program," Bellamy said, speaking rapidly to get the recitation over with. "I was trying to catch the Atheist, the serial killer who's been murdering ministers, rabbis, priests, and nuns in towns along the Mississippi. A self-proclaimed psychic named Waxman, who worked for one of the victims, claimed he could he give me some information about the crimes, proof they were connected to the occult, and asked me to meet him.

"Unfortunately, somebody—Dunn in his beast-man form, I know now—crashed the meeting to silence Waxman. The poor guy was so scared he dropped dead of a heart attack. I shot Dunn, a lucky shot that slowed him down enough to keep him from catching me when I ran away.

"I was just as terrified as Waxman had been, so much so that afterwards, I couldn't remember what had happened. As near as I can make out, Dunn joined SAD to make sure the Bureau never acquired any accurate data on the paranormal, so he wanted to make sure that no one would take my testimony seriously if I ever *did* regain my memory. To accomplish that, he pressured one of VICAP's staff psychiatrists to testify that I'd had a nervous breakdown."

"In a sense, you had," the double said.

Bellamy snorted. "Tell me about it. But just about anyone else in my situation would have had the same reaction. It turns out that creatures like Dunn are inherently terrifying to normal human beings. Anyway, my boss took me off the Atheist investigation. He assigned me to a desk job till further notice. But somehow, I just couldn't believe I was mentally ill, not in the way the doctor claimed I was, and I suspected I'd been side-lined as part of somebody's hidden agenda. Eventually I resumed investigating on my own.

"The trail led me here to New Orleans. Through a fluke, I hooked up with Astarte, who tagged along with me because she's been fascinated by the occult her whole life. Together, we talked to a lot of people." Bellamy wouldn't reveal the identity of Marilyn Sebastian, the transsexual chancellor of the local chapter of the Arcanum, a secret society devoted to psychic research, or of the hideously deformed vampires Mr. Daimler and Miss Paris. He'd promised to protect their anonymity. "And we learned that the supernatural is real." Even now, after all he'd experienced, when he was apparently speaking to yet another paranormal being, he felt sheepish making such a preposterous statement. "More than that, we discovered that there isn't just one Atheist. There's a conspiracy, and at least some of the killers have magical abilities.

"Finally, looking for evidence, Astarte and I broke into an old house owned by an odd group of people from Lafayette, who supposedly have ties to the conspiracy." He felt a twinge of anxiety. For some reason, he was reluctant to say any more, but the words kept tumbling out. "Inside, we discovered proof that they were cannibals. Monsters.

"Then Dunn came in and found us. It turns out that he's one of the group from Lafayette, and he'd come to New Orleans from Natchez to hunt me down. When he changed shape, Astarte panicked and ran. I stood my ground and fought, to give her a chance to get away." Bellamy's uneasiness flared into outright horror. "But now, somehow, I'm here, and Dunn isn't! He could be hunting her right now! He really may be tearing her apart! I've got to—"

"You have to remember the rest," said the double. "It's the only way."

"Later," Bellamy said, peering about. The house was adjacent to the cemetery, but hindered by the fog, he couldn't tell in which direction it lay. "We can fill in the blanks when she's safe."

"What's the substance clinging to your face?" the double asked. "How could your foot plunge right into the ground?"

Bellamy was so distraught and confused, his mind so overloaded, that he'd forgotten those oddities. Now a chill oozed up his spine. "I don't know," he said.

"Yes, you do," said the double, "even if you don't want to acknowledge it. Finish your story."

As if the impersonator's words had unlocked a door, the rest of Bellamy's memories began to trickle into his awareness. "I shot Dunn," he said, "but it didn't do a lot of good. I grabbed a big silver knife that was lying around, hoping that if worst came to worst, and he got close enough for me to use it, it would hurt him worse than the lead bullets had. The confrontation moved out here, we did wind up fighting hand-to-hand, and by dumb luck more than anything else, I managed to stab him in the solar plexus." For a second, he felt an echo of the elation he'd experienced.

"It seemed like he was hurt pretty bad," Bellamy continued. "Like I might actually have a chance of finishing him off. Then he grabbed me and shocked me, like an electric eel, and it—" Suddenly he couldn't go on. He felt stunned, as if someone had clubbed him.

"And the jolt killed you," the double said. "Death by electrocution."

Bellamy violently shook his head. "No. No, obviously it didn't. Otherwise, I wouldn't be here."

The impersonator frowned. "Don't lie to yourself. You don't have time. You know that there *are* such things as ghosts. Dunn told you that Chester, the spirit inside the computer in the house, was one. You remember the moment of your own death, the darkness swallowing you, and now you can stick your body through solid matter. You're a detective. Put the facts together and draw a conclusion."

Bellamy's eyes stung as if he were about to weep, though they didn't produce any tears. "I can't..." He trailed off, not knowing what he'd meant to say.

The double smirked. "You should have made love to Astarte last night when you had the chance. It's too late now. Too late for all kinds of things."

Bellamy felt as if he were drowning in grief. That anguish might shut down his conscious mind just as terror once had. He struggled to stop thinking about his plight. To focus instead on Astarte's situation. He owed it to her, and besides, it might be the only thing that could keep him sane.

"Where is Astarte?" he asked. "Did she get away?"

The impersonator shook his head. "You didn't buy her enough time. You didn't hurt Dunn bad enough. He's hot on her trail, hunting her through the streets. She's pounded on a few doors, but nobody answered. They wouldn't, not at this hour, in this neighborhood. The noise only helps to draw Dunn to her. He's got the senses of a wild animal, as you already discovered."

"Help me find the silver knife," Bellamy said. A gruesome image rose before his inner eye, the bloody weapon clutched in the hand of his own charred and shredded corpse. He tried to push the picture out of his mind. "Then take me to Dunn."

The double shook his head. "It hasn't sunk in yet, has it?" He waved his hand at some tendrils of ivy coiling their way along the side of a tomb. "Pull some of that loose."

"I haven't got time for games," Bellamy said.

"You don't know which direction your girlfriend ran, either," the double replied. "You do what I tell you, or you're on your own."

Bellamy glared at him, considered trying to beat some cooperation out of him, then turned, gripped a strand of ivy, and pulled. To his surprise, he couldn't shift it an iota. He struggled with all his might, strained until his fingers and forearms ached, but it was as if his hands were incapable of exerting any force. Finally, without warning, they became intangible, passing through the substance of the plant without resistance. Thrown off balance, he stumbled backward.

The double laughed. "Get it now? You can't affect the world of the living. You couldn't pick up the knife to stab Dunn. You couldn't even talk to him, or tap him on the shoulder."

Bellamy panted. Anxiety crawled along his nerves. "There must be something I can do. Or that you can."

"As a matter of fact," said the impersonator, "yes. Have you figured out who I am?"

Bellamy shrugged. "Another ghost? A vampire who can change his face to look like whoever he pleases?" Daimler possessed that particular ability. "I don't *care* who you are. Just help me."

"Actually," said the double, "I have your face because I really am you, more or less. I'm the part of you that's in sync with psychic and spiritual forces, and instinctively knows how to get along in the Underworld. I only seem to be a separate person because your Caul—that gunk on your face—is scrambling your brain and making you hallucinate."

"Then I should get rid of it?" Bellamy lifted his hands.

"No," the double said, "not yet. Not until we reach an understanding."

Now bewildered as well as frantic, Bellamy shook his head. If the double was really a part of him, why was the creature wasting time? Why didn't he seem as desperate to rescue Astarte as Bellamy was himself? "What understanding?"

"You have to agree to let me drive," the other man said. "You have to let me be the dominant part of our personality."

Bellamy hesitated. What the double was describing sounded rather like demonic possession. But if the apparition was already an intrinsic part of his own spirit, he supposed that was a false comparison. Heck, if he couldn't trust himself, who could he trust? "I guess that would be all right," he said at last.

"Good," said the double. He stepped forward and pressed his fingertips against Bellamy's temples. Bellamy felt an instinctive twinge of repulsion, and had to make an effort not to flinch. "This should only take a moment. Don't move."

Bellamy felt a cold, sliding sensation inside his head, painless, but such an intimate violation that it was as unbearable as the most excruciating agony. It was as if the double's fingers had lengthened, writhed through openings in his skull, and were slithering around in his brain like snakes.

Their touch released a flood of memories, the ones he'd done his best to bury. The way he'd sobbed when his mother died. The shock and bitter disappointment when his wife had walked out on him. The overwhelming panic when he'd first seen Dunn in the form of a monster.

Somehow he could feel the torrent of anguish eroding the structure of his mind, warping and corrupting his spirit. When the process was complete, he'd be a different person, someone for whom torment and betrayal were the only truths.

He tried to shove the double away from him, but his hands plunged through the apparition's body without resistance. He flung himself backward. Sneering, agile as a great dancer or a champion gymnast, the impersonator effortlessly moved with him, maintaining his touch on his head. Even when Bellamy tripped and fell, it didn't break the contact. The double dove on top of him.

Bellamy thrashed uselessly this way and that. At the same time, he tried to think. If he could neither touch his assailant nor move away from him, then how could he possibly save himself?

The slime on his face! According to the double, it was the reason he could see the apparition as a separate being, and, assuming his attacker had told the truth in any regard, perhaps it was what was making the attempted possession possible. He snatched at the layer of viscous stuff and shredded it away.

The double, the hideous feeling in his head, and the parade of painful memories all vanished at once. Bellamy began to gasp in a grateful breath, and then a host of fresh sensations bombarded him.

He could feel every slight bump in the ground digging into his back. The sounds of the city—car engines, televisions, snoring, groaning pipes, a baby weeping—jabbed into his ears. He could see the tombs and monuments far more clearly than he ever had when he was alive. Strangely, they seemed even more stained and ruinous than they had before, and the vaults emitted a sickening reek of decay.

Evidently, with the removal of the caul, his senses had become inhumanly keen. He wasn't used to such intense perceptions, and in large measure, that accounted for his distress. But there was even more to it than that. It was as if something was *distorting* his sensations in an effort to make the world seem as ugly, corrupted, and unpleasant as possible.

It was one more mystery to ponder when he got a chance. Right now, he still had to find Astarte. Praying that he wouldn't arrive too late, and that he'd think of something he could do to help her, he scrambled to his feet.

When he moved, his garments brushed against his skin, rasping it like sandpaper. He could even feel individual threads in the weave. The unexpected burst of sensation staggered him. As he fought to maintain his balance, he glimpsed a shadow gliding through the fog.

What now? he thought despairingly. He turned, and a lanky, prim-looking black man with graying hair and wire-rimmed glasses emerged from between two tombs. Bellamy recognized Chester instantly, even though, hitherto, he'd only seen a simulation of the other ghost's face on a computer monitor. Dunn's confederate held a snub-nosed revolver in his right hand. Round black crystals bulged from the top of the grip.

"Hold it," Chester said. "Put your hands up."

Bellamy wished desperately that he had a weapon of his own. How was it that his clothing and wristwatch had made the transition into the Underworld with him, but not the Browning or the silver knife? Just more miserable luck, he supposed, the same kind that had dogged him throughout the case.

He had no doubt the revolver could hurt him. Chester presumably knew the ins and outs of being a ghost, and had brought it for a reason. Nevertheless, playing for time, he asked, "Am I supposed to be afraid of getting shot? I'm already dead."

Chester sneered. "You don't know anything. There's a death beyond death, a true annihilation, and darksteel bullets"—he waved the revolver—"are just the thing to send you there. Now put your hands up."

Bellamy obeyed. "Okay," he said mildly, "I guess you got me. But you know, I'm surprised to see you out here, getting your hands dirty. You strike me as a technical man, not a field agent. The FBI is crawling with intellectual types who look just like you."

Chester grimaced. "Dunn is so impressed with your abilities that I thought *somebody* needed to come check on you. And nobody else was available, at least, nobody who can operate on our side of the Shroud. Dunn should have captured you, not killed you. He should have known there was a chance your spirit would enter the Underworld. But that's Black Spiral Dancers for you. Bloodthirsty and psychotic, every one of them, even the few who can pass for human. Now, walk toward me. I'm taking you back to the house for questioning."

By now, Bellamy had sized Chester up. The guy really was an amateur when it came to this kind of confrontation. His penchant for unnecessary chitchat, and the way he waved the gun around, proved it. The FBI agent might even have tried to jump him, except that his newly amplified sensations made his body feel strange and awkward. Until he learned to compensate, he didn't trust his own reflexes.

As it was, he figured his best option was to make a break for it, particularly since the snub-nosed revolver shouldn't be particularly accurate at long range. He took a trudging step toward Chester, trying his best to look cowed and submissive, then whirled and ran.

"Stop!" Chester bleated. "Stop!" After another moment, the gun barked. The blast nearly deafened Bellamy, and he staggered. The bullet whined past his ear. Chester was a better shot than he'd expected.

Doing his best to ignore the disconcerting barrage of his new perceptions, Bellamy sprinted on. With every stride, he was exquisitely aware of the flexing of his muscles and exact position of his legs. It was too much information. If he allowed himself to think about it, he'd forget how to walk.

He heard Chester's footsteps pounding after him. For the moment, the revolver was silent. Perhaps the other ghost simply wanted to get closer before he took another shot. But Bellamy hoped that Chester had lost sight of him. Surely even the eyes of the dead could be blinded by fog.

He zigzagged this way and that, trying to shake his pursuer off his trail, looking for a way out of the cemetery. As he did, he noticed that no matter how he exerted himself, he wasn't getting tired or winded. It was as if he no longer needed to breathe. Nor could he feel his heart hammering in his chest.

At last the cemetery wall, itself a tomb housing multiple rows of vaults, swam out of the mist ahead. Bellamy scrambled toward it, intent on jumping, grabbing the top, and scrambling over. He was flexing his legs for the effort when Chester lunged around a mausoleum ten feet away. The revolver was pointed at Bellamy's torso.

It was obvious that Bellamy couldn't afford to take the time to clamber over the barrier. If he did, Chester would nail him. Praying the maneuver would work, he hurled himself directly at the wall.

Inwardly, he was flinching. Bracing for the impact. But he didn't feel anything. His body became insubstantial and plunged through without impediment. Some sort of ghostly reflex had kicked in.

Behind the wall, the revolver banged, and the bullet cracked against the stone. Bellamy ran on down a narrow, unlit street. He heard Chester scramble through the wall and sprint after him.

Bellamy wondered if he should try dodging back inside the cemetery. If he could count on his newfound ability to slip through solid objects to work every time—a dubious notion—and kept zigzagging back and forth through the wall, it would make it hard for Chester to draw a bead on him. He was still contemplating the advisability of attempting the tactic when three figures emerged from the billowing mist ahead.

Bellamy ran right into them, and realized the collision demonstrated that they too were spirits. Everyone staggered, struggling for balance. A pair of powerful hands grabbed Bellamy's forearms and set him back securely on his feet, then maintained their grip.

Another hand, a black woman's hand, he saw now, brushed his forehead and came away with a wisp of the viscous material that had made up his caul. "An Enfant," she said, sounding pleased, "or near enough."

Chester charged out of the fog, then skidded to a stop when he saw the strangers. "That one's mine!" he cried.

"Is he?" said one of the strangers, a stocky white man armed with a crossbow. Like his black companions, he wore a short, zebra-striped cape secured with an ivory brooch. "Then you should have taken better care of him."

"Just because he slipped away from me," said Chester, a subtle quaver in his voice, "that doesn't negate my claim."

"Doesn't it?" said the black man gripping Bellamy's forearms.

"He doesn't have any claim on me!" said Bellamy, wondering what was actually at issue here. "He's an accessory to murder!"

"Hush," said the black woman. She had the lithe, leggy body of a dancer, which her bottle-green leotard and silver concho belt showed off to good advantage. Her flamboyant, revealing clothing made an odd contrast to the pump shotgun in her hand. "Since I don't recognize him, and he doesn't have one of these"—she touched her brooch, which, Bellamy now observed, was carved with an elegant, fine-boned feminine profile that reminded him of Nefertiti—"I suspect we already know what he is. One of Les Invisibles." She gave Chester a cold smile. "Isn't that right, *mon ami?*"

"No!" Chester yelped. "I'm one of you!"

"Then as a loyal citizen, you shouldn't mind paying a small tax to the Queen," the black woman replied.

"This isn't fair," Chester said. "You can't just steal—"

The black woman jacked a shell into the chamber of her shotgun. The ratcheting sound hurt Bellamy's ears. The white man cocked his crossbow.

Chester trembled, then turned and scurried back into the darkness.

"Thank you," said Bellamy to his rescuers. "I still need your help. There's a girl, a live girl, in terrible danger."

The black woman sighed. "Put her out of your mind, *cheri.* She's no business of yours, not anymore. You're just a poor dead slave now, in bondage to the Queen of New Orleans."

Bizarre as the declaration sounded, Bellamy could tell she wasn't joking. He stamped on the black man's foot. His captor's grip loosened, and he wrenched himself out of his grasp. But at the same instant, the woman clubbed him with the butt of her shotgun.

It was just a glancing blow. Had Bellamy still been alive, he might have shrugged it off. But because of his amplified sense of touch, it hurt worse than any pain had ever hurt before. The blast of agony dropped him to his knees. The woman hit him again, and he passed out.

TWO

Sprawled on a couch built for humans, and thus too small for his towering body, Dunn rubbed the bloody gash in his chest. Lord, it hurt! And because the weapon that had cut him was silver and magical to boot, he couldn't heal the injury in seconds, or, at most, minutes, the way he could an ordinary wound.

Reeking, shredded corpses lay heaped about the gloomy parlor. Black Spiral Dancers didn't devour their prey with any particular delicacy, nor were they much inclined to clean up after themselves. Generally speaking, Dunn was no more fastidious that the other members of the pack, at least not within the confines of one of their strongholds. But at the moment, he wished someone had removed the carrion elsewhere. The rotting flesh bred flies, which were swarming around him, attracted to his cut. Striking with the uncanny agility of his race, he slapped his hands together, crushing the insects between his palms, but no matter how many he killed, there were always more. The clapping sound echoed through the house.

Dunn's cellular phone, which lay on the floor amid the tattered garments he'd shed when he transformed, whirred. Grunting at another jab of pain, he rose, trudged across the floor, and picked it up. Then he realized that unless another werewolf was on the other end of the line, he wouldn't be able to speak to the caller in his current shape. A Crinos throat wasn't made for human speech.

But if he took on Homid form, he'd forfeit his regenerative powers. His wound might become crippling, or even life-threatening. The best he could do was to assume

Glabro shape. His body grew shorter and his fur thinned, though he remained hairier and more muscular than any true human. His ears shrank and moved from the top to the sides of his head, while his muzzle retracted into his skull. Shedding its wolfish characteristics, his face became beetle-browed, the countenance of an ape or a caveman. Ordinarily such transformations were painless, but now the gash throbbed. He silently cursed Frank Bellamy, the cause of his discomfort.

When the change was complete, he answered the phone with a guttural "Hello." The effort made his throat and head ache. The Glabro larynx—and brain—weren't ideally suited for human language either, though they could manage in a pinch.

"Hello," said Chester's voice. Dunn found it odd to reflect that the wraith wasn't simply calling from another phone. In all probability he was actually inhabiting the hunk of plastic and circuitry in the Black Spiral Dancer's hand. It was the only way he had of penetrating the Shroud, the barrier that separated the living and the dead, and communicating. "Did you catch Astarte?"

"No," Dunn growled. He disliked admitting failure, hated admitting weakness even more, but this time, he couldn't see any alternative. "My wound slowed me down too much. I had her scent, but I couldn't catch up with her. Finally I had to come back here. I was afraid I was going to pass out."

"Wonderful," Chester said sourly. "You had them cold, Bill. You could have sneaked up on them and knocked them out before they even knew you were in the house. But no, not you, the mighty manhunter. You had to give them a sporting chance. You had to make it *interesting*."

Dunn swiped his hand back and forth, dispersing another cloud of flies, which re-formed as soon as he quit. "You want to hear me say it? All right, listen carefully, because I'm only going to do it once. I screwed up. And now that particular subject is closed. The important thing is that the girl can't do any real damage. I don't think she learned anything important here, and even if she did, now that she's seen me in Crinos form, odds are she won't remember it. I guess we flesh-and-blood types need to abandon this house, at least for a little while, but except for that petty inconvenience, we're in good shape."

"You don't know that she'll forget," said Chester fretfully. "Apparently she's always had a passionate interest in the occult, and at this point, she's had more than one paranormal experience. She may be getting used to it."

"Maybe," Dunn said, "but frankly, who gives a shit? I *am* going to track her down and kill her, and the rest of her Arcanum buddies too, just on general principles, but I'm not worried about them. It was Bellamy who had the skills and the *cojones* to pose a real threat, and at least I got rid of him."

"That's what you think," Chester said. "Agent Bellamy has joined the ranks of the Restless."

"Are you kidding me?" the werewolf said. He was starting to feel woozy, unsteady on his feet, so he shuffled back to the couch and collapsed on top of it. The springs squealed in protest. "I thought that the vast majority of souls don't become wraiths."

"Is that your expert opinion?" asked Chester cattily. "Didn't anyone ever tell you that if a person dies a traumatic death, with urgent business unresolved in his life, there's a much better chance that he *will* enter the Underworld?"

Dunn scowled. "I suppose," he growled. The longer he spoke, the more the words ground and scraped in his throat. "But I still thought the odds were on our side. Anyway, it's not a problem, right? You found Bellamy stumbling around in a daze with a what-do-you-call-it, a caul, on his face. You captured or killed him without any trouble."

Chester hesitated. "Well, no. When I got to him, his caul was gone, and he was completely awake."

"How did that happen?" Dunn demanded. "Enfants don't usually pull off their own cauls, do they, not that quickly?"

"I don't know how it happened," Chester said. "It just did. Anyway, he ran from me. I tried to shoot him, but I missed. He got out of the cemetery and blundered into one of the Queen's patrols. They could see he was newly dead, and they laid claim to him."

"And you just let them do it?"

"There were three of them and only one of me," Chester replied sullenly. "What was I supposed to do? I was lucky to get away without getting arrested myself."

"Okay," sighed Dunn, "I see your point." He paused for a moment, pondering. "The way I see it, we're still all right. Maybe Bellamy's not quite gone, but he might as well be. He doesn't have any freedom of movement. He's a lowly white Lemure Thrall, and no matter how much he babbles about the Atheist, none of the Queen's people is going to care. They won't connect a bunch of Skinlands murders to their own problems." He smiled. "You know, Chester, when you get right down to it, we must be a couple of nervous nellies, or we wouldn't worry about insignificant loose ends like Bellamy and Astarte no matter what. *Nothing* could derail the plan at this point. The organization's too strong, and we've come too far. A few more deaths, a little disaster here and there, and the river will burn black."

Three

James Graham, in life Earl and Marquess of Montrose, now an Anacreon of the Order of the Unlidded Eye and an advisor to the Smiling Lord, fidgeted with his heavy, richly begemmed and embroidered robes and mantle. He remembered how absurdly rococo and cumbersome these formal garments had seemed when he'd first been granted a place at his master's court. In the many years since, he'd grown accustomed to them. He'd even come to enjoy them as tokens of the prestige and luxury he'd striven so hard to attain. It was strange to think that after today, he might never don them again.

The sonorous note of a gong shivered through the antechamber. Lanky, brown-haired Karl Reinhardt, Montrose's former comrade, fellow inquisitor, and the wraith who'd arrested him and escorted him back to Stygia, said, "It's time, my lord Anacreon." His mask of riveted crimson metal concealed his entire face and thus, of course, his expression. Nor could Montrose glean any hint of his mood from the neutral tone of his voice.

Montrose smiled wryly behind his own glossy black ceramic mask. "You could wish me luck, Karl. For old time's sake. I don't think anyone will accuse you of treason just for that."

"Good luck," murmured Reinhardt, so softly that even Montrose's hypersensitive wraith hearing could barely hear it. "I'm afraid you're going to need it." He directed his gaze at the huge iron doors before him. Crafted by some cunning Artificer, the panels swung silently open in response to his will.

With its high, vaulted ceiling, the somber hall of state beyond the threshold had always reminded Montrose of a Gothic cathedral, and perhaps that was an appropriate comparison. Now that the Emperor was no more, the service of the seven Deathlords, his former ministers, was the closest thing to a religion the militantly godless society of the Hierarchy had. Soldiers of the Order of the Avenging Flame, the Smiling Lord's personal bodyguards, stood along the walls, while torches burned in sconces above their heads. Their hissing greenish flames were largely responsible for the chill in the air. Unlike earthly fire, barrow-flame radiated cold, not heat.

Motionless as a graven image, the Smiling Lord sat enthroned on a basalt pedestal at the far end of the chamber. The sickly jade light glinted on his steel mask, his plate armor, and the darksteel head of the halberd in his right hand. A number of his ministers—Montrose's fellow courtiers and, in most cases, his bitter rivals—stood before the dais. Chiarmonte, the nondescript little Venetian spy master, almost lost in his voluminous robes, the top half of his face covered by a leather domino. And gaunt, loose-limbed Demetrius, the relative newcomer, his head concealed by a carved sardonyx helm.

Montrose started down the long, black marble aisle. His leg irons, invested with a magic that prevented him from using his Harbinger powers in an escape attempt, clinked. Reinhardt marched at his side, and two guards, their assault rifles an anomaly in this ancient place, brought up the rear.

Montrose halted before the throne, bowed deeply, and unmasked. No one else followed suit. In the labyrinthine world of the Onyx Tower, a complex etiquette determined who uncovered his face in any given situation. Generally speaking, in a tribunal such as this one, only the accused was required to do so.

Montrose realized that his mask had left his auburn lovelocks in disarray. He gave his head a slight toss, trying to settle them into place. Then Demetrius intoned, "James Graham, Marquess of Montrose, my lord Anacreon, you stand before our august master the Smiling Lord accused of treason." Evidently the Greek had been selected, or, likely, had volunteered to prosecute the case. "How do you plead?"

"Not guilty," Montrose replied, gazing steadily up at his master. Shadowed by the rings of steel surrounding them, the Smiling Lord's gray eyes were unreadable. On occasion, the accused man had suspected that this aloof and enigmatic presence regarded him as a friend of sorts, but if so, there was no sign of it now.

Demetrius turned to a table. Two slim volumes lay there, one bound in white leather, the other in red. He picked up the red one. "This was discovered among your possessions. A journal in which you declare your intention to renounce your loyalty to the Hierarchy and conquer a kingdom for yourself in the Shadowlands of Earth."

"I didn't write it," Montrose said.

Demetrius looked at Chiarmonte. The gray-haired Venetian, an expert graphologist, said, "It's unquestionably in Lord Montrose's hand." His tone was matter-of-fact.

Montrose took a deep breath. Throughout the journey from Natchez back to the

Isle of Sorrows, he'd wracked his brains, trying to devise an escape plan, or, barring that, a lie that would serve him better than the discreditable truth. He hadn't succeeded at either. "I imagine it looks like my writing because my Shadow penned it to ruin me," he admitted, "during a brief period when it was in control of my body."

Given the heartless character of Stygian justice, it was a poor defense. A high-ranking Legionnaire who'd been possessed by the malignant forces festering in the depths of every wraith's personality was likely to be regarded as a security risk. If he could succumb once, why not again? Wouldn't it be safer to dispatch him to Oblivion, and avoid the possibility?

Chiarmonte cocked his head. "I've known you for a long time," he said to Montrose. "I don't recall you ever having such an episode."

Demetrius looked coldly at the Venetian, as if he resented his usurping a more active role in the proceedings, but made no verbal protest.

"It was a freak occurrence," Montrose said. He looked up at the Smiling Lord again. "Dread Lord, you sent me to the Shadowlands to lead a campaign against the Heretics. One of their leaders turned out to be Louise, the exiled Bohemian princess I once told you about. She whom I loved in life, and who betrayed me. Who sent my army to defeat and me to the gallows.

"When I encountered her in the midst of battle, and captured her, it filled me with rage, and my savagery gave my Shadow strength. But now that I've punished her as she deserved, you can rest assured that my psyche is in firm control again."

The Smiling Lord stared impassively down at him.

"So your dark twin was dominant when you wrote the journal," Demetrius said. "A novel defense. Perhaps it would even be considered a valid one, if it were true."

"It is," Montrose said.

The Oracle picked up the white book. "This too was discovered in your possession. A religious tract. Evidence of Heretical sentiments."

"Don't be absurd," Montrose said. "I'd been persecuting Heretics all along the lower Mississippi as per my orders. Killing and enslaving them and confiscating their possessions."

"But I believe this is the Prayer Book of the old Scottish Kirk," Demetrius said. "Your devotion to the faith it embodies shaped your whole mortal career. And considering your failure to consign this one particular item to the purifying flames, perhaps the creed still has meaning for you today."

Montrose sneered. "I kept it simply as a trophy. A memento." Actually, he wasn't quite sure of his motives, but he supposed he was speaking the truth. Certainly he'd renounced both his Christianity and the lofty ideals which had ruined his life a long time ago.

"You can hardly condemn an inquisitor for coming into possession of Heretical materials," said Chiarmonte to Demetrius, "nor, I would assume, do you claim to be able to read the fellow's mind. Considering that Montrose isn't charged with Heresy anyway, perhaps we should move on to matters of greater substance."

"As you wish," Demetrius replied. "Lord Montrose, you claim that your traitorous ambitions were a transient aberration. But the evidence indicates you were plotting to seize your own independent dominion before you ever left Stygia, and that many of your subsequent actions were meant to further that aim."

"Nonsense," Montrose said. "I didn't even want to go." And that at least was the plain, unvarnished truth. He'd winced at the notion of abandoning the luxuries of the court for the spartan conditions of the Shadowlands, and he'd been reluctant to give his rivals the opportunity to defame him to the Smiling Lord in his absence.

"You sailed with a detachment of Legionnaires," Demetrius said. "According to your report, Soul Pirates attacked your ships deep in the Tempest. Only you escaped."

"That's right," Montrose said. His Harbinger skills afforded him the ability to move with relative freedom through the chaotic dimensions which separated the Isle of Sorrows from the mortal realm, and thus he'd managed to flee the convoy when it had become clear that the battle was lost.

"I submit that you deliberately led your men into an ambush," Demetrius said, "because loyal Legionnaires, soldiers who'd turn on you if they divined your true intent, were a hindrance to your plans."

"You're wrong," Montrose said. "I let Captain Pizarro choose our route through the storm. Why not? He was a far better sailor than I am. Traversing the Sea of Shadows is always dangerous, and what happened to us was bad luck, pure and simple."

"I question that," Demetrius said. "Because when you reached your destination, you raised a new army comprised of the most despicable cutthroats in the region. Precisely the sort of scum who would back you in your treason."

"I needed troops to complete my mission," Montrose said, "and the governors of the province refused to lend me any of theirs. I had to make do with the resources at hand."

"That's not the way Gayoso, Shellabarger, and Mrs. Duquesne tell it," Demetrius said. "They claim they were more than willing to assist you. But you were intent on having your own personal force, and on undermining their authority with the populace."

Montrose shifted his weight. His ankle chain rattled against the marble. "What would you expect them to say?" he replied. "That they refused to honor the wishes of a Deathlord when they imagined they could get away with it? They're locked in a petty little power struggle with one another." In the half century since Charon's demise, during which Stygia's control of its Shadowlands territories had become increasingly attenuated, such intrigues had become more the rule than the exception. "None of them would give me any troops for fear of leaving himself vulnerable to the others. And I daresay they *were* worried that I'd want to stay in Natchez and take control, but that was simply their paranoia.

"Tell me this, Lord Demetrius. If I truly am a traitor, what treasonous act did I commit? What did I actually *do* in the Shadowlands, except carry out my commission to the best of my ability?"

"You weren't yet ready for overt rebellion," the swarthy Greek replied. "You wanted to recruit more desperadoes first." His voice took on a smug, mocking note. "If you recall, you laid out your strategy in detail in your diary."

Montrose turned back to the Smiling Lord. "Master, you know me. I've fought and labored in your behalf for three and a half centuries. Surely you don't believe I'm a traitor."

The Smiling Lord simply stared.

Montrose felt a surge of despair, and struggled to quash the emotion. "During my sojourn in the Shadowlands," he continued, "I discovered that there *is* some sort of sinister plan afoot, though it hasn't got anything to do with me." At last the Smiling Lord shifted on his seat, ever so slightly. The Scot felt an indefinable change in the quality of his master's regard. "There's an ugly mood in Natchez and elsewhere, a feeling of hatred in the air. Wraiths are killing one another over trivialities. By chance, I discovered that many of the veteran local Pardoners have vanished, and new ones are appearing to take their places. But the newcomers practice a corrupt version of the craft. Instead of quelling a wraith's Shadow, they strengthen it, without the victim understanding what's actually going on. That's the source of the unrest."

Chiarmonte frowned. "Who's behind it?" he asked. "Spectres? Heretics?"

"I don't know," Montrose said. "Lord Reinhardt called for me before I had a chance to find out. But I have a hunch that somehow, the disappearance of legitimate Pardoners along the Mississippi has something to do with a series of murders of priests and ministers taking place in the Skinlands of the same region. And if some of our enemies have concocted a scheme large enough to involve hostilities against both the living and the dead, we'd be well advised to uncover it post haste."

He decided not to add that Katrina, the Ferryman who'd helped him escape the Tempest after the loss of his ships, had warned him that a dire threat was looming on the horizon, a menace it was his destiny to confront. The mysterious fellowship of psychopomps to which she belonged had broken with Charon two thousand years ago, when he'd first proclaimed himself Emperor. In consequence, the Deathlords didn't trust them, any more than they trusted any other ghost who refused to accept the authority of the Onyx Tower. Besides, were Montrose to mention the incident, he'd also have to explain that he hadn't taken the warning seriously, and in retrospect, his blindness made him feel like a fool.

"And only you were cunning enough to uncover this diabolical conspiracy," said Demetrius ironically. "Surely, then, only you could get to the bottom of it. So we'd better forget all about these silly charges, hadn't we, and send you back to America to investigate."

"Essentially," said Montrose, "that is what I'm proposing." He gazed up at the Smiling Lord. "Let me return to the Shadowlands, my liege. Under close guard, if you think it necessary. But let me prove my loyalty by ferreting out this threat."

For a moment he had the feeling that the Deathlord was seriously considering it. That the Master of War and Murder might actually spare him. Then the man in the steel mask turned to Demetrius. "Do you think there's any chance at all that there's anything to this?"

The Greek shook his head. "Absolutely not, Dread Lord. Otherwise Gayoso would already have discovered the plot. After all, he knows his domain far better than Montrose. He's resided there for hundreds of years. It's just a lie, a ploy to divert us from our purpose."

"I suppose," said the Smiling Lord. Montrose blinked in surprise. For a moment, there was a faintly querulous, almost *human* note in his master's tone that he'd never heard there before.

The Smiling Lord gazed down at the defendant. "Here is my judgment," he said, his voice cold iron once again. "I find you guilty of treason. Others condemned for the same crime have gone to the torturers, to suffer terrible agonies until Oblivion claimed them. But in recognition of your past services, and because I believe your Shadow may actually be responsible for your transgressions, I choose to grant you mercy. I'm sending you to the Artificers, to have your body smelted into metal."

"Master," said Montrose, "I swear on my honor, you're making a mistake."

"Take him away," said the Smiling Lord. One of the guards grabbed Montrose's shoulder and yanked him backward.

Four

Potter was certain that he and Demetrius were alone. Surely none of his countless servants would dare to spy on the Smiling Lord, and even had they wished to do so, in the small, sparsely furnished scrying chamber, there was no hiding place to spy *from*.

Still, he hesitated, peering about, before drawing off his steel gauntlets, laying them beside the clay figurine, a fleshy nude woman with two faces, on the small, round table, and then, at last, pulling off his visor.

As usual, the crime brought an untidy jumble of conflicting emotions. One was guilt. Charon, whom he'd worshipped, feared, and occasionally hated, had forbidden his Deathlords to reveal their faces or their mortal identities to anyone, even their peers. But along with the shame and anxiety came a defiant joy. It was good to escape the prison of his loneliness. To have a true friend and confidant at last.

"Today was difficult," he said somberly. "I liked Montrose. Are we absolutely certain we've done the right thing?"

"Yes," said Demetrius. Following the tribunal, he'd wasted no time exchanging his formal robes and boots for his customary toga and sandals. "I used my Arcanos to investigate the state of his spirit and his recent activities. The results were consistent with the other evidence against him, even if they weren't admissible in court."

"But was it truly necessary to send him to the Soulforges?" Potter asked. "I could have exiled him."

"Leaving him free to proceed with his conquest of the Shadowlands?"

"No," Potter sighed, "I suppose not. But perhaps we should put him to the question after all. If we don't, how can we be sure that his treachery isn't related to all the other things that have been happening to me?"

Relations among the seven Deathlords had been deteriorating since Charon's passing. Each was striving to amass as much power as possible, either to satisfy his ambition or simply to guarantee his survival. At first the oligarchs of the Restless had confined their rivalry to political maneuvering, at least as far as Potter was aware. But more recently, scrying with the aid of the magical two-faced statue Demetrius had given him, he'd received intimations that one or more of his peers intended to kill him, and then an assassin had actually made an attempt. And though Stygia had a plethora of external enemies, no outsider should have been able to sneak into the labyrinthine complex of palaces and fortifications loosely known as the Onyx Tower. Thus, Potter had no doubt that one of colleagues was to blame.

"I don't think there's a connection," Demetrius said. "One situation involves the petty affairs of the provinces, the other the Isle of Sorrows itself. Besides, if Montrose had been collaborating with your enemies here, he would have mentioned the fact in his journal as freely as he delineated the other aspects of his treachery. Still, you're well rid of him."

"I guess you're right," Potter said. "Are you ready to try another divination?"

"Of course," said Demetrius, waving a hand at the table and the two straight-backed chairs. "Whatever the Dread Lord commands. If you will please be seated?"

Adjusting the folds of his voluminous, ankle-length mantle, Potter sat down. The two faces of the figurine gave him their cryptic smiles. He rested his forearms on the tabletop and his vambraces clinked.

Demetrius sat down opposite him. "I've continued my research, and discovered another ancient Oracular technique."

"Good," Potter said, trying to sound—and feel—optimistic. The trouble with both his visions and his lieutenant's psychic explorations was that they kept yielding incomplete information. They'd never definitively revealed which of his fellow Deathlords were plotting to kill him. At one point Demetrius had hypothesized that his ignorance of Potter's true identity, and of the pattern of his deathmarks, those facial stigmata only Oracles could see, were hampering his efforts. That was why Potter had chosen to unmask for him.

But although the transgression had paid off by creating a true bond of camaraderie between them, and enabling his advisor to Pardon him more effectively, it hadn't solved the problem. Thus, Demetrius had decided to delve into the half-forgotten arcana of the Oracles' guild, dissolved by Charon centuries ago, seeking alternative, and, he hoped, more potent methods of prophecy.

The Greek seemed to catch a despondent note in his master's voice. "I will break through for you," he said. "I guarantee it."

Potter smiled wanly. "I know you will. What's the plan this time?"

Demetrius nodded at the statuette. "With the Dread Lord's permission, I'm going to destroy this ugly piece of bric-a-brac."

Potter cocked his head. "Why?"

"Why not?" said the saturnine Greek, his wide mouth quirking into a momentary smile. "It never tells us everything we need to know, does it, and as long as we use it as gently as its maker intended, I suspect it never will. But if I release all its power at once, perhaps I can finally supply the answers you need."

As a Deathlord, Potter was sufficiently versed in the basics of the Arcanoi of all the guilds to comprehend that what Demetrius was proposing was both theoretically possible and at least a little dangerous. "Very well," he said, "but be careful."

"I always am," Demetrius said. "Please put your hand on the statue."

Potter touched the figure's base and its bare, dainty feet. The baked clay felt cool and dry. Demetrius rested his fingertips on the talisman's misshapen head, closed his eyes, and began to murmur in a language the Deathlord didn't recognize. He suspected that even if he were wearing his mask, an almost sentient artifact possessed of its own memory, a repository of knowledge on which the wearer could draw at need, he might not have understood the words.

A feeling of lassitude came over him. His head swam, and he felt a small portion of his vitality flowing down his arm and into the statue. He recognized the sensation from other magical operations. Demetrius was enhancing the link between him and the statue.

Suddenly the figure's left shoulder shattered. Potter reflexively blinked, but no flying grit stung his face, not did any shower to the tabletop. Apparently that portion of the image had simply disintegrated. A dazzling beam of white light blazed from the jagged hole.

Demetrius grunted and went rigid, then resumed his incantation.

A portion of the figurine's left hip cracked with a noise like a gunshot and disappeared. Another ray of glaring light shone forth. The Oracle's head jerked spastically to the left.

A section of the statue's neck burst into nothingness. Demetrius cried out and clutched at his throat with his free hand. A fierce radiance burned through the cracks between his fingers. Potter realized that his lieutenant had developed a wound in the same place, and with the same bizarrely luminous characteristics, as the image's.

Such an injury would probably have killed a mortal in a matter of seconds. Lacking any blood or true vital organs, wraiths were more resistant to most sorts of damage. Indeed, the resilience and plasticity of their substance lay at the basis of the shape-shifting art of the Masquers. Still, it was obvious that Demetrius was hurt. "What's happening?" Potter asked.

"It's fighting back," the Oracle said through gritted teeth. "It doesn't want to be consumed. But I'll be all right."

He resumed chanting. Another piece of the clay figure exploded into nothingness. An instant later, a shining puncture opened in Demetrius's biceps.

Now nearly hidden by the glow of their injuries, the bodies of the two combatants began to exhibit further changes. Demetrius's substance flowed. At certain moments, breasts and a newly convex belly bulged out the front of his toga, and a second face snarled and gibbered on the left side of his head. Patches of his skin took on the hard, hairless appearance of pottery, while portions of the statue turned to skin. His body shrank, and the talisman swelled. Apparently the figure was trying to trade places with him in some unimaginable way.

It looked to Potter as if the Greek was in serious jeopardy. He wondered if he should remove his hand from the statue and terminate the magic. He dreaded losing his advisor and confessor, his only friend. How could he get along without him? But he also cringed at the thought of forfeiting what might be his only real chance to learn the identities of his hidden foes. His ignorance was a torment. He often felt as if it was driving him mad.

Demetrius's left eye exploded, a white ray blazing out of the socket. The Oracle screamed and thrashed, but somehow maintained his contact with the image.

Enough! Potter thought. *This has to stop.*

But just as he was about to pull his hand back, Demetrius croaked, "No!" The sound came from three sources, his true lips, the ones belonging to a half-formed countenance oozing and bubbling on the side of his head, and the only mouth the talisman currently possessed. "I beg you. I can do this and I will."

Trembling, his mouth dry, Potter left his fingers where they were.

Demetrius chanted rhythmic, grating syllables in yet another unknown language. With its abundance of consonants and paucity of vowels, it sounded as if it had never been intended to issue from a human throat. The pale amber flames in the lamps along the wall flared and guttered in time with his words, while shadows seemed to pinwheel on the floor. Though Potter had locked the door, a blast of hot wind dashed it open to crash against the wall.

The corona of light around Demetrius flared even brighter, like a star exploding into a nova. Startled, Potter had no choice but to avert his eyes and recoil. Just as he began to move, he felt the statue dissolve into nothingness beneath his fingers.

After a moment, the ambient glare dimmed and contracted into a pearly orb. Squinting, still half dazzled, Potter saw that Demetrius, his body whole and unblemished once again, was cradling the ball in his hands.

"Peer into the center of the light," the Oracle said. "Quickly, please. I can't hold the power for long."

Potter stared into the silvery glow. After a moment, a mote of blackness blinked into existence at its heart. The speck expanded rapidly into a picture, a scene, until it became all that the Deathlord could perceive.

Their backs turned to him, two figures crouched over a table in a cramped and shadowy chamber. One was small, stooped, and wrapped in a gray mantle. Her hair white and wispy, she was leaning on a gnarled walking stick. The thin man beside her wore black and white, and over it all a cloak the color of dust. A mechanical silver rat perched on each of his shoulders, ruby eyes gleaming, wire whiskers twitching, hinged feet clutching to maintain their grip.

The conspirators' masks, his a grinning ivory skull face, hers the carved wooden visage of a withered crone, sat discarded on the table. Between the visors lay a large piece of parchment with curling corners.

At first Potter couldn't make out what it was, but then his perspective shifted. Now it was as if he were peering over the plotters' shoulders. The parchment was a map of a portion of the Onyx Tower. Her withered hand trembling, the woman pointed at one of the parks, a painstaking recreation of a Skinlands jungle.

Excited and dismayed in equal measure, Potter took stock of his own sensations and perceptions. This vision was different from those which had preceded it. It didn't feel vague, dreamlike, or unreliable in the least. "I think you've done it," he said.

"What's happening?" asked the now-invisible Demetrius. His voice sounded faint and far away.

"I see the Ashen Lady and the Skeletal Lord," Potter said. "They're alone in a room, unmasked, looking at a map of the Tower. She's pointing to the park where I was attacked. And this time everything is clear. I'm sure I'm witnessing something that actually happened."

"So they're the ones," the Oracle said.

"Yes," Potter said. "And that's bad, though not as—"

The scene shifted abruptly. Potter found himself peering at the summit of one of the castle's tallest towers. Illuminated by flares of jade and azure lightning, the storm clouds of the Tempest churned overhead. Beneath the parapet, their forms half-obscured by the eternal darkness, rose a thousand other gargoyle-encrusted spires. Here and there across the city wavered points of sickly light, barrow-flame lanterns and torches.

In the center of the rooftop, four masked wraiths marched widdershins in a circle, chanting maledictions. A man in a scarlet robe brandished an empty sack.

Another in green dexterously manipulated a pair of crimson dice, clicking them together like castanets in time to the incantation. A one-legged fellow in saffron rags thumped along with the aid of a crutch, a wooden bowl in his free hand. The woman with the tangled mane of raven hair didn't walk so much as caper. Each pace was a step in an antic dance, and the harlequin marionette whose strings she was manipulating mimicked her every move to perfection.

Gradually a translucent figure took shape in the middle of the circle. Potter gasped, because he was looking at his own cloaked and armored form. The four conjurers shouted a word of power in unison. A jagged bolt of black lightning crackled through the image.

Potter felt a stabbing pain in his own chest. He jerked convulsively, and the phantasmal scene vanished. He was back in his meditation chamber. Demetrius's hands were empty. Evidently he'd exhausted his plundered magic.

"Are you all right?" asked the Oracle. "You cried out."

"No!" Potter snapped, trembling. "I mean, I'm not injured. But the vision changed! I saw the rest of them, the Quiet Lord, the Emerald Lord, the Beggar Lord, and the Laughing Lady, working together to lay a curse on me. That must be why I've felt so weak and confused lately."

"Thank goodness that at last we know for certain. Now we can take steps—"

"Are you stupid?" Potter cried. "Don't you understand what I just told you? It isn't just one or two of them. *Every single one of the other Deathlords is out to destroy me.* I can't contend with all six of them at once. If I had any sense, I'd cast myself into the Void right now. It would probably be a less painful demise than the one they have in store for me."

Demetrius laid his hand on his shoulder. "Please, compose yourself," he said.

Potter began to snarl an angry retort and wrench himself away. Then he met his lieutenant's calm, compassionate brown eyes, and a spasm of shame took a bit of the edge off his terror. No matter how hopeless his plight, Demetrius, who'd repeatedly risked his own existence to help him, didn't deserve his abuse. "I'm sorry," he said. "I didn't mean to shout at you. You must flee Stygia tonight. There's nowhere for me to run, nowhere far enough, but they might not come looking for you."

Demetrius scowled. "Do you think I'd abandon you in your time of need? I won't permit you to abandon yourself, either. Think, my lord! The situation isn't as bad as it could be. It isn't six united against one, as it was in some of your nightmares. If I understood you correctly, you saw two separate groups working against you. Isn't it likely that the cabals are scheming against one another as well? And that the members of each are even now plotting to betray their fellows as soon as it's to their advantage to do so?"

Potter ran his fingers through his straw-colored hair. "I suppose. When all's said and done, only one of us can be Emperor. But still, with everyone striving against me—"

Demetrius turned and grabbed Potter's steel visor. Despite the panic still yammering through his mind, the former British soldier felt a jolt of shock. It was a kind of sacrilege, or at least *lese majesty*, for an underling to touch a Deathlord's mask. "This is you," said the Oracle, holding up the face plate for his master's inspection. "The Smiling Lord. Master of the Seat of Burning Waters. A demigod.

An archangel. The incarnation, the pure refined essence, of war and murder."

Potter felt a faint stirring of pride and hope. He didn't know whether to embrace it as the herald of his salvation or reject it as a heart-breaking chimera. "In some sense," he said, a little hesitantly, "I suppose that's true."

"Of course it is," rapped Demetrius. "Charon wouldn't have chosen you if you weren't capable of becoming the entity your office requires. Now I've heard it said that each of the Seven is equally powerful, and I imagine that on an abstract level it's so. Each of the others embodies a particular aspect of death, the same as you do.

"But don't you see, that abstract level doesn't matter. By resorting to violence, they've entered *your* sphere, where none of them can match you."

"So you actually think I stand a chance against them?" Potter asked. "Even though many of the visions foretold my destruction?"

Demetrius waved his hand, brushing such defeatist reflections aside. "The omens reflected your probable fate when you were ignorant and irresolute. Now that we finally have some answers, the weave of destiny has changed. Of *course* you stand a chance, if you muster all the cunning and vast resources at your command, and fight your rivals as mercilessly as they mean to battle you. Dispatch your own assassins. Suborn your enemies' troops. Find ways to manipulate the wretches into attacking one another. And finally, when you've worn them down, trap them and put them all to the Final Death."

Potter nodded slowly. "You know," he murmured, "it might be possible at that, and in any case, what have I got to lose? Better to go down fighting than be slaughtered like a sheep."

"No one's going to slaughter you," Demetrius said firmly. "In a few weeks your so-called peers will be naught but a fading memory, and you, Dread Lord, will be the new Emperor of Stygia."

Five

Astarte made the call from a pay phone outside a 7-Eleven in Slidell. Cars growled up and down the busy street, past tire stores, discount furniture outlets, and fast-food joints, filling the air with the hot stink of their exhaust. People kept brushing past her on their way to and from the store entrance. Some of the locals—the ones who didn't approve of piercings, black lipstick and nail polish, and spiky magenta hair, she assumed—glowered at her. Other rednecks leered at her, checking out her tits and ass, and murmured smutty comments to one another.

All things considered, it wasn't an ideal location for Astarte to touch base with her mother back in Dayton. But she didn't want to do it from the motel where she and Marilyn intended to spend the night. For all she knew, Dunn and the other werewolves and ghosts had tapped Mom's phone, and would trace the call. Or maybe they had some way of monitoring every phone in Louisiana. Such a notion sounded paranoid, but as Astarte had already learned the hard way, it was all but impossible to guess what supernatural creatures could or would do. That seeming lack of any rules or limits was what, even more than the violence and the freakish ugliness of some of the beings they'd encountered, had bothered Frank Bellamy most.

At the thought of Frank, her eyes stung, filling with tears. With his straight-arrow haircut, clothes, and attitude, he was the last person she would ever have imagined herself falling in love with. But once she'd gotten past his FBI-man reserve, he'd turned out to be warm and generous, with a wry sense of humor. Unlike most people of her acquaintance, he really believed he could make a difference in the world. That was part of the reason he'd become a cop. And deep down inside, he'd been lonely, just as she had. Somehow the combination had won her over.

Now he was gone. He'd stayed behind with Dunn in the house off Elysian Fields to buy her time to get away, and she hadn't seen him since. It was remotely possible that the werewolf had taken him prisoner. But she knew that in all likelihood Dunn had torn him apart and feasted on his remains.

The phone on the other end of the line stopped ringing. A sound, so muffled as to be unrecognizable, emerged from the receiver in Astarte's hand.

Astarte blinked away her tears and covered her other ear with her hand, trying to block out the rumble of the traffic. "Mom?" she said. "It's Emily." She hadn't introduced herself that way to anyone since she'd adopted what she thought of as her true, occultist name, borrowed from the Sumerian goddess of love. But at the moment, it felt right to do so. "Are you there?"

Another indistinguishable sound.

Astarte hoped that her mother wasn't too zonked on her pain pills to converse intelligibly. "It's really noisy here. You have to speak up."

"All right, all right," said Mom, comprehensible at last. "I'll shout. But it will be bad for me."

Astarte sighed. Every petty demand and inconvenience was "bad" for her mother, and the fact that she really did suffer from migraines, chronic fatigue syndrome, and a bad back—or at least had found doctors willing to testify to insurance and disability boards that she did—didn't make her complaining any easier to bear. "I don't want you to strain yourself, Mom. Just do the best you can, okay?"

"Okay," said Mom, sounding slightly less sullen. "I miss you. It's hard for me to manage by myself. Are you still in New Orleans?"

Astarte fingered the steel ring in her lower lip. "In a town just outside of it right now." She, Frank, and the Arcanists had decided it was safer to stay in a series of motels beyond the city limits, though they still had to venture inside it to snoop around.

"Are you ready to come home?" asked Mom. On the street behind Astarte, a horn blared, and tires screeched as someone slammed on his brakes. "Because I don't have any money for a bus ticket. You hitchhiked down, you'll have to hitchhike back."

"I don't need money," Astarte said honestly. Marilyn and the other surviving Arcanists had plenty, and they were picking up her tab. "I'm going to stay a while longer."

"Why?" Mom demanded. "What are you *doing* there?"

Astarte was tempted to tell her, just as she'd told her when she'd cut school, smoked marijuana, shoplifted, started having sex, and had her nipple pierced, simply for the somewhat masochistic pleasure of provoking her. She could hear the words in her mind: *I'm investigating a gang of monsters who are committing serial murders. And looking for this guy I like, praying I'll find him in one piece.*

Instead she said, "I'm doing what I told you. Visiting some of the people I met on-line."

"They're *weird*, aren't they?" said Mom accusingly. "They're into all that devil worship and astrology."

Astarte grimaced. "Yeah. They shot Kennedy and put fluoride in America's drinking water, too."

"What?"

"It's a joke, Mom. They're just people. They're nice." In a way, Astarte thought, it was too bad that the Arcanists weren't the sinister coven of warlocks her mother was imagining. Maybe then they'd have a better idea of how to cope with the current crisis. But the truth of the matter was that, despite years of dedicated study, Marilyn and her colleagues didn't seem to know much more about the paranormal than medieval physicians had comprehended about the true nature of disease. They hadn't even realized there was any such thing as a living werewolf until Astarte had escaped from Dunn to tell them so.

"If you stay away much longer," said Mom, "you're going to lose your job at the boutique. Why can't you come home?"

A bunch of reasons, Astarte thought, *even if none of them makes total sense. I can't just run away while there's any chance that Frank is still alive. I have to try to stop the Atheist murders—there's nobody else to do it, nobody who understands.* And despite all the horror she'd experienced, the supernatural still fascinated her. Even now, she couldn't quite let go of the notion that there was something there besides depravity and carnage, a transcendent reality of miracles and passion, and that if she could only become a part of it, she could leave the tedium and disappointments, the fundamental banality, of her mundane life behind.

"I don't want to come home yet," she said. "I don't care about my job. It sucks anyway. And I'm having a good time."

"I'll just bet you are," said Mom resentfully. "I've heard about New Orleans. It sounds like just your kind of place. And what do you care if I have trouble getting up and down the stairs?"

Astarte rolled her eyes. "You get up and down the stairs fine. You have for the last four years."

"You only think I do because you're never home, and when you are, I try not to be a burden. But never mind. I suppose I should let you go. I'm sure you feel that you've wasted enough time and money talking to me. And one of my stories is coming on."

"Wait!" Astarte said. "Don't hang up."

"What is it?" her mother said.

Once again, Astarte's mind insisted on framing the words she wouldn't say. *I called because I don't know if we'll ever get another chance to talk. The Arcanists and I are going to try to beat the bad guys, but deep down, I don't think it's going to work out. We don't even know how to protect ourselves, or where to turn next. We couldn't go to the cops even if Dunn weren't in the FBI. They wouldn't believe us. We can't go to Mr. Daimler and Miss Paris for more information. They've disappeared like they hinted they would. I'm afraid we're just going to flounder around like morons until the monsters find us and finish us off.*

She hesitated, then said, "I just wanted you to know that even though we've had some problems"—she swallowed—"I love you."

"My god," Mom said. For once the whiny note was absent from her voice. "You're in some kind of real trouble, aren't you? What is it, baby?"

Way to go, genius, Astarte thought. *Now she's going to worry.* "I'm fine, Mom. Take care of yourself, okay? Don't take any more pills than Dr. Wilson says." Blinking once again, she hung up the receiver.

SIX

As soon as the scene of the accident came into view, Karen Shaub sensed she had something more than a simple car crash on her hands. The yellow school bus with the text of John 3:16 painted on the side filled the middle of the intersection, its front fender crumpled and the tire beneath it flat. Its grille smashed, a sky-blue Buick sat adjacent to the bus, the fluid from its breached radiator staining the asphalt.

What made the situation look peculiar was that no one was standing near the damaged vehicles. There *were* spectators, but they were gawking from a distance, peeking from the windows of Spaulding's Feed and Hardware Store, the post office, and the diner.

Karen radioed the dispatcher, told him where she was and what was going on, then brought the patrol car to a stop a few feet from the accident. As she swung her long legs out the door, Ben Spaulding, with his round pink face and dainty little Don Ameche mustache, beckoned her frantically from the front window of his business.

She climbed out and gave him an inquiring look. Mouthing words she couldn't hear through the glass, he gestured as urgently as before. She decided she'd better go see what he wanted.

The aluminum barrels of feed made the whole store smell like grain. Tack and a selection of tools—axes, hammers, saws, and wire cutters among them—hung from the walls, while boxes and bottles of wormer, nails, molly bolts, pet shampoo, and flea collars lined the shelves. Spaulding met Karen at the door. His plump hands fluttered before him as if he wanted to grab her and snatch her inside. He did shove the door closed the instant she was clear of it. "Thank God he didn't shoot you!" he exclaimed.

"Who?" she demanded. "What are you talking about?" Was there a sniper taking potshots at people on the street? Was that why everyone was cowering indoors? The notion that she might have been wandering obliviously around with a gun trained on her made Karen's skin crawl.

"Reverend Arnold!" Spaulding said.

Karen frowned skeptically. "The pastor from First Baptist?"

Spaulding nodded vigorously. "He was driving the bus. It was full of kids. I guess he was taking them on some kind of outing. He came flying down the street like a bat out of hell, ran a red light, and Helen Macmillan hit him. She got out of her car, but he didn't. He just popped open the door, screamed something about demons, and shot a pistol at her."

Bizarre as the story sounded, given Spaulding's agitation, Karen had no choice but to believe it. "Did he hit her?" she asked.

Spaulding shook his head. "He took a couple shots at other people who happened to be on the sidewalk, but he didn't hit them either. Everybody ran into one building or another, and then you drove up."

"Where are the children?" Karen asked. "I didn't see anybody on the bus."

"They're still there," Spaulding said. "He must have made them hunker down below the windows."

"It's God's judgment," said a quavering voice with a kind of bitter relish.

Karen turned to meet Gertie Jackson's rheumy eyes, huge and wavering behind the lenses of the glasses she'd worn since her cataract surgery. The stooped old woman was clutching a bag of kitty treats in her shriveled hand.

"I beg your pardon?" Karen said.

"These modern preachers are all corrupt," Gertie said. "They steal and worship the devil and molest little children. You see it on television all the time. Well, the Lord's not going to put up with it. Some of them, He's killing. Others, He's driving crazy, so their wickedness will be plain for all to see."

Karen reflected that lately it was easy to understand how even a devout old woman in a little Southern town like Mayersville, Mississippi, could lose faith in the church, if not in God Himself.

But she had to get to work. "That's very interesting, Mrs. Jackson," she said, turning back toward Spaulding. "No one's called 911. If you had, the dispatcher would have told me what was going on here."

"No," Spaulding said, gesturing helplessly. "Everything happened so fast. I didn't think."

Karen put her hand on his forearm and gave the doughy flesh a reassuring squeeze. "It's okay. But I need to call now. I'm going to need back-up." She took a step toward the counter at the rear of the store, and then a gun barked. Spaulding yelped and jumped.

Karen turned and cracked open the door. As far as she could tell from her vantage point, no one had ventured out onto the street to give Reverend Arnold a target. Which might well mean he'd shot one of the children.

I can't wait for back-up, she realized. *I have to deal with this right now.*

"You make that call for me," she said. "Then everyone stay inside. Keep away from the windows." She drew her Smith and Wesson Model 659 from its holster and looked outside again, studying the bus. Still no one visible inside, but she had the unpleasant feeling that somehow Arnold was watching her, even though she couldn't see him.

I'll be okay, she told herself. *I've actually met the man, and I'm pretty sure he liked me. Once I caught him peeking at my chest. He won't shoot me if I don't make any threatening moves.*

It was a comforting notion. She wished she were certain it was valid. But if Arnold had gone as murderously crazy as those other preachers run amok, as opposed to suffering a garden-variety nervous breakdown, then no one was safe.

Karen took a deep breath, then stepped back out into the afternoon sunlight.

The doors were on the opposite side of the bus. She realized that she hadn't noticed whether either of them was still open when she was driving up. If not, would she be able to force her way in? How securely did a bus door latch, anyway?

Still scanning the windows of the vehicle for any flicker of movement, her mouth dry and her heart pounding, she began to edge around the nose of the church vehicle, sidling between it and Helen Macmillan's beached whale of a sedan.

It abruptly occurred to her that Arnold might have turned his gun on himself. But no. If the children were no longer being held prisoner, surely one of them would have shown himself by now.

Lucky me, Karen thought sourly. *After all, I did become a cop for the excitement, and I'm just about peeing adrenaline now.*

The bus doors came into sight. They were closed.

"Police officer!" Karen called, fleetingly gratified that, no matter how shaky she felt inside, her soprano voice rang out strong and steady. "It's Karen Shaub, Reverend. We met a few months ago, at the high school. Please, let me in. I'm here to help you. Whatever's wrong, I'm sure we can work it out."

"Go away!" shouted Arnold from somewhere in the bus. Karen couldn't pinpoint his exact location. The pastor's voice was too shrill. He sounded panicky.

"I can't do that," Karen said, grateful that at least he hadn't threatened to hurt the kids if she didn't back off. "But I just want to talk."

She pushed on the folding panels of the door. It didn't give, and if there was some easy way to pop it open from the outside, she couldn't see what it was.

With her fine bones and slender frame, Karen lacked the brawn of her male counterparts. Several of them had been kind enough to explain to her that that was one reason among many that women had no business being cops. But she'd learned to use what muscle nature had given her to good effect. Largely it was a matter of releasing her strength in one explosive burst, without flinching from the possibility of getting hurt. She flung herself at the door, ramming it with her shoulder.

It made a snapping sound and buckled. She yanked it aside, clearing herself a path, and smelled the tang of gun smoke. Keeping low, using the square steel divider in front of the first passenger seat for cover, she scrambled up the steps and peered down the aisle.

There seemed to be about twenty-five kids crouching on the floor. Some were merely white-faced and trembling, while others were weeping. If Arnold had shot one of them, Karen couldn't see the victim, but that didn't necessarily mean anything, not with the seats obstructing her view.

The pastor himself was sitting on the floor at the end of the bus with his back against the emergency exit. A thin, thirtyish man wearing spectacles with plastic clip-on tinted sun guards, the kind that swiveled up and down, a green Bible-camp polo shirt, and tan Dockers, he was clutching a .357 Desert Eagle in one unsteady hand and holding a blond little girl on his lap with the other. Karen couldn't tell if he was deliberately using the child as a human shield, but in any case, that was the effect.

"Go away!" Arnold repeated.

"I'm not allowed to," Karen said, "not until I'm sure everything's all right. I heard a shot just a minute ago. Are any of the children hurt?"

Arnold glared at her. "Of course not! Do you think I want to harm them? I'm trying to save them. This thing"—he gave the Magnum a distrustful look—"just went off of its own accord."

"That's an awful lot of gun," said Karen, "particularly if you aren't used to it. Maybe it would be a good idea to put it down before it goes off again."

Arnold sneered. "Right. Leave us all defenseless. You'd like that, wouldn't you?"

Karen suspected that, hiding behind the low metal wall, she must seem like a potential threat. If she wanted to win Arnold's trust, she needed to show herself. She put her pistol back in its holster. Then, trying not to imagine the hole the .357 could punch in her body, wishing she were wearing a Kevlar vest, she slowly rose and stepped up into the aisle.

"I'm not here to make you do anything you don't want to do," she said. "It's just that I don't get it. What do you need to be defended *from?* If you tell me, maybe I can help you. Protecting people is my job."

Arnold stared into her face for what seemed like a long time. At last he said, "I get the feeling you really aren't part of it. But I can't be sure!"

"I promise I'm not," Karen said.

"All right," Arnold said, grimacing. "I'll give you a chance. I have to try *something.* The bus won't start, and we can't just sit here. We have to get away."

"I can take care of that," Karen said. "I can get you transportation. But first I have to understand."

"Okay," Arnold said. "You know about the ministers going insane and killing people?"

A chill oozed up Karen's spine. "Yes."

"Well, they didn't want to do it. They were possessed. I know because for the past few days I've felt a demon trying to take control of me. Sometimes I can hear its thoughts, and I know that when it has me in its power, it's going to turn me into a murderer, too. It wants to make me hurt the children. That's why we all have to get away to somewhere the spirits can't find us."

Karen told herself that Arnold probably wasn't *really* suffering from whatever malady had afflicted his murderous colleagues. He only thought he was. Because the killers hadn't tried to explain their motives to anyone. They'd just done their damnedest to slaughter everyone within reach. Or, if he *did* have the same illness, he must have a milder case of it. Either way, it looked as if she might actually be able to talk him down, if she could exploit his twisted logic to her own advantage.

"Thank you," she said. "Now I see the problem. But if there's a chance a devil will take control of you, then you shouldn't be with the children, should you? It would be better to get you off somewhere by yourself."

Arnold shook his head. "Mayersville is *full* of demons. If I went away alone, they'd just possess other people. I think they've started already. I have to get the children out of town and away from the river."

Karen wondered fleetingly what the river had to do with it. "Okay," she said, "then that's what we're going to do." In the distance, sirens wailed. "Hear that? We've got more cops coming. Enough to drive you and the kids to safety. But for the time being, I'd feel better if you put down your pistol and got off the bus. Just in case. I can stand guard at the door."

Arnold stared at her. She couldn't read his expression. She wondered if she'd said something wrong. If he was psyching himself up to kill her.

"It's the only way," she told him. "I know cops. They won't listen to you as long as you're waving a gun around at a bunch of frightened kids. It'll keep you in town that much longer."

The minister gave her a jerky nod and set the Desert Eagle down. The pistol clinked against the metal floor. Karen shivered as some of the tension bled out of her muscles.

Arnold gently lifted the little girl off his lap and began to stand up. Karen's vision momentarily blurred, and numbness tingled through her body.

Arnold gaped at her. "My god," he whispered, "you *are* one!" Spinning, he made a dive for the Desert Eagle.

Fast and sure as a gunfighter in a Western movie, heedless of the children clustered all around the pastor, Karen whipped out her gun and shot him in the head. Arnold collapsed, convulsing in his death throes.

For a second the police officer thought she'd killed him reflexively but of her own volition. Then her body pivoted and she began to shoot the hostages.

At first she literally couldn't believe it was happening. Something this horrible could only be a nightmare. But no matter how awful it got, she couldn't wake up. Her hand just kept squeezing the trigger. The Smith and Wesson thundered, deafening in the close confines of the bus. Spent brass flew from the breech, and the smoke stung her eyes. Blood splashed, and her victims shrieked.

Finally she could deny the truth no longer. This *was* real. Arnold had been right, even if his insights had driven him a little nuts. There *were* spirits in Mayersville, intent on fomenting a massacre, and one of them had chosen to possess *her*.

Somehow she had to push the demon out. Regain control. *Go away!* she screamed. Not audibly—she could no more use her voice than she could direct the movements of her hands and feet—but inside her head.

When she did, she somehow established a murky contact with the alien mind inhabiting her flesh. Her silent cry gave it a pang of contemptuous amusement. It shot a little boy wearing a mustard-stained Power Rangers T-shirt in the stomach.

God damn you, get out! Karen bellowed. Concentrating fiercely, she willed the numbness away. Commanded her body to feel as if it belonged to her again. Suddenly the deadness gave way to flashes of heat and jabs of pain. She felt the devil's disdain change into surprise.

When she tried to throw the automatic down, she realized she hadn't regained complete control. The clash between her will and the demon's made her muscles spastic. Still, she managed to swing her arm and open her fingers. The weapon tumbled through the air and clanked down on the floor.

"Run!" she croaked. The kids hesitated for a moment. Then most of them scrambled toward the front of the bus, squirming past her and nearly knocking her down.

Karen felt the demon exerting its own willpower, fighting her for dominance. She struggled against it, but to no avail. And what else, she thought despairingly, could she expect? Her opponent was an evil spirit and she was just a human being. Until a few moments ago, she hadn't even comprehended that an atrocity like this was possible. It would have been a miracle if she'd stumbled on a truly effective way to resist.

The numbness flowed back into her limbs. The demon retrieved her Smith and Wesson, exchanged clips, then picked up Arnold's gun as well. It killed the three children who'd been too paralyzed with terror to flee when they'd had the chance, then headed for the door.

As the creature started down the steps, Karen caught a glimpse of her reflection in the chrome on the dashboard. Except for the spatters of gore on her dun-colored uniform, her trim body looked the same as ever. But the head on her shoulders was a scaly, misshapen horror, with two reptilian sets of jaws and pairs of blank amber eyes. The countenance of the monster who'd enslaved her, though she suspected no one else would be able to see it.

Siren keening and chase lights flashing, a second prowl car hurtled down the street. It came to a stop at the edge of the intersection, tires screeching. Ed Morse, a rangy black officer, and Charlie Frink, the watch commander, his coppery crewcut glinting in the afternoon sunlight, jumped out.

Karen tried to shout, *Watch out!* But of course her mouth refused to form the words.

Frink stared at her. "Shaub. God almighty, are you all right?" Then, evidently, something about her—or rather, the demon's—demeanor must have tipped him off that she was about as far from all right as a person could get. His eyes narrowing, he made a grab for his gun.

Inwardly, Karen cringed, expecting the spirit to shoot him. Instead, Morse, still standing on the far side of the car, whipped out *his* gun and fired across the roof. The bullets punched through Frink's skull and blasted chunks out of his face. The redheaded officer dropped.

The devil inhabiting Morse's flesh and the one inside Karen grinned at each other. Then Morse turned and headed for the diner, while Karen's body started toward the feed store.

Surely, Karen told herself, there was nobody left inside. Spaulding, Gertie, and the others should have seen the terrified children run off the bus. They ought to have at least some vague understanding that the police now posed a danger. By now they must be fleeing out the back door.

But she didn't believe it. Nothing else was going right. And she'd told Spaulding to keep people away from the windows. If they'd obeyed, they hadn't witnessed the events of the last two minutes. In which case someone probably *was* still inside, and the devil was about to get another chance to kill.

She had to stop the carnage. But she felt even less able to hinder the demon than she had previously. Her flesh felt even number than before, the link between her will and muscles even weaker. She wasn't certain that she could wrest control away from the spirit again at all, and even if she could, she was sure it would only be for a moment.

But, she suddenly realized, a moment might be enough, provided she picked the *right* moment. She prayed luck would send her the opportunity she needed.

The demon pushed the door and it opened without resistance. Karen winced. She should have told Spaulding to lock it, even though it would probably only have slowed the spirit down for a second.

Her body stepped into the fragrant, air-conditioned interior of the building.

Spaulding, Gertie, a pudgy teenaged employee dressed in a white apron, and a gaunt old farmer in faded bib overalls, his sun-damaged skin like brown, cracked leather, stood in front of the counter at the rear of the store.

"What happened out there?" Spaulding asked. Judging from his tone, he dreaded knowing the answer. "We heard a lot of shooting."

Karen felt her lips stretch into a smile. "You're going to hear some more," the demon said. Using both pistols at once, shooting from the hip, it opened fire. Karen wanted to interfere more than she'd ever wanted anything in her life, but she was all but certain it wouldn't do any good. She forced herself to wait, to stick to her pitiful excuse for a plan.

Gertie fell down. The others scrambled out of the central aisle, using the freestanding shelves for cover. The devil laughed and dashed after them.

For the next minute, the monster and its prey played hide and seek. Karen's body skulked down the aisles, looking, listening, doing its best to keep a watchful eye on the exits. At one point she heard the rubber sole of a sneaker squeak. The devil turned, and she saw that the boy had sneaked to within six feet of the front door. The spirit fired, hitting him in the small of the back, and he went down. It studied him for a moment, making sure he wasn't going to start moving again, then resumed its hunt for the others.

Karen heard stealthy movement in the next aisle over. Her body flung itself around the end of a shelf of grooming brushes. His eyes wide with alarm, the farmer scuttled away from her. The devil aimed the Magnum at his chest, and then its unwilling host heard rapid footsteps pounding toward her back.

The demon whirled. Ben Spaulding was rushing Karen, his plump, pleasant face contorted in a snarl, an ax upraised in his hands. The edge gleamed in the fluorescent light. A yellow price sticker adhered to the smooth oak handle.

It was the moment Karen had been waiting for. For a split second she quailed at the sight of Spaulding's makeshift weapon, then thrust her fear aside.

Don't think. Don't flinch. Just do it.

With one sudden, convulsive exertion of her will, she strove to regain control of her limbs. Perhaps she'd been passive long enough that the devil had assumed she'd given up. Perhaps she'd caught it by surprise. At any rate, pain and heat sizzled along her nerves, searing the deadness away. She felt connected to her flesh again.

She hurled herself forward. Spaulding squealed and swung the ax.

The moment seemed to stretch out for an eternity, the blade looming closer until it was all she could see. She imagined her eyes crossing in an effort to keep it in focus. Then the edged steel slammed into the center of her face.

To her surprise, there was no pain, not yet, but no instant oblivion either. She could feel the heavy, edged steel split her nose and skull and plunge into the tissue inside it. The simple awareness of her mutilation was as excruciating as any physical agony could have been. She yearned to escape it. To have the world go black.

As she dropped to her knees, she heard the demon's silent bellow of rage. The numbness began to flow back into her flesh. Her shaking arms lifted, trying to aim the pistols at Spaulding.

Karen sobbed. She shouldn't have to fight anymore, shouldn't have to exist inside this maimed, violated husk an instant longer. But she couldn't let the devil win, either. She struggled frantically to push her arms to the sides, drawing the guns out of line.

Meanwhile Spaulding tried to pull the ax out of her head. It was stuck, and his frenzied tugging hoisted her knees off the floor. Finally the tool flew free in a shower of gore. Still squealing, he chopped at her again and again, sometimes striking her skull, sometimes her shoulders, shearing off an ear, half severing her arms. Her spurting blood painted his garments red.

The demon screamed in frustration and then she felt it depart. Her shattered body was of no use to it anymore. Perhaps, had it remained, it might even have died with her. She tried to laugh at it, but by that time her jaw was nearly detached from her skull.

She sprawled face down on the wet, red concrete floor. Somewhere, someone else was shooting, a reminder that she hadn't really solved Mayersville's problem, just her own. There were other poor puppets still on the rampage. For a moment she regretted she hadn't been able to do more, wished she knew what the hell this madness was actually all about, and then darkness washed over her and carried her away.

SEVEN

Divested not merely of his insignia of rank but of every stitch of clothing, Montrose felt the unnatural chill of the Soulforges long before the glow of the fires themselves came into view. He did his best not to falter or change expression. He'd never lost his composure during his captivity and execution three hundred and fifty years ago—at least not according to Sir Walter Scott, John Buchan, and the other writers who'd romanticized his mortal career—and he saw nothing to be gained by losing it now. Pride was the only source of satisfaction left to him.

Reinhardt, walking at his side, gestured toward a narrow lane, scarcely more than an alley, that snaked away between massive stone buildings. "This way," he said.

The prisoner glanced over his shoulder, taking a last look at Stygia proper, ponderous, dark, and majestic, rising level on level across the channel. Then he walked deeper into the sprawling complex of warehouses, factories, barracoons, rail yards, and fortifications which, over the last century, the Hierarchy had constructed here on the mainland. The Artificers currently conducted the majority of their operations on this side of the water, an arrangement which suited everyone. It made it easier for the forgers to guard their secrets, and it allowed the squeamish to avoid contemplating the gruesome foundation of their realm's prosperity.

The uneven cobblestones cut Montrose's feet. His shackles clinked, and the boots of his guards creaked as they tramped along behind him. The Legionnaires seemed in high spirits. He wasn't surprised. He could remember a time when, gnawed by envy and ambition, he would have enjoyed participating in the downfall of a high-and-mighty Anacreon himself. He suspected he was lucky that Reinhardt had seen fit to escort him to the Artificers personally. Otherwise the soldiers might well have abused him.

The chill in the air grew even more intense. Montrose tried not to shiver or let his teeth chatter. He heard the hiss and crackle of flames, the rhythmic clank of hammering, and, once, a wail of anguish and despair. Then Reinhardt led him around another bend. A few paces farther on, the street ended at a tall, narrow iron door. Reinhardt pulled a chain dangling beside the frame. Montrose surmised it was a bellpull, though he didn't hear anything ring. After a few moments, a narrow panel slid open. Pale eyes, surrounded by skin burned sooty black, peered from the opening.

"I bring the Artificers greetings and instructions from the Smiling Lord," said Reinhardt, producing a scroll with a black wax seal from the folds of his inquisitor's mantle.

"How may we serve the Dread Lord?" the doorman asked. Judging from his tone, he wasn't inordinately impressed.

"This"—Reinhardt nodded at his prisoner—"is James Graham, Marquess of Montrose. An Anacreon of my order until he was found guilty of treason. Our master has condemned him to be forged."

The Artificer lifted an eyebrow. "Generally the Deathlords condemn traitors to more lingering deaths than that."

"He was a good Legionnaire once," Reinhardt said, "before his Shadow, or sheer ambition, led him astray."

"Well, we'll take care of him," said the Artificer, opening the door. Montrose observed that, contrary to his first impression, the craftsman hadn't dispensed with the Stygian custom of wearing a mask. A molded piece of some glass-like green material clung to the bottom half of his face, while a coin, the symbol of his guild, dangled from the chain around his neck. He wore a pistol on his wide black belt.

Reinhardt's eyes narrowed inside his riveted crimson visor. Montrose suspected that the doorman's casual attitude had irked him. "This isn't some mindless Drone," the Anacreon said. "You have to be careful with him. He's likely to try to escape."

The craftsman snorted. "Trust me, Anacreon, none of them escape. This place is better for that than a roach motel."

"Whatever that means," Reinhardt said sourly. Montrose hadn't understood the reference either. "I'd still recommend you carry out the Smiling Lord's command without delay."

"Sure," said the Artificer. "Whatever." He held out his hand and Reinhardt gave him the scroll.

Montrose favored his fellow Anacreon with a sardonic smile. "Was that last piece of advice absolutely necessary?" he murmured.

"In part, I was trying to do you a kindness," Reinhardt replied, his voice just as low. "It's better to get it over quickly. Apparently conditions in the holding pens—or wherever they keep you—are less than congenial. Good-bye, James."

The Scot gathered that he was about to be conducted into the forge. It was the moment he'd been waiting for. Perhaps now that he was leaving their custody, the Legionnaires would remove the leg irons, thus restoring his Harbinger abilities.

Unfortunately, they didn't. Evidently it wasn't the procedure, or perhaps Reinhardt was too wary. At any rate, he simply motioned the prisoner forward. The Artificer drew his gun—a Luger, Montrose observed—and stepped backward into the shadows, giving the condemned man room to slip through the entry.

Composure, Montrose reminded himself. He mustn't let his disappointment show in his expression. Head held high, he advanced into the building.

Beyond the door lay a small room, bare except for a stool, with a shadowy corridor leading away from it. The thump of the hammers and the whisper of the fires were louder and the air even colder than they had been outside.

The heavy door boomed shut behind him.

Montrose turned. The Artificer was pointing the Luger at his prisoner's chest. By all appearances, he knew how to handle it. "On down the hall," he said. "I'll tell you where to turn."

Montrose saw little choice but to obey. As he walked, he used his preternaturally keen hearing to gauge the Artificer's precise position. The craftsman stayed too far back. There was never a moment when Montrose could have whirled and landed a telling blow before his captor shot him.

The way led back and forth, past scores of branching passages, until it became clear the two wraiths were traversing a genuine maze. Finally multicolored light bloomed in the darkness ahead, wavering along the stonework, growing gradually brighter. Before long, Montrose was squinting. When he reached the end of the passage, he lifted his hand to shield his eyes.

Having done so, he found himself on the threshold of a huge, high-ceilinged chamber, where masses of barrow-flame blazed upward from wells and pits in the floor. Many of the fires were comparable to those employed by mortal blacksmiths. But some were considerably larger, while one, in the exact center of the room, blazed upward like some primordial tree. Noxious vapors hung in the air, stinging his eyes and throat.

Big or small, every blaze had at least one Artificer working beside it. Many of the smiths had skin seared the same sooty black as Montrose's escort. Some toiled bare to the waist or nude altogether, as if they no longer minded the bitter cold, or wanted to convince one another that they didn't.

Their labor, of course, was the grisly business that other Hierarchs preferred not to discuss, the practice that had outraged Heretics and Renegades for centuries, though their qualms seldom prevented them from availing themselves of the fruits of the guildsmen's labors. Beside each fire stood at least one jointed, counterbalanced metal rack, a contraption designed to immobilize a human body and position it at any desired attitude in the flames. Many of the victims hung limply in their bonds, their faces slack, or squirmed sluggishly. But a few thrashed and bucked, their eyes rolling wildly. No doubt, had it not been for the gray iron muzzles, they would have screamed.

When their substance grew glowing hot and malleable, the Artificers placed them on their anvils and began to shape them, pounding them with mallets, chanting incantations, drawing luminous strands of plasm with their forceps, and sometimes slicing a captive wraith into sections. Looking about, Montrose saw some prisoners who looked battered and crushed, but still essentially human, and others all but completely transformed into a selection of the necessities and amenities of Stygian existence: guns, chains, heaps of coins, silverware, artificial flowers. In the latter cases, there was only an occasional sign—a finger oozing from the side of a grandfather clock, a face forming and dissolving inside a propeller intended for some ship—that the article in question had once been an animate soul.

Were the rumors true? Were the transformed ghosts still sentient? Still suffering?

Montrose had no intention of finding out. Ever since his arrest, he'd been waiting for a chance to escape. Thanks to Reinhardt's vigilance, it had never come, and now he was out of time. But with a modicum of luck, he could provoke his captor into shooting him and dispatching him to the Void.

My *last battle*, he thought. He wished he could fight it with a rapier in his hand, and with one of his true enemies—Argyll, VanLengen, Gayoso, or Demetrius—on the other end of the blade. He drew a deep breath, steadying himself—a mortal tic he'd never quite managed to shake—and poised himself to spin around.

"That way," said the Artificer. "Through the doorway in the right-hand corner."

Surprised, Montrose looked in the indicated direction. The exit was a basket arch, the keystone carved in the semblance of Charon's mask. No fires shone in the darkness on the other side.

The Artificer chuckled. "Thought we were going to roast you right away, didn't you?"

"That was my understanding," Montrose said, turning to face his captor.

"Because the inquisitor said to?" The Artificer made a spitting sound. "You're on the guild's turf now, Red. *Nobody* tells us what to do inside these walls, nobody but our masters in the craft. Although to tell you the truth, I'm a cooperative guy. Ordinarily I *would* have chucked your ass on a fire by now. But I don't see a rack available, and we try not to interrupt a job in progress. It usually winds up wasting material."

"Thank goodness for a busy schedule," Montrose said.

The guildsman chuckled. "We'll see if you feel grateful in an hour. Now move it."

The Scot marched forward. Beyond the doorway he found another labyrinth, this one three-dimensional, incorporating a series of staircases and sloping passages. Though the two wraiths climbed upward fairly frequently, Montrose judged that, overall, they were heading down. Finally the way terminated in a natural ledge dimly illuminated by the bluish sheen of tiny phosphorescent crystals in the rock. A colossal, cantilevered machine with toothed jaws perched at the edge of the sheer drop. A crane for hoisting things up from the depths.

In the gloom, even a wraith's eyes could only make out a few individuals among the mass of spirits crowding the pit below. The ones nearest the cliff face appeared to be Drones, slumped motionless or shuffling pointlessly back and forth. But some of the noises echoing up from the cavern—whimpering, curses, mad laughter, the smack of fists battering flesh—attested to the fact that at least a few of the prisoners were still conscious and active, if not necessarily sane.

"Jump," the Artificer said.

Montrose blinked. He'd been expecting the guildsman to lower him with the crane, although on closer inspection, it did look as if it would be difficult for one man to operate the cumbersome apparatus and maintain control of a prisoner simultaneously. "How long a drop is it?" he asked conversationally. "Thirty feet? Don't you lose the occasional captive this way?"

"Only a few," said the Artificer, the blue light glinting on the muzzle of his Luger. "It's more efficient to dump you in this way than to waste the time of several workers doing it gently. You've got to understand, each prisoner is just a little chunk of raw ore. No one of them is important enough to worry about." He grinned through his transparent mask. "Not even you, O royal…marquis, was it?"

"Close enough," Montrose said. He peered over the ledge, looking for a clear piece of rocky ground to fall on. As soon as he spotted one, he leaped, before the random motion of the Drones could cover it over again.

When he hit bottom, he tumbled forward into a shoulder roll, the way his savate teacher had taught him. After he came to rest, the shock of the impact still singing through his body, he cautiously tried to move the various parts of his body. His limbs all performed as required. He was scraped and sore, but nothing seemed to be broken.

Fingers fumbled at his tangled tresses. Startled, he wrenched himself away from the touch and scrambled to his feet. The wraith who'd pawed him stumbled after him, hands outstretched. Lean and sun-bronzed, he had the face and form of a man in his twenties, and a bullet hole—probably a simulacrum of the wound that had killed him—in the center of his chest. "Mama, Mama," he moaned.

Montrose wondered if "Mama" had had wavy auburn hair. "I'm sorry," he said, "but no, I'm not."

The Drone continued forward. "Mama, Mama." He tried to enfold Montrose in a clumsy embrace.

The Scot pushed him back. The Drone tripped over his own feet and fell. Montrose hurried away as quickly as he could. With the leg irons, it wasn't all that fast, but the addled wraith didn't pursue him. He just lay on the ground and blubbered.

Montrose shivered with revulsion and the ghastly chill. For some reason the pit felt nearly as cold as the Artificers' forging chamber itself, as if, in some sense, the inmates were already burning in the freezing fires. Squinting against the darkness, he moved on, grimly intent on charting the precise dimensions of his predicament.

As he'd anticipated, the majority of the inmates did indeed seem to be somnolent Drones. Of the others, some sat sobbing uncontrollably, or, bright-eyed, babbled frantic insanities. Yet another contingent diverted themselves with the torture and rape of their fellows. At first Montrose managed to avoid the predators. Then a lean, crouched man glided out of the shadows. He had a bristling mane of hair like a porcupine's quills and disproportionately long arms. His teeth and nails had metamorphosed into glinting black fangs and claws. Montrose inferred that either the man had already been a Spectre when the Artificers had thrown him into the cave, or else the torments of his captivity had crushed his psyche and warped him into one.

"Fresh meat," said the Spectre, leering. "Bend over, meat. I might not kill you if you behave yourself."

"Back off," said Montrose, raising his fists.

"Too bad," said the Spectre. "And you were such a pretty piece of meat, too." He lunged.

Montrose twisted aside, remembering his shackles just in time to shorten his step and avoid stumbling. As his attacker plunged by, claws missing him by an inch, the Scot slammed the edge of his stiffened hand against the nape of his opponent's neck. Bone, or the ghostly equivalent, cracked.

The Spectre sprawled on his face. Intent on finishing him off, Montrose tried to dive on top of him.

Unfortunately his first blow hadn't hurt the servant of Oblivion as badly as he'd hoped. Just as he sprang, the Spectre scrambled to his knees, pivoted, and lashed out with his talons. The attack caught Montrose in midair, tearing open his belly and tumbling him to one side.

The injury paralyzed the Scot for a moment, and then the reflexes, the grim discipline of an expert combatant, blocked out the shock and the first swell of pain. He thrust up his hands just in time to keep the Spectre from leaping on top of him and pinning him.

Grappling, thrashing, the two fighters rolled over the ground. The Spectre bit at Montrose's head and shoulders and scrabbled at his torso. Finally the Hierarch managed to ram his knee into his assailant's groin.

The Spectre gasped and went rigid. Montrose grasped the creature's head—the quills rattled and pricked the palms of his hands—and dashed it against a rocky bump in the ground.

More bone crunched, and the Spectre's eyes rolled up in their sockets. Montrose kept pounding until waves of shadow began to sweep through the other wraith's flesh, washing it away into the Void. A few more seconds and it was gone.

Now that the fight was over, agony flamed in Montrose's stomach. He clutched at his middle, holding the wound together. He knew that, unlike a mortal, he didn't have any viscera to spill out of the breach, but even so, he couldn't resist the impulse.

He could feel a whimper swelling in his throat, pressing against his lips, struggling to escape. Pride barely sufficed to hold it in. Dignity didn't seem to matter so much without an audience capable of appreciating it, and all he had were the mindless and the mad. He wondered how long it would take for this hellish place to reduce him to their level.

Dear god, how had it come to this? When breathing, he'd embraced the lofty ideals of his family and church, and in consequence suffered betrayal and defeat. Disillusioned, as a wraith he'd followed a different path, committing himself to guile and ambition as fervently as he'd ever striven in the service of God and country. Yet here he was *again*, a condemned man awaiting an ignominious death, while somewhere his foes gloated over his ruin.

Perhaps it hadn't mattered what he'd done. Perhaps some inimical power had decreed it his destiny to suffer and to fail. If he were truly wise, he might as well abandon all hope of anything better and open himself to the lunacy festering all around him. It might be the only way to blunt the pain.

He felt his Shadow, quiescent since it had exhausted its strength possessing him back in the United States, stirring in the depths of his mind. *If you want to end the misery*, he seemed to hear it say, *just let go. Let me out. It will be just like falling asleep.*

"No!" Montrose shouted. He slammed his fist down on the cold, hard floor of the cave, using the shock to drive the terrible temptation out of his mind. Not long ago, he'd thought he'd be well on his way to becoming a belt buckle or a stack of oboli by now. Instead he was here, still in human form and, if scarcely free, at least no longer closely supervised by his captors. Luck had given him one more chance to save himself, and somehow he was going to take advantage of it. Because, despite the grimness and haunting incompleteness of being one of the Restless even at the best of times, on some fundamental level he still valued his existence. Because this time around, he wanted to *win*. And because someone should neutralize the dire threat Katrina had spoken of, and it didn't appear that anyone else was available.

The altruism of that last reflection bemused him. It seemed a sentiment more appropriate to the feckless mortal Montrose than his cynical wraith successor. But he supposed a fellow could purge himself of chivalrous delusions and still take a rational interest in defending the Hierarchy. After all, according to Stygian dogma, the Legions were the only force holding Oblivion at bay. And if the Void ever swallowed the universe, each and every inhabitant would perforce go along for the ride.

Checking his wound, Montrose saw that it had partially healed. He clambered to his feet and stalked on across the pit. As he approached the far wall, he heard something clink.

At first he mistook it for the faint clangor of the Artificers' hammers, audible even here. Then he discerned that the source was closer at hand.

He crept onward, bypassed another trudging, zombie-like Drone, and spotted a narrow hollow in the cavern wall. Within it sat a trio of wraiths, all shackled, methodically pounding their chains with pieces of stone. Four other captives lounged like sentinels before the opening. Two of the watchmen wore leg irons also.

These, Montrose surmised, must be the handful of his fellow captives who were neither Drones, Spectres, nor incapacitated by insanity or despair. They'd banded together for mutual defense and to plot their escape.

Delighted to discover them, the Scot strode forward. He opened his mouth to announce his presence, and then caught his first good look at the features of the slender, honey-blond woman sitting cross-legged at the back of the hollow.

He froze. Because the beautiful wraith was Louise.

Eight

Trembling, Montrose recalled that he himself had sentenced Louise to the Soulforges. The Legionnaires he'd assigned to take her to Stygia would of course have handed her over to Artificers laboring in the service of his and their own master. Thus her presence in this particular dungeon wasn't all that unlikely a coincidence.

But it was both an excruciating torment and a glorious opportunity for a second and more intimate revenge. He felt his mouth contort into a snarl or grin. His hands closed and opened repeatedly.

He vaguely remembered Katrina's admonitions. The Ferryman had foreseen that Montrose would encounter Louise. She'd warned him to be merciful. He hadn't, at least not merciful enough, and his indulgence of his lust for vengeance was, in large measure, what had enabled his Shadow to possess him.

But what did it matter now? The damage was done. At this point, surely he had nothing to lose by raping Louise and rending her flesh as he'd so desperately yearned to before.

No! That was a nonsensical thought, one his Shadow had insinuated into his mind. If he charged out of the darkness and attacked the bitch, her comrades would defend her. They might well destroy him, and even if they didn't, they'd never permit him to join them.

Still, to have his betrayer screaming and thrashing helplessly beneath him, to grind his fingers into her eyes—

He wrenched himself around, blocking out the sight of her, and clawed at the half-healed wound in his belly, tearing open the bloodless white lips of the cuts. The flashes of pain cleared his head to a degree.

When he felt more or less in control, he took a deep breath, let it out slowly, and turned back around.

As soon as he glimpsed her, he felt his muscles tensing, the anger building. Clamping down on it, struggling to smile, he marched forward. "Hello," he called.

The wraiths snapped around and peered at him warily. He realized that from their perspective, neither a human face nor a calm demeanor would guarantee that a stranger wasn't a Spectre or dangerously insane. It was quite possible there were Doppelgängers, minions of the Void all but indistinguishable from ordinary ghosts, roaming the pit, and some lunatics appeared rational at first acquaintance.

Louise gasped.

At her reaction Montrose realized that, muddled by hatred and the blandishments of his dark half, he *still* wasn't thinking rationally. He'd overlooked the fact that Louise was his enemy as much as he was hers. And in all likelihood her friends were Renegades and Heretics too, rebels who'd harbored a bitter hatred for Hierarchs even before their imprisonment. Once she'd identified him as a disgraced Anacreon, she shouldn't have any trouble persuading them to tear him apart. He halted, poising himself for flight.

A scrawny man with sharp, intelligent features, one of the two unencumbered by a chain, gave Louise an inquiring look. "You recognize this palooka, my little crumb cake?"

Louise stared at Montrose for several seconds. He couldn't read her expression. Finally she said, "It's James Graham, isn't it? From that Renegade Circle in Cincinnati."

After a moment's hesitation, Montrose said, "That's right."

"Small Underworld," said the skinny man. "No wonder it's so hard to find a clean rest room. Then I take it the guy's okay?"

"Yes," said Louise.

"Too bad," said the other prisoner. "I hate his hair. He looks like he's got a hunk of cotton candy growing out of his neck." He favored Montrose with a leer. "But what the hey, we'll lower our standards. Welcome, Jimmy. Welcome to our little chapter of the Iron Hills Nudist Association and Future Knickknacks of Stygia. You can call me Artie. Comedian extraordinaire and the slickest abolitionist who ever helped a runaway Thrall along the Underground Railroad, even if my career is in a teeny bit of a slump at the moment." Pointing, he introduced the rest of his companions, coupling each name with a humorous insult.

Still half expecting Louise to denounce him, Montrose walked forward. "I'm honored to meet you all," he said, glancing at his new companions' shackles. Despite the hammering, they were unmarked. "I saw you pounding on your chains. I gather that you aren't entirely reconciled to a future as knickknacks."

"*Au contraire*," said Artie. "I've always had a fantasy about being reborn as a vibrator, a French tickler, or even a humble dildo. People have told me there's already a resemblance. But still, yeah, we have been known to kick around the possibility of escape. You never know, the Artificers *might* turn us into suppositories."

NINE

The drumming throbbed through Bellamy's head. If he hadn't known better, he might have imagined he still had a heartbeat. The words of the chanted litany tugged at his attention, and vague images drifted through his head. Monkeys chattering in a tree. Huge gray elephants on a dusty yellow plain. Towering, shadowy figures—Orishas, living gods, or so he'd been informed—striding through darkness. And the Queen of New Orleans, a slender, striking woman with amber eyes and skin like polished ebony, whom he'd seen only once in reality. In his vision she sat straight and severe on her ivory throne, invested with at least a portion of the majesty of the deities who had supposedly anointed her.

The prisoner beside Bellamy moaned and swayed. Her eyelids fluttered as she succumbed to the spell of the ritual. Bellamy struggled to stay alert while pretending he'd gone under. He scrutinized the drummers, priest, and guards, awaiting his chance.

So far, existence as a ghostly Thrall was nothing like he might have imagined. Logically, a slave should expect to be put to hard labor, but it seemed that, in a place with a paucity of material objects and little industry, a realm where the inhabitants didn't even require food, there wasn't an excess of tangible work to do. Rather than being forced to toil, Bellamy and his fellow unfortunates were receiving an indoctrination intended to make them revere the Queen and believe in the mythology which legitimized her authority.

At first Bellamy had thought the brainwashing was simply intended to make new slaves docile. Then he'd overheard one of the priests remark that their devotion would give the Queen and her agents a kind of magical strength. The notion didn't make a lot of sense to him, but then, nothing else about being dead did, either.

Letting his head nod toward his chest, peering through slitted eyes, he watched the nearest guard slump and nearly drop his spear. The FBI man hastily checked the rest of the captors. They all looked at least a little spaced out, too. That was the problem with the drum magic. It was so hypnotic that even its makers could find themselves slipping in and out of a trance.

Bellamy had taken pains to make sure he wound up standing at the rear of the room. Now he stepped backwards, into the wall. He hoped that, as dark and crowded as the chamber was, no one would notice his absence for some time.

He lurched around. The space he'd entered had no lamps or candles burning, but a bit of faint gray light leaked in from somewhere. Barely sufficient for the hypersensitive eyes of a ghost—or *ibambo*, to use his captors' word—the illumination revealed he was alone in a small, musty-smelling room. A web of jagged Nihil cracks hissed in the far corner.

Bellamy sat down on the floor and attacked the coarse rope hobbling his ankles. At one point the complex knots had been so tight, so resistant to tampering, that he suspected that they, like nearly everything else in this ghastly place, contained some sort of sorcery. But he'd been struggling with them relentlessly since the last time a guard had checked them, and after a minute or two, they yielded.

Rising, he started to toss the rope aside, then stuffed it in his pocket instead. It might come in handy, and in any case, any object which existed on the ghostly side of the Shroud had value. He'd begun to learn that lesson only minutes after his death, when his captors had plundered his belongings. In retrospect, he supposed he'd been lucky they'd permitted him to keep his shirt and jeans.

He crept to the door and cautiously pushed his face through the panel. No one was in the corridor on the other side, though a single barrow-flame lamp radiated wan greenish light and chill from a sconce on the wall, a warning that the Queen's people did traverse this part of the huge old house from time to time. Intent on escaping the ruinous mansion—once, he'd been advised, the palatial home of a filibuster, an entrepreneur who'd fomented revolution in South America to line his own pockets—Bellamy slipped through the substance of the door and glided on down the hall. The floor was cold and gritty beneath his feet.

Actually, the corridor was an option, not a necessity. He could move through one wall and one space after another until he reached the outdoors. But he'd discovered that, novice ghost that he was, each passage through Skinlands matter took a modest toll on his strength. Besides, he was afraid of stepping through a wall and finding himself in the midst of a group of his captors. Whereas skulking down a hall, he should be able to spot trouble from a distance.

Murky portraits of smug robber barons, their dull-eyed wives, and their sullen children regarded him from amid the peeling wallpaper. The drums and chanting still pulsed at his back, while vermin scratched along behind the wainscot. For a moment the memory of some terrible grief jangled his nerves, sickening and invigorating him at the same time. He'd learned that suffering left a residue in the places where it occurred, an energy from which ghosts derived vitality. The knowledge revolted him. It made him feel as much of a vampire as Daimler or Miss Paris.

The corridor led him to a large parlor with a dusty marble mantelpiece. A crystal chandelier hung lopsided, looking as if its weight was gradually dragging it loose from the ceiling. Drop cloths covered the furniture. A rank odor revealed that mice had nested in the cushions of a nearby sofa.

Bellamy peered warily into the open area. Nothing stirred. He started forward.

And *then* something moved, a long, low shape which, in the gloom, he'd mistaken for an ottoman or a table. Its four stubby legs carried it forward with startling speed. Its striped, pointed tail swished along the moldering carpet. Slit-pupiled eyes gleamed behind its scaly snout. Absurdly, it had a bandanna printed with the same zebra-stripe pattern as the capes of the Queen's soldiers tied around its neck.

It's a gator, Bellamy thought. And since it wasn't surrounded by an outline of flickering, multicolored light, the signature of life, the creature evidently existed in the Shadowlands. He'd seen other wraiths who'd used magic to change their appearances, acquiring skull faces or the spotted pelts of leopards, but never one who'd so thoroughly dispensed with the human form. Heck, the gator didn't even have *hands*. Still, he couldn't imagine what else the beast could be.

Bellamy began to backpedal. The alligator hissed. It was clearly a warning, and the fugitive froze.

"Who are you?" the reptile asked. His rasping, guttural voice was nearly as intimidating as his hiss.

Bellamy didn't want to answer truthfully for fear that the gator would recognize his name as that of one of the new slaves. "Bill Dunn," he replied.

The other spirit made a rhythmic barking sound. It took Bellamy a moment to realize the noise was laughter.

"Poor little Lemure," the gator said. "You don't know what you're dealing with. You can't fool Antoine, warmblood. Animals don't lie to themselves, so no one else can lie to them either. Bare feet. Rope marks on your ankles. You smell like a runaway to me."

Bellamy shifted his weight, poising himself for a dash through the right-hand wall.

"Don't try," said the gator. "I guarantee you, I can run you down and rip your legs off. Or better yet, *do* try. I could use the exercise." Though he suspected it was anatomically impossible, Bellamy could have sworn that Antoine's toothy grin stretched a little wider.

"Okay," the fugitive said. "You got me. My real name is Frank Bellamy. I'm an FBI agent."

"Were," said Antoine. "You *were* an FBI agent. It's over now. You don't learn that, you're in for a hard time."

Antoine's remark triggered a swell of misery, which Bellamy struggled to quell. That was how he'd kept his sanity, by refusing to think about all the precious things his death had cost him. "I can't let it be over yet," he said. "I have unfinished business."

The alligator bobbed his head and flexed his front legs. Bellamy realized that the combination of movements was supposed to be a shrug. "Join the club. People who die happy don't wind up in the Underworld."

"But my business is important," Bellamy said. "I died chasing a serial killer called the Atheist." If Antoine had heard about the case, he didn't show it. "I found out that there's really more than one murderer. There's a whole conspiracy, and at least some of the members are ghosts and werewolves." The gator cocked his wedge-shaped head. Bellamy wondered if he'd managed to pique his interest. "And I think the crimes they've committed so far are only the start of something bigger. God knows how many people they might kill if I don't find a way to stop them."

"Death doesn't look like such a big deal from this side of the Shroud," Antoine said. "Still, maybe you should tell one of your trainers."

"I tried. She didn't care."

The gator shrugged again. "Well, so much for that, then, and when you get right down to it, why should we care? Nobody's paying us to watch over the Quick. We have our own problems."

"I've picked up on that," said Bellamy, though he hadn't grasped the details. The priests were intent on painting the Queen as wise and powerful, not on delineating her weaknesses. "But don't you see, if there are ghosts involved in the Atheist killings, maybe everybody's problems are connected."

"Got any proof of that?" Antoine asked.

"No," Bellamy admitted, "but I feel it." In its way, the intuition was as compelling as his dreams of the dark metropolis on the island, the dreams which, as Daimler had warned him, had predicted his death.

The reptile shook his head. "That won't cut it. Some *abambo are* psychic, but the Queen's already got more hot-shit soothsayers and root doctors than you could shake a stick at. Nobody's going to care about your hunches."

"Maybe not," Bellamy said. "But when I died, the girl I love was in terrible danger. I don't know what happened to her. If she's still alive, she may need my help. And I'm just one lousy prisoner. What does it really matter if I escape? So I'm begging you, just pretend you never saw me. I swear to God—to the Orishas, if you want—I'll never tell anyone you helped me."

"Suppose I did let you go," said Antoine. "Do you think you could survive on the streets of the Necropolis all by your lonesome? Let's give you a little quiz. What am I?"

"You're a ghost like me," said Bellamy, "except that a flesh sculptor has given you a makeover."

Antoine brayed, a harsh, derisive screech. After a moment Bellamy realized the creature was imitating a buzzer on a TV game show. "Wrong, warmblood. I *am* a wraith, but not like you. I'm the ghost of a real live bayou alley-gator."

Bellamy peered at Antoine uncertainly. Since the night of Waxman's death, he'd begun to grow accustomed to unnatural creatures and deadly miracles, but for some reason, talking animals, like characters out of a cartoon or a Dr. Seuss book, were just too much to swallow. "You're pulling my leg. Aren't you?"

"Not yet," Antoine said. "That's why it's still attached. Now, why do you suppose you haven't seen a critter like me before?"

Bellamy shook his head. "I don't know."

Antoine made the buzzer noise. "Different places—different belief systems, according to some of the eggheads—serve up different kinds of dead people. In the African Shadowlands, you get as many animal *abambo* as human. On Stygia's turf, you don't get any. By treaty, on the cold side of the Shroud, New Orleans is part of Africa, what the pinhead Hierarchs call the Dark Kingdom of Ivory, and it *should* operate by African rules. But the rest of North America is Stygian, and their reality bleeds into ours, so this burg only gets a few four-legged wraiths. See?"

Bellamy supposed it did make a crazy kind of sense, if a person was willing to forget everything he'd ever been taught about science. Even so, it didn't explain everything. "But how can the ghost of an animal talk and think like a human?"

Antoine snorted. "Watch your mouth, chump. I *don't* think like a two-legger, and I'll gut anyone who says otherwise. As for the talking, well, the hoodoo men say that live animals used to be able to do it. But then one of them let death loose in the world, and as punishment, the Old Gods took their speech away. Sounds like racist propaganda to me, but who knows, maybe it happened just that way.

"Anyway, the point of this little talk is to show you you don't know squat about being dead. You can't help your girlfriend. You couldn't even survive on your own. Here, you're protected, so you'd better calm down and get with the program."

"Maybe you're right," Bellamy sighed. He let his shoulders slump, doing his best to appear beaten and dejected, then spun and sprinted toward the wall.

He heard Antoine scramble after him. The gator's jaws snapped shut on his leg. As he pitched forward, he felt a flash of pain, and heard something snap. His body became intangible when his flailing hands struck the wall, and he fell with the top half of his body in the next room and the bottom half still in the parlor. But the transformation didn't free him from Antoine's grip.

The reptile wrenched him back through the wall. His eyes blazing, he seemed wholly a beast and a savage predator now. Thrashing helplessly, his injured limb on fire, Bellamy was certain his captor would rip his legs off as promised.

Instead Antoine released him and shuffled backward, creating a space between them. He glared at Bellamy for several moments, then rasped, "You shouldn't tempt me, boy. When I was breathing, all I cared about was eating. I miss it. But I'm not a damn Mla Watu. I won't send you to the Void just for the fun of filling my belly."

Bellamy tried to shift his body into a more comfortable position. Another lance of pain stabbed through his leg, and he grunted.

"There's emotion flowing all through the house," Antoine said. "That's why we stay here. Open yourself up to it, and it will heal you."

Bellamy tried. He imagined the echo of suffering he'd felt before, and strained to sense it again. After a few seconds, a sort of pleasurable misery crawled along his nerves. He wondered if masochists like Marilyn felt something akin to this when they were being punished. His leg gradually straightened, and his bloodless lacerations closed, until only the rips at the bottom of his pant leg remained to show that he'd ever been injured.

"Thanks for the tip," he said.

"I didn't do it to help you," Antoine replied. "Do you think I wanted to drag you back to your keepers, tasting you every step of the way? I don't need that kind of frustration. Now get up. You're going home."

Bellamy cautiously rose and tested his leg. It was still a little sore, but it would support his weight without any problem. He started to trudge toward the pulsing sound of the drums. He heard the huge alligator fall into step behind him.

"Why did they make me a slave?" the human asked. He no longer had any real hope of playing on his captor's sympathies, but on the other hand, he had nothing to lose by continuing to try. "I didn't do anything wrong, and I'm pretty sure you people don't enslave every Enfant or Lemure who comes along."

"Some newcomers have *ibambo* friends and relatives to sponsor them," Antoine replied. "Others manage to stay free until it's obvious that, one way or other, they've learned their way around. You didn't fall into either of those categories. Plus, it probably didn't help that you're white. A lot of the Queen's people were slaves back before the Civil War, when they were breathing. Some of them are still holding a grudge."

Bellamy grimaced. "Don't you see that isn't fair?" As they proceeded down the hall, the clattering of the drums grew louder.

"'Fair' is a human idea," Antoine said. "One of the ones that don't have jack to do with the way the universe really works. Look, I'm a pumped-up lizard. And you're right, when I was alive, I *couldn't* think, not the way I do now. I didn't feel guilt or ambition or regret. I was just barely conscious of the fact that I was an individual being, distinct from the rest of the world. Tell me, how can a dumb hunk of meat like that have any 'unfinished business?' It can't. So how come I got stuck in this cold, dark place, always hungry and never able to eat?"

"I don't know," Bellamy said.

"Neither does anybody else," the reptile said. "Because there isn't any reason. Bad things just happen, and there usually isn't anything you can do about it. Existence is a whole lot easier if you accept that, and just float with the current. Forget about your mortal problems and try to fit in. Convince somebody to teach you an Arcanos, so you can make yourself useful. In a few years someone might give you your freedom. Or they might swap you to the Stygians in exchange for—"

The drumming stopped, not with the usual flourish, but raggedly, as if the musicians had been interrupted. Then the screaming and the gunfire began.

TEN

"We're going to go through that gray door up there," Antoine said, "so I can peek through the wall of the room on the other side. We're going to hurry, but we're going to be quiet. Got it?"

Bellamy nodded. "I know the drill."

"You try to run or give me any other kind of hassle and I *will* rip your legs off, warmblood. I guarantee it."

"I understand," Bellamy said. He stalked forward, and the gator shambled after him.

Beyond the gray door was a small room with Spartan furnishings: a single bed, a straight-backed chair, and a dresser with a porcelain bowl and pitcher sitting on top. A faded pink ribbon tied around one of the bedposts provided the only touch of color. Bellamy suspected that the room had belonged to a servant. For a moment another thrill of vicarious suffering froze him shivering in his tracks. He could almost see a thin black girl lying on the bed with her face buried in the pillow, sobbing with loneliness; could almost catch the moist mucus smell of her weeping.

Antoine didn't react to the echo of misery, perhaps because, familiar with every room in the sprawling house, he'd been expecting it. He twisted his head to the side, evidently so he could peek beyond the wall without thrusting the entire length of his snout through it, a maneuver that would scarcely have been conducive to stealth. He stuck one eye into the wainscot, then pulled it out instantly. "Shit!" he growled.

Bellamy hurried to the wall and pushed his own face through. He found himself peeping into the hallway that led to the brainwashing room. Several yards away, two hideous creatures crouched over the motionless bodies of three hobbled slaves, ripping at them. One of the monsters looked somewhat manlike, but with a blank, bald, featureless head like an egg, and sores and boils constantly opening, swelling, and bursting all over its gaunt, naked body. Unlike the dry wounds of the average wraith, these wept blood and greenish pus. The other creature resembled a robotic spider cobbled together from a thousand rusty pieces of scrap metal, but with the prominent, serrated forelimbs of a praying mantis.

Waves of blackness washed through the Thralls, and then they melted away. The two monsters scuttled around a corner, toward the sounds of further fighting.

Bellamy pulled his face back through the wall. Antoine gazed up at him. The FBI agent felt that he could virtually read the gator's mind. Antoine was thinking that he couldn't keep track of his prisoner and defend the Haunt at the same time.

The reptile grunted and crawled through the wall.

Bellamy shook his head, almost dazed by his good fortune. The sneak attack, if that was what was going on, had given him a second chance to escape. Pivoting, he took a step toward the gray door, and another shriek of anguish reverberated through the derelict mansion. Thinking of the poor people he'd seen in the corridor, being clawed and hacked until their bodies crumbled into what wraiths called the Final Death, he faltered. He realized that a part of him didn't want to run away. It wanted to stay and fight the demons.

He scowled. That sentiment was a brainless, inappropriate impulse, birthed by the same protective instincts that had prompted him to become a cop. But unlike ordinary, law-abiding citizens, the Queen's people didn't deserve protection. By kidnapping and imprisoning him, by trying to indoctrinate him as if he were a recruit in some demented cult, they'd proved they were criminals themselves.

Except that that wasn't quite fair. They hadn't broken any laws. Vile as their actions seemed to him, they were only following the customs of their own grim world, and most of them hadn't been *gratuitously* cruel in their treatment of him. Besides, the invaders were slaughtering his fellow captives, too, and they truly were innocent victims. How could he abandon them to die?

Because Astarte was in danger! And compared to her safety, the welfare of the slaves simply didn't matter.

He blinked. That last thought and the accompanying burst of emotion felt...exaggerated, hysterical, partially alien, as if something had inserted them in his mind. Since his capture, a fellow slave more knowledgeable than himself had explained that the Doppelgänger he'd encountered in the cemetery had most likely been a manifestation of his shadowself, a mad, self-destructive aspect which festered inside every *ibambo*. Maybe the same entity was trying to influence him now. Perhaps it wanted him to run away because it thought that would be the wrong or the dishonorable thing to do.

He felt something writhe in the depths of his psyche, a giveaway that his suspicions had been correct. Doing his best to ignore the loathsome sensation, he slipped through the wall.

Except for himself, the corridor was empty. Cries, shots, thuds, and the twang of bowstrings echoed from several directions. It sounded as if the attackers and defenders were fighting throughout the house. It occurred to him that a battle between adversaries who could advance and retreat through walls could easily break up into a series of small, desperate duels and deadly games of hide-and-seek.

He suspected that his best chance of surviving this madness would be to hook back up with Antoine, and that the alligator might well have trailed the junk spider and the faceless man on down the hall. Wishing he had a gun, he crept in that same direction.

A foul smell tinged the air. The stink of the faceless man's sores, Bellamy suspected. He peeked around the corner. He didn't see anyone in the next section of hallway, either, but after a moment, Antoine's hissing roar reverberated from somewhere ahead.

Bellamy sprinted forward. Skidding around another bend, he saw open double doors, and beyond the threshold, a table covered with a miscellany of ritual objects: gourds, rattles, tom-toms, masks, whisks, and bones. Struggling figures blundered back and forth around the table. A man in a striped cape wailed, fighting with the miraculous voice powers a few *abambo* possessed, until a creature like a skeleton cloaked in seething vapor rammed a black shortsword into his back. The jagged claws of the junk spider snapped another soldier's head off his shoulders.

Scrambling forward, Bellamy snatched someone's fallen Vz.58 off the floor. As he darted through the door, he saw Antoine snapping at a vaguely humanoid figure armored in quills like a porcupine. A number of the long magenta spines had broken off and stuck in the reptile's jaws. The bristly figure was trying to chop Antoine with a double-edged ax, while the mist-enshrouded skeleton was skulking up behind him.

Bellamy lifted the assault rifle and fired at the bone-and-smoke monster. The black crystals embedded in the weapon sparkled. The bullets blasted the skeleton off its feet, but it leaped up again and charged him, sword upraised.

Bellamy caught a whiff of its veil of vapor, a sharp ammonia stench that stung his nose. As the creature lunged into striking range, he began to dodge, but, then, at last, the gunfire took its toll. The monster's ribs and spine blew apart, and it clattered to the floor in fragments. These immediately began to fade away, but without black waves of Oblivion pulsing through them.

The FBI agent turned back toward Antoine. The gator and the porcupine creature were entwined together, thrashing around on the floor. Behind them, at the far end of the room, the junk spider gripped in its mandibles a scrawny old man with a painted face. The victim screamed as the metal monster dragged him backward into the wall.

Bellamy started after the spider, then glimpsed a flash of light from the corner of his eye. He spun around. A demon with the body of a voluptuous woman and the head of a malformed baboon ran at him. A halo of golden flame surrounded each of her hands.

Bellamy fired at her. The Vz.58 chattered and then fell silent, out of ammunition. The baboon woman kept coming, her blazing hands poised to seize him.

He sidestepped and tried to club her. Pivoting at the same instant, she grabbed the rifle, wrenching it out of his hands, and flinging it aside, and pounced on him.

The impact knocked him down. He thrashed, battered her with knees and elbows, trying to get away, while she clutched at him. He realized she was trying to set him ablaze. Her crackling flames were searing hot, not cold like barrow-fire.

Her fingers knotted in the fabric of his shirt. He felt the skin beneath it charring. A line of yellow flame oozed upward toward his shoulder.

Then something ripped her off him. As he slapped frantically at his shirt, extinguishing the fire, he saw that Antoine had seized her in his jaws and was lashing her this way and that, breaking her body. Her bones snapped, and finally his teeth cut her into two pieces. One fell to the floor. He tossed his head, casting away the other.

"You all right?" he rasped.

"I think so," Bellamy replied.

Before he'd even finished, the gator was turning, surveying the room, where, the human observed, the fighting had come to a end. The monsters had all perished or withdrawn, leaving a litter of wounded wraiths on the floor. "Damn it!" Antoine said. "I think they got Titus!"

"Who's Titus?" Bellamy asked, drawing himself to his feet. Gunfire and the twang of crossbows still sounded elsewhere in the house. He picked up the skeletal creature's shortsword and stuck it in his belt.

"One of the root doctors," Antoine said. Giving his head a shake, he managed to dislodge some of the quills still stuck in his gums. "One of the most powerful ones we had. I wouldn't be surprised if killing him was the point of the whole raid."

"Was he a bald old man with one half of his face painted red and the other black?"

"Yeah," Antoine said.

"Then they didn't kill him," Bellamy said. He retrieved a fallen pistol and ejected the clip, making sure it still contained ammo, then slammed it back into the gun. "At least, not in here. He was still okay when the metal spider carried him through the wall."

"Then I've get after him pronto," Antoine said, "before they do hurt him."

It occurred to Bellamy that here was a second chance to slip away, but this time he didn't feel even mildly tempted. He suspected the excitement of combat had made him stupid. "Let's do it," he said.

ELEVEN

When they reached the street, Bellamy discovered it was night. Imprisoned in the mansion, he hadn't been able to tell. Hissing faintly, Nihils cracked and pocked the ruinous facades of the old houses. Still not entirely used to the patina of decay the Shroud cast over the world of the living, he winced. Somewhere to the north, a dog was barking. Tinny jazz and rock music sounded from the direction of Bourbon Street, and a warm breeze carried the mud-and-pollution smell of the Mississippi.

Bellamy peered warily up and down. He couldn't see any sign of the junk spider, or any other monsters, for that matter. "Do you have any idea which way to go?" he asked.

"I will in a second." Antoine hunkered down, his posture suggesting intense concentration. Bellamy wondered if the alligator was working some sort of magic. After several moments Antoine said, "Damn it."

"What's wrong?" Bellamy asked.

"Another of those damn quills," Antoine said. "In the back of my tongue. It hurts so much I can't think. Can you get it?" He opened his jaws wide.

Trying not to think about his companion's profound hunger for meat, Bellamy reached deep into his cavernous mouth, gripped the offending object, and tugged it out.

"Thanks," Antoine grunted. He crouched down, and his eyes narrowed. Eventually he nodded toward the river. "The spider took him that way."

They started walking. Gripping his pistol, Bellamy peered ahead, watching for the enemy. "How do you know this is the right way?" he asked, pitching his voice low. He didn't want the spider to hear them coming.

"I smell—and taste—the nasty hot metal of the monster's body," Antoine said. "I smell old Titus, too, except that I'm not *really* smelling them. It's a trick, like an Arcanos, except that nobody had to teach me. I just have the knack." He paused. "I didn't expect to see you again so soon. Why aren't you out looking for your girlfriend?"

"I don't know, exactly," Bellamy said. "I felt sorry for you guys, being attacked by monsters. You enslaved me, but at least you're people." *More or less*, he added silently. "And I sensed that my shadowself wanted me to abandon you, so I figured I should do the opposite." He frowned. "Although now that I think about it, it could have been faking me out with reverse psychology."

Antoine snorted. "That's the worst thing about being one of the Restless. Knowing that a part of your own mind has turned against you. You can never trust even your own ideas and feelings, let alone anybody else."

"How do you stand it?" Bellamy asked.

"I don't know that anybody does," Antoine said somberly, "not over the long haul. Maybe the Void swallows us all in the end, when we run out of the will to carry on."

Bellamy grimaced. He saw no point in dwelling on such a depressing notion, particularly when there were practical issues to consider. "I'd like to hear about the Queen's problems now, considering that we seem to be chasing one of them."

A soft, scuffing sound issued from the shadows ahead. The two hunters froze until a flicker of orange and silver light appeared, outlining the body of a wizened old Quick woman in a long, filthy coat. She tottered out of an alley with a plastic grocery bag stuffed with rags and trash dangling from either hand. The breath wheezed and whistled in her throat, and to Bellamy's horror, he could see a lumpy black mass inside her chest, just as if he had X-ray vision. He realized it was a tumor that would eventually kill her.

Discerning that the bag lady had nothing to do with their search, Antoine slithered forward. "I *think* the Queen's problems come down to one man," he said, "an *ibambo* named Geffard."

Bellamy tore his gaze away from the sick woman. "Who's that?" he asked. "Somebody who wants to be King?"

"Bingo," said Antoine, "but there's more to it. I told you that New Orleans is part of Africa."

"Uh huh," Bellamy said. For a moment, he thought he smelled a putrid odor, something distinct from the complex stench of garbage and wood rot that enveloped this rundown section of the French Quarter, but when he inhaled deeply, it was gone.

"Well, there's another country, another culture, another *reality* of ghosts based in the Caribbean," Antoine said. "In Haiti and places like that. Not all that different from the Queen's gang, but not exactly like them either. We call ourselves *abambo*, and they call themselves Les Invisibles. We bow down to the Orishas, and they worship spirits called Les Mystères." He stopped for a moment, then led Bellamy around a corner and down a street even narrower and shabbier than the one they'd been following. Many of the crumbling houses were dark, with boarded windows, or shutters dangling from a single corroded hinge.

"I think I'm starting to get the picture," Bellamy said. "Some of the Caribbean wraiths live in New Orleans. They'd like to see the city run according to their beliefs. And this Geffard is the leader of the rebels."

"Right again," Antoine said. "Leader and head loa—big kahuna priest. Up until recently, the rivalry between the two groups wasn't too bad. Geffard and his gang defied the Queen when they thought they could get away with it, but subtly, without violence. A lot of the time, she let their disrespect go, like a soft-hearted mama coddling a bratty child. Maybe she figured they couldn't do any real harm, and it might be a good idea to let them blow off steam."

Bellamy paused for a moment to peer into the shadows ahead. He didn't see anything threatening, but intuition warned him that Antoine knew where he was going. The metal spider *was* ahead of them, and not far, either. He swallowed away a dryness in his mouth. "But then things changed."

Antoine nodded. "People began to disappear. Gradually we learned that there were…*things* stalking us. They've been picking off the Queen's most loyal supporters and magicians. Disrupting ceremonies and rituals. Desecrating shrines. Getting bolder and bolder. But they never hit a major Citadel before tonight."

"Attacking holy men and sacred places," Bellamy said. "I was right. Your problems *are* part of the same thing as the Atheist murders."

Antoine shrugged. "I guess it's possible, although I don't know why Geffard would bother to mess with the Quick. How would it help put him where he wants to be? I'll tell you this, though. Belief means everything on this side of the Shroud. It's the fuel that makes the magic work. If the Queen's hoodoo men keep getting whacked, and her gods keep getting insulted, then people will think she's losing her mojo. And once they believe it, it will be true. Geffard will overthrow her and take her throne."

"She should move against him before things get any worse," Bellamy said.

"I think so, too," Antoine said. "But there's a problem with that. He claims that her problems don't have anything to do with him. And the raiders sure don't *seem* like Les Invisibles or any other brand of *ibambo* anybody's ever seen, not even Spectres."

Bellamy remembered the hot fire the baboon-headed woman had wielded against him, and the way the skeletal creature had melted away without the usual ripples of black light. "I noticed that."

"She doesn't want to move against Geffard without proof that he's behind it all," Antoine continued glumly. "There are a bunch of Les Invisibles who don't care about overthrowing the government. But if they think the Queen is persecuting one of their own unjustly, they might decide it's time for a change after all."

"Maybe we'll find the evidence she needs tonight."

"That would be nice," Antoine said. "But I'll be happy if we just get Titus back. We aren't the first guys to chase these new devils into the night. With luck, we *will* be the first ones to survive."

Bellamy smiled. "You really know how to build up a person's confidence. Why didn't they just destroy Titus back at the Haunt? Do they want to interrogate him?"

"Could be. Or maybe one of them is Mla Watu. Maybe they can steal his mojo if they kill him in a special way."

Antoine turned another corner and led Bellamy down another blighted street. The homeless, weirdly beautiful in their shimmering auras, sprawled on stoops and huddled in doorways, reeking of sweat, urine, feces, tobacco smoke, and cheap wine. One gaunt little boy stared at the ghosts for a moment and then began to laugh, a demented, honking sound. No one asked him what was so funny. Evidently he was alone; none of the other unfortunates was taking care of him.

Bellamy sighed and tried to put the abandoned child out of his mind. It wasn't as if he could help him. "You asked me why I'm here," he said to Antoine. "Why are you? What does an alligator care about a conflict between two human political factions?"

"The Dark Kingdom of Ivory has smart wraith animals," Antoine said. "Near as I can make out, Les Invisibles don't. If Geffard takes over, then maybe *zappo!* All of a sudden I'm dumb as dirt again, or maybe I don't exist at all. But really, I guess I'd be here even if my own tail wasn't on the line. You wake up into death and find out you can talk. You're going to be lonely if you can't find somebody to talk *to*. And the Queen's people were decent to me. They made a place for me, and most of them don't treat me like a freak."

Bellamy shook his head. "I'm envious. They treated you better—"

"Quiet!" Antoine snapped. "We're real close now. I can feel it."

The human obediently fell silent. Antoine peeked around another corner. After a moment Bellamy warily did the same. The passage before him was a short, narrow cul-de-sac strewn with sheets of newspaper and other bits of trash. Several jagged-edged Nihils sufficiently large that a person could fall into them seethed and glittered in the brick pavement. A few pieces of litter appeared to float at the top of the pits, because in the reality of the Skinlands, the cavities didn't exist.

Antoine sniffed the air. "I think they're in that building at the end of the alley." He glided forward, using shadows, telephone posts, and the occasional garbage can for cover.

Crouching, Bellamy sneaked after him. He peered this way and that, looking for sentries. He didn't see any, but for a moment he caught a hint of the same fetid odor he'd smelled just outside the Haunt, almost but not quite indistinguishable from the complex stench of the garbage decaying all around him.

A soft rustling sounded from overhead. His head snapped up, and he saw the faceless demon on a rooftop. He just had time to realize that the stink was the smell of its oozing sores, and then its arms whipped through the air. A round, shadowy shape expanded against the sky.

Bellamy shouted, "Look out!" and barely managed to leap clear. Caught by surprise, Antoine wasn't as lucky. Thudding to the pavement, the plummeting net enveloped him, then instantly began to bunch in around him as if it were woven of pythons.

Bellamy snapped off a shot at the faceless thing. The spirit lurched backward. Then something rattled at the end of the passage.

The FBI agent pivoted. The junk spider finished sliding through a wall and charged him, claws upraised.

Bellamy settled into a marksman's stance and fired at it. The darksteel bullets clanged into it and knocked away bits of rusty metal. One shot shattered a mismatched glass eye. But it kept coming. Meanwhile, the faceless man jumped down into the alley.

Still shooting, Bellamy backpedaled toward one of the Nihils. He didn't entirely understand what the holes were—openings into another dimension, apparently—but he'd been warned that large ones were dangerous. He hoped it was true.

Trying to keep his eye on his adversaries, he slightly overestimated the distance to the pit. He stepped backward, and his heel came down on nothingness. Thrown off balance, he flailed his arms. The Nihil seemed to hiss louder. He almost imagined he could feel it sucking at him.

By the time he recovered his equilibrium, the spider was nearly on top of him. He fired his last shot, held himself still for a split second, then ducked its first clawing attack, sidestepped, dropped the pistol, and grabbed the side of its body.

The jagged bits of scrap tore open his palms and fingers. Ignoring the pain, he heaved with all his might. The momentum of the spider's charge helped him tumble it into the pit.

Twisting, scrabbling, the demon caught hold of the edge of the hole. Bellamy was horribly certain it was going to haul itself out. But then its body began to buckle and crumple as if it were being crushed in an invisible vise. One by one, its clutching limbs lost their grip.

Bellamy heard footsteps pounding at him. He whirled. The faceless man lunged at him, intent on pushing him into the Nihil. The FBI agent lurched aside, threw a clumsy punch at the monster, and missed.

The two opponents began to circle one another. Belatedly remembering the shortsword in his belt, Bellamy eased his hand toward the unfamiliar weapon. Just as he touched the hilt, the faceless man pounced at him.

Bellamy punched the demon in the throat. A solid hit this time, but it didn't stop the creature. The monster grabbed him by the shoulders, sinking fingertips as hard as stone into his flesh. Streamers of bloody pus writhed out of its sores and across Bellamy's body, seeking his head. The slimy, reeking tendrils gouged at his eyes, burrowed into his nostrils and ears. One slid down his gullet, choking him. He thought he felt them boring into his brain.

He tried to tear himself free, lost his balance, and fell onto his back without getting rid of his mask of squirming filth. The demon dove on top of him, its knees slamming into his chest.

Bellamy desperately groped for the sword, fumbled it out of his belt, and stabbed blindly.

The blade sunk into something solid, and the weight on his chest disappeared. The pus clinging to his head evaporated.

Sobbing and gagging, he sat up, and saw that when he'd fallen, he'd just missed dropping into the same Nihil that had swallowed the spider. He dragged himself to his feet and staggered over to where Antoine lay thrashing, tail slapping the pavement, still entangled in the net. The mesh had drawn so tight that the gator's scaly hide bulged between the strands. Bellamy suspected that, given time, it could slice his companion apart.

He grabbed a handful of net and sawed at it with the sword. The cords squirmed, trying to avoid the blade, but they weren't nearly as good at defending themselves as they were at crushing someone caught inside their coils. Gradually they came apart, and the more he cut, the more feebly they struggled, until finally Antoine wriggled free.

"Thanks," the gator croaked. He looked Bellamy over. The FBI agent wondered fleetingly just how wild-eyed and frightened he appeared. "What do you think, warmblood? Shall we go on?"

Bellamy took a deep breath. He knew he didn't need it, but the action felt right. "Why not?" he said. "We're winning so far."

"So far," Antoine said sardonically. He crawled toward the door at the end of the alley. Bellamy stalked after him, expecting some other horror to leap out at them at any moment.

But nothing did. Maybe the faceless man and the junk spider had been the only two monsters in the vicinity. Maybe Titus was alone inside the dilapidated building, bound or unconscious. Perhaps Bellamy and Antoine would be able to get him back to the Haunt without any more trouble.

An encouraging thought. But then the two companions heard the soft growling murmuring through the wall.

Antoine looked up at Bellamy. "That sounds like a big, mean dog. Except, not exactly."

Bellamy nodded. "You can hear complicated patterns in the noise, as if the thing is speaking a real language. I told you there were werewolves involved in this mess. I think we're listening to one now." He thought of Dunn in his bestial form, clawing him, finally electrocuting him, and shivered.

"A werewolf," said Antoine. "Son of a gun. I've always wanted to see one. Part man, part beast, it figures I'd be curious, right?" He started up the sagging steps to the tenement's back door.

"Be careful!" Bellamy said. "They're dangerous."

"To the Quick, they're dangerous," Antoine replied. "Your furry friend won't be able to touch us, remember? Odds are, he won't even see us. I just hope there aren't any more spirits around. They're the only thing that guys like us need to worry about."

The reptile slipped into the building. Wondering if his companion actually knew what he was talking about, Bellamy followed him into a foyer with a row of doors lining the wall on either side. The rhythmic snarling issued from one on the left.

Bellamy crept forward, slid his face through the panel, then caught his breath. Beyond the door was a dilapidated apartment, its cracked walls crudely painted with black spirals and some of the other symbols he'd seen in the werewolf stronghold. In the center of the room, too tall to stand erect beneath the low, stained ceiling, crouched another gray-furred beastman, this one with only one external ear, a twisted leg, and a withered, useless-looking third arm sprouting from the left side of his chest. A necklace of long fangs and rough, dimly glowing crystals hung around his neck, and he held a human femur in each of his good hands, slowly twirling them in a way that reminded the FBI man of a tai chi practitioner performing his exercises. His aura was a murky crimson shot through with glittering flecks, and his fur gave off a zoo-cage reek similar to Dunn's. Now that Bellamy had the exquisitely sensitive nose of a wraith, the stench was even fouler.

Bones, feathers, pebbles, and oddly carved pieces of wood radiated outward from the werewolf's feet, defining a complex abstract pattern on the floor. Titus floated in the air before him, motionless, head slumped and hands dangling at his sides. Threads of flickering scarlet light wormed their way across his body, reminding Bellamy unpleasantly of the strands of animate pus that had squirmed into his head. But the crisscrossing bands of radiance weren't the only peculiar thing about the old wizard's unconscious form. After a moment Bellamy realized that Titus was *smaller*. He'd been little before, stooped and shrunken with age when the junk spider had captured him, but now he was only about four feet tall.

"He's *shrinking*," Antoine hissed.

Bellamy glanced down. The alligator was peeking through the door, too. The human took another cautious look at the werewolf, making doubly sure the three-armed horror really didn't seem to sense their presence, even though he obviously perceived Titus, the focus of his ritual. "Yeah. I think you were right, it's a kind of Mla Watu. The wolfman is stealing his power."

"We've got to stop it," Antoine said.

"Can we?" Bellamy asked. "Do you know an Arcanos to affect things on the other side of the Shroud?"

"No," Antoine said. "We'll have to go back to the Haunt and get somebody who does."

Bellamy grimaced. He was afraid Titus would be dead before they got back, but he couldn't see any alternative to Antoine's plan. Feeling helpless, useless, he began to step backward.

The wolfman stopped chanting and snarled. His red eyes blazing, he glared directly at the intruders. Obviously, he had suddenly noticed their presence. He brandished the bone in his left hand.

Twelve

Bellamy felt something sticky touch his face and eyes, as if he'd blundered into an invisible strip of flypaper. He blinked reflexively, lifted his hand to brush the noisome feeling away, and then the phantasmal substance jerked him staggering forward, out of the wall and toward the werewolf, as if he were a fish on an angler's line. Snared by the same magic, Antoine slid thrashing across the floor.

The pulling stopped. Reeling, Bellamy clawed at his face, trying to tear away the stickiness before the magic could yank him forward again. After a second the sensation vanished. He tried to pivot toward Antoine.

And he did manage to flounder partway around, but the motion felt strange and awkward. When he saw that, like Titus, the writhing, hissing reptile was levitating, he realized that his own bare feet weren't touching the cold, gritty floor anymore, either.

Dangling in the air, unable to walk, he could neither flee nor advance on the wolfman to attack him hand-to-hand. Leering at him, the hideous creature made a grating, rhythmic sound. After a moment Bellamy realized the Black Spiral Dancer was laughing.

The human hurled his short sword at the werewolf's face. He was hardly an expert knife thrower, nor was the weapon balanced for use as a missile, but somehow he hit the target anyway. The point of the black blade caught the werewolf squarely in the left eye.

And then it fell away, without doing any damage. Because, of course, it and the monster were on opposite sides of the Shroud. The werewolf laughed again, then resumed his incantations.

Worm-like strands of crimson light began to crawl over Antoine and Bellamy's bodies. The FBI agent slapped and brushed at them frantically, but couldn't touch them, couldn't extinguish them or knock them loose. The tendrils inflicted jabs of pain, as if they were nipping at him with tiny fangs. As he swiped at his left hand, trying desperately to dislodge one of the lights, he saw his middle finger shorten until it was no longer than his ring finger.

Like Titus, he was shrinking. Being devoured. He flailed, alternately struggling to plant his feet back on the floor and to swim through the air to within striking distance of his tormentor. Neither maneuver worked. The werewolf leered at him, baring multiple rows of crooked yellow fangs.

The sight of that mocking, inhuman grin filled Bellamy with hate. He redoubled his efforts to get at the beastman, still to no avail. His rage and desperation swelled and swelled inside him, and then agony ripped through his body. He fell heavily to the floor.

The pain only lasted an instant. As he lifted his head, he saw that the worms of light on his body had disappeared. So had the floating forms of Antoine and Titus, and the hissing, glinting Nihil cracks in the walls.

Bellamy realized that somehow he'd crossed over to the Quick side of the Shroud. Immediately he felt a pull, a suction, not from any definable direction but unmistakable nonetheless. Death was trying to draw him back into its country.

Desperately, without even knowing how, he fought to remain where he was, and felt the force of his will anchor him in place. He *could* stay in the Skinlands for a little while, though only until his concentration wavered.

The werewolf snarled, and drops of his hot saliva spattered Bellamy. The monster started chanting and brandishing the femurs considerably faster than before.

Bellamy wondered why, instead of continuing his sorcery, the creature didn't just make a grab for him. Huge and powerful, armed with vicious fangs and talons, the wolfman couldn't possibly be afraid to battle him hand-to-hand. Indeed, though at least the FBI agent now had a fighting chance, he knew that the odds against him were long indeed.

Then he remembered something Marilyn had told him. Supposedly it was dangerous for a magician to break off a conjuration in the middle. Maybe the werewolf was hurrying on toward a safe stopping point, after which he'd pounce on his opponent.

And just maybe, if Bellamy disrupted the ritual *before* the beastman could babble the proper phrase, it would hurt the creature.

The human grabbed for some of the bones, stones, and pieces of wood arranged on the floor. Even that simple action impaired his concentration, and at once he felt himself begin to slip back into the Shadowlands. He squinched his eyes shut, strained to anchor himself anew, and the pull abated. Struggling to keep his will focused, clenched, he swiped at some of the ritual objects again, jumbling them and effacing a part of the pattern they defined.

Crackling arcs of blue electricity, or something resembling it, danced across the floor. One brushed Bellamy's ankle, convulsing him, flinging him four feet into the air, nearly disrupting his control of his newfound talent and tumbling him back across the Shroud. But the werewolf endured worse. He was at the center of the storm, and the miniature thunderbolts blazed into his flesh repeatedly, like whips, or blades, or striking cobras. His body shuddered spastically, and a smell of charred meat and fur suffused the air.

After several seconds the discharges subsided. Blinking at afterimages, Bellamy waited to see the beastman collapse. Instead the monster took a lurching step, recovering his balance, then dropped the long bones in his hands, and lunged at his human prey.

Though the werewolf's injuries had slowed him down, Bellamy just barely managed to scramble out of his way. He snatched up a length of pointed, intricately carved bone and spun around on his knees, thrusting wildly. A huge, clawed hand ripped at him, shredding his shirt. A split second later his weapon plunged into the werewolf's groin.

The wolfman reeled passed Bellamy, twisting the bone out of his grip in the process. Staggering, the deformed creature pawed feebly at the makeshift weapon, evidently trying to pull it out. Then he made a rattling sound and collapsed.

Bellamy studied the monster warily, making sure he was truly dead, until a surge of pain distracted him. Examining his shoulder, he found white, bloodless gashes. The werewolf's claws had done more than tear his shirt. He just hadn't felt the cuts till now.

A second and surprisingly intense throb of pain served to break his grip on the world of the living. Instinctively he clutched at it with his mind, trying to remain, but this time to no avail. The darkness grew somewhat brighter, and Titus and Antoine swam into view, free of scarlet glowworms and no longer suspended in the air. They'd also regained their proper stature.

The hoodoo man was still unconscious, but Antoine was awake. Tail rustling against the floor, he hurried up to Bellamy. "Good work," the gator said. "Is your shoulder bad?"

"I think it'll be all right."

Something about the human's tone or expression must have concerned Antoine. He cocked his head. "Are *you* all right?"

Bellamy hesitated, not quite certain how to explain. They'd won after all, and he'd discovered a strange new talent in the process. He ought to be jubilant. But for a few moments, he'd been alive again—well, nearly—and now he was mired once more in the cold, hollow realm of the dead. Perhaps his shadowself was tainting his perspective, but at that moment, the anguish and frustration of it were almost too much to bear.

"I'm fine," he said gruffly. "Let's get the old man back to the Haunt before something else happens."

THIRTEEN

Peering this way and that, his gloved hand clutching the revolver in his pocket, Manuel Gayoso de Lemos, Anacreon sworn to the Smiling Lord and one of the three Governors of Natchez, prowled the festering alleys of Under-the-Hill. Allegedly, the riverfront district wasn't as dangerous as it used to be. By enlisting Mike Fink and other notorious outlaws in his crusade against the Heretics, an enterprise which had yielded plenty of loot, Montrose had reduced the incidence of common robbery and slave-taking. Still, under normal circumstances Gayoso would never have come down here without a squad of Legionnaires for protection. In fact, unless he'd been needed to put down an insurrection or repel an invading army, he wouldn't have come at all.

He was sorely tempted to abandon his errand and return to the Citadel. But he'd promised his secret advisor a fee for telling him how to dispose of Montrose, and he was afraid to pay it anywhere near his rival Anacreons. If they ever learned what he was up to, they'd have all the excuse they could possibly need to cast him down. A high-ranking Hierarch could get away with a wide range of cruel and capricious acts, but not with what he had planned.

Frenetic zydeco fiddling and a murmur of conversation sounded ahead. Rounding another corner, Gayoso saw a decaying shack with a green skull and crossbones crudely painted on the side. Presumably this was the tavern known as the Green Head, where Montrose had begun assembling his private army. Beyond it gleamed the black, malodorous expanse of the polluted Mississippi.

Gayoso had been told that the person he sought could generally be found in this vicinity. Peering about, he spotted a narrow lane lit by crimson barrow-flame lamps. Male and female wraiths struck seductive poses in the doorways and windows of the derelict buildings, exhibiting themselves to the riffraff sauntering up and down.

Scowling behind his blue silk hood with the elaborate silver trim around the eye holes, his long leather coat swishing around his ankles, the Governor tramped forward. A burly ruffian with the golden eyes, muzzle, and mane of a lion hailed him jovially. The Anacreon inclined his head, but didn't speak. If he kept silent, no one could identify him by the sound of his voice.

Whores called and beckoned. Many had consulted the Masquers to enhance their erotic appeal. One woman looked like the young Katherine Hepburn, another sported a luxuriant equine tail, and a third employed a red wooden rod to demonstrate the prehensile attributes of her genitalia. One prostitute, a flesh sculptor himself, assumed the form of whoever stopped to look at him, offering potential customers the opportunity to couple with themselves.

The little street was only two blocks long. As he neared the end, Gayoso began to suspect that the object of his search wasn't working tonight. In a way, it was a relief. But at the same time, now that he'd mustered the resolve to perform this particular chore, the prospect of ending the night with it undone, of having the danger and unpleasantness still hanging over his head, exasperated him.

Then the form of a thin little girl, her long black hair done up in pigtails, emerged from the gloom. Unlike the other denizens of the area, she wasn't doing anything obvious to call attention to herself, which was probably why he hadn't noticed her before. Dressed in a white blouse, a plaid skirt, knee socks, and saddle shoes, she sat alone on a crumbling stoop, head bowed, crooning to the Raggedy Ann doll cradled in her lap. Whispers, moans, and the smack of naked bodies bumping together sounded from the rotting brick building at her back.

As Gayoso approached, she lifted her head and gave him a shy smile. But the childish expression wasn't perfect. For an instant a calculating glint shone in her large brown eyes. Evidently, as the Hierarch had heard, she'd died a schoolgirl and retained the form of one, but in the years since, her personality had matured, or at least coarsened. His anticipatory guilt eased slightly.

Leather squeaked on the pavement. Startled, the Governor pivoted. The twin horns of his jester's cap flopping, his expression an odd mixture of eagerness and misery, Valentine was hurrying toward the child prostitute also.

Gayoso hadn't expected to encounter his servant here, but he supposed it made sense that the dwarf preferred a lover of his own stature. The Anacreon quashed an impulse to turn and scurry away. After all, Valentine had already seen him, and evidently hadn't penetrated his disguise.

"Hi, Daphne," Valentine said, eyeing Gayoso a little warily. "If you can, I want to spend the whole night with you. I've got the money." He dug several oboli out of his pocket.

The little girl gave Gayoso a coy smile. "You look like a nice man," she said. "I'd love to have you for my daddy. But you just heard, Vally asked me first."

Gayoso reached inside his coat, removed a bulging pigskin change purse, and tossed it onto the stoop. It landed with a heavy thud and a clink.

Daphne's eyes widened. "Gosh!" She turned to Valentine.

The jester said, "I don't have that much. I wasn't expecting an auction. But I can get you more in a day or two. And I…I really could use your company tonight."

Daphne caressed Valentine's cheek and lips. The little man actually quivered. Gayoso felt a twinge of contemptuous amusement. "You are so sweet," she said. "Come back tomorrow. We'll play then."

"Don't say that!" Valentine said. "I come to you every week. I've given you plenty of money over the years. I thought you *liked* me, at least a little."

"I do," said Daphne. "Except for when you get all icky. So don't be that way. Run along until tomorrow." Her voice hardened. "Or else I won't be able to play with you at all anymore."

Valentine glared at her for a moment. Then he dropped his eyes, jammed his money back in his pocket, and trudged away.

Daphne stooped and picked up Gayoso's purse. "Come inside," she said, simpering, her tone sweet and girlish once more. "I'll show you my special room. My favorite place."

"I have my own place," replied Gayoso, taking pains to speak softly. "Somewhere more private. Let's go there."

Daphne gave him a coy but appraising look. He imagined she preferred to ply her trade in the brothel behind her, where, perhaps, she had allies at hand if someone tried to cheat or hurt her. "I don't know," she said. "I'm not supposed to go farther than the corner. Mama says I'm too little."

Gayoso customarily carried a spare soulfire crystal or two, in case the ones currently powering his gun ran out of energy. He removed one of the black, sparkling orbs from his pocket and tossed that to her also.

She snatched the magical gem out of the air. "Well, okay. I guess I can go. Since I'll be with my *Daddy*." She alit from the stoop and took his hand. Her fingers felt tiny and fragile.

People leered at them as they headed for the corner. Gayoso had sampled a number of exotic pleasures since his induction into the Hierarchy, but he'd never felt any inclination toward pedophilia, and his stomach churned with mortification. He was glad to escape into the less-traveled maze of alleyways beyond.

At first Daphne prattled. Did he like little girls? Did he think she was pretty? Did he like tickles? What about hugs and smooches? Gayoso did his best to enter into the flirtatious spirit of the conversation, but as tense as he was, it was difficult, and the nearer they got to their destination, the edgier he became.

Daphne gave him another speculative look. He was afraid his gruffness had alarmed her, that she'd try to back out of their assignation, but instead she asked, "Are you mad at me, Daddy? Do you think I'm a naughty girl?" Her bubbly manner had turned timid and submissive.

"I saw what you did," Gayoso replied coldly, trying to play along.

To his surprise, she blushed. Lacking blood, most wraiths were incapable of that particular feat. "In the garden with that little black girl," she said, her voice hushed with bogus shame. "Kissing each other's pee-pees. I know it was dirty. Am I going to get a spanking?"

"You'll see," Gayoso said. "This is the place." He glanced about, making sure no one was watching, then led her through the peeling surface of a wooden door and on up a dark, narrow flight of stairs. The interior of the abandoned office building smelled of dust and cockroaches.

Daphne's head turned back and forth. Gayoso presumed she was searching for a bracing jolt of secondhand misery. He knew she wouldn't find it. Unlike many old structures, this one didn't reverberate with the echoes of ancient sorrows. That was why no ghost had chosen the place for a Haunt. Why Gayoso had been reasonably confident no one would discover the room he'd prepared, or interrupt him before he completed his task.

When they reached the second-floor landing, he gestured to the door on the left. "In here."

"Yes, Daddy," Daphne said, still all cowed and apprehensive. She glided through the panel, and he followed.

The sickly green light of several barrow-flame candles glinted on the *conquistador* rapier, cuirass, and morion which Gayoso had left in the corner when he donned his disguise. A large, hissing Nihil, radiating twisting fissures like the tentacles of an octopus, yawned in the middle of the floor. Several darksteel knifes, a rubber-ball gag, a set of chains, and a tarnished silver hand mirror lay on the dusty table beside the pit, while freshly painted sigils and hieroglyphics decorated the walls. The Hierarch had no idea what the symbols represented. He'd merely drawn them according to his benefactor's instructions. But they emanated a palpable sense of malevolence.

Daphne froze, gaping at the menacing scene, and then began to lurch around. *I don't have to do this*, Gayoso thought. *I could still let her go*. But simultaneously he snatched out his gun and slammed the butt down on top of her head. Bone crunched, and she collapsed.

The Hierarch pulled off his hood, strode to the table, and picked up the mirror. For a moment, there seemed to be nothing inside the glass but his own fleshy, hook-nosed features. Then the dark eyes shone more brightly, and the grimace twisted into a wolfish grin.

"Hello, hello," his Shadow said.

"I brought the child," Gayoso said. Not knowing if it was necessary, he tried to turn the glass in such a way as to allow his dark half—if that was what the mirror creature truly was—to peer out at the girl. Like many of the things he said and did in an effort to get along with the Shadow, the action made him feel awkward if not faintly ridiculous.

"So I see," the reflection said. "Scarcely the innocent cherub of my fond imaginings, but she'll do. Chain her to the table and we'll get started."

A few moments after Gayoso strapped the gag in place, Daphne regained consciousness. Spread-eagled, she thrashed, rattling her shackles. Her eyes rolled, and as she struggled to shriek and babble past the mass in her mouth, she sounded as if she were strangling. Feeling queasy, the Hierarch set the mirror on a nearby shelf, once again attempting to position it so the creature inside could see out. That accomplished, he picked up one of the larger daggers, cut off the prostitute's clothing, and discarded his own.

And then it was time to begin.

A fresh wave of doubt assailed him, though it wasn't the prospect of torture and murder that gave him pause. As a high-ranking Hierarch, he'd sent hundreds of people to the rack and the stake, sometimes simply to further his own selfish interests. But he'd never offered a sacrifice to Oblivion itself, never groveled before the implacable enemy of all Creation. According to the laws of Charon—and the codes of most Renegade factions and Heretical sects, for that matter—such worship was the ultimate crime.

Yet if he declined to honor his pact, he risked drawing the wrath of that nearly omnipotent malignancy down on his own head. And after all, he'd spent centuries in the service of Stygia, the Void's eternal foe. Surely no one sin, even an offense as heinous as this, could outweigh that. It couldn't blight his spirit beyond redemption. He'd simply perform the ceremony by rote and get it over with. And then, he vowed, never look in the enchanted mirror again.

"I call to the great emptiness," he said. "The death beyond death. The darkness beyond darkness. I abase myself before Oblivion. Pity your servant, forgive him the foul sin of his existence, and deign to accept his sacrifice." He made the first cuts, carving a cryptic symbol into Daphne's left thigh.

And at that instant, he sensed something stir, something that seemed to be inside him, looming above him, and peering up from the depths of the Nihil, all at the same time. He could feel it gloating over his revulsion and Daphne's terror.

Trying to ignore the ghastly presence, his voice now quavering ever so slightly, Gayoso said, "I prostrate myself before the princes of the Labyrinth, the gods of the Tempest, the angels of annihilation. Gorool of the Claws! Dragon king, mask of the Wyrm, slayer of Charon, give me your blessing." He picked up a small blade like a scalpel and, with a certain amount of trouble—his victim kept tossing her head—slit Daphne's nostrils.

The sensation of being watched became even more intense. Now he could feel the regard of the Void playing across his skin like a hand petting a cat. At first it made him gag, his body shudder and clench, and then, shockingly, it gave him a pang of pleasure.

"Mulhecturous," he gasped, struggling to block out this new sensation. "Mother of plagues and cancers, queen of poisons and putrescence, grant me your bounty! Let me drink from your fountains of corruption." He selected a serrated blade and moved to the other end of the table, so he could saw off one of Daphne's toes.

A sickening joy overtook him once again. He had on occasion relished torture, usually when some particularly impudent rebel or troublesome rival had fallen into his clutches, and now, abruptly, he found himself eager to make Daphne suffer. Reminding himself that he didn't want to become emotionally involved with the ritual, he struggled against the feeling, but to no avail. As he severed the toe, his penis swelled.

"Loki," he croaked. "Mephistopheles. Tezcatlipoca. Count of the Wasteland! God of the thousand faces and lord of liars. Whisper your secrets to me. Teach me to deceive and betray." To his dismay, he found he could no longer drone the invocations mechanically. Like Daphne's mutilation, the recitation had become a sensual pleasure. Every syllable made his lips, his face, his entire body tingle.

Exhilarated and panicky at the same time, he sliced off his victim's right ear. He decided that if he couldn't resist the feelings the sacrifice was inspiring, his best option was to complete it as quickly as possible. He began to chant, and to cut, as quickly as he could.

But his haste merely intensified his excitement. It was as if he were having sex, slipping into the final frenzy, thrusting faster and faster to reach his climax. Visions arose before his inner eye. The Malfeans, the very devils he was invoking, monstrous and alien. The chaotic desolation of the Tempest and Labyrinth, their domain, a realm so immense it made Stygia, the Far Shores, and the other enclaves contained within it seem as insignificant as a single handful of sand strewn across a desert. And underlying that world, and vaster still, the Void itself, a black grindstone wearing away the cosmos, a vortex of absolute nothingness sucking it down.

The vista was too terrifying to contemplate, yet so awesome that Gayoso couldn't turn away. No petty human pretension could stand before it. The Anacreon realized that his dreams, his fears, and his very sense of self were meaningless, and the mighty Legions of the Hierarchy and even the Earth itself were equally insubstantial. Everything he'd ever credited was merely a mirage, a ridiculous phantom pretending to exist for one brief instant before Oblivion swept it away.

For a time—a second? an hour?—he was certain his insights were killing him. How could they not? But as his faith in his own existence shriveled, darkness flowed in to fill the hollow places. He *became* Oblivion, a jubilant destroyer liberated from every sentiment or scruple, an ecstatic avatar of the Final Death. He dimly suspected that no puny human soul could unite with this power for long without being consumed by it, but the notion failed to trouble him. Time was as meaningless as all the other delusions sane minds embraced. In another, transcendent reality, he'd rage forever.

Cackling, crowing his incantations, he capered around the table. Often he carved symbols into his own body as well as Daphne's. His loins throbbed with one orgasm after another. The Nihil beside his improvised altar hissed more and more loudly.

By the time Gayoso reached the finale of the ritual, Daphne was so thoroughly maimed that she could barely twitch. Indeed, her white, vivisected body scarcely looked human anymore. Tittering, pleased with his handiwork, the Hierarch returned to the head of the table to put out her eyes.

As he plunged a stiletto into the second one, the shimmering darkness inside the Nihil shot up into the room like a geyser. For a moment it seemed to swirl like a dust devil, and then, rearing to the ceiling, to *thicken*, becoming as solid and heavy as a mass of granite. Suddenly it toppled at the table, smashing down on diabolist and sacrifice alike.

Gayoso felt a burst of agony, and then he was tumbling through blackness. Certain he was about to perish, to dissolve in the grasp of Oblivion, he yowled triumphantly.

Instead he slammed into a vertical surface, rebounded, and banged his shoulders against another. The double impact dropped him to his knees.

His thoughts crumbled and reassembled themselves in new shapes. Dazed, feeling as if he he'd just awakened from some already half-forgotten but supremely frightening nightmare, he peered about.

He was crumpled at the bottom of a cramped space like a sarcophagus standing on end. A trace of wan green light trickled in from somewhere. Twisting his head around, he saw an oval window set high in the back wall.

What in the name of the Scythe was happening? How could he be, well, fulfilling his obligation—he cringed at a murky recollection of the demented glee which had possessed him—one second, and stuck in here the next? Hampered by the close quarters, he clambered to his feet and shifted around to look through the glass.

An instant later, he gasped and recoiled. Because his own face, looming hugely, a necromantic sigil etched in each cheek, was leering back at him.

"Now that wasn't so bad, was it?" the Shadow said. "You looked like you were having fun."

"What's going on?" Gayoso asked. "Where am I?"

"Can't you guess?" the double asked. "I'll give you a hint." The Governor felt his narrow closet of a prison swivel. Now he could see past his twin into the sacrificial chamber. The pillar of darkness had disappeared, perhaps withdrawn into the Nihil. The table was broken, Daphne's chains were empty, and the black knives lay scattered about the floor.

The view only increased Gayoso's confusion. There hadn't been any iron maiden or upended coffin in the room for him to be stuck inside now. "Stop playing games!" he said. "Just tell me."

The Shadow sighed. "You disappoint me, brother. During the rite, when you yielded yourself to Oblivion, you gave me the opening I needed. It's been a long, hard job, eroding your conscience and will, but I'm finally in control of our body, and you're the one more or less trapped in the mirror."

"No," Gayoso said, his voice breaking. "You can't do this. *I* control the magic. *I'm* the master."

"Then you'd better prove it," the Shadow said.

Gayoso's prison shot upward and over, until he was lying on his back looking at the ceiling. He barely had time to realize that the Shadow had swung the mirror over his head before the creature lashed it down again. One corner of the broken table flashed up at the glass. When they collided, the pane shattered, and Gayoso's mind exploded with it.

FOURTEEN

Montrose's teeth began to chatter with the ghastly chill. Tightening his jaw, he maneuvered through a pack of shuffling, vacant-eyed Drones toward the blue-flecked wall of the pit. Leering as usual, Artie loped along behind him. Montrose had learned that the little abolitionist and his comrades often patrolled their prison, essentially in the desperate hope of suddenly spying some means of escape they hadn't noticed before, and they always did it in pairs. The Spectres and the violently insane made it too dangerous to wander around alone.

The disgraced Hierarch peered upward. High overhead, the huge steel crane crouched like a dinosaur. "Why does this one section of the wall have to be so smooth?" he grumbled.

Artie waved his right hand, a habitual gesture. It looked as if he was brandishing an imaginary cigar. "Because the Artificers polished it to keep us from climbing out, Einstein. I think all those pink curls are smothering what passes for your brain."

Despite his bleak mood, Montrose smiled. Though the two wraiths could scarcely have been more unlike in most respects, Artie's disrespectful manner reminded him of Mike Fink. "It was a rhetorical question. Perhaps, instead of hammering on our leg irons, we should be carving handholds here."

"Tried it," Artie said. "It doesn't work."

A short, black-haired woman skulked out of the shadows, her face a mask of fury, muscles twitching. Montrose met her glare with a level stare of his own. After a few seconds, she hissed and turned away.

"That doesn't make sense," said the Scot. "The stones you people collected are made of the same mineral as the cliff, which means they should be hard enough to chip it."

Artie shrugged. "I guess the forgers used magic to toughen it up. You've got to hand it to the bastards, they know how to slap together a hoosegow."

Behind Montrose, a bare foot brushed the floor. He pivoted, ready to defend himself, but it was only a Drone, trudging aimlessly along and fingering his lower lip. "What about a human pyramid?"

Artie snorted. "For the love of Mike, Jimmy, you're talking to an old vaudeville headliner here. I've worked on the same bill with more acrobats than you could shake a stick at, assuming that's your idea of a good time. But we don't have enough people; we couldn't get high enough. Besides, you can't make like the Flying Rigatonis without attracting the attention of the crazies and the doomshades, and then they do their damnedest to knock the pyramid down. We lost a guy named Amos that way. When he fell, he cracked his head open."

For perhaps the thousandth time, Montrose reflected that, if not for his shackles, he could fly out of the pit. Grimacing, he pushed the frustrating thought aside. "Still, there *must* be a way out of here. We're just not seeing it."

Artie grinned wryly. "Speak for yourself, bubbie. I see it. I did from the start."

Montrose gaped at him, then sighed. "You had me going for a moment there. But I assume you're setting me up for another joke."

"Wrong as usual," the abolitionist said. "All you have to do is pound that ugly noggin of yours against a rock, or let one of our nastier neighbors—one without

Spectre claws and fangs—work out his hostilities on you. When you're hurt badly enough, you'll pop right out of this quaint little bed-and-breakfast."

"And into the Labyrinth," said Montrose. "For a duel to the death with my Shadow." Such an ordeal was called a Harrowing, and was commonly regarded as so perilous that few wraiths would ever consider it as a potential solution to *any* dilemma.

"Bingo," said Artie. "What's the matter, don't you think you're up to the challenge?"

Montrose remembered his Shadow possessing him on Earth, and the way it stirred every time he looked at Louise, and repressed a shudder. "I'd prefer not to find out."

"Me too," Artie said. Suddenly he seemed wearier and more discouraged than Montrose had seen him look before. "Pitiful, isn't it?"

The Scot cocked his head. "How so?"

"You've noticed our hosts didn't make me wear any ankle jewelry." Montrose nodded. "So you figured out I don't know an Arcanos. That's because I never tried to learn."

Montrose glanced around, looking for potential threats. Some sort of brawl had broken out about forty feet away, but so far at least, the melee showed no signs of moving in their direction. "Why not?"

"I was too busy chasing Transcendence," Artie replied. "Meditating on koans, poring over sacred texts, and all that happy horseshit. Trying to understand myself and the cosmos, and master my dark side. After all that preparation, I should be ready to go a few rounds with my Shadow. But I'm afraid to climb into the ring."

Montrose squeezed the smaller man's bony shoulder. "That isn't cowardice. It's prudence."

"Like you'd know," Artie said. "Okay, now it's your turn."

Montrose blinked. "I beg your pardon?"

"I confided in you," said Artie, smirking. "Now you tell me *your* girlish secrets, and we can *bond*."

The Hierarch hesitated. "I don't know what to say."

"Well, there's always the hideous nightmare of your premature toilet training. Or your pathological attachment to your moth-eaten teddy bear Bobo. Or we could start small, with your reminiscences of dear old Cleveland."

"Cincinnati," Montrose said.

"Oh, right," the comedian said. "I used to play Cincy all the time. Is it still the wild, mad pleasure city it used to be? Babylon on the Ohio?"

Feeling increasingly wary, Montrose shrugged. "It's just a town as far as I'm concerned."

"Which Renegade outfit were you with?"

Fortunately, the Hierarch had picked up a good deal of information about American rebels during his sojourn along the Mississippi; he knew the names of many of the Renegade organizations operating in the Midwest. "The Jefferson Brigade."

"No kidding," said Artie. "Then I'll bet you know Debbie Donnelly."

"I'm afraid not," Montrose said.

"Ah," the entertainer said. "Well, that's probably because I just made her up."

"What's this all about?" Montrose asked. "Why would you try to trip me up?

Don't you trust me?"

"Very good," Artie said. "I admire a man with a keen grasp of the obvious."

"Do you think the Artificers would plant a spy in the pit? Whatever for? We're not even people to them, just bits of raw material, and they're absolutely confident we can't escape."

"I don't know what to think," Artie replied. He shivered, and hugged himself for warmth. "But certain things don't add up. For one, you're awfully closemouthed about your past."

"I don't remember too much of my premortem existence," said the Scot. It seemed a reasonably plausible lie. Death sometimes punched holes in a spirit's memory. "And I don't enjoy talking about what's happened since. Too much of it was unpleasant."

"Okay," Artie said. "But back in my salad days, before I hit it big, I played a German, an Italian, an Irishman, a Mexican, and even a Jap on stage. I could do it because I've got a knack for dialects. You've got the kind of no-accent accent a guy gets from traveling and talking to a lot of different people. But underneath it, you don't sound a Midwesterner. I hear a trace of Scots, from, oh, a couple hundred years ago?" He lifted his bushy eyebrows.

"I never said I was born in Cincinnati," Montrose replied. "I emigrated from Scotland when I was seventeen."

"Oh, so you do remember something."

"Of course I do," Montrose said. "Once again, I never claimed otherwise. Is this why you distrust me? These petty anomalies?"

"Oh, there's a little more to it," Artie said. "What particularly bothers me is that you and Louise are supposed to be old buddies. And yet, you never talk. You stay as far away from one another as possible. Sometimes when you look at her, and you don't realize I'm watching, you sneer, and when she peeks at you, she looks miserable."

"But she did vouch for me," Montrose said. Once again, he wondered why. "Don't you trust her, either?"

"I've always found the Sisters of Athena to be honest," said Artie, "so yeah, I trust her to a degree. But when I realize there's something my alleged allies aren't telling me, in a situation where my butt is on the line—"

His shackles rattling, Montrose lunged at the other man.

Artie was quicker, evidently a more practiced combatant than his attacker would have guessed. Goggling in alarm, he nearly managed to leap out of the way. But Montrose snapped a one-two combination to the other ghost's jaw and solar plexus, and the performer reeled. The Hierarch grabbed his arm and tumbled him facedown onto the ground, then dove on top of him and seized him by the throat.

"It would have been safer to confront me in the presence of your friends," Montrose growled. "As the situation stands, I'm certain they can't see us, not in this gloom, from all the way across the cavern, with scores of Drones and madmen in the way. I could snap your spine and send you on to experience that Harrowing after all, and they'd be none the wiser. I could tell them a doomshade jumped us, and slew you before I could intervene." He wrenched Artie's head around. But not quite far enough to break his neck.

"That's what I *could* do," the Scot continued. "What I would do if I truly were your enemy. But happily for you, I want us to be comrades, and work together to free ourselves from this dungeon. I hope that you in turn can find it in your heart to trust in my good will, despite my reticence about my background and any peculiarities you observe in my demeanor."

"Get off me," Artie croaked. "You're as heavy as an ox, and I wish I could say the resemblance ends there."

Montrose rose, and when the little man rolled over, he offered him a hand and hoisted him to his feet. A nearby Drone, a balding, pot-bellied man with a prominent appendectomy scar, peered at them curiously. Perhaps he had just enough intellect left to realize that in this purgatory, a scuffle that ended without grievous injury to someone was a rarity.

Artie massaged his neck. "I think you gave me whiplash," he said.

"Do we have an understanding?" Montrose asked.

"I suppose," said Artie. "Like you said, you could have killed me, but you didn't. Just almost. That really eases my mind."

"One question," said Montrose. "Why *didn't* you question me in the presence of the others? You're clever enough to realize it would have been more prudent."

"I figured there was no reason why *everybody* needed to hear your deep, dark secrets, not if it turned out you really were on the up-and-up." He grinned. "You see what I get for trying to be a nice guy. A haggis-eating gorilla mauls me."

"I'm sorry," Montrose said. "It seemed the only way to make my point." Metal groaned and clinked overhead. Alarmed, he lifted his gaze, but no one was operating the crane. It had shifted slightly on its own, perhaps in response to a stray current of air wafting down from the tunnels.

And abruptly, as he stared up at it, a idea flowered in his mind.

"What?" Artie demanded. "Why are you smiling?"

"I've thought of another way to escape," Montrose said. "And I'll be genuinely surprised if you tell me you've already attempted this one."

FIFTEEN

"It's too risky," said Pierre, squatting at the front of the niche in the cavern wall. He was a lanky, fortyish fellow originally from Quebec, with a remarkably hairy body and one glass eye, a relic he'd managed to carry from life into death. Montrose assumed their mutual captors hadn't noticed the orb was artificial. Otherwise they would have confiscated it as they did everything else.

The fallen Anacreon brushed an errant lock of his auburn hair, now sadly in need of combing, out of his eyes. "I disagree."

"First off," said Pierre, "you don't even know if it will really block out the sound. Chanteur voices are funny. They jab right inside your brain."

"On the other hand, we don't know that it *won't* block it," said Artie, warily studying the horde of wraiths shuffling around out in the pit. Somewhere, someone began to scream.

"But even if it does work, what then?" Pierre demanded. "The Artificers have weapons. We don't, and most of us are wearing shackles. Maybe if we could get by with earplugs, we might have a chance, but—"

"It will be dangerous," Montrose said, assuming his most confident air, "but not impossible. I've seen men who were outgunned, weary, half frozen, and starving prevail against superior numbers. We'll have surprise on our side, and that particular advantage wins a great many battles."

"Maybe so," said Charles, a plump young man with a slight stammer. As usual, he sat with his thighs pressed together, evidently to conceal his genitals. "But it wouldn't be like the other tricks we've tried, where, when it didn't work, we were still alive to think up something else. If we make it to the crane, and then things fall apart, we're finished."

"But we're as good as dead *now*," said Louise from the back of the niche. Even though she seemed to be speaking in support of his plan, her sweet voice scraped at Montrose's nerves. Trying to avert a spasm of outright fury, he avoided looking directly at her. "One way or another, this place will destroy us in the end. We have to take *any* chance to escape, even if it seems foolhardy. And this is the only new idea any of us has hit on in a long time.

"I know James only recently arrived," she continued, "and naturally, you're reluctant to face pain and peril on a stranger's say-so. But I assure you"—her voice wavered slightly—"there was a time when I knew him very well, and he was a war hero. He truly has led armies to victory in circumstances as desperate as this. If he thinks the plan will succeed, I trust his instincts."

"Me too," Artie said, "and I'm a good judge of character, though I admit you couldn't tell it by looking at my ex-wives."

"All right," said Pierre, "I'm in. Maybe it is our only chance." He smiled crookedly. "Besides, I'd feel pretty stupid if you people got away with it, and I was still stuck in this hole."

"I'll go, too," said Charles, after which the other members of the band declared their willingness to do likewise.

Montrose smiled. He'd scarcely dared to hope that all of them would embrace his reckless scheme. With eight fighters on their side, they actually might have a chance.

Once the matter was decided, there was nothing to do but wait, while the hours or perhaps even days crawled by; entombed in a cavern, immune to hunger and the need to sleep, they found it all but impossible to judge the passage of time. They kept two sentries posted outside, watching the summit of the cliff. Everyone else engaged in desultory talk, mostly reminiscing about the joys of mortal existence, or played games like Twenty Questions. At one point Louise looked over at Montrose, set her jaw, rose, and headed toward him.

For a moment, for some reason, he felt hypnotized, fascinated by the way the dim blue phosphorescence gleamed on the contours of her naked body. Then a surge of loathing broke the spell, and he wrenched his gaze away. He jumped up and rushed out into the open cavern.

He feared she might follow, but she didn't. He shuddered, swallowed away a dryness in his throat, and, when he was able, told Charles, "Go inside. I'll stand watch for a while." The young man peered at him uncertainly, as if he'd noticed something odd about his expression or tone, but then did as he'd been bidden.

Perhaps an hour later, something stirred in the shadowy opening behind the crane.

"Quick!" Montrose cried. "It's time!" They had to make their preparations quickly, before the Chanteur started to sing.

Some looking frightened and others grinning fiercely, his fellow prisoners scrambled into the open. Montrose positioned himself in front of Artie, cupped his hands, and lashed them against the comedian's ears, bursting his eardrums. Artie made a choking sound and staggered. Meanwhile Louise, the other expert martial artist in the group, injured Charles in the same manner.

In a few seconds they'd deafened everyone except one another. The crane swiveled slowly, squealing, its jaws creaking open and clanking together, like a drowsy beast awakening from a nap. Her tangled, honey-colored hair flying about her head, Louise scrambled in front of the man she'd betrayed. "Good luck," she said. Montrose slammed his palms against the sides of her head.

Her knees buckled. His fists clenched to strike her again, and with an extreme effort of will, he forced them open. Then, to his horror, a long, ululating cry rose from the ledge and echoed from the rocky walls.

Montrose pressed his hands against his ears, but it didn't do any good. As Pierre had predicted, the Chanteur's voice plunged inside his head, splintering his thoughts and filling him with a mindless compulsion to march toward the crane.

He took two trudging steps, and then something caught his ankle, tripping him and dropping him to one knee. Agony exploded through his ears.

He felt an instinctive impulse to heal himself and end the pain, but managed to quash it just in time. Because he realized he was reasoning again, and that meant his idea had worked. Deaf, unable to hear anything but a noise resembling static, he was immune to the magic of the Chanteur.

Louise hauled him to his feet. The cavern floor seemed to tilt beneath him, and she clutched his arm to hold him upright. His injuries had damaged his sense of balance as well as his hearing.

In the past, he and his companions had survived the coming of the Artificers by racing to the far end of the pit, maximizing the distance between themselves and the crane. Usually the guildsmen stopped scooping up prisoners before any of their band shuffled within reach of the metal jaws. This time, however, they *wanted* to be taken up. So they hobbled forward as quickly as they could.

Hampered by excruciating pain, lack of equilibrium, and his shackles, Montrose soon suspected he wasn't going to make it. Mesmerized by the Chanteur's song, the countless Drones, Spectres, and lunatics were nearly as intent on reaching the base of the cliff as he was. He used every infighting trick he knew to shove and elbow his way through the crowd, praying that none of his captors would peer down and notice one of their victims forcing his way forward with considerably more skill and intelligence than the rest. He lost sight of Louise, Artie, and the rest of his allies within the first few moments.

The farther he advanced, the tighter the suffocating press became, until he could only see a few inches in front of his nose. Finally a long shadow, so vague and ill-defined that only the eyes of a wraith could have discerned it in the darkness, swept over the crowd. He looked up. The immense steam-shovel jaws of the crane hung in the air just a few meters ahead.

Without warning, the head of the apparatus plummeted to the floor, pulverizing the ghosts directly beneath it. Montrose couldn't hear the crash, but the shock jolted up his legs. Prisoners clambered into the gaping gray metal dipper.

Montrose struggled forward, trying to fling himself in. When he was almost within reach, the crane jerked upward. Pivoting, it dumped its burden on the ledge.

For several seconds Montrose was grimly certain he'd missed his chance, that the Artificers had already collected as many captives as they needed. Then the long arm swung outward again. The metal jaws dropped, slamming down to his right.

Once again, he struggled toward them. Just as he wrestled a final animate obstacle out of his path, the crane operators reeled the cable in, and the dipper shot upward.

Montrose leaped for it, landed half in and half out, and immediately slid backwards. He frantically clutched at the bodies of his fellow passengers, striving to anchor himself. Still stupefied by the Chanteur's eerie wail, they slapped and pushed at him sluggishly.

The jaws of the dipper began to close on his waist. Grabbing someone by the neck, he yanked himself forward. The rough metal ridges flayed skin from his knees to his toes, but he got his lower limbs inside before anything was severed.

Now that he was sealed in utter darkness, the writhing mass of the other captives seemed less like a jumble of human bodies than a knot of colossal serpents. Once again he fought the temptation to put an end to the ghastly pain in his ears. Finally the dipper opened, and he tumbled out onto the ledge. Several other prisoners dropped on top of him.

Groaning, dazed, he dragged himself from under the pile and peered about. He spotted Louise, Artie, and Charles right away, but in the gloom and confusion, with people milling about, he couldn't tell if any of his other comrades were present.

Then one of the Artificers held up a long chain attached to a series of iron collars, and Montrose realized it no longer mattered. Even if his force was under strength, they had to strike now, before their captors immobilized them in a coffle. Turning, he shuffled around toward a fat crossbowman with skin burned sooty black. The guard wore a glassy crimson domino, the usual coin around his neck, maroon shorts, and high-laced sandals. A falchion, its hilt wrapped in scarlet leather, hung at his side.

The smith pivoted, also. Doing his best to look hypnotized, Montrose gave him an imbecilic smile. The Artificer's lip curled, and he turned away. The Scot lunged and punched at his kidney.

Another wave of vertigo overtook him in mid-attack. The blow landed, but not solidly. The guildsman skipped backward and raised his crossbow. Staggering forward, Montrose flailed, somehow managed to knock the weapon out of the other man's hand, and then fell to his knees.

The Artificer retreated again, this time to draw his blade. Montrose scrambled forward and flung himself against his opponent's shins. The smith lurched back a final step and toppled over the edge of the cliff.

Montrose sprawled on the ledge for a second, groping for the strength to keep fighting despite the throbbing in his ears and the terrible dizziness. Then he gripped the crossbow properly, lurched to one knee, and shot an Artificer in the back. When that guard dropped, he grabbed the fellow's darksteel saber and engaged another.

By the time he disposed of that one, the crane operators were scrambling away from the heart of their mechanism—a bewildering arrangement of clockwork, pulleys, gauges, levers, a steam engine, gleaming brass pyramids, and pulsing, luminous crystals—to join the fray. Hindered by his shackles, taking small, quick steps, he charged them.

When, rather to his own surprise, he'd cut them down as well, he turned, peering, trying to discern how the battle was going. And was overjoyed to see his side was winning. Evidently his entire force *had* made it to the ledge, caught their captors flatfooted, and nearly finished dispatching them. He grinned.

Then he caught sight of the duel on the edge of the drop.

A mace in one hand and a pistol—presumably out of bullets—in the other, long white gashes on her forehead and left shoulder, Louise struggled to fend off a huge Artificer in a brazen mask. A far better fighter than any of the guildsmen Montrose had slain, the smith swung a poleax with appalling speed and accuracy. Hindered by pain, her shackles, and impaired balance, further handicapped by her adversary's superior strength and reach, the Sister of Athena manifestly couldn't cope with him.

Montrose glanced about. His other comrades were still busy with their own opponents. They hadn't even noticed Louise's predicament, and wouldn't have been able to rush to her aid even if they had. Nor, he thought, smirking, creeping by behind her foe, would they be any the wiser if he didn't help her, either. So why not wait for the Artificer to dispose of her, and *then* drive his saber into the fellow's back? It would be delightful to watch hope flower in her eyes, then crumble into despair when she realized he wasn't going to save her.

But he found he couldn't do it. She hadn't abandoned him when he'd fallen under the spell of the Chanteur, nor did he wish to break faith with Artie, who'd trusted him to stand by every member of their company. Besides, they were nowhere near out of danger yet, and he might need her later. Snarling, he slashed at the Artificer's neck, half severing his head. The big man collapsed, dissolving into ripples of black light before he reached the ground.

Swaying with exhaustion, Louise spoke. Montrose had never studied lip-reading, but it looked as if she'd said, "Thank you." He felt something twist inside his chest, and then someone tapped him on the shoulder.

He lurched around, nearly tripping over his chain. Artie stood behind him, babbling something, brandishing a silvery megaphone.

Montrose surmised that the Chanteur had been using the conical instrument to augment the natural powers of his voice. And if the object was now in Artie's possession, the wretch had presumably been silenced. Gratefully, the Scot allowed his eardrums to heal. The process sent a wave of weakness sweeping through his body. His knees turned rubbery, and he nearly fell. But the pain in his head and his vertigo disappeared. He sobbed with relief.

"—believe we did it!" Artie said.

"I'm just as pleased as you are," Montrose croaked, straightening up and surveying the scene. His troops scavenged clothing and weapons, and Drones shuffled aimlessly about. "But we aren't out of the woods yet. Did we lose anyone?"

Artie's smirk gave way to a grimace. He looked ashamed of his momentary elation. "Yeah. Abdul got shot."

"I'm sorry," said Montrose. "But if only one of us perished, we got off more lightly than we had any right to expect. Thank goodness we were fighting artisans and not trained soldiers. Do you know if any of the enemy escaped into the tunnels?"

Artie shook his head.

"Neither do I," Montrose said, retrieving a green leather vest, matching breeches, and a pair of shoes from the ground. The body that had once been inside them had evidently fallen into the Void. "Considering the confusion, I don't see how anyone could be certain one way or the other, so we'll have to assume the worst. Which is to say, that someone has carried word of our insurrection to the Artificers upstairs."

"Terrific," Artie growled. He flung the megaphone over the drop, bent down, picked up a backsword, and swung it back and forth, testing the weight and balance.

"We should move out quickly," said Louise, "before they have a chance to get organized. But our chances will improve immensely if we can get rid of these leg irons."

"I've got it covered!" Charles cried. Standing beside the crane, his ankles now unshackled and his flabby stomach bulging over the waistband of a yellow kilt, he brandished a ring of keys. "The second guy I killed had these hanging on his belt."

"Good work," Montrose said. Eager to be rid of his chains, he hobbled forward.

"Wait," murmured Louise. His muscles tightening, he pivoted back around to face her. "I..."

"I don't wonder at your hesitation," said Montrose, sneering, but keeping his voice low. It would scarcely help his men's morale to perceive how much he and the missionary despised one another. "What could you possibly have to say to me?" He spied a fallen silver visor, snatched it up, and pressed it his face, where the minor magic woven into the metal held it in position. For some reason, concealing his features made him feel a little calmer.

SIXTEEN

A crossbow cradled in his hands, a quiver of quarrels on his back, and his saber sheathed at his hip, Montrose glanced backward, taking a last look at the Drones trudging aimlessly about on the ledge, or simply staring catatonically. To his surprise, he felt a twinge of guilt. It seemed wrong to abandon any captive who'd made it to the top of the cliff.

Scowling behind his silver mask, he pushed the senseless impulse away. He owed these wretches nothing, and in any case, their idiocy was their ultimate prison. If he couldn't free them from that—and no one could—it would be pointless to imperil his own existence or that of his comrades to herd them through the tunnels.

"I know how you feel," murmured a feminine voice. He hadn't heard Louise creep up beside him, and he gave a violent start. "The poor creatures. I pray that somehow, someday, someone will find a way to heal them."

Why the imposture? he wondered bitterly. *Why pretend to be compassionate when she knows I know her for the ruthless bitch she truly is? Probably for the benefit of Artie and the others, or perhaps her hypocrisy is such that she simply can't help it.* Twisting away from her, he surveyed his other comrades, all now unchained, clad, and armed as well as possible. "Shall we be off?" he asked. "Liberty is just a brisk stroll away." They babbled their assent. "Good. Just remember to be quiet. If there's another force headed in our direction, we want to hear them before they hear us." He led them into the first passage.

With only a few dimly glowing greenish crystals set in the walls for illumination, the tunnels were as dark as the pit. They also had just as many bewildering bends and forks as he remembered. The first time he came to a dead end and had to turn around, Charles muttered something to the wraith beside him. Montrose missed the words, but he caught the anxious tone.

Artie sauntered to the head of the column, his new shotgun cradled on his shoulder. "I was so worried about getting out of the hole, I half forgot what a maze we'd have to run if we did. I'm getting this craving for cheese."

Montrose smiled. "Our hosts' precautions do seem a bit rococo, don't they?"

Artie snorted. "That's Artificers for you. Rube Goldbergs, every one of them. One gadget—or security measure—might do the job, but why stop there when you could build five or ten?"

Two staircases swam out of the gloom ahead. Montrose paused to study them, then rejected both in favor of the arch between them. Some of his companions whispered to one another. They might not know the way out, but they knew they were underground, and would have to climb to escape. The Scot turned. "Patience," he said. "Neither of those is the right staircase. I know because I'm a Harbinger, a pathfinder, just as I told you. I can guide you to the exit, and I will."

"I trust you," Louise declared. "We'd still be stuck in the dungeon if not for you." Montrose led them on down the passage.

"I trust you, too," Artie whispered. The pale jade glow of a wall crystal gleamed on his sharp nose and bushy eyebrows. "Sort of. But I'd feel better if I was sure your talents really apply to the situation."

"They do and they don't," Montrose said, just as softly. "I can perceive twists and fractures in space. That doesn't help me navigate an ordinary three-dimensional labyrinth. But I've also developed an aptitude for choosing the proper direction in any situation. And I tried to memorize our route when my captor marched me in. I recall some of it. Don't tell the others I'm groping my way, all right? It would only rattle them to no purpose."

"I haven't blown your cover so far, have I, even though *you* won't trust *me* with the secret of who you really are. But if you keep making wrong turns, the others'll figure it out for themselves. Any chance of you opening a Nihil? I wouldn't mind being dumped in the Tempest to get the hell out of here."

"Alas, no," Montrose said. He led the column into a tunnel that sloped gently downward. Behind him, someone growled an obscenity. "That particular feat is fairly easy in the Shadowlands, but more difficult in Stygia, where, in a real sense, we *are* inside the Tempest. It's paradoxical, like trying to plunge below the surface of a lake when you're already on the bottom. I'd either need to be one of the great masters of my Arcanos, which I'm not, or exploit a major fault in the dimensional fabric. And I don't sense one anywhere in the immediate vicinity."

The longer they marched, and the more cul-de-sacs they ran up against, the more nervous Montrose's companions became. Though he understood that, having expended precious energy to heal their wounds, they were weary, the Scot still marveled that, armed and tramping away from the hated pit, they seemed more apprehensive than they had when trapped inside it. Perhaps despair had made them reckless before, and now the hope of actually escaping, together with the concomitant reflection that a danger or a wrong move truly mattered, had rendered them timid. Or perhaps their Shadows were chipping away at their resolve.

The Anacreon led them up a staircase into a small pentagonal chamber with a trefoil arch in each wall. Beyond one of them, at the end of a short corridor, was another set of steps, again leading upward. Montrose paused, pondering, and then headed for the opening across from that one.

"No!" exclaimed Pierre. Montrose turned. "I remember this room. We have to keep climbing. Take the next set of stairs."

"I recall the place myself," the Scot replied. "But I didn't come down those particular stairs, and I doubt you did, either. In any case, I sense they won't take us out."

"I don't want to quarrel with you, James," said the other ghost, scowling. "I too am grateful for what you've done. But if your powers were reliable, you wouldn't have us retracing our steps so often. We're running out of time, I say this is the way, and I'm going to use my own judgment." He strode through the arch.

Suddenly Montrose's intuition screamed that the short passage wasn't merely the wrong way, but dangerous. "Stop!" he shouted. Louise, who was closer to the archway, lunged through, hands outstretched to seize Pierre and drag him back.

Dazzling, freezing barrow-flame blasted from a concealed nozzle in the wall, catching Pierre in mid-step, incinerating him. Ripples of shadow, almost invisible inside the glare, dissolved the last vestiges of his substance. The blaze winked out, and a tomahawk, a spear, and a glass eye, all fused by the fire, thumped to the floor.

"Damn it!" said Louise, her arms still uselessly extended. "Damn it! If I'd moved a second sooner!"

Or if I'd realized a second sooner, Montrose thought. Over the centuries, he'd led countless men to destruction. He'd thought he'd grown inured to it, but for some reason, this death galled him. Perhaps because Pierre was no soldier, merely a desperate civilian struggling to survive. Or because his demise might so easily have been avoided.

"Put a maze on top of the pit," Artie said, sounding sick. "Then put death traps in the maze. Rube Goldberg. God, I hate Artificers."

Montrose turned to his companions. "Pierre was right about one thing," he said. "We're probably running out of time. Much as we might like to, we can't stand here grieving. Will the rest of you follow my lead now?"

"Yeah," Artie sighed. The others nodded.

Several minutes later, the party reached a staircase a hair wider than any they'd encountered before. A green crystal glowed in the left-hand wall, about two thirds of the way out. Montrose let out a long exhalation, surprising himself. He hadn't realized he was holding his breath.

"What's up?" Artie asked.

"I *know* I recognize these steps," Montrose said. "What's more, I'm certain I can find the way from here. We've nearly reached the Soulforges."

"Great," said the abolitionist. "And still no guards trying to stop us. Maybe none of the smiths did make it away from the pit, and nobody knows we're coming. Or do you think we really might have slipped past them by going up one tunnel when they were coming down another?"

"I don't know," said Montrose. "Either way, I never believed we'd be this lucky. I assumed we'd encounter opposition, probably at a point like this. If I were trying to neutralize a band of escaping prisoners, I might well have deployed my force at the top of those stairs."

As if on cue, a jumble of noise, shouts and the crackle of gunfire, echoed down from overhead. Charles yelped and jumped backwards. Another man jerked up his rifle, presumably to fire at the top of the steps, though the gun wound up pointing at Artie's skull.

Montrose struck the weapon out of line. "Calm down!" he said. "Can't you tell nobody's shooting at us—not yet, anyway. The sound is still a ways off. Something else is happening."

"It sounds like somebody's attacking the Artificers," said Louise. "Perhaps that's why no one has intercepted us. The hunters rushed back to the surface to oppose the greater threat."

"Maybe it's your Sisters of Athena!" said Charles. "Or some other Renegade army! Somebody who's come to rescue us!"

"Conceivably," said Montrose. Privately he thought it quite unlikely, but on the other hand, he couldn't think of a more plausible explanation. "But the mere possibility doesn't justify dropping our guard. Come on."

They crept up the staircase, the echoing shots, battle cries, shrieks, and clangor of blades louder with every step. As they neared the forging chamber, the air growing steadily colder, it became obvious that the fight was just ahead of them.

Montrose lifted a hand, and the fugitives came to a halt. "It might be helpful to know exactly what's going on before we all blunder out into the midst of it," he said. "So I'm going to scout ahead." He concentrated, straining to invoke his Harbinger abilities.

It was more difficult than he'd expected. Evidently, whether he'd quite realized it or not, he was as exhausted as his companions. Though no longer requiring sleep as mortals did, his body craved rest in some safe and quiet place. Finally cool darkness seeped from his pores and spread across his skin. The others exclaimed as he vanished from their sight.

"It's all right," he said, "I'm still here, merely invisible. Stay put until I return."

He skulked up to the arch leading to the huge, high-ceilinged workshop. Noxious vapors stung his eyes. Beyond the opening raged a chaotic struggle between the Artificers and a band of wraiths in black clothing and armor emblazoned with arcane symbols sacred to the servants of the Void. Each of the attackers wore a full-face mask or a helmet that concealed his features. The prisoners of the smiths hung in the fires, abandoned, their substance burning away to nothing. Even the mindless Drones had begun to scream.

Montrose thought it a strange scene, and for more than one reason. Though some of the Spectres displayed inhuman anatomy—glittering scales, curling ram's horns, or wicked talons—such as a wraith might hire a Masquer to create, as far as he could tell, none possessed the kind of hideous, asymmetrical deformities often manifested by the servants of Oblivion. Nor was any surrounded by a visible aura of dark, malignant energy. Moreover, it was extremely rare, though by no means unheard of, for any foe, Spectre, Renegade, or Heretic, to conduct a raid against Stygia itself.

He grimaced. He'd ponder the oddities later, after he'd extricated himself from this odious place. Dissolving his veil of shadow, he trotted back to his companions.

"What did you see?" Charles asked.

"The Artificers are fighting a war party of Spectres," Montrose replied.

"Is there any chance at all we could slip through the room without getting tangled up in the battle?" asked Louise.

Montrose shook his head. "I don't see how." It occurred to him that, masked in darkness, *he* might be able to do it. But he'd have to abandon the rest of them, and that was out of the question. He was no longer the idealistic fool Argyll had hanged, but he still took pride in being an able general. "I'll just have to find an alternate route through the rest of the maze." He peered about, listening to his intuition, and then conducted the column down another tunnel. The ghastly chill of the fires abated slightly, while the sounds of battle grew gradually fainter.

Before long the fugitives began to pass a series of apartments. Frowning, Montrose noted that the Artificers had profited in the service of the Smiling Lord—indeed, had feathered their own nests far more opulently than their master could have imagined. Even the smallest rooms, presumably the quarters of the humblest apprentices, were crammed with an abundance of furniture and trinkets. Montrose knew ministers housed in the Onyx Tower itself who were less blessed with material possessions. Unlike the amenities they provided for others, many of the guildsmen's goods had frozen, anguished faces projecting from their facades, as if the artisans reveled in the knowledge that their craft required the destruction of living souls.

Montrose rounded another corner. Six feet in front of him, the corridor terminated in a blank gray wall.

"Oh, shit," said Charles. He sounded as if he were struggling not to cry.

"Blast!" Montrose snarled. "I was certain—and by the Scythe and the Lantern, I still am." He stared intently at the surface until instinct told him where to put his hand. A rectangular stone yielded beneath his touch. With a grating sound, the wall slid aside, revealing the darker, narrower passage beyond. The floor was a mosaic of black, white, and crimson stones about eight inches square, seemingly laid down in a random pattern.

"Pretty slick, Jimmy," Artie said. "Of course, we should have figured that if the forgers got a kick out of mazes and death traps, they'd go in for secret passages, too."

Montrose stepped forward. His intuition screamed a warning, and he froze.

"What's wrong now?" Charles wailed.

"This hall is boobytrapped as well," Montrose said. "I'm sure of it."

Charles's face crumpled. "We're never going to get out!"

Louise squeezed his shoulder. "Yes, we will," she said firmly. She turned to Montrose. "Surely the mechanism isn't designed to kill *everyone* who tries to pass through. What would be the point of putting a snare like that in a secret passage?"

"None," the Anacreon replied. "And I believe that if we set our feet on the proper blocks, we'll be all right." Not that he had to tread on any of them. With his Arcanos, he could fly through. But he feared he was too exhausted to ferry them all down the passage, one at a time, and he'd be a shabby excuse for a commander if he asked them to depend on his judgment when he didn't appear to trust it himself. "Everyone, step exactly where I do."

He moved gingerly forward, peering closely at the parti-colored floor. He didn't know if he was actually seeing a difference among the flags, something so subtle he couldn't articulate it, or being guided by pure instinct, but either way, and much to his relief, he found that he *could* distinguish between the trigger stones and the safe ones.

His companions crept after him in single file, their stolen shoes squeaking and scuffing on the floor. Someone panted. Louise murmured a prayer or meditation under her breath. Artie seemed to be reciting both parts of a comedic dialogue, something about "Who's on first, what's on second, and I-don't-know's on third." Montrose wondered if that was *his* notion of a transcendental meditation.

The Hierarch suspected that the Artificers employed a formula to traverse the corridor safely. Now reasonably confident of his ability to spot the trigger stones before he trod on them, he attempted to work out the pattern, but to no avail. Whatever it was, it was too complex to decipher on the fly.

He supposed it didn't matter. Not as long as he could tell—

Crossing his legs, he stepped on a white stone, which yielded infinitesimally beneath his sole. Three barbed darksteel blades, stacked vertically, shot out of the wall. Charles squawked. Invoking his power of flight, Montrose started to hurtle forward, but could already see that he wouldn't get out of the way in time.

Just as they were about to pierce his torso, the blades rang. The middle one snapped in two and the others bent sideways, missing him, as if someone had struck them a mighty blow with an invisible club.

Montrose turned. Artie was clutching Charles, holding him up. Evidently, startled, the pudgy young man in the kilt had lost his balance, and might have stumbled onto one of the trigger flags if the comedian hadn't grabbed him. Trembling, Louise was leaning against the wall. Montrose realized that she'd used her own magical talents to save him.

He didn't know what he felt—surely not gratitude, not after all that had passed between them—or what he should say, but felt he must say *something*. "Are you all right?" he asked gruffly.

"Yes," she wheezed. "That little stunt was hard for me. I'm not really that good a Spook."

"I'm starting to wonder if our pal Pinky here is really all that hot a Harbinger," said Artie, leering, but with a slight quaver in his voice. "Level with me, Natty Bumppo, how many box tops did you have to mail in to get your diploma?"

"I hope you don't begrudge me one little mistake," Montrose said dryly. "But if you're reluctant to follow me any farther, by all means, feel free to navigate your own course back to safer ground." Sure that his companions no longer remembered which stones were safe, he gestured at the yards of hallway behind them.

Artie peered backward as if considering the option, swallowed comically, and said, "Uh, thanks but no thanks, fearless leader. On further consideration, I'd just as soon stick with you."

"I thought you might," Montrose said. "Is everyone ready?" Louise inclined her head. Charles gave him a jerky nod. "Then come on."

They reached the end of the hall without further incident. Another secret door led them into a circular vault, where a carved design of hammers and flames decorated the ribs in the ceiling. Beyond a lancet arch extended another corridor, and at the end of that was a foyer and a tall, narrow iron door.

"That's it," Montrose said. "An exit." The other fugitives jabbered excitedly, and they all surged forward.

A detachment of several Spectres, stepping into view from another hallway, strode into the foyer, blocking the fugitives' way out. A tall doomshade clad in a hood like an executioner's mask and sable robes decorated with the foul emblems of the Malfeans was the first to notice the onrushing party. Startled, he pivoted and stared.

Montrose shot him in the chest. Snatching out his saber, he bellowed a battle cry, one his Highlanders had roared at Alford and Kilsyth, and charged. His companions pounded after him.

Others Spectres lurched around, jerked up their guns, and snapped off shots. The bullets sang past Montrose, leaving him unscathed, though he was grimly certain that not all of his comrades had been as lucky. A final bound carried him into striking distance.

He cut down one foe and instantly assailed another. The second Spectre, a burly fellow whose helm bore a crest cast in the image of Gorool, whipped up his bayoneted rifle to parry. The two blades clanged together, striking sparks.

The doomshade thrust his point at Montrose's belly. The Scot retreated a half step, avoiding the stab, then feinted a slash at his opponent's thigh. As the bayonet jerked down to block, he whirled the saber up and slammed it down on the other wraith's head.

The hideous helmet split in two, revealing a round face with a bulbous, ruddy potato of a nose, pale blue eyes, eyebrows so blond they were nearly invisible, and a receding hairline. His scalp gashed, the rifleman staggered. Gaping in amazement, Montrose finished the fellow off by pure reflex, just as it was sheer martial instinct which prompted him to whirl, searching for another foe. He couldn't find one. His surviving troops—evidently he'd lost another man in the skirmish—had already accounted for the rest of the enemy. He turned back to look at the rifleman again, but by that time the fellow's body had already dissolved into nothingness.

"Come on!" Artie said.

Montrose blinked. "What?"

"Come on!" the abolitionist repeated. "We got the door open! We're free!" He seized the Scot by the arm and half dragged him into a narrow lane. Ugly warehouses and factories towered on all sides. Sheet lightning flickered in the eternal storm clouds overhead, staining the stonework green.

SEVENTEEN

When Montrose slipped inside the boxcar, he found countless scratches on the reinforced wooden walls, floor, and ceiling. Evidently the car had been used to import Thralls, as similar rolling prisons had once carried prisoners to Auschwitz and Buchenwald, and some of the wretches had tried to claw their way to freedom.

The Hierarch grimaced. Having just escaped the Artificers' dungeon, he didn't much care to be reminded of slavery. But the car was sitting on a siding in a seemingly deserted corner of a vast rail yard. It seemed like a good place to hide until he recovered his strength. He looked back out the door. "This will do."

His exhausted companions clambered in, and Charles shoved the sliding door most of the way shut. Though fairly certain no potential enemy was close enough to overhear, Montrose winced at the resulting rumble.

Louise slumped to the floor. "I never imagined it would feel so good just to have clothing, be warm, or see the sky."

"Well, frankly, m'dear I used to pay good money to be chained up naked," Artie said, smirking. "Still, you have a point. And I'm going to feel even better when we put some distance between Stygia and us. Thank God we've got a Harbinger to steer us through the Tempest."

Montrose felt a vague twinge of discomfort. Grimacing behind his mask, he quashed it. "I'm afraid that isn't so. I promised to lead you people out of the guildsmen's fortress. I didn't say I'd shepherd you any farther, and I prefer to take my chances alone from here."

"But then we're still trapped!" said Charles.

"Not so," said Montrose. "The Hierarchy has expended centuries of effort marking and stabilizing certain major byways through the Tempest. Except in unusual circumstances, a person doesn't have to be a Harbinger to follow those roads. Just avoid the patrols and bandits, and you'll do all right. Or better still, stow away aboard an outgoing train. With luck, you could reach the Shadowlands in a matter of hours."

"I know I'm not a soldier," said Charles. "I know I was scared. But I did my best back there, and I'll keep trying—"

Montrose lifted a hand to silence him. "Please, don't disparage yourself. You were fine. You obeyed orders, and fought hard when required. You *all* did well. That isn't the point."

"*I'm* the point, aren't I, James?" said Louise wearily. "You simply can't bear my presence, even knowing you'd be safer with friends to watch your back." Charles, and those other fugitives who hadn't realized Montrose despised her, peered at the two of them curiously.

"True enough," said the Scot. "I desperately want to put some distance between us, and if you have any sense, you ought to feel the same."

"Whatever you say to the contrary," Louise replied, "we both know these others will have a better chance in the company of a Harbinger. If *I* go, will you stay?"

Artie glared at her. "Don't be an idiot. Nobody expects you to sacrifice yourself."

"I'm a Sister of Athena," she replied, "sworn to help others even at the risk of my own existence. Although I have no intention of becoming a martyr. I may not possess James's talents, but I'm a trained warrior, and skillful enough at my own Arcanos. I'll make it back to Earth."

"What a noble offer," Montrose drawled. "And it sounded so sincere. But then, I would have expected no less. Be at ease, you won't be compelled to wrack your brains, thinking of a way to squirm out of it. I'd take my leave even if you weren't here."

"And why's that?" Artie asked.

"Personal reasons," Montrose said.

The little abolitionist made a spitting sound. "You can take your 'personal reasons,' fold them up, and stick 'em where the stars don't shine, hotshot. I didn't mind you holding on to your secrets before, but that was then and this is now. You noticed something just before we ran through that last door, something that flabbergasted you, something that, for all I know, represents some horrible danger to the rest of us. And after all we've just been through together, you *owe* it to us to tell us what it is."

Montrose hesitated. Artie was a presumptuous fool. The Hierarch owed him nothing. If anything, it was the other way around. Yet even so, Montrose *did* feel an obscure impulse to tell. He doubted it could do any harm, and perhaps anyone in his position would desire to share such an immense and calamitous discovery with *someone*. "Very well," he said, making sure his crossbow was still cocked and within easy reach. "I'm not going to relate the whole ugly history of my association with Louise. I daresay she's thankful for my reticence. But I will confide something of more immediate significance. When I first saw the raiders, I thought they made an odd-looking band of Spectres." He explained why. "And when we fought them, I cut one of their helmets in two, and recognized the face underneath. It belonged to a Legionnaire named Ingmar Svensen, a soldier in the service of the Laughing Lady. I fought alongside him against genuine doomshades, in the great campaign of 1832, and encountered him from time to time in the years since. So I'm sure I'm not mistaken."

Charles goggled at him. "You mean you were a Legionnaire yourself?"

"To be exact," said Montrose, "I'm a cashiered Anacreon, wrongly convicted of treason." He found that he rather enjoyed their astonishment. "I hope no one has hard feelings about that, not now, after, as Artie pointed out, we've been through so much together. But if anyone does, well, let's settle it now."

"Calm down," Artie said, sounded annoyed. "Nobody wants to take out his hatred of Stygia on little old you. Especially now that you've given us something more intellectually stimulating to think about. You're claiming that one Deathlord *disguised* her stooges as Spectres and sent them out to fight another's."

"Exactly," Montrose said. "The Seven have been conniving against each other since Charon's demise. Each covets the throne, or at least means to ensure that none of the others gains supremacy. But up until now, they've restricted themselves to political maneuvering. If they've begun conducting covert military operations against one another's minions in the capital itself, it can only mean the Empire is poised on the brink of all-out civil war."

"Well," said Charles, "if it tears itself apart, it'll stop persecuting people like us, and that's good." He faltered. "Isn't it?"

"No," said Montrose, "it isn't. I know you hate the Hierarchy." He smiled ruefully. "Considering what's happened to me lately, even I'm not quite as enamored of it as I used to be. But still, if not for the Legions, the Spectres would annihilate us all, Imperial, Renegade, and Heretic alike."

"It says so right in all the propaganda," said Artie, his bumpkinly tone and wide-eyed expression a parody of naïveté, "so you know it must be true."

"You're a clever fellow," Montrose told him, "correct more often than not. But you haven't been dead anywhere near as long as I have. You haven't witnessed the horrors I saw, fighting Charon's wars. And I assure you that if Stygia ever finds itself unable to continue defending Creation, I can't imagine who else could take up the burden."

Artie smiled. "Don't underestimate us Renegades. If you Stygians had any clue as to just how powerful we're getting, you'd wet your pants. But skip it. If you honestly believe Charon's creaky old dog-and-pony show is indispensable, I'm know I'm not going to convince you otherwise. But even so, you shouldn't worry. Even if the Hierarchy does have a civil war, it probably won't collapse. One Deathlord will grab the throne, and things will settle down. Hell, maybe they'll be more stable than before. The Hierarchy's been slowly losing its grip ever since Godzilla gobbled up El Queso Grande. Maybe a new head honcho could turn that around."

"Perhaps," said Montrose doubtfully, "if any of the Seven is truly fit to wear Charon's mantle. I've seen them all at one time or another, and they're awesome enough to be sure, but none of them exudes quite the same aura of omnipotence their master did. I suspect that now that he's gone, the Empire may very well need each of them, presiding over his proper sphere, to function properly.

"But even if that isn't so, there's still cause for concern. Recently, on an expedition to the United States, I met a Ferryman named Katrina. She cautioned me that some mysterious new menace had arisen to threaten me and countless others. I didn't take the warning seriously. But in time I discovered that Pardoners were vanishing—presumably being assassinated—along the lower Mississippi, and impostors setting up shop in their places. The newcomers practice a corrupt version of their Arcanos, strengthening a client's Shadow instead of binding it. In consequence, an ugly mood prevails throughout the province. People fly into rages and slay one another on the slightest provocation."

"What's more," said Louise, "Heretic priests and missionaries have also disappeared, as if somebody wants to eliminate *anyone* who might provide spiritual guidance to the Restless. I nearly fell victim of an attack myself."

The traitoress cocked her head. "Do you know, James," she continued thoughtfully, "your crusade against the Heretic Circles in the region could be construed as another facet of the same campaign. You and your irregulars were spreading spiritual darkness, also."

"Nonsense," Montrose snapped. "There nothing unusual about Stygia conducting an inquisition."

"Unfortunately," she replied, "I suppose that's so. But the Governors in Natchez didn't request one, did they? If what I heard is true, they initially wanted nothing to do with it. So isn't it interesting that, with all the Shadowlands to choose from, the Smiling Lord dispatched you to that particular part of the American South?"

Montrose frowned, thinking it over. "Perhaps," he said reluctantly. "In any case, I also learned that a murderer called the Atheist is killing mortal priests and ministers, as if to foment terror and disenchantment with religion on *their* side of the Shroud."

"So what does it all mean?" Artie asked.

"I wish I knew," Montrose replied. "I was framed for subversion, arrested, and returned here in chains before I could find out. But if relations among the Seven have so deteriorated that they're about to go to war, that might be another facet of the same complex strategy. They couldn't do much to counter an external threat while fighting one another."

"You two are implying the *Deathlords* are being manipulated," Artie said. "Do you really think that's possible?"

Montrose shrugged. "I wouldn't have said so a month ago. They are virtual demigods, after all. And lord knows, there was never any love lost among them. You don't have to posit an unseen hand to account for their present malice. But I always thought they had better sense than to allow their rivalry to endanger the realm. And for armed hostilities to erupt now, at the same time that sinister forces are at work in the Shadowlands, would constitute quite a coincidence."

"Hm," said Artie, mulling it over. "There's one thing I still don't understand. Well, actually, there are a million things, but one you can explain. Whatever's going on, why don't you want to check out with us? If Stygia's about to become a war zone, that's all the more reason to schlep your keister down the road."

"But I intend to prevent the war," Montrose said. For an instant, the declaration made him feel rather pleasantly like the gallant fool of his youth, the high-minded Cavalier who'd never quailed from any challenge. "By infiltrating the Onyx Tower, reaching the Smiling Lord, or, failing him, someone else in high authority, and convincing that person to do whatever it takes to halt the preparations."

"On the say-so of a supposed Benedict Arnold," Artie said. "Oh, yeah. Good plan, Pinky. That'll happen."

Louise stared at Montrose. "Artie's right. The whole idea is insane. People say that *no one* has ever slipped through the defenses of Charon's palace."

Montrose smiled. "They also said no one had ever escaped the Soulforges. I don't suppose they'll say it anymore."

"I'm sure security is always tight, all over Stygia," Louise persisted. "If the Deathlords are about to go to war with one another, their guards will be more vigilant than usual. And you're a fugitive. Everyone will be watching for you. You'll never even make it across the channel."

"We'll see," Montrose said.

"Well, you're on your own," said a wraith slumped in the corner. "I'm with Artie. I *want* Stygia to crash and burn."

"Well, believe it or not," said Artie, sounding bemused, "I *am* tempted to tag along. This whole thing is so weird, it makes me curious to see what'll happen next. But I can't come, either. I have a responsibility to the Underground Railroad. If the Empire's in danger of falling apart, and something sinister is happening away down south in Dixie, then I've got to tell my friends. Sorry, bubbie."

"That's all right," Montrose replied. "I told you already, I *want* to go alone. None of you can become invisible, so your presence would only be a hindrance. Moreover, if you'll pardon my frankness, given your professed rebel sentiments, how could I trust you not to sabotage the mission? Now, why don't we be quiet and rest? When we've recovered our strength, we'll go our separate ways." He leaned back against the splintery wall and closed his eyes. Muttering to one another, the flooring creaking as they shifted about, his companions gradually settled themselves as well. After a few minutes, the last conversation droned to a halt.

Some time after that, Louise's baggy khaki shorts rubbed softly together as she drew herself to her feet. One sandal squeaked as she crept toward Montrose.

His eyes still shut, the Scot wondered why she thought she could sneak up on him. She'd been dead nearly as long as he had. She ought to be thoroughly accustomed to the keen hearing of the Restless. Perhaps, for some reason, she thought he was Slumbering, although ordinarily ghosts only succumbed to that sleep-like state when grievously injured by darksteel, barrow-fire, or the natural weaponry of certain doomshades.

In any case, he was delighted she'd decided to attack him. The prospect of sparing her had galled him sorely, and now he wouldn't have to. Peering through slitted eyes, he'd wait until she was standing over him with her weapon of choice upraised, then kick her feet out from under her, leap up, and butcher her with his saber. Under the circumstances, no one would blame him for defending himself. Indeed, Artie and the others would finally recognize her for the vile creature she was. For some reason, the thought of exposing her true nature pleased him nearly as much as the idea of her impending demise.

"Oh, James," she sighed. "I was tiptoeing to keep from disturbing everyone else, not because I meant to slit your throat. Dear God, how did it ever come to this?"

He wondered how she'd known he'd heard her coming. He supposed he must have tensed without realizing it. Opening his eyes, he saw that her hands were empty. She'd left her pistol, spiky-headed mace, and long dagger on the floor behind her.

"I'm sure you recall *exactly* how it came to this," he replied. She might have flinched; in the darkness, it was difficult to tell. "If you weren't attempting to slay me, what *do* you want?"

"To talk some more about your plan," she said, squatting down beside him. "Surely there's more than one way to skin this particular cat. Why don't you come back to the Shadowlands and continue striving to discover the enemy's plans and identity there? It would be safer than trying to slip into the Tower."

"Probably so," he said. "But if armed conflict broke out here while I was investigating elsewhere, it would no longer matter what I learned. No, someone needs to address this particular problem immediately."

She was quiet for several moments. At last she said, "Very well, then I'll help you."

Utterly astonished, Montrose gaped at her. "You're joking," he said at last.

"No," she said.

"Then you're mad. I said I wouldn't even trust Artie or these other"—he waved his hand at the remaining fugitives—"staunch comrades who've done me nothing but good. How, then, can you imagine I'd welcome you?"

"Because I protected your identity in the pit, to keep the others from hurting you. And during our escape, I saved your neck."

"For the same reason I helped you: we were in desperate straits, and realized we had a far better chance of getting out if we worked together. Not because you wish me well. Or Stygia either, for that matter. You're a Sister of Athena. You, too, pray for the day when the old order will 'crash and burn.'"

"That isn't *quite* true. I'd be more than content to see it evolve into a more humane system. One that would shut down the Soulforges, strike off the shackles of every Thrall, and reopen the temples of the Shining Ones. I just don't think that's likely to happen without a revolution."

Montrose sneered. "How astute of you."

Her generous mouth tightened at his scorn. "But I agree that the Legions serve a purpose when they hold back the Spectres. I believe that despite our differences, all of us, Stygian, Renegade, and Heretic, share a common interest in resisting Oblivion. And if the same malevolent force is fomenting discord in this place and murdering priests on Earth, then perhaps, this one time, I have a duty to prop up the Hierarchy, corrupt and oppressive as it is."

"What about your professed duty to our companions?"

"Artie's resourceful. He'll get the others back to Earth. You need me more. I may not be able to veil myself in darkness, but you can't deny I have useful skills of my own."

"No, I can't. But that still leaves the issue of your trustworthiness. I don't dare believe a word you've said about your real intentions. For all I know, you *do* want the Deathlords to fight one another. Or perhaps I'm giving you too much credit, thinking you truly care about political and philosophical issues one way or the other. Actually, it seems more likely that you just want to look after yourself. Conceivably you've wearied of the rigors of the missionary life, and have a yen to sample the luxuries of the Isle of Sorrows. You imagine that if you give me up to Stygian justice, someone will reward you with a pleasant sinecure in the Hierarchy. You're probably correct. If you can still feign passion as convincingly as I remember, some Anacreon will likely take you for his whore."

She stared at him for what seemed a long time. Finally she said, "I'm not like that."

"Damn you!" he snarled, his voice breaking, his eyes throbbing as if about to shed tears. "How dare you pretend to any sort of virtue? You, who swore your devotion, then betrayed me to my death!"

She flinched again. This time he was sure of it, and it gave him a pang of vicious satisfaction. "I wish you'd let me explain what happened," she said, her own voice unsteady now.

"No," Montrose said. "I know what you did. Even you haven't had the impudence to deny the essential fact. I'm not interested in hearing you bleat about extenuating circumstances, your motives, or your regrets. Even if I believed what you had to say, it wouldn't change my feelings one iota."

Louise sighed. "All right. I don't blame you for feeling that way. But even if I was a worthless, despicable creature in 1649, isn't it possible that I've changed in the three hundred and fifty years since? Haven't I been a friend so far? Don't I seem sincere?"

He was about to retort that she'd seemed sincere in Holland, which was what had enabled her to ruin him, when a thought struck him. Why was he rejecting her? If he wandered off alone, he might never see her again, might never find another opportunity for revenge. Whereas if he permitted her to accompany him, he could hack her to pieces as soon as he parted company with Artie and the others.

Smirking behind his mask, trying to sound gruff and reluctant, he said, "All right, I admit it, you do seem…reliable. I don't forgive you, nor am I prepared to trust you any farther than necessary. But you're correct, I am going to need help to reach the Smiling Lord, so much so that I'm even willing to accept it from you."

EIGHTEEN

Thin and prim in her round, steel-rimmed spectacles, Mrs. Duquesne sat stiffly erect behind her impressive ebony desk, her smile as cold as it was serene. Gayoso had to admire her. Inwardly the old hag was surely seething with hate and envy, but no one could tell it. In contrast, the green velvet hood veiling his features notwithstanding, it was obvious that Nathan Shellabarger had come to feel profoundly uncomfortable in his fellow Governors' company. The small man kept shifting in his leather chair, and his right hand hovered by his hip pocket, where he evidently had some sort of weapon.

Mrs. Duquesne tapped the sheaf of papers in her gaunt white hands against the desktop, straightening them. "Is that everything?" she asked.

Gayoso hesitated, and then, irked by his own timidity, said, "Not quite. I'd like to discuss the symbol of our regime." He nodded at the black hourglass standing on the desktop to her right, between a wooden bowl containing several oboli—a symbol of her fealty to the Beggar Lord—and the glazed white mask of Tragedy she seldom wore.

Shellabarger tensed. "What about it?" Mrs. Duquesne asked calmly.

"I think I should take charge of it," Gayoso said.

"Surely you remember," the gray-haired woman said, "that by the terms of our covenant, I'm supposed to retain it until Samhain one year hence, at which point I'll pass it to Mr. Shellabarger."

"I know," Gayoso said. "But it's the most valuable object in Natchez, and it just so happens that at the moment, I control more Legionnaires than either of you. Ergo, I could guard it better than you can."

"Ah," said Mrs. Duquesne, "but who would guard us? We're well aware of the size of your personal army, Anacreon. That's precisely why I consider it vital to keep the talisman in my possession. The balance of power, don't you know."

The Spaniard sighed as if her suspicions had wounded him. "My dear lady, you have nothing to fear from me."

"Ha!" Shellabarger interjected.

"I swear you don't," Gayoso continued. "But consider the perspective of our masters in Stygia. For whatever reason, they chose to augment *my* troops. They appointed *me* commander of the current inquisition. One can only conclude that they consider me first among equals, as it were. They'll think it odd if I don't have charge of the supreme symbol of our rule. They might even feel that by hanging on to it, you're flouting their will."

"Oh, I'm reasonably confident that whatever *your* master has arranged in the way of troop assignments and crusades," Mrs. Duquesne replied, "mine would clap me in irons if I conceded preference to the Anacreon of another Deathlord without express instructions to that effect. In other words, if you want the hourglass, you'll have to obtain such orders or take it by force."

"And I'll help her defend it," Shellabarger said. "Do you think your Black Hawks and Grim Riders can defeat both our forces at the same time?"

"Please," said Gayoso, raising his hand, "calm yourself. There's no need for this hostility. I would *never* try to seize the hourglass against your will. I was merely suggesting a more rational arrangement for taking care of it. If you don't think it's a good idea, than we'll forget it. Good evening to you both." The leather straps of his cuirass creaking, the carpet of Stygian iron mesh clinking beneath his high boots, he rose, picked up his rapier, draped the baldric over his shoulder, and opened the door. It wasn't possible to slip through the walls. Chain netting covered them, too, and the ceiling as well, a precaution to keep out assassins.

Outside in the shadowy corridor stood a sentry in a green sash emblazoned with a black hourglass. The soldier held a barghest on a leash. The bloodhound, sculpted by some Masquer into a grotesque, sexless amalgam of man and canine, robbed of its intelligence by its gray iron muzzle, growled when Gayoso emerged. Though its keeper presumably had the creature firmly under control, Valentine had elected to stay well away from it. Sitting at the top of the rusty iron staircase, the dwarf jumped to his feet at his master's appearance. The silver bells on the horns of his red and yellow jester's cap and the upturned toes of his slippers jingled.

"Good meeting?" Valentine asked.

Gayoso felt a surge of rage, and lashed out with a kick. His toe caught the little man squarely in the face, breaking teeth and hurling him backward down the steps. The barghest bayed. Valentine crashed down on the landing below. Rickety as the staircase looked, the impact didn't even make it quiver. Nothing that happened solely on the dead side of the Shroud could do that.

Gayoso stared down the steps, intent on grinding the jester beneath his boots. Valentine scrambled to his feet and on down the next flight, vanishing from view.

His disappearance took the edge off Gayoso's anger. Halting, he closed his eyes and tried to compose himself. He didn't comprehend everything that had happened when he offered up his sacrifice to the Malfeans. The last few minutes, during which he'd apparently smashed his magic mirror, were maddeningly hazy. Still, he knew he'd changed, changed profoundly, but he didn't want everyone else to know it. Not just yet.

Perhaps, he thought, he should procure another child and return to his secret haven for a second session of torture and murder. He sensed that would ease and refresh him as nothing else could. His body quivered in anticipation.

When he felt calmer, he tramped on, soon exiting Mrs. Duquesne's section of the Citadel, a sprawling complex of derelict brick factories and warehouses, and entering his own domain. The labyrinthine Haunt stank of rot and corroding metal, and tiny, glinting Nihils pitted the walls. As he traversed the cavernous rooms and cramped passages, a number of his subordinates saluted him, and he responded tersely. In his present humor, their attentions annoyed him, even though he knew that if they'd been so foolish as to ignore him, their disrespect would have grated on him even more.

At last he reached the top floor, where the echoes of ancient misery were strongest. The rifleman guarding his own door, a Black Hawk with features sculpted into the beaked and feathery visage of a bird of prey, snapped to attention. Gayoso nodded brusquely, then slipped through the wall into his office.

He snapped his fingers and the three white tapers in the brass candelabrum burst into frigid, pale blue flame. And at the same time, he glimpsed a figure from the corner of his eye.

For an instant the intruder seemed naked, scaly, and black as ink, with two pairs of shining, slit-pupiled eyes, and two crocodilian sets of jaws jutting from a single malformed head. But even as the Governor whirled, fumbling out his pistol, the other wraith changed into a plump, round-faced woman with freckles and an impish smile. A potpourri of religions symbols—crosses, stars of David, yin-yangs, mandalas, verses from the Koran in graceful Arabic calligraphy, and countless others—covered her voluminous purple gown. Black stains, the distinctive stigmata of a Pardoner, mottled the tips of her short, blunt fingers. All in all, she looked so normal and innocuous that Gayoso wondered if he'd truly seen her previous form at all.

"Do us both a favor and don't shoot," she said. "I'm on your side. You can call me Prudence."

"How did you get in here?" he asked. The sentry outside was mostly for show. The invisible glyphs on the office walls were supposed to keep out intruders as efficiently as Mrs. Duquesne's spider webs of chain.

Prudence waved her hand at a faintly hissing hairline crack in the floor. "Wherever there's one of those, even a little teeny one, I can generally manage to wriggle through."

"You're a Spectre, then." The Hierarch's finger tightened on the trigger.

"As are you, Manuel. We're brother and sister, you and I."

Gayoso flinched. "No. At the end, I rejected the Shadow. I smashed the mirror."

Suddenly, though he hadn't seen her cross the intervening space, she was beside him, her discolored fingertips resting on his forearm. "You broke it because you didn't need it anymore. You're a different man now, aren't you?"

He felt dazed, feverish, and filled with a compulsion to answer her question. It occurred to him that she was using her Arcanos on him, but the realization had no power to break the spell. "Yes," he said. "When I gave the child to the Malfeans, when I committed what everyone says is the ultimate crime—and *enjoyed* it—I understood that a man needn't be constrained by laws, his supposed masters, or even his own conscience. He can do whatever he wants. And I want to rule Natchez. Not in the name of the King of Spain, Charon, or the Seven, and not as a member of a triumvirate. As its supreme and unassailable lord. I want everyone in the province to cower and grovel before me. After two hundred years of running the place, I deserve it."

"Your contempt for any sort of limits derives from an unconscious comprehension that *everything* is meaningless," Prudence said. Her touch made his skin tingle. "Your urge to mastery is a manifestation of the need to destroy. Open your mind, and see."

For an instant Gayoso perceived a tidal wave of absolute darkness crashing through creation, obliterating everything in its path. And he himself became one tiny droplet of acid at the crest of the tsunami, lending his strength and fury to the devastation.

A part of him quailed from such a fate. Sensed that he'd been given one last chance to step back from the abyss. But the impulse to do so withered at once. For what could be more glorious than to merge with the only pure and valid thing in the universe?

When the vision faded, he found himself sprawled on the floor. Prudence took him by the arm and helped him up. "Do you understand now?" she asked gently.

"Yes," he croaked, awestricken. "I felt Oblivion, working inside me and through me. It was...horrible and wonderful. Will I feel it again? Can I learn to do it without your help?"

She nodded. "Certainly. As the vestiges of your humanity decay, as you come to fathom your new nature, the darkness will possess you more and more frequently, more and more completely, until finally you either fall into the Void or become its perfect avatar."

His vision-induced ecstasy faded, abruptly giving way to a pang of anxiety. Taking stock, he realized his gun was no longer in his hand. It lay on the floor, where he'd obviously dropped it during his epiphany. He stepped away from Prudence, giving himself room to draw and wield his sword. "So I am a Spectre," he said. "Does that mean I have to abandon my old existence? Have you come to lead me away into the Tempest?"

She sighed and shook her head. "No, because you don't *look* like a Spectre. You're a Doppelgänger, like me. Our place is in the Shadowlands, exploiting our human facades to betray and destroy. So for heaven's sake, relax. Poor little lamb. You covet that throne so desperately."

"Yes." He grimaced. "It's foolish, isn't it? The darkness showed me the whole world is filth. And yet I want this one pathetic little piece of it even more than I did before."

"I told you," Prudence said, "your desire is one expression of the yearning for Oblivion, and its fulfillment will further our cause."

"If it ever is fulfilled," Gayoso answered bitterly. "I now control more troops than either Shellabarger or Mrs. Duquesne, but not more than both of them together. Besides which, the old crone currently has custody of our mightiest weapon. And my new recruits are fresh out of Stygia, and loyal to the Smiling Lord. They might fight my fellow Governors if I could convince them the bastards intend to depose me, but under no circumstances would they back me if I tried to rebel and establish my own kingdom. It's maddening, really. I've never had so much power, and yet my goal seems as far away as ever."

"Cheer up," Prudence said. "The apple is about to drop into your grasp. A certain horde of Spectres—my horde—has been working behind the scenes in Natchez for quite a while now. We want to conduct a sorcerous ritual and thus establish a very special base of operations here. It's the first step in a campaign against our ancient enemies."

Gayoso lifted an eyebrow. "'Ancient enemies?'"

"Like you," Prudence said, "we weren't always Spectres, nor did we shed all our human passions when we fell into corruption. Rest assured, our revenge will also advance the cause of Oblivion.

"Before your rebirth, we intended to create so much turmoil and unrest that you and your fellow Hierarchs wouldn't even notice us conducting our real business. Until one day, when we were ready, we'd wrest the territory away from you. Now that you're one of us, however, it would be easier to work *with* you. Let's conquer the place together. You can crown yourself king, and lord it over your present vassals to your heart's content. Just permit us to pursue *our* purposes."

"I don't object in principle," Gayoso said, frowning thoughtfully. "But do you have enough Spectres to overwhelm the resistance you'd encounter if you invaded openly? Every wraith along the Mississippi would take up arms against you, including my own army."

"To be honest," Prudence said, "there *aren't* enough of us to pull it off. But things would be different if your soldiers were doomshades, too. Why do you think I appeared to you in the form of a Pardoner?"

The Governor shrugged. "I don't know."

"Because I am one, brother dear, just as nearly all the other Pardoners hereabouts are Doppelgängers, also. As you might guess, we've been practicing a somewhat different version of our Arcanos. Unbeknownst to our petitioners, we strengthened their Shadows instead of weakening them. The goal was to spread fear and chaos, and demoralize the populace. A necessary preparation for our ceremony.

"With no way to control who consulted us, or how often, that was all our masquerade *could* achieve. Now there are other, more intriguing possibilities. It's a truism, isn't it, that Heresy is a tool of the Void. It follows, then, that your inquisitors are exposed to corrupting influences at every turn. To safeguard their psyches, their commander could order them to visit a Pardoner on a regular basis. Gradually their Shadows will grow stronger and stronger, until, on the night of our coup, my friends and I will contrive to make them dominant. Imagine how surprised the minions of the Beggar and Emerald Lords will be when their fellow Legionnaires suddenly turn on them. Trapped between your troops and mine, they'll crumble."

Gayoso felt a surge of excitement. He almost imagined he felt a heart pounding in his breast, a pulse quickening in his wrists and neck. "If you really can do what you say—"

"We can."

"—I think the scheme might actually might work."

Prudence said, "Then we have a deal."

"One question first. Who are these 'enemies' of yours?" He smiled. "I trust I'm not one of them."

The other Spectre chuckled. "Don't worry about that. We're seeking revenge for atrocities that occurred hundreds of years before you were even born."

Gayoso extended his hand. "Then welcome, ally."

Nineteen

Dunn gazed across the table at the buxom, black-haired woman. Her sensuous lips curved in a seductive, enigmatic smile, her swarthy shoulders were bare, and her necklace of gold coins glinted in the candlelight. Gypsy or not, she looked too young to possess much arcane knowledge. Hell, with her big, brown, bedroom eyes and voluptuous figure, she looked as if she ought to be lap dancing on Bourbon Street, not telling fortunes in a ratty storefront in Metairie.

But even if she was only pretending to occult wisdom, Astarte and the Arcanists might still seek her out. They wouldn't have any way of knowing she was a phony until they got here. The SAD agent took a drag on his hand-rolled cigarette, savoring the pleasant burn of the smoke in his throat and chest, and then blew it out in a blue plume. The fortuneteller wrinkled her upturned nose, but made no other protest. Maybe she was worried that if she objected, he'd tell her to dig his ten-spot out of her cleavage and give it back. Dunn laid his hand on the rickety little table, palm up, beside the wax-encrusted Chianti bottle which served as a candelabrum. "Tell me all about myself," he said.

She picked up his hand in one of hers and slowly stroked the lines in his palm with her fingertip. He suspected that many of her male customers enjoyed the caress. He didn't exactly mind it himself. "I see a strong man with a gentle heart," she said in her Eastern European accent. "I see a deep longing hidden from those around you."

Gentle heart, he thought, amused. *What a crock*. She was a fake, all right. "Would that be a longing to arrest you?" he replied.

Her eyes widened. "You're a cop?" Most of her accent was gone. Evidently she talked like Maria Ouspenskaya to impress the suckers.

"More or less," Dunn replied. No point in telling her too much too soon. Let her worry for a few more seconds. Nervous witnesses tended to be more eager to please.

The gypsy began to sweat. Dunn could smell the perspiration oozing from her pores. "I thought psychic readings were legal in New Orleans," the woman said. "And that's all I do."

Dunn grinned. "No *bujo* for you, eh?" She blinked, surprised to hear him use the Romany word for a con game.

"No," she said. "May my blood spill if I am lying." She gave him a sultry smile. "So if there is a problem, if I've broken some little ordinance without meaning to, surely you and I can work it out."

He chuckled. "I appreciate the thought, darlin', but to tell you the truth, this isn't a shakedown. I'm not the local heat, either. I'm FBI." He reached inside his new blue suede jacket, fished out his Bureau ID, and showed it to her.

She swallowed, and the smell of her sweat grew stronger. "I don't understand. What could the FBI want with me?"

"With you, nothing. But you may have been in contact with somebody we do want." He laid copies of the sketch he'd drawn and the photo he'd obtained from the Louisiana DMV on the tabletop. "Have you seen either of these people?"

She glanced down, then shook her head.

Dunn gave her a frown. "Don't be in such a hurry. *Study* them. The chick with the hardware in her face calls herself Astarte. The guy in the photo is named Marlon Sebastian, but he generally goes by Marilyn. He's a cross-dresser, a pre-op transsexual, actually, and he may have looked like a woman when he came in here."

The Gypsy examined the pictures at greater length. "No," she said, sounding relieved. "I haven't seen them."

"Have you heard from anybody else who claimed to belong to an organization called the Arcanum? Or somebody who wanted to talk about the Atheist murders?"

She shook her head. A strand of her raven hair tumbled across her forehead.

"Well," said Dunn, "if you do, call me." He handed her a card with a phone number written on it. "Help me find them, and the Bureau will pay you a ten-thousand-dollar reward. You'd have to fondle a lot of palms for that kind of bread."

"I sure would," she said. "So yes, of course I'll help you if I can."

When he looked into her eyes, Dunn could see she was lying. Even her greed was no match for her instinctive distrust of the authorities. If he walked away from her now, she'd run like a rabbit. He grabbed her by the wrist and clamped down hard. She gasped in pain.

"Let's get something straight," he said. "For the time being, I own you. You may *not* pull up stakes and disappear until I give you permission. If you try, I'll find you, and I'll make you, your family, and your whole lousy *kumpania* sorry. Sort of like this, only more so." He took a final drag on his cigarette, removed it from his mouth, and pressed the glowing tip into the soft skin on the inside of her forearm. She yelped and thrashed, but couldn't break free of his grip. The odor of charring flesh mingled with the other scents in the air.

"Okay," he said, releasing her, "I think that now we have a real understanding. I'll see you around." He rose and ambled for the door.

Behind him, she trembled, rattling her bracelets and necklace of coins, and whimpered.

The moonlit street outside was a hodgepodge of seedy offices, ethnic restaurants, secondhand shops, and consignment boutiques. Though it was only eight o'clock, many had already closed for the day. Dunn surmised that, though at first glance the area seemed innocuous enough, few people cared to visit it after dark. He wondered if it was a high-crime area, or if the humans sensed the subtle but abiding presence of something more uncanny. Every city contained such disturbing and enigmatic places, and frequently even other supernatural creatures found it impossible to divine what manner of force or entity had polluted them.

As he neared his Land Rover, his cellular phone rang. He lifted it to his ear and said, "Dunn."

"That was inspiring," said Chester sourly.

"Don't you have anything better to do than follow me around?" the Black Spiral Dancer retorted. "Does Geffard know how you spend your time?"

"I think he'd agree he needs somebody to monitor the way you operate. It was pointless to brutalize that woman. Can't you keep your werewolf urges under control, even when you're human?"

Dunn chuckled. "Jeez, what a racist thing to say! And you a member of two different oppressed minorities yourself. You ought to hang your head in shame. There *was* a point. She needed to know who was in control."

"What if she complains to the FBI?"

"A grifter like her would sooner slice off one of her own tits than talk to a cop voluntarily. That was the problem I was solving."

"Well, maybe," said the wraith, clearly unconvinced. "Do you think the Arcanists *will* get in touch with her?"

"It seems like a long shot," Dunn admitted, picking his way through shards of broken glass. The sidewalk beneath the broken bottle reeked of cheap Rhine wine.

"Then it *was* pointless. And we're no closer to catching them than we were before."

Dunn sighed. "I *will* get them, Casper. It's only a matter of time. You play with your computers and leave the man-hunting to the pros, okay?"

"I'd like nothing better," said the ghost in his snottiest tone. "But it seems that we have a new problem. Something else you Dancers have screwed up."

"What are you talking about?" Dunn asked.

"It turns out your Galliard friend Cankerheart kept a journal," said Chester with bitter relish. "Among other things, he wrote about the plan. The document used to be in your safe house by the cemetery. Now it's missing."

"And we're just finding this out now?"

"Cankerheart was in Lafayette when the rest of us decided to clear out. Somebody else moved his possessions for him."

"Great. If it wasn't for bad luck, we wouldn't have any luck at all. Anyway, you think Bellamy and Astarte swiped it."

"It was on the bookshelf in my computer room. They went in there."

"But you didn't notice them taking it. Careful, Chester. You're coming dangerously close to admitting that a glitch might be partly *your* fault, and I know you'd never want to do that."

"He must have grabbed it when I was too busy inside the PC to look out," Chester replied. "My job was to protect the electronic files. I didn't even know the stupid notebook was there, and I couldn't have done anything about it from my side of the Shroud anyway. It wasn't my responsibility."

Dunn rounded a corner and his mud-spattered white Land Rover came into view. One of these years, he reflected absently, he really should get it washed. "All right," he said, "calm down. It was nobody's fault, and even if it was, the important thing now is to assess the damage. Dare I hope that old Cank wrote his girlish confessions in some top-secret mystical script that only Dancer sages are supposed to know?"

"Well, yes, apparently so," said Chester grudgingly. He sounded as if it pained him to admit that the situation might not be an utter catastrophe after all. "But that doesn't mean the Arcanists won't decipher it. That's precisely the kind of thing they're good at."

Dunn unlocked his vehicle and climbed behind the wheel. "They can't decode it if they haven't got it. Let's try to figure out if they do. For starters, let's assume Bellamy was the one who found it."

"Why should we?"

"Because he was a good agent, trained to be observant." Dunn turned the ignition key and the engine roared to life. Tires squealing, the Land Rover shot away from the curb. "If he did pick it up, he would have held on to it, not handed it off to Astarte. Once again, because of his instincts. He wouldn't entrust evidence to a civilian if he didn't have to, not even his girlfriend."

"What about when he decided she should run while he stayed behind to delay you?"

"Maybe if he'd thought of it, but he didn't. I know because I'm observant, too, and I had my eye on them from the moment they realized they were being stalked right up until the second they split up."

"Then where is the journal? You did a lot of damage to Bellamy's body, electrocuting him and then clawing the corpse like a maniac—"

"I had a hole in my chest. It hurt. I needed to express my feelings."

"—but even so, if he had the notebook, some fragment of it should have survived."

"For a little while we were playing hide and seek in the boneyard. He must have ditched it somewhere then."

"If he came back for it—"

"How? He's a slave now, remember, still getting indoctrinated. There's no way the Queen's people would let him run around on his own. And even if they did, he's on the wrong side of the Shroud to so much as touch the damn thing. I'm sure that if we look for it, we'll find it ourselves." He smiled. "You know, we might even be able to turn this to our advantage."

"How?" Chester asked.

"Astarte knows Bellamy lifted the journal. She and the Arcanists must wish they had it. If they thought they knew where it was, it might flush them out of hiding."

"What are you going to do," Chester sneered, "run an ad in the classifieds? *Found: spiral notebook filled with mysterious hieroglyphics?* They'll never fall for that. They'll suspect a trap."

Dunn floored the gas pedal, making it under a traffic signal just before it changed from amber to red. "Then we'll have to be a little more creative, won't we?"

TWENTY

"Again," Titus said.

Bellamy lifted an eyebrow. "So soon? I'm still beat from the last one. And I don't want to be exhausted when we finally get in to see Marie. Speaking of which, what's the hold-up, anyway?"

"She's the Queen, warmblood," Antoine said. "She'll see us when *she's* ready, and that's all there is to it."

"Meanwhile," said the stooped old sorcerer, his wizened features currently painted half blue and half green, "you should practice. You have an extraordinary natural talent for penetrating the Shroud, but raw ability can only take you so far. You must learn to use your Arcanos reliably and precisely, even when you *are* weary. Otherwise it will fail you when you need it most."

"All right," said Bellamy, because after all, Titus was right. It didn't matter how tired he was. He *had* to master the art of crossing over to the world of the living. It would help him in the fight against the Atheist conspiracy, and it was the only way to communicate with Astarte.

He turned to the white, pink-eyed rabbit in the wire cage. The animal belonged to Titus, who evidently used its blood in some of his spells. Bored, the other *abambo* cooling their heels in the waiting room came closer to watch. The cold green light of the barrow-flame lamps gleamed on their faces.

Trying not to let his audience distract him, Bellamy focused his will. Titus had taught him that there were several ways for a ghost to penetrate the Shroud. He'd start with the easiest and work his way up. When he felt ready, he reached into the cage and stroked the rabbit's warm, soft flank with his fingertip.

Startled, the animal lurched away. Bellamy felt a glow of satisfaction, and also a pang of guilt for frightening the helpless creature.

"Good," Titus said. The spectators murmured approvingly.

Next, Bellamy said, "It's okay, boy. I'm not going to hurt you." Though he spoke normally, Titus had told him that in the Skinlands, his voice would sound like a whisper. But evidently it was loud enough. Lifting its ears, the rabbit peered in his direction.

The FBI agent's body quivered with fatigue, and his concentration wavered. Scowling, he struggled to clear his mind, then attempted the next trick, to make himself visible, though not tangible, to the living.

The rabbit recoiled again. According to Titus, it was seeing a semitransparent figure with blurry features floating an inch or two above the floor. Something very much like the average mortal's notion of a ghost. Two of the onlookers began to applaud. Then the double doors to the throne room swung open, and an imperious-looking functionary emerged.

As was the case with many of the Queen's servants, his appearance was an odd blend of modern America and an ancient tribal heritage. Tall and lean, he wore an elegant gray three-piece suit, but with the usual zebra-striped cape on top of it. In his right hand he carried a long assegai, evidently the emblem of his office. Diagonal scars, a shade darker than the surrounding skin, ridged his cheeks, and his front incisors were missing.

"Her Majesty will see you now," he said.

Passing between the sentries guarding the entry, Bellamy, Titus, and Antoine followed the functionary into a long, torch-lit hall which smelled of frankincense. The room fairly throbbed with the memory of ancient sorrow, and webworks of Nihil cracks hissed in the walls. A trio of drummers stationed along the right-hand wall tapped out intricate, murmuring rhythms with their fingertips. At the far end of the chamber, atop a three-step dais, was an ivory throne, and, sitting erect and motionless upon it, the slender, severely lovely woman whose features reminded the FBI agent of Nefertiti. A crown of dyed ostrich plumes rose above her head, while behind her stood two towering idols carved from some dark brown wood, as well as another pair of guards armed with automatic rifles and scimitars.

Bellamy felt a twinge of awe—perhaps a product of his aborted magical brainwashing—eagerness, and, to his surprise, a flash of amusement. Because, oddly assorted as he and his companions were, he was suddenly reminded of Dorothy and her friends approaching the Wizard of Oz.

Reaching the foot of the dais, he salaamed as he'd been instructed. Titus did the same, not quite so deeply. The alligator ostentatiously lowered his head.

"Rise," said the Queen in a husky contralto voice. "Titus. Dear friend. I rejoice to see you safe."

"And yet it took me two days to obtain an audience with you," the old man replied. He didn't sound reproachful. He sounded as if he was worried about her.

"I was petitioning the Orishas," said Marie. "I didn't want to break off in the middle. Though I might as well have, for all I accomplished."

Titus frowned. "Perhaps that's a topic better discussed later."

"Do you think we can hide the problem?" asked the woman on the throne. "Doesn't everyone already suspect that the gods don't speak to me anymore? After all these years, I'm tired, perhaps too tired to raise the power. And maybe the Orishas are weary as well, weary of us, weary of maintaining this one tiny outpost in a hostile land. Perhaps they're ready to abandon it to Les Mystères, the Deathlords, or anyone else who wants it."

"Your Majesty!" Antoine said, sounding so scandalized that, in other circumstances, Bellamy would have been hard pressed to repress a grin. "If your magic's not working, it's because our enemies are messing with us. Once we beat them, everything will go back to normal. You can't give up!"

She sighed and gave him a sad little smile. "No, of course not, not as long as faithful subjects like you want me to carry on. At least we'll go down fighting, eh?" She turned to Bellamy. "You're the warrior who rescued Titus."

"Actually, Antoine and I did it together," the FBI agent said. "But yes."

"And as your reward, I raise you from Thralldom," the black woman said. "Henceforth you will serve me as one of my guards. Kneel to recite the oath of fealty." The functionary stepped forward with the assegai extended. Bellamy inferred that he was supposed to touch the long, broad spearhead as he swore.

He remained standing. "Your Majesty, I'm grateful for your generosity. But I don't think this is going to work for me. Especially if you're thinking of sending me off to boot camp, or making me stand watch around the Haunt." He smiled at the impassive sentries behind the throne. "No offense, guys."

Marie gave him a stony stare. "For the moment at least, I'm still the monarch of New Orleans. It's perilous to defy me."

"I don't mean to defy you," Bellamy said. "But your difficulties are one facet of a bigger problem, a bigger mystery. I've vowed to crack the whole thing, and as an FBI agent and, I'm told, a natural Proctor, I have the skills to do it. I want to help you as an ally, not a buck private in your militia. I want to help you plan your strategy. And when the time comes to deal with an aspect of the overall situation that doesn't have anything much to do with keeping you on your throne, I want you to help me with that, not get mad at me for deserting my post."

"What 'bigger problem'?" asked Marie.

Bellamy began to relate a condensed version of his experiences, beginning with the night of Waxman's murder. He wondered fleetingly how many more times he'd have to lay out this story, and for whom. He'd already told it to a transsexual occultist, a pair of hideous vampires, and now ghostly royalty. His audiences couldn't get much stranger than that.

When he finished, the Queen said, "You've walked a dark path and made some strange discoveries. But I don't understand how they fit together."

"I don't either," Bellamy said. "But they must, because there are two threads that run through everything. The attacks on priests and shrines, and the werewolves."

"Who turn out to be the guys sending those nasty new spirits against us," Antoine said. "By the way, what are those things, Titus? Now that you've seen 'em yourself, I'll bet you know."

The old man grimaced. "Not precisely. But I can tell you that our Underworld—the Shadowlands, the Ocean, the Lost Kingdoms, Stygia, and all the rest of it—is only a part of a greater metaphysical domain. Creatures we *abambo* rarely encounter, demons and elementals, inhabit the other levels. Quick sorcerers know how to conjure such entities into the mortal sphere. Evidently the werewolves have discovered how to inflict them on us."

Antoine nodded, mulling it over, his toothy snout bobbing up and down. "You don't suppose that three-armed mutt Frank killed was the only one who knew how to open the door, do you?"

Titus smiled sardonically. "What a pleasant thought. But I certainly wouldn't count on it."

"And so," said the Queen, "in all likelihood, the attacks will continue." She looked at Bellamy. "I'm a hard woman. I've had to be, to climb from slavery to a throne and hold it this long. What I take, I keep. If I gave you, a lowly Lemure, the liberty you want, treated you like a counselor, a chieftain, an ally, people would say I'd gone soft. It would erode my authority still further. Particularly since you're white."

His mouth tightening, Bellamy struggled to swallow his irritation at the racism. It was obnoxious, but irrelevant to the discussion. "I just want an understanding between you and me, Your Majesty. We don't have to advertise it."

"You'd be surprised how difficult it is to keep secrets in this place," said Marie ruefully. "I suppose it's one more sign of the decay of my rule. But never mind that. If you want to be my strategist, Mr. Bellamy, what *is* your advice?"

"For one thing," Bellamy said, "you have to help me locate Astarte and the Arcanists. I'm sure Dunn and his friends are hunting them too, to finish them off. We've got to find them first."

The Queen sighed as if he'd disappointed her. "Waste precious manpower searching for a band of fugitive mortals. I'm sure you'd like to see your lover protected, but that won't help me win the war."

"Yes, it will," Bellamy said. "I told you about the notebook. Titus sent somebody to retrieve it. We've got it now, but he can't read it, either. Maybe the Arcanists can."

"And perhaps they can't," said Marie. "Or perhaps it doesn't contain any pertinent information."

Bellamy grimaced. "We're short on clues, Your Majesty. We have to make the most of what we do have, hoping it will lead us to the answers."

"I suppose," said the Queen. "Still, to divert warriors to search the city when our Haunts are under assault...but perhaps we can spare a few. What else do you propose?"

"Attack!" Antoine rasped. "We're never going to win unless we go on the offensive."

"That may be," said Marie, "but first we'd have to locate the rest of the werewolves."

"Screw the werewolves!" the gator said. "They're working for Geffard. Destroy him and they'll leave us alone."

Marie shook her head. "We don't *know* they're in league with Geffard. We merely suspect it."

"According to Titus and Antoine," said Bellamy, "the hostile spirits always menace your strongholds and never those of Les Invisibles. That's suggestive to say the least."

"What's more, the devils strike at specific targets," Titus said. "A certain prized fetish, or one particular priest. Granted, the werewolf sorcerers have some ability to peer into the Underworld. Still, the accuracy of their operations indicates they have someone feeding them intelligence from our side of the Shroud."

"But all that's simply conjecture," said Marie. "I can't act without proof."

"Why not?" Antoine demanded. "You're the Queen. You can do whatever you want."

"Once, perhaps," she replied. "Not anymore. The people would rise if they thought I'd acted unjustly. Despite all the pomp and ritual, they don't hold me in awe as they once did. Nor do I dare move against the enemy without a better understanding of the resources at his disposal. Not when he's been winning all the battles." She wearily rubbed her eyes with her thumb and forefinger, and as she did, a band of darkness flowed upward from her feet to the top of her head, like dusky pigment streaming beneath her skin.

Bellamy stared in horror, expecting her to vanish into the Void. She didn't. Evidently she wasn't quite ready to give up her hold on existence. But it was obvious that fear and despair were eating away at her like a cancer, just as they were preventing her from striking back at Geffard.

The FBI agent glanced at his companions. Titus shook his head. Obviously the hoodoo man had observed the wave of shadow also, but didn't want Bellamy to mention it. Perhaps he thought that pointing it out would plunge Marie even deeper into her funk.

How much longer, Bellamy wondered, *before she just melts away? A week? An hour?* He had no reason to love the woman, but he couldn't help pitying her. Besides, if the Atheist conspiracy wanted her destroyed, that was reason enough to help her.

"If you had proof and solid information," he asked, "*then* would you act?" It was obvious that she had to break through her paralysis of doubt and confront her enemies. Nothing else could save her.

Realizing that he'd impugned her courage, she frowned with at least a measure of her accustomed hauteur. "Of course."

"Then I'll get it for you," Bellamy said. "By going undercover in Geffard's operation. He has his own corps of soldiers and flunkies, right? And since I have this natural talent for jumping across the Shroud, he ought to be glad to add me to the payroll."

"Maybe," Antoine said. "But I don't know if this is a good idea, warmblood."

"I hope you aren't going to tell me again that a poor little Lemure like me couldn't survive on the mean streets of the Necropolis," said Bellamy impatiently. "I handled myself okay when we rescued Titus."

"I admit," the alligator said, "you're tough. But even so, you're going to run into situations that'll surprise you."

"That always happens when you go undercover," Bellamy said. "You just have to stay cool and bluff your way through."

"But that guy Chester will recognize you," Antoine said.

"Not if one of your flesh sculptors changes my face," Bellamy said. "He can turn my skin black while he's at it. No one will expect a newly dead white man to do that, and I'm guessing that it'll make it easier to ingratiate myself with Les Invisibles."

"It could work," said Titus, nodding thoughtfully. "No Masquer can change your deathmarks, but I'm somewhat familiar with this Chester, and he can't have seen them. His talents run in a different direction. Unfortunately, it's still conceivable that if someone with psychic abilities chose to study you, he could sense that you weren't what you claimed to be."

"I'll risk it," Bellamy said. He gazed up at the woman on the ivory throne. "What do you think, Your Majesty?"

"If I could see the face of my enemy," said Marie, "if I could know what forces he commands and what he intends, perhaps I could finally discern a way to save myself.

At least it's a chance. So yes, do it."

"We'll begin immediately," said Titus. He salaamed, Bellamy followed suit, and Antoine inclined his head. Then they turned and retreated from the throne.

"You surprised me," the alligator murmured. "I was sure you'd want to comb the city for your girlfriend."

"I do," Bellamy said. "I want it more than anything in the world. But this job has to be done, and as a trained detective, I'm best suited to do it, especially since the bad guys won't be expecting me. The last time Chester saw me, I was being clubbed unconscious and dragged off into slavery.

"And since I am going, I'm counting on you guys. Don't let Marie sit around and brood. Make sure she sends out search parties. Find Astarte."

"We'll do our best," said Antoine. "But New Orleans is a big city."

TWENTY-ONE

When he reached the river-front park at the end of Canal Street, Bellamy stopped to marvel. It was clearly the same place he'd visited with Astarte just a few days ago, yet it seemed utterly transformed. Thanks to the distortions of the Shroud, the two-story facade of the Aquarium of the Americas appeared to be crumbling into ruin. Nihil cracks seethed and glittered in the brick walkways. The grass was sparse and brown, the oaks twisted and withered. The wilting roses smelled of decay, the stench mingling with the sharp reeks of oil and acid rising from the Mississippi. It was as if he'd returned to the site after some terrible disaster.

And indeed he had. Except that the disaster hadn't happened to the park but to him. Dunn had ripped away his life.

A swell of grief rose up inside him. Scowling, he quashed it as best he could. He might be dead, but at least he still existed. And somehow he was going to smash the Atheist conspiracy and reunite himself with Astarte.

When he had himself under control, he strode on through the darkness. Cold, green barrow-flame torches marked the way toward a structure so bedizened with multicolored lights that it resembled a Christmas tree. The sight was sufficiently dazzling that he'd nearly reached the water's edge before he began to determine the structure supporting the lamps.

Geffard had docked his steamboat the *Twisted Mirror* just a few yards away from the *Cajun Queen*, as if to invite comparisons with the Skinlands vessel, and why not? His sidewheeler was longer and broader, and its twin smokestacks towered higher. A carved skull face grinned between them. This, like the rest of the macabre, rococo gingerbread—tangles of bones and serpents, capering gargoyles—covering virtually the entire exterior of the boat, was black. A Strauss waltz sounded from the decks. Bellamy paused for a moment, taking in the spectacle, and then headed for the gangplank.

Two hulking, bare-chested guards armed with machetes stood at the top of the movable bridge. They didn't challenge him, nor had he expected them to. The *Twisted Mirror* was open to all, a floating pleasure palace extending lavish hospitality to every free ghost in New Orleans. Which likely meant that Geffard conducted any illicit business elsewhere. Still, it was a place to make contact.

"Is the loa here this evening?" Bellamy asked.

"Last time I looked," said the sentry on the right, "he was in his cabin. But he'll come down eventually. He always does."

"Thanks," the FBI agent said, stepping aboard. He sauntered down the deck, through a set of double doors, and into the lounge.

The decor in the expansive central cabin reflected a sort of split personality. Most of the space was given over to the kind of furnishings which had graced authentic antebellum steamboats: rich carpeting, crystal chandeliers, and a mirrored bar, where Sandmen dispensed hallucinatory intoxicants along with what appeared to be the occasional glass of genuine liquid. Gamblers wagered at poker, faro, and roulette, dancers waltzed, and the twenty-piece orchestra played atop its platform. Except for the grotesque aspect of the gingerbread and many of the oil paintings, Samuel Clemens would have felt right at home in such surroundings.

But the far end of the chamber was different. An abstract design of circles and straight lines, drawn in some sort of yellow powder, decorated a section of bare floor. Behind it was a long, low altar covered with a white tablecloth, and atop that reposed a carved wooden serpent on a pole, crucifixes, polished stones, necklaces strung with beads and snake vertebrae, earthen jugs, bottles of amber rum, candles, wicks burning in coconut shells filled with oil, skulls, small packets of cloth, a pair of crossed sabers, an egg, and cigars. To the left of the altar were three drums of different heights and materials not unlike the ones in Marie's throne room, while to the right was a stool. Two more sentries guarded the display. Evidently Geffard sometimes converted the salon into a temple, and revelry gave way to the worship of Les Mystères.

The waltz swirled to an end, and the dancers clapped. The conductor, a small *ibambo* with a magnificent, flowing mane of silvery hair—Bellamy wondered if he'd paid a flesh sculptor to create it for him, so as to look like the popular image of a maestro—inclined his head, acknowledging the applause, and lifted his baton once more. But then, instead of giving the downbeat, he pivoted toward a door in the right-hand wall. Others looked in the same direction, and Bellamy peered along with them.

A tall, slender, youthful-looking wraith sauntered into the cabin. From the description he'd been given, Bellamy recognized him as Geffard. The rebel leader wore a blue uniform with gold piping and braid which the FBI agent assumed to be a copy of an authentic Mississippi riverboat captain's outfit. Somehow it looked odd with his plaited dreadlocks.

His white grin dazzling in his dark face, Geffard looked up at the conductor. "Please, don't stop," he said. "You sound marvelous, and our friends want to dance." Instantly, the orchestra launched into the "Blue Tango." Meanwhile, a score of wraiths clustered about their host. Geffard had a handshake and a clap on the shoulder for each of the men, a kiss on the hand or the cheek for each of the women. Once a ghost with a desperate look in his eyes approached him. Geffard whispered something in the *ibambo*'s ear and pressed what appeared to be a phosphorescent red marble into his hand. The supplicant was so grateful he began to weep.

In short, Geffard looked like a born politician taking an ebullient joy in his ability to work a crowd. Pushing his way forward through the press, Bellamy reflected on the contrast to the Queen, isolated and morose on her seat of ivory.

Finally he got near enough to make himself heard. Up close, the loa smelled pleasantly of cologne. "Mr. Geffard?"

Other wraiths glanced at him curiously. Geffard lifted an eyebrow. "Generally, people call me *Doctor* Geffard," he said coldly. "Or Père. Or Captain." Abruptly he smiled, revealing that he hadn't really taken offense. It had only been a pretense. A joke. "But Mister is fine. And who are you, my friend?"

"My name is John Oliver," Bellamy said.

"I don't believe I've seen you around before."

"You're right," Bellamy said. "I only got to New Orleans a few weeks ago. I'd always wanted to see it." He grimaced. "If I'd known I was going to die here, I wouldn't have been so eager."

"I'm sorry," said Geffard. "But don't despair. Existence in the Mirrorlands can be just as happy as what you've left behind." He waved his hand at the dancers, the gamblers, and the drinkers at the bar. "Look at them. They're enjoying themselves, aren't they?"

"Yeah," said Bellamy, "at the moment, thanks to you. But I've been dead long enough to find out that not everybody has fun all the time. Some people never have any, because there aren't enough toys and goodies to go around. That's why I wanted to talk to you."

"I'm listening."

"In private," Bellamy said.

Geffard shrugged. "All right. It's a nice, balmy night for a stroll along the decks." He waved Bellamy toward the exterior doors. One of the guards by the altar started forward. "No, that's all right, Jacques. I'm sure I won't need a bodyguard." Given that the loa had surely noticed the shortsword hanging at his waist, Bellamy was impressed by the other wraith's self-confidence.

Outside, the river smelled more of silt and water, and less of pollution. Bellamy chalked it up to a shift in the current, or perhaps the vagaries of the Shroud. Out on the black water, vague shapes spangled with points of light glided along. Sometimes the agent could tell which were mortal vessels and which belonged to the dead, sometimes not.

Geffard led him up a narrow staircase to the uppermost deck. "The view is better up here," the loa said, resting his hands on the ornately carved rail and gazing out across the Mississippi. "Now, what's on your mind?"

"I want a job," Bellamy said.

Geffard snorted. "You didn't have to take me away from the party for that. People ask me for that kind of favor all the time."

"I don't mean some kind of scut work," Bellamy said. "When I was alive, I moved contraband. That's why I was in New Orleans, to swap guns for cocaine. The deal went south—damn crazy Colombians!—and I wound up taking a bullet in the neck. Now I'd like to put my talents to work for you."

"What makes you think I'd be interested in the services of a professional criminal?" asked Geffard.

"People say you want to take over the city. If so, you're going to need soldiers. Guys willing to get their hands dirty."

Geffard extracted two long, thin cigars from the interior of his jacket. Bellamy caught a whiff of pungent tobacco. "I don't imagine you've seen too many of these on this side of the Shroud."

"I hadn't seen any until I looked at the altar downstairs," Bellamy said, "and I wasn't sure if those were real."

"Of course they are," said Geffard. He handed one cigar to Bellamy. "It would be a terrible insult to offer anything less to Les Mystères. And just between you and me, making such a sacrifice isn't truly a terrible hardship anyway. I gather that you didn't grow up with the mortal version of our faith."

Bellamy shook his head. "I'm from Albany. Not much voudoun there."

Geffard lit his own cheroot, then Bellamy's. Grateful that he'd taken a token puff on a few cigars in his time, to celebrate the successful conclusion of a case or the birth of a colleague's baby—it wouldn't create much of an impression if he coughed and choked—the detective sucked in a little smoke. Cold like the barrow-flame that birthed it, it chilled his mouth and lungs.

"Well," the rebel continued, "we have a closer, fonder relationship with our Quick counterparts than the Morts—the Queen's people and the Stygians—have with theirs. Our living friends and relations welcome us into their bodies. We can possess them without a struggle, whenever we feel nostalgic for the genuine pleasures of the flesh. What's more, our mounts sacrifice to us, just as we make offerings to Les Mystères, and sometimes, when they perform the ritual properly, the sacrificial object—a magnum of champagne, perhaps, or a pistol, or a box of cigars—passes into the Mirrorlands."

"If your people have the lion's share of the wealth," said Bellamy, "then it makes sense for you to run things."

"I'm inclined to agree," said Geffard, blowing out a plume of cool, fragrant smoke. "For that reason and others. It's preposterous for a woman even to attempt to govern a large, tumultuous state like New Orleans. Particularly when I still talk to my gods, and it's whispered that Marie has lost touch with hers. And now a new menace, some unfamiliar breed of Baka—what the Stygians call Spectres and the Africans, Sinkinda—is threatening the Queen's people, whereas my magic protects my friends. If I were King, I could muster even more power and defend everyone, but as it stands..." He shrugged.

"As it stands, it doesn't break your heart to see the Baka tearing the hell out of your enemies."

Geffard smiled. "People say that when a Creole passes from life into death, he leaves his conscience behind. And I certainly have my pragmatic side. I *can* tolerate the thought of a little carnage, if it opens my path to the throne.

"But it's one thing to turn someone else's mayhem to your own political purposes, and something else to initiate violence yourself. Rumor often speaks falsely, my friend. Just because I want the crown, it doesn't automatically follow that I intend to commit murder to get it. Perhaps I'm hoping Marie will see reason and abdicate for the good of the realm. And even if I did intend something sinister, an assassination or an armed coup, I hope I wouldn't be reckless enough to confide my plans to a stranger."

"Come on," Bellamy said, injecting a note of annoyance into his voice. "It's good to be careful, I guess, but according to your reputation, you can read people like a book. If that's true, you ought to be able to tell I'm being straight with you. I want to get rich and powerful working for the next boss of New Orleans. I'm willing to do whatever it takes to help put you on top. And I *can* help. Not only do I know how to handle myself, I recently found out I have the power to jump across the Shroud."

"Really," said Geffard. "That is a rare and valuable talent. Show me."

Bellamy concentrated and felt the Arcanos power rise within him. He began to shift himself into the mortal world, then realized that if he did, the riverboat would vanish beneath his shoes, dropping him into the Mississippi thirty feet below. He let the magic dissipate. "I'll be glad to demonstrate on dry land," he said.

Geffard laughed. "Believe it or not, I've seen far more experienced Proctors than you make that same kind of mistake. It's good that you're not a fool. I don't hire idiots."

"Will you hire me?" Bellamy asked.

"I don't know yet," the Creole said. "Look at me, and stand still."

Bellamy did as he'd been told. Geffard peered intently into his face. After a moment the FBI agent realized the other wraith was subjecting him to some sort of psychic probe.

Titus had warned him that such an examination could render his disguise worthless. He felt a jolt of anxiety, a wild urge to lash out at Geffard, kill him or take him hostage. Instead he stood still, and kept his expression impassive.

At last Geffard said, "Interesting."

"What is?" Bellamy asked.

"Your deathmarks," the loa said. He tossed the stub of his cigar over the railing. "Generally speaking, they seem consistent with your account of yourself. They tell me you've fought and killed in your time, and that you died at the hands of another. I see anger, loneliness, determination, and ambition. Yet there's something odd about the configuration. It isn't quite what I'd expect to find in the face of an outlaw. Too much morality, I think."

Bellamy knew his ectoplasmic body couldn't break out in a sweat. At that moment, his forehead and armpits felt clammy anyway. He shrugged. "I was a criminal," he said, "but I always kept my word. I was always loyal to my bosses. If you give me a chance, I'll be just as loyal to you."

"All right," said Geffard. "but my organization is like any other. No one starts at the top. You'll have to prove your usefulness, and earn my trust. There are plenty of routine chores that need doing to keep our community running smoothly. Do them well, and I'll consider involving you in more sensitive matters. Ultimately, you just might wind up as one of my right-hand men."

Bellamy's muscles tightened in frustration. God only knew how long it would take him to convince Geffard to involve him in the Atheist conspiracy. Meanwhile the murders would continue, the Queen might fall into the Void, Dunn would hunt Astarte—

He pushed the unpleasant possibilities out of his mind. Geffard was offering him a chance to find the answers he needed, and he had no real option but to take it. He held out his hand. "It's a deal."

TWENTY-TWO

The one-story stucco house stood behind a trio of oaks bearded with Spanish moss. Plastic toys, a Big Wheel and robotic action figures from a TV cartoon series, lay in the monkey grass in the front yard, gleaming in the moonlight. The place wasn't far from Bucktown, New Orleans's commercial fishing community, and a piscine odor, so faint that only a wraith could smell it, tinged the cool night air.

Bellamy noticed that the home didn't appear as dilapidated as most Skinlands buildings. Perhaps the Shroud—or the Surface, as Les Invisibles called it—was particularly thin here. If so, that would make it easier to accomplish the task at hand.

"Come on," said Louis, skulking up the driveway, his ratty black raincoat flapping. A Masquer who'd sculpted his body into the form of a withered corpse, complete with artificial maggots writhing sluggishly inside the gaps in his tattered flesh, he was Bellamy's boss on the current errand, and would presumably report to Geffard concerning his performance.

The FBI agent followed the other *ibambo* through the substance of the front door. Inside, a pulse of pure happiness sang along his nerves. When the exhilaration faded, he blinked in surprise. It was a rare building that accumulated such an atmosphere of joy that a ghost could actually feed off it.

Louis's shriveled features were essentially incapable of expression, but Bellamy sensed that the other spirit was sneering at him. "Enjoy that, did you?" the Masquer asked.

Bellamy realized he was smiling foolishly, and wiped the expression off his face. "It was a fix," he said, shrugging. "We all need a jolt of emotion now and then."

"Be patient," said Louis. "In a few minutes you can drink your fill of the good stuff." Turning, he placed his skeletal hands against the wall and murmured something under his breath. Bellamy had heard that his companion had mastered other Arcanoi beside flesh sculpting, and now he sensed some sorcerous power streaming through the substance of the house. Exterior doors groaned in their frames. Windows turned grayish and translucent.

"That's got it," said Louis. He strode toward the back of the darkened house. As Bellamy followed, he caught a glimpse of a copy of the *Times-Picayune*, the sections scattered on the floor beside a recliner in the living room. His *ibambo* eyes could make out the headlines, even in the gloom. Evidently a team of Baton Rouge fire fighters had gone berserk, chopping up people they should have been rescuing, and kindling new conflagrations.

Bellamy repressed a grimace. First the Atheist murders had served to shake people's faith in religion. Then priests and ministers, the Atheist's potential victims, had gone on killing sprees themselves, undermining everyone's trust still further. Now cops and firemen were going crazy. If it kept up, it wouldn't be long before the average mortal would feel that he couldn't depend on *anything*.

Bellamy still didn't understand the point of it all, but he was convinced the Atheist conspiracy, of which Geffard and his royal ambitions appeared to be only one small part, was behind every bit of it, and that if their plan advanced unchecked, it would unleash the ghastly catastrophe Milo Waxman had foreseen. He had to stop it, no matter what the cost. Which meant he couldn't shrink from the chore Geffard had set for him, no matter how unsavory it was.

Louis halted in front of a door. The soft, slow respiration of a sleeper sounded on the other side. "We can start here," he said.

The two ghosts slipped through the panel into a little boy's bedroom, with a baseball bat leaning in the far corner, a row of Super Nintendo cartridges on a shelf, and a stray white sock peeking out from under the bed. The child himself lay tangled in the covers, with only one foot and the top of his head protruding.

Bellamy's eyes narrowed. He and Louis had come because one of Les Chevaux—Les Invisibles' mortal worshippers—had a grudge against the man who lived here, and had petitioned his ghostly patrons to punish the offending party. Evidently, in New Orleans, there was nothing illicit about such harassment of the living. It was common practice, a fact which served to lower Bellamy's opinion of the society of the *abambo* yet another notch. But, unpleasant as the prospect seemed, he'd supposed he could throw a scare into some poor Quick guy for the sake of his mission. He hadn't bargained on tormenting children.

Turning to Louis, he said, "We're in the wrong place. I imagine we want the master bedroom."

"No, this is good," said the skeletal ghost. "The whole family has to suffer. It's all part of Villiers's punishment." He laid his hand on the blankets covering the boy.

Masses of gray fungus spread across the cloth, until it looked as if some parasitic growth was consuming the mortal. His shoulders shifted restlessly. "Now wake him," Louis said.

Swallowing his distaste, reaching across the Shroud, Bellamy gingerly touched the child's cheek. The mortal twitched, but didn't wake.

"Again," Louis said impatiently.

Bellamy obeyed. The boy suddenly sat upright; for an instant, Bellamy's hand was *inside* the child's torso. Startled, he snatched his arm back.

The boy—now that he could see him better, Bellamy judged him to be about eight or nine years old—peered about, blinking. When he noticed the patchwork of mold on his covers, he caught his breath. Louis touched his pale blue pajama shirt and tendrils of puffy, damp-looking fungus oozed along the cotton fabric.

The boy screamed, his fear a palpable force vibrating through the air. Bellamy winced. Louis tittered.

In another room, bedsprings squealed, and then rapid footsteps thumped down the hall. The door flew open, and the boy's parents rushed in. His mother flipped on the light.

The adult mortals were graying, in their late forties, older than Bellamy had expected. Mrs. Villiers, a short-legged, chubby woman in a long, white nightgown, stopped short at the sight of the mold, then rushed to the boy and took him in her arms. Her husband, a sallow, round-shouldered guy wearing green silk boxer shorts, peered about as if he dimly suspected the presence of the ghostly intruders, then followed her to their son's bedside.

"Hush," murmured Mrs. Villiers, "hush. Mommy and Daddy are here, and everything's all right." She looked at her husband. "What *is* this stuff?"

"I don't know," he replied. He stripped the covers off the bed, dumped them on the floor, then reflexively wiped his hands on his shorts. "Some kind of fungus. Don't touch it any more than you have to. Put your hands over your head, Davy. I need to pull your shirt off."

"Kill the light," said Louis. Bellamy flipped the switch down, plunging the room into gloom. Only the wan moonlight leaking through the curtains afforded any illumination. The mortals jumped. Mrs. Villiers squawked.

Louis cackled. "Man, I love this job." He capered about the room, touching the striped beige wallpaper, leaving hand prints of reeking black decay.

"What's happening?" Mrs. Villiers cried, clutching Davy tightly against her.

"That's your cue," said Louis to Bellamy. "You're the one who can talk to them."

Feeling sick to his stomach, the FBI agent approached the bed. "You've offended the dead," he said, imagining the sepulchral whisper the mortals were hearing. "Now you have to pay."

"Who are you?" said Villiers, peering wildly about, his voice quavering. "Where are you?"

"I'm right beside you," Bellamy said. He touched his fingertip to Villiers's right eye.

It was a light touch. Using his most rudimentary Proctor abilities, he couldn't have exerted much force even if he'd wanted to. But Villiers still screamed, flailed, and lurched backward to slam into the wall.

Davy shrieked, too. "What happened?" his mother wailed.

Villiers sucked in a deep, shuddering breath. "Nothing," he moaned. "Just…nothing. Somebody's playing a trick on us, that's all. But we've got to get out of the house. Get up, Davy." Evidently paralyzed with fear, the boy didn't move. Villiers lifted him in his arms, and then he and his wife crept warily toward the door.

"We'll leave them alone until they reach the front door," Louis said. "Give them hope that nothing else is going to happen. Then, when we start messing with them again, it will hit them all the harder."

The ghosts followed the mortals to the front door. Mrs. Villiers unlocked it, then pulled on the brass knob. The door didn't move. Louis's magic had jammed it in its frame.

"Laugh," Louis said. "That always shakes them up."

Still feeling disgusted with himself, Bellamy forced a cruel laugh, like a villain in a corny old movie. No doubt it sounded genuinely diabolical on the other side of the Shroud. "There's no escape," he said. "Not until the dead have had their way with you."

"What do you *want*?" Mrs. Villiers wailed.

"Your fear," Bellamy replied. "Your blood. Your souls." He pushed a spindly porcelain vase off a marble-topped table. When it shattered, Davy shrieked and thrashed in his father's arms.

Mrs. Villiers struggled to open the door again, still to no avail. Her husband scrambled into the living room, dropped Davy on the couch, and pounded his fists against the window. Hardened by the power of Louis's Arcanos, the glass wouldn't shatter. Villiers bashed it with an end table, but that didn't work either.

For the next few minutes the mortals dashed around and around the house, trying desperately to escape. Occasionally one of them would pick up a phone to call for help, but Bellamy always broke the connection. He also snarled threats, poked his victims, and upset objects light enough for him to shift. Meanwhile the gleeful, capering Louis spread fungus and decay throughout the home. Sometimes he fondled the mortals obscenely. They couldn't actually feel his touch, but they cried out in loathing as patches of their nightclothes melted into cold, stinking slime.

Soon they were staggering, their hearts pounding and their breath rasping in their throats, the smell of their sweat filling the air. For a time Bellamy wondered why, when they manifestly couldn't escape, they didn't simply stand their ground and defy their tormentors to do their worst. Granted, the ghostly harassment was unpleasant, but it hadn't done them any bodily harm, and repetition should have rendered even the most disturbing tricks less frightening than they'd been initially.

Then he realized that his victims literally *couldn't* get over their panic. He was a supernatural creature now, and his visitation was inspiring the same irrational, irresistible terror that he himself had experienced the first time he saw Dunn in werewolf form. He wondered if his discernible presence would have the same effect in any circumstances, on any living person, even Astarte. The possibility made him feel hollow and sick with dismay.

The mortals stumbled up to the front door again. Sobbing, Mrs. Villiers heaved on the knob with all her strength, then battered the panel with bloody hands.

Desiccated arms uplifted, Louis twirled around. "They are *so* frightened!" he crowed. "And it tastes so good! Thank you, Legba! Thank you, Damballah! Thank you, Gbo and Tokpodu!" He turned to Bellamy. "Time for the *coup de grâce.* Appear to them."

Bellamy hesitated. As hard as the older mortals' hearts were thumping, he was afraid they might go into cardiac arrest if he gave them another shock. But he had no choice but to obey. How else could he learn what he so urgently needed to know?

"We've toyed with you long enough," he said to the Quick family. "Now I'm going to destroy you." Concentrating, his arms upraised to look menacing, he made himself visible on the warm side of the Shroud.

Mrs. Villiers made a tiny whining sound and sank to her knees, clawing at her own face with her pink, lacquered nails. Her husband's eyes rolled up and then he fainted, carrying Davy to the floor with him. Pinned beneath his father's bulk, the boy stared wide-eyed and shuddering at the apparition before him.

Bellamy realized that this ugly little scene didn't have much in the way of a punch line. It would be anticlimactic when his phantasmal image simply disappeared. Not that he cared. He just wanted to stop torturing the poor mortals. He turned to Louis. "I guess we're done, aren't we?"

Louis chuckled. "Not quite. Pop all the way through the Surface and kill the boy."

Bellamy gaped at him. "Are you serious? Geffard didn't say anything about any killing. He only said we were going to frighten Villiers."

"If you yank the kid out of his father's arms and strangle him in front of his mother's eyes, that should do the trick, don't you think? Look, I've been working for the loa a long time. I know him, and when he wants somebody punished, he wants them punished *hard.* Besides, the bastards are only Mounts, just puppets for us to play with. And I shouldn't have to *convince* you anyway, because he put *me* in charge. Now, are you going to follow orders, or what?"

Bellamy wondered fleetingly if he could pretend to throttle the boy and whisper to him to play dead. But no, it wouldn't work. With his supernaturally sharp ears, Louis would overhear him. And even if he didn't, Davy was far too terrified to cooperate with the object of his dread.

The agent allowed all aspects of his presence to slip back to the dark side of the Shroud. "Or what, I guess," he said.

Louis shook his withered, hairless head. "Too bad you're squeamish. Screwing up one of the first jobs Geffard gives you is a bad career move."

"I'll bet you're right," said Bellamy. "So I think I'll try my luck in another town. If Geffard is this much of an SOB, I don't want to work for him anyway." As suddenly as he could, he made a grab for the pistol in his jacket.

Unfortunately, he failed to catch Louis by surprise. The Masquer's bony arm stretched like taffy, lashed at him, and struck his wrist. His hand flew open, and the gun tumbled across the room.

"That was a stupid move, too," Louis said, his sunken eyes glittering. As his arm retracted, his hands swelled to twice their previous size, and yellow talons extended from their fingertips. Lunging, he raked at Bellamy's eyes.

The agent sidestepped and blocked. Louis's nails ripped his sleeve and gashed his forearm. Bellamy snapped a punch into his skeletal opponent's side, and felt one of the fleshless ribs break.

As Louis reeled past, Bellamy lifted his foot to kick the other wraith in the knee. He should have had a second to execute the attack before his adversary could wheel back around to face him. But the flesh sculptor's malleable body simply twisted one hundred and eighty degrees at the waist, bringing his hands into position to rake at the FBI agent once again. His talons flashed at Bellamy's torso.

Bellamy was caught off guard. The attack ripped open his chest and knocked him onto his back. Another wraith would have had to drop on top of him to continue clawing, but Louis merely lengthened his arms.

Bellamy shook off the shock of his wounds, struggled desperately to keep Louis from rending him again. In response, the Masquer stretched his limbs still further, looping the extra lengths around the downed man, entangling him. Straining, Bellamy fumbled his sword from its scabbard, but Louis knocked it out of his grasp. The weapon spun across the floor.

Bellamy could hear his Shadow in the depths of his mind, cackling over his imminent defeat. Behind the writhing, shifting form of Louis, he glimpsed the mortals. Now unable to sense the presence of the ghosts, evidently daring to believe the haunting was over, Mrs. Villiers had crept to her loved ones and was ineffectually trying to comfort Davy and rouse her husband at the same time. Her ministrations made a bizarre contrast to the desperate battle just a few feet away.

Bellamy felt himself beginning to weaken. If he was going to turn the fight around, it would have to be in the next few seconds, and he could only think of one more trick to try. Turning his head, he sank his teeth into one of Louis's tentacular arms. The thin layer of desiccated flesh tasted rotten and foul. The phony maggots squirmed against his tongue.

The flesh sculptor's limbs jerked, loosening their grip. Bellamy thrashed frantically, freeing one leg from the coils that held it and scooting himself a few inches across the floor. He whipped his foot up at Louis's crotch.

Since Bellamy didn't know what was under the grubby black raincoat, he had no idea how effective the attack would be. If Louis had withered his genitals as he'd shriveled the rest of his flesh, the kick might not hurt him at all. But evidently the Masquer's perverse desire to resemble a rotting corpse had stopped short of a willingness to emasculate himself. He made a choking sound, and, staggering, doubled over. His elongated arms flailed spastically.

Bellamy thrust-kicked at Louis's ankle. Bone cracked, and the Masquer fell. The FBI agent swarmed on top of him and started battering his ghastly skull face. The Invisible tried to fend him off, but his movements were still too feeble and clumsy with pain. Bellamy slammed a punch into the bridge of his opponent's nose. The blow sent a burst of pain through his own hand—evidently he'd broken a knuckle or two—but Louis abruptly stopped struggling and lay inert.

Gasping needlessly but compulsively for air—he wondered how long it would take him to shed the habit—Bellamy scrambled across the floor, picked up his gun, then straddled Louis's chest. Meanwhile, Mrs. Villiers tried the door knob. This time, it worked. Weeping softly, clinging to one another, she and her family stumbled out into the night. Bellamy sent a silent apology winging after them.

He was pretty sure he hadn't hurt Louis severely enough to dump him into the Labyrinth. If the flesh sculptor were going to vanish, he would have done it already. Bellamy just had to be patient, and wait for him to awaken. And after a few minutes, the skeletal *ibambo* groaned, and his lidless eyes shifted in their bony sockets.

Bellamy aimed the pistol at the other ghost's face. "Welcome back," he said. "I've got darksteel bullets in this thing, so if I were you, I wouldn't try anything too macho."

"Why are you doing this?" Louis croaked.

"I work for the Queen," Bellamy told him. "I have orders to infiltrate Geffard's operation."

"You won't get away with it," Louis said.

"Apparently you're right," said Bellamy. The bloodless cuts in his chest and arm began to close. "I didn't count on your boss sending me on such nasty errands that no decent person could stomach them. So it's time for Plan B. I'm going to interrogate you. If you give me the answers I need, you might survive the experience."

Once again, Bellamy *felt* the Masquer's perpetually leering countenance sneer. "I'm not going to tell you shit."

"Then send me a postcard from the Void." Bellamy slowly tightened his finger on the trigger.

"Wait!" squawked Louis. "I'm just a peon. I don't know anything!"

"Then that's your tough luck." The gun was almost ready to fire. Bellamy wondered if he should ease the pressure. A few days ago, he would never have contemplated murdering a prisoner. But now that he was buried in the cold, dark realm of the dead, his wounds throbbing, his Shadow still squirming in the back of his head, his mortal life and scruples seemed dim and far away.

"All right!" said Louis. "Maybe I know *something*. I'll tell you what I can."

"Good," Bellamy said, shifting his weight. Louis's frame was far too bony to make a comfortable seat. "Let's start with the basics. Geffard wants to be King."

"Sure. Everybody knows *that*. People say that when he was a young *houngan* in

Haiti, he had problems with his mother, who was also his teacher and sponsor in voudoun. She accused him of walking the Left-hand Path, of joining the *culte des morts*, and wanted to strip him of his magic. He tried to fight her, but he wasn't strong enough. He had to flee to New Orleans to keep his powers.

"He hoped he could be top dog here, like he wasn't on the island. And New Orleans has had a lot of powerful hoodoo men, guys like Doctor Cat and Father Byron. But it's always been the priestesses, the Laveaus and Latours, who really run things. I've heard that eventually one of the *mamaloi* got tired of his uppity ways, stole one of his suits, and dressed a corpse in it. Geffard looked all over Louisiana for that body, but he couldn't find it. As it rotted, so did he.

"And of course, when he passed over, he found a Queen ruling the dead half of New Orleans, too. Must have made him crazy. But eventually he went down into the Abyss, found the Island Beneath the Sea, made a pact with one of Les Mystères, and became more powerful than he'd ever been in life. And when he came back to the Mirrorlands, he swore that the third time was the charm, and he was finally going to knock one of the bitches off her throne and take it for himself."

"How does he plan to do that?" Bellamy asked.

"How should I know? Do you think he spills his guts to every guy on the payroll?"

"I think you're the kind of creep who keeps his ear to the ground," the agent said. "I think that even if Geffard hasn't confided his plans to you, you've probably discovered some of them for yourself. And I'm absolutely certain that if you dry up on me, I'm going to put a bullet into your head."

"Okay," Louis growled. "But all I know is what I hear. I can't promise any of it's true."

"Just tell me."

"The word is, Geffard made a deal with a horde of Baka."

Bellamy thought of his shadowself, the foulness festering inside him. And supposedly Baka—Spectres—were *all* Shadow. He grimaced in disgust. "And that particular piece of information didn't bother you. You kept working for him anyway."

"Fuck you," Louis said. "We Invisibles have a more realistic outlook than you Morts. We wouldn't try to wipe out the dark side of existence, even if we could. It's there for a purpose. We get along fine by keeping the dark and the light in balance."

"Whatever," Bellamy said. "Tell me about the deal."

"The Baka gave Geffard control over some kind of spirit nobody's ever seen before, to attack the Queen's flunkies and desecrate their shrines. That would mess up her *gris-gris* and make people lose faith in her. And because the creatures were so weird, the royal guards would have trouble fighting them, and it would be hard for anybody to link them to Les Invisibles."

"What did the Spectres get in return?"

"We Creoles are really good at possessing the Quick. The Baka needed to learn how to do it, and Geffard taught them."

"And now they're making mortals kill for them," Bellamy said. "Preachers. Cops. Fire fighters. Why?"

"Just the usual Baka meanness?" Louis said. "If that's not it, it beats the hell out of me."

"Do you know the motive behind the Atheist murders?"

"No. How would I? Are you trying to blame those on the Baka, too?"

"I'll ask the questions. Tell me about the werewolves."

"What werewolves? Look, I've given you everything I've got."

"Let's hope that isn't true," Bellamy said. "Because it hasn't been enough to save your neck. Geffard must have a hideout. A place where he and his fellow conspirators meet to do the things they can't do openly. Where is it?"

Louis hesitated.

"You have till the count of five," said Bellamy, "and then I'm going to shoot. One, two, three—"

"Stop!" the Masquer cried. "There's supposed to be a big old house on Barracks Street, between Chartres and Decatur. I can't tell you which one it is, because I've never been there."

"All right," said Bellamy. "That's it for now." Glad to ease his aching rump, keeping his pistol trained on his prisoner, he stood up cautiously.

"Look, I really have told you everything," said Louis, clambering to his knees. "Why don't you give me a break and let me go?"

"Sorry," Bellamy said. "I won't kill you, but you can't just walk away either. I'm taking you to the Queen, to tell her what you told me."

"No," said Louis, "you can't do that. Geffard is going to find out I ratted on him. He'll put a curse on me. If I'm going to survive, I have to get out of town right now."

"Maybe in a few hours," Bellamy said. "But for now—"

A tentacle of gray, desiccated flesh and yellow bone, extruded from the substance of Louis's back, whipped over his shoulder and lashed at Bellamy's face. The FBI agent jumped backward, but the unnatural limb still clipped him a glancing blow to the temple. Louis scrambled up and charged him, talons outstretched.

Off balance, Bellamy had no choice but to fire. The shot blasted a hole in Louis's brow and blew out the back of his head. The skeletal wraith collapsed at his captor's feet, waves of black light washing through his body.

"You were no loss to anyone," murmured Bellamy, watching the Masquer melt away, "but I still wish you hadn't done that. There was no need for you to die." He wondered if Louis's Shadow had prompted the suicidal assault. If so, perhaps Les Invisibles weren't as good at managing their inner darkness as they thought. Perhaps it couldn't be placated, only opposed, the same way that good people were obliged to stand up to all the *external* violence and savagery in the world.

Frowning, Bellamy pushed such philosophizing aside. He had more pressing matters to think about. Like reaching the Queen as soon as possible. Now that Bellamy had answers for her, she'd mobilize her army to arrest Geffard. Wouldn't she?

Maybe not, the agent thought glumly, remembering the darkness which had rippled through Marie's body. Even though he'd rescued Titus, he was still essentially an unproven stranger, and a white one at that, in her eyes. Would she find his fragmentary, secondhand information, extracted under duress from a shifty, unreliable character who'd subsequently evaporated into thin air, sufficiently compelling to shake her out of her fear and indecision? He had an unpleasant suspicion she might *still* refuse to act.

But Bellamy did have an option. He could scout out the house on Barracks Street himself. Maybe he could find some physical evidence to support his allegations, or learn enough about Geffard's resources and strategy to help Marie through her paralyzing dread of making the wrong move. But if he was going to do it at all, it had to be now, before the loa noticed that he and Louis had gone missing. The detective retrieved his gleaming black shortsword, then strode out into the night.

TWENTY-THREE

Marilyn removed her blond wig, revealing the dark crewcut beneath, set the hairpiece on its black, vaguely skull-shaped plastic stand, and fussily began to comb it out. To Astarte, the monotonous swishing had grown as wearily familiar as the nondescript decor of the motel room, which miraculously never seemed to change, even though the fugitives never slept in the same place two nights running. "I hope you don't think that thing looks real," she said irritably.

Turning, the occultist arched a plucked eyebrow. "Is that the reason for the magenta stripes in your own coif, and all those piercings? Your devotion to the natural look?"

"That's different," said Astarte, touching her finger to the ring in her lower lip. "This isn't supposed to look like part of my mouth. A wig *is* supposed to look like your real hair. But it doesn't. It looks like some kind of animal crawled onto your head and died."

Marilyn simply looked at her for a moment, and then, lowering her voice, said, "I know this whole enterprise is difficult. Also painful, frustrating, and frightening."

Astarte's annoyance abruptly gave way to a surge of dismay. Her eyes stung, and she blinked furiously. "I don't want to give up hope. But I keep thinking, if Frank was alive, he would have contacted us by now. He would have thought to leave a message on Grailnet."

The transsexual put down the comb, got up from the vanity, sat down on the bed beside her companion, and took her hand. Up close, she smelled of Obsession and the garlic chicken she'd eaten for supper, and Astarte could see the tracks on her inner arms. "Perhaps he's alive but a prisoner."

"I guess that's the only hope," Astarte said. "But you didn't see the half-eaten dead bodies heaped up in the house. If you had, you'd have trouble believing the werewolves could scrounge up the willpower to leave any human prisoner in one piece, even if they wanted to."

"If you're convinced Agent Bellamy's gone," Marilyn said, "there's still time for you to walk away from this. We're glad to have you, of course, but you're not a member of the Arcanum, you don't have any special expertise, and I suppose that if we have to, we can carry on without you."

Scowling, Astarte twisted her hand out of Marilyn's grip. "Forget it. I'm staying, no matter what. If I can't get Frank back, I'll make the bastards sorry they killed him. I just wish you people would crank up your 'special expertise' and *do* something."

"But we are," Marilyn said. "Joan Crosby is studying some suggestive fluctuations in the local ley lines. Alan Fong is consulting the Tarot and I Ching. Tom Kincaid is meditating, trying to contact a benevolent spiritual entity who, he believes, has counseled him twice before in times of danger. Others prowl the city every night, visiting sites with a history of paranormal—"

"I *know* all that," Astarte said, "and none of it is getting us anywhere. You keep fiddling around with your experiments and observations, kidding yourself that you're getting closer to the truth, wasting time, when meanwhile, for all we know, the end of the world is coming!"

"And what would you have us do?" Marilyn asked patiently, sounding as if she was certain she already knew the answer to her question.

"I don't know exactly," Astarte said. "But you can work magic, even if you say you're not a wizard. You sure put a spell on Frank and me."

"A parlor trick," the occultist replied. "Jumped-up hypnosis. And even that required days of grueling preparation. It no more resembled true magick than the flame of a single match resembles a forest fire."

"Whatever," Astarte said. "The point is, you *can* do stuff. So maybe we should come out of hiding. Draw Dunn and his buddies into a trap."

"Confront the devil head on," said Marilyn. "That was R. J.'s way, and it got him killed."

"At least he got to look the supernatural in the face before he died," Astarte replied. "You claim you want to do the same thing. Learn real sorcery and uncover the secrets of the universe. You've spent God knows how many years puttering around with grimoires and Ouija boards. But you're never going to get anywhere if you flinch whenever it's time to take a risk. Hell, to you and your buds, I'm just some kind of ignorant Goth New Age groupie. But since I came to New Orleans, I've seen more paranormal shit than you have in your whole life."

For a moment, Marilyn looked as if she were going to snarl some angry retort, but then she sighed and lowered her eyes instead. "Perhaps you're right," she said in a troubled voice. "Maybe I have been too cautious. Lord knows, eager as I am to experience the occult, it terrifies me, too." Her painted scarlet lips quirked into a crooked smile. "It's what one of my psychiatrists called an approach-avoidance conflict. I wish I did have your single-minded determination to explore the darkness, no matter what horrors are waiting inside it.

"But it doesn't matter whether I'm courageous or a coward. The simple fact of the matter is, we Arcanists are scholars and scientists, not mages, saints, or even soldiers. Our adversaries are the spawn of Hell, or any rate, something comparable. We couldn't possibly confront them and live to tell the tale, not at this stage of the game. Our only hope is to study them from a safe distance, using the best tools at our disposal, and pray we discover data which *will* allow us to foil their schemes."

Astarte could see she was never going to change her friend's mind. And for all she really knew, Marilyn's perspective was the right one, even if she did find it hard to swallow. "All right," she said. "We'll play it your way. But when time runs out, and the disaster happens, remember I told you so." She picked up the remote control from the night stand. "I suppose we should watch the news. Find out if the Atheist has killed anybody else."

"I suppose," Marilyn said, rising. She returned to the vanity, unscrewed a jar of cold cream, and began to remove her makeup.

Astarte clicked on the television. The screen displayed what appeared to be the climactic scene of a medical drama, a surgical team laboring frantically while monitors bleeped and blinked behind them. Sneering, she muted the sound.

As she watched the chief surgeon massage his patient's wet, crimson heart, she wished she were as fearless as Marilyn thought she was. In truth, she'd recoiled from the hideous Nosferatu Mr. Daimler, while Dunn's transformation from man into beast had driven her mad with terror. Evidently such paralyzing dread was an all but inescapable part of a normal human's first encounters with the supernatural, but people could get past it if they tried. Frank had done it, and so, she vowed, would she.

A string of commercials—for pickup trucks, sugar-frosted breakfast cereal, and scented douches—finally led into the news. A slender young blonde in a lacy white blouse and an avuncular, ruddy-faced, gray-headed man in a navy business suit sat behind a desk. Just as Astarte turned the sound on, the words MYSTERY DEATH IN CEMETERY appeared on the screen behind the reporters.

"The body of a man in his twenties or early thirties was found in the Gates of Serenity Cemetery Number Two about an hour ago," said the blonde. The TV displayed a collection of cops, some uniformed and others in plain clothes, clustered around an indistinct form on the ground. Yellow crime-scene tape, strung from tomb to tomb, fluttered in the breeze.

Astarte made a tiny sound in her throat. Her face older, more angular and masculine without cosmetics, Marilyn jumped back up and put her hand on her companion's shoulder. "I'm sorry," she murmured.

"The cemetery isn't maintained, and apparently the body lay undiscovered for several days," the blonde continued. "As yet, the police have been unable to identify the victim. But Channel Six has learned that he died of violence, though the precise cause of death is undetermined. The body was virtually shredded, as if slashed repeatedly or mauled by a large animal, and also extensively burned."

Two men in coveralls hoisted the corpse onto a gurney and rolled it toward the camera. Marilyn gently tried to turn Astarte's head away from the screen. "Don't look," she said.

"I have to," Astarte said. "We still don't *know* it's him."

The gurney rolled closer. She felt herself growing tenser and tenser. Meanwhile time seemed to slow down, until she imagined the interminable wait would make her scream.

And then, at last, the dead man's face swung into view.

His features were tattered and charred, puffy and greenish, with fluids leaking from the mouth, nose and ears, and bumps like blisters studding the skin. Astarte discerned that insects and rats had been nibbling at him, though she couldn't have said exactly how she knew. She told herself that death had so ravaged and rotted the corpse's features that no one, even his would-be lover, could possibly identify him.

Yet even as she framed the thought, she realized she was deluding herself. The dead man *was* Frank, beyond any shadow of a doubt. She recognized him even through his mask of decay. And all the mental work she'd done to prepare herself for this moment didn't soften the blow at all. She whimpered.

Marilyn hugged her, tried ineffectually to turn her head. "You've seen what you needed to see," the occultist said. "Now look away."

"No!" snarled Astarte, her grief warping into a seething rage. She wrenched herself free. "I want to remember. Remember what they *did* to him." Bellamy's body moved off screen, and then a paunchy black policeman carrying an evidence bag sauntered past the camera. Inside the clear plastic container was a spiral notebook.

"My god!" Astarte exclaimed. The two reporters reappeared on the screen.

"What is it?" Marilyn asked.

"The notebook. The one Frank stole from the house. The cops have it."

"How is that possible?" Marilyn asked. "Why didn't Dunn retrieve it?"

"Maybe Frank dropped it somewhere before Dunn caught up with him," Astarte said. "Or he had it stuffed inside his clothes, and Dunn never noticed it. You have to remember, he didn't know we took it." She grimaced. "Look, it doesn't matter how he missed it. The important thing is that there it is, and we have to get it. Now, before the police identify Frank. Once they do, they'll call the FBI, Dunn will get involved, and our chance will be gone."

"Slow down," said Marilyn. "Breathe. You're jabbering a mile a minute."

"What difference does that make?" Astarte demanded, baffled and annoyed by the Arcanist's lack of enthusiasm.

"You're almost hysterical," Marilyn said gently. "I think you're getting all worked up about this to sidestep the pain of Frank's death."

As if on cue, Astarte felt a swell of immense, debilitating sorrow. Clenching her fists, trembling, she fought to will it away. "What if I am? The notebook really is important, isn't it? God, this is so typical of you people, worrying about what's going on with my fucking *feelings* in the middle of an emergency! You've got money and pull, right? You can find out where the cops took the notebook. Maybe you can even bribe somebody to turn it over to us, or make us a photocopy."

"It's conceivable," Marilyn said. "But we need to think more about this. Why would the police have any difficulty identifying Agent Bellamy?"

"He was on leave from his job. Nobody had filed a missing person report or anything."

"But wasn't he carrying ID?"

Astarte shrugged. "I don't know. Maybe he didn't have it on him."

"We didn't find it among his effects."

"Then Dunn lifted it. Maybe because he didn't want Frank identified."

"Possibly," said Marilyn, frowning. "I suppose he wouldn't want his colleagues in the FBI poking around next door to the werewolf lair. But in that case, why allow the body to be found at all? Why not bring it into the house with the others?"

"Probably Dunn didn't want to take the time. He was eager to get after me."

"But why not later?"

"Maybe after I got away, they decided they'd better clear out of the house, in case I called the cops, and then it didn't matter anymore."

"Perhaps," Marilyn said, sounding unconvinced.

Astarte scowled. "All right, Sherlock, what do *you* think is going on?"

"I don't know. Possibly nothing more than meets the eye. On the other hand, you wondered if we could lure the enemy out into the open. Perhaps they're trying to do the same to us."

"I don't *believe* you," Astarte snarled, drops of spit flying from her lips. "Frank gave his life to get that notebook. It may have all the information we need to stop the Atheist. And all the magic secrets you've been looking for your whole life. But you won't go after it. Because you're worried we might be walking into a trap, even though there's no solid reason to think so, and like always, you're too gutless to take a chance. But no problem. You can always shoot up and *dream* that you're not pathetic!"

Her jaw tight and her eyes troubled, Marilyn gazed at her companion. "I never said I wouldn't try to get the notebook," she said at last. "I just said we should discuss it. Now that we have, I'll make some calls."

TWENTY-FOUR

His Mag-10 Roadblocker shotgun dangling casually from his enormous fist, a long ax slung across his brawny back, Mike Fink prowled through the dark, ruinous, high-ceilinged room, moving from one cluster of guerrillas to the next. Answering their questions. Inspecting their equipment. Sympathizing over the pain of their wounds and the loss of fallen comrades. Doing his best to assess their mood, which was unquestionably more sullen than it had been a few weeks before.

Though he would have sooner have been torn apart by doomshades than admit it, Fink felt somewhat out of his depth. Hitherto, he'd never commanded anything grander than a keelboat crew or a band of desperadoes. Even serving as Montrose's lieutenant, he hadn't quite realized how onerous it would be to bear the ultimate responsibility for leading the Grim Rider's ragtag army himself.

The thought of Montrose made him frown, which in turn caused the freckle-faced archer he was currently palavering with to twitch in apprehension. The boatman would never have admitted he could miss anyone, either. In the eyes of the Underworld, Mike Fink was a raging force of nature, a titan who could shatter a Deathlord's head with a flick of his finger and gag the sucking maw of Oblivion with his cock, not some weakling who craved the companionship of lesser men. Still, he'd gotten used to the auburn-haired inquisitor. Sometimes he found himself regretting that he hadn't tried to rescue him from the Legionnaires who'd shown up so unexpectedly to arrest him.

Fink snorted the thought away. If he'd tried to buck those odds, he would only have wound up destroyed or manacled himself. Sometimes discretion *was* the better part of valor, even for the King of the Mississip.

"Mr. Fink?" said a diffident voice.

Fink turned and saw Valentine, Gayoso's nominal jester and general flunky. The dwarf's homely face displayed a couple of shiny patches, the ghostly equivalent of bruises.

Fink didn't much like the little man, particularly now that he'd become so furtive and morose. His new demeanor reinforced the former outlaw's suspicion that Valentine had somehow participated in Montrose's fall from grace. "What the hell do you want?" he growled.

"Governor Gayoso would like to see you," Valentine replied.

Fink gave the archer a reassuring clap on the shoulder, staggering him, and then twisted his face into a menacing leer. "I wonder why the Spanish son of a whore always sends you to fetch me," he said to Valentine. "Every time I see your ugly little monkey carcass, I get the urge to see how far I can kick you."

"That probably is why," Valentine said. "He'd enjoy seeing you do it. He has some pretty crude notions of entertainment, particularly lately. He also doesn't like to be kept waiting, so shall we go?"

"Sure," Fink answered. "Maybe I want to talk to him, too."

As they set off through the labyrinthine corridors and gloomy chambers of the Citadel, he noticed Valentine was limping. He quickened his long stride, making it that much more difficult and, he hoped, painful for the servant to keep up with him. "Do you *like* being knocked around?" he asked contemptuously. "Is that why you're spending your afterlife licking Gayoso's boots? Is that what you pay that little girl down in Under-the-Hill to do for you?"

Valentine peered up at him. To Fink's surprise, the dwarf didn't look angry or insulted, just miserable. "You know Daphne? Have you seen her lately? Do you know what's happened to her?"

Fink whipped his shotgun in a horizontal arc. The end of the barrel caught Valentine across the ear and threw him stumbling through the wall. When the jester reappeared, his face screwed up as if he was struggling not to cry, Fink said, "Do I look like a pervert? No, I don't know—or care—what happened to the bitch."

Valentine lifted his hands in a pleading gesture. "I just thought that with all your connections, you could—" Abruptly all the desperate hope in his expression withered, replaced by a kind of bleakness. "But why would you? Sorry I annoyed you."

They finished the walk in silence. Fink felt vaguely uncomfortable. If he hadn't known himself incapable of shame, he might almost have wondered if that wasn't what he was experiencing.

Illuminated only by the trio of milk-white tapers burning blue and cold in their brass candelabrum, a bracing echo of ancient misery thrumming in the air, Gayoso's office seemed much the same as ever. Except that the last time Fink had visited here, the Anacreon hadn't had bodyguards armed with Skorpion Model 61s and cutlasses watching vigilantly from the shadowy corners, nor had Prudence, the plump, matronly Pardoner, sat lounging on the sofa beneath the equestrian portrait of Robert E. Lee.

Gayoso had set aside his helmet and cuirass, but, as usual, retained his steel domino. He frowned. "You're out of uniform," he said, referring to the green sash emblazoned with a black hourglass, emblem of the Citadel's military forces, which he'd given Fink the week before.

Fink shrugged. "It gets in my way. Anyway, my boys and I are mercenaries, not Legionnaires. That was the deal we made with Montrose when he recruited us."

"The traitor is gone," Gayoso replied. "I'm in charge of the crusade now, and I'd appreciate it if you'd accommodate yourself to my way of doing things."

"I know things have changed," the river man said. He hesitated for a split-second, then decided that, as long as Gayoso had summoned him here, he might as well speak his mind. "The trouble is, they've changed for the worse."

Inside the steel mask, Gayoso's eyes narrowed. "If there's some sort of problem," he said, his voice full of what Fink assumed to be bogus concern, "please, tell me about it."

"All right," said Fink. "You keep sending us farther and farther north, and farther and farther away from the river."

"Of course," the Spaniard said. "When you've stamped out Heresy in one region, it's time to move on to the next."

"The farther we travel from the capital, the more danger we're in. There's always the chance a big bunch of god-lovers will circle around behind us and cut us off. Meanwhile, we're getting less and less support from the Legions. It's like Grand Gulf every damn time."

"I thought you irregulars boasted that any one of you is worth twenty Legionnaires."

"We are," Fink growled. "That doesn't mean we want to go on suicide missions. I'll tell you, Anacreon, if I weren't such a gentle, trusting sort, I might even think you're worried that since Montrose hired us, *you* can't trust us. And you figure, now that you have a fresh levy of soldiers from Stygia, the smart thing is to send us into tough situations until you get us killed off."

"That's absurd!" Gayoso snapped. "I care about the welfare of *all* my troops. Even insolent former criminals. If I didn't understand the stress you've been operating under, I'd be tempted to have you bastinadoed for suggesting otherwise.

"The truth is, I've been depending on you and your force to spearhead the campaign against the Heretics for one simple reason. Your men *are* formidable. Under Montrose's leadership, they accomplished miracles. If you're not the general he was, or if you've lost the belly for hard fighting, feel free to step down from your position. I'll find someone else to place in command."

The keelboatman drew himself up straight. "You think you can find a better man than *me*? I'm *Mike Fink*, you spic son of a bitch. I can outrun, out-jump, outsmart, out-fuck, out-voudoun, or drag out, throw down, and lick any wraith on the river. Spectres and death mages piss themselves when they see me coming. When I fart, I blast holes in the Shroud. I'm a Salt-River roarer and I'm chock-full of fight.

"Don't worry, I'll head up your lousy little crusade for you. I'll slaughter every Heretic from here to Hannibal. You just make damn sure you deal square with me."

"Absolutely," Gayoso said. "If you feel you need more support from the regular troops, I'll see that you get it. Now that that's settled, let's discuss what I actually invited you here to talk about. As you presumably recall, I ordered all my soldiers to consult Mother Prudence and her colleagues here in the Citadel at least twice a month. You haven't, nor have most of the fellows under your command."

"Montrose warned me that a lot of the Pardoners along the river are really Spectres in disguise," Fink replied. After the Hierarch's arrest, he'd intended to investigate the mystery himself, but he hadn't made any headway. The inquisition had kept him too busy.

Gayoso's jaw tightened. "Despite your notoriety, Mr. Fink, I've given you the benefit of the doubt. I've assumed you were Montrose's dupe, not a willing collaborator in his treason. Still, now that he's been unmasked, it would behoove you to stop parroting his lies.

"My agents have checked, and there's absolutely no evidence to support such a preposterous claim. And even if there were, that would be all the more reason for you to seek out Prudence and the other Pardoners on my staff. I can personally vouch for every one of them."

"Isn't that peachy," Fink said. "But I've never been to a confessor and I don't see any reason to start now. My Shadow doesn't bother me. I think my soul chewed it up, swallowed it, and crapped it out a long time ago."

"Exposure to Heresy weakens the psyche," Prudence said. "So do the brutality and hardships of warfare. Even if you're immune, Mr. Fink—which, in all honesty, I doubt—your subordinates aren't. Darkness is eating them up inside. Yet they avoid the ministrations of those who could help them, because they're emulating you."

"Bull," Fink replied. "They just don't feel like they need it. Why would they? How often does the average ghost visit a soul-shrinker? Two or three times a year?"

"Perhaps," said the fat woman, "but that's inadequate, particularly for front-line soldiers in the war against Oblivion. We have to do better."

"I order you to commence treatment tonight," said Gayoso to Fink, the sapphire candlelight gleaming on his domino. "And to make sure all your men do likewise within the next seventy-two hours."

"What if I say no?" asked Fink.

"This isn't a trivial matter, like wearing a strip of cloth," Gayoso replied. "I need soldiers I can depend on. Between your outlawry and your friendship with Montrose, you already have two black marks against you. If you won't permit the necessary precautions to keep Oblivion from gaining a foothold in your soul, then I'll take it that you have resigned your command." He gave Fink a contemptuous little smile. "I suppose that if you *do* feel inadequate but can't bring yourself to admit it, this is a good way to save face."

Fink glared back at him. His instincts told him to tell the Anacreon to go screw himself. As a rule, he resented taking any kind of orders from anyone, and this one galled him more than most. He'd always regarded the role of penitent as inherently weak, effeminate, and undignified. In fact, the thought of revealing his innermost thoughts to a Pardoner, of allowing a stranger to tamper with the essence of who he was, revolted him.

But if he didn't play along, maybe people really would think he'd abandoned his new command because he'd lost his nerve. They'd start to doubt his *legend*, and the prospect of that was simply intolerable.

He supposed a person could talk to a confessor, yet refuse to disclose anything personal. Surely the bastard wouldn't be able to *do* anything to him if he declined to open up.

"All right," he grunted. "It's a waste of time, but I'll do it once, just to prove I'm right."

Beaming, her voluminous purple gown with its miscellany of religious symbols swishing around her, Prudence hauled herself laboriously to her feet. "I'm so glad," she said.

TWENTY-FIVE

Montrose carried his crossbow in his left hand. The fingers of his right opened and closed repeatedly. He imagined he could feel the hilt of his saber inside them. Soon, he knew, he'd draw the weapon from his scabbard and cut Louise to pieces.

He would have attacked her already, except for one consideration. Back in Grand Gulf, he'd realized he didn't dare torture her, richly as she deserved it. He couldn't succumb to the temptation without strengthening his Shadow to an intolerable degree. Which left him only one way to prolong and savor his revenge: skulk along beside her through the dark streets and claustrophobic alleys as if he truly had accepted her as an ally. Feast his eyes on her slim form and honey-blond hair until the lust to slay her became irresistible.

As they neared an intersection, a column of silvery fire shot up above the row of gray gable-and-valley roofs on the buildings to their right, like a response to the multicolored lightning flashing in the storm clouds overhead. The boom came two seconds later, shivering the grimy, uneven cobbles beneath their feet.

Her mace cocked over her shoulder, Louise studied the pillar of flame. "I wonder which Deathlord's agents blew what up," she said, "and whether the saboteurs were disguised as Spectres, too."

Her voice was dulcet even when she whispered. At the sound, Montrose suppressed a fresh shiver of loathing. "It's not important," he replied. "What matters is that the explosion wasn't particularly close. With a modicum of luck, we shouldn't encounter anyone fleeing or rushing to the scene."

They peered both ways before crossing the avenue. No one else was in sight. Off to the left, however, stood a barracoon, its high walls capped with coils of razor wire and its iron gates decorated with complex designs of woven chain. With his preternaturally sharp hearing, Montrose caught the sound of a few voices murmuring inside, proof that, appearances to the contrary, the area wasn't actually deserted. He supposed most people realized there were raiders about, and were prudently keeping indoors.

Louise gazed at the fortress-like enclosure. "I wish we could liberate those poor souls," she said.

Montrose's mouth tightened. "I don't," he said, with rather more fervor than he'd intended. "And even if I shared your sentiments, we have more important matters to attend to." Or rather, he did. She was only minutes from Oblivion.

The fugitives prowled on, past factories and warehouses, many of them drab stone boxes, but others encrusted with statuary, gargoyles, and carved facades, sometimes jumbled together in a jarring clash of periods and styles. At one point Montrose spotted a small, round keep overlooking the road ahead, with riflemen standing watch along the battlements. He and Louise detoured to avoid it.

Eventually the ground began to slope downward, and Montrose caught the sound and scent of the Sea of Souls. The monotonous roar of the surf coupled with a noise that at first resembled the screeching of gulls, but on further hearing blurred into the muffled wailing and lamentations of countless human tongues. The odor of salt water uncontaminated with seaweed or algae, as much like the smell of tears as that of any Earthly ocean.

Evidently realizing what she was about to see for the first time in her afterlife, Louise began to recite some prayer or meditation under her breath. Meanwhile, Montrose wondered what would happen if he decapitated her. Would sentience linger for an instant afterward? Would her severed head stare up at him in anguish? Would he have time to blow her a mocking kiss before she melted away?

They rounded a bend, and the narrow street terminated abruptly on a stretch of rocky beach. Despite her efforts to steel herself, Louise gasped.

At certain moments, the gray waves with their foaming crests looked like water and nothing more. But when the lightning flickered, one noticed the myriad human forms, elongated, constantly changing shape, tumbling and streaming over one another, trapped inside the surf. Or perhaps the captive souls *were* the water. Montrose had never been quite sure. Either way, he was surprised to discover that the sight of the Weeping Bay made him slightly uneasy himself.

"Dear God," said Louise. "It's even worse than the Artificers' pit. There we at least knew our torment would eventually come to an end. James, how could you bear to dwell in sight of this, decade after decade, century after century?"

For some reason, the question made the Scot even more uncomfortable. Scowling, he pointed across the channel, at Stygia. At the docks, where Viking longships, biremes, clipper ships, and aircraft carriers floated at their moorings. The ornately carved stone buildings, climbing level on level up the flanks of the island to the labyrinthine splendors of the palace. The Onyx Tower proper, jutting high above the surrounding structures like a darksteel dagger extending from a fist. "For the sake of that. The greatest city—and the capital of the greatest empire—that ever existed or ever will. A treasure that *must* be defended, no matter what the cost."

"Why? To provide luxury and privilege for the Marquess of Montrose?"

He glared at her. "Yes, as a matter of fact. But also because it's the pinnacle of human achievement. And because it represents the only hope for *anyone* to have a tolerable afterlife, no matter what rubbish you Heretics babble about the Far Shores and Transcendence. If not for the Legions, the Void would devour us all. Not even the Quick would be spared. I explained as much in the rail yard, and you claimed you understood. Why are you baiting me about it now?"

Crimson lightning flared, thunder boomed, and a gust of breeze stirred her hair. "I imagine I'm trying to wake the kindly, gallant poet I once knew. I have faith that he's sleeping inside the cold and merciless Stygian lord who stands before me. Once in a while I catch a glimpse of him—"

"How dare you judge me?" Montrose snarled. "You, who betrayed me. Who made me whatever I am today." He whipped out his sword. The blade hissed as it cleared the scabbard. The waves sobbed like a mother weeping over the corpse of her child.

Louise recoiled a step. The trained reflexes of a warrior swung her mace into a guard position. "Stop!" she said. "I apologize. You're right, I *don't* have the right to criticize you, and I won't do it again."

He glided forward. "How very generous of you."

She continued to back away. "Remember, we have a quest, to keep the Deathlords from making war on one another. You agreed to let me help you."

"Only to lure you away from your fellow subversives, my love. Only to entice you to the killing ground." Seeking to disarm her, he cut at her wrist.

She parried the blow, the spikes of her mace clashing against his blade. "This is mad," she said, still retreating. "Someone will hear. A patrol will come. Your Shadow is controlling you!"

"Why are you so dismayed?" he asked, feinting a slash at her head, then cutting at her forearm. Jumping backward, she avoided the real attack, but only barely. "Don't you like the setting I chose for your demise? I know you don't have a crowd looking on, the way I did in Edinburgh, but the view is picturesque."

"Please," said Louise, her face full of despair, "I beg you, don't let it end like this."

"Fight back," he told her. "Fight or die like a sheep." Lunging, he thrust at her stomach. She parried the stroke, then, finally, lashed out at him, snapping a kick at his groin. He twisted and caught the blow on his thigh. Grinning, delighted she'd decided to give him some sport, he returned to the attack.

As they battled back and forth, striking, parrying, and dodging, occasionally kicking, grunting with effort, the sand crunching and slipping beneath their feet, he waited for her to make a grab for her gun. Exultant with hatred, he had no fear of the firearm, and when she finally snatched it from its holster, he simply shot the crossbow one-handed, without taking conscious aim.

The quarrel plunged into the elbow of her pistol arm, the gleaming black head punching out the other side. Her mouth twisted, ripples of darkness streamed up and down her arm, and the gun tumbled from her grip.

"I won the silver arrow at St. Andrews two years running," Montrose said, flinging the crossbow at her. "Did I ever tell you that?" The stock of his makeshift missile struck the shoulder of her wounded arm, staggering her. Springing forward, he hacked at the long haft of the mace, chopping it in two.

She backpedaled frantically, but judging from her expression, she was bracing for the death blow. Instead of delivering it, he halted his advance. "You mustn't lose hope," he said, his voice dripping mock encouragement. "You still have your knife."

"James, please—" she panted, reeling, a band of shadow flowing across her face.

"Draw your knife!" he snapped.

She dropped what remained of the mace and fumbled for the hilt of the dagger. He stalked forward.

Her eyes narrowed in concentration. Montrose realized she wasn't as weary and weak with pain as she was pretending, but the insight came too late to do him any good.

Energized by the power of her Arcanos, a cloud of sand and pebbles lurched up from the beach and hurtled at him, blinding him and knocking him off balance. The stones rang against his sword and silver mask.

Afraid she'd stab him before he could recover, he invoked his own powers and flew upward, trying to climb beyond her reach. She didn't attack again. When he had rubbed and blinked the grit out of his blurry, stinging eyes, he glimpsed her dashing back toward the street.

He flew over her head and landed in front of her. "I almost forgot your Spook tricks," he said. "Not that it matters. *Allez!*" He cut at her shoulder. She blocked the blow and leaped at him, aiming a flying kick at his head. He dodged and gashed her calf as she flashed by.

When she landed, she staggered. For a moment it looked as if her wounded leg could no longer support her weight. He sprang forward in a balestra, thrust, and she floundered frantically backwards. His point missed her breast by a hair.

He kept attacking without pause, never allowing her the split-second required to activate her Arcanos. She fought well but, now limping, unable to kick, one arm disabled and her one remaining weapon considerably shorter than his own, was unable to seize the initiative. He realized he could kill her whenever he liked.

Seeking to draw out the moment, he made sure she knew it too, flicking the saber past her guard, inflicting one superficial cut after another. "How do you like knowing you're going to die?" he asked. "I grew quite familiar with the sensation after you tossed me into Argyll's clutches. I didn't much care for it."

As she fought, she began to recite the creed of the Sisterhood of Athena. "I am dead, and death is a journey. Spirit clothed in light, risen and sundered—" Suddenly her eyes widened. "James! Behind you!"

Montrose laughed. "The oldest trick in the book, my darling. You can hardly expect me to fall for that one." His blade nicked her shoulder.

She threw the knife. Her aim was off, it wouldn't hit him, but he swatted it out of the air anyway, just for fun. Arms outstretched, she lunged forward.

All he had to do was extend his saber in a stop thrust and she'd impale herself. And he supposed he'd hurt and humiliated her sufficiently; it was time to consummate his vengeance. He began to straighten his arm, then perceived that she wasn't coming straight at him, any more than her knife had. She was attempting to scramble around him.

Halting his attack, he whirled, an instant too late to defend himself from the immense claw poised to snap shut around his neck. But Louise managed to grab the creature's arm and hinder the attack. Hissing, the thing thrashed and flung her aside.

The monster somewhat resembled an immense, chitinous serpent with a body as thick as a man's torso. But it had jagged-edged pincers like a crab, and with its antennae, mandibles, and round, compound eyes, its head, reared eight feet above the ground, was more ant-like than reptilian. Its sharp, acidic smell stung Montrose's nose.

Evidently the thing was a Spectre or some other hostile spirit, emerged from the Tempest in search of prey. Lacking a natural moat to protect it, the Iron Hills complex was far more vulnerable to such incursions than the Isle of Sorrows. As Montrose cut at the beast, he marveled that it had slithered so close unnoticed. Perhaps it too had some ability to become invisible. Or perhaps he and Louise had been so utterly intent on one another that even a gigantic horror like this one had had difficulty capturing their attention.

The saber crunched through dun-colored chitin into the wet, black flesh beneath. The creature screamed, a thin, high-pitched sound like the wail of a terrified child, and struck at him with its chelae.

Montrose jerked his weapon out of the monster's breast and sprang backward. Pincers clacked shut just in front of him, at eye and knee level. He dived between them, rolled, scrambled to his feet, and drove his point at the wound he'd opened before.

With no chitin blunting the force of the thrust, the saber plunged deep into the snake-thing's chest. The monster shrieked, its arms flailed, and then its upper body collapsed toward the ground. Montrose sprang aside just in time to avoid being pinned beneath it.

He watched the carcass until it began to dissolve, making sure it was really dead, then turned toward Louise. She still lay where the monster had hurled her, evidently too spent to rise.

Montrose retrieved the saber from the last wispy remains of the monster's body, then advanced on her.

She looked up at him calmly. "I warned you that if we fought, the noise would bring something," she said.

"You said it would bring Legionnaires," he replied. He lifted the sword, then drove it down into the sand, just missing her. She twitched, but only slightly. The movement scarcely qualified as a flinch. It was, he reflected bitterly, a most unsatisfactory finale to his grand revenge.

TWENTY-SIX

"I gather," said Louise, "that you've decided to let me live."

"Yes," he said. "You could have let the serpent snip my head off. I daresay you could have made your escape while it occupied itself with me. Instead you risked your own existence to save me. And in consequence I don't have the stomach to destroy you anymore."

Teeth clenched, she drew the crossbow bolt from her elbow. "I wonder if you ever really did," she said. "When we fought, you could have killed me many times over. But you held back—"

"Don't flatter yourself," he spat. "I'm no longer fond of you, madam. I'll never forgive you for what you did to me in Holland. But honor compels me to concede that your actions today must be considered an atonement."

She smiled wanly. "'Honor.' You used to speak of it all the time, but I think this is the first time I've heard you use the word since we encountered one another in Grand Gulf."

The observation irked him. "Because it's a useless, archaic notion. But I was saddled with it as a youth, and once in a while I still feel obliged to indulge it. Thank your Heretic gods for my foibles as you make your way back to the Shadowlands."

Her gashed, bloodless hand trembling, Louise brushed a strand of hair out of her eyes. "I'm not going back. I'm going to the Onyx Tower with you."

He stared at her in amazement. "You're joking."

"Not at all. I said I'd help you and I will."

"But I just tried to kill you."

"And then you relented."

Montrose shook his head. "Even so, I can't believe that you still want to accompany me."

She looked at him for what seemed a long time, until her stare began to make him uncomfortable. "Let's just say that *I* don't feel I've atoned," she said at last. "And that I accept your thesis that open war among the Deathlords would be disastrous for Hierarchs, Renegades, and Heretics alike."

"That may be," said the Scot. "But I never actually meant to take anyone with—"

She scowled. "Don't start that again! I've proved I'm trustworthy, and you need me. I just saved your neck!"

He could have retorted that if he hadn't been drunk with the hatred her presence inspired, the monster could never have sneaked up on him. But now that the feeling had subsided to a dull loathing, and he'd abandoned his intent to destroy her, he supposed it was time to focus on his mission. And the truth was that she had demonstrated her reliability, and her talents might indeed prove essential. Moreover, it wasn't as if he'd never fought alongside a comrade he detested before. For a Legionnaire determined to rise through the ranks, surrounded by rivals with similar ambitions, such situations were more the rule than the exception.

"All right," he said grudgingly, "we'll do it together."

"Such enthusiasm," she said, smiling crookedly. "You certainly know how to make a lady feel welcome." She attempted to clamber to her feet, but her knees buckled.

He gripped her forearm and held her up. "What's wrong?" he asked.

Slumped drunkenly against him, Louise chuckled. "He cuts me to ribbons with darksteel, then wonders why I'm so weak. I'm sorry, James, but I need to Slumber. It's the only way I'll heal."

"All right," he said. He pulled the saber from the sand, returned it to its scabbard, then lifted her in his arms. "Go ahead. Sleep. I'll take care of you."

Her golden head lolled on his shoulder. She snored, the same faint buzz he remembered from their nights together in The Hague.

Peering warily about, he carried her down the strand, past iron towers and long stone warehouses. The surf muttered and whimpered; once it almost seemed to call his name. Before long, turquoise lightning flared, illuminating a dismasted sloop beached in the gloom ahead.

He approached the vessel cautiously, but no one was about. He laid Louise on deck, where the topsides hid her, then trotted back down the beach to retrieve the pistol, knife, and crossbow. Once that was accomplished, there was nothing to do but sit down beside his companion and keep watch.

The surf moaned and the thunder rumbled, but he didn't hear any more shots, outcries, or explosions. Perhaps the internecine raids had ended for now. Sheet lightning wavered in the clouds, staining Louise's ivory face with a succession of colors: violet, amber, chartreuse…

One by one, her wounds closed. Then her eyes began to roll behind their lids, and her limbs to twitch. The trouble with Slumber was that a wraith's Shadow invariably seized the opportunity to torture him or her with nightmares.

Remembering the ghastly visions he'd suffered in similar circumstances, Montrose felt a twinge of pity. He reached out to stroke her tousled hair, then snatched his hand back with a grimace.

What was he thinking of, seeking to comfort the bitch? She was probably reliving her sins, her betrayal of himself and God knew how many others.

Turning his back on her, he gazed across the bay at what should have been a considerably more pleasant sight: the Isle of Shadows. Even at this distance, in the perpetual darkness, he could make out the great bowl of the amphitheater and several other structures nearly as impressive. He told himself that Stygia truly was a kingdom of wonders and delights, and when he regained the Smiling Lord's favor, they'd all be his to savor once again.

But his mind played a prank on him. Though he wanted the vista to inspire him, for the first time in centuries, his thoughts of the capital were tainted by the young, Quick Montrose's sensibilities. He saw the buildings as dark, cyclopean, and oppressive, the carvings as grotesque, morbid, and overtly sadistic. A few minutes ago he'd claimed the city was the apex of human achievement, but now he wondered if genuine human beings could ever have built or chosen to inhabit such a forbidding place. Perhaps wraiths were deluding themselves when they imagined they were still essentially the same people they'd been in life. Perhaps death inevitably twisted them into something alien and vile.

Scowling, Montrose pushed the disquieting thought away. Louise's eyes fluttered open a few minutes later.

"How do you feel?" he asked.

"The usual," she said, sitting up. "Shaky. My head is full of ugly thoughts and pictures. But they'll fade. The important thing is that my wounds are healed. How long was I unconscious?"

Montrose shrugged. "Several hours, I think. Long enough for the tide to come in."

She peered at him quizzically. "Are you all right? You seem strange. Melancholy."

"I'm fine." He rose and climbed out onto the sand. "It's simply that I don't find your company conducive to high spirits." She tried to reply, but he pressed on without a pause, denying her the opportunity. "We should cross the channel without any further delay. The raiders were a stroke of luck. The chaos they created may well have prevented anyone from reacting to our exodus from the Artificers' stronghold. But surely someone's hunting us by now."

"I imagine you're right." She picked up her knife and gun from the deck, returned them to their sheaths, and, moving a little stiffly, clambered out to stand beside him. "Well, fortune has provided us with a boat."

"I doubt we'd elude the patrol cruisers, not in a craft as slow as this."

She looked out at the spans of iron extending over the channel. "Could we use one of the bridges? I'm sure there are sentries, but perhaps we could wear disguises."

"That might work on another occasion, but not when everyone's on general alert, and the guards at those stations are looking for me specifically. I doubt I could even slip past them veiled in shadow. They'll have barghests with particularly keen noses."

"Could you fly all the way across the bay, carrying me?"

"Probably," Montrose told her, "but the Artificers have some sort of magical radar monitoring the sky, along with winged Masquers who fly considerably faster than a Harbinger."

"What, then?" Louise demanded impatiently. "Back in the boxcar, you were confident you could reach the Tower. You must have had some notion of how to begin."

Enjoying her perplexity, Montrose smiled. "To tell you the truth, I was half hoping to find Katrina waiting on the strand to take me across. She exhorted me to try to sort out this imbroglio, so it seems only fair that she should at least assist to the extent of furnishing transportation. And with her powers, she probably could deliver us to the island safely. But alas, she isn't here."

Louise snorted. "Never count on a Ferryman to do *anything* he hasn't explicitly promised to do, that's what they teach us in the Sisterhood. The hooded ones sometimes seem benevolent, but nobody knows their true agenda."

"Then your sorority of harpies and the Hierarchy agree on one subject," Montrose said. "At any rate, if we can't fly, avail ourselves of one of the bridges, or sail to our destination, there's only one course of action remaining. We'll have to swim across, or wade along the bottom."

She gaped at him. "Through *that?*"

"Yes. It's not as if we have to breathe."

"I know, but..." She gestured at the myriad translucent, unstable human forms, streaming over and through one another, shredding as they flowed onto the sand. "We'd be moving through a mass of souls. It might destroy them."

"I thought you believed they were in such hellish torment that the Final Death would be a blessing."

She grimaced; as he recalled, it had always particularly vexed her to have her own words turned against her. "It might kill us, too. According to legend, it's fatal to bathe in Weeping Bay."

"It didn't seem to inconvenience Gorool."

"Gorool was a Malfean."

"Granted, but consider this. When I was a Regent, newly come to the Isle, I was curious about many of its mysteries, including the ghosts imprisoned in the harbor. As it happened, no one could much enlighten me on the subject. Charon had worked that particular miracle himself, and I was scarcely on intimate terms with him. So one day, I studied the waters myself.

"When I looked at them, I felt the same instinctive revulsion you're experiencing now. I forced myself to transcend that initial reaction and regard them objectively. And I observed that the prisoners appeared soft and flimsy, as liquid as ordinary water. Certainly the ships of the Imperial fleet cut through them as readily as they would through the currents of any other harbor. Finally, when I was fairly certain they were harmless, I leaned over the side of my skiff and immersed my left hand in the current, my rapier poised in my right in case my hypothesis was faulty. Nothing threatened me. The bay felt unpleasant against my skin, but that was simply because it was a bit more viscous, more jelly-like, than common water. Later I even swam a few strokes away from my boat, and survived that experience also."

"Didn't you tell anyone what you'd discovered?"

"For all I knew," Montrose replied, "Charon himself had fostered the tale that the bay was deadly, to forestall submarine attacks. He might have been unhappy with anyone who disconfirmed it. Besides, ambitious courtiers are reluctant to share secrets. You never know when you might be able to use a particular piece of information to discomfit a rival."

Louise frowned as if his final remark had disgusted her. "There is another possibility," she said. "Perhaps the bay truly is perilous, and you were merely lucky."

"I've considered that," Montrose said. "But it seems reasonable to choose a path that may indeed be safe, or at least only minimally dangerous, over those I have every reason to consider deadly. Will you accompany me, or would you prefer, your heroic declarations notwithstanding, to turn back?"

She scowled at him. "I'll go. When?"

"There's no time like the present." He held out his hand. "We don't want to become separated."

She twined her fingers in his. His body tried to shiver at her touch, a spasm of revulsion, he supposed. He led her toward the foaming, whispering surf.

TWENTY-SEVEN

Despite his previous experience with the bay, Montrose had to force himself to step into the water. Its touch, soaking his stolen shoes and streaming around his calves, was as viscous, tepid, and generally unpleasant as he remembered. Louise gasped when she entered the surf. Her fingers clenched convulsively on his.

"Are you all right?" he asked.

"Yes," Louise replied. "It's just...unsettling. Let's keep moving." Pink lightning flickered overhead, tingeing a leering face floating on the surface with the color of life. As the waves surged, it rippled, flattened, and split in two.

Montrose and Louise waded deeper. Moaning and sobbing, warping, tearing and interpenetrating, liquid souls streamed around their torsos. Shorter than her companion, the Sister of Athena had to submerge her head first. She clenched his hand again as she went under. Strands of her yellow hair floated on the surface like seaweed.

After another few steps, it was Montrose's turn to immerse himself fully. The salt water stung his eyes, but only for a second. Beneath the waves, the gray waters seemed faintly phosphorescent, but with a sheen that only illuminated the flowing, tumbling shapes imprisoned inside them. The Scot could barely make out the woman beside him or the patch of sand immediately beneath his shoes, and he couldn't see beyond the interface of sea and air. Had he not been a Harbinger, he could have lost his bearings with terrible ease.

He supposed that the deeper he and Louise went, the safer from detection they were likely to be, so he led her on across the bottom. Once they emptied their lungs, their clothing and weapons provided sufficient ballast to keep them from bobbing to the surface.

After a time Louise relaxed her grip, and though he remained vigilant, Montrose began to feel more comfortable himself. Nothing had tried to hurt him. The wretched creatures in the water afforded a ghastly spectacle—indeed, when a person submerged himself among them, their garbled cries sounded even eerier than before. But the Stygian grew steadily more convinced that they truly were feeble, fragile, mindless things, incapable of harming other wraiths, just as his investigations had suggested.

And then the captive souls began to nuzzle and caress him.

The consistency of the water changed so slowly that at first the alteration was nearly imperceptible. But gradually portions of the current *thickened*, differentiating themselves from the rest of the flow. The whorled contours of someone's ear slid down his forearm. Fingers pawed feebly at his neck. A woman's torso grazed along his calf.

The tangible body parts were only a little more solid than the water that birthed them. They squashed into nothingness at a touch, and posed no impediment to progress. But the phenomenon was repulsive nonetheless. Louise gave Montrose an alarmed, questioning look.

He didn't want her panicking. He squeezed her hand, trying to convey reassurance, and guided her onward. Phantom lips kissed the corner of his mouth, then oozed away.

As the seemingly random touches continued, he became somewhat inured to them, and acute disgust gave way to a dull loathing. He trudged onward, trying to ignore the noisome fondling, his awareness contracting into a dogged determination to keep moving.

As if to reflect his resolve, a rectangle of relative brightness appeared in the gloom ahead. The sight was almost like peering through an arch. Feeling suddenly, inexplicably weak, Montrose hurried toward it.

After a few more steps, he saw that he wasn't really heading toward an arch. The brightness was merely the sunlight, framed by the oaks and pines growing thickly on either side of the narrow dirt road.

The road he'd taken, abandoning his home, friends, and cobbler's workshop, to escape the famine. Pray God there was food left somewhere in Tuscany, and that he could find it before the dregs of his strength gave out. His stomach had stopped aching, but his vision was blurry, his ears buzzed, and he could no longer feel his feet.

Suddenly his knees buckled, pitching him to the rutted ground. He tried to stand up again, but shuddered and died instead.

The next thing he knew, an archer in a mask was snapping shackles on his wrists. He tried to protest, and then to struggle, but found himself unable to do either, as if death had broken his mind.

The archer and his comrades marched him away from his stinking corpse with its withered limbs and bloated belly, through a nightmarish wasteland, and finally to a black stone city on an island. Even reduced to imbecility, he was awed by the place, grander than any work of mortal men, but was given little opportunity to admire it. The soldiers locked him in a lightless pen with a host of other addled wretches like himself.

And there he languished until a figure in a mask made of seven different materials came to view the prisoners. Wrapped in a dark mantle, a scythe with a gleaming black blade cradled in his powerful hands, the stranger was no more than six and a half feet tall. But he radiated a power, a majesty, which made him seem larger than any mere human; he loomed like a titan, or Death himself. Surely he was the master of the dark city, and the prisoners worshipped him from the moment they laid eyes on him. As one, they abased themselves before him.

On the masked lord's command, the soldiers marched the prisoners to the shore, then herded them on into the surf. The Thralls were frightened, but none could muster the defiance to oppose the will of an archangel. The titan brandished his scythe and shouted an incantation. Montrose felt his body began to liquefy, screamed as his substance merged with the surging waters of the bay.

Even after his transformation, he retained his helpless adoration of the god of the scythe. Decade after decade, tumbled back and forth by the tides, he babbled repentance for his crimes, whatever they were, and whimpered for the masked lord's mercy. Until one day, a scaly leviathan smashed through the seawall—

No! Montrose thought abruptly. None of this was right. He *had* seen Gorool invade the bay, but from the ramparts of the Smiling Lord's citadel, not from beneath the waves. Evidently the memories of one of the captive ghosts had somehow infiltrated his own mind.

He noticed he was still slogging forward with Louise in tow. Apparently the possession, if that was the appropriate term, had only lasted a second. Perhaps it was inherently an evanescent phenomenon, with no capacity to do him lasting injury. Nevertheless, he resolved to make sure he didn't lose himself again.

But a second trance seized him without warning, a chaotic barrage of images and sensations which blasted his own thoughts apart. Sunlight glinting on the minarets of the mosque. The taste and feel of fresh, juicy dates, squishing between his—or was it her?—teeth. The agony of childbirth. The pink, cherubic face of an infant son. And then the years of bitter disappointment, as, despite all attempts to nurture and guide the boy, he grew up cruel and selfish. The final quarrel, when the lad snatched out the dagger and plunged it into—

Montrose's mind balked. That particular memory was too painful to relive. Better to surrender to the endless but more endurable torments of the bay. To allow one's thoughts to crumble into shapelessness. To cry for the mercy of the marid in the mask, the sultan of the island.

Once again, like a sick man retching up tainted food, Montrose's mind strained to purge itself of the alien perspective. Eventually it more or less succeeded, but the visions left a dreadful blankness behind. At first he couldn't remember his name, couldn't tell if he was male or female, didn't know where he was, or why.

In a moment some of the information returned, in another jumbled rain of images, phrases, and sensations. Magdalen and the children, smiling and chattering in the happy days before his dedication to Kirk and King tore the family apart. Argyll slamming the shutter closed, too craven to look him in the eye, even though he was bound and helpless in the hangman's cart. The Smiling Lord leading his Legions into battle, slaughtering scores of Heretics with his halberd and Arcanos.

But Montrose could tell that he hadn't fully recovered his identity. Many of his memories were still obscured—the gaps ached like rotten teeth—and even the ones he had regained weren't locked down tight. Another surge of alien thoughts might well obliterate them.

The ghosts of the bay swirled around him, fumbling at him, mewling and whining in his ears. He tried to shoot one, but found that his hands were empty. Evidently, at some point he'd dropped the crossbow. He whipped out his saber and laid about him. But the darksteel edge divided the watery ghosts without causing them lasting harm. They simply shredded and reformed, just as they did when the tide pulled them to pieces or ground them against the shore.

False memories seethed in his head, competing for his attention. A flint-headed spear in his hand, naked except for a coating of woad, he danced around a menhir. His arms and shoulders aching, he trudged along behind an ox and plow. Wracked with cramps, huge swellings in his armpits, he begged his father to come and ease his pain. But Papa hadn't stirred from his chair in days. He wouldn't even raise his hand to shoo away the big black rat nosing about in his lap.

Montrose realized that now multiple minds were invading his own. He suspected the effect could be even more disorienting, more devastating to his sense of self, than the assault of a single foreign personality. As he fought to push them out, numbness tingled in his sword hand, up his arm, and through the right side of his body. With a twinge of pain, the saber fell out of his grasp, shearing his fingers in two in the process. The sections oozed back together, mending themselves sluggishly, but meanwhile the afflicted half of his body stretched and rippled. Some of the liquid ghosts slithered through his flesh. Each such violation intensified the alien memories, scrambled his own thoughts, and threatened to annihilate his reason.

The Scot thrashed and screamed, choking momentarily on the water. Somehow this expression of outrage resolidified his flesh, at least for the time being. But visions of strangers' lives kept eating holes in his mind.

He realized that if he didn't put a stop to it, he'd become a creature like his tormentors, another demented, helpless slave forever chained to Weeping Bay. Heedless now of the threat of patrol boats or winged sentries, he tried to fly up into the air, but found that his mind was already too damaged to invoke his Harbinger abilities. He struggled to swim to the surface—if he at least got his head out of the water, perhaps that would help him resist—but somehow the fumbling hands of the captive spirits, awkward, weak, and fragile as they were, contrived to hold him on the bottom.

His identity crumbled. Names—the Covenant, Kilsyth, Venture Fair, Demetrius, Mike Fink—bubbled into his awareness. He clutched at them like a drowning man snatching at a lifeline, only to find himself unable to recall what they denoted. He felt a surge of terror and despair, and in the depths of his mind, his Shadow crowed.

And then he thought of Louise.

She'd played key roles in his life and his postmortem existence as well. Perhaps if he could keep her in sight, it would help him remember who he was.

Evidently he'd let go of her hand at the same time he'd dropped the crossbow, but she must be nearby. Fearful that he'd forget who she was before he located her, he mentally chanted her name as he floundered through the gray water.

The seconds dragged by, until he began to fear some trick of the current had swept them far apart. But at last he glimpsed a vague silhouette, thrashing spastically in the gloom. Charon's prisoners drifted around their victim, pawing at her.

Montrose clawed his way through the watery ghosts and threw his arms around her. Her mind disordered, Louise struggled against him as frantically as she had against the captive souls. But her movements no longer reflected even a vestige of martial arts training, and he found it relatively easy to hold on to her.

He grasped her chin and tilted her head up, so he could gaze down into her face. Blessedly, the alien images and voices dimmed, supplanted by flashes of his own memories:

The first time he'd seen her, at a reception at the Dutch Court. He'd been hell-bent on impressing the assembled dignitaries, on accomplishing the difficult diplomatic task of persuading them to provide troops, ships, and treasure to put young Charles on his father's throne. Impoverished exile that she was, Louise had worn a hand-me-down gown reflecting the height of last year's fashion. Still, he could hardly take his eyes off her.

The morning she'd begun painting his portrait. Frowning in concentration, specks of pigment on her hand and cheek, intent on her beloved art, she'd so captivated him that after an hour he simply couldn't stand there posing any longer. He'd had to go to her and kiss her. She'd protested that someone could wander into the studio at any moment, but ultimately they'd made love at the foot of the easel.

The hours he'd spent striding back and forth beside a table with a map of Britain spread out on it, discussing his plans for the campaign. She'd listened gravely, offering encouragement and sometimes shrewd suggestions, never voicing the concern for his safety which he'd imagined he saw lurking in her eyes.

The evening VanLengen had come to him in Skibo Castle. Sneering, his mask of camaraderie discarded, the mercenary had taken cruel pleasure in telling the weakened, feverish prisoner how he'd betrayed the Royalist force to Strachan's cavalry, and that he and Louise had intended the treachery from the start. Somehow Montrose had maintained his composure, but he'd felt as if the man had driven a sword into his breast.

And the night in Grand Gulf when Louise had lain chained and helpless at his feet, at his mercy at last. The terrible ecstasy of beating her unconscious.

Fighting to reestablish his sense of self, Montrose savored *all* the memories, the pleasant and excruciating alike. When Louise stopped struggling, he ran his fingers over her face, exploring its contours by touch as well as sight.

He felt his mind stabilizing, but judging from the condition of her body, Louise wasn't faring as well. Her head stretched upward as if it were made of dough, simultaneously becoming translucent. One of Charon's prisoners floated past, and the creature's trailing, elongated toes dragged through her temple.

Montrose wondered why she wasn't deriving the same benefit from their renewed contact that he was. Then she groped at his face, feebly but frantically, and he remembered his mask. He pulled the silvery visor off and let it drop to the seabed.

Her body returning to its normal shape and solidity, Louise stared into his eyes for a second. Then she hurled herself against him and pressed her lips to his.

Caught by surprise, he made no effort to resist. Her kiss was as electric as ever. It suffused him with a bitter anger, but for an instant, despite himself, a keen pleasure as well.

In any case, that contact too reinforced his mental defenses. Louise drew back and waved her hand. Somehow he comprehended that she was suggesting they move on.

And indeed they'd better, or the captive wraiths would surely wear them down in the end. Unfortunately, Montrose had become completely disoriented during the psychic assault. He had no idea where the Isle of Sorrows lay in relation to their present position. Praying that his Harbinger instincts, if not his actual powers, were still functional, he groped for some sense of his bearings. When he felt he'd achieved it, he put his arm around Louise's shoulders, and she wrapped hers around his waist. Clinging to one another, they blundered on.

Periodically false memories burst into Montrose's consciousness faster than he could push them out, at which point he stopped and tugged Louise around to face him. At other moments, no doubt similarly beset, she did the same to him. Then they gazed into one another's eyes, ran their hands over one another's features, until they felt strong enough to press onward. On one such occasion, Louise tried to kiss him again, but he gripped her forearms and held her back.

The captive souls flowed around them. Now that he and Louise were resisting them more successfully, Montrose half expected them to fumble at their intended victims more energetically, or their distorted sobs and moans to turn to howls of frustration. But the spirits' behavior didn't change. Perhaps they weren't sadists or predators after all. Perhaps they truly were the dazed, sluggish creatures they'd initially seemed, simply acting according to their natures, no more consciously desiring to harm their victims than fire consciously wished to consume its fuel.

Finally, unexpectedly, the Stygian took another step, and in so doing, thrust the top of his head above the surf.

He desperately wanted to bolt for the shore and bring the psychic torment to an end. But Stygia was teeming with foes who could destroy him just as handily as the ghosts in the bay. So he forced himself to remain in place and survey the vista before him.

The Isle of Sorrows towered against the churning storm clouds, the multicolored lightning glinting on the structures encrusting its slopes. The oldest buildings were modeled on colonnaded temples and palaces from ancient Greece and Rome. Others—castles and edifices resembling Gothic cathedrals—dated from the Middle Ages, while the skyscrapers had risen within the last hundred years. But most of the buildings, whatever their period, sported hideous gargoyles, ornate tableaux celebrating death and decay, and a variety of other grotesque architectural details which served to differentiate them from their Shadowlands counterparts as surely as the dull black stone and iron of their construction. And there were a great many—cyclopean, bizarrely shaped, reared and held erect only by Artificer magic—unlike anything which had ever existed on Earth, or ever could.

A complex of docks serving a miscellany of vessels occupied the shoreline to Montrose's right. But the section of beach immediately before him appeared deserted. A shattered, fire-blackened shell of a temple stood beside the groaning water, its statuary defaced, many of its pillars toppled, and its dome of a roof half fallen in. Two sagging piers, equally ruined, projected into the surf.

The Scot smiled. He'd been aiming for this particular landmark, and despite the worst that the water ghosts could do, he'd hit the bull's-eye. Perhaps he was an even better Harbinger than he'd imagined.

Another stab of alien memory—the nasal wail of some woodwind instrument—extinguished his glow of self-satisfaction and goaded him into motion. Leaning on one another, he and Louise staggered out of the surf, picked their way through an expanse of rubble, and entered the derelict house of worship. There, utterly spent, they slumped down on the cracked marble floor.

Twenty-Eight

Some time later, Montrose's eyes fluttered open. He'd only meant to rest, remaining on guard while he did, but now he wondered if he'd actually been Slumbering. He had a brittle, unpleasant feeling in his head, but couldn't tell whether it was an aftereffect of his ordeal in the bay or of tortures inflicted by his Shadow.

Grimacing, he decided it didn't matter. What did was that no one had intruded on him and Louise while they recovered. Of course, people seldom visited his current refuge or the other seaside ruins like it. The sites were generally considered accursed. That was why he'd chosen this particular spot to come ashore.

He hauled himself to his feet and peered about, scanning the rubble and the shadows. After a moment he noticed Louise standing before the remains of the altar. Something—magic, he assumed—had blasted it to pebbles.

Evidently hearing him rise, she turned in his direction. "This was one of the Temples of the Shining Ones, wasn't it?" she said.

"Yes," he replied, approaching her, his damp shoes squelching.

"It's been so thoroughly desecrated that I can't even tell what faith it belonged to."

Montrose shrugged. "Originally, who knows? At the time of their insurrection, the Shining Ones were nearly all Christians of one stripe or another."

"As were you, James. Yet the thought of their destruction doesn't trouble you?"

He sneered. "Why should it? It happened centuries before I was born, and more to the point, the Fishers brought it on themselves. All they had to do was pay their taxes and acknowledge Charon's sovereignty. He in turn would have permitted them to continue to carry the gullible away to their fraudulent Far Shores paradises, which was supposedly their only reason for abiding in Stygia in the first place. Instead they chose to mount a rebellion. And lest you forget, I am emphatically not a Christian anymore." Abruptly, with a spasm of irritation, he wondered why he was justifying his sentiments to a treacherous creature like Louise. "I don't see much advantage in discussing Imperial history. Let's focus on the present, shall we? How are you?"

She smiled. "I feel as if my mind has been shattered and glued back together, and the glue isn't dry yet. But I'll be all right." She hesitated. "James..."

He sensed she wanted to discuss the intimacy they'd established at the bottom of the channel. It had been essential to their survival, but he had no desire to perpetuate it now. Indeed, the thought inspired a pang of something that almost felt like fear. "Then you're ready to move on," he said briskly, cutting her off.

She sighed. "Yes, I suppose." She unclipped the knife from her belt and held it out to him hilt first. "To replace your saber and crossbow."

He took the weapon. "Thank you. I hope your pistol will still fire after its immersion."

"If not, I can use it as a club." She moved to a jagged crack in the wall, just wide enough to squeeze through. He followed a pace behind. Pausing at the opening, she gazed up at the city on the mountain.

"I studied this view quite a bit while you were sleeping," she said in a troubled tone.

"Stoking the fires of your hatred?" he asked sardonically.

She snorted. "*I'm* not like that, whatever you choose to believe. Not that there isn't a lot to despise. Surely even a Deathlord's lieutenant can see how monstrous it is. But magnificent, too, in a horrible kind of way. It's so *huge*, and *intricate*. Viewing it, I can almost believe it is the supreme creation in the universe, the great bastion of order that holds the Void at bay." Her generous lips twisted. "Speaking as a Heretic, I don't like feeling tiny and insignificant before the works of my would-be oppressors."

Montrose felt an urge to pat her on the shoulder. He quashed it, but drawled, "Come now, it isn't all *that* impressive. It doesn't even have a golf course."

Her blue eyes widened in surprise, and then she chuckled. "That peculiar Scottish game you used to go on about. I remember."

"Golf is not peculiar," he said with feigned hauteur. "It's the finest sport in the world, but I was never able to convince the Smiling Lord to allocate sufficient land and manpower to build me a place to play, though I would have settled for a humble nine holes."

"I guess even the lords of the Onyx Tower don't get *everything* they desire."

"Indeed not, and we're more than a little disgruntled about it. But here's my point. Stygia *is* immense, but how sophisticated can it be if it lacks such a basic amenity of civilized existence? Two wily adventurers such as ourselves shouldn't experience any difficulty outwitting the local bumpkins and reaching our objective. So don't heed any inner voice that tries to persuade you differently. It's just your Shadow, trying to demoralize you."

Louise smiled at him. "All right," she said, then, twisting her shoulders, stepped out under the open sky. Montrose wriggled through behind her.

Senses straining, he peered about, looking for hostile presences. The soft, ceaseless drone of the island metropolis—a sound compounded of the sobbing of the bay, the babble of countless conversations, the slap and scuff of myriad footsteps, the clink and rattle of a million chains, and the hiss and crackle of a host of barrow-flame torches and lamps—a hum which somehow seemed to overlay a deeper, unbreachable silence, murmured in his hypersensitive ears. But as far as he could determine, no one was stirring close at hand. He led Louise toward the mouth of a narrow, crooked street at the foot of the slope.

Their route carried them upward between rows of grimy tenements. The builders had decorated the buildings' keystones, cornices, and friezes with a crown-of-thorns motif to denote that this precinct lay under the authority of the Emerald Lord. Blank white faces peered from shadowy doorways and narrow windows. Other wraiths lay motionless on the cobblestones, not Slumbering but inert, or shuffled aimlessly up and down. Some seemed blind to obstacles in their paths, and Montrose and Louise learned to sidestep to avoid collisions.

The Scot frowned. The wretches seemed scarcely more sentient than the ghosts imprisoned in Weeping Bay. He'd heard vague rumors of districts like this, appearing like cancers since Charon's demise, populated chiefly by souls declining into senility, but until now, he'd never seen one firsthand.

"Is much of the city like this?" asked Louise.

"I hope not," he replied, stepping around the motionless form of a nude woman with varicose veins and curly gray hair. "None of it should be. The Deathlord in charge of the area is supposed to do something about it. Give the inhabitants a festival, force them to work, or impress them into the army. Anything to strike a spark of vitality." He hesitated. "And those who can't be helped should go to the Forges."

She grimaced. "Oh, now there's a wonderful solution."

"It's better to put them to productive use than to allow them to fall into the Void," he said, feeling momentarily defensive. "That would give Oblivion a foothold on the island."

"As if it doesn't have one already," she replied.

The street turned sharply to the left, then ended at the base of a tower like an iron spike, its base narrower than its top. A ramp spiraled up the side of the building like the thread of a screw. Grateful that the Restless were far less susceptible to ordinary muscular fatigue than their mortal counterparts, Montrose began the dizzying ascent, and Louise climbed along beside him. The metal surface clinked beneath their feet, and gaunt cadavers capered beside them in an endless procession. Graven on the dusky metal wall, the *danse macabre* was invisible most of the time, but withered grins and skeletal hands sprang from obscurity whenever the lightning flared.

Eventually Louise looked over the side, gasped, and hastily stepped backward. Montrose grabbed her by the arm as if she'd been in some genuine danger of falling over the side, then released her instantly, annoyed at himself.

"I know we've been climbing for a while," she said, "but we can't possibly be as high as we seem to be."

"Stygia is like that," Montrose said. "Sometimes, when you peer down from a high place, the drop seems to extend forever. It may result from spatial distortion, some vestige of the Tempest Charon couldn't purge. Or it may be an illusion he crafted himself, to make the city seem even grander. Either way, it's simply a trick of perspective. It can't harm you."

"I know that," she said, sounding irritated. He remembered that she'd always bristled at any hint of condescension. "It simply startled—"

Above their heads, metal made a faint, shivering sound.

Montrose and Louise looked up, at an arched bridge linking their tower to a gargoyle-encrusted basilica of a structure across the way. Evidently someone was creeping around on it.

The Scot considered veiling himself in darkness, or soaring up to the bridge to survey the situation. But if he drew on his Arcanos every time he heard a suspicious noise, he'd exhaust himself before he completed a fraction of the trek which lay before him. So he simply loosened the knife in its sheath, and then he and Louise tramped on.

As they stepped up onto the foot of the bridge, a pleasant baritone voice said, "Halt, if you please, milord and lady." On the center of the span stood a lanky man clad in lace, a cocked hat, and a crêpe mask. A rapier hung at his side, and he grasped a flintlock pistol in either hand. Despite the threat of the leveled firearms, Montrose was momentarily bemused by the spectacle of what appeared to be a highwayman from the era of his own life. The knight of the road had a henchman standing on either side. The one to his right, a short, bare-chested, bearded man with green skin, aimed a blowgun at Montrose. The one on the left, clad in a gray trench coat, slouch hat, and a metal visor the dull color of lead, pointed a crossbow.

Montrose said, "I believe the traditional greeting is, stand and deliver."

The man in the crêpe mask grinned. "I'm mortified. You seem to have us confused with common thieves. We're the bridge keepers, gentle sir. The tollmen."

"Indeed," said Montrose. "You don't look like Legionnaires."

"Most of the soldiers have withdrawn higher up the mountain," the highwayman said. "Positioning themselves to defend the grander precincts of the city from marauders and saboteurs, or so they say. Keeping a distrustful eye on one another, if you believe the more outrageous and seditious rumors, which, I hasten to say, I don't. Either way, in their absence, it falls to humble citizens such as ourselves to maintain public services like this bridge. And sadly, that necessitates our collecting a modest user's fee from passersby."

Montrose levitated several inches into the air. "Actually, we don't need to use the bridge."

None of the robbers seemed impressed by Montrose's display of power. "A Harbinger," their leader said. "How interesting. But I regret that you still have to pay, even if you now choose to fly across. The tax pertains to usage of the path up as well as the span itself."

The Scot settled back onto the platform. "I understand. But unfortunately, my associate and I haven't an obolus between us. Surely there's some charitable provision for the needy."

The man in the crêpe mask nodded. "Of course. Anything less would be barbaric. But I fear, my lord, that you and your companion don't meet the criteria for such a dispensation. You see, if a traveler can't pay in specie, we're prepared to collect the toll in goods and services. You have clothing. The weapons which, acting with commendable prudence, you've chosen to leave in their sheaths. And you, dear lady, have your charms. We get lonely up here, selflessly laboring—"

Montrose decided he'd stood bantering long enough to blunt the edge of the robbers' alertness. He shrouded himself in darkness and tapped Louise on the arm, hoping she'd understand he was signaling for her to attack.

She did. Gripped by her Spook power, the crossbow spun in an arc, wrenching the wraith in gray around with it. With a twang, the weapon discharged its bolt into the highwayman's ribs. He staggered and his flintlocks barked, the shots ringing against the bridge.

Wild-eyed, pivoting toward Louise, the green robber inflated his cheeks. Montrose sprinted toward him. The blowgunner couldn't see his attacker coming, but must have heard his footsteps bonging, because he spun back around to face him. The long wooden pipe made a coughing sound.

Montrose dove onto his belly and the dart whizzed over his head. He scrambled up again and knifed the green man in the stomach. The bandit collapsed.

A blade hissed out of its scabbard. Montrose whirled. Despite the quarrel in his side and his target's invisibility, the highwayman thrust out his darksteel rapier with deadly accuracy. The Scot only barely managed to leap back in time to avoid being spitted. His backside slammed into the guardrail.

Possibly orienting on the resulting clang, the highwayman lunged at him again. Montrose frantically flung himself to one side, then kicked the swordsman in the knee. The robber leader fell. Montrose booted him once more, this time in the temple. The rapier slipping from his grip, the bandit sprawled unconscious.

Montrose turned just in time to see Louise hit the man in gray three times. First the heel of her hand mashed in the nose of his leaden mask. Next her fist thudded into his solar plexus. And finally, bellowing a fierce *kiai*, she punched him in the throat. The masked man reeled against the railing, would have pitched over it if she hadn't grabbed him by the sleeve and yanked him back. She cocked her arm to hit him again, perceived he was already unconscious, and allowed him to fall onto the bridge.

"Why didn't you shoot him?" Montrose asked.

Louise shrugged. "I don't know. He came at me unarmed and I defended myself the same way." The Scot remembered when such chivalrous behavior had come naturally to him as well, and felt what might nearly have been a twinge of admiration, or at least nostalgia. "Besides, I don't have that many bullets." She smiled. "Compared to fending off the spirits in the bay, that was almost fun."

He scowled. "Productive, anyway. We can use additional weapons, and fresh disguises as well." Turning his back on her, he stooped, yanked off the highwayman's mask, and tied it around his own head. The black fabric felt soft and soothing on his face.

TWENTY-NINE

The great bowl of the Coliseum, with its Corinthian pilasters, round arches, and half-columns, was still hundreds of feet away. But Montrose could already hear the audience roaring inside. Indeed, he'd been hearing them for blocks.

A Legionnaire patrol, resplendent in burnished cuirasses and crested helmets, appeared in the press ahead. Struggling against the current of wraiths rushing toward the amphitheater gates, the soldiers headed in Montrose's general direction. Suppressing an impulse to veer away from them, the Scot told himself he wasn't a fugitive from the Smiling Lord's justice but an upstanding Stygian gentlemen turned out in a fine cloak, cocked hat, and lace to enjoy the games. And Louise was simply his companion, a bit eccentrically dressed perhaps in her leaden mask, trench coat, and slouch hat, but what did that mean in a metropolis whose sartorial styles reflected a hodgepodge of influences from the last few thousand years?

And sure enough, the warriors passed them by without a second glance.

Montrose and Louise had been climbing the mountain for five days, following a circuitous route which the Scot, drawing on his knowledge of the city and Harbinger instincts, judged to be the safest. Sometimes it snaked along the ground and sometimes scaled the towers, leading them across elevated bridges from one roof or balcony to another. Along the way, the fugitives had dodged countless patrols, watched the Laughing Lady's soldiers quell a riot with brutal efficiency, and seen a hideous structure resembling a colossal iron scorpion, one of the Skeletal Lord's lesser fortresses, vibrate until, with a deafening clangor, it shook itself apart. Another act of sabotage, evidently, accomplished with sorcery rather than explosives.

Despite the length of the journey, at odd moments Montrose still felt self-conscious in his new attire. He hadn't worn true seventeenth-century clothing in decades. The outfit felt surprisingly *right*, evoking a bittersweet nostalgia, but for some reason, dangerous as well.

"Considering all the evidence of unrest we've seen," said Louise, "I can't believe the Deathlords are putting on a gladiatorial exhibition." She switched the crossbow from her right hand to her left, then tugged the brim of her fedora lower.

"What better time?" Montrose replied. "With luck, the entertainment will take people's minds off the problems, and reassure them that the Seven have matters well in hand."

"Bread and circuses," she said distastefully. "Just like imperial Rome."

He twisted his shoulders to avoid jostling a heavy-set man in a crimson ceramic domino and a checked ulster. "And imperial Rome endured a long time, so it would seem their techniques of governance had merit."

"Mere survival isn't the be-all and end-all of existence, even for embattled spirits like us, who spend our days resisting the tug of Oblivion." She paused, and somehow, despite her visor, he sensed she was smiling wryly. "Don't cringe, I'm not commencing a sermon, just making an observation. Do you truly think the games will provide us a passport into the Onyx Tower?"

He shrugged. "It's the most promising scheme I've hit on so far, but obviously there are no guarantees. We'll just have to see how it goes."

A colonnade ran around the exterior of the amphitheater. Beneath the arches, prostitutes, tumblers, jugglers, souvenir vendors, Masquers, Sandmen, Chanteurs, Oracles, and even a Pardoner plied their trades. But few stopped to patronize them. Most people kept pushing toward the gates, intent on claiming whatever seating remained, or, failing that, standing room on the uppermost tier. Montrose and Louise shoved and squeezed their way in with the rest.

A dark corridor with an arched ceiling led to the interior of the stadium, a monument resembling the Flavian amphitheater in its heyday, or so Montrose had been informed by wraiths who had seen both, but considerably larger and grander. Ornately carved fountains in the forms of nymphs, chimeras, satyrs, dragons, skulls, and leering cadavers jetted sweetly scented water into the air. A moat ringed the white sand floor, where blind men, with blank expanses of skin where their eyes should have been, fought with tridents and sabers. Electric floodlights—an innovation much decried by traditionalists, the Scot recalled—shone down to illuminate the action. From the cages beneath the arena sounded the roars and howls of captive Spectres and Phantasies.

The tiers of marble seats rose so high that from his position Montrose had to tilt his head far back to see the top. Many of the spectators ensconced in the rows or squatting in the aisles were animated to the point of frenzy. They screamed encouragement and invective at the fighters, or brayed with laughter when the sightless men did something comical, like tripping over a fallen rival, or backing into one another. Here and there, some masturbated, fornicated, clawed their own flesh, or collapsed and thrashed like epileptics. Hawkers worked their way through the throng, selling programs and cushions, while bookmakers clambered from one level to the next, shouting the current odds.

The general hysteria was a palpable miasma, fouling the air. Louise shuddered. Recalling occasions when he too had relished the games, Montrose felt a pang of shame, or at least discomfort. Annoyed with himself, he quashed it.

"Pull yourself together," he said gruffly. "It's just a mob relishing the sight of someone else's misfortune. Surely you've encountered such things before."

"Not when the mob was so huge," she said. "It's going to be an effort to keep the psychic fallout from driving me crazy, too." She waved her hand impatiently. "But I'm all right. Let's get on with it."

Montrose turned, surveying the seats reserved for the grandees of the Tower. Predictably, none of the Deathlords had chosen to put in an appearance. They might wish to reassure the masses that all was well, but not enough to expose themselves to the threat of assassination. However, some of the ministers of the Beggar Lord were present, as were those of the Ashen Lady, each contingent warded by a substantial bodyguard of glowering Legionnaires.

The Scot frowned. Desiring to reach his own master—despite recent events, he still thought the Smiling Lord more likely to heed him than were the other potentates of the Seven—he'd hoped to find officials from the Seat of Burning Waters in attendance. Theoretically, that would have enabled him and Louise to gain immediate access to the proper part of the Tower complex. As things stood, the two of them would wind up in either the palace of Golden Tears or the manse of Shadows.

"Ah, well," he said, "if there were no challenge, it wouldn't be any fun, would it?"

Louise chuckled. "Judging by the way events have fallen out so far, I don't think we need to worry about *that*."

The Beggar Lord's minions were the closer of the two groups, so Montrose led his companion toward them. As they neared the reserved seating, he was concerned that the *locarii*, as the old-timers insisted on calling the ushers, would demand to see their tickets, but none did. Perhaps his fine new sword and attire were responsible; now that he'd plundered the highwayman's possessions, he looked like he belonged with the other aristocrats. Or perhaps by this time the attendants themselves were too caught up in the spectacle unfolding on the sand to perform their function.

Montrose could feel it tugging at him as well. Louise was right, the atmosphere in this place would addle anyone who permitted it. From the corner of his eye, the Cavalier glimpsed a new battle.

A *bestiarius*—a monster fighter—equipped with a roaring chain saw sheared away pieces of a Spectre. The doomshade looked and smelled like a nine-foot statue made of dung and slime; Montrose caught the vile stink of it even though the ambient haze of perfume. At first the monster seemed to move too sluggishly to have any hope of defending itself. Then, with a metallic scream, the saw struck something solid hidden inside the monster's mucky torso. The weapon rebounded and slipped from its wielder's grasp. As he fumbled for it, trying to catch it before it tumbled to the ground, the doomshade raised its brown, crumbling hands and slammed them down on his shoulders. The *bestiarius* dropped, his face coming down on the dancing teeth of his blade.

The mob roared. A sickening, intoxicating wave of emotion swept through Montrose, filling him with vigor. He had to force himself to tear his eyes away. He hoped Louise hadn't noticed him yielding to the spell of the display.

She gripped his forearm. "Look there!" she said.

Clad in saffron hooded robes decorated with vertical rows of topazes, a pair of the Beggar Lord's ministers proceeded to the aisle separating them from the Ashen Lady's vassals. There, swaying like drunkards, clutching at one another for support, they began to make their way down the steps. Three soldiers, their artfully tattered yellow surcoats and the stocks of their assault rifles decorated with the outstretched hand emblem of the Legion of Paupers, fell in behind them.

Montrose had hoped that some of the dignitaries would separate from their party at some point, to visit a whore, buy a hallucinatory cup of wine from a Sandman, or pursue some other amusement. "There are too many of them for my liking," he said. "On the other hand, this could be our best opportunity."

"I'm game," said Louise. "Let's do it."

Suddenly feeling bold, he grinned. "Very well. Come on."

They pushed forward along the crowded aisle, striving to move quickly enough to keep their quarry in view yet remain relatively inconspicuous. They reached the stairs just in time to see the Beggar Lord's servants vanish into a doorway positioned beneath the lowest tiers of seats.

"Where does that go?" asked Louise.

"Underground," Montrose replied. "It's like a maze down there. Hurry, or we'll lose them." They strode on.

Beyond the doorway, a narrow stairway descended, illuminated by a single cold, hissing barrow-flame torch. Voices babbled and rushing feet pattered in the darkness below. The draft rising from the depths smelled of earth, stone, and the fetor of abominations.

A beefy woman in a latex Marilyn Monroe mask and baggy coveralls sat on a stool just inside the opening. A truncheon lay in her lap, and she held a slim volume of verse in her callused hand. Her gray eyes narrowed as if in annoyance or mistrust.

Montrose quickly extracted a few oboli—more bounty plundered from the robbers—from his purse. "We're aficionados," he said. "We'd like to go backstage to view the Spectres at close range."

"Well, you can't," the gatekeeper said brusquely. "If it were a normal show, and I liked the looks of you, then maybe. But we had to kick this *extravaganza*"—her husky voice infused the word with a wealth of sarcasm—"together at the last minute, on orders from the high mucky-mucks in the Tower, and everybody's frantic down below. Too frantic to put up with rubber-neckers getting underfoot."

"I just saw you let some other people pass," Montrose said.

"Big shots from the House of Golden Showers," growled the woman in the rubber mask. "Them, I couldn't stop. You, on the other hand, don't look to be anything but the usual idiot fan, so why don't you get the hell—"

Louise grabbed the gatekeeper, yanked her off her stool, and slammed her against the wall. The club bounced clinking down the steps.

The larger woman tried to break free, but Louise did something—from his vantage point, Montrose couldn't see precisely what—that made her go rigid and helpless with pain. "We *are* going into the tunnels," the Sister of Athena said. "You're going to take my friend's money and not give us any more trouble, isn't that right?"

The gatekeeper gave a jerky nod. Louise released her, Montrose dropped the coins on the stool, and the two fugitives bounded down the steps.

"That was a bit rough, wasn't it?" Montrose said. "Particularly coming from a kindly missionary. I was considering offering a larger bribe."

"You said we were in a hurry," replied Louise.

Alighting from the stairs, they found themselves in a large but crowded room, where teams of gladiators armed and costumed like medieval knights, World War II soldiers, and comic-book superheroes milled about, along with a brass band of Chanteurs. Getting in some last-minute practice, a Sandman conjured the illusions he'd be using to turn the floor of the arena into a cratered moonscape. The flickering phantasms made the scene even more chaotic.

Montrose peered about, but saw no sign of the Beggar Lord's servants. He turned toward a gladiator dressed as a gaudy Hollywood fantasy of a cowboy, with a white Stetson, an elaborately embroidered Western shirt, chaps, boots, silver spurs, and two pearl-handled Colts slung low on his hips. Appearing more at ease than most of his fellows, the performer absent-mindedly twirled a lariat.

"Two ministers and three soldiers," Montrose said, "all wearing yellow. Have you seen them?" The cowboy nodded toward an opening in the back wall.

The fugitives hurried on, past wheeled cages full of hissing, gibbering horrors, lined up to enter an elevator and thence the arena as their presence was required. Then something whimpered up ahead.

Montrose raised a hand to halt Louise's advance. Masking himself in darkness, he crept on down the shadowy corridor. Small rooms, scarcely more than cubicles, opened off the hallway to either side. In one, an eyeless gladiator, perhaps the sole survivor of the combat in which he'd fought, lay on a table, his body riddled with punctures and gashes, shuddering and gasping. Their cowls thrown back, the Beggar Lord's ministers hovered over him, exploring his pale, bloodless wounds with their tongues and fingers. The three bodyguards stood by stolidly. The bespectacled little man in the corner, however—a Usurer, judging from the delicate brass scales he carried, no doubt present to give the injured wraith a suffusion of vitality—seemed to be struggling to conceal his disgust.

Still veiled in shadow, Montrose skulked back to Louise. "We've found them," he whispered, startling her and making her jump. "Let's do this quickly and with a minimum of noise. No gunfire unless you have to."

The Heretic nodded. "You hit them first. Use your invisibility to take them by surprise. I'll jump in."

Montrose drew his rapier, then led Louise back down the hall. As they neared the doorway, the blind man began to blubber and plead for mercy. *Courage*, thought Montrose, *deliverance is at hand*. He realized he was glad he'd caught the officials practicing their perversion. Though he'd witnessed far worse, generally without it troubling him in the slightest, for some reason, this time around, the depravity disgusted him, and that was good. It would transform what had seemed a noisome extremity into a pleasure.

He stalked through the door and began the killing.

His first thrust took the nearest Pauper in the left eye. The Legionnaire's body dissolved instantly, before it had even begun to fall. Pivoting, the Scot stabbed a second soldier in the breast. The darksteel point struck armor, but punched on through. Bands of darkness writhed across the soldier's anguished features, and then they crumbled in on themselves.

The remaining Pauper frantically pointed his gun in Montrose's general direction. Louise's crossbow twanged. The bolt slammed into the bodyguard's chest, and he fell thrashing to the floor.

The ministers looked up from their pleasures. One froze, his mouth falling open. The other thrust his hand inside his robes, no doubt snatching for a weapon. Thrusting over the cot and the blind fighter's body, Montrose opted to slay the more dangerous man. Louise darted around the bed and knifed his stupefied companion.

Becoming visible once more, Montrose leveled his rapier at the cowering Usurer. He'd thought Louise wise to intimidate rather than kill the doorkeeper. Someone might have missed her. But he doubted that anyone would look for this scrawny little healer, not for hours to come, and it seemed only prudent not to leave any witnesses to the slaughter.

And yet he hesitated. Perhaps it was because the Usurer was a fellow Stygian, a countryman who'd never offered him any harm. Or perhaps he simply didn't want to listen to Louise decry his cold-bloodedness. At any rate, contemptuous of his own squeamishness, he said, "The grandees sent you away so they could practice their vice without the distraction of your disapproving stare. Thus, you never saw any of this. Get out."

The Usurer scrambled through the door.

Louise rested her hand on the blind man's brow. "It's all right," she murmured. "They can't hurt you anymore. Sleep, and heal." Rather to Montrose's surprise, the gladiator stopped shaking and twitching.

The Sister of Athena stooped and picked up one of the now-empty begemmed robes. "I saw what those sadists were doing," she said to Montrose. "'Vice' is a mild term for it. I thought before that it would trouble me to strike them down by surprise, but now I doubt that guilt will overwhelm me."

For a moment, Montrose wanted to assure her that, while he had on occasion attended the games, he'd never engaged in any practices like the one she'd just observed. Grimacing, he wondered why he kept experiencing these witless urges to justify himself. "The audience comes here to *feel*," he said. "Rage and triumph, terror and pain. But some people aren't satisfied merely to soak up the secondhand emotions from the stands. They desire a more intimate communion with the principals."

"I understand," she said. "Just as I know that wraiths of all persuasions engage in the same sort of cruelties in the Shadowlands. But somehow they seem even worse in such a grandiose setting, and when the evil appears to be so thoroughly *institutionalized*."

Not knowing how to respond to that, he picked up the other robe. With the topazes weighing it down, it was heavier than he'd expected. He tried it on and was pleased to discover just how voluminous it actually was. He'd have to discard his hat—otherwise, he wouldn't be able to pull the cowl over his head—but it looked as if the habit would conceal his sword and cloak.

Louise folded up her fedora, stowed it in one of her robe's internal pockets, and buttoned the garment up over her raincoat. Montrose eyed the Paupers' assault rifles wistfully, but decided not to push his luck by trying to hide one of those under his golden disguise as well. He peeked out into the hallway. He didn't see or hear anyone rushing to intercept them, so he and his companion headed back the way they'd come.

"I still don't know about this," she said. "Two ministers and three Legionnaires leave their seats. The two ministers come back alone. Are you certain no one will be suspicious?"

"By no means," he said, striding past a cage containing a beast like a two-headed leopard with vermilion spots. The monster snarled at him, spattering him with fine drops of saliva. "But I'm prepared to gamble on it. It's a large group, they're all masked, and everyone's drunk on destruction. The euphoria will almost certainly linger while they travel back to the Onyx Tower. And even in these unsettled times, the guards are likely to pass the party through all together. They won't look closely at each individual the way they would if you and I tried to enter by ourselves."

"When you explain it that way, it makes sense." They made their way through the gladiators gathered in the waiting room, then headed up the stairs. "I'm starting to believe we might actually pull this off."

Smiling, he opened his mouth to remark that they made a good team, then suddenly remembered that this was the Lorelei who'd betrayed him to his death, who might yet betray him again if he didn't keep his guard up. Any inclination to make pleasant conversation with her died in a spasm of loathing.

As they passed the doorkeeper, who had recovered her bludgeon and sat back down on her stool, the crowd in the amphitheater cried out. Somehow the noise sounded different than the cheering and gasps of excitement Montrose had heard before. Suddenly apprehensive, he quickened his pace, and Louise trotted to keep up with him. A ragged volley of shots rang out.

The fugitives broke into a run. As Montrose scrambled into the interior of the stadium, a centurion of the Iron Legion, clad in the traditional gray garb and armor of the Ashen Lady's warriors, blundered around to face him, gaped, then fired a .45 automatic.

The shot whizzed past Montrose's ear. Wishing that his rapier and flintlocks weren't buried out of reach beneath his cumbersome robe, he lunged at the centurion and kicked him in the groin. The Legionnaire doubled over. Montrose slammed the edge of his stiffened hand down on the back of his opponent's neck. He hit the warrior's gorget, sending a jab of pain through his own flesh, but the man in gray fell unconscious.

Montrose peered frantically about, first making sure no one else was about to attack him, then trying to determine what was going on. The scene was so chaotic, and his vantage point at the mouth of the passage so inadequate, that for a moment he couldn't make sense of what he was seeing. Finally he discerned that the Iron Legionnaires and the Paupers were fighting one another. It was hard to imagine that any commander had planned such an engagement. There was no conceivable tactical point to it. It was more likely that, inflamed by the slaughter in the arena, aware that the Deathlords were preparing for civil war, some hothead had simply succumbed to the urge to lash out at the servants of one of his sovereign's rivals, thus sparking a general melee.

But whatever had triggered the conflict, it was happening with a vengeance. Legionnaires fought hand to hand or blazed away at one another, heedless of the danger to noncombatants. Shrieking civilians streamed down the tiers of seats, fleeing away from the soldiers' battle and toward the exits, crushing and trampling one another. Others, maddened by their own combative impulses, attacked those around them. Daggers rose and fell, Masquers ripped other wraiths apart as if their bodies were made of paper, Chanteurs wailed, and brilliant arcs of Haunter lightning flared and crackled, drenching the air with the smell of ozone. Perhaps the rioters, all of whom were pledged to one Deathlord or another, imagined that they too were waging war on the partisans of their masters' rivals, though in reality, they appeared to be lashing out at random. On the sand, twenty swordsmen and as many spearmen stared up at the stands in astonishment, their own interrupted conflict quite forgotten.

The Beggar Lord's ministers were attempting to escape the Coliseum also. In fact, aided by several Paupers who'd stayed out of the battle, and who shot or stabbed anyone who impeded their charges' progress, they seemed on the brink of success. In another few seconds they'd disappear into one of the tunnels leading outside, and

Montrose's best hope of infiltrating the Onyx Tower would vanish with them.

The Anacreon snatched up the Iron Legionnaire's pistol. Trying to skirt the soldiers' battle, he clambered up several tiers, then plunged down a row, with Louise scrambling along behind him.

Despite his best efforts to avoid the maddened warriors, a soldier in gray charged him, a dirk in one iron gauntlet and a .45 in the other, bounding from one tier of seats to the next as if they were stair steps. Montrose leveled his own gun, but before he could pull the trigger, the Legionnaire fell backward as though he'd run into an invisible wall. Evidently Louise had bashed him with her Arcanos.

The fugitives drove onward. A smiling, slender Haunter, wrapped in the traditional inky cloak of her fallen Guild, reached out for Montrose. He brandished the pistol in warning. But the other ghost, student of an esoteric art notorious for driving its practitioners insane, simply gave him a friendly pat on his hooded cheek, then continued to peer about, taking in the mayhem. If her serene expression was any indication, she found the spectacle soothing.

Suddenly the crowd surged, lifting Montrose off his feet like an ocean swell. He glimpsed Louise helplessly falling as well, and then he crashed down with his feet on one row of seats and his shoulder on the next one down. The impact stung, but that pain instantly gave way to a host of greater ones, as running feet stamped down on his body.

Terrified, he fired the automatic upward until it was empty, trying to drive the stampeding crowd away. Unable to shift his feet beneath him, he struggled to use his Harbinger powers to levitate. Finally there came a moment when no one was treading on him, and his battered, pain-ridden body lurched into an upright posture.

He spun. Curled into a ball, Louise was using her arms to protect her head. She also employed her telekinesis in an effort to clear a space for herself, but couldn't thrust the onrushing Stygians away fast enough. Montrose dropped the pistol, seized a man who was about to trample her, swung him away, and flung him on down the tiers. Then he made a desperate grab for Louise's arm, and, catching hold of it, wrenched her off the floor.

He peered ahead. The Beggar Lord's minions were gone. He wondered if the grandees would make it through the passage without being crushed. Assuming they did, there was only one chance of catching up with them now.

He put his arms around Louise. Perhaps grasping his intention, she embraced him as well. He soared upward.

It was a dangerous maneuver. He and Louise wore the robes of the Beggar Lord's officials, which presumably made them desirable targets to many of the frenzied combatants and, flying, they were bound to draw people's attention. Still, for a second he exulted, simply because he'd lifted himself clear of the crush.

Then a Chanteur shrieked at him. His head throbbed, for an instant the world went black, and he felt himself falling. Something—an arrow?—pierced his thigh, and he felt waves of Oblivion, alternately cold and hot, pulsing away from the wound.

"Fly!" screamed Louise. "Fly!"

Grimly he focused his will. Pulled out of his fall inches before he would have crashed back down on the heads of the crowd. Rose once more. Archers and gunmen shot at him. Zigzagging, he dodged some of the missiles, and, her muscles bunching,

Louise deflected the rest.

Then the barrage ceased. He realized he'd flown high enough to lose himself in the floodlights' glare; no one in the stands could draw a bead on him. He soared on out of the stadium. Green light flickered in the bellies of the storm clouds overhead.

"Are you all right?" asked Louise.

"Probably not," he said. Clenching his teeth, he pulled the missile—a crossbow quarrel, he saw now—out of his flesh and dropped it into the darkness below. "But I can function. What about you?"

"About the same," she said. "I got kicked in the head a few too many times, but I'll manage. What do we do now?"

"Wait for our friends in yellow to emerge, then join their party. With luck, in their haste and confusion, they won't realize we weren't with them all along."

They peered down at the panicked throng pouring out of the arena. After a few seconds, a clump of shadowy figures in voluminous robes and ragged surcoats struggled into the open. Praying that none of them would look up, Montrose swooped like a hunting owl, landing silently at the rear of the procession.

A Pauper Marshal with a pistol in either hand turned toward them. "Move it!" he snapped. "I mean, please hurry, my lords. We have to return to the palace without delay."

"We're coming," said Louise.

With many a fearful backward glance, the party fled up the mountain, in the process leaving the last of the tenements and apartment complexes behind. The ornate—though often bizarre and grotesque—edifices looming on either side were often as huge as the hive-like structures on the slopes below, but in most cases each was the house of a single master, a wealthy merchant or luminary of the Court who, for whatever reason, chose to maintain a residence apart from its splendors.

Then the procession rounded a corner, and suddenly the Onyx Tower itself came into view, its outermost walls dwarfing the mansions clustered around them as if they were doll houses. Looking tiny as ants, sentries patrolled the parapet, and behind them, countless spires pierced the sky. In the center of this forest of stone rose the mightiest structure of all, the colossal cylinder that was Charon's donjon, lightless and vacant since the Emperor's exequies.

It was a greater castle than any which had ever existed on Earth, perhaps the greatest which had ever existed anywhere in the universe. Louise, who hitherto had only glimpsed it from afar, froze and stared. Montrose seized her arm and tugged her into motion once again.

Their bodyguards herded them on toward a sally-port, insignificant as a mouse hole at the base of the prodigious enceinte. A guard stepped into view on a balcony fashioned in the shape of an outstretched hand. "Halt! Who goes there?" he cried.

"Open up, idiot!" the Marshal snarled. "Don't you know another riot's broken out? We have to get these people inside immediately!"

"Yes, sir!" said the guard, his voice breaking. The postern swung open.

The procession hurried into a long, shadowy tunnel with inconspicuous murder holes dotting the ceiling. A few dim amber electric bulbs burned along the walls. The gate boomed shut again.

The enceinte was so thick that it seemed to take forever to traverse the passage.

But at last it opened on a small courtyard with a sculpture of a black marble question mark standing in the center, and faux rosebushes, the fragrant yellow flowers a miracle of the Artficer's craft, ringing the perimeter.

Montrose had worried that once everyone was safe, his companions might try to engage him and Louise in conversation, but no one did. Rather, the group began to disperse immediately. Perhaps they were all scurrying to their posts in this time of crisis.

The fugitives slipped through a trefoil arch and down a narrow passage that no one else had taken. "We made it!" said Louise. "We're inside!"

Montrose smiled sardonically at the excitement in her voice. "Indeed we are. Now for the *difficult* part of the plan."

Thirty

Footsteps clicked up the marble corridor beyond the door. Potter reflexively sat up straight on his throne and made sure the head of his halberd pointed directly at the ceiling. As always, it was his task to look majestic and enigmatic, like a steel statue of some dark and terrible god.

Two figures appeared at the entrance to the chamber. The first was Demetrius, wrapped in his toga, his sardonyx helm reflecting the chill, greenish lamplight. Beholding him, Potter felt a sort of relief, an easing of the anxiety that gnawed at him day and night. The Oracle's companion was a hulking man shrouded in the red and yellow layered cloak of the Order of the Avenging Flame, with a matching beret perched on his square-jawed, crewcut head.

Doffing his cap, the stranger bowed deeply, sweeping his mantle open in the process. Potter noted with satisfaction that the man's scabbard and holster were empty. Demetrius quickly closed and locked the door, then inclined his head as well.

"Come forward," Potter intoned.

The newcomers advanced up the length of the Lesser Gun Room, past display cases full of matchlocks, flintlocks, carbines, revolvers, pistols, shotguns, and automatic weapons. At the foot of the dais, they bowed once more. The man in red and yellow lost his balance and took a quick, lurching step to regain it.

"Are you all right?" Potter asked.

"Yes, Dread Lord," the other man replied, smiling wryly as he removed his scarlet, gold-trimmed domino. The vestige of a Scots accent reminded Potter of Montrose, inspiring a fresh twinge of regret that the Grim Rider had chosen to turn traitor. "I'm simply not used to being this tall. I'm not one of those fellows who asks the flesh sculptors for a new body every month, just for the novelty of it. But in these unsettled times, it wouldn't do for anyone to observe Robert Fitzroy, Anacreon of the Penitent Legion and legate of the Laughing Lady, slipping into the Seat of Burning Waters."

Fitzroy's demeanor was cool and composed. Though he almost certainly felt a measure of awe at being in the Smiling Lord's presence, he possessed sufficient *savoir faire* to mask it. Nor could Potter discern any telltale glint of insanity in the diplomat's eyes, for all that the fellow served the patron demigoddess of those who perished by dint of madness. The Deathlord couldn't decide if that was good or bad. A rational man might be more predictable, easier to read, yet harder to deceive.

"Conditions *are* unsettled," Potter agreed. "As is my sworn duty, I intend to put an end to the current troubles before they damage the Empire beyond repair. Unfortunately, it seems plain that any such intervention will require fundamental alterations to the structure of the government."

Fitzroy's eyes widened slightly. "How so, my lord Ares?"

"I suspect you comprehend," Potter said. "When Stygia had a single monarch, the state was strong and healthy. Under the Council of Seven, it's sickening by the day. The present system is simply too cumbersome and rife with inconsistencies. It wouldn't work even if several of my colleagues weren't actively undermining it to further their imperial ambitions."

The Penitent hesitated. "You're speaking with great candor, my lord, particularly considering that this is our first discussion. May I be forthright as well, without giving offense?"

"Speak," Potter said.

"My lady has heard rumors that you're scheming to seize the Emperor's throne yourself. Needless to say, these tidings alarm her, and thus far, your statements this evening have offered nothing to allay her concerns."

"Then I'll try to do so now," Potter replied. "I *don't* aspire to be Emperor. My powers are formidable. You should hope that you and your Penitent comrades are never required to face them. Yet I know I'm no Charon, nor are any of the other Deathlords. None of us could hold the Hierarchy together by himself."

"Then what are your goals?" Fitzroy asked.

"First, to preserve my existence, by casting down the traitors who have been trying to destroy me. Second, to restore peace and order to the realm by establishing a *smaller* group of oligarchs, who can govern efficiently, without constantly finding themselves at cross purposes, and who will be content with their offices. They ought to be, wouldn't you agree? After all, the fewer the surviving Deathlords, the more power each will wield."

Fitzroy fingered his dimpled chin. Potter wondered fleetingly if the new face itched, or if it was simply a mannerism. "You provide an interesting perspective," the diplomat said. "Exactly who do you envision presiding over the new regime?"

"Your mistress and myself," Potter said. "It's only fitting. By the Emperor's ancient decree, she rules all souls who died of lunacy, while those slain by their fellows come to me. And for the last two centuries, our domains have grown enormously. The Quick are going mad in droves—their whole civilization is deranged—and modern strife slays millions.

"In contrast, consider the provinces of the other Deathlords. The Skeletal Lord rules pestilence. Once a major instrument of death, but today science is poised to eradicate it. One could argue that even now, were it not for the folly and wrath of nations—your lady's sphere of influence and mine—disease and starvation would reap far fewer victims than they do. By the same token, the forces which the Laughing Lady and I embody often *produce* the mysterious fatalities, lethal happenstance, and suicidal despair from which the Beggar, Emerald, and Quiet Lords derive their vassals. By what justification, then, do the other Deathlords claim parity with us?"

"You neglected to mention death by senescence," Fitzroy said. "Surely the Ashen

Lady too might reasonably claim that with the decline of disease, her office has waxed increasingly important."

"That's true," Potter replied. "And I would have no qualms about sharing supreme authority with her. Provided, of course, that she's willing to support my strategies. Should she oppose me, I would have no choice but to humble her with the rest of my foes."

"And might I inquire your plans for the Lady of Fate?"

"She's not truly a Deathlord," Potter said, "and thus far, she's given me no reason to believe she covets the throne. Does your mistress think otherwise?"

Fitzroy hesitated, evidently deliberating whether to give up this particular piece of intelligence. "No," he said.

"Good. Then I predict the Isle of Eurydice will hold itself aloof from the struggle, just as it always has, and if so, I'll have no quarrel with its inhabitants."

Fitzroy nodded. "Well, then, the matter comes down to a proposal of alliance between you, my queen, and possibly the Ashen Lady if she'll throw in with you. Which obliges me to pose another delicate question. Your argument as to why you and my mistress *deserve* a higher estate than the other Deathlords seems sound enough, but pragmatically speaking, what guarantee can you offer that your cabal will emerge victorious?"

"For one thing," said Potter, using the icy, reverberating voice he could draw at need from his enchanted visor, "I am the Master of War and Murder." The lamps dimmed, flooding the room with shadow. Blanching, Fitzroy took an involuntary step backward. "I'm not so foolish as to belittle the magic of my fellows, but by taking up arms, they've entered *my* arena, where none of them can match me. I can annihilate all six of them, your lady included, if necessary. But despite the injuries she's done me in recent weeks, it pleases me to offer her a chance to redeem herself."

Fitzroy swallowed. "I assure you, Dread Lord, the Laughing Lady has never attempted—"

"Enough!" Potter snapped. Three of the glass display cases shattered. "You can't lie to one of the Seven, nor need you worry that you'll harm your mistress's interests by telling the truth. I'm willing to forgive her the harassment, provided we reach an understanding now."

The emissary quivered. Potter sensed that the fellow wished he could look away, but wouldn't permit himself to do so. "Forgive me, Dread Lord," Fitzroy said, his voice slightly unsteady, "I intended no disrespect. Nor do I doubt the efficacy of your Arcanos. However, as you yourself observed, the other members of the Council command potent sorceries as well. Despite your martial prowess, if the conflict were to come down to you and my lady against the other five, it does seem at least conceivable that your enemies would overwhelm you."

"Does it?" Potter replied, permitting the aura of fear he'd evoked to dissolve. "Then consider this. Your lady has little hope of weathering the coming storm without any allies at all, and I daresay she's already learned that, despite any and all assurances to the contrary, she can't trust anyone else. As proof, consider the railroad incident. A train bearing a rich harvest of souls to the Seat of Succor was derailed and looted crossing the Tempest. Ordinarily one would attribute such a calamity to Spectres, bandits, or rebels, but you Penitents found evidence that the Emerald Legion was responsible."

Fitzroy lifted an eyebrow. "May I inquire *how* you know this, Dread Lord?"

"You may not," Potter said. "There have been other such calamities as well. A fortress taken by stealth and the garrison put to the sword; the sole surviving witness implicated the Paupers. One of your mistress's most valued advisors, perhaps the finest Monitor on the island, vanished from the Agora bare minutes after exchanging words with soldiers of the Gaunt Legion. I could go on, but I think I've made my point."

"Quite," Fitzroy said. "Once again, you present a strong case for alliance. Still, I must reiterate, before binding her fate inextricably to yours, the Laughing Lady will wish to be convinced that the two of you have some reasonable hope of prevailing."

Potter simply sat motionless, as Demetrius had advised him to do at this juncture in the parley.

After a while, Fitzroy said, "Dread Lord?"

"I'm deliberating," Potter replied grimly. "You ask much of me, Anacreon. Why should I expose my hidden strengths to you? For all I know, your mistress has no genuine interest in my friendship, and if that's the case, I'd be supplying her with information she could use against me."

Fitzroy spread his hands in an eloquent gesture that somehow seemed more natural for a man with a smaller frame. "I appreciate your dilemma, Dread Lord. In your place, if I may presume to imagine such a thing, I'd feel exactly the same way. Nevertheless, my mistress's perspective is as I've presented it. If you want her to stand with you, you must demonstrate that such a course is in her best interest."

Potter paused again. Finally he said, "Very well. I'll give you one morsel to carry back to her, in the hope of whetting her appetite for more. You are of course aware that, much as he taught us Deathlords, Charon reserved his most potent magicks for himself. At one point it seemed that his secrets had perished with him. Happily, that impression has turned out to be unduly pessimistic."

The Penitent's eyes narrowed. "Are you saying you have the Emperor's missing mask?"

"No," Potter said, "but I have something equally useful. Unfortunately, I can't exploit its full potential by myself. As I said, no one Deathlord can perform the miracles Charon did. Two, however, are a different matter."

"Would you care to be any more specific about this new source of power?" Fitzroy asked.

"No," Potter said, "I would not. Not until I hear your mistress's reaction to what I've said so far. Go confer with her, then return here at this time tomorrow."

"I'll show you out, milord Anacreon," said Demetrius. The two courtiers bowed at the foot of the dais and again before exiting the chamber.

Potter laid his pole arm across his knees, slumped back on his throne, and shifted his shoulders restlessly. His plate armor seemed to weigh him down and chafe him. He watched the door impatiently, willing Demetrius to reappear through it.

And eventually he did. Potter pulled off his visor. "What did you think?" the Deathlord asked.

"That it went well," the Greek replied, removing his own stone mask.

"I don't know," said Potter, massaging his face. His gauntlet felt unpleasantly cold and hard against his skin, and with a grimace, he yanked it off as well. "In Fitzroy's place, would *you* believe we know about all the raids simply through superior intelligence? Wouldn't you suspect we know because our agents executed them themselves, and manufactured evidence to make it appear that the other Legions were responsible?"

"Not necessarily," said Demetrius. "Don't forget, the other Deathlords *have* been plotting against one another for decades. It's entirely plausible that a number of them would choose to escalate the conflict in this manner. Indeed, some of them *are* doing so, even if it is in response to our terrorism against them. Besides, Chiarmonte's talents as a spymaster are all but legendary."

"Then why can't we take him fully into our confidence?" Potter grumbled.

"You know why," the Pardoner answered. "We decided it would be safest to dole out information to *all* your lieutenants solely on a need-to-know basis. Moreover, you yourself insisted that the Venetian, for all his acumen, wouldn't grasp the justification for all our raids and acts of sabotage. He wouldn't recognize that an armed struggle for the throne is now inevitable, and your best hope of survival is to make certain the conflict unfolds according to a scenario we devise."

"I know," Potter sighed. "God damn it, I never wanted this! A war among the shepherds of the dead is an abomination! Why couldn't the rest of the Council be satisfied with what Charon bequeathed them? Why couldn't they leave me alone?"

"I don't know," Demetrius said somberly. "I suspect their Shadows are to blame."

"Do you think the Laughing Lady will want to combine forces with me?"

"Probably, though with the intention of betraying you when the time is right."

"Did it seem to you that Fitzroy believed I've stumbled onto one of Charon's secrets?"

"I think he withheld judgment," the saturnine Oracle said. "You must remember, my lord. The beauty of our scheme is that it offers your fellow Deathlords more than one reason to do what we desire. Some will appear at the appointed rendezvous because they believe you truly have unearthed a piece of Charon's wizardry, and aspire to share or steal it. Others will be less credulous, but still interested in discussing an *entente* with you face to face. And others will come with their deadliest warriors in tow, seizing on what they imagine to be an unparalleled opportunity to assassinate you. Their motives don't matter in the slightest, just as long as they show up."

"I don't know that they all will," Potter said. "They aren't like me, fumbling novices in their roles. Centuries of near-godhood have made them wise and inhuman in ways I can't begin to understand. They'll smell a rat."

"Arrogant as they are, confident of their ability to deal with any situation, some of them will come," said Demetrius placidly. "I guarantee it. And after you make an example of those, the rest may well have the good sense to bend their knees to you. If not, we'll simply devise a stratagem to eliminate them as well."

"Which ones will come?" Potter asked. "Prophesy for me, Demetrius."

For an instant, the Greek smiled wearily, like a father whose child had demanded the same bedtime story for the thousandth time. Potter had a sense that the hint of disrespect ought to enrage him, but instead it made him feel mortified and weak.

"I scried for you only this afternoon," Demetrius said. "How rapidly do you think the tree of destiny puts forth new branches?"

"I think the future changes every time I talk to one of these mealy-mouthed emissaries," Potter said. "Every time one of my rivals communicates with another, or two of their partisans start a brawl down in the city. And our only defense is to discern what's coming! I'm sure our foes would have annihilated me already if it hadn't been for you."

Demetrius sighed. "All right. One more divination, but that will have to suffice until tomorrow, unless you feel you can dispense with my less esoteric services while I recover my strength." He reached into his brown leather satchel.

Potter leaned forward, eager to see what would happen next, and felt a bit let down when Demetrius brought out a pack of cards. Cartomancy was a legitimate means of divination, but the Deathlord would have preferred a more exotic technique, something the Greek had unearthed in the ancient tomes of the Oracle's guild. Those, after all, were the methods which had hitherto yielded the most critical information.

Demetrius smiled as if he sensed his master's disappointment. "It looks like an ordinary deck, doesn't it?" he said, sounding almost like a stage magician. "But watch." He pivoted, flinging out his arm and scattering the cards.

Instead of tumbling to the floor, they hung in the air, and then, slowly at first, began to rotate on their central axes, like revolving doors. At the same time, pasteboard and printer's ink turned to glass, flashing as it caught the lamplight.

For a moment, this dazzling display was all that Potter could see. Then he discerned that each spinning, gleaming rectangle held tiny images, as if it were an enchanted speculum or window. One showed the Isle of Sorrows with thunderheads massed behind it, another, the Emerald Lord's crimson dice tumbling across green felt, and a third, a grotesquely decorated black steamboat with a carved skull-face mounted between its smokestacks, moored beneath a starry Shadowlands sky.

Potter tried to glean some central theme or portent from it all, but the task was hopeless. There were too many separate visions to take in, now whirling so fast that it was all but impossible to make them out.

Demetrius studied the display with his bare, olive-skinned arms outstretched. Presumably, as the seer who'd conjured the effect, he was drinking in its import as no one else, not even a Deathlord, could. Suddenly, he grunted.

Concerned, Potter looked where the Greek appeared to be looking. He glimpsed a wink of coppery red and honey yellow inside one of the whirling glasses, and then, so abruptly it made him blink, the rectangles were all cards again, drifting to the floor like a rain of pigeon feathers.

"What did you see?" the Deathlord asked.

"Victory," said Demetrius quickly. "Our snare will catch the Skeletal Lord, the Laughing Lady, the Quiet Lord, and perhaps others as well."

Potter said, "That's glorious. But...there at the end, you seemed, I don't know, startled."

"By just how extraordinarily positive the auspices are, I suppose," Demetrius said blandly.

For just an instant, Potter suspected there was something the Oracle had decided not to tell him. Grimacing at his own paranoia, and what it implied about the condition of his nerves, he quashed the feeling.

THIRTY-ONE

Alice Mason looked up at the night sky. There wasn't a cloud in sight, just stars and the Milky Way, shining like a scatter of pearl dust on black velvet. Yet the prickling on her face and hands suggested a storm was imminent.

Perhaps something hanging in the air, some effluent from a tile factory or a creosoting plant, was responsible. In any case, dedicated walker though she was, she was beginning to regret turning down Harriet Oswald's offer of a ride home from their step aerobics class.

Well, she could be in her house in another minute. Then a cool, damp cloth would wash away the crawling on her skin, and a glass of iced raspberry tea would quell the vague anxiety nibbling at her nerves. A slim, sixty-two-year-old woman in a blue and yellow sweat suit, her silver-rimmed bifocals perched on the bridge of a long French nose, she clambered over the rail fence, taking a shortcut through the park. The area supposedly closed at sunset, but she'd begun taking evening strolls within its confines thirty years before some bureaucrat made that particular rule, and though not usually a scofflaw, she felt that seniority entitled her to an exemption.

Pines and oaks, their shapes blurred by the darkness, rose before her. Beyond the trees, she knew, was an assemblage of playground equipment, swings, seesaws, and the like. She wondered fleetingly just how many hours she'd spent supervising children romping on such devices, cautioning them to be careful and drying their tears when they scraped their knees anyway, and then someone whimpered.

Startled, Alice froze, then grimaced at her own reaction. It was true that terrible things were happening throughout Louisiana and Mississippi. The newspapers described the atrocities every day. But a woman, particularly a widowed senior citizen with no one to depend on but herself, mustn't let such stories spook her, lest she find herself too timid to leave the house. Even in this modern world, which seemed so much colder and crueler than the era of her youth, the chance of a criminal harming a given individual was too remote to fret over, at least in a quiet neighborhood in a pleasant town like Slidell.

Squinting against the gloom, she moved forward. "Is someone there?" she called. "Do you need help?"

The whimper sounded once again. Alice listened intently, but couldn't home in on the source.

Frowning, she pushed between two fragrant longleaf pines. The needles rustled against her sleeves. The playground opened out before her. She thought she saw the merry-go-round begin to revolve, but when she pivoted toward it, it was motionless.

Turning this way and that, wishing the park were lighted, she peered into the shadows. Finally she caught sight of a small form huddled beneath a sliding board.

Indistinct in the darkness, the shape might almost have been a basketball. Alice had to move within ten feet of it to be certain it was really a little girl sitting with her back against the ladder, her legs drawn up against her chest and her face hidden behind them.

Grasping the ladder, Alice lowered herself to one knee. "Hello, little one," she said in her most soothing voice, "what's wrong?"

The child made a snuffling sound, then sobbed, paying no attention to Alice whatsoever. For a moment the adult had the odd feeling that the little girl literally couldn't hear her.

"Young lady," she said, a bit louder and more insistently. The girl still didn't acknowledge her presence. Alice gently laid her hand on her shoulder.

For a second the girl *still* didn't react. Then her body jerked as if she'd received an electric shock. Her thin, tear-streaked face whipped around toward Alice. Her dark eyes enormous, the child started to shiver.

"Don't be afraid," said Alice. "Whatever's wrong, we'll make it better. My name is Mrs. Mason. What's yours?"

Still shuddering, the child just stared at her.

"Did your mommy and daddy tell you not to talk to strangers?" Alice asked. "That's usually very wise, but you can talk to me. I'm a teacher. Are you hurt?"

The girl's mouth twitched.

"That's right," Alice said, "talk to me. Are you lost?"

The child's pale lips worked, but Alice couldn't make out what she was saying. She turned her head, positioning her ear in front of the girl's mouth. Even then, the halting whisper was barely audible.

"—the fire," the child concluded.

Alice wondered if someone's home was ablaze. But surely she would have seen the glow of the conflagration in the sky. "Please say that again," she said. "I didn't catch the first part."

"Black fire," said the girl. "Strings and dots of it, floating all around."

Frowning in perplexity, Alice said, "There is *something* nasty in the air. But it's just smoke from some factory. It can't hurt us."

"I thought it would be worse inside," said the child. "Because the house has bad things in it, even if Mommy and Daddy and Brad can't feel them. A mean man hurt the girl who lived there before us. So I went out the back door when nobody was looking."

At last Alice felt she was on familiar ground. "You slipped out without your parents' permission."

"But it didn't help," said the girl. "The fire was just as bad outside. It burned me just as bad, and no matter where I went, I couldn't get away from it. After a while I tried to go home again, but nothing looked right."

Alice nodded. "It's easy to get lost in the dark. But if you can tell me your name and address, it will be just as easy to get you back home."

The girl began to shake more violently. "I walked for a long time, and then I saw the park. I came in because it was a place I knew, and it still seemed the same. But when I looked at one of the picnic tables, I saw…I saw…" Without warning, she threw back her head and screamed.

Alice took the girl into her embrace. The child thrashed, trying to break away. "Little one, little one, listen to me!" the teacher said. "Whatever you saw, it's over and done with. Nothing can hurt you now."

After a few seconds, the girl slumped inert in her arms, all but catatonic once again. Then blades of radiance slashed through the night, and running footsteps pounded the ground. Fearful that whatever had alarmed the child was now charging toward her, Alice held her breath until two masculine silhouettes emerged from the darkness, each gripping a flashlight.

One of the beams flowed across the child and Alice, compelling the latter to flinch from the glare. "Ruthie!" cried a teenage voice, breaking on the second syllable.

"Are you the child's family?" asked Alice. Laboriously—as usual after a workout, her joints had stiffened up as soon as she'd stopped moving—she hauled herself to her feet. "Thank goodness."

"That's us," said another voice, deeper, older, and rougher. "I'm Tom Parker. Who are you?"

Alice's mouth tightened at the brusqueness of the question, but perhaps the man she assumed to be the girl's father was too upset to be polite. "My name is Alice Mason. I was walking through the park when I heard your little girl crying."

"Huh," grunted Parker, lumbering closer. With the light out of her eyes, Alice could see that he was a burly, moonfaced man with a baseball cap jammed down over a head of dark, greasy-looking curls. An oval patch on his coveralls said SHELBY BRICK CO. He bent over the child. "Ruthie, are you okay?" The child didn't answer, or even look up at him. He scowled at Alice. "What's the matter with her?"

"I don't know," Alice replied. "She was like this when I found her, until I managed to coax her into speaking. What she said made very little sense but was quite upsetting to her, so much so that relating it made her hysterical. I assume you came running because you heard her scream. After that, she became withdrawn again. Is she under a doctor's care?"

"No!" the big man answered. "What's that supposed to mean?"

"Nothing derogatory," Alice said. "It's just that she seems confused, so I wondered if she had a history of similar problems."

"Not really," said the teenager, a lanky boy with hands and feet too large for the rest of him. "Sometimes she says she sees things, but I always thought she was just playing. She's always had a big imagination."

"Shut up, Brad," said Parker. "There's nothing wrong with Ruthie. She's a normal kid."

"Then has she had some sort of shock?" Alice asked. "She alluded to bad things happening in your house. Another little girl being abused."

"Are you accusing me of something?" Parker asked.

"No," Alice said quickly. "What Ruthie told me was very cryptic. I just thought it might reflect—"

"Because I don't even *have* another girl," the big man said. "Just Ruthie and her brother here. Isn't that right?"

Brad nodded. "Yeah."

"What's more," Parker said, "she was fine an hour ago. Playing with her Sailor Moon dolls, happy as a pig in shit." He hunkered down beside his daughter. "What's the matter with you, sugar cookie? You can tell Daddy."

Ruthie didn't answer.

"I don't know if it's a good idea to question her now," Alice said. "Even if you could get her talking, it might just agitate her again. Let's take her to the hospital. The emergency room. I'm sure they have a psychiatrist on call."

"I told you, she isn't crazy," Parker said. He rose, lifted Ruthie in his arms, and handed her to Brad, who received her a little awkwardly. "Take care of her."

"I didn't say she was mentally ill," Alice replied. The longer they talked, the stranger the big man's attitude seemed. She wondered if he *had* been mistreating Ruthie, but actually didn't think it likely. In her experience, abusive parents in fear of detection were far more likely to turn on the charm than to become hostile. "But it's obvious she needs medical attention, don't you agree?"

"Oh, we'll look after her," Parker said. "You can count on that. But first you're going to answer a couple questions. What were you doing here?"

Puzzled, Alice cocked her head. "Walking home. I thought I told you."

"The park is closed at night."

"Then I suppose I'm a trespasser," Alice said impatiently. The irritant in the atmosphere stung her forehead. "You can alert the authorities if you think it necessary, though your daughter might still be lost if I hadn't happened along."

"Yeah," said Parker. "But I'm thinking, if I wanted to carry a kid off somewhere and mess with her, I might take her to a dark, lonely spot just like this."

The statement was so bizarre that for a moment, Alice thought she'd misheard it. Parker couldn't really mean what he seemed to be implying. "Are you suggesting that *I* abducted this child? Broke into your house and spirited her away?"

"She wouldn't go out at night alone without a word to anyone. She knows better."

"Something frightened her. It may have had something to do with this nasty vapor in the air."

Parker snorted. "Right. That sounds real likely. Stupid me, I was thinking that maybe a *person* scared her. Maybe even a person who got caught at the scene of the crime. And tried to throw suspicion off herself by making out that the poor little kid is crazy."

"I understand how terrified you must have been when you discovered Ruthie was missing," Alice said. "I'm sure you're still distraught. But you're being ridiculous. I'm a teacher at Long Elementary. I sing in the choir at First Methodist. I'm an old lady, for heaven's sake."

"That doesn't mean you can't be a pervert or maybe even a devil worshipper," Parker said. "Kids are getting molested in schools and daycares all over the world. You see it on TV all the time. Hell, lately, *everybody's* going nuts. The crazy preachers and teachers and cops have just about killed off all the good ones."

The contaminant fouling the air seemed to be thickening. It coated Alice's mouth with a vile taste and tied a knot in her chest. "I'm not going to debate this any further," she said. "It's too silly, and more importantly, Ruthie needs to go to a hospital without any further delay."

Cradled in her brother's arms, Ruthie murmured, "Needles."

Parker lurched around toward her. "What?"

"Needles," the little girl croaked. "The monkey man on top of the table was made of needles, and he stuck them in, one after another, until—" Her words dissolved into sobbing.

Parker glared at Alice. "What did you do to her, you bitch?"

The teacher struggled against the impulse to shrink before his anger. "Are you even listening to what the child is saying? In the first place, she talked about a monkey *man*—"

"So you had a friend. With sense enough to run when Ruthie finally let off a scream."

"No. Will you just *think*? Does it sound as if the child is describing anything real?"

Parker's massive form quivered. "I told you, she isn't crazy."

"Fine," Alice said. "Believe whatever you like. Just get her to a doctor and then you can report your suspicions to the police. Make a jackass of yourself to your heart's content."

"Sure," said Parker. "And by the time they come after you, you'll be in another state."

"If you like, I'll stay with you until they arrive to take your statement."

"Then I guess you're all in it together," Parker said. "They must like to hurt little kids, too. So I think we'll just settle this right now, by ourselves." He slapped his flashlight against the palm of his hand. The long metal cylinder landed with a meaty smack.

Alice attempted to speak, but no sound came out. She swallowed and tried again. "This is ludicrous. I was at an exercise class until just a few minutes ago. Twenty people can vouch for me."

"Oh, I'm sure your pervert buddies will give you an alibi." The flashlight whacked into his left hand.

"Whatever you believe," Alice said, "you can't just *batter* a person. You'll go to prison."

"It's dark, and we've got trees blocking the view from the street. I'm willing to take my chances." The flashlight thudded against his palm.

"This is insane," said Alice. She gazed at Brad beseechingly. "For God's sake, do something!"

The boy grimaced, hitched his shoulders as if his sister's weight was growing uncomfortably heavy, and finally said, "I don't know about this, Dad. We got Ruthie back safe, that's the important thing, isn't it? Whatever happened, there's not a mark on her. Maybe you *could* talk to the cops."

"No," Parker said. "You're a good boy, son, but you don't understand. There's a sickness loose in the world, and now it's broken out here. You can just about taste it every time you take a breath. And until it runs its course, we won't be able to trust anybody outside the family. We'll have to protect ourselves, any way we can. Now you get Ruthie away from here. She doesn't need to see this."

Brad peered at his father with troubled eyes, then turned his back. "No!" Alice cried. "Please, you mustn't let this happen!" The teenager walked away.

Parker smiled, slapped the makeshift weapon into his hand, and lifted it over his head. Moving without haste, almost casually, he started forward.

At first Alice simply stared at him, not quite able to believe that she truly was in mortal danger. She'd stopped to *help* Ruthie, and Parker had no reason to suspect otherwise. Then a surge of terror jolted her out of her daze. She wheeled, fled, and heard the big man break into a run as well. His feet seemed to shake the ground, but perhaps that was really the pounding of her heart.

She sprinted past a jungle gym. Sensed Parker closing the distance between them, and fought the urge to look over her shoulder. Strained to run even faster instead.

Then she lurched forward, her feet no longer beneath her, her balance gone. As she slammed down on her ground, she thought she'd tripped. Then she belatedly felt a throb of pain in the back of her skull, and realized Parker had clubbed her.

She tried to scramble back up, but a second blow caught her on the shoulder. The impact snapped bone and smashed her back onto the grass.

"Please," she moaned, "I didn't do *anything*."

Parker dropped to one knee and grabbed her forearm, anchoring her in place. "Bitch," he gasped, evidently winded from the brief chase. The flashlight rose over his head. "Nobody"—the flashlight hammered down on her breasts—"hurts"—another blow smashed her glasses and crushed her nose—"my kids!"

Alice struggled to protect herself for as long as she could, but it wasn't long before she couldn't even move anymore. Her lack of resistance did nothing to deter Parker. He went on beating her as savagely as ever. Her eyes full of blood, she almost imagined she could see the shreds of black fire Ruthie had spoken of, floating all around her. The tatters multiplied until they formed a single mass, an ocean of acid drowning and dissolving the world. She felt her heart judder and rip, and the darkness howled.

Thirty-Two

Astarte rubbed her eyebrow. Her face felt strange with the steel jewelry removed from her piercings. Hell, *she* felt strange clad in bright colors, with the spikes and magenta highlights gone from her hair. But Marilyn had thought it best that they come to the police station in disguise.

Dressed as a man tonight, in a loud plaid polyester jacket utterly different than her usual elegant masculine attire, the Arcanist studied the four-story brick slab of a building on the other side of the parking lot. "I guess it looks all right," she said at last.

"It looks like a cop shop," Astarte said impatiently. "Are we going in or what?"

Marilyn smiled sourly. "Apparently so." She pushed up the nerdy plastic black-rimmed glasses she'd donned to further alter her appearance. "Come on."

They started across the brightly illuminated ring of asphalt encircling the station house. The amber lights atop the tall poles made Astarte feel exposed and vulnerable. With a twinge of sardonic amusement, she reflected that recent events had made her afraid of the dark as well. She guessed a girl knew she was really in trouble when she no longer felt safe *anywhere*.

Marilyn led her companion through the public entrance into the reception area, a long, narrow room with greasy-looking gray linoleum and bilious yellow walls. Backless wooden benches flanked the doorway. The dozen people sitting on them looked sick and weary in the harsh fluorescent light. The air smelled of cigarette smoke and disinfectant.

A fresh-faced cadet behind the Information and Complaint Desk drew herself up straighter on her stool. Ignoring her, Astarte and Marilyn scanned the people slumped on the benches as if they were looking for someone, then sat down themselves. Looking disappointed, the cadet returned to the hefty criminology textbook she was reading.

A round white clock with black numbers hung above the candy machine. The red second hand crawled around the dial with agonizing slowness. By the time it completed its fourth circuit, Astarte felt edgy enough to explode.

"Can't we just go for it?" she whispered.

"I'd rather not," Marilyn replied. "I told you, I'm not a mage, and assuming this trick works at all, it isn't going to function as it would in a movie. Let's choose our moment carefully, so as to maximize our chances."

Six more minutes crept past. Then the door flew open and a voluptuous black woman staggered through, clutching her temple. Blood streamed through her fingers and stained the shoulder of her pink knit pullover. Several other people, some battered and bleeding also, rushed in after her. Charging to the desk, they all started jabbering at once. The senior patrol officer and his trio of cadets converged on them to sort out the chaos.

"Perfect," Marilyn breathed. Slipping her hand into her hip pocket, she rose and ambled toward the door at the right-hand end of the desk. The sign on it read, AUTHORIZED PERSONNEL ONLY.

Astarte stood up and followed, trying to match the Arcanist's air of nonchalance. She reached into her own pocket, took hold of the little cloth bag Marilyn had given her, and squeezed it hard.

From her perspective, the results were less than spectacular. She didn't feel any surge of magic power sizzling through her flesh. She could still see her own body, just as she could still see Marilyn walking a pace ahead of her. But supposedly, if the charms worked, other people would tend not to notice them, particularly if some commotion was providing a distraction.

Astarte held her breath as Marilyn opened the door, and cringed when the senior patrol officer glanced over directly at them. But the cop didn't appear to register their presence, or the fact that the door was now ajar. He just grabbed a clipboard and pen and turned back to the disheveled, babbling crowd in front of him.

The intruders quickened their stride, hurrying past the Communications Center, a glassed-in area housing telephones, computers, radios, fax machines, and two harried-looking dispatchers. Beyond that was a deserted hallway.

Marilyn let out a long exhalation. "Thank God," she said. "If I'm not mistaken, we became visible almost as soon as we passed through the door. I was sure one of the dispatchers was going to look up and see us." Suddenly, to Astarte's surprise, the Arcanist smiled, not her former grimace of nervous resolve but a genuine expression of glee. "Still, it worked well enough, didn't it? That's sorcery, my dear, or at least a faint echo of it. How do you like being the one *wielding* the supernatural powers for a change?"

"I like it a lot," Astarte said, grinning back. "It's what I've wanted all my life."

The exhilaration in Marilyn's face withered abruptly. Now her features looked haggard and apprehensive again. "Well, we can savor the memory later. Let's do what we came to do and get out of here. I'm not sure the charms will work a second time, so don't use yours unless you feel you absolutely have to. Now that we've made it past the gatekeepers, we should be all right. Anyone who sees us will assume we have legitimate business in this part of the building. Just try to look as if you belong."

Astarte scowled. "Right. We went over this already. Jeez, you treat me like I'm stupid, just like Frank—"

At the mention of Bellamy's name, a wave of anguish swept through her. Her eyes burned, and a sob caught in her throat.

Marilyn tried to lay a comforting hand on her shoulder. Astarte twisted away, avoiding the contact. "I'm okay," she growled. "Let's just do this."

Marilyn nodded. "All right," she said softly. "According to my information, the Evidence Room is on the second floor. Let's find a way up."

In a minute they came to a wooden staircase. Marilyn glanced back at Astarte, evidently making sure she wasn't having a nervous breakdown. The solicitude made her angry. She was afraid that if her friend kept fussing over her, she *would* fall apart. She glared and gestured impatiently. Marilyn started up the steps, which creaked beneath her scuffed Hush Puppies.

As she set her foot on the fifth riser, she froze.

"What's wrong?" Astarte asked.

"I don't know," Marilyn replied. "Perhaps nothing. Do you feel something in the air?"

"No."

"Well, I suppose that since you aren't a natural sensitive, and haven't undergone any mystical training, you wouldn't. But all of a sudden, I do. A kind of psychic pressure or heat, coming in waves from the northeast." She pointed in what Astarte assumed to the appropriate direction.

"What does it mean?" Astarte asked.

"I have no idea," Marilyn answered, still standing where she was.

"Does it hurt?"

"No, it's merely...disturbing."

"Well, that's too bad, but if your head isn't going to explode or anything, can't you just put up with it?"

"I could," Marilyn said. "But it's a mystery. An anomaly. Possibly a sign that we should turn back."

"But you don't know that," Astarte said. "It might not have anything to do with us at all."

Marilyn spread her hands. "True enough. Perhaps it isn't even real. Perhaps I'm simply imagining it, because I'm afraid. As usual, I can't tell you anything for certain." She sneered in manifest self-contempt.

Astarte sighed with mingled sympathy and exasperation. "It's okay. You got me inside. I'll handle the rest. You get out of here and I'll meet you back at the motel." She climbed past her companion.

Marilyn gripped her forearm. "No," the Arcanist said. "I said I'd do this and I will. I'm *not* going to flinch, not this time." Marching upward, nearly shouldering Astarte aside, she took the lead once more.

They reached the second floor and prowled on down another hall. Astarte couldn't help noticing how empty and dark most of the station house seemed to be. No one else was traversing the corridors, and except for the faint buzz of the commotion down in the reception area, no voices disturbed the silence. She guessed that most of the cops working the night shift were on patrol or answering calls. God knew, these days there were plenty of crimes and disturbances to keep them busy.

Astarte and Marilyn turned down another hall. At the other end, an acrylic sign hanging above a Dutch door read EVIDENCE ROOM. The lower section of the door was closed, the upper, open. Behind it, just barely visible at this angle, slumped a man with his head cradled in his arms on his Formica-topped desk.

Astarte smiled. The guy was obviously napping on the job. He might be a little dazed when they woke him up. Maybe he'd believe the phony paperwork they'd brought, supposedly ordering him to release the werewolves' notebook to them. Maybe they wouldn't have to dope him.

The intruders headed down the shadowy passage. Halfway to the Dutch door, Marilyn halted, sniffing.

"What is it now?" Astarte asked. Then she caught it too. A sickening odor of decay. "Never mind, I smell it. But it's probably just somebody's lunch rotting in a wastebasket." Her companion didn't move. "Come on, Marilyn, we're *here*, and nothing's happening. Let's finish what we started, okay?"

Her face sweaty, Marilyn gave a jerky nod. "All right." She walked on.

The clerk in the Evidence Room still hadn't moved. Astarte still couldn't see him very well, but she could tell that he seemed to have a terrible case of acne. Bumps studded his mottled skin on the neck and hands, and moist sores pitted it. He looked almost as chewed up as—

Now it was her turn to falter. Her mind balked too, reluctant to complete the ghastly train of thought it had begun. Then Bellamy lurched up out of the chair, and, his head and limbs flopping, leaned out into the hall to leer at her.

Astarte tried to scream, but the sound jammed in her chest. For a moment she believed that Bellamy's corpse truly had returned to a kind of demonic life, and the idea of such a desecration was the worst horror yet. She felt her mind recoiling, twisting in on itself, then noticed the huge, black-furred hand gripping her beloved's shoulder, its claws sunk deep in his ravaged flesh, and realized the truth.

Bellamy's body was inert. Hidden behind the door, Dunn was manipulating the corpse as if it were some sort of crude puppet. Perhaps it was his idea of a joke.

The werewolf flipped Bellamy into the hallway. When the mangled corpse struck the wall, its right leg fell off. Eyes shining like lanterns, crouching to avoid bumping his head on the ceiling tiles, Dunn bounded through the door.

THIRTY-THREE

Bellamy skulked along Barracks Street, gliding from one bit of cover to another, studying the houses. Many were obviously still occupied by the Quick, and consequently unlikely to be Geffard's secret Haunt. But there were also a number of dilapidated, seemingly abandoned structures. He supposed he could search them all, one after another, until he found the one he was looking for. But that could be dangerous if he accidentally encroached on some other *ibambo*'s domain. It could also take time, and some instinct warned him that time was running out.

A hot, almost slimy presence hung in the air. Sometimes it seemed to beat against his face like a poisonous wind gusting in from the north. It wore at his nerves and intensified his sense of foreboding. If there was one thing he didn't need, he reflected sourly, it was another mysterious phenomenon to worry about.

But much as it annoyed him, his shadowself obviously thrived on it. He could feel the parasite bloating in the depths of his mind, moving around, laughing at him. The Nihils seemed to like the polluted atmosphere too. A webwork of fissures in the street hissed more loudly. A glittering black pit in the hood of a white Dodge Neon parked at the curb swelled until it looked as if the front end of the vehicle had virtually disappeared.

Bellamy frowned as a thought struck him. Nihils. He still wasn't sure he entirely understood what they were—doorways to Hell, evidently—but they seemed to be associated with evil, and with certain kinds of ghostly magic as well. Queen Marie's throne room contained a lot of them, and Geffard's stronghold might, also.

He turned and retraced his steps. Soon he spied a crumbling antebellum mansion with flaking cream-colored walls, gray doors and trim, and a stable, slave quarters, and a Creole kitchen in the fenced, overgrown yard behind it. The house was markedly more infested with Nihils than the buildings around it, so much so that it seemed as if it ought to collapse into a thousand pieces. Lopsided shutters and rotting curtains prevented him from peering in the windows.

Okay, Bellamy thought. Assuming he really had found Geffard's hideout, what now? He doubted that it would be easy to approach the place unobserved. The loa must surely have lookouts posted, even if the FBI agent couldn't spot them from his vantage point.

What he needed was a diversion. He hurried to the next corner, where he'd seen a grubby little bar with neon beer logos in the window. Outside it, frowning in concentration, he projected himself through the Shroud. The patina of grime and corruption imposed by the metaphysical barrier vanished. The neighborhood seemed less seedy, the air far sweeter than it had before. He took a deep breath—now that he was here, he was suddenly afraid he'd forget to breathe, and someone would notice—and then, his nerves jangling with anxiety, stepped through the door.

The bartender and some of the customers perched on stools turned to look at him. The fleshy, graying man behind the stick frowned and cocked his head. One of the patrons, a stooped old man in a checked shirt, suspenders, and bow tie, snorted in amusement, scorn, or disbelief.

Bellamy felt a surge of gratitude. He didn't care that, with his clothing in tatters and his black shortsword hanging at his hip, he looked peculiar. What mattered was that, unlike the Villiers family, these mortals weren't quailing in terror. He *could* pass for one of the living when he wanted to.

It occurred to him that if he really desired it, if he fought with every bit of willpower he possessed, he could leave the horrors and frustrations of being a ghost behind and remain in the world of the Quick forever. Granted, he hadn't managed the trick before, but then he'd been surrounded by spirits and monsters. Now he was among ordinary people in a nondescript little neighborhood beer joint, where the air was hazy with pungent cigarette smoke, a boar's head sporting sunglasses and a derby hat hung behind the bar, and a *Baywatch* pinball machine glowed in the back corner. The utter normalcy of his surroundings would anchor him here until he was completely alive again.

But no. Deep down, he knew that it couldn't possibly be that easy to break the grip of Death, or no wraith would ever remain a phantom. Already he felt the remorseless undertow of the Shadowlands, trying to drag him back. Perhaps his dark side was tempting him with this fantasy of resurrection to trick him into wasting his time in the mortal world. Or maybe he'd simply fallen victim to wishful thinking.

"Are you all right?" the barman asked. "You look a little spaced out, if you don't mind my saying so."

Bellamy smiled ruefully. "You don't know the half of it. Could you please give me a book of matches?"

"Sure." He reached under the bar.

The elderly man in the bow tie sneered at Bellamy. "Wandering around in a stupor with a big knife and your clothes torn to rags. Smoke a little crack, did you? Get in a little fight? You ought to be ashamed of yourself. Punks like you are the reason this country's going to Hell in a wheelbarrow."

"You guys don't know the half of *that*, either," the wraith replied, taking the matches from the bartender's outstretched hand. "Have a good night." He turned and exited the bar.

As he stepped back onto the sidewalk, he felt the insistent pull of the Underworld increase. He hurried down the street to a point where, he judged, he was too far from Geffard's Haunt for anyone there to observe him, but close enough for his diversion to attract plenty of attention.

Using the shortsword, he cut strips of cloth from his jacket, knotted them together, then unscrewed the gas caps of three parked cars. He inserted the makeshift fuses in the vehicles' fuel tanks and struck a match.

The teardrop of fire was warm and golden, like yet utterly unlike barrow-flame with its coldness and unearthly colors. For a moment Bellamy stared at the match, almost hypnotized, as if he could see all the pleasures and wonders of mortal existence swimming in its glow. Then, grimacing, he lit the fuses, allowed himself to slip back into the Shadowlands, and dashed away.

He ducked behind a considerably more modest home on the far side of Geffard's stronghold. Cheerful voices and the scent of spicy food issued from inside. The former sounded unpleasantly shrill and the latter smelled subtly rancid.

Time seemed to creep by, until he wondered if the fuses had gone out. Then three blasts thundered in rapid succession, and a flickering orange light tinged the sky. Debris clanked and banged as it showered down.

Hoping that his ploy had gotten all of Geffard's thugs looking in the wrong direction, Bellamy charged the house. He plunged through the rusty wrought-iron fence and immediately felt a nauseating jolt of energy. Evidently an echo of suffering permeated the entire property. Shrugging off the sensation, refusing to let it slow him down, he sprinted on between two of the crumbling slave cabins.

"Halt!" spat a deep male voice with a Caribbean accent.

Bellamy turned. A lanky black wraith wearing a black leather slouch hat and mirror sunglasses stood in the doorway of the shack on the left, pointing a crossbow at him. Perhaps the explosions had distracted the sentry, but not enough to make him overlook the intruder dashing right past his station.

"I came to warn you," Bellamy said, advancing on the other ghost.

"I told you to halt," the guard replied.

"They're about to attack," Bellamy said, not breaking stride. "From that direction."

He gestured back the way he'd come. "The blasts were a diversion. Oh, God, look!"

The sentry reflexively turned his head a fraction. Bellamy knew it was the only break he was going to get. He sprang.

The crossbow clacked, and the bolt flew past his shoulder. He punched the guard in the throat, then rammed the heel of his palm into the base of the other wraith's nose, flattening it. Either blow might well have killed a living man. The guard didn't disintegrate into the Labyrinth, but he did fall down on the rotting stoop, unconscious.

Bellamy quickly dragged him into the cabin, a cramped, filthy box stripped of all furniture but a straight-backed chair. As he might have anticipated, the aura of misery was even stronger here.

As long as the guard was still around, there was a chance he might awake and raise the alarm. Bellamy felt a momentary impulse to dispatch the helpless *ibambo* with his darksteel blade. But death and desperation hadn't made him quite *that* ruthless yet. Scowling, he pushed the temptation away.

He peered out of the shack. No one else was in sight. He ran on to the verandah, swarmed through the railing and up onto the shadowy porch itself.

An instant later he heard voices murmur and the front door of the mansion creak open and bump closed. His mouth dry, he drew his pistol from its holster. Careful to stay below the windows, he crept along the verandah until he could peek out toward Barracks Street.

Three men were ambling toward the gate that opened on the thoroughfare. One, possessed of a murky aura laced with ugly strands of black, was clearly alive and possibly another werewolf, or a Mount with a spirit riding inside him. The other two were ghosts.

They seemed to be going to investigate the explosions, but judging by their casual demeanor, they weren't unduly concerned. Why should they be, when the disturbance had occurred half a block away? In all likelihood, it had nothing to do with them.

Bellamy watched them disappear, the mortal unlocking the gate and the spirits melting through the metal bars beside it, then he warily slipped his face through the mansion's exterior wall.

On the other side was the dusty, ruinous husk of a once-lavish parlor. Two ghosts sat playing backgammon, the sickly greenish light of a barrow-flame lamp gleaming on the oboli, rings, and bracelets they were wagering. Judging from the bolt-action Springfield rifles leaning against the inlaid table, they were soldiers, too.

Bellamy hastily withdrew and moved on, peering into one gloomy, decaying ground-floor room after another. He saw three more of Geffard's henchmen loitering around, but nothing else of note.

All he'd established so far was that the mansion was one of the rebel leader's strongholds, and that wasn't good enough. He needed evidence that something treasonous was going on here, and that meant he was going to have to sneak inside and search. He shifted his shoulders, trying to work the tension out, and took a deep, steadying breath. Then he glided through the wall into what had once been a library. The room still stank of reeking paper, but the moldering books had mostly vanished from the shelves, replaced by someone's collection of human and animal skulls. The empty eye sockets stared at him, and then someone moaned.

Raising his pistol, Bellamy whirled, but no one was in sight. After a moment, the whimper sounded a second time, and he discerned that it was coming from upstairs.

He wondered if someone was being held prisoner up there. Some poor soul who might be able to divulge the details of Geffard's perfidy to his rescuer. He moved to the doorway, peered warily out, then stalked on down the corridor. He had to slip past the parlor to reach the staircase, but fortunately the backgammon players didn't glance up at the doorway. The rattle of dice followed him on his way.

As Bellamy ascended the stairs, the groaning suddenly changed to a string of softly articulated syllables. He had no idea what the words meant. He didn't even recognize the language. But something about the sibilant, hateful sound of them made his skin crawl. It was like the auditory equivalent of the hot, greasy feeling in the air.

Okay, maybe it wasn't a prisoner. Bellamy skulked on, even more cautiously than before.

Ragged scraps of wood littered the landing. Some agency had crudely demolished the ceilings and interior walls of the first three bedrooms on the right, possibly to create a chamber wide and high enough to accommodate occupants larger than a man.

Nevertheless, to all appearances it *was* a man, albeit a hunchbacked, naked, freakishly deformed one, who stood in the middle of the cleared area, his aura threaded with dark, pulsing veins, string warts dripping from his upraised, twisted arms. Croaking and chanting, he swayed back and forth, and a shimmering in the air before him, like the sheen of a floor-length mirror with the glass itself missing, shimmied with him as if the two of them were dancing. Crystals, bones, and symbols drawn in reeking blood and dung surrounded his splayed, blemished feet in a complex pattern.

Crouching near the top of the steps, peeking through the newel posts in the banister, Bellamy was all but certain that the freak was a werewolf sorcerer like the one he and Antoine had encountered, except that this specimen was currently wearing what passed for his human form. What's more, the FBI agent had a hunch that the column of glow was a gateway such as Titus had spoken of, which allowed the alien demons to pass from their native dimension into the Underworld.

He grimaced, because, although he was confident he was right, it was only supposition. He still needed more to break Marie out of her paralysis of indecision.

It looked as if, by ascending the steps, he'd come to the right place to find it. Evidently this was where the conspirators worked their black magic, and conceivably did much of their plotting as well. Unfortunately, to continue his search, he'd have to pass through the hunchback's field of vision, and not just for an instant, either. He had at least ten yards to cover.

Would the deformed man see him? The other shaman had, but he'd been in his monster shape, and also intent on devouring Titus. He'd adjusted his inhuman senses to perceive ghosts, and even so, it had taken him a few moments to detect Bellamy and Antoine's intrusion. Whereas the hunchback was currently human, and presumably not looking for wraiths. In fact, he seemed to be in some sort of trance. Maybe Bellamy could slip right past him as easily as if the warlock were an ordinary person.

Or maybe not. Ultimately, there was only one way to find out. Bellamy swallowed, stepped up onto the landing, and strode forward.

For the first few paces, nothing happened. Then the hunchback clenched his fists, threw back his head, and howled like a beast. Intent on shooting the werewolf before he could cast a spell, Bellamy started to shift himself across the Shroud, then realized the outburst had nothing to do with him. The hunchback was still staring at whatever it was he saw inside the shimmer. Slowly, his wavering cry fading, he dropped to his knees.

Hoping that this craziness was a common occurrence, and no other Restless would come running to find out why the sorcerer was making so much noise, Bellamy hurried on down the gloomy corridor until a wall cut off his view of the other man, and, theoretically, vice versa. He cautiously slipped his face through a heavy oak door with a cut-glass knob, then stiffened in surprise.

Once, presumably, the chamber had been a spacious bedroom belonging to one or more children. A small wooden horse on wheels and a toy chest, their paint faded and worn, sat abandoned in a corner. But currently the place was a shrine somewhat reminiscent of the one on Geffard's riverboat. A table with a red and white checkered cloth served as an altar. Atop it were skulls, bones, a crossed shovel and pick-ax, a garishly painted cross wreathed in a feather boa, and rows of crudely made brown candles, burning with a sickly green and radiating chill.

Unlike the altar on the *Twisted Mirror*, this one emanated a palpable feeling of sickness and malevolence. But that wasn't what had startled Bellamy. Rather, it was the life-sized statue of Marie standing in the center of the room. The Queen's willowy form, crown of ostrich plumes, and severely beautiful face were unmistakable. Her features were contorted in agony, her knees were giving way, and she was fumbling ineffectually behind her back, trying to pull out the dagger stuck between her shoulder blades.

Smaller images, dolls and puppets, some lying on the floor and others reposing on tables and shelves, radiated outward from the central figure in yet another intricate pattern. Some were crudely made, but it was obvious that each of them depicted Marie also, always in a position of torment and humiliation. One version was being raped by a creature like a hideous monkey, another had had its eyes torn out, and a third hung impaled on a spit. Occasionally black light flowed sluggishly through one of the images, or leaped crackling from one to another.

Bellamy was sure they were voudoun dolls, designed to exert a destructive influence on the Queen, and that they were responsible for her inability to contact the Orishas. He'd finally found the evidence he needed.

He wondered if he should destroy the display while he had the chance, but his ignorance of ghostly magic made him hesitate to tamper with it. He stepped into the room, then stood irresolute, trying to decide. The hunchback resumed his howling.

Finally Bellamy approached one of the smallest images, a clay portrait of Marie with her hands and feet cut off, and gingerly picked it up from the dusty floor to examine it. His hand prickled and itched. Then, abruptly, voices sounded on the other side of the door. The sorcerer's wail had masked them till now.

Bellamy frantically scrambled through a closet door. Old clothes on wooden hangers penetrated his insubstantial flesh, stinging him. Their musty smell tickled his nose and made him want to sneeze.

He didn't hear the door open, but the voices came closer. Evidently the speakers were *abambo*. "—yowl like that for hours on end," said a man. Though he'd only spoken to Chester on one occasion, Bellamy was almost certain he recognized the computer operator's prissy, petulant tones. "It's excruciating. How are the rest of us supposed to get any work done? You never should have included them in the plan."

"We needed helpers who exist naturally on the bright side of the Surface," said a deeper, richer voice, sounding amused. "We couldn't do everything with possession and psychokinesis. You have to admit, the Black Spiral Dancers have been abundantly useful to the loa."

"The Banes they conjure into the Underworld are useful," Chester replied. "But whenever they try to do anything else, they mess it up. Take Dunn. He's been chasing the Arcanists for days now. He claims he's going to trap them tonight, but you watch, he'll foul that up, too."

Bellamy twitched in shock.

"Don't be such a pessimist," said the other ghost. "Every important aspect of the grand design is proceeding nicely. This marvelous engine of destruction, for example. Can you perceive how much stronger the curse has grown? It won't be long before Marie is too feeble to rise from her throne or think a coherent thought."

"I hope so," Chester said. "Is there anything else you want to see?"

"I guess not. I hope you don't feel I was checking up on you. It's just that I get nervous if I don't touch base with my allies once in a while. Thank you for indulging me."

Bellamy realized the other wraiths were about to leave. Without divulging where Dunn had laid a trap for Astarte and the Arcanists. He put the clay doll into his pocket, and then, gun leveled, stepped back into the room. Chester and his companion, a plump, bald, bearded black man with the inky stains of a Pardoner on his fingertips, were already moving toward the door to the hall. "Hold it," the FBI agent said.

Chester jumped and lurched back around. The Pardoner turned more slowly. "What is this?" Chester quavered. "Who are you?"

"It's your friend Agent Bellamy," the Pardoner said. "He found a Masquer to change his appearance."

Bellamy frowned. "How do you know that?"

The plump wraith shrugged. "We can discern a lot of things."

"Well, you'd better *discern* that I'll kill you if you don't tell me about Dunn's trap."

"At least we'll have company on the road to the Void," the Pardoner said. "The sound of the shots will bring our friends down on your head."

"With Fido screaming his lungs out down the hall?" Bellamy replied. "Maybe, but I'll risk it. Now talk. Or do I have to kill one of you to convince the other I'm serious? If so, then this is your unlucky night, Chester. I got pretty darn sick of you back in the cemetery."

Trembling, Chester opened his mouth to speak. "Don't you say a word!" the Pardoner growled.

"Dunn arranged for the New Orleans Police to find your remains," the computer operator said, ignoring his fellow prisoner. "He got the discovery reported on TV.

And—"

In the blink of an eye, the Pardoner changed form. Now he was naked and hulking, his ebon scales gleaming with an iridescent sheen, as if they were coated with oil. Twin reptilian faces jutted from his single head. Hissing, ivory fangs bared, he raised a peculiar weapon, a length of wood edged with bits of black stone, and rushed Bellamy.

The FBI agent recoiled, firing. He *thought* he'd hit his assailant—with the massive creature virtually filling his field of vision, it was difficult to imagine how he could miss—but the strange sword hurtled at his throat anyway. He threw himself to one side, and the stroke missed him by a hair. He staggered, recovered his balance, and fired again, emptying the magazine.

The reptile man reeled backward. Concentric rings of shadow streamed outward from the holes in his chest.

Bellamy spun toward Chester. He expected to see the wraith in the wire-rimmed glasses pointing his snub-nosed revolver at him. But instead the Creole was fleeing through the wall dividing this room from the next. Maybe he wasn't carrying his gun tonight.

The FBI agent gave chase. Plunging through the partition, he found himself in a computer room much like the one in the werewolves' lair. The scrawny, gray-headed Creole lunged at the Pentium on the desk beside the window and laid his hands on the casing. Instantly his body became translucent, while his hands slid into the plastic as if they were being taken up on rollers. The hard drive chattered.

Bellamy realized that in another moment Chester would vanish into the machine, beyond his reach. He grabbed for the Creole's arm, but to no avail. His hand passed right through his enemy's flesh, just as a mortal's fingers would slide unimpeded through his own.

In desperation, Bellamy leaped across the Shroud. Fortunately the barrier was thin here, as it was in most Haunts, and he accomplished the shift in an instant. He swept the PC off the desk, then popped back into the Shadowlands.

Falling, the computer dragged Chester's arms down with it as if his hands were sealed in a concrete block, wrenching him off his feet. When it crashed to the floor, he gasped in pain.

Bellamy made another grab for him, and this time found solid flesh to seize. He jerked Chester across the floor, away from the damaged machine. The Creole's hands flailed out of the casing. For a moment they were as flat as sheets of paper.

Bellamy dived on top of him. The other *ibambo* thrashed, trying to get away. His struggling filled Bellamy with rage. He battered Chester with his pistol, then dropped it and snatched out his shortsword, poised the blade for a thrust at the Creole's throat.

Astarte's face, with its piercings, black makeup, and customary provocative half sneer, flashed before his inner eye. If he killed Chester, there'd be no one left to tell him where Dunn was lying in wait for her. He hammered his opponent's forehead with the pommel of the sword, stunning him momentarily, then pressed the blade up under Chester's chin.

Bellamy's Shadow writhed in disappointment.

Ignoring the unpleasant sensation as best he could, the FBI agent said, "Stop fighting or I'll cut your throat."

His glasses lost, his face a patchwork of shiny scrapes and bloodless gashes, Chester glared up at him. "All right."

"Dunn's plan. The local police found my body." The thought of such a thing, of *himself* lying cold and inert in a drawer in a morgue, made him queasy. "The story made the news. Tell me the rest."

"He also made it appear that the cops recovered the notebook you and the girl stole from my office."

Puzzled, Bellamy frowned. "What made him so sure Astarte didn't have it already? Never mind, that's not important. What was the point of all this?"

Despite the blade pressing into his neck, Chester smiled a nasty little smile. "Isn't it obvious? To lure your Quick friends out into the open. Dunn believes they'll go to the police station to steal the notebook. If so, they'll do it tonight, before the city authorities can identify your remains and involve the FBI in the case. Your Dancer colleague is lying in ambush."

Surely, Bellamy thought, his mortal allies weren't dumb enough to blunder into such a snare. But deep down, he knew otherwise. They *weren't* stupid, far from it, but by now they must be utterly desperate to get a line on the Atheist conspiracy before their supernatural enemies finished killing them off. Moreover, Astarte could be reckless and impetuous at the best of times, and at the moment she was no doubt distraught with rage and grief over his murder. *She* might well go after the notebook, even if Marilyn and the other Arcanists had sense enough to stay away.

The air seemed to grow hotter and thicker. The hissing of the Nihils took on a rhythmic, pulsing quality, as if they were laughing. "Which station house?" Bellamy asked.

Chester hesitated. "Give me your word that you'll let me live."

Bellamy pressed harder with the shortsword, slitting his captive's skin. Chester gasped and went rigid. "You'll live," the FBI agent said, "but only if you tell me within the next five seconds."

"All right!" Chester said. "It's the one on Elysian Fields, just a few blocks from the cemetery."

"I remember seeing it," Bellamy said. He wished he could stay and interrogate Chester a while longer. The little weasel undoubtedly had a lot more to tell him. But Astarte might already be in mortal danger.

His shadowself whispered that she was probably already dead.

Scowling, thrusting the ghastly thought out of his mind, Bellamy bashed Chester once again. The Creole thrashed and then went limp, his head lolling to the side. His captor watched him for another moment, making sure he was really out, then sprang to his feet.

The shaman's howling died away. New voices murmured from the same direction. Evidently someone else was ascending the stairs.

Perhaps somebody had heard the fight, or missed Chester and the two-faced creature, and was coming to investigate. In any event, it was clear that Bellamy couldn't exit the way he came in, not right now, and with Astarte in danger, he couldn't hide and wait until the coast was clear, either. He ran at the exterior wall and leaped through it, out into the night.

He plummeted as fast and hit the ground as hard as a mortal. He tried to roll out of the fall, but something went wrong. With a burst of pain, his right leg snapped.

For a second, panic yammered through his mind. Grimacing, he suppressed it. He knew how to fix this. Antoine had taught him. Trying not to think about the sentries who at any moment might notice him sprawled on the grass, he drank in the residue of sorrow which pervaded the property, then willed the energy to heal him.

His leg straightened. He seemed to feel the two ends of a broken bone align themselves and fuse together. When the pain dwindled, he scrambled to his feet and then through the bars of the wrought-iron fence.

No one shouted after him, or fired a shot. He'd gotten away free and clear—

The sky roared.

Startled, Bellamy looked up. Waves of blackness streamed out of the north, occluding the stars. Then the wind smashed into him, nearly knocking him off his feet. Bits of hot, flying grit, so tiny he couldn't see them, cut him as if he were caught in a sandstorm.

At first he thought a tornado had touched down, or that a hurricane had blown ashore. Then he noticed that the trees weren't writhing, nor was the litter skittering down the street. Whatever the nature of the storm, it only existed in the Underworld.

Which was good. It would make it easier to get where he was going. Leaning into the wind, his ragged coat streaming out behind him, he staggered forward.

Then his shadowself flowed into the forefront of his consciousness like a tide of sewage surging down a pipe.

Appalled by the malice and perversity, the sheer insanity that he now perceived dwelling inside him, Bellamy dropped to his knees, his throat and belly clenching with the dry heaves. He felt his awareness dwindling as the parasite fought him for control of his body. He tried to scream, *Not now!* But his mouth wouldn't form the words.

Thirty-Four

Shuddering, her heart pounding, Astarte stared down the hall at the huge, black beast that was Dunn. Emotions ground together in her mind. Terror. Hatred of Bellamy's killer, and outrage at seeing his body used for a plaything. Guilt that this situation was a setup after all, and she'd pressured Marilyn to march right into it.

Instinctively she clutched at the latter feelings, embracing them to hold total panic at bay. She slipped her hand into her pocket and gripped the cloth bag.

Dunn's inhuman leer stretched wider.

"Even if the charm has any magic left," Marilyn quavered, "that one won't work on a creature like him."

Astarte fumbled with the catch on her purse, which stubbornly refused to yield and grant her access to her pistol. Dunn still just stood and watched, toying with them, drawing out the moment. "Oh, Marilyn," Astarte said, "I'm sorry!"

"How comforting," Marilyn sneered, slipping her hand inside her garish plaid sports coat. "No, forgive me, I didn't mean—"

Dropping to all fours, transforming in an instant, Dunn became a creature more akin to a true wolf, but six feet tall at the shoulder. He charged, fast as a cheetah.

Astarte had once stood on a railroad crossing while an Amtrak train hurtled at her, frantically blowing its horn, just to see what it would feel like. She flashed on that moment as she recoiled.

But Marilyn stood her ground. Her hand whipped out of her coat with *another* hand, a brown, twisted claw like the appendage of a mummy, clutched inside of it. To Astarte's amazement, the severed hand grasped a stubby white candle, and somehow, the taper was alight. As she recognized the grisly artifact for what it was, a talisman called a Hand of Glory, the occultist brandished it over her head and jabbered something in Latin.

The black wolf stopped suddenly, stumbled back as if he'd struck an invisible wall. Astarte remembered the story Bellamy had told her, of how Marilyn had fended off another supernatural attacker with a mystical device called the Cross of Hermes.

Still grinning, his pale eyes gleaming, Dunn drove forward again, more slowly this time, struggling against the power Marilyn had raised against him. He moved as if he were shoving his way through a thick hedge. His heavy claws dug into the dingy linoleum for traction. Astarte smelled his musky, zoo-cage scent.

The flame burned dazzlingly bright, consuming the candle with unnatural speed. Molten wax flowed down over Marilyn's hand, but she didn't seem to notice the blistering heat. "Run," she said. "The ward won't hold for long."

"I can't," Astarte said. She finally managed to tear her purse open and take out her gun. Her hands were still shaking so badly that she had trouble releasing the safety. "This is all my fault."

"Don't be stupid," Marilyn said. The mummified hand began to crumble, showering flakes of dried flesh. Dunn pushed a yard closer. "There are police downstairs. Send them up here."

Astarte shook her head. The cops would never arrive in time, and even if they did, they'd probably freeze or run away as soon as they got a look at Dunn, just like everybody did the first time. Holding her automatic in both hands, the way Bellamy had taught her, she sighted down the barrel. After a moment her hands stopped shaking, and then she fired.

The gun barked. She hit the black, leering beast about half the time. Dunn twitched at the impacts, but didn't go down, or even falter in his efforts to close the remaining distance. Blood only flowed from the holes in his shoulders and muzzle for a few seconds, and then the wounds closed.

Why, thought Astarte despairingly, hadn't she and the Arcanists equipped themselves with silver bullets? But it simply hadn't seemed feasible, not while they were on the run. And for all she knew, it wouldn't have made a difference anyway.

The pistol was empty. She ejected the spent clip and rooted in her handbag for the spare. The candle blinked out, and the Hand of Glory disintegrated into dust. Dunn lunged forward, and, strangely calm in that final moment, she realized there wasn't enough time left to reload.

Flecks of foam flying from his gaping jaws, his ivory fangs gleaming, Dunn sprang at Marilyn. The occultist reflexively thrust out her hands to fend him off. And something exploded into existence inside and around her, like a halo.

Astarte didn't know what it was, or how she was even perceiving it. She had a muddled impression of a momentary blaze of light and a noise like trumpets blaring, but knew that in actuality, neither had occurred. But it was obvious that *something* real had happened. Because when Dunn ended his leap, he landed beside Bellamy's mangled body, back down by the entrance to the Evidence Room. He hadn't been slammed through the intervening distance, either. Somehow, he was simply *there*.

Marilyn stared down the corridor, and then at her own hands, with an expression of utter astonishment on her sweaty, bespectacled face. "What's happened?" Astarte demanded.

Marilyn said hesitantly, "Something—the stress of the moment—finally woke up my power."

His pale eyes glowing, Dunn snarled. To Astarte, it sounded like a challenge, as if the werewolf had decided that Marilyn was an adversary as opposed to mere prey. The monster charged.

Extending her arms again, Marilyn jabbered words and phrases in what, to Astarte's untrained ear, sounded like a miscellany of foreign languages. Now, fast as Dunn's legs were moving, he didn't appear to be covering any more ground. It was as if he were running on a treadmill.

Astarte abruptly recalled that she was a combatant too. And damn it, one properly placed shot *could* incapacitate Dunn. That was how Bellamy had escaped him on the night of Waxman's death. She rammed the fresh clip into her gun.

Sighting down the corridor, she found it surprisingly difficult to shoot. At certain moments the hallway looked a mile long, and Dunn was only a tiny speck at the end of it. At others, she felt as if she were moving in slow motion, and needed a minute to pull the trigger or shift her aim an iota. Evidently Marilyn was playing tricks with both space and time to keep Dunn from reaching them, and unfortunately, the fallout was affecting her as well.

What was even worse was that, despite the Arcanist's best efforts, Dunn was gradually driving forward. By the time Astarte exhausted the clip, she could see, during those instants when the corridor looked relatively normal, that the werewolf had covered half the distance. "Can't you just nuke him?" she asked.

"No," Marilyn croaked. "I don't know how. I don't know how I'm doing *this*. I have the talent, but not the training to use it effectively. So run while I delay him. You've got a chance now."

"Fuck that," Astarte said. She dropped her empty gun, slipped her hand under Marilyn's hideous jacket, and pulled the Arcanist's pistol from her shoulder holster.

She resumed firing. Missed three times in a row. Wondered fleetingly why the noise didn't draw the cops. Maybe Dunn or one of his buddies had magically soundproofed the area so he could make his kill undisturbed.

Every stride seemed to bring the werewolf a little nearer, his jerky, flickering progress resembling motion in a silent film. Marilyn said, "I can't—"

The distortions of space and time ceased abruptly; everything looked normal again. Dunn pounced, and his jaws snapped shut on Marilyn's shoulder. Tossing his head, hurling spatters of blood around the hallway, he jerked the Arcanist up and down like a terrier shaking a rat. Now shooting at point-blank range, Astarte fired bullet after bullet at his head.

Some hit him, but once again, it wasn't enough. Dropping Marilyn's shredded body, Dunn leered at his remaining quarry with pink, bloodstained fangs.

Whimpering, wet with her companion's gore, Astarte stepped backward and squeezed the trigger. The automatic clicked, out of ammunition.

Thirty-Five

Kneeling in the howling wind, Bellamy retched at the spite and lunacy, the fantasies of destruction, torture, and masochism, boiling in his head. Chopping up his ex-wife with an ax. Returning to FBI headquarters and blowing away Hanson, Byrd, and every other condescending bastard who'd doubted his sanity. Tying Astarte to a bed and ripping the surgical steel rings and pins out of her piercings, one at a time. Burning his own genitals with a cigarette lighter.

Dear God, if this was who he was...

But no. It wasn't. His shadowself was force-feeding him these feelings and images, to distract him while it wrested control of his body. He had to focus past them and fight the parasite off. Already bereft of his voice, he lurched up and down, pounding the pavement with his fists in a mute gesture of defiance.

His vision swam, and the night grew darker. The Shadow was claiming his eyes for its own exclusive use. Trying to spur himself to fight even harder, Bellamy imagined Astarte dangling helpless in Dunn's talons. The thought of it filled him with desperate fury, though an undercurrent of gloating pleasure oozed beneath his outrage. He hammered his hands to pulp.

At last something—the thought of Astarte in danger, the physical pain, or the combination of the two—blunted the force of the psychic attack. Barracks Street wavered back into focus, and he felt firmly in control of his limbs and voice once more. Giggling, satisfied because at least it had hurt him, and might even have delayed him long enough to cost the woman he loved her life, his shadowself scuttled back into its hiding place in the depths of his soul.

Unwilling to take any more time to quiet the pain in his hands, Bellamy climbed to his feet, then staggered as the wind nearly knocked him down again. Though as forceful as before, it no longer gusted exclusively from the north but changed direction from one moment to the next. The shifts made it even harder to maintain his balance. Squinting against the barrage of invisible grit, he ran up the street.

A Nihil in the pavement ahead of him yawned, and a Spectre resembling a huge white octopus began to squirm through what, for it, was a narrow opening. The doomshade's body was composed entirely of human heads, fused together and gibbering cacophonous pleas for deliverance.

Desperate to get past the creature before it finished heaving itself from the Tempest into the Shadowlands, Bellamy put on a burst of speed. As he circled the Spectre, it lashed a tentacle at him, the heads comprising it opening their mouths to bite. He ducked, the attack whizzed over his head, and then he was out of range. The Spectre's myriad voices screamed curses after him.

A few strides farther on, a female ghost in a golden mask and a long crimson gown struggled toward the refuge of a derelict three-story house. Other wraiths peered out the windows, beckoning and crying encouragement, until a particularly powerful blast of wind caught her. She twirled like a top and then her body frayed into streamers of ectoplasm, which disintegrated in the gale.

Horrified, Bellamy stared at the empty space she'd occupied. Evidently the abrasive properties of the storm itself, what he'd ignorantly taken for the sting of airborne sand, could flay an *ibambo* to pieces and send him to the Void. Dashing on, he tried not to imagine the same thing happening to him.

Intent on making headway despite the wind and the horde of Spectres slithering into the Shadowlands, he had little attention to spare for events on the warm side of the Shroud. But eventually he noticed the disturbances breaking out in the houses he passed. Shouting. Sobbing. Dogs barking and dishes smashing. Farther afield, car horns blared. Though the living couldn't experience the storm directly, they were reacting to its presence nonetheless.

Every time Bellamy reached an intersection, he peered up and down the cross street. To get to the station house quickly, he was going to have to hitch a ride. But it was late, there was little traffic, and the few occupied vehicles he did see were traveling too fast for him to board, or to cross over into the Skinlands and attempt to flag them down.

His face and hands smarted as if they'd been dipped in acid. Worse, he felt a numbing trickle of Oblivion flowing inside him, eroding the bonds that held him together.

For all he knew, Astarte had been wary enough to avoid Dunn's trap, and in any case, Bellamy couldn't help her if the wind tore him to pieces. Maybe the only sane course was to take shelter from the storm.

No. Some instinct told him that Astarte *did* need him, and right now. Ignoring the urgings of his fear, he staggered on, and finally, a few yards beyond Dauphine Street, spied an old white rust-dappled Thunderbird with rocketship tail fins just pulling away from the curb.

He flung himself at it, willing his body to become completely insubstantial. With a shriek, the gale shifted direction. The blast of wind caught him in midair, nudging him to one side, and for a second he was certain it would spoil his leap. Then he plunged though the side of the car onto the stained, ripped upholstery of the back seat, which to his hypersensitive nose reeked of cats. He nearly tumbled on through it before he managed to solidify himself. As it was, he wound up with an arm and a leg stuck inside it. The interpenetration hurt for a second, until his body adjusted.

To his surprise, he could still feel the wind, but at least the T-bird's body blunted its force. He no longer had the impression that his substance might unravel at any moment. Sitting up, he looked at his unwitting chauffeur.

She was a tall, brown-haired woman in her thirties, not fat, but big-boned and solidly built. She had a pretty face, with clear skin and apple cheeks, and something about her gave Bellamy the impression that she probably had a pleasant smile, though she was glowering now. She snapped on the radio, then punched the buttons, unable to find anything she wanted to hear. Animal-rights leaflets, bundled together with rubber bands, sat on the seat beside her.

Concentrating, Bellamy projected himself across the Shroud. The upholstery remained just as torn but didn't look nearly as filthy on the mortal side of the barrier. "I need your help," he said.

She slammed on the brakes, and, as the Thunderbird lurched to a halt, twisted around to gawk at him. "Get out of the car!" she said.

"I can't. This is an emergency. I need—"

She jumped out of the T-bird, tore open the back door, grabbed him, and started to drag him out. When he tried to push her away, pain exploded up his forearms. He'd forgotten injuring his hands.

In that instant of paralysis, she hauled him halfway through the door. He bashed at her with his forearm, breaking her hold, then, forcing his sore, stiff fingers to obey him, yanked his shortsword out of its scabbard. Seeing the weapon, she turned to run. He leaped out, grabbed her by the shoulder, and pressed the sword against her neck. She froze.

"I'm sorry," he said. "I truly don't want to hurt you, but I have to get to the police station north of here on Elysian Fields, right now, and you're going to drive me."

"You're kidnapping me so I can drive you to the *police?*" she asked incredulously.

"Believe it or not," Bellamy said wryly.

"Why don't you just take the car?"

He wished he could. It would spare her the stress of the journey and him the hassle of keeping her under control. But he was afraid he wouldn't be able to hold himself in the mortal world long enough to drive the entire distance. "I've got my reasons. Now, we're both going to get back in, very slowly. If you give me any trouble, I'll cut you."

They climbed in, and she put the old Ford in gear. Bellamy moved the shortsword a couple inches away from the woman's throat. "Drive fast," he said.

"Don't worry," she said, accelerating. "I want to get this over with. What happened to you anyway?"

Prompted by the question to take stock of himself, Bellamy noticed that, flayed by the storm, his hands were covered with tiny scratches, and that on this side of the Shroud, the cuts *bled*. For some reason, the sight of the blood captivated him, just as the hot Skinlands flame had. He had to wrench his gaze away. "Let's just say it's been a rough night."

"How did you get into the car without me seeing you?"

"I'm a ghost. I'm invisible to the living most of the time."

She hesitated, then said, "Okay." Obviously humoring him.

"When I was alive, I wouldn't have believed it either. But you will in a minute, because I'm going to disappear. I'm warning you because I don't want you to freak out and lose control of the car. Or to think I'm gone. I'll still be right behind you, ready to hurt you if you deviate from the program."

"I understand," the animal-rights activist said. Her jaw dropping, she goggled dramatically at the rearview mirror. "Oh my God, oh my God, you *did* disappear!"

The atrocious overacting made Bellamy laugh. After hours of apprehension punctuated with interludes of outright terror, the release of tension came as a blissful relief. "Sorry," he said, "but I haven't done it yet. *Now* I'm doing it." Relaxing his will, he allowed the persistent tug of death to whisk him back into the Underworld.

Despite his warning, she jerked the steering wheel. The T-bird almost crashed into a parked Isuzu pickup before she got it under control again. "Oh, shit, oh shit," she chattered, her face white as paper. Her aura flamed bright orange, and waves of dread poured off her. Feeling like a ghoul, Bellamy nevertheless drank in the emotion, using the power to heal his lacerated skin and broken hands. Then he reloaded his gun.

"I can't believe this," the driver said abruptly. "You think *you're* having a bad day. First, my landlord wants to evict me for having too many cats. There's nothing in the lease that says I can't have cats. They aren't hurting anything. Next, my editor orders me to stop writing so much about cruelty to animals, or the paper will drop me. It's the *pet* column, what did they expect? Then I find out that the shelter wants to start gassing strays after just a week, and nobody else on the committee even has a *problem* with it. And last but not least, a ghost, a fucking *ghost*—"

As she rambled on, her fiery orange halo faded. Bellamy guessed that her monologue was helping her control her fear. Now that he'd healed and refreshed himself, he was all for it, particularly if it kept her from having an accident. He peered through the windshield, looking for the station house, but the streaming, roaring darkness kept him from seeing very far ahead.

"—think I must be nuts," the woman continued bitterly. "I'm wasting my life on this, and nobody gives a damn. Nothing changes. Well, screw it. Screw all of them." She flipped up the turn-signal lever and stepped on the brake. Abruptly Bellamy spied the station house immediately ahead. The animal-rights activist pulled into the parking lot, then drove up to the public entrance.

To avoid stepping out into the full force of the storm, Bellamy crossed the Shroud. The driver flinched at his reappearance. "Thanks for the ride," he said. He climbed out, sheathed his sword, and then, after a moment's hesitation, added, "Don't give up on your cause if you really care about it. It turns out that caring is just about the only thing that matters." He strode toward the doors.

After a moment, the activist jumped out and hurried after him. Her heels clicked on the tarmac.

"What are you doing?" he asked. "I can pretty much guarantee that it won't do any good to report me to the cops."

"I know that," she said. "I'm not a *complete* idiot. I just want to see what happens next."

"Unfortunately, from your vantage point, not much," Bellamy said, opening the door for her. Inside the reception area, an excited crowd was jabbering at the sergeant and cadets behind the desk and at one another. "I'm just going to blink out—"

Gunshots banged faintly somewhere above his head. He expected the mortals to react, but nobody did. Evidently a person needed the sharp ears of a wraith to hear the muffled sound, at least with half a dozen people yammering in the foreground.

In any event, his instincts had been correct. Astarte needed him right now. He gripped his companion's forearm. "Hey!" she said.

"Listen to me," he said. "Somebody's being murdered on one of the upper floors. Get every cop in the building up there. Don't take no for an answer." Making sure no mortal would try to stop him, he slipped back into the Shadowlands, then dashed deeper into the building.

It seemed to take forever to find a staircase. As he scrambled upward, he smelled gun smoke, Dunn's animal reek, and a foul, rotten stench. Heard breath rasping, hearts pounding, and Marilyn chanting an incantation in what might have been Greek or Latin. After a hiatus, the shooting recommenced.

He rounded another corner, then faltered, taking in the vista before him.

Despite their disguises and the fact that he'd come up behind them, Bellamy recognized Astarte and Marilyn instantly. The former was doing the shooting, and, her arms thrust out, the latter was seemingly working magic. The length of hallway in front of her appeared to stretch and flicker from one moment to the next. Like Astarte's, the Arcanist's aura burned orange, red, and purple, but it was also shot through with brilliant sparkles, evidently a side effect of her display of mystic power.

Just a few feet further on, dwarfing the humans, loomed a black-furred creature, perhaps a prehistoric version of a wolf, with pale, luminous eyes. Bellamy had never seen anything exactly like it before, but he was all but certain the thing was Dunn, wearing a shape that could operate comfortably in the relatively cramped confines of the corridor. Evidently Marilyn's magic was supposed to hold him back, but it wasn't doing the job. The grooves and punctures his claws had left in the linoleum revealed his arduous progress toward his prey. His ivory fangs bared, he struggled forward another step.

Bellamy reached for his pistol, and then, for some reason, his eyes locked on what should have been the least significant element of the scene, a stinking, mangled cadaver lying at the far end of the hall, near the sign that read, EVIDENCE ROOM. He stared at it, repelled yet captivated, and after a moment, despite the burns and bloating, the blisters studding the greenish skin, recognized himself.

He shuddered, and then, his mission forgotten, started toward the corpse. To touch it. To cradle it in his arms. To caress it and gaze into its milky eyes as if his love and anguish could wash away its injuries and restore it to life.

He scrambled past Marilyn and Dunn. For a moment the corridor looked a mile long. Then the occultist said, "I can't—" and the passage snapped back to normal.

Bellamy heard the Black Spiral Dancer pounce. Heard the creature seize Marilyn and lash her about, rending her flesh and breaking bones, while Astarte plinked desperately away. Smelled the rich, coppery odor of the Arcanist's blood.

The *ibambo* faltered. What has happening was terrible, and it was precisely what he'd come to prevent. He should do something about it. But it was his *body*, the vessel of his *life*, in easy reach now that Marilyn's spell had dissolved. Feeling as if he were dreaming—for after all, he couldn't *really* be committing such a selfish, treacherous act—he continued forward.

Marilyn's body thumped to the floor. Astarte's gun clicked, out of ammunition, and she whimpered.

That tiny sound, so fraught with terror and despair, snapped Bellamy out of his trance. He whirled, leaped across the Shroud, whipped out his gun, and fired.

The first bullet took Dunn in the hindquarters. The werewolf yelped, staggered, lurched around, then faltered as if in surprise. Bellamy had the distinct impression that Dunn recognized him despite the alterations to his appearance. Taking advantage of the monster's hesitation, he squeezed off a second shot. That one hit Dunn in the chest.

The colossal wolf sprang. Trying to dodge, Bellamy also threw up his arm to shield his throat and head. Dunn's enormous fangs snapped shut on the limb, shearing through skin and muscle, and the ghost tumbled down with the beast on top of him.

Bellamy kept firing. Dunn's body jerked with every shot. Though evidently less deadly to werewolves than silver, perhaps the darksteel bullets were doing more damage than less exotic ammunition.

But it wasn't enough. Dunn kept attacking as fiercely as before. In another second or two, he was going to sever Bellamy's arm. The wraith tried to escape back across the Shroud, only to discover that he couldn't make the transition. Perhaps his Shadow had momentarily usurped control of his Arcanos and was using it to hold him in harm's way.

As he fired his last shot, Astarte ran up to Dunn and started battering him with her gun. For a second Bellamy hated her. While he distracted the werewolf, she should have run away. As it was, they were *all* going to die.

Then he heard rushing footsteps, rumbling up the stairs. The animal-rights activist had evidently managed to convince the officers on the ground floor that something was amiss.

Releasing Bellamy's mangled forearm, Dunn raised his enormous head and peered in the direction of the noise. Ordinarily he probably wouldn't be afraid of ordinary humans armed with conventional weapons, but with the malignant power of darksteel now searing his wounds, perhaps he questioned his ability to handle them.

He glared down at Bellamy as if evaluating whether he had time to finish him off. Trying to look as ferocious as a supine man with a shredded limb could, the *ibambo* brandished his pistol, reminding Dunn of its existence. He hoped the monster hadn't been counting his shots.

Dunn snarled, wheeled, and dashed away. His form blurred and became increasingly translucent. After a few seconds Bellamy couldn't see him at all.

Bellamy clutched his arm in an inadequate attempt to stanch the spurting blood. Despite the severity of his wounds, he didn't feel a tremendous amount of pain, just a cold shakiness that warned him he was going into shock. He tried to heal himself, but nothing happened. Maybe some wraith powers were more difficult to use on the bright side of the Shroud.

Her aura glowing orange, pink, and blue, Astarte dropped to her knees beside him. "Frank?" she breathed.

Pleased that she'd recognized him despite his disguise, and that she wasn't shrinking from him, Bellamy did his best to give her a reassuring smile. "Yeah. I can't stay. I have to go where I can fix my arm, but I'll be back. You have to get out of here. If the police take you into custody, Dunn and the other Atheists will know where to find you."

At that instant, excited voices sounded from the far end of the hall. Astarte looked wildly about, obviously realizing that, with officers approaching from both directions, she was boxed in. "Shit!" she said.

"Give me your talisman," Marilyn croaked.

Startled, Astarte and Bellamy jerked around. Lying in a pool of her own gore, the Arcanist extended a trembling hand. "You're alive," the FBI agent said stupidly.

"You, on the other hand, are *dead*." Marilyn replied. "Amazing. After all these years of groping, I'm seeing everything, learning everything, all at once. But there's no time to talk about it. The charm."

Astarte fumbled a little brown cotton bag out of her pocket. Bellamy caught a pungent aroma of spices leaking from inside the cloth. Marilyn produced a similar pouch of her own. Pressing the two together between her bloody palms, she mumbled.

The glittering motes in her aura, which had never vanished entirely, now multiplied and shone dazzlingly bright, particularly around her hands.

When she opened them, the bags were gone. An instant later, the first contingent of cops dashed around the corner. Bellamy winced, but the officers ignored him and his companions, stepping around them without seeming to notice they were doing it, directing their attention exclusively to his corpse, the spatters of blood, and the claw marks on the linoleum.

"Now *this* is an invisibility spell," Marilyn said. "Unfortunately, it won't hold for long. Help me up."

No doubt realizing it could be fatal to move her friend, Astarte grimaced and hauled the Arcanist to her feet. They wrapped their arms around each other.

"Can you really walk?" Astarte asked.

"Yes," Marilyn gasped. "No problem. Just help me to the car."

"You won't see me, but I'll follow you out," Bellamy said. "And then I'll take you somewhere safe." Astarte and Marilyn staggered away, leaving a trail of the Arcanist's blood behind them, and he tried once again to reenter the Underworld. This time, it was easy. He drank in some of the emotional charge crackling in the air and directed the energy into his arm. After a few seconds, his wounds began to close.

Thirty-Six

Still spotted with a few stray spatters of Marilyn's blood, Astarte paced back and forth across the musty music room, treading obliviously on the top of a pothole-sized Nihil. The white Skinlands candles which one of the Queen's servants had found grudgingly doled out a measure of wavering light, barely enough for a mortal to make out the shape of the grubby cello case in the corner, or the features of the bust of Mozart on the piano. The withered orchids in the porcelain vase on the table still gave off a trace of perfume so faint than even a wraith could barely smell it.

His wounded arm itching, Bellamy stood and watched the mortal girl. He wanted to talk to her as much as he'd ever wanted anything, but he was afraid to. Afraid that now that the desperation of battle and flight was over, she'd cringe from the creature he'd become. Finally he projected himself across the Shroud, materializing behind her back. He felt shy about popping out of nowhere in her view, even though she'd seen him do it before. "Hi," he said.

She jerked, but it was hardly perceptible. She'd suppressed the reaction just as he might have expected, knowing how she hated appearing rattled or vulnerable. She turned, looked him up and down, and said, "I've finally done it. This is going to kill my mom."

"What?"

"I'm dating a black guy."

"It's a disguise," he said. "My friend Titus will turn me back—"

She threw her arms around him. Embracing her in turn, he kissed her. The moment held the promise of exquisite pleasure, but he found that he couldn't experience it fully. If he surrendered to the sensation, his control of his Arcanos would waver, and death would drag him back into the Shadowlands.

After a time he realized she was shuddering, and lifted his mouth away from hers.

"Are you all right?" he asked.

"Yeah," Astarte stammered, her teeth chattering, "it's just that you're so *cold*."

He felt a pang of shame and confusion. "I'm sorry." He released her from his arms, but she only moved back slightly and took his hands in his.

"It's okay," she said. "I kind of like it."

Not knowing what to say to that, he asked, "How did you recognize me?"

She snorted. "After all the shit we've been through together? What a moron question."

"If you say so. Anyway, I see you've got a new look, too. I like it."

"Well, tough. As soon as I get my stuff back, I'm going to change back into my old self, too." She hesitated. "Marilyn was right, wasn't she? You are a ghost."

"My new associates say *ibambo*, or Restless. But yes."

"What's it like?"

At a loss for an adequate answer, he shrugged. "It's like existing in two worlds at the same time, the living one and the land of spirits. They overlap. So far, the wraith world is full of black magic and demons, but I'm hoping I just arrived at a bad time."

Her eyes shone. "I'll bet it's great. And this is really the Ghost Queen's palace?"

"One of them. It's full of *abambo*, going about their business by the greenish glow of their lamps. You just can't see them or the light either. But they'll protect you and the Arcanists too, as soon as they get here. Ordinarily ghosts don't have much use for occultists and parapsychologists, but they're frantic to get the werewolf notebook translated."

Astarte's mouth twisted. "I just wish they could have started protecting Marilyn a few hours sooner. She finally gets what she's wanted her whole life, and then Dunn tears her apart a minute later."

"I thought she was going to die in the car," Bellamy said. "Since we made it here, she's got a chance. Titus, one of the Court magicians, gave her an infusion of life energy, the same way he healed my arm."

Astarte turned Bellamy's forearm, inspecting the raw-looking scars. "It doesn't look like he did that great a job."

"Apparently werewolf bites are tough to fix. They're poison or something. But I'm okay. The marks will go away when I get a chance to sleep."

"I feel like such a piece of garbage," Astarte said.

"Why?"

"*I* goaded Marilyn into walking into the trap. *I* got her hurt. I shouldn't feel anything but worried and rotten. And I do feel that way, but I'm happy too, because I found you again."

Bellamy remembered how he'd stood idly by, entranced by the sight of his corpse while Dunn mangled the Arcanist, and experienced his own pang of guilt. "I understand what you mean. But nobody's infallible. You made what you thought was the right move, and Marilyn chose to make it with you. I don't think she'll hold you to blame for the way it worked out."

"I hope not," Astarte said, shivering, "even though I do myself." She extricated her hands from Bellamy's grip and rubbed them together. "Sorry. I need these back for a little bit."

"It's okay," Bellamy said, doing his best to conceal a foolish sense of loss. The relentless pull of the Underworld intensified. "Uh oh. I don't know how much longer I can stay visible to you."

"Don't go yet," Astarte pleaded. "It's only been a few minutes. You've hardly told me anything."

"It isn't something I can control," Bellamy said. "Not yet. But I'll learn. I'll fix things so we can be together all the time."

"You'd better," she said, opening her arms. He tried to hug her, but his limbs passed right through her, and vice versa. She scowled. "Oh, great, Frank. Great timing."

"I'm sorry," Bellamy said, even though he knew she could no longer hear him. He kissed her softly on the cheek.

"Sickening," rasped a guttural voice. "Thank the Orishas I'm not a mammal."

Bellamy jerked around to see Antoine and Titus standing in the doorway. The gator seemed to leer. The hoodoo man, his wizened face painted half gold and half silver, regarded his fellow humans with a somber expression.

"What are you people, voyeurs?" Bellamy asked sourly. Evidently surmising that he wasn't going to rematerialize in the next few seconds, Astarte stalked to the piano, sat down on the bench, folded back the lid, and started glumly depressing the yellowed keys. About half of them still produced a note, the others, a dull click.

"All *abambo* spy on the Quick," Antoine replied. "And if you insist on hanging out on the other side of the Shroud, we'll peep at you, too. Get used to it."

"We only arrived a moment ago," Titus said. "We had to find you because the Queen is ready to hear your report." He led his fellow wraiths into the corridor.

"It's about time," Bellamy said.

Titus glanced about, making sure no one else was in earshot. "The Maelstrom had a bad effect on her, even here in the Haunt, where she should have been immune. At first she experienced something like a crippling migraine, and later, it was more like epilepsy."

"It all just keeps getting better, doesn't it?" Antoine growled.

"Maelstrom," Bellamy said. "I assume that was the storm. The wind that could cut us to ribbons and called the Sinkinda out of their holes."

"Yes," Titus said. "The raw power of Oblivion, streaming out of the Tempest and across the Shadowlands. Caught outside a Haunt, you were lucky to survive it. Of course, that was only a little one."

"You're kidding," Bellamy said. "What triggers it, anyway?"

"No one knows for certain," Titus replied. "Or at least my teachers didn't. The huge storms tend to occur at times of great upheaval and calamity. The most devastating one in recent memory began when the atomic bomb fell on Hiroshima. Before it ran its course, a dragon rose from the Labyrinth and killed the Emperor of Stygia himself, not that we Africans were inclined to mourn for *him*. Some sages believe that when hordes of souls cry out as one in fear, misery, or despair, the Void answers, and a Maelstrom is its reply."

"My god," Bellamy said, moving to one side of the corridor to allow a cloaked warrior with a rhino horn jutting from his forehead to pass, "could that be it?"

"Could what be what?" Antoine asked.

"The Atheist atrocities are creating 'fear, misery, and despair.' Shaking people's faith in God, the government, and their neighbors. Maybe the point of it all is to create these storms."

"Hm," said Titus, frowning. "No, I can't see it. Even though Les Invisibles claim to enjoy a special understanding with the Spectres, Maelstroms are just as dangerous to them as they are to us. I can't imagine how such a ploy would help the loa seize the throne."

"I keep telling you," Bellamy replied, "your local rebels are hooked in to something bigger. The masterminds heading up the conspiracy brought them in because they wanted their expertise at possessing the Quick. That's one of the things I learned tonight. I'm guessing it's the *real* Atheists who need Maelstroms. It's just our bad luck that their goals are such that they mesh well with Geffard's ambitions."

"I suppose it's possible," said Titus dubiously. Antoine grunted.

They turned down the passage leading to Marie's throne room. Drumming pattered in the distance, and Bellamy caught the fragrance of incense, sandalwood tonight. The guards flanking the entrance, one male, one female, both armed with sabers and CAR-15 assault rifles, stood up straighter upon glimpsing Titus.

After a few more steps, Bellamy said, "Did you hear me promise to fix things so that Astarte and I can be together like a normal man and woman?"

"Yes," Titus said.

"Can you teach me how to do it?"

Titus hesitated, then said, "As you gain skill with your Arcanos, you'll be able to journey to the bright side of the Shroud for longer periods. Your appearance there will become increasingly lifelike. And yet, there will always be differences that set you apart. Even if you steal some poor mortal's body, or somehow manage to reanimate your own, the scent of death will cling to you."

Bellamy grimaced. "But you just said yourself that there are spells and secrets you don't know."

"That's true," Titus answered, "but—"

"Then I'll find a way. I hope you'll help me."

Titus sighed. "I owe you my life, my friend. I'll do whatever I can for you. But first we have to save the Queen."

They stepped through the substance of the doors into the long, torch-lit hall. The Nihil cracks in the walls hissed louder than on Bellamy's previous visit, perhaps an aftereffect of the Maelstrom. Enthroned before the two dark idols, Marie sat as erect and impassive as usual. But Bellamy sensed a fragility, a brittleness about her, as if a loud noise might shatter her into a thousand pieces.

He, Titus, and Antoine salaamed at the foot of the three-step dais. "Rise," said Marie, her husky voice rougher than usual. "You came back quickly, Mr. Bellamy. I thought it would take weeks to infiltrate Geffard's counsels and uncover his secrets."

"Actually," the FBI agent said, "that plan fell apart. Antoine was right, I ran into a situation I hadn't anticipated and couldn't bluff my way through. But I managed to go on investigating anyway, and I found out quite a bit." He gave her a terse account of his adventures.

By the time he finished, Antoine's tail was twitching back and forth, and his clawed feet dug at the floor. Had he not been a wraith, they would have gouged and splintered the wood. "Those back-stabbing bastards!" he snarled.

"Your orders, Your Majesty?" Titus asked.

Marie raised her hand, gestured vaguely, and let it fall again. "I don't know. I…I have none as yet."

"*What?*"Antoine exploded. Bellamy was similarly aghast.

"I told you," said Marie, "I need detailed information before I can decide anything."

"I established that Geffard and the werewolves are working together to take over the city," Bellamy said. "I found their base of operations. What the heck do you want?"

"Don't take that tone with me," snapped the Queen.

"I'm sorry," Bellamy replied, his jaw clenched. "No disrespect intended. But—"

"Can you tell me how many werewolves there are? How many of these Bane demons they can conjure into the Shadowlands? How many *abambo* Geffard commands? Or the true nature of the two-faced spirit you encountered? If not, then our tactical disadvantage is nearly as great as before. Perhaps we should hold off acting until your Arcanist friends translate the notebook, or until I try again to petition the Orishas."

Though he knew her hesitancy was the fault of her enemies' magic, at that moment Bellamy could have slapped her. "Try to understand, Your Majesty. We can't afford to wait on that or anything else. Chester saw me poking around Les Invisibles' stronghold. When he comes to, he'll tell Geffard we're on to him."

Marie frowned. "You should have destroyed the man."

"Maybe," said Bellamy, "but it's a moot point now. What matters is that if you give Geffard a chance to act, he'll move the voudoun dolls somewhere else, somewhere we can't find them, and then the curse will go on making you sick. He might even launch an all-out assault on us thinking we're about to do the same to him. Trust me, no matter how spotty our intelligence is, we'll be a lot better off if we hit him before he has a chance to deploy his troops for battle."

The Queen looked at Titus and Antoine. "What do you think?"

"I'm with Frank," Antoine said. "Shit, I'll go farther. If we don't get rid of Geffard right now, within the next few hours, we might as well take a running jump into the Void and save him the trouble of sending us there."

"I agree," Titus said.

"But will the people stand for it?" Marie asked. "They love Geffard." Her mouth twisted. "He gives them *entertainments*. And we still don't have any proof."

"If the testimony of a lowly white Lemure like me isn't good enough," Bellamy said sardonically, "then maybe this will help." Hoping the sight of the ugly thing would jolt her out of her funk, he pulled the tiny clay figurine out of his pocket, strode up the first two steps of the dais, and held it out to her.

Her eyes widening, she flinched, then, slowly, her hand trembling, reached out to take the maimed caricature of herself. The figure quivered in Bellamy's palm. His skin prickled.

"Stop!" Titus shouted.

Bellamy tried to snatch the doll back. Moving just as quickly, possessed by the malevolent power of the image or her own shadowself, Marie lunged out of her seat and grabbed it anyway. Dark flame exploded from her hand, hurling Bellamy backward. She screamed once, then tumbled headlong down the steps, to sprawl unconscious on the floor with the figurine clenched tight in her fist and black waves of Oblivion streaming through her body.

Thirty-Seven

Fluid pattered into fluid. Evidently, Montrose thought, he and Louise were approaching another fountain. Like his own master's stronghold, the Seat of Golden Tears contained an abundance of them, the difference being that the ones here dripped ordinary water instead of gushing cold, crackling liquid flame.

He warily led his companion around another corner. The passage opened out into a chamber with rough, irregular walls, rather resembling a cave. It even had a dank, earthy smell. Beads of water oozed through the center of the floor, then shot upward, collecting in a pool on the ceiling.

"The water's lighter than air," Louise said, her voice slightly muffled by the hood of her saffron robe.

"Perhaps, perhaps not," Montrose said, waving his hand at a large trapezoidal window to the left. Storm clouds churned in the bottom of the glass. Above them was a topsy-turvy view of the Beggar Lord's artificial gardens, and, beyond that, the ramparts which defined the perimeter of his domain.

To the Scot's amusement, Louise gave a start, her reflexes insisting that she was about to drop on her head. He might have reacted similarly once, before the practice of levitation had all but ground the fear of falling out of him. "Then *we're* upside down?" the Renegade asked. "Walking on the ceiling like flies? You'd think we would have felt the magic shift us around as we entered."

"If that's what happened," Montrose said, gesturing toward an octagonal window on the other side of the chamber. Beyond it shone beds of orange and yellow tulips, and these, from his perspective, were right side up.

Louise shrugged, the topazes on her heavy robe clinking. "Well, then something here, some aspect of this, is an illusion."

"That's what I would have thought, but supposedly *nothing* in this labyrinth is an illusion in the ordinary meaning of the word, no matter how paradoxical or contrary to common sense." They walked on toward the exit at the far side of the room. He noted with satisfaction that the soreness in his wounded thigh had all but disappeared.

"Why was the maze built?" asked Louise. "What purpose does it serve?"

"Theoretically, the Beggar Lord rules over those souls who meet mysterious deaths. Some such find themselves driven to discover how and why they perished, or even to penetrate the fundamental secrets of the universe. Areas like this—I'm told there are many—were constructed to aid the seekers in their quest. Contemplating the enigmas here is supposed to unlock the mind and afford it glimpses of hidden truths."

"Like trying to unravel a koan," said Louise thoughtfully.

"I suppose," he replied. "Perhaps it works. Many of the greatest philosophers and metaphysicians in Imperial history owed their allegiance to this Seat, and few of them were renowned as thinkers or savants on Earth."

Stooping, the fugitives stepped through a low doorway. Though the wall outside had been made of stone, they now found themselves in a round glass chamber with a high, domed ceiling, like a bell jar. Montrose glanced around, then, startled, caught his breath. Outside the room, visible from the waist up, loomed two giants in saffron robes. Peering upward, the taller one aped the Hierarch's movements to perfection, while the shorter mimicked Louise. To all appearances, the gargantuan figures had just stepped into a bell jar themselves, and outside its transparent confines towered two more titans, who dwarfed them as they dwarfed the wraiths. Though he couldn't actually see any farther, Montrose had the feeling that that pair was gaping up at an even huger duo, the progression extending onward to infinity.

In the exact center of the room stood a table with a bell jar on it. No doubt when he gazed into it, he'd see a minuscule incarnation of himself, looking down at another tinier still.

"Disconcerting, isn't it?" said Louise, a trace of humor in her voice. Evidently she was enjoying his discomfiture as he'd enjoyed hers in the previous chamber.

He nodded. "A bit. I think I'd be more comfortable if I were either the largest Montrose or the smallest, assuming there are such. There's something particularly unsettling about being merely a link in the middle of the chain." His robe swishing, he started for the exit across the room.

"I know what you mean," she said. "It undermines our certainty that we're the real ones. Tell me, where are all the mystics this wonderland was intended to serve? Why haven't we come across anybody meditating?"

"I imagine they're busy with their duties," he said. "You don't think the Beggar Lord would allow his vassals time off for contemplation when he's preparing for civil war, do you? That's why I thought this would be a good place to rest and ponder our next move." Nearing the jar on the table, he observed that it did indeed contain two minute figures scurrying along, and felt a sudden desire to experiment with it. If he opened it and squashed the tiny Louise, would a giant hand descend from above and crush the woman beside him? If he smashed it, would the walls around him shatter too? Grimacing, he pushed the perverse impulse away. Most likely his Shadow had slipped it into his mind. He doubted that his dark half would ever stop troubling him as long as his betrayer was at hand to agitate it.

"Still," said Louise, "everybody can't be on duty all the time. You'd think we'd see someone."

"Since Charon perished," he said, struggling to keep a fresh attack of loathing from roughening his voice, "the Beggar Lord hasn't limited himself to harvesting the victims of Mystery. He grabs whatever souls he can, just like the rest of the Deathlords, so in all likelihood many of his newer subjects feel little need to frequent this particular facility. Nor, I suspect, are they encouraged to do so. In good times, the Empire has been known to smile on the pursuit of spiritual insight, at least via approved channels. In bad times, however, the ruling powers tend to suspect all such endeavors of being inherently Transcendental."

Louise snorted. "Occasionally I see some marvel here that makes me think Stygia isn't a complete hell after all. But then it always turns out that you've wasted or corrupted it."

He felt a pang of defensiveness, which instantly flared into a blaze of fury. "Who are you to judge us, traitoress?" he snarled. "Who are you to disdain anyone?"

She halted, turned to face him, pulled back her cowl, and removed the mask beneath it. Above her, colossi did the same, revealing the same taut, lovely features.

Montrose felt a flicker of dismay at the pain and anger in her face. "May I *finally* tell you what happened back in The Hague?" she asked.

"Thank you, no," he said coldly.

"Damn it, don't say that!" she snapped. "You *do* want to know. You want to know so badly that it's grinding you up inside."

"Conceivably so. But even so, knowing you to be a liar, why should I listen to whatever new falsehoods you've concocted?"

"I haven't deceived you on this side of the Shroud," she replied. "I have no intention of starting now, especially not here, in a temple devoted to truth. Nor do I expect you to forgive me. But as long as we don't talk about it, it will gnaw at us, ruining every peaceful moment we might otherwise have had. Perhaps once you know the truth, we'll be able to work together without my presence being such a torment for you. And even if it *doesn't* clear the air, at least you'll have your curiosity satisfied."

He stared at her for several seconds, then, said, "I already tried to slay you once. Should your story enrage me, I might do the same again. But if you're willing to run the risk, then say on."

"First unmask," she said. "Don't make me confess to a blank expanse of cloth."

Reluctantly he threw his cowl back, then pulled off the black crêpe mask beneath it. The air felt cold against his skin.

"Thank you," said Louise. She swallowed. "Let me start by saying that I truly did love you."

"I cringe from even imagining how you would have treated a fellow you disliked."

She glared at him. "Just be silent! You can scoff and sneer after I'm done. I loved you with my whole heart. I would have died for you. I wished you could be with me every night.

"But you couldn't, of course. You were busy planning the invasion of Scotland, and even an exiled, bankrupt princess has to be discreet. And one night, when you couldn't visit my bedchamber, someone else did."

Despite all that had passed between them, all that he'd surmised about her true character, the declaration cut him like a knife. Grinning to conceal the hurt, he said, "How fortunate that you were adaptable enough to make do with a substitute. Who was it, VanLengen?"

"I told you to be quiet! No, it wasn't him, or anyone human."

"I beg your pardon?"

"The maid had already gone," said Louise. Her voice and blue eyes took on a subtly remote quality as memory possessed her. "I read another few pages of Erasmus, then blew out the candles beside the bed. And for some reason, that was when I saw him, when the light was gone.

"He was waiting in the corner, watching me. His long, bony face shone pale as the moon, and his dark, deep-set eyes glittered like soulfire crystals. I could barely make out the shape of his gaunt frame; draped in black, it blended with the shadows.

"Though not handsome in any conventional sense, he looked beautiful and dangerous. I opened my mouth to scream, but he shook his head and the cry withered in my throat. Unable to tear my gaze away from his, I groped for the candelabrum, thinking to use it as a club. I grasped, it but then suddenly he was beside me. He caressed my hand, my fingers spasmed with terror and pleasure, and my weapon thudded to the floor.

"He held me and he raped me, though only with his touch and mouth. I knew I should cry for help or do something else to stop him, but I didn't. It was as if I'd been drugged." Her voice turned harsh with self-contempt. "Or perhaps it simply felt too good. At the end, he bit my inner thigh and drank a measure of my blood, slurping like a child guzzling porridge, and that felt the best of all."

"A vampire," Montrose said.

"Yes. I fainted while he was drinking. When I awoke hours later, he'd gone, leaving nothing behind to prove that he'd ever been there. Even the marks of his fangs had healed without a trace.

"I decided it had only been a shameful, lascivious dream. Perhaps he'd commanded me to think so. At any rate, I clung to the belief as long as I could, but eventually, after several visitations, I realized the truth.

"Yet even then, my thoughts were murky. I'd forget all about him for hours or even days at a time. Often, when I did remember, I could only think of the rapture he gave me. I couldn't recognize that he was a demon, that he'd enslaved me and imperiled my soul, nor that when I yielded to him, I was being unfaithful to you, the one I truly loved. Occasionally, briefly, I *would* perceive exactly what was happening, but even then I did nothing to end it. My horror didn't energize me, it paralyzed me.

"As the weeks dragged on, and the day of your departure drew near, the vampire told me I must do him a favor to repay him for all the nights of bliss he'd given me."

"Convince me to make VanLengen one of my lieutenants?" Montrose asked.

She nodded. "He said the man was his ghoul, whatever that means. By then my thinking was so twisted that I did it without even considering the implications. Afterwards, gloating, the vampire informed me that I'd planted a Judas in your company. I begged him to permit me to undo what I'd done, but he only laughed. When he'd had his fill of mocking me, he vanished, and never came to me again.

"I vowed to tell you the truth, but I couldn't. The vampire was still inside my head, muzzling me, making me smile and laugh and paint, forcing me through my normal routine as if I were an automaton. I spent long hours praying, and earnestly discussing theology with my mother's chaplain, hoping that my acts of piety would break the spell." She smiled bitterly. "But obviously, they didn't."

"No," Montrose said. "This can't be true. I adored you. I spent every spare moment with you. If some devil had turned you into his puppet, if you were secretly in agony, I would have noticed."

"You were working round the clock, making your final preparations to sail. Your spare moments were few and far between, and then you were weary and preoccupied."

"I still can't believe—" he began, and then, abruptly, his certainty crumbled. The quest to recover the throne for young Charles had consumed him. Perhaps he *had* been too intent on his mission even to notice that the woman he loved was languishing under an undead monster's spell. The realization brought a pang of shame.

"After I learned of your death," Louise continued, "I left my mother's house in secret, became a Catholic, and took the veil. Did you know that?"

"No. Even after I made it back to the Shadowlands, well into the 1700s, I never checked to find out how your life had turned out. It occurred to me, but for some reason, I didn't truly want to know."

"I felt a need to dedicate myself to God, to atone for the hideous thing I'd done. I even gave up my art as a part of my penance. In time I achieved a measure of serenity.

"Death took it away again, of course. I discovered what all we Restless discover, that this afterlife of ours is nothing like what my religion had taught me to expect. But for some reason, unlike many wraiths, I didn't become cynical. I still had faith that a soul could find God, or at least goodness and wisdom. Eventually my search led me to the New World and the Sisters of Athena."

Feeling befuddled, Montrose shook his head. "You said you weren't telling me this to gain my forgiveness. But surely the point of the story is that what happened wasn't your fault."

"No!" she said fiercely. "That *isn't* what I'm saying. If not for the perverse, masochistic part of my spirit, the part that relished my debasement at the vampire's hands, perhaps I could have found the will to resist him. At any rate, I should have been strong or clever enough to do *something*."

"Why did the vampire want the expedition to fail? Was he Argyll's agent? Or his secret overlord?"

"He didn't say," Louise replied. "You have to understand how it was, James. All those hours pressed together in the dark, all those intimate things he did to me, his icy flesh burning mine, and he never even told me his *name*."

Montrose shook his head. "I don't know what to say."

"Just tell me how you feel. Has this helped to ease the pain at all, or have I only given you new reason to despise me?"

"Well," he said hesitantly, "assuming that any part of your tale is true—"

She grabbed him by the forearms. "Don't hide from me like that. It *is* true. You know it is. Now you be honest with me."

He glared at her. "All right. The truth is, I wish you hadn't told me. Because hatred isn't the most troublesome emotion a man can feel. It's less crippling than confusion and ambivalence, and suddenly I don't know what I feel, or ought to feel, about you or anything else.

"*Could* you have broken the vampire's spell if you wanted to badly enough? Have I been right to hate you all these years? I'll never know, just as I'll never know who your undead lover was. I knew my mortal life was a fiasco, but at least I imagined I understood who my enemies were, and how and why they brought me down. Now, suddenly, I discover that there were forces arrayed against me that I never even suspected. But I'll never, ever comprehend them, not three hundred and fifty years after the fact."

"I'm sorry," she said softly. "I didn't realize it would affect you this way."

"I'm sure you didn't," he said, sneering, stepping back to distance himself from her. "You flattered yourself that it was *your* betrayal that set me on the path I've walked in the Underworld. That made me a fiendish Legionnaire as opposed to a stalwart Renegade or a saintly Heretic. You imagined that if you could persuade me that you were actually worthy of my devotion all along, my ruthlessness and selfishness would fall away from me. I'd renounce the Hierarchy and revert to the gallant ass you knew.

"Well, it's not going to happen. Even if you didn't mean to betray me, plenty of others did; even, at the end, my King himself. It *all* helped to teach me the true shape of the world, and so has everything I've experienced in the afterlife. I couldn't turn back into the fool you knew, even if I wanted to. And I *don't*. I'm happy as I am."

"I wasn't trying to change you!" she said, then hesitated. "Or perhaps I was. Maybe I don't know what I was trying to accomplish. I just needed to explain."

"Well, I hope it made *you* feel better," he spat. They stared at each other in helpless, excruciating silence, she evidently having no more idea what to say next than he did, until the tramp of booted feet and the jingle of metal shattered the moment. It sounded like a group of armed men, moving briskly in their direction.

Montrose nearly smiled. The threat of a band of soldiers was a welcome distraction from the bewildering knot of emotions aching in his chest. Hastily pulling his cowl over his head, he whispered, "Come on, this way."

The passage beyond the bell jar divided at a Y intersection. Montrose and Louise skulked down the left-hand branch, and soon found themselves in an octagonal room where three geometric forms, each roughly the size of a medicine ball, sat in a line on the middle of the floor. At one end was a bright blue tetrahedron, clearly smaller than the yellow sphere in the middle, which was in turn smaller than the red cube. Yet Montrose's eyes simultaneously insisted that the tetrahedron was larger than the cube. He could already tell he'd contract a splitting headache if he looked at the tableau for very long.

He strained, listening for the warriors. To his relief, they sounded farther away than before. Evidently they'd moved off in a different direction.

"Do you think they're looking for us?" asked Louise.

"Who knows? It's possible that what we heard was simply a routine patrol. On the other hand, perhaps someone noticed that the original owners of these robes have gone missing. Perhaps he then quizzed the Legionnaires who escorted us into the gate, and they swore they brought all their charges back. If so, he surely deduced that there are two intruders roaming the Seat in disguise, and started the Paupers hunting us."

"That doesn't sound like an easy job," she said, "not in a place where most of the civilians wear more or less identical hooded robes. Maybe learning to tell your associates apart was originally an exercise to sharpen your perceptions, too." Montrose sensed that she too was grateful for an excuse to shift the focus of their conversation to less intimate concerns.

"Perhaps so. At any rate, I daresay the Beggar Lord's guards are up to the challenge, and I think it's time we departed from here and made our way to my own master's fortress."

"How?"

"Clearly, we'd be unwise to assume the sentries here will simply let us pass through a gate unchallenged. I'd rather fly over the wall. If we pick the proper place, we may be able to slip away without anybody spotting us. The defenses here are primarily intended to keep people out, not in."

"I assume the defenses at the House of Strife are intended to keep people out, too," she said. "Have you figured out how to get through them?"

"I'm working on it," he said.

Thirty-Eight

With its pale marble flagstones, the plaza was like a huge mirror reflecting the teal and ochre flickers of lightning overhead. Every so often a thunderbolt blazed brightly enough in the proper quadrant of the sky to cast the prodigious shadow of Charon's donjon across the square. In the perpetual night of the Underworld, the band of deeper darkness resembled a chasm plunging into the earth.

The last time Montrose had seen the Plaza of Lost Stars, so named for the cyclopean statues scattered across it, each depicting one of the constellations of the Earthly sky, the area had been full of people. Messengers scurrying from one Seat to another. Ministers and lackeys strolling at their leisure. Artificers hauling some new creation to a Deathlord or grandee. Overseers with snapping whips herding coffles of trudging Thralls.

Now, like the rest of the squares, markets, parklands, and thoroughfares which the Seven held in common, the space was silent and deserted. Everyone was keeping to the stronghold of his own master. Everyone but the patrols, looking for signs that someone else's sovereign was readying an attack, or collecting intelligence to aid them in launching one of their own.

Terse voices muttered off to the right, where the faceted ramparts and spires of the Seat of Thorns, a structure reputedly carved from a single monstrous emerald, glowed against the sky, illuminated by some magic bound in the stone. Glad to be rid of the hindering folds of his saffron robe, Montrose drew his flintlock pistols, cocked them, and ducked behind the pedestal of a stoic if not bovine Andromeda chained to her rock. Her crossbow ready, her slouch hat and leaden mask concealing her features, Louise crouched beside him.

A moment later a dozen female soldiers prowled into view. Though their choice of clothing and weapons was eclectic—the one on point wore only a short deerskin dress and carried a lever-action rifle, while the next one in the procession had opted for mail, a pike, and a brace of Colt .45s—each sported a copper mask-of-comedy badge, a token of allegiance to the Laughing Lady. They'd all received bald heads, fiery red eyes, and pointed goblin ears from some Masquer, too, evidently to express their devotion to their particular unit. Montrose took them for Storm Maidens, an elite corps specializing in the destruction of Spectres. If the Mistress of Lunacy was calling them to Stygia from their outposts in the Tempest, that was one more indication that all-out war could break out at any time.

Not, Montrose reflected grimly, that he needed another sign. The indications were everywhere.

To his relief, the Amazons stalked by without noticing him and Louise. "How many scouting parties have we dodged?" the Sister of Athena asked wryly. "I'm losing count."

"Five, I think," he said. "It's a miracle they haven't all started fighting each other." In point of fact, he and Louise had heard cries and crackles of gunfire as one such skirmish erupted in the direction of the Ashen Lady's castle.

"At least that would make it easier to slip past them. I thought for sure those

Mutes were going to notice us."

"Chin up," Montrose said. "We've nearly reached my master's citadel."

"I hate it when you call him that," she said.

He scowled, his hostility welling up anew. "Why? That's what he is. You didn't scorn me for giving fealty to Charles as my King."

"Back then, we all had lords, unless we were the lords. We assumed it was the natural order of things. But the mortal world has changed since then. I don't know how much of it you've seen—all this time we've been traveling together, and we've told each other so little!—but the Quick have new philosophies and systems of government. The old authoritarian notions that were showing their age even in our day have no currency at all anymore, at least not in Europe or America."

"As it happens, I *do* know something about present conditions in the Skinlands." Actually, given that he'd spent most of the modern era in the Onyx Tower, his knowledge was unquestionably more superficial than hers, but he wasn't about to admit it. "And whatever rights the living have proclaimed for the common man, and whatever systems they use to ratify their laws, the strong and the cunning still control the destinies of the weak and the dull, just as they do here. Nor are you Renegades and Heretics any different, with your field marshals, first citizens, popes, and ayatollahs. Human societies inevitably organize themselves into hierarchies."

"No," she said. "I don't agree. But let that go. The real point is that your devotion to your King was different from your service to the Smiling Lord. You fought for Charles Stuart and his son because your principles required it; earlier in your life, when the father tried to tamper with your church, you opposed him with equal fervor. In contrast, your fealty to the Seven with all their cruelty and oppression seems so…" She waved her hand, groping for the right word.

"Expedient?" he supplied. "That's precisely what it is. It elevated me from a wretched foot soldier battling Spectres in the bowels of the Tempest to a peer of the realm dwelling in the luxury of the Imperial Court, and when we sort out our current difficulties, it will do the same again."

Despite her mask, he could *feel* her frown. "And that's all that matters to you."

To his annoyance, he hesitated a beat before answering. "Short of preventing the Void from swallowing all Creation, yes. You know, I thought we'd about had our fill of intimacy back in the Beggar Lord's palace. If you can suppress your penchant for personal observations, I'd prefer to concentrate on the task at hand."

"All right," she sighed. "I'm sorry."

He led her onward, skulking past towering stone images of Taurus the Bull and Orion the Hunter brandishing his sword, using the statuary for cover. The cold wind gusted, toying with his cloak.

Beyond the plaza was a patch of artificial woods, a stand of fragrant evergreens trilling with recorded bird song. A road ran through it, but for concealment's sake, the fugitives chose to stalk among the trees instead. The ground, carpeted with brown, dry needles, was soft and springy beneath their feet.

Nearing the end of the miniature forest, they glimpsed the Seat of Burning Waters. Louise caught her breath, and small wonder. Every Deathlord's residence was imposing in its own way. Each, even those that should have seemed fragile—like the Seat of Shadows, which crumbled into ruin during the course of every day, renewing itself in the blink of an eye at midnight, or the Skeletal Lord's castle of bone, which looked as rickety as a latticework of matchsticks—projected an aura of preternatural strength. But as befitted the personification of war, the Smiling Lord's fortress was the hugest and most forbidding of all. Constructed of dark basalt, it stood on a motte in the middle of a wide, barren clearing, where searchlights swept over a crazy-quilt of ditches and razor-wire fences devised to hinder any enemy's advance. Rounded towers protruded from the enceinte, ensuring that any foe who did dare to approach could be subjected to constant fire, usually from more than one direction. Almost invisible behind the merlons of the battlements high overhead were cannons, mortars, trebuchets, rocket launchers, mangonels, and insectile darksteel artillery pieces with no counterpart in Earthly history, products of Artificer ingenuity capable of discharging deadly magics. Of all the structures Montrose had ever seen, in Stygia, in the Shadowlands, or in the Tempest, only the Onyx Tower itself was more impressively ominous.

Montrose took cover behind a thicket. Studying the landscape, he said, "The spotlights are a new touch. Considering all the defenses that were already in place, it seems like a prime example of gilding the lily."

"It reminds me of every old prison movie I ever saw," Louise replied.

"And have you seen many? Do you like movies?" He realized that it was the first question about her current tastes and casual pleasures he'd asked since they'd crossed swords in Grand Gulf. Somehow it had just slipped out.

"Yes," she said, a hint of laughter in her tone. "Even Heretic nuns don't spend *all* their time chasing Transcendence and plotting against the Legions. I was actually stationed in Los Angeles during the silent era. In my free time, I watched DeMille shoot—"

Its rotors chopping, anti-tank guided missiles jutting from its nose, a Defender helicopter rose from behind the castle walls. Montrose held himself absolutely motionless until it became obvious that the gunship wasn't coming after him and Louise. Like an angry wasp, it droned off in the direction of the mainland.

"Speaking of shooting," Louise said ruefully. "I guess this isn't the time to pause and reminisce, is it?"

"Possibly not."

"*Can* you get us inside, James? I'm no defeatist, but the place looks impregnable."

"I think we have a chance. Remember, I resided here as a high-ranking officer. I learned the defenses." He pointed to the left. "Do you see that relatively clear, rectangular patch of ground, more or less leading up to that sally-port?"

"Is that where we're going to make our approach?"

"No. It's a minefield, and the gate is only a blind door, a lure. But can your Arcanos reach that far? Could you apply pressure to the ground and set off the explosives, walking the blasts away from us?"

"I think so."

"Well, once you get all the guards looking that way, we'll fly in the opposite direction, toward that hexagonal tower with the frieze of carrion crows around the top. We'll be moving under and through a web of invisible light. Should we break any of the strands, we'll set off an alarm, so keep your arms and legs in close. Don't let yourself brush the ground, either, even though at times we'll only be a few inches above it."

"I take it that there are a few mines over there, also."

"Unfortunately, yes. Once we make it through the net, we'll slip over the wall, and that will be that." He gave her the grin which had always heartened his ragtag army of Highlanders, and later, the wraith soldiers he'd commanded. "The whole thing's childishly simple, now that I come to think about it."

"Childishly," she said, an answering smile in her voice. "Are we ready?"

He unfastened his cape. He couldn't afford to have it billowing and flapping around him. "We are now."

She took off her fedora, folded it up, and stuffed it in her pocket. That done, she stared at the minefield, taking slow, deep breaths, her body occasionally tensing, then relaxing once more. At first, nothing happened. Frowning, Montrose decided she'd overestimated her range, that they'd have to move closer to the explosives and thus dangerously extend their approach. Then, with a boom, a pillar of crimson fire shot upward, followed by a second several yards beyond it, and a third more distant still.

"That's it," gasped Louise. "I can't reach any farther."

"That's good enough," he said, taking her in his arms. Pressing close, she wrapped all four of her limbs around him, almost as if they were making love. He floated off the ground, then flew out into the clearing.

He couldn't grope his way as he had in the Artificers' labyrinth. Louise's diversion had only bought them a few seconds. He had to travel fast, climbing and diving suddenly, trusting that his memory of the pattern of the web, augmented by his pathfinder's instincts, would see him safely though. And as if that weren't demanding enough, he had to avoid slamming into more tangible obstacles as well.

A circle of light swept across his path. Decelerating frantically, sacrificing a precious second, he kept himself from hurtling into the illumination. As soon as the beam slid by, he shot forward, made a ninety-degree turn, dove through the narrow opening between a portion of the web and coils of glinting darksteel wire. Black barbs snagged Louise's coat, then tore free.

"You're doing it," she said.

Yes, he thought, by God, he was. Unlikely as it seemed, they'd negotiated more than half of the net already. Grinning fiercely, still flying low, he zigzagged onward toward a ditch, and then a dark, glistening shape heaved up directly in front of him.

He started to veer left, remembered that if he did he'd break the web, and tried to swing right instead, but by that time it was too late. A scaly tentacle thicker than a big man's thigh flailed at him. It only grazed him, but even a glancing blow was sufficient to smash him and Louise to the ground.

Montrose slammed down on top of his companion. Striving desperately to shake off the shock of the sudden attack, he scrambled to his feet and snatched out his pistols. Meanwhile, whistling like a tea kettle, the moat monster clambered out of its den.

In the gloom, the huge beast was only a vague mass with an acrid stench, gleaming fangs, and perhaps a dozen thrashing rubbery limbs. Montrose had no idea where its vital organs might be located, any more than he could tell whether it was a captive Spectre, a Phantasy, or some poor slave, lobotomized and flesh-sculpted into a horror.

Praying for a lucky shot, he fired the flintlocks.

The black beast faltered for a split-second, then kept coming. Wishing he still had the automatic he'd picked up in the Coliseum, Montrose dropped the single-shot guns and whipped out his rapier. With a grunt, still dazed, Louise struggled to her feet, raised her crossbow, and stumbled sideways, trying to flank the creature.

Intent on the creature's advance, Montrose could only see Louise from the corner of his eye, but even so, his Harbinger's intuition suddenly warned him that she mustn't take another step. "Freeze!" he shouted. "A mine!" Then the monster lunged at him.

All he could see was a shining black confusion of coiling, flailing limbs. He did his best to thrust past them, at the beast's central mass. He felt his point plunge into flesh, and then the monster heaved, tearing the sword out of his grasp. Tentacles whipped around him and crushed him to the ground. Huge saurian jaws dipped toward his head. He struggled madly but impotently to break free.

Then the beast lurched and fell over as if someone had swung a wrecking ball into its side. A muffled blast jolted it and hurled chunks of its flesh skyward. Its tentacles spasmed, nearly tearing Montrose limb from limb, and then relaxed. As he squirmed free, retrieving his rapier in the process, he realized that Louise must have used her Spook powers to knock the creature onto the mine he'd warned her of.

Clutching her head, the Renegade swayed from side to side. Evidently shifting such a heavy mass had strained her psychokinesis to its limits. "Don't move!" Montrose snapped.

"Another mine?" she said.

"Just to your left." Sheathing his blade, he struggled to invoke his own mystic talents once again. After a moment, he felt the power rise. He floated upward, lifted her in his arms, and flew on toward the Seat. Perhaps, he thought, no one had noticed the creature coming out of its hole, the mine blowing it apart, or anything else. Perhaps he and Louise were still all right.

Then guns blazed from the battlements.

Well, at least he didn't have to worry about breaking the damn web anymore. Swooping unpredictably back and forth to throw off the sentries' marksmanship, he raced on toward the castle. "Shield us!" he said.

"Trying," Louise croaked. A second later, several arrows whizzed out of the darkness, then stopped and broke as if they'd hit an invisible wall. She shuddered violently.

Automatic weapons chattered, spotlights flitted around the fugitives, and then suddenly the enceinte was directly in front of them. Flying at maximum speed, Montrose barely managed to pull up in time to avoid crashing into it. He rocketed toward the stormy heavens, weathered tiers of huge basalt blocks streaking past only a foot away.

Now that he was next to the wall, many of the defenders could no longer see him. Even so, bullets hammered the stonework, stinging him with flying chips. A magenta fireball exploded on his left, buffeting him sideways.

He doubted that he was going to make it to the top, but then, abruptly, the battlements were beneath his boots. The guards on the wall-walk gaped up at him, frantically swung their weapons up to shoot him. One, a Harbinger himself, levitated straight upward, three-round bursts erupting from his rifle.

Montrose swooped lower, hurtled onward over the jumble of courtyards, chemises, towers, and other outbuildings which lay between the perimeter defenses and the primary keep. Searchlights, gunfire, and sizzling bolts of magic pursued him across the rooftops. Other Harbingers soared upward to intercept him.

He plummeted, dodged around a barbican, and sped on toward a low, sprawling, ruddy sandstone structure resembling a gargantuan temple from the ancient world, a flat roof with pediments at either end supported by rows of corinthian columns. Unwilling to waste time decelerating fully, he touched down hard on the cobbled path outside the structure. The shock jolted up his legs.

He hastily set Louise on her feet. Her knees buckled. He grabbed her and gave her a shake.

"You have to walk," he said, "and right now!"

She drew herself up straight. "All right."

"In here." Drawing his rapier, he led her between two of the pillars. A scarlet mist smelling of blood and excrement sprang into existence around them, concealing all but the nearest columns and any trace of the world outside. Louise gave a start of surprise.

"Keep moving," he said, "we have to get farther in." He stalked on, peering about, reflexively counting his steps. In the old days, he'd never taken more than nine before the ordeal commenced.

This time, he only managed six. Then a man in the red coat and conical helmet of an eighteenth-century English soldier stepped out of the fog, bayoneted musket shouldered and ready to fire. Montrose sidestepped, and the ball whizzed past his head. Sword extended, the Hierarch charged, used a coupe to deceive the apparition's attempt to parry his blade, and stabbed him in the chest.

The soldier fell backwards, shuddered violently, and lay still. The corpse remained for a moment, giving its slayer a chance to contemplate it, then blinked out of existence.

"Stay alert," Montrose said to Louise. "He was only the first of many." They hurried on.

Thirty-Nine

The red mist turned gray, and Montrose found himself walking arm and arm down an alley beside a stocky little man in an opera hat and cloak. The night smelled of burnt coal oil, rotting produce, and horse droppings, whispered with the tinny strains of the bawdy song leaking from a music hall somewhere nearby.

Montrose sensed Louise several yards behind him, strolling along with a newfound companion of her own. He wondered if his escort and hers were identical, but not enough to twist around and look. Better to devote his energies to trying to finish this encounter with a minimum of pain and inconvenience.

Pivoting, he attempted to punch the little man in the kidney, only to find that his arm had lost much of its force, speed, and accuracy. The blow glanced harmlessly off. The little man grabbed him and thrust him backwards, slamming his head into a brick wall.

"Whore," the man in the top hat said, his breath redolent of brandy and tobacco. "Whore." Gripping Montrose by the throat, he reached inside his coat and brought out a long knife.

Knowing he had no chance, that the insult to his head had completed the job of rendering him defenseless, the Hierarch still scrabbled feebly at the other man's face. Until the knife opened his belly and his viscera came sliding out, at which point his arms flopped down, inert. The murderer dumped him on the ground, knelt beside him, and kept on cutting.

Montrose felt unavoidable agony and dread, but beneath them he seethed with impatience. *Very well*, he thought, *you won. Kill me. Get it over with.*

At last his pounding heartbeat stopped. Despite himself, he silently screamed his terror and denial, then toppled into darkness. An instant later, shaken but intact, he was standing among the columns once again. The scarlet mist now smelled of burnt gunpowder and mustard gas.

"Dear God," moaned Louise.

He turned. Despite her mask, he could tell from the way she carried herself that she was on the verge of collapse, and small wonder. She'd strained herself using her Arcanos to get them inside the Seat, fought three battles since, and just now presumably endured a ghastly albeit temporary demise.

"Sit down," he said. "I think we're far enough inside the pavilion to take a rest. We won't have to contend with any more phantoms until we start moving again."

She flopped down onto the stone floor. He looked and listened for pursuing Legionnaires, detected none, then squatted beside her.

"I gather I just met Jack the Ripper," she said.

"Or a facsimile of him."

"Lucky me. But what *is* this place?"

"The Beggar Lord's vassals have special retreats in which to contemplate Mystery," he replied. "The Smiling Lord's subjects, all of whom theoretically perished violently, need an academy where they can study war and murder, and this, the Crimson Gallery, is it. Here we wander in the mist, killing and being killed, absorbing the lessons to be learned thereby. Even if you don't attain any sort of esoteric insights—and I must confess that *I* never did—it's superb martial training."

She snorted. "My *sifu* would have loved it, but I'm not quite that dedicated. Why did you bring me here?"

"I planned to slip into the fortress unobserved. Alas, the beast in the ditch made that impossible."

"I take it you didn't know the creature was there."

He grimaced. "No. And people are always tinkering with the defenses. I should have been on the lookout for something that had been added since the last time I reviewed them. I apologize for my stupidity."

"Don't be silly. You did your best, and you got us in. No one could have done any better." She lifted her hand and let it drop again, as if she'd wanted to touch him but thought better of it. He felt grateful for her forbearance, yet for a moment regretted it as well.

"Thank you for your tolerance," he said. "At any rate, after the soldiers spotted us, our task of infiltration became more complicated. I had to shake them off our tail. And the best way to do that was to duck in here."

"Why?"

"Well, for one thing, we could scarcely afford another second out in the open, and the Gallery was close at hand. But I had another reason, too. I'm hopeful that the guards lost sight of us when we flew around the barbican, and didn't see us enter. In which case they'll have to mount a search of the general area. Still, they'll follow us in here eventually, but when they do, they too will have to cope with the mist and the apparitions. That should enable us to stay ahead of them."

"There's no way to turn the magic off?"

"Not if we're lucky. Charon created this place himself. I suspect that even the Smiling Lord doesn't know how the enchantment works."

"Then our situation does sound promising," she said. "As long as we're not bottled up inside here."

"We shouldn't be. The place is disorienting—it's much bigger inside than out, and the fog dampens sound almost as much as it hinders sight—but I've spent a lot of time in it, and I have my Harbinger's senses to guide me. There are patterns of warped space here, similar to those in the Tempest. Nothing I can manipulate, but useful as signposts. We should be able to find our way through to a secret passage I know of, and that in turn will take us into the palace."

"But first we have more slaughter to endure."

"Yes." He hesitated. "I always visited the Gallery alone before. That was how you were supposed to do it. I can't predict exactly how the magic will deal with the two of us being together. Sometimes we may share the same encounter, as when the musketeer came at us. Sometimes the power may separate us so we can each have our own private version of the same experience, as happened with Jack. Or it may conceivably whisk one of us away into some artificial environment and leave the other behind.

"Either way, when a threat appears, kill it instantly. Should the Gallery cast you in the role of a murderer, dispatch your victim with the same urgency, no matter how sickening the prospect. Your only goal is to conclude the experience as quickly as possible, so we can move on."

"And besides, the apparitions aren't real," she said. "I understand."

"When an encounter kills you, remember that your death isn't genuine, either, no matter how much it feels like it. The pain and fear are probably inevitable, but don't let them unhinge your mind."

She chuckled. "You don't expect much of a girl, do you, James?"

He smiled. "Of an ordinary lass, no. But I should think that ferocious rebel leaders take such petty annoyances in stride. Now, if I vanish—"

"Don't panic. Stand and wait until the magic has had its way with you and sends you back." She started to clamber stiffly to her feet. Straightening up himself, he thought of offering her his hand. But he hesitated, and then it was too late.

"Are you ready to move on?" he asked.

"I'd better be, don't you think? Your Legionnaire friends are going to turn up eventually. Which way?"

He gestured. "That one. I'll go first."

"My hero," she said, her voice dripping good-natured mockery.

They stalked on, weapons at the ready. Now smelling of charred flesh, the red vapor swirled, alternately shrouding and revealing the rows of pillars. Suddenly, hooves drummed on the sandstone floor. A man-at-arms on a destrier hurtled out of the murk, lance couched. Montrose leaped out of the animal's path. Louise's crossbow twanged, and the bolt caught the war-horse in the throat.

Mount and rider went down with a tremendous clangor of armor. Montrose darted toward the lancer, intent on finishing him, but both phantoms, man and animal alike, disappeared before he could. Presumably the fall had broken the medieval warrior's neck.

"Drat," said Louise. "When the horse went, it took my quarrel with it." She extracted a fresh one from her quiver.

When she'd reloaded, they prowled on. Though her departure was silent, Montrose sensed it when the Gallery carried her away. He whirled, and sure enough, she was gone.

All he could do was await her return, struggling to curb his impatience and anxiety. What if she was gone for hours? Or what if the magic subjected her to such a protracted, excruciating death that no one could emerge from it with sanity intact? Perhaps he didn't truly comprehend the forces at work in the Crimson Gallery any better than he'd grasped the hazards of Weeping Bay. For all he actually knew, the hall might subject her to the *final* death.

An indistinct, muffled noise sounded off to his right. He turned, peered, saw nothing. He hoped his ears were playing tricks on him. Then, without warning, Louise blinked back into view, kneeling, clutching her chest, the crossbow resting upside down on the floor beside her. "Are you all right?" he said.

She lifted her head. Gazed out of her mask with tortured eyes. "I was a zoo keeper," she whimpered. "I took care of the elephants. And Sadie just nudged me off my feet, put her head on my chest, and *pressed*."

"Take a deep—"

"I loved her. I took good care of her. Why would she want to hurt me?" Louise sobbed, her head lurching downward.

Montrose grasped her chin and compelled her to look at him. "It wasn't real," he said. "You *aren't* the zoo keeper. You've never so much as laid eyes on Sadie. It's entirely possible that neither the brute nor her victim ever truly existed. The encounter pulled you in deep—they do that sometimes—but you have to be Louise again. I'm afraid the guards may already be inside the hall."

The Heretic shuddered. "Yes. I'm fine. Let's go." Montrose took hold of her forearm and helped her up.

Peering this way and that, senses straining, they crept forward. The dank mist fingered their faces, bringing them the stench of corpses bloating in the sun. Montrose sensed something he'd never felt in the Gallery before, an indefinable change in the atmosphere, almost as if a storm were building. Then, abruptly as always, swirling red gloom gave way to the wan sunlight of a rainy summer day.

Looking down at a sea of upturned faces, he recognized instantly where and when he was. He was standing on the scaffold by the Market Cross on the morning of his execution, clad in the same clothing he'd worn then. White gloves. A red suit richly trimmed with silver and Brussels lace. He remembered thinking that it looked well with his auburn lovelocks.

His situation stunned him, evoked a profound, unreasoning horror that, he suspected, no other scenario could have matched. Why was the Gallery forcing him to relive an actual event from his own career? It never had before.

There was no way to know. All he could do was endure the experience, preferably while maintaining his composure. According to his biographers, he'd managed it admirably the first time around, so surely he could do the same again. He just hoped he could avoid making the same asinine declarations he'd uttered in 1650. Forgiving his tormentors. Praying for young Charles. How could he say such things without bursting into bitter laughter?

Or rather, how, he thought suddenly, surprising himself, could he repeat them without withering in shame, given that he'd so thoroughly betrayed the ideals which had inspired them? Scowling, he pushed the ridiculous thought aside. Perhaps his Shadow had slipped it into his mind.

Looking for the hangman, he turned, and then gave a start of surprise. In place of his original executioner, a tender-hearted fellow who'd wept as he performed his office, *VanLengen* stood before him, flanked by a pair of frowning soldiers. And the traitor's normally ruddy, well-fed face was pale and slack with fear.

It was the Dutchman's manifest dread, along with the position of the guards, which alerted Montrose to the truth of his situation. This wasn't an exact recreation of his execution after all. This time, *he* was the hangman, and VanLengen was the one about to dance at the end of three fathoms of rope.

The Hierarch reminded himself that it was all an illusion. Still, it was a taste of revenge, the only one he'd ever know. And he had to play out the scene in any case. Smirking uncontrollably, he advanced on VanLengen. The prisoner tried to recoil, but the soldiers grabbed him and held him in place. The spectators growled at his display of cowardice.

"Would you care to kneel and pray?" Montrose asked with bogus solicitude. "I seem to recall that it made me feel a little better."

"Please," VanLengen said, "I beg you, don't do this. I was his *ghoul*! I didn't have a choice."

"I meant, pray to God," said the Scot. "I can assure you, you'll have no mercy from me. Give me your hands. Quickly! Or the guards will assist you, and most likely cause you pain in the process. Either way, the result will be the same."

Shaking, VanLengen obeyed. Montrose picked up a length of rope and knotted the prisoner's wrists together, tying them as tightly as possible, making the cord bite painfully deep. Then he hung the manifesto—the death warrant—around the traitor's neck. Finally, in a parody of courtesy, he waved his arm at the ladder. "After you, my faithful lieutenant."

"No, please—" VanLengen whined.

"Climb it or I'll fetch the noose down and strangle you slowly."

The Judas mounted the rungs, and Montrose followed him up. At the top, shivering now himself with eagerness, the Scot seized the dangling halter and placed it around his victim's throat.

"My hangman bade me nod to signal when I was ready for him to turn me off," Montrose said. "Permit me to extend the same courtesy to you."

"Please," said VanLengen. "I'll give you anything, I'll do anything—"

"Too late," the Hierarch replied. "We haven't got all day." He shoved the prisoner off his perch.

The rope thrummed and then jerked taut. VanLengen's neck cracked, and the gibbet groaned. The Dutchman's legs pumped for a moment, as if he were running through the air, and then he hung inert, swinging back and forth.

The crowd cheered. Montrose threw back his head and raised his arms, quaking with exultation. Illusory or not, this was one of the most ecstatic moments of his long existence.

The world turned dim and scarlet. Through coiling strands of vapor, he glimpsed Louise peering warily about. Though he knew he should rejoin her as expeditiously as possible, his heart cried out in protest. He wasn't ready to depart. Couldn't he remain just a few more seconds to gloat over VanLengen's corpse?

As if in response to his wish, the red murk vanished. Abruptly he found himself on the platform at the foot of the ladder once more. Despite his joy, he felt a twinge of anxiety. He'd made his kill, so why hadn't the encounter ended?

He couldn't even guess. He'd just have to continue to play his part and hope for the best. He turned toward the condemned man, expecting to see VanLengen, but this time it was the Marquess of Hamilton, with his flowing black hair and thin, straight mustache, who stood, looking dazed and sick, between the guards. The Stygian felt his lips stretch into a grin.

As he proceeded with the second execution, Montrose struggled to remember that he had cause to be on his guard. To act with detachment. But the pleasures of slaying another of his betrayers proved irresistible. By the time he had herded Hamilton up the ladder, prodding him on with the point of a knife he'd borrowed from one of the soldiers, he was giggling like a madman. And when the prisoner hit the end of the rope, the resulting burst of ecstasy was even more intense than before. For a moment the Hierarch thought he'd faint and plummet from the ladder himself, but he didn't care.

The Edinburgh square dissolved into a dim view of Louise and her environs. He could tell from the hunch of her shoulders and the way she twisted back and forth, like an animal at bay, that now she was genuinely frightened. Perhaps he'd been gone a long time, even though it only seemed like a few minutes to him. Or perhaps she heard the Smiling Lord's soldiers drawing near.

In a dull, fumbling way, he still remembered that he was supposed to return to her. Yet at the same time, giddy with bloodlust, he yearned to see if the magic would deliver another of his enemies into his hands. He was, he thought with a momentary flicker of insight, like a drunkard who knows he shouldn't imbibe yet gropes for the bottle anyway, but the realization failed to dampen his desire.

The Sister of Athena vanished. Finding himself at the base of the gibbet, Montrose turned toward the prisoner, then crowed in delight. This time it was Archibald Campbell, the Marquess and Eighth Earl of Argyll himself, with his sour, intelligent face and fleshy beak of a nose, who'd come to die. Argyll the schemer. Argyll the coward. Argyll, the cruelest and most relentless of his enemies. Argyll, whom he'd humiliated repeatedly on the battlefield, yet who'd laid him low in the end with lies and double-dealing.

Smiling pleasantly, Montrose sauntered toward him. "Good morning, my lord," he said. "I hope you enjoyed your ride in the cart."

"Spare me," Argyll said, "please! I know we didn't see eye to eye, but everything I did was to uphold the Covenant, and for the benefit of Scotland."

"First VanLengen, then Hamilton, now you. All of you sniveling for mercy. I always knew you would, had fate chosen to send *you* to the gallows." Montrose drove his fist into the other man's solar plexus, then, when he doubled over, slammed the blade of his hand against his neck.

Argyll fell heavily to the plank floor. Snarling, Montrose kicked him repeatedly. The traitor curled into a ball and wrapped his arms around his head in a pathetic attempt to shield himself. The spectators on the ground laughed and cheered.

Suddenly the Hierarch remembered the last time he'd beaten a helpless prisoner. That time, back in America, it had been Louise. Louise, who was counting on him to reappear and guide her out of the Gallery.

For a moment his savage exhilaration collapsed into shame and confusion. What was wrong with him? What was actually transpiring here? He had the sudden, disquieting suspicion that the jaws of a trap were closing on him. That if he didn't find a way to break free—which seemed to require regaining control of his emotions—the magic might never let him go of its own volition. Consumed by vengeance, no longer cognizant that he was mired in unreality, he'd torment and exterminate his old enemies over and over again.

Argyll shifted his bloody hands to peek up at his nemesis. When Montrose saw the wretch's eye, his fists clenched in hatred.

Surely it wouldn't hurt to drive one more man up the ladder and turn him off. Surely not when it was *Argyll*! Then afterwards, if Montrose still didn't return to the Gallery, he'd look for a way out when the scenario began anew.

"No!" he cried, wrenching himself around. It helped, but only a little. Even with his back turned, he still *felt* Argyll's presence drawing him like a magnet, beckoning him to continue his revenge.

"You're not real," Montrose groaned. "All of this is over. Over and done for three hundred and fifty years. I shouldn't *care* about it anymore!" He ran at the edge of the scaffold and threw himself over the railing.

Gaping, wide-eyed faces hurtled up at him. In his near delirium, he'd forgotten that people were standing directly beneath the platform. He crashed down on their heads, tumbling them to the cobblestones.

Sprawled on top of them, he took stock of a new collection of pains. He felt the stab of a broken finger, the throb of a wrenched back, but nothing that signaled a mortal wound. He'd wanted to slam headfirst into the ground, dashing out his brains or snapping his spine, but the onlookers had cushioned his fall.

Well, he'd just have to find another way to die. His sword—no, that was gone for the moment. He scrambled to his feet, then, screaming the filthiest obscenities known to the land and era of his birth, began punching and kicking the people around him, doing his best to strike a lethal blow. One of their deaths might end the scenario, too, and if not, he needed to provoke them to retaliate in kind.

For a second, the throng seemed to freeze, as if the enchantment that had spawned them, caught off guard by his eccentric behavior, required time to reprogram them.

Then, with a roar, they started fighting back.

At first, as fists flew and open hands snatched at him, he struggled frantically to defend himself. He wanted to be slain, not subdued. Then, from the corner of his eye, he glimpsed a gleaming blade. Pivoting, throwing his arms high to expose his entire torso, he lunged toward the hulking, curly-haired fellow who held it.

The dagger plunged into his chest, glanced off a rib, and punctured his right lung. He dropped, yanking the weapon from its owner's grasp in the process. For a moment the press was too tight to allow him to fall all the way down, but then people lurched backward, making room for him to slip onto the cobbles.

His breath wheezing in his throat, blood bubbling out around the knife, he waited for a tide of darkness to sweep him away. It didn't come, nor did the people goggling down at him seem inclined to finish him off. He spat at them, cursed them, feebly kicked and clawed at their legs, until at last they began to stamp on him in return.

He felt his bones breaking, his flesh tearing and pulping, his inner organs bursting. A coldness welled up inside him, creating a space between him and his agony, and the sunlight dimmed. He clenched his jaw, concerned that otherwise a reflexive spasm of terror would make him whimper.

Everything went black for an instant, and then he was standing in the crimson mist again, his sword in his hand and the highwayman's garments on his back. His body uninjured but still beset by the memory of pain, he stumbled and nearly fell.

Louise grabbed him by the arm, steadying him. "Are you all right?" she asked.

"Yes." He put his hand over hers and squeezed it.

"It seemed like you were gone for at least an hour."

"The Gallery kept putting me through alternate versions of the same scenario. I had to experiment to find a way to break free."

"Do you have any idea why?"

"I'm afraid not. Perhaps we bollixed the works by coming in together. Or perhaps, now that Charon is gone, the wonders he crafted are breaking down."

"He pretty much 'crafted' your whole Empire, didn't he? Maybe we're risking our necks to preserve a system that's destined to crumble no matter what."

It was a grim notion, and over the course of the last few days, they'd seen plenty of evidence to support it. But for some reason, it neither daunted nor angered him. Despite all the problems and perils confronting him, for the moment at least, he felt strangely confident and blithe. He grinned at his companion. "What a thoroughly demoralizing idea. I thought you were supposed to be the high-hearted optimist, and *I*, the dour cynic."

"Oh, is *that* how it's supposed to work? My apologies." Her tone became more serious. "I truly am sorry. The last thing either of us needs is discouragement. It's just that waiting for you to reappear grated on my nerves. Periodically, I imagined I heard our pursuers. Off in the distance, but inside the hall."

"It's possible you did," he said. Drawing on his Harbinger talents, he oriented himself. "So we'd better get moving." He led her onward.

After several paces, a machine-gun nest, protected by mounds of sandbags, appeared in the scarlet mist. The wraiths scrambled for cover behind the pillars, but they were an instant too slow. Sweeping in an arc, stuttering atop its tripod, the belt-fed weapon riddled them with bullets. They fell and died. And then, resurrected, they peered ahead, making sure their slayer had disappeared, rose, and continued on their way.

A pair of identical Vikings with horned helmets and long yellow braids charged out of nowhere brandishing axes. Louise shot one of them through the heart. Dropping into a crouch and thus allowing the other twin's weapon to whiz harmlessly over his head, Montrose thrust his point into his assailant's throat and up inside his skull.

The corpses vanished, and the fugitives pressed on. "Is it much farther?" Louise asked.

In point of fact, it wasn't, but Montrose didn't get a chance to tell her so. Abruptly, leather creaked, and despite the stench of the billowing mist, which currently reeked of blood, he caught the scent of oiled metal. Pivoting, he saw three riflemen emerging from the murk. Each had had his mouth sculpted into a fixed, exaggerated grin as a token of his allegiance to the Smiling Lord.

Spying the fugitives, they shouldered their weapons, then vanished. Evidently the Gallery had whisked them away into one of its more elaborate fantasies. Montrose and Louise strode on.

The Scot heard other hunters prowling on either side. He struggled against the growing suspicion that he and his companion weren't going to escape after all. And then, all at once, the world wasn't red anymore. He was standing at the end of the Gallery, looking out between two of the outermost columns at another building, this one carved all around with scenes from the Trojan War. Immediately across the way, Ajax was hurling his stone at Hector. Which meant that Montrose had navigated his way directly to the entrance to the secret passage.

Grinning, he started to rush out into the open, and only then noticed the half dozen Legionnaires standing several yards away on the path that ran between the two structures, waiting for him to emerge. Frantically, he grabbed Louise's arm and jerked her behind one of the pillars.

"Are we in the right spot?" she whispered.

"Yes."

"Then don't worry. I'll divert the guards' attention." She stared at her crossbow until it drifted upward out of her hand. Suspended just below the ceiling, where no one looking in from outside could see it, the weapon floated along until it passed beyond the sentries. Then it flew into the open, dashed itself at the ground, and bounced banging and clattering down the path.

The guards all lurched around in the direction of the racket. Two of them snapped off shots at it. The fugitives darted out of hiding, and Montrose pressed down on Ajax's missile.

For an instant, the carved boulder didn't move, and he had the sickening feeling that someone had seen fit to render the catch inoperable. Then the rounded shape sank into the surrounding stonework, and the tableau swung silently inward. He and Louise scrambled into the darkness beyond, then hastily closed the door.

Forty

Like the Artificers' maze, the secret passage was dimly lit by a few phosphorescent green stones set into the walls. Montrose and Louise rushed along it until they were sure the soldiers hadn't followed them inside. Finally the Scot raised his hand, signaling a halt. "We seem to be in the clear," he said. "Let's relax for a moment."

"That suits me," she said, the edge of her mask catching the sickly viridian glow. "Thank the Bright Powers our pursuers didn't know about the secret door."

"I was reasonably certain they wouldn't. You can't tell many people about a hidden path, not even your own retainers, lest its existence become known to all. In my glory days, I had the Smiling Lord's confidence as much as anyone, but I'm sure I only know a few of the clandestine ways in the Seat, and some of those—including this one, now that I think about it—I discovered on my own. Unfortunately, I *don't* know a secret route which will take us all the way to my...master"—to his momentary annoyance, he found himself stumbling over the word—"or one of his inner circle of advisors. At some point, we'll have to move back into the open."

"Now that we've penetrated the outer ring of defenses, could we simply surrender to some officer or other, and *ask* to see the Smiling Lord?"

Montrose shook his head. "We're condemned felons. We killed loyal Hierarchs during our escape from the pit. What's more, everyone here is on edge, waiting for the beginning of the war. I'm still afraid the guards might slay us on sight. Better to reveal ourselves only to someone we actually want to talk to."

"And hope *he'll* listen."

"I'm banking on the fact that the Smiling Lord and his lieutenants have known me for decades and in some cases centuries. They'll be amazed I didn't have the good sense to flee Stygia when I had the chance, instead of thrusting my head back into the lion's jaws. Especially if I'm not bent on spying, sabotage, or assassination, and when I intrude on them begging for a hearing, it should become obvious that such is not the case. They ought to be curious enough at least to listen before sending us to the block, and after that, it will all come down to my eloquence." Which hadn't saved him at his trial, but having chosen his course, he saw no point in dwelling on that now.

"That sounds reasonable," she said, "particularly since you always had a silver tongue." She tossed her slouch hat away, discarded her quiver, shook out her tousled honey-blond hair, and shrugged off her trench coat. He found his eyes drawn to her slender form, now clad only in the sleeveless white shirt, shiny blue sash, baggy khaki shorts, and sandals she'd donned in the dungeon beneath the Soulforges. "With luck, the soldiers will assume that we couldn't possibly have slipped into the palace itself. Still, the whole citadel will likely be on the alert for a lady bundled up in gray and a redheaded gentleman in black Cavalier finery. Therefore we should change our appearances." She reached for her visor.

"Leave that. It's not particularly distinctive by itself, and even if it were, no one but a Thrall would walk the corridors of the Seat unmasked. But otherwise, changing our looks is a good idea." He stripped down to his breeches and high boots. "Hm. Even though people walk around in all sorts of outlandish outfits, we're underdressed for Court, and thus too conspicuous. Still, we're better off than we were before. We'll just have to filch other attire at the first opportunity."

She gave him a mischievous smile. "*You* still look way too much like the Montrose everyone in this castle knows. But I can fix that. Take off your mask and go down on your knees."

When he obeyed, she drew her knife and began deftly shearing his long hair off close to his scalp. To his own amusement, he felt a reflexive pang of dismay, even though he knew his cherished lovelocks would reappear soon enough. Every wraith body possessed one innate shape, to which it would always revert unless fixed in another by a Masquer's Arcanos.

In any case, there was something pleasant about the cool, light touch of her fingers on his skin. He nearly regretted it when she stepped back and peered at him critically. "That will have to do," she said. "I don't trust myself to cut off the mustache without amputating your upper lip along with it."

"I appreciate your restraint," he said, rising and replacing his mask. He considered his rapier for a moment, then hung the baldric over his shoulder once more. He and Louise could alter their appearances still further by abandoning their weapons, but he couldn't quite bring himself to press on into danger unarmed. "Shall we finish up this little errand?"

"Why not?" she said.

The tunnels had a musty smell and a general air of disuse, as if no one had entered them in years. Still, Montrose and Louise traversed them warily, senses probing the darkness for signs that someone else was present. As far as the Scot could tell, they were alone.

At odd moments he continued to experience the buoyancy, almost a giddiness, of spirit that had been bubbling up inside him ever since his escape from the illusory Edinburgh. Trying to account for it, he noticed that his Shadow seemed shrunken, almost quiescent. It made him feel as if he'd carried a heavy burden a long way and finally been permitted to set it down.

"Are you aware," Louise murmured, "that you're beaming like an idiot?"

"Perhaps I'm on the brink of achieving Transcendence," he replied. "Wouldn't you be irked if the condition truly existed, and a Hierarch scoundrel like me got there ahead of you? No, seriously, I simply feel exhilarated. I suppose it's a natural reaction to having overcome so many obstacles, even when we know there are more to come."

"I wasn't really complaining," she said. "Even a somewhat simpleminded smile is more pleasant than that closed, haughty Anacreon face you tend to put on whenever you aren't actually scowling and glaring at me."

They walked on quietly until they turned a corner and started up the steep, narrow staircase that would take them into the palace. Then he said, "You shouldn't have renounced your painting. Honthorst told me you were the most gifted student he'd ever taught."

Louise looked at him as if she didn't quite know how to take his remark. "I told you why I did it."

"Yes. But in the end, you did struggle to break the vampire's hold on you. And it was no disgrace to fail. You were merely one of the Quick, and he, a creature with supernatural powers. Suppose you saw fit to use your Spook abilities to injure some unfortunate mortal. How much of a chance would he have against you?"

She sighed. "Naturally I've told myself that countless times. So have my friends and superiors in the Sisterhood. But sometimes you know a thing in your head and still don't feel it in your heart." She paused, then asked, "Do you still write any poetry at all?"

"No, but unlike the empty canvases you might have filled, my virgin sheets of parchment represent no great loss to anyone."

"I don't know about that," she said. "At the very least, your verses gave pleasure to you and those who loved you. Why, then, did you give them up?"

He shrugged. "You remember my customary subject matter. Honor. Duty. Stainless knights embarked on glorious quests. When I attained a wiser perspective, I lost my muse. 'Look out for yourself first, last, and always, because that's what all the other lads are doing' may be the only sensible principle on which to base one's existence, but I could never figure out how to make the sentiment sound sublime in rhyme and meter."

"Perhaps that's because, deep down, you never truly believed it."

He expected her remark to evoke the usual twinge of irritation, but it didn't. Instead he felt a murkier emotion, something that might almost have been sorrow. Halting, he turned to look her in the eyes. "My lady, as you may have discerned, I don't seem to hate you anymore. Somehow I've put what happened in The Hague behind me. But that still doesn't mean I've miraculously reverted to the Montrose who wooed you then, or that I ever could. My current mode of existence has served me well. By committing what you would no doubt deem crimes and atrocities, I've won myself as desirable an existence as any ghost attains in this bleak, cold *demimonde* of ours. You mustn't expect anything different of me, or you'll be cruelly disappointed."

"Very well," she replied. "But notice, I didn't *ask* you to change, not this time. You're arguing with yourself."

He snorted. "You're being disingenuous. The call to virtue was clearly implied. And now we'd best be quiet for a bit. We're approaching our entry into the great keep."

The stairs led to a gray door with a peephole in the center. Peering through the fish-eye lens, Montrose saw a long, narrow chamber, almost a corridor, that someone had seen fit to turn into a portrait gallery. Electric illumination gleamed on oils of Omar Bradley, the Duke of Wellington, Saladin, and Hannibal.

As far as he could tell from his vantage point, no one was on the other side of the door. He pulled a lever and the panel cracked silently open. He and Louise scrambled through, then pushed it shut. From this side, it was a picture of a scowling Ulysses Grant. Montrose had always thought that the artist had made the Union commander look hung-over.

"Where now?" whispered Louise.

"That way, I think," he said, turning to the left.

It had always been impossible to walk through the Smiling Lord's palace without being reminded periodically of violence. Even the brightest, airiest halls, given over to the most peaceful and frivolous of pursuits, celebrated mayhem in one way or another. Nazi banners hung above the indoor tennis courts. A howitzer sat on display in the middle of an arboretum, and many of the residents, even those performing the least martial of duties, carried weapons and affected the uniforms of one military force or another, hoplites and pilots from von Richthofen's Flying Circus rubbing elbows with dragoons and condottieri.

Now, however, the simple realization that one was inside a vast fortress, indeed, a shrine to armed conflict, had changed to a chilling feeling that actual strife was imminent. The dance halls, theaters, natatoria, and other recreational facilities were nearly as deserted as the commons beyond the castle walls. Servants and minor officials *scurried* through the corridors under the cold, watchful eyes of a plethora of sentries and patrols. Whenever Louise and Montrose neared a party of guards, he tensed, expecting them to order him to halt, or simply to open fire. But though some eyed the fugitives curiously, they allowed them to pass unchallenged.

Finally the pair reached one of the many apartment complexes where the Smiling Lord's lesser minions made their homes. The Scot rapped on a black door with a brazen skull-face knocker. Receiving no response, he glanced up and down the hall, making sure no one was watching, then twisted the handle. The door was locked, so he lifted his foot to kick it.

"Let me try," said Louise. She stared at the lock for a moment, and then the tumblers clicked. "*Voilà*. Sometimes I can do that, when it's a simple mechanism."

Montrose opened the door on a parlor containing a snooker table, a rack of cues, a stained-glass chandelier, and little else. Beyond it were two considerably smaller chambers, one of them crammed full of the chairs, sofa, stereo, bookshelf, and other amenities, which in another residence, might have occupied the front room.

"I know the officials who dwell here," Montrose said, heading for the rear of the flat. "A married couple, so there should be clothes for each of us." He opened an ornately carved armoire.

They began rooting through an eclectic collection of garments. She pulled out a pair of jeans, a matching denim jacket decorated with brass rivets, and a cotton work shirt, casual, modern garments such as she'd worn when he'd encountered her in America. "So even wicked Stygians sometimes marry," she said.

"A few," he replied, coming upon a bottle-green suit tailored in a style from the Restoration era. It was similar enough to the clothing he'd worn in life to be comfortable, yet different enough from his black highwayman outfit that no one would mistake the one for the other. He lifted it out.

"But you were never even tempted?"

He thought of the many lovers, Thralls and courtesans mostly, he'd known since his arrival in Stygia, women whose innate sensuality had been sculpted into a dazzling and sometimes unhuman erotic perfection. Each unique, yet somehow just the same as all the others. Beauties as intoxicating as sweet liqueur, and just as cloying once one had had one's fill. "No. The Restless can theoretically endure forever. That's a long time to bind yourself to one person, particularly with no possibility of children."

"And especially when your selfish beast of a husband insists on taking up most of the space in your home with an enormous toy."

He grinned. "Actually, Maria is the selfish beast, a fact which shouldn't surprise an Amazon like you. The table is her diversion." He started to unbuckle his belt, then faltered. For an instant, it had felt wholly natural to undress before her eyes, no doubt because they'd been naked together as mortal lovers, and again in the Artificers' dungeon. But now perhaps it wasn't appropriate. Flustered, he turned his back, and heard her do the same.

As he donned his new mask, a cool, smooth piece of carved jade that left his lower lip and chin uncovered, Louise said, "I'm decent." He turned. The domino she'd chosen was highly polished gold. He could see the reflection of his face smeared across the front of it. "Are we ready to press on?" she asked.

"As ready as we're likely to get, I suppose. Unfortunately, it isn't going to be easy."

"You mean, unlike all the other hurdles we've jumped to come this far?"

"I didn't mean it will necessarily be *more* difficult. God forbid. But you saw that the palace is crawling with guards. They didn't challenge us because we weren't trying to go anywhere important. But the suites of the Smiling Lord and his chief officers are a different matter. No one will be allowed in without giving a full accounting of himself."

"So how do we proceed?"

"Scout around. With luck, we'll spot a hole in somebody's security. And if not, we'll figure out how to make one."

She nodded. "Let's do it."

For the next two hours, they prowled through the Seat, past innumerable displays of armor, weapons and battle flags, and countless grotesquely shaped fountains spewing cold, hissing liquid flame, inspecting the portals leading to the more august personages of the fortress. Soldiers of the Order of the Avenging Flame stood before every entry, guns at the ready. Frequently barghests in iron muzzles crouched at their feet, eyes burning, nostrils snuffling and flaring.

"What do you think?" murmured Louise at last.

"I don't know yet," Montrose admitted. "I'm confident we could fight our way past one of these groups of sentries, but the noise would bring a host of others down on our heads. We need to pass through with a minimum of commotion, and I can't see how to do it."

"Perhaps I could divert them while you slip through."

"Conceivably so, but unless you managed your subsequent retreat with extraordinary cleverness, they might well destroy you. I'd prefer to stick together."

She smiled crookedly. "What's my paltry little existence, against the survival of all Stygia? You said that the Imperium is the only thing that keeps Oblivion at bay."

He grimaced. "Be that as it may, we're not going to offer you up like some sort of sacrificial lamb. I think your career as a nun and a Heretic has given you a morbid craving for martyrdom."

"No, I'm just getting more and more apprehensive. Time is passing. Open war could break out at any moment. What's more, sooner or later one of these patrols is going to accost us, just making a random check. We have to make some kind of a move. I can't bear the thought of you coming this far, only to—" She faltered, staring at the tall, arched double doors at the end of a branching passage. A lone Legionnaire, an AK-47 clasped in his mail gauntlets, stood before them. "Is *that* anyplace important?"

"Yes," Montrose said, excitement thrilling along his nerves. "As a matter of fact, one of the Smiling Lord's most trusted ministers occupies that suite. He must have refused anything more than a token guard. Of all of them, he's the one who would. He's always eschewed ostentation. Defended himself by blending into the background."

"Then this is it. Our best chance."

"Yes. Keep walking. We don't want the guard to notice our interest." They sauntered on, and then, when they'd passed beyond the soldier's view, Montrose invoked his Harbinger abilities. Cool darkness welled out of his pores and flowed across his body. "Keep watch here until I call you."

"Be careful," she said.

He slipped back around the corner and skulked on toward the double doors. It occurred to him that the occupant of the suite might have declined an abundance of armed guards because he had less obvious defenses in place. Booby traps. Alarms. Magical wards. That would be thoroughly in character also. But it was too late to worry about the possibility now.

He was two yards away when the Legionnaire somehow sensed his presence. Wide-eyed, the soldier pivoted toward him, lifting his assault rifle. Lunging, Montrose punched him in the jaw.

The Legionnaire reeled backward, thumped against the double doors, and collapsed. Montrose grabbed for him and somehow managed to keep both the armored wraith and his firearm from clanging down on the polished marble floor. Lowering them gently, he listened for the sound of reinforcements rushing to the scene. As far as he could tell, no one was coming. "Louise," he breathed, just loud enough, he judged, for her hypersensitive ears to hear.

She hurried down the corridor, and he dissolved his cloak of shadow. "I heard you hit him," she said, "but I was close by, and expecting to hear something. I doubt anyone else noticed."

"Good," Montrose said. He tried the doors. They were locked, and the unconscious sentry didn't appear to have any keys. "Can you get these open?"

"I can try." She stared at the lock, but nothing happened. "All right, then, so much for finesse." With a sharp *crack!* the panels lurched inward. Montrose winced at the additional noise, but with luck, no one would notice it, either.

They dragged the Legionnaire into a dark, high-ceilinged, sparsely furnished antechamber. From deeper in the suite came the whir of a computer, and then the rustle of old parchment. The fugitives readied their weapons and crept toward the sounds, through one gloomy, spartan chamber after another.

Within a few paces, Montrose perceived that they were also proceeding toward a fracture in space. Frowning, he wondered what it portended, hoped it was nothing that would complicate his plans.

Wan illumination flickered through an arched doorway. He and Louise skulked up to it and peeked inside. In the center of an austere study sat a clerkish little man in a gray tunic and breeches, alternately studying the monitor of a PC and an ancient map of the Isle of Sorrows drawn in faded bronze-colored ink. Heaps of books and papers lay atop his enormous oak desk, along with a leather domino and a darksteel dagger. The air smelled of dust, and barrow-flame candles burned coldly in the sconces along the walls. The disturbance in space emanated from a large freestanding mirror in the far corner. With its richly carved golden frame, capped with Charon's mask glaring out above a pair of crossed scythes, it looked utterly out of place in the otherwise drab chamber, but Montrose was certain its owner hadn't installed it for decoration. It was something akin to a Nihil, a magical gateway to another place, possibly intended to serve as an escape hatch.

Well, he'd just have to make sure his fellow Anacreon didn't get a chance to scramble through it. He nodded to Louise, and the two of them rushed into the study. In an instant he had his rapier poised at the other man's throat, while she had her pistol aimed at his head.

"Hello, Chiarmonte," Montrose said.

Forty-One

As the Cavalier might have expected, the little spy master looked momentarily startled, but afterwards, didn't betray so much as a hint of fear. "Lord Montrose," he said. "My compliments on your flair for disguise. Chopping off all that red hair thoroughly transformed your appearance."

"For the worse, I suspect."

"Sadly, yes, but one must sacrifice to excel at any art. I hope you're going to present me to the lady."

"My name is Louise," she said. "I'm a Sister of Athena."

Chiarmonte lifted a thin gray eyebrow. "Is this the same Heretic," he asked Montrose, "you spoke of at your trial? She who betrayed you in life, and whose appearance in the Underworld inspired such overwhelming hatred that your Shadow seized control of you?"

"Yes," said the Scot. "Our relationship has changed since then."

"Evidently."

"We didn't come here to hurt you," Montrose said. "If we had, we could have done it already. We simply need to talk to you. If we put up our weapons, will you give us a hearing before you reach for an alarm button or shout for aid?"

"You have my word," the Venetian said.

Louise returned her gun to its holster, and Montrose lowered his blade. "You'll recall," said the Scot, "that I warned the Court of unknown enemies plotting against the Empire in the vicinity of the lower Mississippi."

"Of course," Chiarmonte said. "They were supposedly murdering Heretic priests and Pardoners, and dispatching corrupt confessors to poison people's psyches."

"Well, I'm convinced that the same conspiracy is at work here in Stygia," said Montrose. "It's manipulating the Seven to go to war with one another."

"How is that possible? How could one manipulate the gods?"

"Fairly easily, perhaps, considering that they were already predisposed to believe the worst of one another. A cunning enemy could use his own troops to convince each Deathlord that his colleagues were raiding his holdings. Whereupon each of them would retaliate in kind, escalating the hostilities without any further impetus from outside."

"But how would said foe insinuate his warriors into Stygia and keep them hidden long enough to initiate the process?"

"I don't know," Montrose said. "But you once told me that no security system is impregnable, and I daresay our presence here in your quarters demonstrates just how right you were."

"I see your point," said the Venetian. "Still, do you have any hard evidence to support your hypothesis?"

Montrose grimaced. "No. But doesn't it make sense? The Seven have been maneuvering against each other for half a century, but none of them has ever dared to wage actual war on the others. Because each had every reason to doubt he could win, and knew that in any case such a conflict might well cripple the Empire beyond any hope of repair. Why, then, is it happening now? Conceivably they've all gone mad, but I think someone has gulled them into believing that war is coming whether they desire it or not."

"And consider this," said Louise. "Even if the coming civil strife doesn't destroy Stygia, it will almost certainly prevent you from acting to quell the trouble brewing in the Shadowlands. Do you honestly think the simultaneous emergence of the two threats is a coincidence?"

The intelligence officer frowned. "I confess, I'm not a great believer in coincidence."

"Then let's talk to the Smiling Lord together," Montrose said. "He'll listen if you ask him to. We'll convince him to stop the hostilities before they go any further."

"Even if he believed you," said Chiarmonte, "I don't know that he could arrest them now."

"He has to," the Cavalier replied. "Look, you and I know how the seraphim customarily communicate with one another. About the same way they condescend to us. They're haughty, aloof, mysterious, hoarding every secret and jealous of every advantage. That's partly why they distrust each other so, why this ludicrous situation could arise in the first place. If the Smiling Lord speaks openly for once, if it's clear that he's concerned for the entire realm and not just his own personal welfare, he can cut through everyone's paranoia. Particularly if they all privately dread the prospect of war, and unless they've gone utterly insane, they must."

"It's an interesting idea," said the smaller man thoughtfully. "But I'm not sure it would be the best way to proceed. You see, though you've done an admirable job of piecing together a theory, there are aspects of the current situation of which you remain altogether ignorant."

"What are they?" Montrose asked.

Slowly, as if he feared a sudden move still might provoke the intruders to attack him, Chiarmonte pushed his chair back. The legs squeaked on the gleaming stone floor. Rising, he gestured toward the mirror behind him. "That's a doorway, Sister, as Lord Montrose has no doubt already perceived. If the two of you will follow me through, I'll show you something you really ought to see."

Montrose frowned. The discussion seemed to be going as well as he could realistically have hoped, and he trusted Chiarmonte as far as he trusted any of his fellow courtiers. Still, he was reluctant to step from this quiet room, where he and Louise at least appeared to hold the upper hand, into the unknown. "Whatever it is, can't you just tell us about it?"

"It wouldn't have the same impact," the Venetian said. "My friend, I'm a good judge of character, and I'm inclined to believe in you. I always doubted you wanted to carve out your own shabby little Shadowlands kingdom, whatever that ass Demetrius imagined. I think it equally unlikely that you've returned to our master's stronghold in the desperate hope of tricking him into embarking on some disastrous course of action, knowing full well he'll keep you close at hand to chastise if it goes awry. I think that, despite the company you keep—pardon me, Sister—and all other appearances to the contrary, you truly are a loyal vassal of this Seat, striving to save your master and the entire Hierarchy from a calamity. But a show of faith on *your* part would help assuage any lingering doubts."

Turning to Montrose, Louise said, "We knew we'd have to relinquish control to someone eventually."

"True," the Scot replied. "We'll accompany you, milord Anacreon."

Chiarmonte nodded, turned, and walked into the mirror, vanishing the instant he came into contact with it. Ripples of light streamed across the glass. For an instant Montrose thought he could still see the spy master's shadowy image on the other side, and then that too was gone.

"I'll go next," said Montrose. As he stepped through, he felt a stab of bitter sorrow, a twinge of hunger, and the sensation of hurtling upward like a rocket. Then he stumbled from the magical doorway into a cave illuminated only by a barrow-fire lantern in Chiarmonte's hand. Louise arrived a moment later.

"Where are we?" Montrose asked.

"Deep below Charon's keep," Chiarmonte said. "Follow me, and watch your heads. The ceiling dips low in places." He moved away from the portal—visible on this side as a rippling in the air—and through an opening in the left-hand wall.

As the three wraiths proceeded down the passage, Montrose perceived more zones of warped and fractured space. Indeed, the distortions were more easily discernible than any he'd ever encountered, even in the most chaotic reaches of the Tempest. They blazed like bent and braided lengths of white-hot iron, dazzling, nearly blinding his Harbinger's sight. He wondered what could possibly be responsible.

Something hissed. A flickering light, possessed of a disquieting, indefinable quality, tinged the gloom ahead. Then the passage ended, depositing the trio on a ledge. Montrose gazed outward, then gasped.

The ghosts stood partway up the craggy wall of a gargantuan basalt chamber, beneath a lofty dome of a ceiling graven with immense runes, and at the summit of a narrow path spiraling downward. Far, far below, seething like boiling oil at the bottom of a cauldron, was a lake of darkness. Montrose had the impression that it was swirling like a vortex, though he couldn't actually be sure. Though its depths were black as pitch, pale sparks and flames danced across its surface, the source of the stark, vaguely nauseating illumination.

Montrose loathed the sight of the pool, yet simultaneously yearned to throw himself in. Or to push his companions in. With an effort, he wrenched his eyes away.

"Dear God," Louise whimpered, "what is it?"

Montrose pivoted. The Heretic was leaning far out into space, staring down into the abyss. When he took hold of her arm, she tensed as if she meant to fight him, but then suffered him to draw her back and turn her away from the spectacle below.

"One could call it the largest Nihil ever seen," he said, "but even that wouldn't do it justice. Because it's not just an opening into the Tempest. It's a window on the Labyrinth, or perhaps even the heart of the Void itself."

Chiarmonte nodded like a teacher indicating his approval of a clever student. "It is indeed." He strolled on down the path. The fugitives followed more carefully, fighting the irrational urge to look at the black whirlpool again.

"Did Charon build his city on top of it, knowing it was here?" asked Louise. "I can't imagine that."

"He may even have opened it himself," the Venetian said. "Oblivion is the ultimate threat, but it's an extraordinary source of power as well, and those"—he waved his hand at the cabalistic symbols carved in the stone high above their heads—"allowed him to tap it to work his wonders."

"Rotting his soul in the process," she said.

The Venetian shrugged. "All monarchs do that anyway, one way or another." He ambled on.

Montrose wished they could turn around and return to the fortress. He didn't want to remain in the vicinity of the vortex another moment, let alone descend closer to it. But evidently Chiarmonte had more to show them. "This is all very interesting," said the Scot. "But what does it have to do with the present crisis?"

"What," said Chiarmonte, "if someone else were able to use the energies of the pool to influence the course of the war?"

Montrose's eyes narrowed. "Has the Smiling Lord figured out how to do that?"

"Well," said the smaller man, a hint of laughter in his voice, "not exactly. He certainly can't manipulate them with anything like the facility the Emperor undoubtedly acquired." He stepped over a knobby outcropping of rock. "But here's what's going to happen. Our master has invited each of the other Deathlords to a clandestine meeting in the Tower, supposedly to seal an alliance. I'm certain that, for one reason or another, at least some will attend. Alas, they won't find Prince Ares—he'll be many levels above them—but they will, to their dismay, encounter one another."

"And then, you hope, attack and destroy each other," Montrose said, "as opposed to simply withdrawing. I wouldn't count on it. They're too wary, too calculating, to act so precipitously."

"Ordinarily, you might be right," Chiarmonte said. "But suppose the Lord of Violence weaves a spell to infuse them with homicidal rage. Suppose he augments the innate powers of his office with Charon's secret source of magic. Don't you think his rivals might stand and fight then?"

Montrose frowned, pondering, wondering if the sovereign to whom he'd sworn allegiance actually had a chance to seize the Imperial throne. If so, then his lieutenants, Montrose included if he could win back his favor, would rank as high as the Seven did now!

Louise touched him on the arm, dispelling his momentary fantasy of glory. "James," she murmured.

He grimaced. "I know. You're right. Chiarmonte, it doesn't matter who's best positioned to win the conflict. The point is that the Seven shouldn't be fighting in the first place, not at the instigation of a foe who means to exploit our internal conflicts to his own advantage. I respect the Smiling Lord. I daresay he's as wise and powerful as any of his peers. But do you honestly think he's capable of taking Charon's place? Or of putting a war-ravaged Stygia back together, with Fate only knows how many of the Legions destroyed, and the other Deathlords slaughtered or driven into hiding?"

At last Chiarmonte halted. He turned, smiled, and said, "Frankly, no. I think that the Imperium is in for a long, bleak time of weakness, disorganization, and hardship at the very least. My true masters conceived my mission in Stygia as a diversion to draw attention from the offensive in America, just as you hypothesized. But they had no idea just how much I could achieve. I think that one day, in the last bloody hours before the death of all things, people will look back and recognize that mine was actually the more significant victory of the two."

Louise snatched for her pistol, and Montrose raised his sword. "Your 'true masters?'" he said. "Are you saying that *you're* part of the conspiracy?"

"Yes," said the other Anacreon. "You would never have suspected it of shrewd, responsible Chiarmonte, would you? So perhaps it will comfort you to know that I'm not him. I killed him and took on his shape just a little while ago." His body grew tall and gaunt, his skin darkened, and his gray medieval attire became the folds of a white toga. A sardonyx helm clasped casually under his arm, he gave the other wraiths an ironic smile.

"Demetrius!" Montrose said.

"If you like," the Oracle said. "Although actually, that identity is a mask as well. Haven't you ever wondered how, after centuries as an obscure functionary, the Greek abruptly developed the talent and ambition necessary to attract the notice of the Smiling Lord? Simple. I murdered him and usurped his place."

"James," Louise said tensely, "he impersonated Chiarmonte because he guessed that that was who you'd turn to, especially if there was only a single guard watching the door to the suite. He *planned* to bring us here."

"She's right," said Demetrius. "You seem to be a man of almost infinite resourcefulness, milord Anacreon. You've certainly accomplished feats I would never have expected of the jaded debauchee I remember, whoring, gambling, and sidestepping all but the least onerous of duties. But you've been operating under an insurmountable handicap from the start, namely, my divinatory powers. I assure you, no true Stygian can match them. They warned me early on that you alone might foil my schemes. Unlikely as that seemed, I took steps to ensure you wouldn't get the chance. I persuaded the Smiling Lord to dispatch you to the Shadowlands, and passed along the intelligence which enabled the Soul Pirates to intercept your convoy. Naturally I hoped they'd destroy you, but even when they didn't, it was all right. On the Mississippi, unwittingly advancing our agenda through your persecution of the Heretics, you couldn't interfere while I got on with the task of clouding your master's mind."

"And how did you do that?" Montrose asked.

"I'm afraid you give him too much credit for sagacity," Demetrius said. "Employing my Art, I long ago determined that he was the weak link among the Seven. Not in terms of might—he can more than hold his own on that score—but with regard to his personality. He's by far the youngest of them, and accordingly sees himself as vulnerable and despised. I enhanced his anxieties by various means, mystical and psychological, and made him increasingly dependent on me. In due course one of my minions pretended to try to assassinate him.

"Naturally he assumed that one of the other Deathlords was responsible. After that, it was an easy matter to persuade him to attack his colleagues' holdings in a way that would cause them to blame one another. As it happens, my lord, though I'm proof that a single enemy agent can infiltrate the Onyx Tower, and even sneak an occasional confederate in, I don't think an entire armed host *could* conduct operations in Stygia without somebody finding out about it. But with the Smiling Lord's soldiers at my disposal, I had no need of other troops.

"Soon open war appeared inevitable, and your sovereign was well on the way to luring his peers into their perilous rendezvous. I'd cast the necessary enchantments to channel the energies of the vortex to him at the proper time—since he has no idea this place exists, his amplified magical prowess should come as a pleasant surprise at first—and to feed the mystical forces unleashed by the battle back into the pool, with, I hope, useful or even spectacular results. In short, I thought I could relax. Imagine my chagrin when, scrying, I observed two fugitives, an auburn-haired swordsman and a lovely blond woman, making their way to the palace.

"The omens indicated that you could *still* ruin my schemes, Montrose. Foreseeing that you'd enter the Crimson Gallery, I tampered with the magic there in the hope of causing it to swallow you forever. But by whatever means, you escaped that trap as you'd evaded so many other hazards. Luckily I also had a backup plan—impersonating Chiarmonte—in readiness. You see, uncertain of how much you knew, I couldn't simply let the palace guards deal with you. There was at least a slim chance they'd arrest rather than slay you, and then you might have spoken to someone who would listen. So I opted to defuse the threat you represented by luring you away to a secluded spot like this."

"To kill us, one would assume," Montrose said, wondering if the saturnine Oracle was insane. "But we three appear to be alone here, milord Anacreon. It's two against one, you're unarmed, and we have the drop on you. However potent your various Arcanoi, we can slay you in an instant should you force our hands."

"But Spectres don't fear Oblivion," Demetrius said, leering. "I certainly won't mind going down into the darkness now that I know my people will be avenged. And they will. I explained my scheme—bless you both for providing me an opportunity to strut and gloat at last—but perhaps I didn't make it clear just how rapidly it's racing to fruition. Maddened by Prince Ares's magic, the other Deathlords will be at one another's throats within the hour. And rest assured, my friends, whether you dispatch me or not, you'll be in no position to mar the festivities."

The whisper of the shadowy maelstrom changed. For an instant Montrose had no idea how, then realized a portion of the sound was now emanating from the rocky wall above him as well as from the abyss below. Perhaps the hissing overhead had been there all along, but he hadn't been able to pick it out until it changed timbre.

With a ghastly sense of foreboding, he raised his eyes. Nihils no larger than pinpoints dotted the escarpment. *I should have seen them!* he thought, hating himself, though he knew that, with Demetrius and the repellent yet fascinating vortex to occupy his attention, no one else would have noticed either. The tiny, glittering openings lengthened into fissures, and scores of horrors, the majority creatures with dark, gleaming scales and two reptilian faces, flowed through.

"Dear Jesus," Louise breathed.

The sound of her voice pierced Montrose with an excruciating pang of love and anguish. Demetrius laughed, and his fellow doomshades streamed down the cliff like a black torrent.

The Obsidian Blade

Dark Kingdoms: Volume Three

Dedication

For Kendall, Micky, and Jade

One

The horde of Spectres surged down the wall of the gargantuan basalt vault in a black wave, clinging to the vertical surface almost as easily as if it were level, charging the wraiths on the narrow path which spiraled into the depths.

Though she must have realized it was a futile gesture, Louise lifted her pistol and started firing at the doomshades. Her honey-blond hair and golden domino gleamed in the eerie light flickering up from the bottom of the chamber. James Graham, onetime Marquess of Montrose, thrust his darksteel rapier into the breast of Demetrius, the traitor who had led them into this trap.

The gaunt, swarthy man kept laughing brokenly as his knees buckled and black waves of Oblivion pulsed through his form. His barrow-fire lantern shattered on the ledge, while the sardonyx helm slipped from beneath his arm, fell, and rolled over the drop. His human body warped into a black, scaly horror with two reptilian faces—a creature resembling many of the Spectres hurtling down the path—and then dissolved altogether.

Invoking his Harbinger abilities, Montrose wrapped his arm around Louise's waist and flew off the ledge, an instant before the hissing, gibbering doomshades swept over the path like a torrent.

The dark whirlpool at the bottom of the vault was the largest Nihil Montrose had ever seen. He sensed that the rift opened not merely on the chaotic dimensions of the Tempest, but into the Labyrinth, the very heart of that hellish realm, or even into the ravenous nothingness of the Void itself. He struggled not to look at it. To hurtle upwards.

But it was impossible. The wound in space silently called to him, and without consciously willing it, he halted his ascent. Peered down at the pale flames dancing atop the swirling, churning darkness. Plummeted.

Louise screamed his name and pummeled him, snapping him out of his trance. He struggled to rise again but his powers of levitation were unequal to the task. He felt as if the Nihil had augmented the force of gravity to drag him down with brute force. Straining his abilities to the utmost, he managed to slam down on the path at a point considerably lower than the one he'd taken off from.

"I can't fly us out," he said. "The vortex won't let me."

"I figured that out," said Louise. She gestured at the Spectres, charging them again, streaming down the twisting path. "Here come our friends. Let me see if I can slow them down." She peered intently up the slope, her hands closing into fists, and he realized she was invoking her psychokinetic abilities.

With a crash, a portion of the cliff crumbled. An avalanche poured down, crushing doomshades and sweeping them into the gulf, arresting the forward momentum of the charge. Taking advantage of the enemy's momentary consternation, making sure he didn't veer out far enough or rise high enough to catch a glimpse of the vortex, Montrose flew up the path, dispatched three Spectres in as many seconds, then made a hasty retreat when the monsters poised themselves to strike back at him.

Alighting back at Louise's side, he said, "Nice trick. How many times can you do it?" Her Spook abilities were really only intended for moving loose objects around. A display of force like crushing a mass of solid basalt strained them to the utmost.

"Not nearly enough to destroy them all," she wheezed. "It would be helpful if you could think of a trick or two of your own."

"I'll give it a try," he said. Employing his Harbinger senses, he scanned the area, seeking a trans-dimensional warp he could use to transport them to another place. Ordinarily one wouldn't expect to find such things within the borders of Stygia or any of the other islands of stability inside the Tempest. But due to the proximity of the vortex, space was fractured here, so much so that the walls were riddled with tiny Nihils, a phenomenon normally encountered only in the Shadowlands of Earth. But he couldn't locate a gateway large enough for his purposes. Only Demetrius's magick mirror, inaccessible in the cave at the very summit of the path.

Montrose picked Louise up and flew farther along the descent, keeping ahead of their pursuers, landing about two thirds of the way down the chamber wall. He wondered grimly how much deeper they could retreat without succumbing to the impulse to fling themselves into the vortex. The closer they got, the more difficult it became to block out its beckoning presence, loathsome yet infinitely fascinating.

He wondered if it might not be preferable to let the Spectres have them, or better still, to slay each other, then angrily thrust the thought aside. Undone before by treachery, he'd lost the war he'd fought in life. Somehow, this time around, he was going to win. The welfare of all the Restless and perhaps even the Quick depended on it. Louise was right, he had to think of a trick—

Up the path, four Spectres vanished into the cliff face. Montrose peered frantically about, spied the hissing Nihil holes pocking the expanse of basalt above his head. A split-second later the openings lengthened into fissures, and the creatures flowed out of them. As Louise had warned him, this particular breed of doomshade was particularly adept at moving from normal space into the Tempest and back again. The monsters could squeeze through warps so small that they were impassable to most spirits, corrupt or otherwise, and exploit the distortions of their native realm to traverse distances elsewhere with uncanny speed.

Its twin sets of dragon jaws hissing, the lead Spectre swung its sword, a length of bone lined with razor-sharp chips of obsidian, in a two-handed blow at Montrose's head. He sidestepped the swing and counterattacked. His point took the monster in the throat.

As the Spectre began to dissolve, filling the air with a momentary stench of putrefaction, it toppled off the wall and onto the path, and its comrades sprang down behind it. Its four slit-pupiled eyes blazing, one lunged and raked at the Scot with glistening ivory claws. He levitated above the attacks and stabbed the monster in the back, where its double necks joined together. The Spectre fell forward, nearly dragging his blade out of his hand in the process.

Louise's pistol banged. Montrose whirled, just in time to see a third doomshade reel over the drop. The last one, a hulking creature with lines of iridescent scarlet scales forming geometrical patterns and cryptic symbols among its black ones, pounced snapping and clawing at the Sister of Athena. She tripped it with a foot sweep, then drove her knife into its chest. Montrose simultaneously thrust his rapier into the Spectre's spine, and the servant of Oblivion vanished like a bursting bubble.

Montrose looked back up at the Nihils, saw that no more Spectres were swarming through as yet, and then a thought struck him. "Do your trick again," he said, "on this piece of wall."

She cocked her head quizzically. "Wouldn't it be easier just to retreat away from the Nihils?"

"If you break up the rock and move the pieces," he said, "you can move the Nihils inside them. Merge them into a single rift large enough for *us* to pass through."

She frowned. "That won't be easy, if it's even possible."

"Give me the pistol. I'll hold the Spectres off and buy you the time you need."

She handed him the gun, then gazed intently at the Nihils. The basalt around them began to crack. Chips rattled down onto the ledge and bounced over the drop.

Rapier in one hand and pistol in the other, Montrose looked up at the scores of horrors racing down at them. A pang of dread lanced through him. What could he do against so many? They'd overwhelm him in an instant.

He scowled the demoralizing thought away. No, damn it, they wouldn't. He'd promised to defend Louise and he was going to keep his vow. He drew on his Harbinger's abilities and cool, gray shadow oozed from his pores to flow across his skin. With luck, the Spectres would have difficulty targeting an invisible man.

Intending to stop the creatures of Oblivion well before they reached Louise, Montrose flew several yards up the path. When the Spectres came in range, he fired until the pistol was empty, dropping four of them. Then the vanguard of the charge hurtled into striking distance.

The Cavalier attacked madly, again and again, flying in and back, up and down like an enraged hornet, relying on his veil of darkness to keep the doomshades' blows from landing, scarcely perceiving his foes as individual creatures. They seemed a single yammering, screeching, reeking mass of shadow, equipped with countless sets of luminous eyes, rending talons, and gnashing fangs.

Alighting on the path, he lunged and drove his point into the belly of a creature with six tentacles and the face of a diseased bat. Stumbling backwards, ripples of black light washing through its chancrous flesh, the Spectre began to dissolve. But its death throes would hinder the advance of the doomshades behind it for at least one precious moment. Springing forward, Montrose thrust over the eroding corpse at the club-wielding minotaur just behind it. His point tore a gash in the horned Spectre's shoulder.

Louise bellowed a *kiai*. Montrose pivoted toward the sound. Two Spectres had somehow gotten past him. Perhaps they'd clambered along the sheer walls instead of using the path, or perhaps they'd emerged from Nihils below the Heretic's position and then climbed back up to her. Now armed only with a knife and her kung fu, the Sister of Athena was fending them off as best she could.

Something smashed into Montrose's back, staggering him. Addled by pain, he murkily realized that, despite his invisibility, the minotaur had managed to bludgeon him. Then he reeled over the edge of the drop.

He frantically shut his eyes but caught a glimpse of the vortex anyway, and after that the image burned inside his mind, freezing him with terror, enticing him to a perverse but seductive consummation. He strained to supplant it by visualizing Louise's lovely face, and to reactivate his levitation abilities.

For a moment that seemed to stretch on forever, nothing happened, and he was certain he was going to continue to fall. Then the Arcanos power stirred inside him. Keeping his eyes shut, relying on his pathfinder's instincts to guide him, flying as awkwardly as a bird with an injured wing, he lurched toward the path.

His mystic powers faded abruptly, and he fell more than landed on the ledge, his knees slamming down painfully on the stone. Opening his eyes, he saw that he'd landed right beside Louise. She'd disposed of the Spectres which had been attacking her, but now their hideous companions were pounding down the path. The foremost were only a few feet away.

"I need more time," the Sister of Athena said. Montrose realized that she could see him. He'd lost his veil of darkness.

"I'll see to it," he groaned. He scrambled up, raised his sword, and his injured back throbbed. But he didn't have a moment left to heal himself, or to attempt to reactivate his Harbinger abilities either. Ignoring the discomfort as best he could, he hurled himself at the doomshades.

He advanced, retreated, sidestepped. His narrow blade dropped, rose, shifted back and forth, deceiving attempts to block it, then flashed forward in lethal thrusts. For a few moments it almost appeared as if his prowess, coupled with his boldness, might actually be enough to see him through. He dispatched the minotaur with an attack to the groin, then slew three of the doomshades with the double reptilian faces. The remaining Spectres seemed to falter. To flinch.

Then the whole mass of them roared as one, and plunged forward. Forced irresistibly backwards, unable to go back on the offensive, Montrose ducked and parried frantically. A bone-and-obsidian sword whizzed by an inch from his temple. Iron claws streaked at his eyes, and came close enough to tear his jade mask off. The follow-up attack sliced open his left forearm.

"I've got it!" croaked Louise. She scrambled unsteadily to his side. Her dagger wove shaky defensive patterns in the air.

Trusting her to guard his back, Montrose wheeled to inspect her handiwork. A lump of basalt about three feet across, composed of several smaller pieces fitted together like a jigsaw puzzle, lay amid the scree beneath the fresh gouge in the cliff. In the center of the stone hissed a glittering Nihil the size of a man's skull.

Montrose grimaced. He'd never tried to pass through such a small rift. But Adrain, his mentor in the mystic arts, had once told him that if a Nihil was undersize but not *too* tiny, a skillful Harbinger could sometimes force it to admit him, and now he was going to have to try.

"Now *I* need time," he said. He called on his powers and stared at the pocket of seething darkness, struggling to impose his will on it. After several seconds his Harbinger perceptions reported that the rift had dilated, although to normal vision it was the same size as before. The contradictory impressions made his head ache and his stomach twist.

"Come on!" Montrose shouted, hastening back to Louise. Fighting side by side, they retreated to the stone, the Spectres slashing and battering at them every inch of the way. "Go through. You first. It's bigger than it looks."

She whirled and scrambled into the Nihil. Watching from the corner of his eye, Montrose saw to his relief that the opening did indeed admit her entire squirming body. Her legs seemed to flop around at impossible angles as she wriggled through, as if her limbs had turned to rubber.

Her feet disappeared. Montrose drove the Spectres back a pace with a lightning series of feints, then threw his rapier at them, whirled, and dove for the Nihil.

When he inserted his hands and arms, pain spiked through them, as if they were being crushed. Not allowing the sensation to deter him, he struggled on. Once his head slipped inside, he beheld a phosphorescent emerald tunnel extending ahead of him with no apparent end in sight. The air had an acrid smell, and stung his eyes.

The pain kept grinding at his body, as if the extra-dimensional passage were clenching around him, constricting his flesh. Nevertheless, crawling frantically, he made headway anyway. Until fingers grabbed his right ankle.

He kicked backward with the foot that was still free. His boot heel slammed into something solid, and the grip on his other leg slipped away. Realizing that he had, at most, only another second or two to drag himself beyond the Spectres' reach, he wriggled forward again.

Though he couldn't see anything ahead but more blank tunnel, he felt small, strong hands grip his wrists and heave him forward. An instant later, the Nihil passage seemed to vanish, though he could still sense the mouth of it suspended invisibly in the air behind him. He lay on his stomach in a desert of bluish sand, from which crooked towers of gnarled, eroded stone rose against a stormy sky. An icy wind blew veils of grit across the landscape, and high overhead, in the churning thunderheads, humanoid figures solidified, and then, mewling and whimpering, melted back into swirling vapor once again.

The Tempest had rarely looked so good to him.

TWO

Louise hauled Montrose to his feet. "Hold the gate for a moment," he said.

The Sister of Athena was still unsteady from her exertions, but she gave him a game smile. "We could hold it forever," she said, "since they have to come through one at a time."

"Don't count on it," he said, concentrating to activate his Arcanos. "Remember, they're better at passing through Nihils than we are. Besides, I sense a number of rifts in the immediate area. They're liable to pop out of any one of them. However, now that we're away from the black whirlpool, I should be able to fly freely."

Fifty feet away, a patch of air shimmered, and a trio of doomshades leaped out of it. But at the same moment, he felt the Arcanos power rise inside him. Grinning, scarcely able to believe that he and Louise had escaped after all, he felt a giddy urge to tease the monsters. To let them charge almost close enough to assail their prey before he and his companion soared out of their reach.

But of course it was a mad idea. Far better to play it safe. He put his arms around Louise, and his battered back throbbed in protest. Tightening his jaw against the pain, he carried her upward. The frigid wind tore at their garments. The Spectres screeched, hissed, and brandished their peculiar swords in impotent fury.

Louise laughed down at them. "So long, suckers!" she cried.

Montrose chuckled. "That's not very refined language for a princess, or a woman of the cloth either."

He wended his way among the columns of weathered stone, keeping a wary eye out for any of the dangers infesting the Tempest, perils which could assume an infinite variety of forms. A creature with a lion's head and veined, transparent insectile wings, crouching on a ledge, roared at the wraiths but chose not to fly up and attack them. Streamers of amber gas, somehow moving against the howling wind, corroded whatever they touched. A gurgling fountain of red wine suffused the air fifty feet away with its rich bouquet. The scent was so enticing it made Montrose's head swim, but, certain that the liquid was either deadly in its own right or the bait in a snare, he forced himself to turn and go in the opposite direction.

Finally he found what he was searching for, and touched down on a ledge near the top of one of the columns. "No lurking beasts here," he said, "nor, as far as I can tell, are there any spatial rifts within a hundred yards. So we ought to be able to rest without any Spectres popping out at us."

"That sounds good to me," said Louise. With a twinge of reluctance, he let go of her, and she slumped down against a boulder. After a moment, pale, scraped patches on her hands and jaws—the ghost equivalent of bruises—began to disappear. Her cuts and scratches faded as well, but more slowly. Wounds inflicted by the claws and fangs of Spectres were generally more difficult to heal.

Montrose took another look around, making absolutely certain that nothing was creeping up on them, then sat down on an outcropping and set about mending his own injuries, relishing the sensation of the ache in his back ebbing away.

A bolt of crimson lightning cracked through the clouds overhead, destroying the vaporous figures once and for all. A drizzle of blood began to fall.

"What shall we do after we refresh ourselves?" asked Louise.

"Return to Stygia and stop the Deathlords from slaughtering one another," the Scot replied. "Despite this little detour, our objective hasn't changed."

"Of course not," said Louise, "but *can* we get back in time? Demetrius said that the Smiling Lord was about to lure the rest of the Seven into his trap, and I doubt we can return to Charon's vault the way we came. The Spectres won't leave that portal unguarded. The rest of the Nihils opening into the cavern are too small for us to pass through. And we're not likely to find any other rifts that lead to Stygia at all, are we?"

"We have one chance," the Scot replied. "Demetrius's mirror."

She cocked her head. "I thought that only connected Chiarmonte's study with the vault."

Montrose peered about. Far off in the distance, on the ground, a pack of enormous wolf-like creatures pursued a humanoid figure with an enormous eyeball for a head, but nothing was stirring in the immediate vicinity. A drop of blood splatted against the Scot's face, and he wiped it away. "It's possible that there's an opening here in the Tempest, also. Even if there isn't, the two ends must connect *through* the Tempest. That's the only way the magick could work. If I can find the tunnel, I might be able to force another opening." He grimaced. "Listen to me. 'If.' 'Might.' You can tell that I'm out of my depth. Adrain, my teacher, told me that I had the capacity to become a very good Harbinger, but I never really tried to fathom the deeper mysteries of the craft. I just took what I needed to lead my Legionnaires and advance my career in the Hierarchy. And after I secured a permanent position at Court, I was too busy enjoying my pleasures and jockeying for preference even to practice what I had learned. What an ass I was, to fail to appreciate the gift I'd been given."

She rose stiffly, crossed the space that separated them, and put her scratched, abraded hand on his shoulder. "Don't be discouraged," she said. "You've mastered every challenge so far. We both have. We escaped the Artificers' pit and slipped into the Onyx Tower when both those feats were supposed to be impossible. And we're going to keep rising to the occasion until we accomplish what we set out to do."

His chest ached, and his throat felt clogged. He had to swallow before he could speak. "When Demetrius's trap sprang shut on us and the Spectres flowed out of the wall, I realized something. I still love you."

She hesitated. He wished she weren't wearing the golden mask, so he could see all of her face. "Despite the fact that I betrayed you?" she asked at length.

"It wasn't your fault. I know that now."

"I'm glad, because I still love you as well."

He stared at her, half suspecting she was mocking him. "Even though I tortured you, sent you to the Soulforges, and then tried to kill you with my own hands?"

She smiled mischievously. "All couples have their little tiffs. I understand you were upset."

He shook his head. "I can't believe this."

"Why did you think I accompanied you on your mission? I mean, after you were finally convinced that I didn't mean to betray you."

"To preserve the Hierarchy and thus prevent the Spectres from overrunning the entire Underworld."

She rolled her eyes. "Well, if you must be technical, that was part of it too. But I thought we were trying to be amorous."

"Then by all means," he said, rising, "let's be amorous." He took her in his arms and kissed her.

He felt that he could have clung to her forever, and she seemed just as avid for his embrace, but eventually, as if responding to a common signal, they loosened their arms and moved slightly apart. Louise was breathing heavily, if needlessly. For his part, Montrose almost imagined he felt a heart pounding in his chest.

"This isn't really the time or the place for this, is it?" the Heretic said.

"Alas, no," Montrose said, cautiously surveying their surroundings. "We have to move on soon. Do you feel strong enough?"

"Yes," she said. "You know what they say about the Restless. We derive our vitality from pure emotion. And the last couple minutes were *extremely* emotional."

He picked her up in his arms, then levitated. Flying among the pillars, soaring high and swooping low, he made his way from one dimensional distortion to the next. Some rifts were imperceptible to ordinary sight, while others were visible as white ovals hanging unsupported in space, inky tunnels opening in rocky walls, or a wavering like air shimmering above hot pavement. Sometimes, probing them, he formed some psychic impression of what place lay on the other side, but other times, not. In the latter cases, he relied on pure pathfinder's instinct to decide whether he'd found the passage he wanted. He didn't dare start trying them at random. Aside from the danger—one never knew what predator might be lying in wait on the far side—some gates only worked in one direction, or blinked out of existence after a single transit. He and Louise could wind up stranded a thousand realities away from Stygia, with no possibility of making their way back in time.

Once they flew over a quartet of scaly black Spectres with double faces, who gave chase until Montrose lost them by flying behind a pillar and doubling back on the far side. "I'm surprised we haven't seen more of them," said Louise.

"I'm not," said the Scot. "They don't think we can get to the Isle of Sorrows, either. And since their goal was to keep us from interfering with the impending conflict there, they think they've won. Thus, malice aside, they see no reason to hunt us with extraordinary zeal."

"It's going to be satisfying to prove them wrong."

"I hope so," said Montrose grimly, swooping down toward another rift, this one an octagonal pit in the desert floor with tongues of flame licking around the edges. There were so many distortions to check, and no way to be certain he was spotting them all. Or even that time was passing at the same rate here as in Stygia. Perhaps he and Louise would return only to discover that the Deathlords' battle had been over for hours.

Floating above the pit, he sensed that it led to a benighted swamp in the Shadowlands, an unwholesome place infested with mosquitoes, water moccasins, and quicksand. He scowled at the portal's uselessness, and Louise gave his shoulder a comforting squeeze. He flew on, heading for a dark fissure halfway up one of the rocky columns.

En route, he sensed a tiny flaw, like a hairline crack, marring the fabric of reality about forty feet above the ground. He approached it, probed it, but received no impression at all of what lay on the other side. He started to turn away and his wayfarer's intuition froze him in place.

"What is it?" asked Louise.

"It's little more than a hunch, but I think I may have found it. If so, the mirror passage *doesn't* have a branch opening into the Tempest. But the channel is right in front of us. Behind an invisible wall, so to speak."

"Can you break through?"

He shrugged. "Generally I can only punch holes from the Shadowlands into the

Tempest. But since there's already a weakness here, perhaps I have a chance. Let's find out."

Drawing on his Harbinger energies, willing the tiny scratch on the surface of space to shatter into a true rift, he hammered it. Nothing happened. He lashed out again, even more forcefully. The flaw popped slightly open and instantly sealed itself again, like an eyelid blinking up and down, affording him a tantalizing glimpse of the pearly hyperspatial passage on the other side.

"Well, there definitely is *something* here," Montrose said. "I can discern that much." Grunting as if he were using every iota of his physical strength, he willed the fracture to open.

Space tore, and the luminous tunnel swallowed them. For a moment they hurtled down it as if they'd been shot out of a cannon. Then the channel spat them back into the Tempest, and they started to fall. Teeth gritted, Montrose arrested their descent and levitated back up to the flaw, which was once again as impassable as it had been originally.

"You nearly made it that time," said Louise.

"Nearly," said the Scot, assessing the depleted state of his powers. "I may succeed next time, but it's going to take everything I have, and if I fail, I doubt I'll even be able to stay aloft." Given the resilient nature of wraiths, a fall to the sand below might not destroy them. But it would almost certainly leave them maimed and broken, helpless to defend themselves against any hostile entity that chanced upon them.

"You won't fail," said Louise. "Do it."

He thrust at the flaw. Reality burst and re-formed in an instant. They plunged along the glowing tube, then tumbled into darkness and onto a hard, cold, uneven surface.

Louise tore herself from Montrose's embrace and scrambled to her feet. He heard hissing, a long blade whizzing in an arc, the rustle of his beloved's garments, and then an inhuman screech of agony.

"A doomshade," said the Sister of Athena, "hanging around here for some reason. I got him."

"It's a good thing *you* were able to sense him," Montrose said, clambering to his feet. "I'm too weak and addled from forcing the passage."

"Are we in the vault's antechamber?"

"Yes, thank fortune, and the portal should function normally now that we're not trying to compel it to do anything unusual. Let's hurry through before the Spectre's death cry draws its comrades down on our heads." Unhindered by the darkness, his Harbinger perceptions revealed the exact location of the gate. Groping, he caught Louise's arm and led her to it. "The opening is right here in front of us. After you."

She stepped forward and vanished. He waited a moment for her to move away from the door on the other end, then followed her. For an instant he felt parched with thirst, and that his body was stretching as if it were made of rubber. Then he emerged into Chiarmonte's office.

He'd been half afraid he'd find a contingent of doomshades or Legionnaires awaiting him, with Louise already writhing helplessly in their clutches. But the study was just as he'd seen it last, a dusty-smelling room lit by barrow-fire candles burning coldly in sconces along the wall. A computer and stacks of ancient books sat atop the massive oak desk, among with a darksteel dagger and a leather domino. The magick mirror, an ornate creation with the mask of Charon decorating the top of its golden frame, stood in one corner.

Louise gestured to the glass. "Should we smash it?"

"To stop the Spectres from pursuing us? Absolutely." They overturned the mirror and it shattered on the floor. Montrose wondered without much caring if any Stygian would ever find his way to the Emperor's secret place of power again.

He strode to the desk and picked up Chiarmonte's mask and knife. The weapon would serve until he acquired a sword and firearm. "All right," he said, "the best way to get to the Onyx Tower—"

Thunder cracked repeatedly, like a rapid series of gunshots, and the earth rumbled. The room lurched and shook, tumbling tapers from their sockets and demolishing the stacks of books. The ancient tomes scuttled off the edge of the desk, plummeted, and burst apart against the floor.

"Oh, no," whispered Louise. "The Deathlords' battle has already started."

Three

The guards behind the ivory throne hastily shouldered their automatic rifles. Staring in horror at Marie, the wraith Queen of New Orleans, sprawled motionless at the foot of the dais with black waves of Oblivion washing through her body, Frank Bellamy noticed the warriors aiming at him an instant too late to have any hope of diving for cover.

At that moment, he almost didn't care if they shot him. He'd lost his mortal life investigating the Atheist cabal, a conspiracy of supernatural beings committing atrocities against both the living and the dead. As an *ibambo*, a spirit, he'd finally been ready to strike back at them, but now, thanks to this one ghastly mistake, he'd blown his chance.

Titus, the wizened little shaman, his face painted half gold and half silver, shouted a word in a language Bellamy didn't recognize. The guards squeezed the triggers of their rifles, but the guns didn't fire. Startled, they faltered, then reached for the hilts of their scimitars.

"Stop!" said Antoine, scuttling forward to place himself between Bellamy and his assailants. His scaly alligator's tail dragged along the floor. "It was an accident. He didn't mean to do it."

"No," said Titus, stooping to pick up the tiny clay voudoun doll which had blasted Marie with magick, a likeness of the Queen with its hands and feet cut off. "He didn't. *I* knew he'd brought the image into Her Majesty's presence, I'm supposed to be knowledgeable about such things, but I didn't foresee that, separated from the other mannequins, it would pose a danger. So if you must avenge her, slay me."

The bodyguards looked uncertainly at one another, then released their swords.

Antoine turned to peer at the willowy black woman still lying inert on the floor. "If we're done saving Frank's ass," he rasped, "hadn't somebody better do something for the boss lady?"

"Yes," said Titus. He turned to the three drummers stationed along the Nihil-riddled wall, who were gaping at the catastrophe unfolding before them. "Resume your playing. It may strengthen her." The musicians obeyed. Once again, intricate rhythms murmured through the frankincense-scented air of the gloomy hall.

The old sorcerer cast the clay doll away, then squatted to examine Marie. "How is she?" Bellamy asked, feeling wretchedly guilty. It was all very well for Titus to claim responsibility for this disaster, but it was the FBI agent who, hoping to shake the spell-stricken Queen out of her paralysis of indecision, had put the malignant talisman in her hand. Not that he was any expert on voudoun, but still, somehow he should have sensed the danger.

"Well, at least she's not *fading*," Titus said. "But she will, if I don't leech some of the dark fire out of her." He shifted to a kneeling position. Then, scowling, he rested his hands on Marie's shoulders and muttered under his breath.

The waves of black light racing through the unconscious woman's flesh surged up Titus's arms as well. His scrawny frame vibrated as if he'd grabbed hold of a live wire. After several seconds, he cried out, threw up his hands, and fell over backward.

Bellamy bent over him. "Are you all right?"

"I'll survive," the old man groaned, trying unsteadily to rise. Bellamy took hold of his arm and helped him up. "But I didn't do her as much good as I'd hoped." Marie still lay inert, with bands of shadow oozing down the length of her body, though the ripples flowed more sluggishly than before. "I'm afraid she can't endure much longer."

Bellamy strained to thrust his guilt and anguish aside. To think constructively. "She was sick already, from Geffard's curse. This just exacerbated her condition, right?"

"Yes," Titus said.

"So if we break up Les Invisibles' doll collection, she can still get well."

"Possibly," the old man said, "but—"

"Then in a sense, nothing's changed," Bellamy said. "We came here to tell her that we *abambo* have to attack the rebels immediately, before the Loa learns that I found the dolls and moves them. And that's still the plan. In fact, this clears the deck to implement it. Don't get me wrong, I'm not happy that Marie has gotten worse. But the curse was affecting her mind and keeping her from doing what needs to be done. Now you can take command, Titus, and—why are you shaking your head?"

"The people wouldn't follow me to war."

"Why not?" Bellamy demanded. "They respect you."

"I hope so," the sorcerer said, "but that doesn't make me a monarch, anointed by the gods to rule the city. Remember what's been going on here. On one level, it all comes down to public relations. Two rivals have been fighting over the hearts and minds of the populace, each striving to demonstrate that he or she possesses more spiritual power and is thus better suited to rule. Thanks to the recent raids on our Haunts, Marie's malaise, and her consequent inability to commune with the Orishas, it's a battle she was already losing."

Bellamy frowned. "And therefore, if we're going to strike at Geffard, she has to lead the troops herself."

"Yeah," Antoine rasped. "Otherwise people will either figure out that she's sick to death, or assume she's afraid to face him. Either way, they'll lose what little faith in her they have left."

The gator's toothy grin seemed to stretch a little wider. "But you know, warmblood, when I talked about 'the people,' that's not everybody. I can round up a few more hard cases like you and me. Guys too ornery to roll over for Les Invisibles even if they are sure to win. We could put together a force big enough to at least do some damage before they take control of the city. What do you say we loyal vassals of the Queen go out in style?"

Bellamy hesitated.

After a moment Antoine grunted. "Never mind. It's okay. I was forgetting, you didn't even know us *abambo* until a few days ago, and the first thing we did was make you a slave. You don't owe us anything, and you've got other stuff to worry about."

"Well, yeah. I have to protect Astarte. And Marilyn, and the rest of the Arcanists. If they can get the werewolves' notebook translated, it might finally tell me what I need to shut down the *whole* Atheist conspiracy, not just the part of it that's menacing New Orleans." Bellamy grimaced. "Still, I said I'd help you, and I want to. If we could just think of something better than a suicide mission, a plan with *some* kind of a chance—hold on a second."

"What is it?" Titus asked.

"Since we can't give the people a Queen, let's give them an impostor." One of the zebra-caped bodyguards gasped. Bellamy gave him a wry smile. "Hey, it worked in *The Prisoner of Zenda*. And Titus, I know from personal experience that you can turn whoever we pick into an exact double of Marie." Thanks to the sorcerer's Arcanos magick, the FBI agent was currently disguised as a black man.

"It's...an interesting idea," said Titus, frowning. "Unfortunately, it's also *lese majesty*, and a kind of sacrilege."

"I don't believe this," Bellamy said. "Marie's dying, and you people are more worried about respecting her queenliness than restoring her to health."

"I'm not," Antoine rasped. "He's right, Titus, our backs are against the wall. Screw tradition."

"There's more than tradition involved," the old man said. "Many would regard it as a deadly insult to the Orishas."

"The Queen hasn't even been able to dial up the gods in months," the alligator wraith replied. "That's why we're in this mess. So I can't say that I'm worried that they're hovering over us, just waiting to slap down any impostor who puts on the ostrich-plume crown. If only they *did* watch over us that way."

"I didn't mean that *I* thought it would be an unpardonably blasphemous act," Titus said, "simply that many others would. I don't know if we can find a volunteer in the short time we have left."

"I'll do it," said Bellamy, though the thought of having his male body turned into a female one provoked a pang of queasiness which the prospect of changing from white to black had not.

Titus shook his head. "It would never work. I can alter your form and voice, but your body language would still be masculine, and give you away in an instant. We need a woman. I'll just have to start making inquiries, and pray that Her Majesty's condition doesn't become common knowledge as a result."

"Do you think that's likely?" Bellamy asked.

Titus shrugged. "Lately it seems that nothing discussed outside the Queen's inner circle remains a secret for very long."

"Great," said the FBI agent, "just great. Still, if we're agreed that this is our only shot, you'd better get started."

"Hold on," Antoine said. "I know somebody who'd be glad to volunteer, if everything you've told me about her is true."

"What are you talking about?" Bellamy asked.

"How about your girlfriend?" Antoine said.

Bellamy gave the gator a flinty stare. "Astarte's *alive*, Antoine, on the wrong side of the Shroud to do the job. I hope you're not suggesting—"

"Shit, no," rasped the gator. "What kind of guy do you think I am? But Titus knows magick that will yank a sleeping soul out of its body and let it run around in the Shadowlands for a while. I'll bet he can give it a new face, too, just like it was a real *ibambo*."

"Conceivably," said the shaman. "As far as I know, no one has ever attempted such a transformation."

"And no one's going to try it now," Bellamy said. "This is a bad idea."

"I disagree," Titus said. "Since Astarte isn't one of us, she won't feel she's breaking a taboo by impersonating the Queen. And even in the land of the dead, the aura of life will cling to her. I can enhance that, to create the impression that she's cloaked herself in some potent sorcery. That should encourage our warriors and alarm Les Invisibles."

"I'm telling you, we have to find somebody else."

Titus sighed. "I understand your wish to keep the woman you love out of harm's way. But she's your comrade as well as your lover, isn't she? She *wants* to help you in your struggle. And how safe will she be in any case, if our enemies defeat us and overrun the Haunt?"

Bellamy grimaced. "All right. I'll talk to her."

Four

Bellamy held Astarte's hands in his. To his dismay, he could tell his touch was chilling her again, though she was doing her best not to show it. "Are you sure?" he asked. "It's dangerous. You'll be the enemy's primary target, and unlike the real Marie, you don't have magick powers to protect yourself."

Astarte snorted. She hadn't had a chance to restore the spikes and magenta streaks to her hair, or to exchange her brightly colored clothing for her customary black leather jacket and jeans, but the steel rings in her right eyebrow, left nostril, and lower lip were back in place, along with her raven lipstick. "From what you told me, her magick didn't protect her anyway."

"That's right, it didn't, and that's more or less my point. You're going to be even more vulnerable than she was."

She rolled her eyes. "Yeah, right, it's dangerous. I get it already, and I'm not scared. I'd do anything to get even for what Dunn and the Atheists did to Vulture and Marilyn, and I've been waiting my whole life to see the spirit world." Her aura shone with excitement.

"Okay," Bellamy said. He took her in his arms and she kissed him passionately.

He tried to ignore the shivers that wracked her slender body. "Sit down so you won't fall when Titus puts you to sleep. I'll see you soon."

"Okay." She flopped down on the middle step of the dais. He allowed the relentless magnetism of death to draw him back to the dark side of the Shroud.

When it did, the empty hall became the throne room he remembered. Drumbeats whispered through the air. An ivory stone and two tall wooden idols stood atop the dais. Still unconscious, with waves of shadow washing sluggishly through her flesh, Marie lay at the foot of her chair, while Titus, Antoine, and the two bodyguards were gathered around the pedestal. The sentries glared at Bellamy, perhaps because they still blamed him for the Queen's collapse, or because they resented his efforts to warn Astarte of the perils she was about to face.

"It's about time," Antoine growled.

"I had to explain what she was getting herself into," Bellamy said defensively. "It was only fair."

"If you say so," the gator said. "Get moving, Titus. We're on the clock."

"I'm aware of that," the old shaman said testily. "You're not the only one who understands the urgency." He crouched in front of the oblivious Astarte, who was peering about, impatiently waiting for something to happen, and stroked her face with his fingertips. Her eyelids drooped shut, and she slumped back against the steps.

"Now he has to coax her soul out," Antoine muttered to Bellamy. "It generally takes a minute. He could just *yank* it out, but that would hurt her."

The *ibambo* sorcerer crooned incantations. His withered hands made intricate passes over Astarte's body. And despite his misgivings, Bellamy felt a thrill of anticipation. It seemed intrinsically wrong to draw any living person into the bleak, savage country of the dead, and yet…"When I asked Titus if there was a way for Astarte and me to be together," he said, "why didn't he mention this?"

Antoine bobbed his wedge-shaped head in the odd gesture that was his attempt at a shrug. "You'd have to ask him."

Astarte's flesh began to glow. Still chanting and gesturing, Titus slowly rose from his crouch, and the radiance followed him upward, from the Quick girl's body into the open air. At first it was merely a haze of light, but it rapidly took on form and definition, its face and limbs emerging from the sheen until it appeared altogether solid, though still surrounded with a trace of the aura of life.

Astarte's spirit form sported the full array of Goth trappings she normally affected. But her face seemed somehow younger, open and unguarded, without the slightest trace of her customary sneer. She peered eagerly about, as if trying to take in everything at once.

"Are you all right?" Bellamy asked.

"Oh, *yes*!" she replied. Laughing, she threw herself into his arms. "You did it, you did it, I'm really here!"

"Actually, Titus did it," Bellamy said, clasping her to him. This time, he thought with a surge of joy, he didn't have to worry about giving her frostbite. "He's the gentleman with the two-tone face."

She smiled at the sorcerer. "Thank you. This is everything I ever wanted." She smiled up at Frank. "Well, almost."

"It's for us to thank you," Titus said. "You're the one endangering yourself to help us."

"Theoretically," said Antoine. "If we ever get on with it. Will you transform her already?"

"Next crisis," Titus said, "you do the magick, and I'll goad and harass you. I need a minute to recover my mystical energies, and then we can continue."

Astarte slipped from Bellamy's embrace and took his hand. "If we've got time, then show me around. Show me everything."

"Good idea," Bellamy said, though he wished he could simply go on holding her. "There are things you need to know. Uh, here's your body. You can see you're still breathing."

In her place, he would have been eager to verify that his mortal shell was in fact still alive, but she barely gave it a glance. "That's good, but I already know what I look like. Show me this world. Show me something magick."

"Okay," Bellamy said, "watch this." He pushed his free hand through the substance of the dais. "Ordinarily you can't shift or break objects in the world of the living, because they exist on a different level of existence. If you choose, you *can* move right through them as if they weren't there."

Astarte thrust her hand inside the dais, pulled it out, slipped it in again. "This is so cool!"

"Not if you need to affect things on the far side of the Shroud and don't have any way to do it. Then it will drive you crazy. Anyway, don't try moving through solid objects while other *abambo* are watching, not unless you absolutely have to. Since you're new to the Underworld, you might not do it right the first time, and that would blow your disguise."

She rolled her eyes. "You worry too much. I've got the hang of it. Look." She moved her hand rapidly in and out of the pedestal, and then, seeing that he wasn't going to change his mind, sighed. "Oh, all right. I'll be good. Show me more." She turned toward Marie, and her smile faded. "Oh. This is obviously the Queen, and those black stripes are the Oblivion poison sloshing around inside her."

"Yeah," Bellamy said.

Astarte gently touched the comatose woman's face. "We'll help you, Your Highness. I promise." She lifted her gaze to the glowering wooden statues, and the excited smile flowed back onto her lips. "Who are these guys?"

"Two of the Orishas. The gods of the African wraiths."

"They're awesome," Astarte said. She studied them for another moment, then wheeled and hurried to one of the torches burning along the wall, tugging Bellamy along behind her. "It's cold," she said, grinning, the wavering green light staining her features. She reached for the flame.

"Be careful," Bellamy said. "It can still burn you."

She held her hand just outside the hissing barrow-fire as if savoring the ghastly chill, then hauled Bellamy onward to a web-work of seething cracks in the wall. "What are these?" she asked.

"Nihils," said Bellamy. "Openings into another part of the Underworld. Hell, or someplace equally unpleasant. Some of the holes are big enough to fall in, or for evil spirits to pop out of. You don't want to go anywhere near those."

Perhaps hoping to peek into that other realm, she leaned close to the Nihils.

Bellamy fought the urge to yank her back. As far as he knew, openings this small were harmless, but still, he was no more comfortable watching her bring her face close to the nasty things than he would have been seeing her play Russian roulette with an unloaded gun.

"They're beautiful," she said at last, pivoting toward him. "Everything is."

The happiness Bellamy had felt when she came into his arms was giving way to frustration. When he'd visited her in the country of the living, the chill of his touch and the knowledge that death would soon snatch him back into the Shadowlands had kept the experience from being as joyful as it should have been. And now that she'd come to him, her exuberance was having the same effect. Not that he wanted her quailing in horror at her surroundings, but it was hard to feel truly close to her when their perceptions were evidently so different.

"'Beautiful,'" he said wryly. "When *I* look around, I see dirt and damage. Sometimes sounds hurt my ears, and things smell rotten. The Shroud makes the whole world ugly. I was afraid that when you entered the Underworld, the same thing would happen to you, but I guess live people are immune no matter where they are."

"Oh, I noticed that it's darker here, even though, somehow, I can see better anyway," Astarte replied. "Just like I noticed that the mansion seems like even more of a ruin. But that doesn't mean that things aren't beautiful, just that it's a weird, spooky kind of beauty." She grinned. "And that's the way the spirit world *should* be."

Bellamy shrugged. "Maybe so, but most of the ghosts don't like it that way."

"I'm ready now," Titus called.

Bellamy and Astarte hurried back to the dais. "What do you want me to do?" the latter asked.

"You, stand clear," said Titus to Bellamy. The FBI agent reluctantly released Astarte's hand. "You, young lady, sit down and try to stay still. The ritual may cause you some discomfort. I've never attempted to sculpt a living soul before."

The Quick girl touched the ring in her eyebrow. "I can take a little pain."

"Good," Titus said. He reached into a pouch at his belt, brought out a pinch of dust, and tossed it into the air. The grains flashed and popped, disintegrating before they reached the ground. The sorcerer then held out his hand and a bronze scalpel appeared in it, as if an invisible nurse had placed it there. Humming softly, Titus began to caress Astarte's features with the blade, indenting her skin but not quite breaking it.

"Why is she like this?" Bellamy whispered, looking on.

"Like what?" Antoine replied.

The FBI agent hesitated, groping for the right word. "Giddy. Like a kid at Disneyland."

"How do I know?" said the alligator wraith. "I'm not a hoodoo man or even a two-legger, to understand how you warmbloods think. But maybe it's got something to do with the fact that she hasn't really died. Her mind hasn't split into pieces like ours, so she doesn't have a shadowself working to twist and spoil every wholesome thought like we do."

"Maybe that's part of it," said Bellamy, "but I suspect it's not the whole story."

"Well, then, how about this? She's asleep, right? So to her, this is a dream, not quite real. That lets her mind file off the rough edges. I don't know what you're complaining about. You ought to be glad she likes it here."

Bellamy grimaced. "Not if her judgment's so impaired that she can't look after herself."

"*We'll* look after her," the reptile said. "Seeing as how it's either that or listen to you whine. Hey, she's starting to change."

Although Titus had appeared to focus on Astarte's face, the transformation first affected her legs. With a series of cracks and pops, they grew longer, first the left and then the right. The Quick girl twitched repeatedly, her halo flickering, and Bellamy winced in sympathy.

"Are you all right?" Titus asked.

"Fine," she said, her voice rougher. "Don't stop, get it over with."

The shaman began to chant and to shift the scalpel around Astarte's face more and more rapidly, until the bronze blade was a blur. Bellamy waited for the knife to gash her, but somehow, even when she gave an involuntary jerk, it never did.

Her pale skin darkened, then lightened again. Scowling, brandishing the scalpel, Titus spoke four words. His sharp tone reminded Bellamy of a dog handler bringing a disobedient animal to heel. Astarte gasped and stiffened. Her skin blackened, but only for a few seconds.

"Stop," Bellamy said. "It isn't working, and you're hurting her."

"I'm okay," Astarte grated. "I can feel the change *almost* taking hold. I just need one or two more zaps."

"So shut up," Antoine said to Bellamy. "Let Titus do his stuff."

Bellamy grimaced. "All right. We'll give it another minute."

Ignoring the FBI agent's outburst, the old man continued his magick. His voice dropped to a cajoling murmur as he recited a rhyming incantation. The cadence of the unknown words had a soothing quality which reminded Bellamy of a nursery rhyme. The scalpel stroked Astarte's face slowly and gently, and she stopped flinching.

Somewhat reassured by the changes in the ritual, Bellamy relaxed slightly. Then, suddenly, Titus bellowed and slashed the bronze knife across Astarte's eyes.

Her aura blazing orange, the mortal screamed and clutched at her face. Fearful that Titus would cut her again, Bellamy launched himself at the shaman, but something snapped shut around his leg, tearing his skin and dumping him on the floor. Twisting his head, he saw that Antoine had him in his jaws. The FBI agent reached for his gun.

"Stop it!" Astarte cried. He turned and saw Marie's golden eyes gazing out of the Quick girl's face. This time, the new color didn't bleed away. "He didn't do any permanent damage."

"I had to use a drastic technique to break through the resistance," Titus said. "The rest of the change should be less stressful."

"I'm...sorry I assumed the worst," said Bellamy gruffly. He felt his Shadow writhing in the depths of his mind, enjoying his discomfiture. "It's just—"

"Just that it's difficult to stay calm while someone's ripping out your beloved's eyes," Titus said. "I understand, but now be quiet." He turned back to Astarte. He stroked her cheek with the tip of the scalpel, and her features flowed into new shapes.

Antoine released Bellamy's leg. "That's the second time I've gotten a taste of you," the gator said. "If you make me bite you again, it'll be your own fault if I eat you."

"Am I that delicious?" asked the human, climbing to his feet. His leg throbbed, and he reached out with his mind, found one of the echoes of ancient sorrow still reverberating through the Haunt, and tapped the energy to heal himself. "Hard to believe. But I won't say you didn't warn me."

In another minute, Astarte had Marie's body. She was as tall as a tall man, with skin like gleaming ebony and a face like Nefertiti's. Stepping backward, weaving his hands in mystic passes, Titus put the finishing touches on his work. The black leather jacket, tank top, and faded, tattered jeans became a snowy, floor-length, off-the-shoulder gown. A crown of ostrich plumes shimmered into being on the Quick girl's head. Her halo faded until it was less a visible corona than an indefinable impression of strangeness.

Titus's incantations droned to a stop. Astarte asked, "Is it—"

And then faltered, no doubt because what had emerged from her throat were the richer, more measured tones of the Queen. "Done?"

"Yes," Titus said, "and it's a perfect copy if I do say so myself."

Grinning, the pain of the transformation evidently forgotten, Astarte scrambled to her feet. "Where's a mirror? I've got to see."

Titus winced. "A perfect mask, but everyone will see through it in an instant if you don't behave like Her Majesty. She would never bounce up like you just did, or speak with such unbridled enthusiasm. She's dignified. Aloof. Some might even say haughty."

"A bitch," said Astarte. "I can do bitchy, can't I, Frank?" She winked at him.

"Marie is a monarch struggling to protect her people in a desperate time," Titus replied, anger lacing his voice. "She's also the voice of the gods."

Astarte shrugged. "Whatever."

"Just look cold and arrogant and let Titus and Antoine do the talking," Bellamy said.

"No problem," she said. "Honest. Just because I'm acting like me right now, that doesn't mean I can't be her when the time comes."

"It has come," Bellamy said. "We have to get on with this. Let's go muster your troops. The guards will watch over Marie and your body until we return."

"I'm sure we can find a mirror on the way," Antoine said sardonically.

Five

"Get him!" a deep voice shouted. His horned cap flopping, Valentine whirled, irrationally certain that someone was after him.

But no. For a change, someone else was being harassed. A lanky wraith in a top hat, cravat, and cutaway coat dashed down the moon-lit street, bounding over a seething pothole-sized Nihil in the pavement. Six other ghosts were hot on his heels, but it looked to the dwarf in motley as if their prey might have a chance of outdistancing them. But then, howling, a ghost in the lacquered armor of a samurai sprang through a tenement wall and landed square in the fugitive's path. The newcomer's skin had a lemon-yellow hue and his blue eyes and long, upswept eyebrows an exaggerated slant which could only be the product of a flesh sculptor's magick.

Like Valentine, he probably had no idea *why* the miniature mob was chasing the man in nineteenth-century clothing, but he also didn't care. Swinging his katana like a baseball bat, he hacked open the fugitive's stomach. The stovepipe hat tumbled off and rolled across the cracked, pitted pavement.

The wounded man stumbled a few more paces and collapsed in a heap at Valentine's feet. "Help me," he moaned. "I didn't do anything."

The dwarf *wanted* to help, but was afraid that if he tried, the mob would hurt him too. Fear froze him in place until the other wraiths overtook their prey, laid hands on him, and dragged him back up the street. The bogus samurai marched along beside them, looking smug, his curved sword on his shoulder.

"Why are you doing this?" wailed the captive. "Why? Why?" He kept asking until someone silenced him.

Valentine peered about, looking for Legionnaires. After a moment he spied three of them, two common soldiers and a Centurion, all wearing black raptor patches, a token of their allegiance to the Fifth Legion and to Governor Gayoso, and the green sashes, emblazoned with an hourglass, which were the uniform of the entire ragtag army of Natchez. The trio were casually examining a selection of jewelry—grave goods most of it, cherished mementos which newly deceased wraiths had managed to carry into death with them—on display in an open-air market.

The Centurion, a small, sharp-featured woman, her graying hair chopped short and restrained by a braided leather headband, turned in Valentine's direction. The dwarf gestured toward the mob and its victim. The Centurion sneered as if Valentine were an imbecile for thinking that she and her comrades might bestir themselves to investigate such an insignificant disturbance.

You useless bastards! Valentine thought. Quivering with disgust, he turned and tramped on down the hill.

He'd only gone a few paces before his fury at the Legionnaires crumbled into disgust with himself. He hadn't lifted a finger to help the man in the cutaway coat, either. He told himself that, puny freak that he was, he *couldn't* have helped. Had he tried, the pursuers would have squashed him like a bug. But that reflection only made him loathe himself the more, because it underscored the point that he was the genuinely useless one, too feeble and stupid to help a man in trouble, or locate his beloved Daphne either. The last time he'd seen her, the child prostitute had turned him away in favor of a larger man proffering a larger fee, but he scarcely blamed her for that. He wished he could turn *himself* away and be reborn as an altogether different person.

He trudged on past another decaying brick house. Behind a cracked, grimy window, two naked wraiths sat playing gin. One, a redhead with a raw white wound where her left ear should have been, crowed and laid the rest of her cards on the table. Her companion, a pudgy brunette who was missing both ears, her eyebrows, and her nose, cursed, tossed away her cards, picked up an iron knife, and took her left nipple between her thumb and forefinger.

Valentine hastily averted his eyes. He supposed that he shouldn't be shocked. The Restless were notoriously prone to bizarre and even perverse amusements. Probably their Shadows were to blame.

But a few months ago, the upright citizens of the Necropolis surrounding the

Citadel had practiced their less savory diversions furtively. Now, increasingly, the deviance was all out in the open. The climate in the supposedly respectable district seemed little different than that in the lawless quarter called Under-the-Hill. It was almost enough to make a person believe that some amorphous but terrible danger really was threatening the entire territory, as the more paranoid members of the populace had been whispering for some time. As Montrose had claimed when the Stygians came to arrest him.

Montrose. Valentine's eyes stung as if they could still shed tears, and he furiously blinked the sensation away. The inquisitor's downfall still weighed heavily on his conscience. Montrose had befriended him and he'd repaid him with treachery, stealing the Cavalier's journal at Gayoso's behest.

No! he thought. It *hadn't* been a betrayal. Montrose had been the traitor, a false servant of the Hierarchy scheming to conquer his own kingdom in the Shadowlands. It had been Valentine's duty to help his master bring him down.

But no matter how hard he tried, the jester couldn't quite believe that, because he'd *known* Montrose. When he'd first arrived in Natchez, the Stygian had wanted nothing more than to complete his crusade against the Heretics as rapidly as possible and return to the luxuries of the Onyx Tower. Later, possibly without even realizing it himself, he'd begun to enjoy his sojourn on Earth, but that was because he relished the challenges and excitement attendant upon his mission, and the camaraderie of desperadoes like Mike Fink. It didn't mean he'd coveted a throne here. No, damning as the journal seemed, there must be another explanation for its contents.

Nor could Valentine delude himself that he'd actually stolen the book out of loyalty to anyone or anything but himself. He'd taken it because Gayoso commanded him to. Because otherwise the Anacreon might have cast him out. And while his court jester position could be humiliating, and even painful when the Spaniard chose to kick him around, it still afforded him the only security he'd ever known in his brief, squalid life or since. The prospect of losing it terrified him.

God, Valentine thought, he was pathetic.

His path led him into one of the precincts of the Quick, a warren of tenements scarcely less rundown than the derelict buildings of the Necropolis. An overturned and burned-out ambulance blocked one intersection. On the next street over, the bloated corpse of an old man hung by its neck from a lamppost. Judging from the stink of putrefaction, it had been there for some time.

Unlike some ghosts, Valentine wasn't inordinately interested in the affairs of the Quick, but he had heard that the mortals dwelling along the lower Mississippi had been having their problems too, the so-called Atheist murders and countless outbreaks of senseless, savage violence. What in Charon's name was happening? Was all this unrest a sign that the last days had arrived, and the Void about to devour all the universe at last?

Sighing, the dwarf struggled to push such thoughts aside. It was ludicrous for him to speculate about the vast, hidden forces at play in the world when he was helpless even to manage his own petty existence with any dignity or honor. He trudged on, into Under-the-Hill. The breeze carried the silt-and-pollution smell of the river.

The streets were crowded as usual, as Fink's irregulars swaggered about pursuing their pleasures, and merchants and entertainers pandered to them. Montrose was gone, but the prosperity his crusade had brought to Natchez—an affluence based on slave-taking and plunder—remained.

Squirming through the throng, Valentine finally came to the black expanse of the river. About forty wraiths had assembled on the bank to repair an assortment of keelboats, skiffs, powerboats, and catamarans. Presumably the vessels had been damaged by the recent Maelstrom.

Beside the improvised boatyard stood the tavern known as the Green Head, a tumble-down shack with an emerald skull-and-crossbones sloppily painted on the wall. Next to it a narrow lane lit by crimson barrow-fire lamps ran into darkness.

Valentine took a breath, steadying himself, then headed down the street of brothels, peering at the figures posing in doorways and windows. A voluptuous quadruple amputee propped up on a mound of satin cushions. Telltale wisps of light playing about her stumps revealed that her limbs had begun to reform. By morning she'd probably be whole again. A John Wayne look-alike wearing only a white Stetson, a neckerchief, and a leather vest. A black woman with a second face between her legs, winking and lasciviously licking its lips. No Daphne. By now most of the denizens of the area knew the jester was searching for her, and by and large, they found his desperation funny. They called out taunts as he passed by.

Eventually he reached the rotting brick tenement where Daphne had been accustomed to ply her trade. Inside, voices moaned and begged for release, and bodies smacked and slurped together. Tonight Cassius the bouncer, a hairy, hulking bear of a man dressed in steel-toed work boots and bib overalls, sat on the porch in a rocking chair with his ax handle lying across his knees. Spying the dwarf, he grimaced. "No," he said, "she hasn't come back."

Valentine shook his head. "It just doesn't make any sense. She wouldn't just go away without a word to anyone."

"Oh, hell, no," Cassius drawled, "not if it meant running out on a stud like you."

"I'm just saying, one of her friends must know something, even if she doesn't realize it. If I could just talk to everyone again—"

"You got some more cash, to pay the girls for their time?"

"Not yet."

"Then get lost."

"Daphne worked in this house for years and now she could be in trouble. Don't you people care?"

"No. And we're all sick of you whining and sniffing around. It's bad for business. So get."

Valentine groped for the magic words that would win the bouncer over. He couldn't think of any.

"Don't make me come down there," the big man said, lazily brandishing his club. "I'll play hockey with your teensy little midget ass."

Valentine remembered how Montrose had effortlessly disarmed a sentry at the Citadel gate, and battered Fink, whose ferocity was a legend along the river, into submission. *Real* men, people who weren't stunted little freaks, could do things like that. They didn't have to back down when somebody threatened them. He turned and shuffled on down the street. A woman watching from a third-story window brayed a raucous laugh.

There were a few more strolling prostitutes and crumbling whorehouses between Daphne's former Haunt and the corner, but Valentine didn't have the heart to look for her anymore. He just wanted to lose himself in the tangle of alleys beyond the intersection, a desolate little cyst in the body of the city, seldom visited by either the living or the dead.

Away from the mocking eyes of the whores and their customers, he tried to feel less worthless and humiliated, but in vain. Unlike many wraiths, he was rarely conscious of his Shadow laboring to hurt and corrupt him. Often he'd thought he was lucky, but now he almost wished his dark self would rise and consume him. So what if he became a Spectre? He'd rather be strong and evil than weak and ashamed. And if he didn't turn into a doomshade, if he simply fell into Oblivion, well, that would be all right too. At least the misery would be over.

But the psychic parasite didn't rise to the bait of his despair. Maybe, he thought glumly, it was a *dwarf* Shadow, impotent and useless as his host.

Ahead of him, around a bend, two sets of footsteps scuffed on the filthy asphalt. He still didn't want anyone else looking at him, so he hastily stepped behind a splintery telephone pole.

A pair of wraiths strode into view. The one in the lead was a petite, sharp-featured young woman clad in bellbottoms, an embroidered peasant blouse, and love beads. She peered avidly this way and that, looking for something, prompting Valentine to shrink back half an inch farther. Her companion, a hunched, scrawny teenager, slouched along a pace behind her. He wore what was likely a facsimile of the conservative navy-blue suit and white shirt his family had buried him in, though he'd discarded the tie and opened his collar.

"Are you sure this is the right place?" the woman asked nervously. "It seems so deserted."

The teenager took his own look around. "That's why we're here," he said, and slammed her fist into her back.

Valentine flinched. The woman tumbled to the pavement. The boy kicked her three times, then pulled a length of rope from inside his coat.

She tried to scramble away from him, but only managed to writhe in place. For the moment, pain had immobilized her. "No," she whimpered, "please. You said you'd help me if I paid."

"I can't help you," said the boy, giving her another kick. "But you're going to help me. You're going to put some *real* money in my pocket. There are slavers who'll buy you, no questions asked." He straddled her, punched her twice, then grabbed her wrists and tried to force them together.

Dear God, Valentine thought, *please, not* more *violence. Don't make me watch again.* As before, he yearned to come to the victim's aid. And her attacker was just a single skinny kid, an aspiring tough guy who evidently didn't even possess a weapon or the guts to join Fink's band of cutthroats, where most of the genuine hard cases in Natchez were currently making their fortunes.

Yet Valentine's every instinct screamed that while the punk might pose little threat to an ordinary man, he was more than capable of disposing of a dwarf. He didn't even dare try to creep away in search of help, for fear that the teenager would hear him move. All he could do was cower in the shadows, flinching and averting his eyes every time the boy struck his victim, then helplessly peering out once more.

The boy tied the woman's arms together. Bucking and twisting suddenly, she caught two of his fingers between her teeth. Squealing, the teenager wrenched himself free and backhanded her across the jaw. She slumped back onto the asphalt, stunned.

"Bitch," the teenager snarled, rubbing the bite marks in his flesh. "You're going to be sorry for that." He tore her blouse open. The little white buttons clinked on the pavement. Valentine felt a sudden surge of nausea, and, unable to control himself, made a tiny retching sound.

The punk's head snapped around. "Who's there?" he asked, his voice breaking. He rose and stalked toward the telephone pole.

The dwarf knew it would be futile to run. With his stunted legs, he could never outdistance the other ghost. His bowels watery, he stepped out into the moonlight. The boy's eyes widened in surprise, and then he sneered.

"Shit," he said, "it's a fucking *chimp*."

"Maybe," said Valentine, striving to keep his voice steady, "but it's Governor Gayoso's chimp. I don't imagine an ignorant lowlife like you gets up to the Citadel very often, but even you must have heard that one of the Anacreon's aides is a dwarf."

"'Aides?' The way I heard it, you're his *clown*."

Valentine wished he'd worn conventional clothing instead of motley, wondered fleetingly why he never did, even on his own time. "You should learn not to judge by appearances," he said, smiling contemptuously. "In a world full of flesh sculptors and shape-shifters, it'll get you killed. I may tell jokes for the Anacreons and their guests on special occasions, but generally I'm responsible for other duties." It was true as far as it went, though the chores in question were those of a lowly gofer.

The teenager hesitated, then said, "Whatever. You're in the wrong place at the wrong time." Crouching, hands poised to grab, he edged nearer.

Valentine fought the urge to recoil. "One of the nice things about being a Legionnaire," he said, "is that we have genuine Stygian mystics to teach us the Arcanos. Do you honestly think a man of my importance would be wandering Under-the-Hill unescorted if I couldn't defend myself? Trust me, I could rip you to shreds or toss you into the Tempest with a wave of my hand. But I'm feeling merciful tonight, so I'm going to offer you a choice."

The punk's gray eyes narrowed. "What kind of a choice?"

"You can march your pimply ass up to the Citadel and enlist in the service of one of the Governors. It's possible that the Legions can make a man out of you, though I admit it doesn't seem likely. If that option doesn't appeal to you, you can submit to arrest, go to trial, and probably be reduced to Thralldom yourself. Or you can resist, in which case I'll destroy you. Decide now. I'm tired of fooling with you."

The boy gnawed his lower lip. "I'd be just like any other soldier? They wouldn't treat me different because of why I came in?"

Dear God, thought Valentine incredulously, *the brainless son of a bitch is actually buying it*. "You have my word on it. The lady mentioned that she'd paid you?"

The teenager hesitated again, then fished a black change purse out of his hip pocket. When he held it out, Valentine had to resist another impulse to cringe away. "It's just a few oboli," the boy said sullenly, as if that would justify his keeping it.

"Which aren't yours," said Valentine, taking the money. Its touch stung his fingers, even through cloth. "Now get moving."

The boy frowned. "How do you know I won't just run away?"

"Try if you like," Valentine replied, "but I don't advise it. The Hierarchy has a million eyes and a very long reach."

The punk sighed. "Maybe the army won't be so bad. At least they'll give me a gun and some different clothes, right?" He turned and headed in the direction of the Citadel.

Valentine watched him for a moment, making sure he wasn't going to spin around and charge him, then hurried to the woman and knelt beside her. White scrapes and bruises covered most of her face, but she wasn't fading away, nor were there ripples of shadow moving under her skin. He judged that she ought to recover fairly quickly, and as he untied her hands, her eyelids fluttered open.

Instantly she began to thrash, and took a clumsy swipe at him. He caught her arm. "Easy!" he said. "The kid's gone. I'm a friend."

She stopped struggling. "I…I'm sorry."

"It's okay. Just lie still. Give yourself a minute to finish healing."

A shiny patch on her forehead faded, and her swollen lower lip shrank. "Who are you?" she asked.

"Valentine. Governor Gayoso's jes—uh, man."

"What happened to Rudy?"

"Was that the punk?" She nodded. "I convinced him to leave you alone. Bluffed him into thinking I was some kind of Hierarch grandee with hot-shit magical powers. I can't believe he was stupid enough to believe it." He repressed a giddy urge to giggle.

"Thank you. Thank you from the bottom of my heart."

He remembered that, given a choice, he would have stood idly by while Rudy raped her and sold her into bondage, and his momentary elation died in a spasm of shame. "It was no big deal," he said gruffly. "I just talked to him."

"You saved me," the woman said, touching his hand. "Only now—" Her half-healed face twisted, and she sobbed.

"Hey," said Valentine, awkwardly patting her shoulder, "hey, everything's okay now. He's gone."

"You don't understand. Rudy said he could help me find my little girl. I was really counting on him."

A chill flowed up Valentine's spine. "Your little girl," he repeated.

"Yeah. She disappeared last week."

"Was she a prostitute?" Valentine asked.

The woman stared at him incredulously. "*What?* She's a *child.* I mean, we died in 1967, but she still has a child's *mind.* What kind of a question is that?"

"I'm sorry," Valentine said. "I wasn't trying to be nasty, but I had a reason for asking. Look, why don't you tell me exactly what happened, and then I'll tell you why I was running around Under-the-Hill tonight."

"Okay." Frowning, the woman sat up and wrapped her arms around her knees. "It won't take long. I'm Belinda, Belinda Talley, and my daughter's name is Starshine. We've been drifting around the Underworld since we died in a plane crash, trying to get along and looking for Transcendence too, I guess."

"So you're Heretics." Given the current campaign of persecution, he felt oddly touched that she trusted him enough to tell him.

Belinda shrugged. "Maybe. We just listened to the different gurus and meditated once in a while. Took the right kind of psychedelics when we could find them. We never joined a cult or wanted to overthrow the government or did anything that would get us in trouble. Starshine and I never had any hassles with anybody until..." Her fists clenched, and her face twisted.

Valentine gingerly squeezed her shoulder. "It's okay. Take a deep breath and then tell me the rest of it."

She gave him a jerky nod. "All right. We came to Natchez about six months ago. I got a job at the Nightlight Theater. I can do a little bit of the Sandman Arcanos, not enough to *be* a Sandman, but enough to work as a helper to a real illusionist. Anyway, while I was doing that, Starshine would play in the street outside."

"In Under-the-Hill," said Valentine, his voice flat with amazement at her lack of caution.

Belinda glared at him. "I know this place has a bad reputation, but we've always stayed in what was supposed to be the bad part of every Necropolis, and it was always okay. I always thought that if your karma's clean, you'll do all right no matter where you are. Besides, Starshine knew not to go far, and the people on the block knew us. I thought they'd watch her!"

"I'm sorry," Valentine said. "Whatever's happened, I didn't mean to say that you're to blame."

Belinda slumped and shook her head. "No, you're right, I am. I never should have let her out of my sight. Because one night she was just *gone*."

"Didn't anyone see anything?"

"No. Not really. Jules the gunsmith said he saw a guy in a long leather coat and a blue mask with silver trim hanging around earlier, but bunches of wraiths go up and down that block all the—why are you looking at me like that?"

"Daphne spent some time with a man dressed that same way on the night *she* disappeared. I saw him myself."

"Who's Daphne?"

A bit reluctantly, Valentine told her his story. He was afraid that the revelation that his lover had had the mind of an adult but the body of a child would revolt her. But if it did, she hid it well. Perhaps she was too worried about her own kid to worry about a stranger's sexual quirks.

When he finished, Belinda asked, "Have you tried to find this man?"

"Some," Valentine replied, "but I didn't look too hard. I concentrated on hunting for Daphne herself. You have to understand, I didn't have any special reason to suspect him of anything. As far as I was able to find out, she, uh, entertained him in her room in the whorehouse like she usually did, and no one could hurt her there. She had protection. What's more, a couple people told me they were pretty sure they saw her hours later, just before dawn, outside the Green Head." He grimaced. "I wonder if they really did, or if they just thought it was funny to get the freak all worked up."

"If this man kidnapped Starshine," Belinda said, "then I've got to find him. And

I don't know how. I've never had to do anything like this before. Will you help me?"

Doubtful that he could actually help anyone do anything important, Valentine hesitated, but then, unexpectedly, a surge of impatience flushed his misgivings away. He'd saved her from Rudy, hadn't he? That showed he wasn't *completely* useless. Maybe he could locate the man in the blue mask too, and in any case he owed it to Daphne to try.

"Yes," he said. "We'll find the son of a bitch."

Six

A feathery sensation tickled Montrose's ears and neck. Startled, he brushed at it and discovered that his auburn curls had abruptly regrown to their normal length. He was reasonably certain it didn't matter. Every corridor in the palace seemed jammed with wraiths rushing from one point to another, but at this point they were all too distraught to take notice of a fugitive, even one with distinctive red hair. He drank in their panic, unpleasant though the sensation was, using it to replenish his own depleted strength.

Clinging to Louise's hand, he shoved his way into an atrium with a fountain of gushing liquid flame at its center. Ringed with elevated promenades, the walls rose four stories to a vaulted ceiling, at the apex of which was a blue and red stained-glass skylight. Flares of lightning made it glow.

On the third-tier walkway stood a gesticulating grandee in a silver visor and begemmed robes. He was haranguing the milling, yammering crowd below. Because of the din, Montrose couldn't hear a word the nobleman was saying, but he assumed the fellow was urging everyone to remain calm.

The earth bucked, and the Smiling Lord's castle lurched with it. The skylight shattered, showering the chamber with glittering blades. The grandee staggered forward and tumbled over the railing before him. The fountain crumbled, and waves of icy, fluid fire swept outward across the arcane symbols inlaid in the marble floor. Wraiths screamed and flailed as their garments ignited.

Montrose wrapped his arm around Louise's waist and levitated, his empty hand upraised to ward off falling glass. On his way up, he noticed the crimson and yellow uniform of a warrior of the Order of the Avenging Flame lying empty on one of the elevated walkways. Perhaps, terrified, convinced the end of Stygia was at hand, the soldier had lost the will to endure and vanished into the Void, leaving, as sometimes happened, his possessions behind.

Possessions which luckily included two Walther P38s and a smallsword with a gold and ebony hilt. Montrose detoured to the gallery, grabbed the elite bodyguard's weapons belt, then flew upward once more, through the broken skylight and out into the open air.

The howling wind ripped at his clothing and hair, and he tightened his grasp on Louise. Thunder roared, and jagged bolts of multicolored lightning split the sky. Towers swayed, and soldiers scurried about the baileys and battlements of the immense fortress like frenzied ants.

Still ascending, Montrose soon gained a view of the entire Isle of Sorrows. The colossal sea-wall, built of steel, iron, and the twisted, frozen forms of countless Thralls, shuddered, while the earthquake whipped the Sea of Souls to froth. Sailors labored to keep the heaving ships of the Imperial fleet from dashing themselves to pieces at their moorings.

Here and there, structures began to fall to pieces. One of the ruined Temples of the Shining Ones. A gleaming gray bridge linking the island to the warehouses, factories, rail yards, and fortifications in the Iron Hills. An apartment building in the form of a gargantuan statue: a slender, skull-faced dancing girl poised on one foot, which smashed two other edifices when it fell. Finally, as the quake grew ever more violent, portions of the Deathlords' palaces themselves began to collapse. A barbican of the Skeletal Lord's ivory castle disintegrated in an avalanche of bone. A graceful amber minaret inside the Seat of Golden Tears shook itself to pieces. Bizarrely enough, the wind carried the fragments away as if they weighed no more than autumn leaves. The Beggar Lord's citadel maintained its reputation as a realm of impossibilities even in the throes of its destruction.

"Look!" said Louise, screaming to make herself overheard above the roar of the storm. "Look up!"

When he did, he quailed. The thunderheads above the island marked the boundary of the Tempest, and as a part of that chaotic realm, sometimes churned and twisted into peculiar forms, affording disquieting vistas to the wraiths below. But Montrose had never seen them as they appeared now, bunched into the semblance of a host of gargantuan faces, many so hideous and sickeningly alien as to be almost unrecognizable as visages at all. The assembly of titans filled the sky, diminishing the City of Dark Echoes to a child's plaything. In the forefront of the gathering leered a creature with two draconic sets of features mounted side by side on a single head.

The giants were too huge, too ghastly, and radiated an overwhelming sense of malevolence. Montrose had the feeling that if he looked at them for very long, the sight would shred his reason. His eyes aching and his stomach churning, he wrenched his gaze away. "They must be Malfeans," he said.

"Come to gloat over the death of Stygia."

"How disappointed they're going to be," Montrose said, striving to believe it. Taking care not to look up at the dark gods again, he flew on, riding the wind when it blew from behind him, fighting it when it shifted and tried to drive him backward.

The statues in the Plaza of Lost Stars had begun to topple. Heedless of the danger, a crowd clustered around the huge black cylinder that was the Onyx Tower proper. Dazzling lights flashed behind the meurtrières and narrow, shuttered windows as if a raging storm were trapped within the donjon. A number of the onlookers had chosen to kneel with their arms raised in supplication. Montrose suspected that they hoped the display inside the keep heralded the return of its imperial master, just in time to preserve his city from destruction.

"The tower is so *big*," cried Louise into Montrose's ear. "Can we find the Smiling Lord in time?"

"I hope so," he replied, ascending past rank after rank of windows and machiolations. "Judging from the flashes, the other Deathlords are fighting on the lower levels. If I were Prince Ares, I'd hide on one of the upper ones, where they wouldn't be likely to stumble across me. That's also where Charon's maintained certain private areas, forbidden to all others, including, I'm certain, chambers for working his greatest mag—"

The section of wall in front of them exploded. Huge chunks of stone hurtled through the air like a cloud of buckshot. Montrose reflexively spun around, shielding Louise's body with his own. Bits of rock stung his shoulders and rump, but all the fragments large enough to do real harm streaked past him.

Turning again, still rising, the Scot peered into the ragged-edged breach. Beyond it was the ruined husk of what had once been an opulent ballroom. The crystal chandeliers had shattered into the glittering grit on the floor, the stately Corinthian columns were melting like snow, and sparks of the black fire of Oblivion danced about the interior walls, eating holes wherever they touched. At one end of the chamber loomed the Emerald Lord in his jade crown of thorns, verdigris-encrusted androgynous mask, and wheel-of-fortune amulet, chanting words of power. Suddenly he rolled his crimson dice, which tumbled as if bouncing along an invisible table, came to rest, and then flew back into his white-gloved hand. Something which could be sensed but not truly seen sizzled into existence before him, then leaped at the archangel on the other side of the room. Gaunt to the point of emaciation in his suit of black and white, a cloak the color of dust hanging from his narrow shoulders, the Skeletal Lord grunted, clutched his belly, and doubled over, aping the distress of a starving man, and the creature or spell plunging toward him winked out of existence. Meanwhile, the ruby-eyed mechanical silver rat which usually rode on his shoulder, now grown as large as a war-horse, savaged three luckless members of the Legion of Paupers. Their comrades broke and ran.

Shadow seething in the eye sockets of his ivory skull mask, the Master of Famine stalked toward the Prince of Chance. At which point Montrose soared above the hole, cutting off his view of whatever would happen next.

Drawing on his Harbinger senses, he studied the lofty expanse of tower still above him. Three levels beneath the roof, portions of the black stonework shimmered and writhed. According to Demetrius, there was supposed to be an exchange of energies between the Smiling Lord and the subterranean vortex. With any luck, the spatial faults were a manifestation of the transfer, and a signpost pointing to Montrose's goal.

The Cavalier alit on a small balcony. Even this high above the ground, a sturdy crenelated rampart protected the platform. The stonework shivered beneath his boots, a warning that if the earthquake and the battle of the Deathlords raged on unchecked, even the mightiest fortress in Stygia would shake itself apart in time.

Louise twisted the handle of the iron-bound door. It didn't budge. "Locked," she said, and stared at it intently. With a crack, the panel flew open, revealing a room dominated by an ornately carved black oak armoire and matching canopy bed. "But not anymore."

"We're lucky it was *only* locked," Montrose said. "The tower has been magically sealed since the Emperor's disappearance. Either he did it before he sailed out to fight Gorool, or the Seven did it afterwards. I suppose they needed to dissolve the ward to get in themselves." They stepped inside. He gave her Chiarmonte's darksteel dagger to back up her other weapons. "I'm sure you remember what to do."

"Hang back out of sight."

"Exactly. The Smiling Lord is more likely to hold off lashing out if he doesn't feel outnumbered. And if we do wind up having to fight him, surprise may be the only chance we have." For the sake of her morale, he hoped she didn't realize what a remote chance it actually was.

She touched his arm. "I love you," she said.

"And I you," Montrose replied. "Shall we go preserve the Empire?"

He stalked through the bedroom and down an almost lightless corridor decorated with a collection of coffins and sarcophagi standing on end in niches along the wall. Louise was presumably trailing him, though creeping along so silently that, strain as he might, he couldn't hear her.

His pathfinder's intuition led him up a narrow staircase. After a few paces, he discerned a soft greenish radiance shimmering down from above. The smell of bitter incense stung his nostrils, and he caught the voice of his liege lord, snarling syllables which, though the Scot had no idea of their meaning, made his skin crawl.

At the top of the steps was a trefoil arch capped with a carving of crossed scythes, and beyond that, an enormous, shadowy chamber with a high, fan-vaulted ceiling, lit by the chill, wavering light of barrow-flame torches. Pentacles, their lines, arcs, and arcane runes inlaid in gold, silver, ruby, and jet, adorned the floor, while shelves laden with the tools of a supreme master of the Arcanoi—grimoires, wands, talismans, alembics, censers, ritual daggers and masks—stood along the walls. Probably evoked by the Smiling Lord's conjurations, worms of phosphorescence crawled on the magick circles and the sorcerous implements.

At the far end of the chamber, before a lofty onyx altar which, judging from the triptych of carved scenes adorning it, Charon had raised in his own honor, Prince Mars chanted his spell while simultaneously performing a sort of martial exercise. The images of the other Deathlords shimmered into existence around him, and, reacting instantly, he struck and dispersed them, the steel solerets of his plate armor clinking on the pale marble floor and his halberd whizzing through the air. Space bubbled and fractured as he moved, and though he couldn't truly discern it, Montrose got a vague sense of the fearsome power flowing in and out of the rifts, and even of the black whirlpool churning on the other side.

He removed Chiarmonte's domino and stepped out into the open. "Dread Lord," he said, "I've come to talk to you. To implore you to stop what you're doing."

His pole arm whirling into a guard position, the Smiling Lord pivoted toward the intruder. Montrose could tell that the Deathlord meant to charge him. The Cavalier's arms trembled with the urge to snatch out his pistols. He held himself motionless, harmless, instead. "Please," he said. "Despite what you've been told, I'm your loyal vassal, as I've always been. I beg you, just listen to me."

The masked demigod settled into a defensive stance. Unlike lesser beings, when he stopped moving, he stopped *completely*, suddenly becoming as inhumanly still as a metal idol, his cold, unblinking gray eyes, perfect balance, and the impeccable line of the halberd as intimidating as a cocked and leveled gun. Though by no means a true sorcerer himself, Montrose sensed the intricate mechanisms of the Smiling Lord's ongoing magick slowing a bit. Without the fuel of his conjurations, they would eventually grind to a halt.

"Begone," the angel said. "I condemned you, but I have more important matters to attend to. Flee *now* and you may survive."

His mouth dry, Montrose suppressed a craven impulse to do precisely that. "I'll go when I've had my say. Surely you can suspend your enchantments for a few moments without your peers recovering their senses. From what I saw below, they're completely berserk."

The visor hid the Smiling Lord's mouth, yet Montrose could *feel* him smile. "Are they? How wonderful."

"It won't be wonderful if the fallout from your magick destroys the entire Isle of Sorrows. Don't you feel the tower quivering? Extend your awareness. Look outside. Buildings are collapsing!"

The Smiling Lord stood silent for a moment. Perhaps he actually was clairvoyantly peering beyond the walls. "Remarkable," he said at last. "To be honest, I had no idea the spell would do that. But war always entails a certain amount of destruction. And perhaps it will even be better this way. Charon built the capital to his own tastes. Why shouldn't the new emperor remake it in his own image, even more glorious than before?"

"You can't remake it if you scour everyone and everything away, right down to the bedrock," Montrose said. "Look at the Malfeans, laughing down from the storm because they think our doom has come at last. Have you truly examined the vortex that's feeding you power? Can't you feel that it's wielding you like a weapon?"

"You're mad," said the Avatar of War, a hint of pity in his voice. "I thought as much when you first betrayed me. I don't perceive any Malfeans or any vortex either."

Montrose felt a surge of despair. His erstwhile master was more befuddled than he could have imagined possible. "They're there, nonetheless. You're the one who's not entirely in his right mind, Dread Lord, through no fault of your own. You've fallen prey to subtle enchantments and cunning lies."

"That's rubbish. Apparently you've forgotten who and what I am."

"A Lord of Death," Montrose replied. "A seraph. But that doesn't make you immune to deception. If you can't *see* your true enemies, then *think*. No doubt some of the other Council members do covet Charon's crown, but would any of them be so reckless as to try to seize it by armed force? It would be one against six, and besides, the Imperium is still struggling to recover from the Emperor's disappearance and the Fifth Maelstrom. A civil war could cripple it for all time. You princes are supposed to be wiser than that."

"Indeed we are," the Smiling Lord replied glumly. "Fate knows, *I* had better sense. I was content with my station. But sadly, the others weren't. They sent raiders and assassins against their fellows, myself included."

"No," said the Scot, "they didn't. Not until they believed they had to strike back in self-defense, as you do. Spectres committed the first few atrocities to set you against one another."

"Impossible," said the man in armor. "I had visions of the other Deathlords conspiring against me."

"Visions engineered by Demetrius, himself a Spectre."

"The longer you blather on," said Prince Ares, "the more ridiculous your story becomes. Demetrius is my *friend*. The only true friend I've found since Charon anointed me."

"He was a Doppelgänger," Montrose insisted. "He murdered Chiarmonte. When I slew him, his corpse turned into an abomination with black scales and a double face. Similar creatures—"

"'Slew him?'" the Deathlord repeated, his voice breaking. "*Slew him?*" He bellowed a battle cry and charged.

SEVEN

A hot, greasy feeling hung in the air. Creeping up Governor Nichols Street with his allies, Bellamy wondered if another Maelstrom could be on its way so soon, and winced at the thought of trying to fight while one was raging. But if they had to, they had to. Marie couldn't wait for better weather.

He glanced at Astarte, stalking along beside him with an oval shield on her left arm, an assegai in her right hand, and a golden-hilted saber hanging at her hip. To his annoyance, she winked at him. By dint of holding herself stiffly erect and glowering while Titus did the talking, she'd carried off the first phase of her masquerade successfully. But as far as Bellamy was concerned, she still wasn't taking her situation seriously enough.

He peered about, looking for enemy sentries, and didn't see any. Halting, he raised his hand and the other ghosts, perhaps sixty altogether, gathered around him. "The Haunt is directly on the other side of this place," he said, pointing at an old apartment house on the east side of the street. The usual cryptic graffiti—GENERATION LAST, RAT MONDAY!—covered its dilapidated gates, and the first gray light of dawn tinged the sky above its gables. Stinking garbage bags, the majority torn open and their contents scattered, sat heaped on the curb.

"We'll sneak in as close as we can," Antoine rasped. "Once they spot us, give them everything you've got. We don't know how many guys they have, or what kind. They may have brought in reinforcements since Frank paid them a visit, but on the other hand, maybe they haven't gotten around to it yet. Les Invisibles don't like moving around in a shadow storm any more than we do. Those of you who can reach across the Shroud, make sure you kill any wolfman you see. Just because they're in the Skinlands, that doesn't make them harmless. Their hoodoo men can cast spells on us, or send those weird Sinkinda after us."

"And," Titus added, his wrinkled face painted black and white and a Thompson submachine gun enormous in his withered hands, "though I trust it goes without saying, each of you will defend the Queen, even at the cost of your own existence. Though I hope that you, Your Majesty, will make such sacrifices unnecessary by not taking extraordinary risks."

Astarte's mouth tightened. Certain she meant to argue, Bellamy tensed. But then she inclined her head.

"Okay," Antoine said, "time for a little revenge." He crawled around the piles of trash and slipped through the weathered wooden panels of the gate. His companions followed.

Beyond the gate was a courtyard with a magnolia tree rising in the center of it. Birds perched in the branches were beginning to sing. Distorted by the Shroud, the twittering had a harshness to it, just as the late-model Audi, Mercedes, and Lexus parked on the turnaround looked battered and soiled.

The spirits stalked on, into an apartment where a television and a collection of tennis trophies lay broken on the floor. As they glided through the back wall, a woman in one of the bedrooms began to scream. Bellamy grimaced. He had no doubt that with their hypersensitive ears, the Creoles would hear her screeching. He'd just have to hope that the cries of one of the living wouldn't alarm them.

As he and his friends approached the rusty, wrought-iron fence, he studied the crumbling antebellum mansion on the other side, a dingy white house with gray trim, so riddled with seething Nihil cracks that it looked as if it was about to disintegrate into a million pieces. The slave quarters, stable, and Creole kitchen in the overgrown yard were almost equally infested. Two guards with rifles stood atop the mansion roof. Fortunately, at the moment both had their backs turned and were gazing out at Barracks Street. An orange and white rental truck sat parked near the front door, with two more riflemen watching over it. A pair of Les Invisibles carried images of a mutilated Marie from the house toward the waiting vehicle. A hunched little Quick man, his aura murky as thick smog and his face a mass of warts and lesions, stalked along behind them, exhorting them to be careful. Given his ability to perceive the dead, he was probably a werewolf shaman.

"Drat," Titus whispered, "they're already moving the dolls."

"The hell they are," Antoine replied. He melted through the fence, racing forward faster than a human could run. The rest of the company dashed after him. The alligator had nearly reached the truck when one of the men on the roof turned and cried a warning.

One of the Queen's zebra-caped warriors lifted her crossbow and put a quarrel through the sentry's throat, but the damage was done. Creole wraiths leaned through the walls of the mansion and began to shoot. One cupped his hands around his mouth and wailed, whereupon one of Bellamy's companions screamed and staggered, his left shoulder and half his face dissolving into iridescent bubbles.

Titus bit one rifleman to pieces while his lashing tail knocked down the other. Whirling, he snapped the second man's head off, then rounded on the *abambo* with the statues. They frantically dropped the images, smashing one, and reached for the blades sheathed at their sides. The ugly little man raised his arms, hooked his fingers into claws, and jabbered ugly-sounding syllables. Points of light sparkled in his muddy halo.

Bellamy surmised that the werewolf was about to throw a spell at Antoine. Sprinting through a hail of arrows and gunfire, he vaulted across the Shroud. From his perspective, everyone but the shaman vanished. As he raised his gun, the ugly little man wheeled and scrambled back into the house, his body swelling and sprouting fur as he ran. The agent snapped off a shot, but missed.

Bellamy opened the cab of the rental truck. As he'd hoped, the keys were in the ignition. He grabbed them, threw them into the darkness, then allowed Death to snatch him back into the Underworld.

One of the ghosts who'd carried the statues had disappeared, fled or lost to the Void. Tossing his head, Antoine tore the other rebel's arm off. The Queen's warriors were melting through the walls of the mansion.

"Astarte," Bellamy said.

Antoine spat out the shredded limb. "Already inside. She went this way." He charged up the front steps, onto the verandah, and through the one of the double doors. Bellamy followed.

Inside was a spacious, high-ceilinged foyer which Bellamy had seen before. Wraiths were fighting everywhere. Blades rang, guns banged, and the wounded screamed. A number of Les Invisibles had opted to make a stand on the stairs, evidently defending the upper floors of the house. A ghastly howling sounded through the ceiling.

To Bellamy's dismay, the disguised Astarte was in the forefront of the African soldiers trying to fight their way up the steps. A Creole near the top shot a crossbow at her, and the Queen's shield leaped upward to block the quarrel. To the FBI agent, it looked as if the protective device had yanked Astarte's arm up rather than the other way around. She laughed, her other arm cocked and straightened with one fluid motion, and the assegai flew upwards. The spear pierced the crossbowman through the chest, and his body burst into black flame. The weapon lurched out of his flesh and whizzed back into Astarte's hand. She caught it effortlessly, without even looking.

But even magick weapons couldn't provide perfect protection against every danger. As the rebels on the steps shifted about or perished in waves of shadow, a space opened up in front of her, and she sprang up onto the risers. Instantly the enemy pressed in all around her, stabbing and slashing. The shield couldn't possibly swing itself around quickly enough to deflect every attack.

Bellamy lunged forward, firing into the melee, praying he wouldn't hit Astarte. Antoine lunged into the thick of the fight and started snapping off people's legs. Titus backed out of a doorway, his Tommy gun shaking and rattling, then pivoted toward the stairs and whispered a word. Given the circumstances, it should have been completely inaudible, but Bellamy heard it plainly, even from ten feet away. Slivers of pale light resembling icicles appeared around Astarte's opponents, and, darting and spinning, began to harass the Creoles like a swarm of angry hornets.

The rebels faltered. Bellamy caught Astarte by the arm and hauled her backward. Striking, he trusted, of its own volition, the assegai jabbed at him, and he barely jerked his head aside in time to keep from losing an eye. His gray hide gashed and punctured in several places, Antoine also scuttled out of the fray.

Bellamy looked Astarte over. To his relief, she was only scratched. "Titus told you to hang back," he said.

"Don't take that tone with the Queen," she said, smirking. And then, more softly: "Come on, give me a break. Even if I didn't want to help, I *have* to fight since that's what Marie would do."

"You don't have to be reckless," he snapped. "This isn't a game." More eerie howling reverberated from overhead, and he grimaced in frustration. He wanted to stay with her, protect her, but if he did, their side might lose the battle. He turned to Titus. "I told you about that Nihil kind of thing upstairs. I think it's the door to the place where the demons live, and the werewolf shamans are opening it now. Somebody has to get up there and stop them."

"There's another set of stairs," the old man said. Perhaps warned by some sixth sense, he pivoted and shot a rebel who'd been drawing a bead on him. "Unfortunately, I perceive rebels defending it as well." His mouth twisted. "I *can* get up there, but it sounds as if there are at least two wolfmen. I don't know if I can cope with them by myself."

"Then I'll have to go, too," Bellamy said. "Cover me, then join me when I make it to the top." He projected himself across the Shroud.

The battle vanished. To all appearances, he stood in a dark, abandoned house. The sudden silence rang in his ears until shattered by another howl from above.

Trying not to think about the horde of invisible, intangible enemies standing in his path, Bellamy started up the stairs. Something hit him hard in the chest. Gasping, reeling, he clutched the banister for support. The railing dropped out from under his hand as if someone had smashed the support posts with an ax. Bellamy started to topple into space, but somehow, arms flailing, managed to wrench himself back to safety.

He braced for another blow, but nothing happened. Perhaps Titus or one of his other allies had disposed of the ghost who'd been using Spook powers against him. He scrambled on.

Halfway up the steps, a sudden weariness turned his legs to rubber. Dropping to his knees, his thoughts turning vague and dull, he almost lost his grasp on the world of the living before snapping fully awake again. Six risers farther up, a voice groaned, and an excruciating terror made him cringe, but the unseen Chanteur fell silent an instant later.

Bellamy bounded onto the landing. Someone had crudely demolished the interior walls and ceilings of the first three bedrooms on the right to provide the werewolf sorcerers with a spacious workplace. Two of them—thank God it was *only* two—both in wolfman form, swayed and capered at the center of a complex design of crystals, bones, and symbols drawn in stinking gore and feces on the floor. One monster had four yellow eyes set asymmetrically in his skull, and vermin like tiny, pale green scorpions crawling through his russet fur. His companion's multiple rows of fangs were so long and crooked than he couldn't close his jaws without lacerating himself. His muzzle was a patchwork of scabs, perforations, and scars. Bellamy couldn't tell which of them, if either, was the Black Spiral Dancer he'd fired at outside. Toward the rear of the open area shimmered the sheet of light the FBI agent had seen on his previous visit, but now it seemed more active, with waves of brightness rippling rapidly across it.

Bellamy hastily dragged his shoe across the floor, knocking crossed femurs apart and smearing a bloody mandala. Effacing a part of the ritual pattern. The last time he'd tried this trick, it had spoiled the werewolf's magick, triggering a backlash which nearly fried the creature. This time, however, nothing happened. Scowling in disappointment, Bellamy lifted his Browning and fired.

The darksteel bullets caught the four-eyed Dancer in the spine. Roaring, he spun around and charged, and the other monster followed suit. Bellamy kept firing, his shots now punching holes in the lead wolfman's chest.

Huge hands with long yellow claws shot out to seize the wraith, and then, at last, his bullets had some noticeable effect. The wolfman stumbled and fell headlong. Bellamy sprang backward so the giant creature wouldn't land on top of him, then opened up on the beast with the malformed teeth.

He hit him twice, once in the sternum and once in the stomach, and then, hurtling forward like a high-speed train, the towering horror came into striking range. His talons streaked at Bellamy's shooting arm. The human snatched it back in time to keep it from being shorn off, but the blow caught the pistol and slapped it out of his grasp.

Bellamy backpedaled, ducked a strike at his head, and whipped out his gleaming black shortsword. The monster lunged, claws upraised and ribbons of viscous brown saliva streaming from his gaping jaws. Holding himself in place till the last possible instant, the ghost twisted aside and drove his blade at the Black Spiral Dancer's midsection.

The sword plunged deep into the werewolf's flesh, but at the same instant the monster's elbow struck Bellamy a glancing blow to the jaw. Given the Dancer's prodigious strength, even that accidental brush was sufficient to send him reeling. The back of his head slammed into the wall, stunning him, and he crashed to the floor in a heap.

Blood spurting from the gash in his flank, the werewolf with the misshapen fangs rounded on his attacker. Meanwhile the other beast-man reared up from a crimson pool, roared, and lurched to his feet. Still dazed, Bellamy tried to stand up as well, but his legs wouldn't obey him. His heels scraped uselessly at the floor. He raised the shortsword. His arm shook.

The werewolf with the oversized teeth emitted a hideous, rhythmic growl which might have been laughter. He flexed his legs to pounce, then shrieked and clutched at his temples. Knots on his head began to palpitate, splitting his skin. The squirming bone made a crunching, grinding sound.

The other monster peered madly about, then, orienting on a patch of floor in front of a cracked, grimy window, snarled a rapid incantation, to no apparent effect. His companion's skull exploded, showering blood, bone chips, and scraps of flesh and brain.

The four-eyed werewolf clawed deep gashes in his own chest and repeated his magick words. Titus appeared, his form vague and translucent, shadowy strands like coils of barbed wire writhing about him, tearing his skin and entangling his limbs. He lost his balance, fell, and mouthed an incantation of his own. The strands faded for a moment, but then darkened again. The werewolf raked his fingers through his fur, collecting a handful of green parasites, and hurled them at the African wizard. The tiny scorpions vanished in midair, reappeared on Titus's body, and started to sting him.

Meanwhile, the dimensional portal dilated.

Bellamy tried again to rise. This time, he made it. Sword extended, he ran at the surviving wolfman.

Caught by surprise, the monster wheeled an instant too slowly. The bloody darksteel blade punched into his side, scraped over a rib, and almost certainly punctured a lung. The beast-man reeled backward and fell, nearly wrenching the weapon from Bellamy's grasp. Aware of the Black Spiral Dancers' regenerative powers, the wraith crouched over the thrashing giant and kept stabbing.

Titus's shadowy bonds melted away. He waved his hand in a mystic pass and the scorpions dropped off his skin, stunned or dead. Beginning to fade from view once more, he staggered to his feet and glared at the widening portal, his muscles bunching.

Gory punctures riddling his torso and neck, the werewolf finally stopped writhing. Maybe he wasn't dead even now, but he certainly didn't look as if he'd regain consciousness any time soon. Bellamy permitted Death to pull him back across the Shroud.

Now he could see monstrous forms and faces swimming inside the gate, perceive the insectile rustling and the sulfurous stench wafting from its depths. A huge black serpent with white, faceted eyes began to slither out. Then Titus shouted a word of power and the portal blinked out of existence, cutting the snake in two. The front section squirmed and flopped around the floor.

Looking for the next opponent, the next danger, Bellamy pivoted toward the stairs. To his amazement, Antoine stood fighting on the landing. The Creoles had nearly ripped the gator to pieces, but he was still savagely biting and lashing out with his tail.

Bellamy rushed forward to help him, but at the same instant, a roar resounded up the stairs. With Astarte in the lead, the Africans charged up the steps, smashing through the opponents still blocking their path.

Bellamy crouched beside Antoine. "How are you?"

"How do I look?" the reptile croaked irritably. "It's bad, but I think Titus can fix me up."

The human pivoted. "Get over here, Titus!" He turned back to the gator. "No offense, but are you crazy? You weren't supposed to follow me up the stairs."

"I thought maybe I could make it. Being built low to the ground helps when you're trying to move through a bunch of enemies packed in tight together. Even if people notice you, they may not be able to get into position to take a poke at you. And you needed somebody to watch your back. Jeez louise, warmblood, did you think that all the Creoles who could reach across the Shroud would just forget about you once you made it up the steps?"

Bellamy shook his head. "I guess I didn't think. Thank you."

Titus squatted beside them. "I'll help Antoine," the old man wheezed, his wrinkled, chocolate-colored skin mottled with pale cuts and punctures. "You mind our business. This affair isn't over yet."

Bellamy patted Antoine's scaly neck, then rose and hurried to Astarte. She looked all right, though something had shorn two of her ostrich plumes away. The FBI agent tried not to imagine how the blow might just as easily have split her skull. Grinning, her amber eyes alight with excitement, the bogus queen was conferring with two of her lieutenants.

"What's our situation, Your Highness?" Bellamy asked.

"Great!" Astarte crowed. The caped warriors eyed her quizzically. "This was the main battle right here, and we won it. Our other guys wiped out the rebels on the back stairs. Now we just regroup, mop up, and go kick the ass of Geffard himself."

"I'm glad you're having such a good time," Bellamy said sourly. He looked around, located his Browning, and exchanged the spent clip for a fresh one. "The room with the dolls is down this way. I'm going to check on it."

"I'll go with you. I want to see it."

Bellamy's mouth tightened. He would have preferred that she stay in a secured area, surrounded by guards, not go scouting down a dark corridor with him. But it looked as if the battle really was over. Any rebels still at large had probably run away. "All right, Your Highness." He turned to the soldiers. "You guys come along, too."

Bellamy taking point, the foursome headed down the shadowy hallway. Tiny Nihils hissed and glittered in the walls. The FBI agent strained his senses, looking for potential threats, reminding himself that a wraith ambusher could pop out of a solid wall as easily as through a doorway.

As before, the room housing the voudoun fetishes gave the FBI agent the creeps. About half the dolls and puppets were already gone, yet he could still discern a pattern in the arrangement of the remaining figures radiating outward from the life-size wax image in the center, as if the Creoles and werewolves had been taking care to move the magical artifacts in a particular order. Black light still rippled through the talismans, or leaped sizzling from one to another, and the altar against the wall, with its skulls, bones, and crossed shovel and pick-ax, still gave off a sickening aura of *wrongness*.

Judging by their scowls, the two soldiers found the display as disquieting as Bellamy did. To some extent, Astarte seemed to share the feeling, yet she was fascinated as well. "This is awesome," she breathed, reaching for a crude rag doll representing the Queen with her body split open from throat to crotch.

Bellamy grabbed her and yanked her back. Granted, the evil magick contained in the images was aimed at the real Marie. But Astarte was wearing the Queen's shape, and had been told that simply touching one of the talismans had plunged the wraith monarch into a coma. Didn't the Quick girl have any sense at all?

"Sorry, Highness," he said, trying to keep his annoyance out of his voice. "But it would be better to leave this stuff alone until Titus can defuse it."

Astarte sighed. "I guess," she said, and then Bellamy heard a tiny noise, perhaps the rustle of clothing as someone shifted position, whispering through the wall.

He strode through the surface into the next room, where the remains of Chester's Pentium still lay broken on the floor. The scrawny, gray-haired ghost himself jerked backward, simultaneously lifting his snub-nosed revolver. An instant later, Astarte and her guards glided into the room, weapons at the ready. Outnumbered four to one, the Creole lowered his weapon and placed it on a table.

"Well, Chester, hello again," Bellamy said. "Were you hoping you could hide out here until my friends and I cleared out?" He wondered why the ghost in the wire-rimmed glasses hadn't concealed himself inside an inanimate object. Maybe he could only possess electronic gadgets like working computers.

"Are you going to kill me?" Chester asked, his voice quavering slightly.

"No," Bellamy said, "not if you cooperate."

Chester sighed. "Well, why shouldn't I? I suppose I should be happy to switch to the side of someone competent. I always knew that Dunn and his pack were idiots, but I thought that at least the loa and his Baka friends knew what they were about. But if they had, their curses would have worked, and Her Majesty wouldn't have been able to lead her troops against us."

Astarte chuckled. "Life's a bitch."

Bellamy shot her a glance, trying to remind her to stay in character. "Now that we aren't quite so pressed for time," he said to Chester, "I want to know all of it. First off, where's Geffard?"

"Probably aboard the *Twisted Mirror*," Chester said. "That's where the wolves were going to take the dolls."

"Makes sense," the FBI agent said. "If he carried them out into the middle of the river, we'd have a tough time getting to them. Now, we know your boss's objective. He wants to be King of New Orleans. But what are the Spectres and the Black Spiral Dancers trying to accomplish? What's the point of the Atheist murders and all the other crimes against the living? Are your friends deliberately trying to stir up Maelstroms?"

Chester grimaced. "You're pretty clever, particularly for a Lemure. That's a part of it, in a sense."

"What's the whole answer?" Bellamy demanded. "Why—"

Chester pivoted and lunged through the exterior wall.

Caught by surprise, Bellamy faltered for a precious instant, then gave chase. Once outside the room, he found himself on the roof of the verandah. The Creole was dashing along it toward the corner of the house.

"Stop!" Bellamy shouted. He squeezed off a warning shot. Chester leaped into space.

With Astarte and the two warriors pounding along at his heels, the FBI agent ran to the corner and looked down. His leg twisted at an unnatural angle, the rebel lay on the roof of the rental truck feet below. Bellamy's alarm gave way to a pang of pity. Chester was a computer nerd, not a man of action. He should have known he'd only get hurt if he tried to make a break for it.

Chester's skinny body melted into the body of the truck. The engine roared to life, the loading ramp retracted, and, the rear doors swinging and banging, a couple of dolls tumbling out, the vehicle lurched into motion.

Now Bellamy understood why the rebel hadn't concealed himself inside some object in the Haunt. He'd been conserving his mystical energies to merge himself with the truck, which had already been loaded with many of the voudoun fetishes—quite possibly enough to finish the job of destroying Marie.

Bellamy leaped, and slammed down on the rear of the rental vehicle. Astarte and the soldiers jumped after him, but fell short.

The truck hurtled out onto Barracks Street. Evidently conscious of his unwanted passenger, Chester began to swerve unpredictably back and forth. The motion threatened to tumble Bellamy from the roof. He peered about, looking for something to cling to, but there was nothing. Lying spread-eagle, he held himself in place as best he could.

Until he realized with a twinge of irritation that he was thinking like a mortal. He wasn't trapped on the roof. Willing his body to become completely intangible, he fell into the cargo compartment, landing on an image made of crossed sticks and clothes stuffed with straw, like a scarecrow. He banged his knee, and his left hand plunged on through the floor, giving his shoulder a painful wrench.

Lurching to his feet, he wondered what his next move ought to be. Throw the fetishes out onto the road? He was leery of damaging them, for fear that whatever befell them might also, in some measure, happen to Marie. But he suspected that breaking a few was less risky then allowing Chester to deliver the lot to Geffard. He grabbed the scarecrow doll and carried it toward the rear of the compartment.

The doors clanged shut and latched, plunging Bellamy into darkness. He was sure that Chester had done it on purpose. Groping his way now, the floor shuddering beneath his feet, the FBI agent tried to shove the image through the steel panel. The maneuver seemed like it ought to work. After all, the voudoun doll existed in the Shadowlands, just as he did. He could carry other objects, like his clothing and weapons, through walls without any problem. But the fetish wouldn't penetrate the metal. Maybe Chester was responsible for that, too.

Bellamy ran his hands over the double doors. Found a lever that should open them. He projected himself into the Skinlands and pulled it, but it didn't move. He tried again, grunting and straining, the metal bar cutting into his hands, with no better result. He kicked the doors, and that didn't budge them, either.

He felt his shadowself stir in the depths of mind, laughing at his impotence. Ignoring the parasite as best he could, he discarded the scarecrow, stumbled to the other end of the compartment, and hurled himself at the front wall.

He smashed into the surface, rebounded, and fell. Hauled himself to his feet and tried again. Antoine had told him that in the realm of the dead, belief was power, and he strove to believe that, unencumbered with any of the images, he *could* pass through. That Chester's magick was too feeble to hold him back.

For a split second he thought he felt himself flowing through the steel, and then it thrust him backward. His wrist throbbed as if he might have broken it.

He flung himself forward a third time, and his body penetrated, though not without resistance. The Skinlands matter felt like knife points dragging and snagging along inside him. Then he lurched into the cab.

His flailing, outstretched hands plunged inside the dashboard, the interior of which seemed to clamp down on them like a trap snapping shut. Bellamy barely managed to yank them out in time to keep them from being crushed. He made sure his entire body was inside the cab, then positioned himself in the driver's seat and vaulted across the Shroud.

With a click and a crackle of static, the radio switched itself on. "I'm in control," said Chester's voice. "There's nothing you can do. Jump out now and I'll let you live." The door swung open.

"Forget it," Bellamy said. He stamped on the brake. The pedal wouldn't budge. He kept fighting the resistance, then suddenly floored the accelerator and jerked the steering wheel to the left.

As Bellamy had hoped, Chester didn't seem able to concentrate his force of will equally in all the controls at once. The wheel felt sticky, but it turned, while the gas pedal didn't resist at all. The truck hurtled at a parked Hyundai.

The accelerator bumped Bellamy's foot upward, and the steering wheel spun, as Chester barely managed to avoid a collision. The FBI agent yanked the emergency brake, nearly bringing the vehicle to a lurching halt before the lever snapped off in his fist.

The truck sped forward. Bellamy put his foot on the brake pedal, then instantly shifted it to the accelerator, propelling the van onward even faster. At the same instant he seized the gearshift and rammed it from Drive into Reverse.

The transmission made a grinding, crashing sound. Chester's voice screamed from the radio as if the insult to his borrowed mechanical body had wounded him, too. Hoping that it had, Bellamy wrenched the steering wheel.

The truck jumped the curb and slammed into a cornstalk fence. Bellamy jolted forward into the wheel. The steering column collapsed beneath his weight and he hurtled onward, driving his head through the windshield. Writhing, razor-edged shards of glass tightened around his neck like a noose, and then he passed out.

EIGHT

At first Marilyn Sebastian could neither wake up completely nor sink deep enough into unconsciousness to escape every vestige of pain. She didn't know which was more annoying, the gray fog smothering her mind, or the pangs wracking her body. She only knew that she wanted to be rid of both. Exerting her will, she struggled to push them away, or perhaps to propel herself free of their grasp. She heard a sharp click.

An instant later she was standing naked in a bedroom. Judging from the ornate furnishings, the dark, musty chamber might have been considered luxurious a century ago, but now everything was grimy and festooned with filthy cobwebs. An oil lamp shed a wavering greenish light—strangely, the fire seemed to be shedding chill instead of heat—and black cracks seethed in one corner of the ceiling.

On the canopy bed lay a tattered body, reeking of blood. As soon as Marilyn saw it, she began to remember the battle in the police station, and understood that the mangled husk belonged to her. For a moment she felt a twinge of horror, but then the sensation withered into a disinterested curiosity. She calmly surveyed the wreckage. Much of her face shorn away. Both breasts shredded, her cherished implants burst. Three fingers cut short, and it looked as if Dunn might have given her a head start on the final phase of her sex change, too.

She looked down at the luminous shape she was wearing now. Slender but muscular arms. Small breasts. A narrow waist. A penis with no external testicles, and beneath it, a vagina. She'd become a true hermaphrodite, the perfected being the alchemists and cabalists had extolled. Running her hands over her smooth, unblemished flesh, she laughed with delight.

A white light flowered in the corner.

Fearless, curious, her radiant form gliding with the easy grace she'd possessed as a boy of twenty, she moved closer. Images formed in the pearly glow. Each lasted only an instant, but she had no difficult assimilating them.

A baby boy entering the world, bloody and squalling, in Amsterdam. An exuberant childhood spent skating, playing soccer, and frolicking along the canals with a host of friends. And when the friends were absent, learning yoga, meditation, and ultimately how to conjure spirits and rouse dull, dead matter to fluid, obedient life. Because the boy's parents were mages, and he'd inherited their gift. Indeed, he possessed it in far greater measure than they did. Grown to handsome, vigorous manhood, a master of his art, he worked miracles with a snap of his fingers and explored a hundred extra-dimensional worlds. Lesser sorcerers begged him to accept them as disciples.

That's me, Marilyn realized. *That's my next life, waiting for me to start it up.* She stepped forward.

"Stop," said a woman's voice.

Startled, the Arcanist turned, to see that the wall behind her had disappeared. The room now opened on a benighted stretch of rocky beach. Some distance out to sea, four mounds of rock jutted above the surface, and closer in, breakers hissed as they crumbled into white foam. A chilly breeze carried the scent of the salt water.

A glowing lantern hanging from its ornately carved prow, a small lateener sat beached at the edge of the surf. Beside it stood a tall woman, her dark, multi-layered cloak sodden from the waist down, its cowl shadowing her features.

"Who are you?" Marilyn asked. She was still unafraid, but a hint of disquiet blunted the edge of the bliss she'd been feeling a moment before.

"I'm called Katrina," said the woman in the hood. "A Ferryman, though I doubt that title means anything to you."

"It makes it sound like you help people travel to wherever they're going. Are you here to take me to my new life?" Marilyn didn't actually feel as if she needed an escort. She sensed that another step or two into the light would suffice to unite her with the fetus inside her new mother's womb.

"No," Katrina said, "I wish I were. Ordinarily I'd rejoice to see a soul move on to another reincarnation. Every such transmigration cheats the Void."

"Then what's the problem?"

"The Atheist conspiracy. Your unfinished business."

"Unfinished or not," Marilyn said, "I'm dead. It's somebody else's problem now."

"You're only dead if you choose to be," the Ferryman replied. "You uncoupled your soul from your body voluntarily, to escape your discomfort. Many mages can do it, or so I'm told. You still have time to return before your heart and lungs stop pumping."

Marilyn frowned. "If I go back now, will I still move on to the life in the light whenever I do die?"

"I'm sorry," Katrina said, "but no. The universe never stops changing. Unclaimed opportunities disappear."

"But at least I'm finally a genuine sorcerer in my present life," Marilyn said. "I'll learn to do all the things I saw him do."

"No," said the woman in the hood. "His genotype would be perfect, his parents would be superb mentors, and he'd begin learning in his cradle. In your current incarnation, you possess less native ability, may never find any sort of teacher, and are already middle-aged. At best, you'll acquire a fraction of his abilities. And before you ask, I'll confess it's unlikely that you'll ever be altogether free of disfigurement and pain. The werewolf savaged you too badly."

"Then to hell with it," said Marilyn, "I'm going forward."

"Even though people need your help?"

"You seem to be some sort of angel or Buddha or something," the Arcanist replied. "*You* help them."

"I swear to you," said Katrina, "I am, to the extent I'm able. I have vows to keep, no matter what the cost, obligations you wouldn't understand."

"How convenient for you."

"I assure you," Katrina said, an undertone of anger in her voice, "it's far from that. I don't want to see millions of souls suffer, or the world blighted."

Marilyn's eyes narrowed. "It's really that bad?"

"Yes," Katrina said. The cold breeze gusted, stirring the topmost layer of her cloak. The surf whispered. "I can't see precisely what's coming, but I can tell it will be disastrous. What's more, it will create an ongoing menace, which, by all the laws of karma, the young warlock in your vision will almost certainly have to confront."

"Better him than the current edition," Marilyn said. "You said it yourself: he'll be more powerful."

"But the agents of Oblivion will have had decades to increase *their* strength. And what about all the spirits, living and dead, who will perish in the interim? What about your colleagues in the Arcanum, and your other friends?"

Marilyn grimaced. "I care about them, of course. I care about 'the world,' for that matter. But what makes *me* so important?"

"You may be a fumbling, unschooled mage, but mages of any sort are thin on the ground, and you have an urgent task to perform."

"Damn it, I don't even know you! What if you're a demon, trying to trick me?"

"You can *feel* that that isn't so," Katrina said, and in fact, Marilyn did. "Do you recall what Astarte told you? That as much as you wanted to embrace the supernatural, you always wound up flinching from the danger it embodied?"

"How could I forget?" Marilyn said sardonically. "She taunted me with my cowardice to shame me into going after Bellamy's notebook. Because I listened, we walked right into Dunn's ambush, and he ripped me to pieces."

"Yet it was that confrontation which unleashed your powers," the Ferryman said. "By defying your fears, you won the prize you've always dreamed of, even if you did pay a heavy price for it. Now be bold again. Don't take the easy, selfish path. Stand by your allies. Do what you know is right."

Marilyn turned and gazed into the light. Something twisted inside her breast, and then she wrenched herself back around. "All right," she said, her voice breaking, "you win. I'll stay and fight." The radiance at her back died, deepening the ambient gloom. "Now what exactly am I supposed to do?"

The far wall popped back into existence, cutting off Marilyn's view of Katrina and the surf. "Hey!" the Arcanist yelped. "Come back!" Nothing happened.

Snarling curses, Marilyn stalked over to her ravaged body, put her strong but delicate hands on its gashed, bandaged shoulders, and willed it to admit her. After a moment a circle of golden light appeared on its forehead, and she spun dizzily into it like water swirling down a drain.

NINE

Geffard glared at Denis, the wounded soldier, in disbelief. "You must be mistaken," the loa said, though the watery feeling in his guts told him otherwise.

"No, Captain," the other wraith said, shaking his head. A ring of shadow oozed outward from the bloodless hole in his forearm. Probably he still had a darksteel bullet or arrowhead stuck inside his flesh. "The Queen made a sneak attack on the house on Barracks Street. We tried to defend the place, but they drove us out. I don't know how many others besides me got away."

Fearful that his face would betray his dismay, Geffard turned away to compose himself. Resting his hands on the railing encircling his steamboat's uppermost deck, he gazed out at the broad expanse of the Mississippi, stinking of silt and pollution, the color of charcoal in the pre-dawn gloom. Far out in the water, the lights of a small boat, one violet and one green, drifted silently along. His instincts told him that the craft belonged to one of the dead.

Try as he might, Geffard couldn't comprehend how this debacle had come to pass. All right, this Bellamy person had invaded the Haunt, made it out again, and somehow even survived the Maelstrom that arose immediately thereafter. None of that altered the fact that Marie had been too weak and addled to lead an assault, and her troops wouldn't have marched without her. Geffard would have staked his very existence on that; he'd only decided to move the fetishes on the principle that it was foolish to run even a tiny risk if it could be avoided. Yet now, inexplicably, it seemed that his meticulously crafted scheme had fallen apart.

Grimacing, he abruptly decided it didn't matter how Marie had escaped the curse. What was important was to turn the situation around. Molding his handsome features into a confident smile, he pivoted. "I know you didn't have an easy time of it, bringing me this news," he said. "I won't forget. Go tell one of the officers to summon our supporters. Then find yourself a healer to tend your wound."

Denis frowned. "Captain," he said hesitantly, "we've already lost a lot of men. The rest are scattered through the city, and we don't know how many of them will arrive here in time. You're on a boat. Maybe you should get out on the river. It will give you time to make new plans."

Geffard quivered with fury. His own mother had driven him out of Haiti after he joined the *culte des morts.* The *mamaloi* of New Orleans had subjected him to a slow, agonizing, humiliating death for challenging their power. And now this fool was advising him to let a woman humble him *again?* The loa's power stirred inside him. The force of his will tightened around Denis's neck like a noose, then jerked him into the air. The other Creole kicked and pawed frantically at the insubstantial tether holding him aloft.

"Coward," said Geffard. "You faithless, stinking coward. We lose one battle and you're ready to run away? I should—" The magician's rage deserted him in mid-sentence, or rather, he realized that Denis wasn't its proper target. The man was neither timid nor disloyal, or he would never have trekked wounded through the streets to warn his commander. Nor would it profit Geffard to alienate any of his followers, particularly at this juncture.

He hastily set Denis down, and then, when the wounded ghost's knees buckled, grabbed him and held him up. Begrudging the expenditure of spiritual force—he was likely to need every iota of it over the course of the next few hours—the *houngan* willed a bit of his vitality to tingle from his hands into Denis's body. With a creak, the soldier's neck straightened, and the raw groove beneath his chin disappeared.

"I'm *sorry!*" said Geffard, suffusing his musical voice with horror and self-loathing. Meanwhile, his mind reached out to Denis's, kneading it like clay. "I don't know what came over me. I'll do anything, anything at all, to make it up to you."

Denis stared back at him with dread and loathing in his chocolate-colored eyes. Then Geffard felt his magick take hold and twist the other wraith's emotions. Denis blinked. "It's...it's all right, Captain," he rasped. "I know you didn't mean it."

"You're as generous as you are brave," said Geffard, his voice breaking, all gratitude and humility. "The gods know, I don't deserve friends like you. But since I'm lucky enough to have them, we *are* going to beat the Queen. I promise you that. Now, do you feel strong enough to carry my orders to an officer?"

"Yes, Captain."

"Then go, please. Time is of the essence. Tell them I'll be down directly."

Denis hobbled to the companionway and started down the steps. Geffard strode to his cabin, whispered the word which dissolved the seal on the door, and went inside.

On a sidewheeler like the *Twisted Mirror*, even the captain's quarters were none too large, but Geffard had done to his best to made them luxurious, with an ornately carved featherbed, armoire, and dressing table of gleaming cherry. On the sideboard gleamed crystal decanters of bourbon, cognac, and rum. Like the humidors of fragrant Cuban cigars and marijuana, the liquors were offerings from Les Invisibles' mortal worshippers, translated by magick into the realm of the dead. A stereo system powered by soulfire crystals and a rack of CDs lent an anachronistic touch to a room which otherwise reflected the nineteenth century.

On the instructions of his patron deity, Geffard had raised his personal altar in the darkest corner of the cabin. The space had seemed even darker since. Somehow neither the lamplight nor whatever natural illumination leaked in from outside could clearly illuminate the skull, crossed Bowie knives, candles, crucified serpent, miniature coffin, and other ritual objects swimming in the gloom.

Geffard would have preferred to use the grand altar in the central cabin below. Empowered by countless rituals of mass devotion and sacrifice, it had more energy in it. But since he needed to confer with his god in private, that would have entailed banishing all his troops and supporters from the salon for the duration, and that didn't seem like a good idea. He didn't want to shake their confidence by making them wonder if he had something to hide.

He knelt before the altar, grimacing for a moment at the chill that shrouded it. He raised his arms and said, "Héviyoso! Piè Jupité-Tonné! God of the thunder and the lightning, father of storms, please, come to me."

Nothing happened.

"Father," said Geffard, "it is I, your son, who calls. The plan has gone wrong. The bitch has broken the spell. She and her followers are marching against me. I need your wisdom."

Still nothing.

Since the night they sealed their covenant in the god's palace on the Island Below the Sea, Héviyoso had always come when he called. Geffard struggled to quash the fear that something was terribly wrong. "Master," he said, "I beg you, accept this sacrifice and reveal yourself to me." He picked up one of the heavy knives and lifted its point to his right eye.

The wraith's plaited dreadlocks and the strands of golden braid attached to the epaulets of his riverboat captain's uniform stood on end. Abruptly the cold air smelled of ozone, and almost seemed to buzz against his skin. Something laughed, a rumbling like rhythmic thunder. "You can keep your eye," a bass voice said.

Geffard looked up. Above the altar loomed a vague figure seemingly composed of black, churning storm clouds, its long, narrow eyes flickering, its murky features constantly seething and changing with the roiling of the vapor. Though logic suggested that to fit in the corner between altar and ceiling it could be no larger than a child, Geffard's mind insisted on perceiving it as vast, huge as a skyscraper or a mountain.

"Master," said Geffard. "Father. Thank you for speaking to me. But why the delay? Did Marie's gods try to block your path?"

"No," said Héviyoso. "I just thought it would be amusing to see you squirm. Did I unsettle your faith in me?"

"No," said Geffard, struggling to mask a pang of annoyance, "of course not."

It was strange. Before he had ventured in search of Les Mystéres, he'd imagined the storm god to be as primal and straightforward as the force of nature he personified. Certainly that was the way in which the myths depicted him. But Héviyoso had proved to possess a sly, malicious side, almost as if his nature derived less from the clean, elemental cloudbursts of the physical world than from the hellish tempests perpetually raging in the Abyss.

But Geffard didn't have time to ponder such ambiguities now. "Do you know what's happened?" he asked.

Héviyoso chuckled. "Better than you."

You don't have to sound so happy about it, Geffard thought bitterly. "Many of my men are gone. The Black Spiral Dancers lost some of their shamans as well, but not all of them. If the ones who are left can conjure up enough Banes in time, I can still muster a force as large or larger than Marie's."

"You're forgetting," the storm god said, "even the majority of your own warriors are unaware that you've made common cause with Baka, wolfmen, and demons. Certainly the general populace has no notion that you're behind the recent attacks on the Queen and her supporters. Should they find out, they'd turn on you in an instant. No, your allies must stay hidden."

"I follow what you're saying," Geffard replied, "but then how am I supposed to win?"

"Ah," said Héviyoso, "that's the question, isn't it? I wonder if we can stumble on an answer."

"Please," said Geffard, "don't toy with me, not now. You gave me your blessing to ally myself with the Spectres. You said the plan was a good idea."

Héviyoso chuckled. "And if you can't trust me, who can you trust?"

"Well...yes."

"Do you ever recall your descent into the Abyss?"

Geffard frowned. "Of course, Father. It was the most important event in my existence. I reflect on it constantly. But—and I ask this with all respect—is there a reason for us to talk about it now?"

"It was a bold undertaking," the storm god said. "The Abyss is a fearsome, bewildering place, a maze and a trackless wilderness with hurricanes blowing through. And you'd never set foot in it before. Granted, you had your magick to sustain you, but still, few neophytes would have wandered in so deep without a guide."

Geffard held in a sigh. If Héviyoso insisted on squandering precious time chatting, there wasn't much his priest could do about it. A further display of impatience would probably only amuse the god, prompting him to draw out the consultation even longer. "Tradition says that the supplicant *has* to descend alone, Father. And I was desperate to make my pledge."

"Indeed you were," said Héviyoso, his vaporous countenance writhing. "Desperate to teach all the arrogant ladies a lesson. But I'm curious. Were you *never* troubled by the suspicion that you may have gotten lost and never reached the Island Below the Sea at all?"

Geffard blinked. Swallowed away a sudden dryness in his throat. "I don't understand."

"And here I thought you were such a clever fellow. The Abyss is full of tricksters and shape-shifters. What if one of them showed you the landscape you expected to see? Appeared to you in the guise of one of the entities you hoped to find? What if you didn't give yourself to Les Mystéres but to something else?"

The Creole hesitated, then said, "My father is teasing me. Testing my faith again. I *know* you're Héviyoso, lord of the rain. But just for argument's sake, suppose I learned otherwise. You would still be a great and generous god, the patron who gave me true power and has aided me countless times since. I would worship you no matter what."

Héviyoso laughed. Lightning flickered through his roiling body, and sparks danced popping and crackling on the knives atop the altar beneath his feet. "That's a good answer, my child. A wise and dutiful answer. I chose my servant well. Such being the case, let's discuss how to plant your posterior on the ivory throne."

"Yes, please," said Geffard.

The god chuckled. "The tension in your voice! Relax, little *bocor*. Your situation isn't so desperate, quite the contrary. The Africans are playing directly into your hands."

"In what way?"

Héviyoso explained. Geffard's lips stretched into a grin.

TEN

When the Smiling Lord charged, Montrose backpedaled, simultaneously drawing his smallsword with his right hand and one of the Walthers with his left. "Halt!" he cried.

The Master of War kept coming, his steel soles clanging on the pale marble with its inlaid pentacles, his purple mantle billowing out behind him. Montrose opened fire.

Without breaking stride, the Smiling Lord spun his halberd. Metal rang on metal. Impossible as it seemed, the demigod was deflecting the bullets. And if any did streak past his guard, they glanced harmlessly off his armor.

The pistol clicked, out of ammunition. Dropping it, still retreating, Montrose invoked his Harbinger Arcanos. Cool shadow welled from his pores and flowed across his skin, and he shifted to the left.

The Smiling Lord veered to follow him. Montrose wasn't surprised. He would have been amazed if any of the magics at his command could hinder one of the Seven.

The Deathlord hurtled into striking range. The halberd whirled at Montrose's skull. Ducking, dodging, and jumping back, parrying only when necessary lest the heavy weapon break his lighter one, the Scot narrowly evaded the first flurry of blows. Finally, taking advantage of what seemed an opening, he lunged past the halberd's spiked ax head and thrust his point at one of the eye holes in Prince Mars's visor.

The Smiling Lord skipped backward so quickly and cunningly that Montrose barely perceived it. The thrust fell short by two inches. The lengthy halberd should have been too cumbersome for any man to wield easily at such close quarters, but the seraph spun it over his head and then it flashed at Montrose's groin.

The Scot leaped back. Before his boots touched the floor, the halberd's point was streaking at his belly. Parrying, he jumped back again, reeling until he could catch his balance. He saw that the pole arm had notched the forte of his blade.

The Smiling Lord glided forward. "You fight well," he said. "I always said so. You've already lasted longer than most men would."

"I don't want to fight you," Montrose said, retreating. He allowed his useless mask of invisibility to dissolve. Perhaps his powers of levitation would prove more useful; although, a master Harbinger himself, the Smiling Lord could fly right after him. "I only opened fire in self-defense. I've come to help you. Probe my mind if you don't believe me."

"Demetrius—my *friend*—already did that." Pouncing, closing the distance which separated them, the Smiling Lord attacked.

Once again, Montrose gave ground. The halberd grazed his thigh, just a nick, but enough to send ripples of Oblivion, alternately burning hot and numbing cold, streaming down his leg. Meanwhile he feinted, disengaged, probed, striving to find or create an opening in the other wraith's seemingly impenetrable guard.

At last a beat in sixte followed by a deceive appeared to make the spinning halberd falter. Montrose levitated straight up, as if he meant to soar over the Smiling Lord's head and strike him from behind, then he plummeted into a crouch and drove his point at his liege lord's groin.

The Deathlord twisted, and the darksteel smallsword glanced screeching along the tassets of his armor. One armored foot lashed out with a snap kick. Had it landed, the attack might have broken Montrose's neck, but, still using his powers of flight, he bounced backward, out of range. The Smiling Lord's toe rang against the Scot's blade and nearly knocked it from his grasp.

The Lord of Murder halted, once again becoming so still that he seemed altogether inhuman. Montrose took advantage of the pause to ready his remaining automatic. "A waste of time," said the Smiling Lord, a hint of mockery in his voice. "You're better with a sword than with a gun; not that your blade will save you either." He glided forward.

Montrose retreated, squeezing the trigger. As the Smiling Lord had warned, the shots did no damage. Where, the Scot wondered desperately, was Louise? Why didn't she attack?

The halberd swept up and plummeted at Montrose's head. He sidestepped and parried in prime, only then discerning that, now, impossibly, the pole arm was striking at his ankles. He sprang upward and the spiked head whizzed under his soles.

He extended the smallsword and hurtled forward in a sort of aerial flèche attack, simultaneously squeezing off the last shot in his gun. His point punched between two of the overlapping rings comprising the Deathlord's gorget, then popped back out as he rocketed by.

The demigod took a lurching step, catching his balance, and for an instant Montrose dared to hope that either his sword or his final bullet had done some significant damage. Then the halberd flew out of nowhere and the spear point slammed between the ribs under his left arm.

Pure reflex carried him racing onward, directly away from the attack. Otherwise the spike would have passed through his entire torso. Still, he could tell the wound was bad. Waves of black fire washed through his substance, eroding his strength and awareness. When he touched down on the floor, his left leg tried to buckle beneath him. Without meaning to, he dropped the Walther.

"Now that," said the Smiling Lord, "was a jolly good try. It's time to put an end to this." He swung the halberd into a high guard. Montrose raised his sword, and then a soft thump sounded from the direction of the onyx altar.

The Smiling Lord pivoted toward the noise, and, blocking out the pain of his wounds as best he could, Montrose rushed him. Turning back instantly, the Prince of Bloodshed struck at his opponent's knees. Levitating above the blow, Montrose tried to continue his charge, but the Smiling Lord's weapon instantly leaped up into his path. The outlaw had to freeze to avoid impaling himself.

The Deathlord stalked forward, feinting and striking with blinding speed. Giving ground, Montrose desperately looked for an opening, an opportunity for a riposte or a counterattack. At first the seraph didn't give him one, but then something rustled off to the left.

The whirling halberd seemed to slow a bit. Montrose darted to the Smiling Lord's left and thrust at his leg. His master parried the blow, striking sparks from his blade.

Expecting an immediate riposte, Montrose leaped backward, but the Smiling Lord didn't seize the initiative. Evidently he was still trying to determine the source of the noises.

The Cavalier could have told him. Louise must be making them with her telekinesis, hoping to distract him. And the trick was working to a degree, but not enough to turn the tide in Montrose's favor.

But perhaps the Scot could enhance the effect. "If I were you," he said, "I'd surrender now. You may not get another chance."

His master laughed. "Such bravado, even with the poisons of Oblivion gnawing your flesh to rags. I wish you hadn't turned traitor, James. I truly am going to miss you."

"You really don't understand, do you?" said Montrose, trying to inject a note of pity into his tone. "I assumed that if you could see through my veil of invisibility, you could penetrate theirs, but evidently not. Nevertheless, it's obvious, they're here."

"No one is here," the Smiling Lord replied. Montrose thought he heard a hint of uncertainty in the other ghost's voice. He prayed that he hadn't imagined it. "No one but you and me."

"You're mistaken," Montrose said. "Did you think I came here to slay you? I knew I couldn't single-handedly defeat the Avatar of War. But I did hope I could divert you from your conjuring long enough for your spell to weaken. I suspected it wouldn't have to fade very much for the other Deathlords to break its grip, and now they've come to settle accounts with you."

It was a preposterous bluff. Anyone capable of perceiving mystical forces could discern that the intangible mechanisms of the Smiling Lord's ritual were indeed spinning out power a bit less efficiently than before. But the floor was still vibrating beneath the Prince of Murder's feet, the wands, talismans, and alembics still rattling on their shelves, proof that the earthquake still raged, and thus, that the other Deathlords were still fighting on the lower levels of the donjon. A moment of coherent reflection should have sufficed to assure the Avatar of Violent Death that Montrose was talking nonsense.

But as Montrose had hoped, Louise didn't permit the archangel time to think. Her psychokinesis cast down the black altar, shattering it. A shelf of scrolls and grimoires toppled. A section of floor banged and cracked, the fissure splitting a crimson pentacle in half. Three barrow-fire torches jerked themselves from their sconces, whirled about like green comets orbiting an invisible sun, and then flew at the Smiling Lord.

And, maddened by the paranoia Demetrius had so cunningly and persistently induced in him, Prince Ares believed the worst. That, shrouded in cloaks of darkness so cunningly woven that even he couldn't see through them, his peers had assembled to destroy him. He brandished the halberd and the torches simply ceased to exist. He barked a word of power and the space the brands had circled exploded in a burst of dazzling white light.

Montrose took a deep breath, steadying himself, then charged the Smiling Lord. The Scot beat the other man's weapon, whipped his sword over it in a coupe, and lunged. The Smiling Lord skipped backward, and the attack fell short. Montrose redoubled, trying to take up the distance, then realized he was plunging into a trap just in time to keep the halberd from gutting him.

Yet when he wrenched himself frantically backward, the Smiling Lord didn't pursue him. He was too busy lashing out with his sorcery at the sundry noises and disturbances Louise created. As far as the Deathlord was concerned, there were far greater threats than Montrose assailing him, and striking at them took priority.

The Scot was certain that Louise's tricks couldn't deceive the Smiling Lord for long. Befuddled or not, Prince Ares would soon realize that if his peers had truly gathered to destroy him, their assault would have been far more deadly than anything the Heretic had thrown at him.

Teeth gritted against the pain of his injuries, Montrose circled around behind the Smiling Lord. The demigod's armor clanked as a hail of ivory, silver-bound staves, wavy-bladed ritual daggers, golden, begemmed chalices, and alchemical glassware battered him. None of it did any noticeable damage or even made him flinch or stagger, but it served to draw his attention to the barrage's point of origin. He chanted, and space folded in on itself, grinding a section of shelving and a piece of floor to rubble.

Montrose floated off the floor and hurtled forward, sword outstretched. He expected the Smiling Lord to whirl and strike at him. Instead his point plunged through the other wraith's voluminous purple cloak and slammed deep into his back, either punching through his armor or sliding through the narrow gap between his backplate and the taces encircling his hips.

Sure that he'd landed a killing blow, Montrose felt an instant of exaltation. Then the Smiling Lord spun around, jerking the outlaw's smallsword out of his grasp in the process. Montrose tried to float backwards and up to give himself sufficient room for a full-force savate kick to the other ghost's head, but the Smiling Lord seized him in a telekinetic grip and smashed him to the floor.

Pain screamed through Montrose's injured body. He struggled to break through the shock, to scramble to his feet, but the Smiling Lord's Arcanos held him down like a butterfly mounted for display. Evidently deciding his lieutenant posed a significant threat after all, the Avatar of War raised the halberd to behead him.

Demented laughter shrilled through the air. A black shape like a huge bat—or someone shrouded in a flapping hooded cloak—swooped through the doorway.

The Smiling Lord uttered a word *sotto voce*, and the dark shape flew apart in a blast of flame. Montrose gasped in horror, then saw that Louise hadn't been wearing the cape—which she'd evidently snatched from one of the shelves—after all. She'd been charging *behind* it, using it to shield her advance, and now she opened fire. Her bullets rang and whined as they ricocheted off the Deathlord's plate.

Prince Ares glared at the Sister of Athena. Montrose struggled frantically, but still couldn't tear himself free of his liege lord's grip. Coils of shadow coalesced, then closed around Louise like a clenching fist. But at the same time, she reached out with her psychokinesis, seized a blazing tatter of cloak, and dropped it atop the Hierarch's head.

Even War Incarnate couldn't contend with an infinite series of threats and distractions. Eventually, if his foes kept the pressure on, his dominance of one aspect of the battle or another had to falter. And now, at last, as the Smiling Lord fumbled at his burning blindfold, Montrose felt the crushing pressure on his body diminish. Drawing on both his waning strength and powers of levitation, the Cavalier jerked himself to his feet and whipped his arm around in an elbow strike to the Deathlord's head.

Prince Ares lurched a step backwards. Montrose grabbed the halberd and wrenched it from the other wraith's gauntleted hands, then rammed the spearhead through his breastplate. The bands of constricting shadow dissolved, and Louise emptied her gun into the Deathlord. This time the shots punched holes in his plate.

But the Smiling Lord still didn't go down. He yanked the burning rag off his head and snapped it at Montrose like a whip. The flames exploded outward in a blast like some colossal dragon's breath, smashing Montrose backward, stunning him, burning him, and chilling him to the bone. His eyes swimming with afterimages from the flash, he murkily saw the Prince of Bloodshed pounce after him, his steel-jacketed hands stiffened into karate swords.

Scrambling backward, Montrose tried to menace the Smiling Lord with the head of the halberd, but the armored wraith pressed him too closely for him to bring the weapon to bear. The best he could manage was to clutch it across his body like a quarterstaff and use the shaft to block his master's strikes. An unexpected kick to the shin of the Cavalier's wounded leg bought a flash of pain and nearly knocked him down.

Bellowing a *kiai*, a knife flashing in either hand, Louise rushed in and attacked the Smiling Lord from behind. The Prince of Murder whirled to face her, and mystic energies rippled the air around him. She sidestepped just in time to avoid a bolt of sizzling light which blasted a hole in the far wall. Meanwhile, Montrose finally managed to step back, point the halberd, and thrust it into the Deathlord's spine.

The Smiling Lord lurched forward and fell to one knee, his genouíllère clanging against the floor. Montrose leaned on the halberd, driving it deeper. Louise stabbed the Hierarch monarch in the neck, slamming one dagger through his gorget and then the other.

Montrose couldn't see through the Smiling Lord's plate, but he could feel the eruption of black fire in his master's flesh. A bit of the power resonated up the halberd's shaft to sting his hands. The armored form toppled forward. Judging from the hollow rattle when it struck the floor, and the way it sprawled motionless afterward, limbs twisted at unnatural angles, there was no one inside it anymore.

ELEVEN

As Montrose stared down at the empty, battered suit of plate, a bewildering knot of emotions churned inside him. Sorrow that he and Louise had been compelled to slay the lord to whom he'd vowed his allegiance, a generous master till Demetrius poisoned his mind. Sheer disbelief that the two of them had managed to destroy a god.

Louise touched him on the arm. "Are you all right?" she said. "Your wounds..."

When he turned and saw the love and concern in her blue eyes, saw that she'd come through the struggle relatively unscathed, he felt a swell of gratitude which momentarily drove every other feeling from his mind. "The wound under my left arm is bad," he said. The fury of battle had enabled him to shut out much of the pain, but now it throbbed. "I'll just have to cope with it for the time being."

"What happened to the spell?" she asked. "I can't see it. My Arcanos doesn't deal with such things."

He tried to open his Harbinger senses. In his injured, depleted state, even that simple operation was difficult, but after a few seconds he dimly discerned the magical structure the Smiling Lord had created. "It's disintegrating," he said. "The channels to the whirlpool have all but closed."

"Thank the Bright Powers," she said. "I don't think the tower is shaking so much, either."

He realized she was right. He listened, straining, and caught the muffled boom of an explosion and a faint rat-tat-tat of automatic weapons fire whispering through the floor. "Yes, the earthquake is subsiding. Unfortunately, the other Deathlords are still fighting on the lower levels."

"Won't they stop?" asked Louise. "Now that the enchantment is broken."

Montrose sighed. "I hope so. But it's possible they don't realize they were bewitched in the first place. And even if they do, they still don't understand how the doomshades sowed mistrust among them. Each still regards his peers as implacable enemies, and therefore, at least some of them may think that now that open war has broken out, the wisest course is to fight it through to the end."

Louise frowned. "You're saying we have to go down there and convince them to break it up."

"I suppose I am," Montrose replied. It certainly didn't seem fair, when they'd done so much already. When his wound was hurting worse with each passing second. "And it might be a good idea to bring along something to capture their attention." A bit reluctantly, knowing it was a crime for a lesser being to touch it, he bent over, reaching for the Smiling Lord's visor.

As soon as he started to move, agony flared down his left side, and he fell atop his former master's armor. Waves of ravenous shadow licked at his substance. Louise cried out and crouched beside him.

He rolled over and tried to smile at her. It seemed to take all the strength he had. "I'm all right," he said. "I just lost my balance."

"You're *not* all right," she said, "and you shouldn't move. I'll go to the Deathlords, then bring you a Usurer."

Montrose shook his head. "The Seven think I'm a condemned traitor, but at least they know me. They're more likely to heed me than you." He took hold of the Smiling Lord's mask, and a sort of shock sang up his arm. Though he hadn't established telepathic communication with it—he assumed he'd have to put it on for that—he was perceiving the powerful, inhuman intelligence dwelling inside the steel. "Help me up."

Louise hesitated.

Montrose wondered just how badly hurt he looked, how badly hurt he *was*. Rumor claimed that the Smiling Lord's halberd was far more poisonous than common darksteel, that any wound it made festered with a dreadful malignancy. As far as Montrose knew, he was the first of Prince Ares's opponents to survive long enough to assess whether the story was true. "Please. In your place, I wouldn't want to do it either. But we knew we were risking our existences when we embarked on our mission. I can't flinch now, not after coming so far."

"Like you didn't flinch from invading Scotland," she said grimly, "even know that the young King had sold you out, and you were marching to your death. All right, but you aren't going to perish this time. I won't allow it." She dragged him upright and put her arm around him. It would have been easier if she could have used her psychokinesis, but no doubt, like his, her mystical abilities were entirely depleted. "Lean on me."

"I'm afraid I'll have to." Afraid that his numb, trembling hands would drop the Smiling Lord's mask, he stowed it inside his shirt. "Let's go."

They limped toward the doorway. His pain ebbed, but now time seemed to be skipping along, as if existence were a film with sections missing. "Stay awake," said Louise. "Talk to me."

"All right," he mumbled. His head seemed full of mud, and he had to grope to find something to say. "You waited a long time before you took any action against my…against the Smiling Lord. I was worried that something had happened to you."

They trudged through the trefoil arch and headed down the stairs. His flesh began to ache again, though without dispelling the cottony feeling in his mind. "I didn't want to risk revealing my presence until I thought of something genuinely useful to do," said Louise. "You see, from the moment the fight began, it was obvious you had no chance at all."

Montrose laughed, then stiffened at the resulting jolt of pain. "That isn't a very charitable assessment."

"Don't get huffy," she replied. Her arm began to slip from around him, and, with a grunt, she shifted her grip. "You're one of the most formidable fighters I've ever seen. But he really did move like the god of war, quick and sure, yet with no sense of urgency at all. He didn't even bother to raise his Arcanos against you."

"Probably because if he'd activated his mystical powers, it would have leeched a bit of energy away from his spell. Still, I grudgingly concede your point. Dueling one on one, my situation was hopeless."

Louise half lifted him off the bottom riser. "I don't suppose you'd better try to fly us back down the tower," she said.

"Not unless you're prepared for an exceedingly hard landing."

"Then we'll look for an elevator." They shuffled down the gloomy corridor, past the caskets standing upright in their niches. For a moment Montrose had the mad notion than one of the boxes might open its lid, inviting him inside.

"We were saying that the Smiling Lord wasn't likely to have any difficulty killing me," he said.

"Yes," she said, "and I could see that he wouldn't have any trouble slaughtering the both of us, either, not if I just jumped out and had at him. Our only chance was to play on his paranoia. To rattle him. I'm glad you had the presence of mind to pick up on what I was doing. It wasn't until you told him that the other Deathlords had come to get him that he really went over the edge."

"You did the difficult part, driving him to the precipice." His legs went rubbery, and she nearly dropped him. "I just gave him the last little push. I love you."

"And I love you. It's galling to think of all the time we wasted apart, neither knowing the other had joined the Restless. But it's all right. Now we can be together forever."

He tried to promise that they would indeed, but a wave of faintness stole the words away.

The two ghosts stumbled around a corner. Before them, the corridor terminated in a staircase. The flights spiraling endlessly into the gloomy depths seemed to swirl. For a moment, Montrose thought that he and the Heretic nun were back in Charon's secret vault, peering down at the black whirlpool.

"Well," said Louise heavily, "we didn't find an elevator. Just this."

"There may *be* an elevator," said the Scot, "behind a secret door or something. But this time I can't see the path. I'm too muddled. I'm sorry." His incapacity made him feel worthless and ashamed. His eyes pulsed as if they could still shed tears.

"It's okay," said Louise. "If we have to walk down—" Suddenly her knees buckled, and they both fell to the cold, hard marble floor.

Montrose fumbled at her with hands gone numb and dead. "Louise!" he croaked. "Louise!"

"It's my turn to be sorry," she gasped. "I'm out of strength. I used so much, performing all those Spook tricks, and then the Smiling Lord hurt me with those steel gauntlets and his magick. But I just need a minute!"

Black fire burned inside him, hollowing him out. He felt as fragile as an eggshell, or a smoke ring. "When you recover," he said, "go on without me. I'm afraid I've gone as far as I'm *ever* going to go."

"Don't say that!" she cried. "Don't give up!"

He tried to think of a proper farewell, something that might give her a measure of comfort, then noticed just how deep the silence was. "Either I'm losing my hearing," he said, "or the Seven *did* had the sense to stop fighting, even without a scolding from you and me."

Phosphorescence flowered in the hallway, and the Emerald Lord and the Skeletal Lord materialized inside the glow. The silver rat riding his shoulder once again, the angel in the ivory skull mask knelt beside Montrose and laid his hand on the wound below his arm. The fires of Oblivion guttered out. The Scot felt his body take on substance, and the puncture closed.

Twelve

By the time the Queen's army reached Woldenberg Riverfront Park, the sun had crept above the horizon, only to lose itself behind a rampart of gray clouds. Despite the overcast, many of the *abambo*, both the zebra-caped warriors who had participated in the raid on Barracks Street and the supporters who'd swelled their ranks on their march across the French Quarter afterward, had chosen to don sunglasses to protect their hypersensitive eyes. To Bellamy, they looked as if they were striving to be the hippest collection of ghosts around. Had he not been so tense, he might have found the sight amusing.

He supposed he had a right to feel edgy, after Chester had nearly decapitated him. When he'd awakened with his head still sticking through the broken windshield, he'd found that he'd slipped back to the cold side of the Shroud, but he knew that that alone couldn't have saved him. Had the Creole still been functional, he could have uncoupled himself from the rental truck and finished his enemy off with his hands. Bellamy could only assume that the bespectacled ghost had abruptly succumbed to injuries sustained when the vehicle crashed.

And whether it nourished his shadowself or no, he couldn't help feeling a cold satisfaction at the thought of Chester's demise, though it was nothing to the pleasure he'd feel when he finally took revenge on Dunn.

Thanks to the distortions of the Shroud, the park looked as ruinous by day as by night. The aquarium seemed to be crumbling into rubble, Nihils hissed and glittered in the brick walkways, and the plants were either brown and withered or else spotted and foul-smelling with black, mushy decay.

Despite the dawn, the lines of tall, barrow-flame torches still burned, lighting the way to Geffard's gingerbread-encrusted black riverboat. The carved skull leered between the twin smokestacks. A throng of spirits had gathered before the sidewheeler, and more crowded the decks. Many appeared to be unarmed, and even those who clearly were warriors hadn't arranged themselves into any sort of battle formation.

The FBI agent lifted his hand. "Hold up a second."

Astarte turned. She was still having trouble staying in character. On the trek to the river, she'd smiled and waved at some of the *abambo* they passed, more like a beauty-pageant winner riding a Mardi Gras float than a grim warrior queen hunting down her archenemy. "What's up?" she asked merrily.

"By now, somebody must have told Geffard that we were on our way," Antoine rasped. "But he hasn't gotten ready to fight, or run away either."

"Maybe he's going to throw himself on our mercy," said Astarte.

The gator snorted. "After laying a death curse on M—on you, Your Majesty? No way. He knows better."

"From the looks of things, he's spent his time gathering as many *abambo* as possible, irrespective of their martial prowess or political sympathies," Titus said. "To serve as witnesses, perhaps. But to what?"

"I don't know," Bellamy said, "but I'm not thrilled about it. He's trying to set us up for something. Even so, having come this far, we can't just turn and slink away. It would convince everybody that Your Majesty *is* weak and afraid, and Geffard would just start building a new doll collection."

"So let's go arrest the son of a bitch!" said Astarte, grinning. "You show us how you Junior G-men take care of business." She brandished her spear and strode forward. Her soldiers followed.

Bellamy quickened his pace to catch up to her. "Calm down," he whispered. "Stay alert, stay in character, and let Titus and Antoine do the talking."

She rolled her eyes. "I know, I know, for the thousandth time, I know. Chill already."

As the procession advanced, the mortals in their path—joggers, commuters hurrying to their jobs, and shuffling, ragged, malodorous homeless people—paled, gasped, and scurried out of the way, though in all likelihood, none of them could have explained why. Bellamy caught the drone of the wraiths ahead, chattering to one another, and the bouncy strains of the orchestra playing a Cole Porter song in the *Twisted Mirror*'s central cabin.

The mass of spectators split in two, clearing a space before the gangplank. Antoine glowered up at the two burly, bare-chested guards at the top of the ramp. "We've come for Geffard," he said.

"I'll see if he wants to talk to you," said the bodyguard on the left. Marie's supporters growled at the show of disrespect. Other wraiths murmured in shock, or in some cases, amusement. The warrior turned and ascended a companionway, his machete dangling from his massive fist. He climbed to the uppermost level of the vessel and entered the wheelhouse. After half a minute he reemerged, and Geffard stepped out after him.

The loa looked particularly respondent in his ornate captain's uniform. Somehow, even the wan gray sunlight was enough to make the gold braid shine. He paused in the doorway to light a cheroot, kindling it by magick, and the scent of cherry-flavored tobacco tinged the air. He smiled down at the spirits assembled on the quay. "Your Majesty," he said. "I'm delighted to see you up and about. I'd heard you were suffering some sort of malaise."

"You're under arrest for treason," said Antoine. The Creoles in the crowd muttered to one another. "Come down and give yourself up."

"May I ask," said Geffard, "precisely what form this treason supposedly took?"

Titus gave Bellamy a glance, silently asking whether they should keep talking or storm the boat without further ado. After a moment's hesitation, Bellamy gave him a nod, signaling his preference for the former. He couldn't imagine how Geffard thought he was going to turn the tables on them, yet the traitor must have some sort of notion. But perhaps the loa simply overestimated his powers of persuasion; during his career in law enforcement, Bellamy had met a number of con artists who believed they could talk their way out of anything. And it would be worth letting the Haitian protest his innocence to all and sundry if it enabled the Queen's men to take him into custody without the necessity of another battle.

"You made a pact with Spectres and werewolves," the wizened old shaman called up to Geffard. "With their aid, you created fetishes to destroy the Queen, and conjured demons into the Shadowlands to harass her subjects and so undermine confidence in her rule."

Geffard chuckled. "And whyever would I do that?"

"To seize the throne yourself," Antoine said.

"An interesting notion," said the loa, "and you have to wonder, who would blame me? Who truly belongs on the throne? A senile old woman teetering on the brink of the Void, hiding in her Haunt, helpless to protect her people from marauding Baka or, rumor has it, even commune with her gods? Or a man in the full prime of his power, who looks after his followers, reaps bounty from the Visible, and shares it with all who care to enjoy it?"

The spectators babbled and shouted, some in approbation and others in condemnation. Bellamy couldn't tell which group was larger.

Titus raised his reedy voice to make himself heard above the din. "Then you admit your guilt."

Geffard grinned. "Heavens, no. I was merely speaking hypothetically. What evidence can you offer to prove your accusations against me?"

"Evidence!" Antoine cried incredulously.

"Yes, Monsieur Lizard, evidence. Does your animal brain recognize the concept?"

"We found your voudoun dolls in the Haunt on Barracks Street," Antoine said.

"Has anyone besides the Queen's sworn men seen the fetishes?" asked Geffard. "And even if some impartial witness has, do you a have a wisp of proof that I helped create them, or even knew of their existence? I ask everyone here, have any of you ever observed me hobnobbing with Spectres or wolfmen? I think not."

Bellamy stepped forward. "We're not going to try your case here and now, Doctor. Surrender, and you can present your defense at your trial."

"I wonder," said Geffard. "Perhaps, once you have me in your clutches, I'll simply vanish. You can tell everyone that, invigorated by my terrible wickedness and my fear of my inevitable conviction and punishment, my Shadow devoured me, and I fell into the Void."

"You have our word," Bellamy said, "that won't happen. We'll give you a fair and public trial. Now come down, or we'll come up and get you. You can see we have a lot more men than you do, and they're better armed to boot. Even your magick can't protect you from all of us."

"So it appears," said the loa, puffing on the cheroot. "And might makes right, eh, and to Hell with the sensibilities of Les Invisibles, compelled to watch one of their own clapped in chains and hauled away on the flimsiest of pretexts, like some poor darkie in the bad old days. But if I have to go to prison, I at least want to hear as much from the Queen's own lips. A prominent citizen, to say nothing of an anointed priest, deserves that much consideration, wouldn't you agree? What about it, Your Majesty? You dragged yourself off your sickbed to attend this lynching. Don't you want to denounce me yourself?"

Inwardly, Bellamy winced. But for once, her expression scornful and austere, Astarte imitated the real Marie to perfection. "I'm content to let my lieutenants speak for me," she said. "I have no desire to converse with a despicable creature like you."

"No," said the loa, "I'm sure you don't, but I won't take it personally. I imagine you'd rather avoid talking to almost everyone here. And I know why." He snapped his fingers.

For a split second, Bellamy thought he glimpsed a giant figure, its body composed of gray clouds and its eyes pale, radiant slits, looming in the sky above Geffard's head. Then the crowd gave a collective gasp.

At first Bellamy thought they were shocked because they'd all seen the huge apparition, too. Then he noticed where they were staring. At Astarte.

When he turned, he felt as if someone had punched him in the stomach. Though still wearing the battered ostrich plume crown and carrying Marie's shield, assegai, and saber, the Quick girl had reverted to her own form, fair skin, spiked, magenta-striped hair, piercings, and all. Somehow Geffard had undone Titus's transformation in the blink of an eye. Perhaps the apparition had been the Creole's patron deity, and had augmented the power of his magick.

"It's a trick!" Antoine bellowed.

"The devil it is," Geffard replied. "My friends, I think we can all see who the real plotters and deceivers are, and what's really happening here. I never conspired against the Queen. But, too frail to bear up under the burdens of her rule, she fell gravely ill nonetheless. Perhaps by now she's even perished. Either way, those closest to her recognized that I'm her logical successor, and they feared they'd lose their power if the monarchy passed from the Dark Kingdom of Ivory to Les Invisibles. And so they conceived an elaborate scheme to discredit and destroy me. A scheme which required them to raise up a false Queen. To profane the crown and blaspheme against their own gods!"

Some of the crowd still looked stunned, while in other faces, astonishment was giving way to anger. Even many of the Queen's own soldiers were goggling at Astarte in dismay, drawing away from her in disgust, or readying their weapons.

It was obvious that if Bellamy and his comrades didn't turn this fiasco around right now, it was going to be too late. The FBI agent raised his Browning and opened fire on Geffard. Titus swirled his hands in an intricate pattern and jabbered an incantation.

The cloud titan flickered momentarily into view, its immense gray hands poised protectively over Geffard's head. Sparks flashed in front of the rebel leader's chest, and Bellamy realized that some power was deflecting or disintegrating his bullets. Nor was Titus's sorcery having any appreciable effect.

"Seize them," said Geffard. The crowd surged in at the African leaders. The majority of Marie's soldiers surrendered their weapons without a struggle. Those who resisted were quickly overwhelmed. Hands battered Bellamy, tore his pistol and shortsword away, and finally immobilized him.

Geffard beamed down at the quay. "Thank you," he said to his supporters. "Thank you for your courage and your good sense. It seems that these traitors are going to experience *our* justice, instead of the other way around. What shall we do with them?"

"Feed them to the Void!" a Creole soldier shouted. In an instant, everyone had taken up the cry. Bellamy thrashed in his captors' grasp. He knew that even if he broke free, the mob would only subdue again an instant later, but he had to try *something*. Meanwhile, Antoine writhed, trying to fling off the wraiths who were keeping him on his back and holding his jaws shut.

"So be it," the loa said. "Dispose of the sorcerer, the fellow next to him, the gator, and the warriors who tried to defend them as you see fit. But leave the woman to me. By daring to put on the crown, she's committed a particularly heinous crime, and I feel a responsibility to provide a fitting punishment."

"Screw you!" Astarte shouted.

Geffard laughed. An invisible force tore the Quick girl away from the wraiths who were gripping her arms and up into the air. Suspended ten feet above their heads, she clawed desperately at her neck, as if there were a noose around it.

Bellamy wrenched himself around toward Titus. The two-tone paint on the old man's face was smeared where someone had roughed him up. "Do something!" the agent said.

"I'm trying," Titus said. "But with his god and the adoration of the crowd feeding him power—"

One of the shaman's captors, a huge, moonfaced woman wearing a dozen strands of jade and garnet beads, pressed a darksteel dagger against his throat. "Shut up and stand still," she said. "Don't let me hear another word out of your sorcerer's mouth. Don't let me see your fingers so much as twitch."

Holding his cheroot between thumb and forefinger, Geffard poked it lightly in Astarte's direction, like a painter dabbing motes of color onto a canvas. Each gesture seared a round black dot on the mortal girl's forehead. Bellamy smelled scorched flesh. Saw that the diagonal trail of burn marks appeared to be leading toward Astarte's left eye.

Raising his mystical power, the FBI agent prepared to leap across the Shroud. At least that would free him from his captors' grasp, and then he could shift back and do…well, *something*. But, either divining his intention or simply to be cruel, someone clubbed him from behind him, driving a spike of pain through his skull. His body went limp, and the magick slipped away from him.

The next jab would put out Astarte's eye. Geffard lifted the cheroot higher, like a conductor flourishing his baton. Then the prisoner hurtled backward, away from the riverboat, as if something had ripped her from the Haitian's psychokinetic grip. His dazed view blocked by the crowd, Bellamy lost sight of her instantly. Still half stunned, he struggled feebly against his captor's restraining hands, but was still unable to see what had become of her.

Then the mob gasped, babbled, and parted as they had before, clearing a path. One hundred feet away, Astarte sat slumped beneath an oak, shaking and gasping, with three figures clustered protectively around her. Two of them were African soldiers armed with bolt-action rifles and bayonets. The other was Marilyn, slouched in a motorized wheelchair, bundled up in a blanket, a man's voluminous gray overcoat, and a slouch-brimmed hat. The garments concealed most of her bandages but couldn't mask the reek of blood which wafted from them. Like the smell, her aura—red, pink, and glittering with white sparks—gave proof that she was still alive, yet it was equally obvious that she could perceive her ghostly companions.

Though the Arcanist cut a remarkable figure, none of the wraiths near Bellamy paid much attention to her. Rather, they fixed on the thirteen figures advancing on the *Twisted Mirror.* A wedge-shaped formation of warriors with Marie striding along at the point. She'd seemed arrogant and formidable before, even with Geffard's curse sapping her strength and will. She moved like a stalking panther now.

If the Creole leader was dismayed at her arrival, he did a good job of hiding it. "Well, well," he said to Marie, "just how many of you are there? Has Titus put you into mass production?"

"I'm the real Queen," she said. "You aren't the only one with allies, *bocor*. The Quick mage came to me and woke me from my cursed sleep. If you doubt my identity, look at my deathmarks."

"You never did have much of a sense of humor," said Geffard. "I was teasing. Of course I can tell you're the genuine Marie, fragile and faded from your illness but still quite recognizable. As to whether you're still the genuine monarch, or at least, whether you deserve to be, well, that's another question."

She smiled. "Is it?"

"Yes. You accuse me of scheming to overthrow you. It's a lie, but even if it weren't, what would it matter? How did *you* claw your way onto the throne, woman? How does anyone seize and hold power? Not without a little sharp practice somewhere along the line. No soul endures long in the Mirrorlands before discovering that.

"That being the case, the only thing that truly matters is that you're weak. You admit that you can't even protect yourself, let alone the people of the city. Something was able to render you unfit to perform your duties. If your Quick healer hadn't taken pity on you, you might have remained unconscious indefinitely. And while you were indisposed, your lieutenants committed genuine acts of treason and blasphemy, setting up a false Queen and allowing her filthy white hands to profane the holy royal regalia."

"Desperate circumstances require desperate measures," Marie replied. "My servants did no wrong."

"I disagree," said Geffard, "and so will many others." Peering about at the faces of the mob, Bellamy could see that the Creole was right. "But the central point is that if not for your incapacity, your flunkies wouldn't have had to do anything. Step down, woman, for everyone's sake. New Orleans needs a real monarch. A King who can drive back the Hierarchs the next time they try to annex us, and keep the Spectres from overrunning us."

"And that's supposed to be you?" Antoine shouted. At some point during the interchange, the gator's captors had released him and allowed him to stand, though two Creoles were still pointing crossbows at him. "The Sinkinda have already bought and paid for you!"

Geffard sneered at him. "Be still, you ignorant beast, or I'll hire some Stygian smith to turn you into a belt and a pair of shoes."

Marie ran her cold amber gaze over the crowd. Many wraiths refused to meet her eyes. It looked as if the majority, civilians and warriors alike, were uncertain which leader they ought to support. Such being the case, it would be dangerous for either to command his followers to attack. It was impossible to know who would wind up with the weight of numbers on his side, and in any case, with everyone now mingled together, the battle would be utterly chaotic.

Marie stared back up at Geffard. "You say it all comes down to strength," she said. "Then let's settle our quarrel once and for all, just the two of us, without hazard to anyone else. I challenge you to measure your power against mine. But I warn you, facing your anointed ruler in a duel will be more dangerous than whispering curses behind her back."

"Oh, I don't think so," said Geffard. "Not when the ruler is only a female, and a spent, haggard shell of a woman at that." He tossed the cheroot away and raised his arms.

"Be careful!" Bellamy shouted to the Queen. "His god is here!" As if on cue, the cloud giant flickered momentarily into view behind Geffard. Thunder boomed and crackled, and a fierce wind began to blow. Marie's long, white skirt flapped madly in the gale.

She waved her hand almost casually, and the wind died as abruptly as it had begun. She stared at Geffard, and the deck beneath his feet shattered into splinters.

The Creole's body bobbed, dropping partway through the hole and then levitating back out. He held out his hand and a gourd rattle materialized inside his fingers. He shook it as if he were pounding a nail with a hammer, each clattering beat as loud as the thunderclap had been.

At first the rattling seemed ineffectual. Unfazed, the Queen kept her eyes locked on Geffard. Patches of greenish barrow-flame blossomed on the loa's blue, gold-trimmed uniform.

The cloud titan swam into view behind the Haitian, and this time, it didn't vanish again a moment later. The giant apparition shifted its gray, vaporous hand, and the fires consuming its protégé's coat went out. Its lambent eyes pulsed in time with the rattling, which was suddenly even louder.

Marie cried out and stumbled backward. Her left arm withered into a fleshless stick, and bands of shadow rippled beneath her skin.

"I'm the King!" Geffard shrieked, his voice nearly inaudible above the deafening pulse of the rattle. "The crown belongs to me! Say it, bitch, and I'll let you live!"

"No," croaked Marie. She chanted in a language Bellamy didn't recognize, perhaps the same tongue Titus used to work his magick. Her golden eyes blazed.

In one section of the park, the gray daylight turned to darkness. Intricate drumming, the voices of three instruments of different sizes twining together, pattered out of the gloom. The sound wasn't nearly as loud as the grinding beat of the rattle, but for some reason it made the fine hairs on the back of Bellamy's neck stand up in awe nonetheless. A gust of breeze brought him a scorched, dusty smell, and then the rich perfume of an abundance of flowers mingled with the stench of vegetable decay. Though he'd never visited Africa, somehow he knew the former was the odor of the veldt in drought, and the second, the complex scent of a rain forest.

Elephants trumpeted inside the darkness. Monkeys chattered. A towering shadow strode toward the threshold where night met day. Its white, striped headdress reminded Bellamy of images of the Pharaohs. Though it was difficult to see the figure clearly, he knew what *it* was, too. An Orisha. He'd experienced visions of the African gods when Marie's slave-trainers had tried to brainwash him.

Geffard laughed wildly. "Fine!" he cried. "The Orishas against Les Mystéres. We'll decide once and for all whose reality is—"

The words caught in his throat. He lurched around and peered upward, confirming what Bellamy now observed as well. The vaporous giant had summarily disappeared.

The Orisha advanced to Marie's side without ever crossing into the light of day. Rather, the darkness of his native realm flowed along with him and engulfed her.

Meanwhile, Geffard shrieked at the sky. "Héviyoso! What are you doing? Come back!"

Marie laughed. "It would seem that *my* gods are stronger, at least in New Orleans. Certainly your patron fears to face them."

Geffard lurched back around, his dreadlocks flying about his head. "I don't need Héviyoso," he snarled. "I'll destroy you myself, and your quaint tribal spirit there as well. I *won't* lose, not again!" He shook the rattle. It was still louder than was natural, but not as loud as it had been with the voudoun god lending it power. The contrast made it sound almost pathetic, and it did no further damage to the Queen.

"Die," said Marie. Fresh green flames erupted across Geffard's body. He swirled his hands in a mystic pass, and the flames burned low for a moment, but then flared up even more fiercely than before.

The Haitian began to scream, flail, and stagger about, finally toppling over the rail. Perhaps he'd thrown himself over on purpose, in the desperate hope that the river water would quench the fire, but he never reached it. He burned to nothingness halfway down, like a meteorite disintegrating as it plummeted through the atmosphere.

Marie turned and knelt to the Orisha. The shadowy figure lifted her back to her feet, touched her forehead, eyes, and lips in a gesture which Bellamy took to be a blessing, and rested its long-fingered hand on her shoulder. The waves of blackness beneath her skin faded, and her arm swelled back to its normal shape. The Queen pivoted back toward the crowd, and then it was everyone else's turn to kneel. The FBI agent noticed that the rebels and their sympathizers did so with particular haste.

THIRTEEN

A vile, acidic aftertaste clung to Bill Dunn's tongue, and his stomach churned. It was remarkable that anyone could brew a potion so nasty that it could sicken a guy accustomed to feasting on raw, rotting human flesh, but Cankerheart had accomplished it. Still, Dunn couldn't deny that the drug worked. If he squinted, he could dimly see into the ghost world. Make out the black riverboat and the figures gathered around it.

Not that the view was any treat. Quite the contrary. When Geffard perished in a ball of fire, Dunn turned to his companion on the aquarium rooftop. "Shit!" he said.

Cankerheart grinned, revealing yellow, pointed teeth. As was the case with most Black Spiral Dancers—Dunn was a rare exception who could easily mingle with humans without attracting notice——each of the sorcerer's five forms was deformed to some degree. In addition to its dental abnormalities, his man shape sported pointed ears, black nails, and orange eyes with diamond-shaped pupils. "Does it pain you to see our noble ally fall?" he cooed, all false solicitude. "Such a tender sentiment! A Dancer shouldn't feel loyalty to anyone or anything except the Wyrm and the Tribe as a whole. And a Ragabash, to play his appointed part, must make himself particularly callous and treacherous."

Dunn grimaced. Cankerheart might be a hotshot hexer, but as far as the rogue FBI agent was concerned, he was also a bore and a condescending fool. "I don't give a rat's ass about Geffard," he said.

Cankerheart smirked. "Or your friend with the computers either?"

To his surprise, Dunn *had* felt a slight regret that Chester evidently hadn't survived the battle on Barracks Street. God knew why, the prissy, nagging ghost had always gotten on his nerves. In any case, he knew better than to reveal such a sentiment to the warlock, or any other Dancer for that matter. "Or him either. It's the principle of the thing." He waved his hand at the scene below the rampart. The African super-ghost, or whatever the hell it had been, had vanished, taking its patch of unnatural darkness with it, but the assembled spooks were still on their knees. Dunn had a hunch that snotty Queen Marie might keep them there a good long time before allowing them to rise. "*The enemy won.* I know that Geffard himself warned us off, and I understand why. But still, if the rest of us conspirators had jumped in the thick of this, it might have worked out better than it has."

"Or perhaps we would have died along with Geffard. There aren't many of our Spectre friends in New Orleans. I seem to be the only Dancer wizard left in the city, and with the portal in the Barracks Street house lost to us, I couldn't have transported Banes into the Underworld quickly enough to make a difference. And few of the other Dancers can reach through the Surface to attack a ghost at all."

Dunn glumly had to admit that all that was true. He himself was cut off from events in what Les Invisibles called the Mirrorlands. It infuriated him to watch Bellamy bopping around the park and know there was no way of getting at him. What a shitty world, where you couldn't rid yourself of a pest even by electrocuting him and ripping the corpse to shreds. "I should at least kill Sebastian," he said, "if only so we can say we got a lick in. It's a hell of a long shot for a pistol, but I can make it." He reached inside his suede jacket for his Desert Eagle.

"Wraiths have senses as keen as ours," said Cankerheart. "They'd discern where the shot originated, and come after us."

"And you're afraid that your hoodoo is no match for theirs?"

The shaman scowled. "Of course not, but there are hundreds of them down there. I'd have to contend with the Queen and Titus both, plus whatever powers the others might bring to bear. For all we know, the *god* is still lurking about, just beyond the limits of my perception. And through it all, *you'd* be no help at all."

No, thought Dunn wistfully, but he was willing to bet he could do a first-rate job of slipping away while Cankerheart drew the enemy's fire. "But doesn't it bother you to see those bastards win?"

"Why should it? *I'm* not the one they've made a fool of, time after time." Dunn's muscles ached. His body wanted to grow into wolfman or dire-wolf form, and gut this impudent ass who dared to mock him. "Besides which, it doesn't matter who rules New Orleans."

Dunn struggled to quash his anger, and the pains in his flesh subsided. "And you accuse *me* of not toeing the Dancer party line. To hear the Philodoxes tell it, no battle, no chance to destroy, is unimportant."

"In the greater scheme of things, this one is. We needed Les Invisibles to teach our Spectre partners to possess the living. Subsequently we had to give Geffard the help we'd promised, or he might have told someone what he knew about our intentions. But since the fool had little else to offer us, we're well rid of him and our obligations to him."

"We'd be a lot farther ahead of the game if we were rid of Bellamy, the girl, and Sebastian," said Dunn. "They aren't going to quit sticking their noses in our business, you know."

"Who cares? Let them poke around New Orleans to their hearts' content. We'll be in Natchez, completing our work."

"I'll bet you they trail us there. One way or another."

Cankerheart cocked his slightly lopsided head. "I think you've lived too long among the humans. You're whining like a querulous pup. If I didn't know better, I'd think you were afraid of Bellamy."

The ache pulsed in Dunn's limbs and shoulders. His skin tingled as fur tried to sprout there. Once again, he resisted the change. "Keep needling me, old man. Keep it up, and see what it gets you. I'm not afraid of that son of a bitch. I'm just sick of his luck. Sick of the way he keeps slipping out of my jaws and popping up again. I want to be done with him."

"You nearly are," said Cankerheart. "We have Natchez firmly under control. If Bellamy and his friends show up there, we can deal with them easily, even before the ritual. And afterwards, well, if you want revenge, that will be ideal. He won't be able to hide behind the Surface then, will he? It will be so thin that you'll be able to reach right in after him, just as our Spectre friends will be able to molest any mortal they please. Though in single combat, I wouldn't put it past him to kick your mangy backside again. But with a few hardy Ahroun warriors backing you up, you can finally send him to what the ghosts call Oblivion and regain what passes for your honor."

Dunn grinned. For some reason, Cankerheart's mockery had gone from annoying to amusing. Perhaps it was because the FBI mole liked the notion of Bellamy being trapped on the same level of reality with him. Then Dunn could hunt him at his leisure, toy with him, maim him a bit and set him free to run again. "Okay, I admit, that does sound like a plan. Maybe while I square off against Frank, you can go one on one with Sebastian. It would be a hoot to watch a decrepit old witch doctor like you try to throw down on a genuine Awakened human mage."

"The hermaphrodite may have been awakened, as you put it," said Cankerheart, "but it hasn't been schooled in the proper uses of its power. When the time comes, I'll crush it like a gnat." He peeked over the rampart again, and Dunn followed suit.

Below, the wraiths were finally vacating the park, in what seemed to be a victory procession. Someone began to chant in what the werewolf spy assumed to be an African language, and over the course of the next few seconds, nearly everyone joined in. Dead or alive, the hairless apes loved to babble.

"Guess the show's over," said Dunn. "We'll give the ghosts a couple minutes to clear completely out, then take off ourselves."

Killing time, he took out his pistol and sighted in on Sebastian, Astarte, and especially Bellamy, over and over again. "Pow," he whispered. "Pow. Pow. Pow."

Fourteen

As usual, the attack, if that was the proper term for it, began as a simple act of perception. Manuel Gayoso de Lemos, Anacreon in the service of the Smiling Lord, one of the three Governors of Natchez and the surrounding territory, and commander of the current crusade against the Heretics, looked at the brass, triple-branched candelabrum and recognized it for the fragile piece of junk it was. With his newfound strength, he could twist it apart with his bare hands.

His desk and other pieces of office furniture were just as flimsy. A good kick or two would smash them to kindling. Nor could the puny, sluggish Legionnaire bodyguards in the corners withstand him should he choose to assail them, their cutlasses and Skorpion Model 61s notwithstanding. He could rend them to tatters of ectoplasm in the blink of an eye.

Awareness swiftly gave rise to the desire to act. To the conviction that items so worthless and contemptible, non-sentient or otherwise, *should* be destroyed. The urge was like a nagging itch, one which, at this moment, he couldn't scratch. How glorious it would be when he was finally the sole and absolute ruler of Natchez, and could indulge every whim, no matter how outrageous, the instant it entered his mind.

Another sentry stepped into the gloomy office. "The dwarf is here to see you, milord," he said. "Along with some vagrant girl from down in the Necropolis."

Gayoso grimaced. It was too bad it wasn't Prudence who'd turned up. Using her Pardoner's Arcanos, the Doppelgänger had had a fair measure of success in helping him control the desires he'd developed since his transformation. As a general rule, he could at least defer their satisfaction until it was safe to let himself go. He wondered what Valentine wanted, and promised himself he'd give the little man a beating if it wasn't important. "Show them in," he said.

The Legionnaire stepped aside. Valentine shuffled into the room, followed by a small woman in bellbottoms, love beads, and a hand-tooled leather headband decorated with peace signs. At the sight of her, Gayoso felt his free-floating hatred wax a notch stronger. He hadn't cared for the Quick hippies of the 1960s, and as a rule, he liked their ghosts even less. Most of them flouted the authority of the Hierarchy whenever they could get away with it. Of course, Gayoso was now in the process of flouting it himself, but that bit of irony failed to blunt his resentment of a group that had proved an irritant for the past three decades.

"Good evening, milord," said Valentine. "This is Belinda Talley. She works in Under-the-Hill."

I'll bet she does, the Anacreon thought. *As a slut of one sort or another*. Perhaps

Valentine had become infatuated with her. After all, she wasn't *too* much taller than he was. He wondered how the dwarf would react if his master grabbed the bitch, tore her clothes off, raped her atop his desk, and then drove his rapier between her legs, up through her torso, and out her mouth, right here and now. His lips tried to twist into a leer, and he did his best to push the fantasy from his mind. "What do you want?" he asked.

"You remember when I talked to you about Daphne," Valentine said.

The Spaniard's muscles clenched in annoyance. He struggled to quash the feeling and think of an innocuous response. "Of course. Has she turned up?"

"No."

"That's too bad," Gayoso said, remembering how the child prostitute had thrashed in her chains and grunted through her rubber-ball gag as he cut her apart. How he'd felt Oblivion staring at him and simultaneously looking out his own eyes. That first time, he'd felt a horror which, despite his efforts to resist, had inexorably warped into ecstasy. At the end, the Void had claimed him for his own, and his subsequent sacrifices had been *all* pleasure. "But as I explained before, having looked for her once, there's really nothing more we can do. It's an unfortunate truth that people disappear from Under-the-Hill rather frequently, for all sorts of reasons. If you've found a new...*friend*"—he glanced at Belinda—"I think you may as well forget about the old one."

The woman's mouth tightened. "I'm not a hooker, my lord Anacreon, and Valentine and I don't have that kind of relationship. We came to you because we found out *something* about what happened to Daphne, and it ties into the disappearance of my daughter."

Gayoso felt a pang of dismay. If he'd abducted and butchered the whore's child, perhaps she and Valentine *had* pieced together something, though obviously not the whole story, or they would have run to one of his fellow Governors, not to him. "What do you mean?" he asked.

"If you recall," said Valentine, "I saw Daphne with a man in a trenchcoat and a blue mask."

"I also remember you decided he had nothing to do with her disappearance. He was just another customer."

"That's the way it seemed," the jester said. "But people saw someone answering the same description hanging around outside the Nightlight Theater, just before Starshine—Belinda's child—disappeared from there."

"Once we found that out," said Belinda, "we did some checking around. A couple other kids have disappeared. And slavers have sold some child Thralls to a guy in a long coat and a blue, silver-trimmed hood. A man who barters with gestures, and never speaks, as if he *really* doesn't want anyone to recognize him. None of those kids has been seen again, either."

Given that the Void aspired to devour the entire universe, Gayoso had sometimes wondered why he could only quiet his most insistent urges by sacrificing child wraiths. He supposed the answer had to do with some buried kink in his own nature, but his existence would have been simpler had the situation been otherwise. Thanks to modern medicine, the ghosts of prepubescent youths were relatively scarce, a circumstance which had compelled him to purchase some of his victims in the city's slave markets. And as a result of that, Valentine and his new tramp were virtually certain they comprehended what was going on.

Still, Gayoso told himself, he shouldn't panic. It was one thing to figure out what the man in the blue mask was up to. It would be quite another to divine the killer's true identity, especially if a certain high government official made it his business to scuttle the inquiry.

"It's no crime to purchase Thralls and do whatever you want with them," the Governor said.

"No, milord," said Valentine. "But it is to kidnap and kill free citizens. Don't you see, we may have a serial killer who preys on children running around loose. Sometimes he preys on Thralls, but sometimes on kids he snatches off the street."

Gayoso heaved a sigh, like a wise man striving to be patient with the prattling of fools. "That's a bit of a reach, don't you think? Do you know how many fellows there are wandering around in long coats and blue masks?"

"Not just a blue mask. One with fancy silver trim." Gayoso realized he'd better adopt another disguise. Or rather, a number of them; it was obviously risky to wear the same one twice in a row. "And this guy never talks, or hardly ever. That sets him apart from the rest."

Gayoso imagined himself tearing out Valentine's babbling tongue with a pair of pincers. He could almost feel the cold, hard iron in his fingers, feel the failing resistance as the flesh tore free. "I'm afraid I'm still not convinced that you, Señora Talley's friends, and the slave vendors all saw the same man. Or that he's a murderer even if you did."

"Why the hell not?" Belinda asked.

"For one thing," said the Spaniard, "it's quite conceivable that, eh, Moonlight, was it?"

The hippie scowled. "Starshine. My lord."

If her disrespect became any more overt, Gayoso thought, he *would* have an excuse to hurt her. "Yes, please excuse me. It's possible that Starshine simply ran away."

Belinda shook her head. "She wouldn't do that."

Gayoso thought she very well could have if she'd gotten tired of watching her mother go down on her knees for every ruffian with an obolus in his pocket, but he supposed it would impolitic to say so. "Then perhaps she simply lost the will to continue and fell into the Void. In our world, a youthful shape can house an old and weary spirit."

"No, my lord. I'm sorry to argue, I'm not trying to give you a hard time, but I knew her, and you didn't. She was a little girl, inside and out."

That's true, Gayoso thought, struggling to conceal a sudden, unexpected mirth. *I know. I* saw *her insides.*

"Sir," said Valentine, "I know we can't *prove* we're right, but on the other hand, we might be. We're hoping that you can help us check out our suspicions."

Gayoso's amusement abruptly skewed back into annoyance. It was remarkable just how labile his emotions had become. He'd heard that erratic mood swings were a symptom of insanity, but the concept of madness had little meaning and certainly no terrors for a being such as himself. Ultimately, rationality was simply another meaningless phantasm of the intricate lie called Creation. "We already police the Necropolis," the Anacreon said. "Considering the—forgive my candor—larger issues confronting us, the Inquisition and all our other problems, I don't see how we can do any more. Even if I were willing, the other Governors would never authorize it."

Belinda scowled. "I should have known—"

"Sir," said the dwarf, raising his voice to cut her off, "if we do have someone running around killing kids, he could easily be a Spectre, or on the verge of becoming one. *That's* important, isn't it?"

The Governor shrugged. "To some degree, but he would hardly be the first doomshade to establish a lair in Under-the-Hill and commit atrocities. We always find and destroy the creatures sooner or later."

"Once or twice," said Valentine, "you flushed out really nasty ones by conducting a building-by-building search."

Such a search might locate the derelict structure where Gayoso conducted his sacrifices, even though the place was outside the Necropolis proper. He saw no point in allowing that to happen. "And wasn't that a nightmare, with all the thieves and Renegades complaining every step of the way."

"But you *were* able to do it," said the dwarf, "when you decided it was necessary. And I'm thinking, what if Daphne and the kids are locked up somewhere, still alive? What if the guy in the blue hood wants to torture them for a while?"

Gayoso heaved a sigh and removed his steel domino. He had to force himself. Even before his transformation, he'd seldom been comfortable unmasking in front of anyone, and the aversion was even stronger now. Valentine's jaw sagged at the unprecedented intimacy. "Old friend," the Spaniard said in his most sympathetic tones, "I knew you were going to say that eventually. Logistical considerations aside, it's the *other* reason I don't want to turn the city upside down looking for this mysterious stranger of yours."

"I don't understand," said the dwarf.

"Whatever happened to Daphne and Starshine," said Gayoso, "it's overwhelmingly likely that they're gone for good. You have to accept that, and move on. By clinging to the notion that they might be languishing in some makeshift dungeon somewhere, or even the fantasy of exacting vengeance from their supposed murderer, you're merely prolonging the pain."

Looking a little befuddled, Valentine shook his head. "But if there is a murderer, he'll keep on killing."

"If so, then eventually we'll catch him. I didn't say I wouldn't do *anything*. I can advise the watch to look out for suspicious fellows in blue masks with silver trim. But I don't want *you* to worry about this anymore. You have bigger fish to fry. How would you like a promotion to quartermaster and Centurion?"

Valentine goggled at him. "You...you're not teasing me? You really mean it?"

"Certainly. You're too clever to spend your days as a menial entertainer." What a pity, thought Gayoso, that he couldn't summarily destroy the dwarf for daring to poke his ugly nose into his master's business. But until the Spaniard was king, he couldn't just go around slaughtering his own household servants, not without some sort of pretext, and at the moment it would almost certainly require less effort to divert Valentine than to frame him for a crime.

The little man swallowed. "Then...I accept. And thank you!"

"You accept?" Belinda exploded. "You're going to let him buy you off?"

Valentine spread his hands. "It's not like that. The Governor said he'll have the soldiers keep a lookout, all through Under-the-Hill. That's more than we could do."

"I assure you," said Gayoso, "I'll take every action I can justify, given the speculative nature of what you've told me." He imagined how it would feel to flay the face off her skull with a dagger.

"I can tell you're not going to do anything!" the hippie said. "Fat cats like you never do, do they, not to help outsiders like me." She glared at Valentine. "But you! I trusted you. I need you. But tough on me, right? I guess you didn't really care about Daphne after all." She wheeled and strode toward the exit. Gayoso waved his hand, signaling the soldiers to let her go. It was unlikely that such an insignificant vagabond, a nonentity who had chosen to exist outside the Hierarchy, could cause him any trouble on her own.

Valentine's homely face twisted as if he were about to cry. "Maybe I should go after her," he said.

"I wouldn't," Gayoso said. "She was hoping for a miracle, and she needs some time alone to come to terms with the fact that her expectations were unrealistic. If you feel the need, you can look her up in a day or so. For now, why don't we discuss your new duties? And why don't you take off that ridiculous cap?"

Fifteen

Montrose looked up at the churning thunderheads. Inside them, lightning flickered as rapidly as a strobe light, tingeing the air with the scent of ozone. Unless he missed his guess, a Maelstrom was in the offing.

A good reason, he reflected, to be glad he and Louise were safe in Stygia. And to enjoy the garden while they could, before the breaking storm drove them back into the guest villa they'd been given. The Deathlords—who were presumably collecting themselves after their battle, and who were supposed to summon him for a full debriefing by and by—had advised him not to return to his suite in the Seat of Burning Waters. They were concerned that some of Prince Ares's vassals might divine the fate of their master, and attempt to avenge him.

Montrose fancied that someone had laid out the garden in conscious imitation of one he'd visited while touring Europe as a young man, that of the Villa Lante in Bagnaia. At the entrance was a water-parterre and at the center of that, a gushing fountain, where a black marble Charon leaned on his scythe. Box-edged flower beds, some laid out in scrollwork and some in geometric patterns, blazed with an assortment of fragrant roses, pansies, hyacinths, lilies, and poppies. Orange and lemon trees flourished in earthen pots, and glowing golden orbs set on tall poles gave the illusion of sunlight. "It's lovely, isn't it?" said the Scot.

"Yes," said Louise, squeezing his hand. Unlike him, and rather to his disappointment, she hadn't chosen to dress in seventeenth-century clothing. She'd opted for comfort in the form of sandals, jeans and a chambray shirt. "And very restful compared to the Artificers' pit, the Crimson Gallery, and all the other places we barely escaped. Not a single soul has tried to destroy us, or even drive us mad."

Montrose smiled. "I hope you won't grow bored."

"Fortunately," she said, "we seem to be able to make our own excitement." She took him in her arms, and they kissed.

Eventually, breathing heavily, Montrose ended the kiss and placed his lips beside his ear. "Do you see the hill?" he whispered. At the rear of the garden rose a terraced slope, with a stream cascading down the center.

"Of course," said Louise.

"Then notice the grove of ilex at the top. Look how thick the trees are. If we walked to heart of it, no one could see us. It would be as private as a bedroom."

"You," she said, "are a wicked man. Let's head that way."

He offered her his arm, and they strolled onward. The image of Charon in the center of the fountain seemed to glower at them in disapproval.

Bees—or rather, automata fashioned to resemble them—droned among the flowers. An alabaster faun smiled slyly from the center of a bed of narcissi. "It's almost like being back in The Hague, isn't it?" Montrose said. "In our own time. Not that the Dutch gardens were precisely like this, but they gave me much the same feeling."

"Do you miss the world of our youth?" asked Louise.

"A few weeks ago, I would have given you an emphatic no. After all, my mortal career ended in disaster. But now that we've found one another again, I've discovered a certain nostalgia for the good times. Perhaps what I really miss is simply being alive."

She squeezed his arm. "I feel more alive now than I have since the moment I learned of your execution."

Montrose smiled at her. "I know what you mean, and truly, I'm not melancholy. I'd a hundred times rather be one of the Restless and your sweetheart than Quick and bereft of you. I was only thinking, if you like the villa, perhaps the Seven would grant it to us permanently when we return."

"'When we return,'" she repeated, her voice flat.

"Yes," he said, surprised at her seeming incomprehension. "You know we have to travel back to America to deal with whatever else the Spectres have planned. But afterwards—" He abruptly realized what she was getting at. "Don't you want to come back?"

"I'm a Sister of Athena," she said. "I don't belong here."

He snorted. "Considering that you kept Demetrius from destroying the Deathlords and the entire city along with them, I daresay that people will make you welcome."

They climbed a flight of stone stairs, past a topiary sculpture of the Emperor's mask. "It's not that simple," said Louise. "I swore an oath. I have duties."

"Aren't women allowed to resign from your sorority?"

"Yes," she said, "but I don't know that I want to. I believe in the search for Transcendence. To tell you the truth, I was hoping that after all we've experienced together, you'd look at Stygia with fresh eyes and decide that *you* didn't wish to remain."

"I would have sworn you were beginning to like it here."

"Primarily I'm enjoying being with you, though I can appreciate all the wonders and luxuries as well. Still, many of them feel hollow and unnatural, like some kind of conjuring trick." She waved her hand at a bed of scarlet carnations. "They look alive, but they're not. Some Artificer *made* them."

"Your paintings were artificial, also," said the Scot. "All of civilization is unnatural, if one cares to look at it that way. That doesn't make it any the less worthwhile. At least Stygia *has* beauty and pleasures. Did you prefer existence in the Shadowlands, with the Shroud making everything ugly, and most of the world forever out of reach?"

"The Shroud doesn't distort everything. And even when it does, at least one knows that the natural world is there. But I'm not primarily concerned about aesthetics. What troubles me is knowing that all the jasmine and hollyhocks in this garden were forged from *souls*, and that all the towers and ramparts beyond were raised through the toil of countless Thralls."

Montrose sighed. "I should have known that eventually you'd have more to say on that subject." He led her on toward the wall girdling the foot of the terrace. At the center of it, the water gurgling down from the crest of the hill jetted upward from a second fountain.

"Doesn't it bother you that your precious Empire is built on slavery and mass murder? Can you ignore that, even now?"

Montrose sighed again. "No, not entirely, not anymore. In many respects, Stygia seems a darker place than it did before. But at the same time, I have a renewed appreciation of the purpose the Legions serve. If we don't hold back Oblivion, who will?"

"I don't know," said Louise. "Perhaps everyone, all the Restless, working together." They started up one of the two staircases which ran diagonally up the wall. The spray in the fountain hissed and sparkled. A stray drop gave Montrose an icy-cold kiss on the cheek.

"That's easy to say," said the Scot, "but you Renegades and Heretics have no way of guaranteeing it would actually happen. So perhaps we shouldn't bet the universe on it. And perhaps I, having sworn my own vows to the Hierarchy, have a duty to stand by it and help defend Creation."

"I understand," said Louise. "But Spectres aren't Oblivion's only weapons. I suspect they aren't even the most dangerous. If we tolerate cruelty and corruption, even in the service of some supposed higher good, then in the long run, we strengthen the Void. Eventually the Imperium must either renounce its sins or be overthrown to make way to something better. If I honestly thought it likely that I could promote change from within, perhaps I *could* stay here."

"But you don't."

She hesitated. "Do you?"

He grimaced. "I suppose not. Even though I'd do all I could to help you."

They hiked up the hill, staying close to the chuckling stream. Dense *boschi* of evergreen oaks and plane trees stood to either side. By the time the wraiths had climbed halfway, they could see beyond the confines of the garden to the seven Seats, Charon's towering donjon, and the cyclopean curtain wall encircling the entire Onyx Tower complex.

After a time, Montrose said, "I'm surprised you don't question my motives."

"What do you mean?"

"I claim I feel that honor obliges me to cleave to Stygia. But what if it isn't that at all? What if I'm simply unwilling to forfeit my rank and all the privileges that go with it?"

"Not you," she replied, her tone one of affectionate mockery. "Not my 'verray parfit gentil knight.'"

"How can you be certain of that? When we embarked on our mission, that was *precisely* my motivation. I *believe* I've changed, that I've shed a measure of my selfishness, but perhaps that's only a rationalization. In all honesty, a part of me *would* grieve to give up my position. I struggled and schemed for three and a half centuries to get it. I just now risked my neck to win it back."

She patted his shoulder. "Don't worry, I'm sure, even if you're not. Even when you were doing your best to be hateful and ruthless, when you would have jeered at the very idea of conscience and morality, I could always see the old gallant James inside you, struggling to break free." She grinned. "Well, maybe not when you were trying to kill me on the beach. But *most* of the time."

He put his arms around her. "I can't lose you again. It would destroy me."

"I feel the same way."

"Good. Then let's resolve that, come what may, nothing will ever tear us apart. You may feel you can't bear to ally yourself with the Hierarchy, and I may feel I can't forsake it. We may have absolutely no idea how to solve the problem. But promise me that we'll never stop trying."

"I promise," she said, and they kissed. "Now let's stop talking about it, at least for now. I don't go strolling in gardens with redheaded poets to be serious." She twisted out of his arms. "If you want to enjoy my favors, you'll have to catch me!" She sprinted toward the ilex.

"Easily done!" Montrose cried, giving chase. He wondered if they could find a way to stay together forever. He wanted it desperately, and could tell that she did, too. But he knew only too well how matters of conscience could divide kinsmen, friends, and sweethearts. They'd certainly blighted his marriage to poor Magdalen.

Scowling, he pushed such somber reflections out of his mind. Louise had the right idea. The two of them were together *now*. They had a respite from the peril which had dogged their every step. They should savor the moment.

On the hilltop, twin pavilions bracketed the spring. Beyond the source of the rivulet, paths radiated outward into the trees. Louise started down one of the tracks, and then a shadow glided across the ground.

Startled, Montrose reflexively reached for his rapier. But the newcomer was only a Centurion of the Black Hawks, a Masquer possessed of magnificent avian wings with inky plumage. Furling them, he touched down lightly beside the bubbling spring. Louise turned and trotted back to the basin.

"Madame," said the Legionnaire. His steel helm, cast to resemble the beaked head of a bird of prey, left the lower part of his smooth, boyish face bare. As if to compensate for his appearance of youth, his voice was solemn, and the set of his downy jaw, stern. "Milord Anacreon."

"Hello, Centurion," Montrose said. "I take it that the Seven are ready for us at last."

"Yes, sir. They command the two of you to attend them atop the Pinnacle of Lamentations."

Montrose frowned. He'd assumed himself acquitted of all the charges which Gayoso and Demetrius had leveled against him. Certainly, in the wake of his struggle with the Smiling Lord, everyone had treated him as an honored public benefactor, not a prisoner.

Yet the Pinnacle of Lamentations was a place of judgment.

SIXTEEN

The air felt hot and dirty on Beverly Schott's face. According to the six o'clock news, scientists said that the pollution in Natchez, and all along the lower Mississippi, for that matter, was no worse than usual, even if countless people had complained about it. All Beverly knew was that *something* was giving her a headache.

She should be home in her air-conditioned house, not sitting in the stuffy waiting area of a tacky commercial building. With its grayish linoleum, institutional green walls, and fluorescent light fixtures, the place looked as if it might once have been a tire store, or a branch office of the DMV. Heaven knew, the molded plastic chairs were uncomfortable enough. She scowled at Pete, her clueless loser of a husband. How much of her time had he wasted over the years, making her sit through sales pitches for impractical get-rich-quick schemes and other deals too wonderful to be true? Make a million in real estate with no money down. Raise ostriches. Install an Olympic swimming pool for pennies a week. Apparently such dubious calls to the good life had an irresistible attraction for men who couldn't land decent jobs. At any rate, if not for Timmy and Paul, the beautiful boys Pete had miraculously managed to give her—thank God they didn't take after his side of the family!—she might well have felt he was wasting her entire *life*. "How much longer?" she asked.

A short, somewhat tubby maintenance man who'd insisted on wearing his one and only suit to the interview, Pete rolled his eyes to signify that she was the bitchiest woman on Earth. What a grumpy little bastard he could be, even though he rarely had the guts to express his distemper straight out. "I don't know," he said.

"I thought you had an appointment."

"I did. They must be running late. We'll just have to be patient."

"Wonderful," she sneered.

"Darn it," whined Pete, "why do you always have to be so mean? This is important, and I'm doing it for you and the kids."

"Oh, give me a break. I know that terrible things are happening all over the state, and I worry about it, too. Who doesn't? But don't you know this is going to turn out to be some kind of scam? Like when you thought the nice salespeople were going to give us a big-screen TV just for listening to them blab on and on about the time-shares. Honestly, you are so gull—"

Someone cleared his throat.

Startled, Beverly jerked around. While she'd been busy setting Pete straight, four people had emerged from the rear of the building. Three of them were clearly a family: a husband in his early twenties, with muscular arms and a trim waist—like Pete had possessed before he'd dedicated his leisure time to Budweiser, Doritos, and TV—his pretty blond wife, and a sleeping infant girl cradled in her daddy's arms. Bev assumed that these people too had come for an interview, and that the other member of the quartet was the person who'd talked to them.

He was a tall, thin man of about her own age, in his mid-thirties. His chestnut hair with its widow's peak showed a sprinkling of white at the temples. He had a long-nosed, pleasant, intelligent face, and, to Bev's surprise, wore the black suit and clerical collar of a minister.

Pete scrambled to his feet.

"Hello," said the preacher, shaking hands. "I'm Matt Harper, and you must be the Schotts. I'm sorry you had to wait." He turned to the couple with the baby. "Very nice meeting you. Keep your beepers switched on, memorize the information in the handout, and everything will be fine."

"Thank you," said the young mother, giving him a warm smile. "I think I might finally get a good night's sleep tonight." She and her family headed for the door.

Pivoting back toward the Schotts, Harper gestured toward the hallway. "Will you step into my office? It isn't much—I threw it together in a hurry—but the chairs are more comfortable than the ones out here."

He was right on both counts. The little office was unimpressive. There were no curtains hanging in the window, nor any pictures on the walls. But the seats did have cloth cushions, and Bev settled onto hers with an appreciative wriggle.

As he sat down behind the small metal desk, Harper said, "I couldn't help overhearing what you were saying, Mrs. Schott."

"She didn't mean anything by it," said Pete. "Really."

Harper smiled. "Please. It's all right." His right hand opened and closed on the desk top, as if he were trying to work a cramp out of his fingers. "You folks have every right to be cautious. I respect you for it."

"Then you won't mind if I ask some questions," said Bev.

Pete winced, but Harper said, "Absolutely not."

"Are you really a minister?"

Harper chuckled. "As a matter of fact. Would you like to see some identification?" He reached inside his jacket, produced an oxblood leather wallet, and tried to open it. For a moment, he had difficulty, as if his hand were still stiff, numb, or sore. Then the billfold came apart, and he laid it on the desk in front of her. On one side was his Mississippi driver's license, on the other, a picture ID card issued by the Presbyterian church.

"This says that you're the pastor at the church on Concord Avenue," Beverly observed.

"That's right," Harper said.

"Then why are we talking here instead of there?"

Harper smiled ruefully. "I wish we could. It would save me running back and forth. But the synod wouldn't approve of what my friends and I are doing."

Pete shifted in his chair. "Which is helping people protect themselves, right?"

Harper nodded. His fingers curled and uncurled. "Exactly. We're putting together a fellowship of decent, reliable citizens who can call on one another in an emergency. If one of us finds himself in a desperate situation, all he has to do is make a phone call, and everyone else will come running. We're concentrating on recruiting parents because our first priority is protecting children."

"Our boys are at their aunt's," said Pete, making sure Harper understood they *had* children, even though the minister had just made it clear they wouldn't have been invited otherwise. *Moron*, Beverly thought.

For her part, she had to concede that the comment about putting children first made sense, but that didn't mean that any of the rest of it did. "This sounds like one of those crackpot militias," she said. "Why would we need it? Why wouldn't we just dial 911?"

Harper opened a fat manila folder and handed her several glossy photographs. When she saw the heap of bloody bodies in the top one, she had to swallow away a sudden clog in her throat.

"The *police* massacred those poor people," said the minister, "in Mayersville. Look at the next picture." Beverly did. It contained images even more gruesome than the first. This time, the corpses had been hacked apart. "Firemen in Houma were responsible for that. They used their axes. The photo under that shows what some demented doctors and nurses did in the county hospital in Vicksburg. And as a member of the clergy myself, I'm ashamed to say that the next one shows what happened when a nun went berserk in a parochial school in Clarksdale."

Bev could hardly bear to look at the bodies of the butchered children. They were only *little boys*, about the same age as her own. Sickened, she hastily handed the photos back to Harper. She thought he'd return them to their folder, but instead he spread them out across the desktop, placing the one from the school directly in front of her.

"I know you've already heard about these atrocities on the news," Harper said. His right hand twitched. "Just like I realize that these pictures are awful to look at. But I'm trying to get you to think seriously about what's going on in the world. There's a terrible hysteria cropping up everywhere, infecting people like a plague. Nobody really understands why. Some people claim it's God's judgment on our sinful society, others talk about some toxic chemical in the atmosphere, and a few are even blaming transmissions from Russian satellites. But we all know it's turned scores of people into mass murderers, including any number of public servants. In fact, for some reason policemen and EMTs and, yes, even preachers seem to be more susceptible than the average person. It's tragic, but most people can't trust *anyone* anymore."

Bev kept her gaze fixed on the minister's face so she wouldn't inadvertently look at the photos again. And thus couldn't help noticing what compelling green eyes he had. They almost seemed to glow, yet with motes of darkness drifting behind the luminous irises like shadows falling on a stained-glass window. Something about them eased the ache in her temples, yet made her lightheaded as well.

She tried to cast off the feeling. "Maybe that's true—"

"You know darn well it is," said Pete somberly. "I'm afraid to send the boys to school anymore. I'm afraid to let you or them out of my sight."

He really *did* sound afraid. As if he loved their sons, and conceivably even her. For a moment, Bev felt a twinge of grudging affection for him. But he *had* interrupted her, so she shot him a withering glare anyway. "As I was trying to say," she continued to Harper, "if a person can't depend on anybody, if ministers are turning into maniacs just like cops and doctors, then why should we trust you and your gang of gun nuts?"

"That's a good question," Harper said, his eyes shining. "Here's how we operate.

Someone who already belongs to the organization recommends another family, like yours. Then I meet with the potential recruits. I have a degree in psychology and a lot of experience counseling, and I consider myself pretty darn good at sizing people up. If I'm not certain that the members of a family are of good character and mentally stable, they don't get in. This way, we make sure that our members really can depend on one another. That none of them is likely to let us down when we need him most, or fall prey to the hysteria and turn into a lunatic himself."

"It sounds great," said Pete.

"Listen to Mr. Keen Judgment," Beverly sneered, although, really, it seemed as if Harper actually had put at least a *little* thought into what he was doing. "As I recall, the Yugo sounded great to you, too." Her head began to swim again, and she strained to will the sensation away. "But even if Mr. Harper can keep the nut cases out of his club, well, let's say that a member really did have a pack of mad-dog killers chasing him, and dialed the hot-line number. What are the odds that the other Boy Scouts and Campfire Girls would actually get to him fast enough to save his butt?"

Harper sighed. "I have to admit, they might arrive too late. After all, we aren't any of us Superman." His fingertips quivered on the desk top. "But on the other hand, someone *might* show up in time. And it could be the only chance the poor victim has. Besides which, there's another advantage to belonging."

"What's that?" asked Pete, eager as a puppy.

"Well," the minister said, "you have to remember that we don't know how bad the plague of craziness is going to get. When it started, you had lone individuals running amok. Now there are groups of people flipping out together. I hate to say it, but it's possible that before this thing runs its course, we could get to a point where there are so many psychotics on the rampage that they threaten all of Natchez. If that time comes, we have a refuge prepared. A kind of fortress, if you want to call it that. You can bring your children there and be safe."

Except for his eyes, the minister's features blurred. Bev blinked to bring him back into focus. A part of her still wanted to mock the whole idea of Harper's fellowship. To do otherwise would imply that Pete had been right and she'd been wrong, and Lord, that would rankle! Yet even so, the clergyman made a certain amount of sense. The world *was* crumbling into craziness and chaos. She *would* want someone to depend on if the madness threatened her family.

But there was one more question she needed to ask. "And what is this going to cost?"

"The fellowship provides the beepers," Harper said. "Somebody made a donation that covers those and the switchboard. If it's not a hardship, we'd like you to be responsible for your own guns, ammo, and your own store of blankets, bottled water, and non-perishable food in the shelter. Beyond that, there isn't any cost."

"In that case," she said slowly, "maybe it isn't a *totally* stupid idea."

Harper smiled. "I'm happy you feel that way. May I ask my questions now?"

"Shoot," said Pete.

As it turned out, Harper wanted to know a lot of things, about their family backgrounds, their medical histories, the jobs they'd held, and God knew what else. Still feeling a little dizzy, Bev let Pete field most of the questions. As he babbled on, dropping in the occasional fib about his beer consumption or church attendance, her gaze dropped to the photo of the murdered boys, then hastily skipped away to land on Harper's hand.

The hand trembled, then floated up from the desk top in a way that reminded her of a helium balloon. It extended its index finger and drew a straight vertical line, followed by an attached arc on the right. Together the two movements defined a capital D.

For an instant she had the oddest notion that the hand had a mind of its own, altogether separate from Harper's, and that it wanted to tell her something. Then the minister scowled and clenched it into a tight fist.

"I see you noticed my tic," he said, smiling once again, his jade eyes bright. "Nerve damage from a car crash a few years back."

"I'm sorry," said Bev, feeling so flustered that the odd fancy popped right out of her head. "I didn't mean to stare."

"It's all right. I know it looks peculiar sometimes. Like I have the DTs or something." He opened a desk drawer and removed a pair of beepers and a stapled sheaf of white paper. "I believe we've discussed everything we needed to cover. Welcome to the Family Mutual Protection Association."

Pete grinned like the fool he was. "We're in? Just like that?"

Harper smiled back at him. "Just like that."

Somewhat to her own surprise, Beverly felt almost as gratified as Pete looked, though, unwilling to give him any more satisfaction that she had already, she did her best to hide it. For a second, a final hint of *something*, some residual distrust, skepticism, or uneasiness, squirmed deep inside her mind, but it faded before she had a chance to recognize it for whatever it had truly been.

SEVENTEEN

When Bellamy found Astarte, she was restlessly prowling the corridors of Marie's Haunt, inspecting the grimy portraits and landscapes on the wall by the light of a stubby white candle. The sharp scent of the smoke stung his hypersensitive nose. Unbeknownst to Astarte, several *abambo* had gathered around her to gawk at the Quick girl who'd had the audacity to impersonate the Queen.

"Hi," said Bellamy to the other ghosts. "Could you guys give us some space? I want to talk to her, and I'd really appreciate a little privacy."

A lanky warrior in a zebra-striped cape, his cheeks and forehead ridged with ritual scars, nodded respectfully. "Sure, Agent Bellamy. No problem." He and the others moved on down the gloomy hallway. Bellamy wondered if they'd actually stay gone. Many *abambo* were shameless when it came to spying on events on the warm side of the Shroud. They seemed to regard all of mortal life as nothing more than a show provided for their entertainment.

But there was little Bellamy could do about it if they did decide to pry. He wouldn't even know they were watching. So he went ahead and jumped the Shroud, noticing with satisfaction just how easy the crossing had become, at least here in the Haunt where the barrier between the worlds was thin. His Proctor powers were growing. "Hi," he said.

Astarte turned and threw herself into his arms. Her leather jacket creaking in his embrace, they kissed until, finally, shivering, she drew away from him. "It's about time you showed up," she said. "I'm bored out of my mind. There's nobody to talk to except the Arcanists, and they don't want to. They're too busy trying to translate the notebook."

"I'm sorry," Bellamy said. "I've been busy too, helping Antoine and Titus interrogate Geffard's lieutenants. Unfortunately, none of them seems to know any more about the overall conspiracy than we'd figured out already. Wouldn't you know it, they claim that Chester was the only one who did. We've also been hunting out hunting for werewolves, or suspicious Pardoners who might be Sinkinda in disguise, but we didn't find any. Either they're lying low or they've pulled out of New Orleans altogether."

"To Lafayette? That's supposed to be where the werewolves came from in the first place."

The FBI agent shrugged. "Maybe. It seems plausible, but my intuition tells me different. Lafayette is too far from the Mississippi. Most of the Atheist murders occurred in towns along the banks. So have most of the other atrocities. I think whatever the conspirators are planning next will happen in that corridor as well."

"Makes sense," said Astarte, hugging him again. "How long can you stay with me?"

"A while," he replied. "I seem to have a lot of psychic strength tonight. I feel the Underworld trying to tug me back, but I always feel that. It isn't pulling hard yet. I'm not straining to anchor myself in place."

"But probably not for more than an hour? Maybe even less?"

He sighed. "Well, yes."

"In that case, it would be better to have Titus put me to sleep and yank me over into your dimension."

Bellamy hesitated. "I'm not sure that's a good idea."

Astarte cocked her head. "Of course it is. We can be together longer. You won't have to worry about keeping your brain clenched, or whatever it is you do to hold yourself here, and I won't freeze my ass off when we touch."

"I know, but I hate to drag you over here where everything's dangerous and ugly."

She snorted. "Like I haven't run into any danger on this side of the wall."

"I know, but—"

"And it wasn't ugly to me. Everything was magick. *I* had magick, at least sort of, when I was using the Queen's weapons."

Bellamy scowled. "Did the spirit world seem all that wonderful when Geffard was about to burn your eyes out?"

"I admit, that was a little scary. But I got out of it, so what the hell. Anyway, so what if he'd burned them out, as long as he didn't kill me? I wouldn't have stayed blind, would I?"

"I don't know. Even Titus isn't sure. A real *ibambo* wouldn't, but maybe you would, even after your spirit returned to your body. You might have wound up with a lifelong case of hysterical blindness."

"A pack of rabid guinea pigs *might* attack me the next time I walk down the street, but I'm not going to waste time worrying about it."

Bellamy grimaced at her flippancy. "What really concerns me is that when you were out of your body, you didn't worry about *anything*. You were in danger every moment, but it never even fazed you."

"Ever since we've been together, you've been telling me I'm reckless. Poor Marilyn said the same thing. So if I was taking chances, that wasn't anything new."

"The difference is that when you were over here, you took your recklessness to a whole new level. You acted like you were high, or drunk, or a little crazy."

"Because I was excited. It was the peak experience of my life."

"I think there's more to it than that. I think the living don't belong in the land of the dead."

"You might just as well say that ghosts shouldn't jump the Shroud and visit the living. Because if they were meant to do it, it wouldn't be so hard for them. If we start worrying about the way things are *supposed* to be, we're going to lose each other. And I don't want that."

Bellamy hugged her tight. "Neither do I. I think I'd fall right into this Oblivion the other Restless talk about. But we have to find another way."

She held him as tightly, as lovingly, as he was holding her, but her voice held its familiar edge. "How do you know there is another way? And even if there is, how come *you* get to decide what *I'm* going to do?"

"Well, for one thing, I doubt Titus will bring you across if I ask him not to."

She squirmed from his embrace and stepped back to glare at him. "That is so fucking typical. You always have to be the big cop boss of everything, don't you? Well—"

Bellamy glimpsed motion at the corner of his eye. He pivoted, his hand shifting reflexively toward his pistol. But it was only Titus, materializing on the bright side of the Shroud. His wrinkled face crimson on the left and blue on the right, the old man looked a little uncomfortable.

"Forgive me for intruding," he said. "But the Arcanists have deciphered a part of the notebook. I thought you'd want to come and hear Marilyn explain what they've discovered."

"Yeah," Bellamy said, "I guess we'd better." Titus turned and headed back down the hall. The younger ghost and Astarte fell in behind him.

The mortal girl took Bellamy's hand. "Our conversation *isn't* over," she murmured.

EIGHTEEN

Marie's followers had installed the Arcanists in the old mansion's cluttered library, then illuminated the place with an assortment of candles and kerosene lanterns, though they'd hadn't bothered to sweep away the sheets of filthy cobweb. The air smelled of dust, old paper, tobacco, and Marilyn's blood. Evidently her bandaged wounds were still bleeding at least a bit. The transsexual sat slumped in her wheelchair beside a large globe, her legs and torso swaddled in blankets, the notebook resting in her lap beneath her mangled hand.

Bellamy noticed that neither the very pregnant Joan Crosby, chain-smoking Alan Fong in his garish Hawaiian shirt and Yankees baseball cap, nor any of the other surviving Arcanists had elected to sit particularly close to Marilyn. Perhaps her injuries repelled them, although that didn't seem likely. Surely the occultists had seen their share of carnage in the course of their investigations into the supernatural. Maybe they were in awe of the colleague who'd moved beyond them. Who'd *become* a supernatural being in her own right. Or maybe they were jealous of Marilyn's newfound magick, despite the grisly price she'd had to pay for it.

When, still unaccustomed to the presence of the dead, they saw Titus and Bellamy, the Arcanists abruptly fell silent. Astarte scurried to Marilyn's side. "How are you feeling?" she asked softly.

Half of Marilyn's mouth was visible through her facial bandages, enough to show her smile. "I'm fine, dear. You have to stop clucking over me like a mother hen. Guilty or not—and you shouldn't be—the role doesn't suit a truculent little smart-ass like you."

Titus turned toward the far wall and salaamed. Marilyn inclined her head. Surmising that Marie must have entered the room, Bellamy offered his own show of respect. He was surprised that the Queen had come to the Arcanists rather than summoning them to the throne room, but perhaps, haughty though she was, she'd wanted to spare Marilyn any unnecessary moving about.

"Hm," said Titus. "This is rather awkward, isn't it?" He opened a leather pouch at his waist, extracted a pinch of dust, tossed it into the air, and whispered a magick word. The bits of powder flashed and barked like a string of firecrackers going off.

The forms of Antoine, Marie, and two of her zebra-caped bodyguards wavered into view, intermittently transparent but visible nonetheless. Titus had made it possible for the living to see and presumably hear things on the cold side of the Shroud. The occultists gasped and gaped. Some of them flinched.

"Bow like I did," Bellamy told them. "That's the Queen."

The Arcanists scrambled to obey. "Be at ease," said Marie. "You fancy yourself hunters of ghosts. Over the centuries, your kind has sought to enslave, torment, and murder mine, all in the name of scholarship, as if you had some intrinsic right to our secrets. But we're allies now, and as long as that condition holds, you are welcome here."

"Provided you behave yourselves," Antoine rasped.

"Wow," whispered Astarte to Bellamy, "that would sure make *me* feel right at home."

Evidently she'd forgotten the inhumanly sharp hearing of wraiths. Marie gave her a frosty smile. "I don't mean to frighten anyone, child. I appreciate the aid that you, Mr. Bellamy, and Marilyn have given me. I simply think it's important that we all understand one another."

"I imagine we do," said Marilyn, shifting on her seat. Bellamy wondered if her wounds were paining her. "Shall we discuss the notebook now?"

"By all means," said Marie, settling onto a dilapidated leather armchair. She sat straight and tall, just as she did on her ivory throne. Her bodyguards took up positions behind her.

"The person who wrote the journal," said Marilyn, her voice falling into a dry, pedantic tone, "used several different languages or ciphers, God knows why. Perhaps he considered particular scripts appropriate for particular subjects."

Titus nodded as if he considered this a good guess.

"That being the case," Marilyn continued, "we haven't been able to translate everything. But we believe we have figured out the gist of several passages. Some of them use characters derived from the ancient languages of Northern Europe—Norse runes, Pictish pictograms, and that sort of thing—and the rest are based on a lexicon of symbols once employed by quasi-Gnostic cults throughout the Mediterranean and the Middle East. Luckily, Ms. Crosby is an authority on the former, and I've dabbled in the latter. Joan, would you care to report on our findings?"

The pregnant woman pushed her wire-rimmed glasses back up her nose. "I can," she said, though judging from her rather nervous expression, she would just as soon have left the lecturing to ghosts to Marilyn. "Does everyone know who the Aztecs were?"

"I have a vague idea," said Marie dryly.

Astarte nudged Bellamy in the ribs. "We saw clay figures that looked Aztec in the werewolf house," she whispered.

Bellamy nodded. The black pyramid on Chester's computer screen had reminded him of the Aztecs as well. But in the press of subsequent events, he'd nearly forgotten about it, not that he was sure he'd have ascribed any special significance to the Mesoamerican stuff in any case. He'd seen too many weird symbols and artifacts, derived from too many disparate cultures, in the course of this investigation. Werewolf hieroglyphs and pentagrams. Voudoun dolls. Marie's murmuring, hypnotic drums and towering African idols. Marilyn's Hermetic rituals. And now the Arcanists were blithely throwing Vikings, Picts, and quasi-Gnostics—whatever *they* were—into the mix. It was enough to make his head swim.

"Well," Joan said, "it seems that when white people sailed to the New World, their ghosts made the crossing with them. The spirits were fleeing from a king or an arch-devil who was persecuting them for their beliefs."

"Of course," said Marie. "They were Heretics escaping the yoke of Charon of Stygia and his seven ministers, who forbade them to worship any gods but themselves. Everyone knows that."

"Everyone dead may know it," said Marilyn. "It was news to us. Go on, Joan."

"The, uh, Heretics wanted to found their own kingdom," the pregnant woman continued. "So they set out to conquer the Aztec ghosts, just as the Spaniards were out to conquer the live ones. In the final battle, the European spirits somehow opened a big hole into nothingness—"

"The Void," Titus murmured.

"—right under the Aztecs' feet. They were supposed to fall to a death beyond death. An ultimate annihilation."

Antoine cocked his wedge-shaped head. "'Supposed to?' They did. Everybody knows that much, even people who are bored stupid by history, like me. Once you take a header into the Big Zero, nothing can save you."

"According to the notebook," Marilyn said, "you're wrong. *Most* of the Aztecs perished, but as they plunged screaming down the Abyss, one of their gods caught a few of them in his hand. Our historian identifies the deity as Loki, the Norse god of mischief. Obviously we can't take that literally. The designation may be an artifact of the language he's using. I suspect he really means Tezcatlipoca, or Smoking Mirror. The Aztec god of the sun and music and the very personification of treachery."

"If they encountered this god at the edge of the Void," said Marie, frowning, "then whatever they *thought* he was, he must really have been one of the pharaohs of the Sinkinda."

"Perhaps," said the mage. "In any case, he offered them a bargain. He'd save them from Oblivion and help them take revenge on their conquerors, but there was a price to pay. They'd have to bind themselves to him more closely than ever before, forsaking all their other gods, and be utterly transformed in the process."

"In other words," said Bellamy, "become Spectres." Death tugged at him, trying to draw him back into the Shadowlands, and he exerted his will to resist.

"Apparently so," Marilyn replied. "As you will have guessed, they took the deal, and now they've risen from the netherworld to crush their enemies."

Antoine crawled closer to Marilyn. The end of his translucent tail dragged through Alan Fong's sneaker-clad foot. The scholar goggled at the phenomenon, and, when the reptile had passed, surreptitiously fingered the affected extremity.

"I don't get this," Antoine said. "For one thing, the Dark Kingdom of Obsidian got itself trashed maybe three hundred years ago—"

"Almost five hundred, actually," Marilyn said.

"Whatever," Antoine growled. "My point is, why didn't the Aztec Sinkinda come back until now?"

"The Ocean is the realm of primordial chaos," Titus said. "It can play tricks with time as well as space. It's also possible that the Sinkinda needed five centuries to lay their plans and gather strength. But actually, my guess is that they were waiting until the Hierarchy was vulnerable. Charon is gone now, his satraps are squabbling with one another, and their grasp on their Shadowlands holdings has grown relatively weak."

"There's something else that doesn't make sense," the gator said. "The Aztecs wanted revenge on the Heretics, not the Stygians. But they missed their chance, because the Heretic nation didn't last. The Legions crossed the Atlantic and took it over."

"As near as I can make out," Marilyn said, "the Aztecs aren't discriminating between one group of white spirits and another. Why should they? Being Sinkinda, they pretty much hate all of existence anyway. At any rate, they blame every ghost of European descent. They want to obliterate them from the Americas and reclaim the hemisphere for themselves, though I imagine that, given their transformation, their new—what did you call it?—Dark Kingdom of Obsidian would be a far nastier place than their old one. Eventually they hope to destroy every Caucasian ghost in existence anywhere, and then, if they ever complete that special vendetta, I suppose they'll throw themselves into the general Sinkinda jihad against all Creation."

"Jesus Christ," Astarte said.

"At least they think big," said Bellamy wryly. "What we still haven't heard is what the Atheist murders and all the possessed cops and kindergarten teachers going on killing sprees are supposed to accomplish. Does the notebook shed any light on that?"

"A bit," Marilyn replied. A red dot swelled on the white gauze masking her cheek. "They've been terrorizing and corrupting live and dead souls both. Destroying their faith in God, their governments, and everything else. The idea is to pollute the psychic atmosphere in preparation for a great work of magick which will somehow help them conquer a piece of North America. A beachhead from which to attack the rest of it. Their werewolf friends will set up shop there, too. The spiritual climate of depravity will enhance their power."

"Do you know where this ritual is supposed to happen?" Bellamy asked.

"No," Marilyn said.

"Well," the FBI agent said, frowning, "if I were going to conquer a piece of Stygian territory, I suppose I'd devote special attention to knocking out the most important Hierarchy enclave in it. Where's that?"

"Natchez," said Titus. His body took on a shadowy look and his voice grew a hair fainter as he allowed himself to slip back across the Shroud. "The capital of the province immediately to the north."

"Which is also right in the center of the Atheists' kill zone," Bellamy said. "Until we learn differently, let's tentatively assume that the enemy will make their move there. The next question is, when?"

"The notebook isn't clear about that, either," Marilyn said. "But I suspect, soon."

"So do I," said Titus. "If their purpose was to foul the psychic landscape, well, I can't imagine that they could get it much dirtier than it is already. Upriver, mortals are barricading themselves in their homes, rioting, and lynching their neighbors, while the Restless duel and murder one another on the slightest provocations. We can feel a difference even here, at the periphery of the effect. If I'm not mistaken, another Maelstrom will rise before the night is through."

"It sounds to me," said Bellamy, "as if we'd better get ourselves to Natchez quick."

"Which 'we' is that?" asked Marie. "Are you referring to all the occupants of this room, together with the warriors you led against Geffard?"

"I suppose I was," said Bellamy. "After all, this is everybody's problem. The Aztecs may have a special hatred for white people, but I doubt they're all that keen on letting you Africans hold onto your little piece of America, either. And even if they would, do you want a nest of Spectres on your border?"

"No," said Marie. "But I would be rash indeed to leave the city now. I've just regained my strength and put down a revolt. I must be seen to rule, or others may question my fitness and rise against me."

Bellamy could see from her expression that he wouldn't be able to talk her out of it. "I understand, Your Majesty."

"Nor may you take my army. I may need it to control the remaining Creoles, or even to defend the city against Sinkinda if your mission fails."

"You wouldn't want 'em anyway," Antoine said. "New Orleans has fought the Hierarchy a bunch of times. The Stygians kept trying to steal little pieces of our turf, or even gobble up the whole city. And to be honest, we've raided their Haunts and their shipping a time or two. Since they have Soulforges and we don't, it was always a big temptation to slip across the border and score some loot. So the two sides aren't exactly best buddies. We aren't at war right now, but if you march a New Orleans army up the river, they'll take it as an invasion, and do their damnedest to wipe it out."

"I understand," said Bellamy again. He turned back to the Queen. "Your Majesty, I'm picking up that you no longer consider the conspiracy your most pressing concern. I think that's shortsighted, but even if it's not, I thought we had an understanding. If

I helped you, you'd help me."

Marie's amber eyes smoldered. "Do not presume to tell me what I pledged to do. Nor to imply that the Queen of New Orleans would renege on a debt of honor. I never intended that you should go to the Stygians alone. Titus, old friend, will you accompany him?"

"Gladly," the shaman said. He shot Bellamy a smile. "I've traveled there as an ambassador before, The three Governors—Gayoso, Shellabarger, and Mrs. Duquesne—know me, even if I'm not their favorite person. We'll call on them, explain the situation, and enlist the services of *their* army. They should be only too happy to help us, considering that it's their heads on the chopping block."

"Thank you," Bellamy said.

Antoine's jaws opened a fraction, as if he meant to speak, then closed.

"I'll give you Geffard's steamboat for the journey," said Marie. "As my envoys, you ought to travel in state."

"I wish I could ride on it," Marilyn said wistfully. "But I guess I'll have to travel by some more pedestrian conveyance."

Astarte peered at her. "Are you sure you're up to it?"

Marilyn smiled. "Remember my lifestyle, darling. One of the nice things about SM is that it teaches you how to handle pain. Look, I admit, I only have the vaguest notion of how my magick works. I don't know why I could suddenly see and hear wraiths when I woke up from my coma, unless that was a gift the Ferryman gave me. I don't understand the instinct that led me to Her Majesty's sickbed, or exactly how I managed to heal her. But the fact remains, my powers *have* come in handy, and they may again. And even if they don't, the Spectres have helpers in the mortal dimension. So should Frank and Titus."

Astarte grimaced. "Okay. At least your wheelchair is electric. I won't have to push the fucking thing."

Antoine's tail twitched back and forth. "I guess I'll tag along, too."

Bellamy smiled. "I was hoping you would."

The gator bobbed his head in his approximation of a shrug. "I guess the five of us are alike, warmblood. None of us is the kind to quit on his pals in the middle of a fight."

"That's true," Titus said, a hint of worry in his voice. "But are you sure you shouldn't stay and help organize the defenses of the city? Someone needs to attend to that as well."

"Somebody else can handle it," Antoine rasped. "You guys are liable to need me worse, so you've got me." He shuffled around toward the Queen. "If Your Highness will let me go."

Marie hesitated, then inclined her head.

Alan Fong cleared his throat. "I don't know how much more we Arcanists have to contribute. I mean, we're not commandos or wizards—"

"I think you've done your part," said Marilyn gently. "Stay in New Orleans for the time being. You should be safe here now. We'll send for you if we need you."

"It would appear that we've laid our plans," said Marie, "but before you all commit yourselves irrevocably to this venture, there's something you should know."

Bellamy felt a pang of pure annoyance. How much stranger and more complicated were things going to get? "What's that?" he asked.

"You saw Geffard's god. You watched it abandon the Haitian to his fate."

"Yeah," said Antoine. "It was too weak or too chicken to go up against the Orisha."

"No," said Marie. "I wish that were the case, but I sensed that it wasn't. The spirit was cunning and powerful. It simply saw no advantage in fighting another god merely to defend a pawn who had outlived his usefulness."

"Was it Smoking Mirror?" Astarte asked.

"Geffard probably didn't realize it," said the Queen. "He would have taken it for one of Les Mystéres. But I suspect so, and if I'm right, you're likely to encounter it again. Without my god and me there to help you."

"Great," Bellamy said sourly. "Anybody want to back out?" No one spoke up. "Me neither. Because I'm no expert on the Aztecs, but even I know that they sacrificed victims by the hundreds, to make the sun shine and the crops grow. And it's a safe bet that Aztec Spectres are even more bloodthirsty. Poor old Milo Waxman was right. The doomshades are planning a massacre, something that will make everything we've seen so far look trivial."

NINETEEN

Belinda Talley inspected the gleaming assortment of weapons on the racks and counters of the stall before her. Stilettos, bowie knives, and sabers. Spiky-headed maces. A miscellany of firearms, flintlock and pepperpot pistols lying next to pump shotguns, automatic rifles, and even a rocket launcher. It all gave her a queasy feeling in the pit of her stomach.

She thought of Starshine and thrust her distaste aside. She pointed to a stubby little revolver, one that looked as if it would fit her hand. "How much is that?" she asked.

The merchant grinned at her. He was a plump, apple-cheeked little man with an upturned nose. Some Masquer had accentuated the natural impishness of his appearance by giving him pointed ears, a pair of small, blunt horns, and a long prehensile tail with a fleshy arrowhead on the end. "Ah, the Model 12! Excellent choice. Someone carried it over when he died, so it's a *real* Smith and Wesson, not a copy. But notice that I've fitted it out with soulfire crystals. You won't have to feed it juice to make it fire."

"How much?" Belinda repeated.

"For you, because it's a lovely evening and I like your smile, thirty oboli."

She stared at him. "You're kidding."

The merchant's grin slipped ever so slightly. "Natchez is a prosperous town these days. Like any successful businessman, I charge what the traffic will bear." He waved his hand at the wraiths—swaggering Legionnaires and mercenaries, most of them, bristling with weapons and decked out in green sashes—drifting among the stalls of the open-air market with beggars, pimps, and whores following at their heels. "I guarantee you, most of these people would jump at the price I quoted."

Belinda understood that she was expected to haggle, but if he was starting at thirty, she'd never argue him down to a price she could afford. She only had six oboli left in her change purse. She pointed to a flintlock pistol, the curve of its brown wooden stock reflecting the greenish light of the barrow-flame torches. "How much is that one?"

"I could let it go for, oh, nineteen oboli."

"For something that old?"

"A classic, in perfect condition."

"Maybe, but it only shoots one time, doesn't it?"

"If you ever have to defend yourself from a Spectre or a Renegade terrorist, you'll discover that one shot is quite a bit better than none."

Provided she could hit her attacker on the first try, Belinda thought, which, given her lack of experience, wasn't all that likely. Still, she supposed that for her, any sort of firearm was a better bet that a knife or tomahawk. She could, in a vague, cringing sort of way, picture herself pointing a gun at someone and pulling the trigger. She couldn't imagine ramming a blade into anybody. She was certain that she'd only freeze if she tried.

"Nobody else is going to buy this," she said. "Not when you and all the other gun vendors have modern pistols for sale. I'll give you one obolus."

"One!" he cried. "You must be crazy. Go away and stop wasting an honest man's time. I couldn't possibly let the gun go for less than eighteen."

They argued for a quarter of an hour, during which overseers armed with snapping bullwhips and buzzing electric cattle prods drove a coffle of Heretic prisoners toward the slave market on the other side of the square, and an itinerant Sandman entertainer wandered by, filling the air with illusory swirls of fragrant, multicolored vapor. In the end, Belinda couldn't convince the weapon seller to go below eight oboli.

She pulled off her love beads and leather headband. "Will you take these to make up the difference?"

The merchant snorted. "My customers are Legionnaires and soldiers-of-fortune. Professional killers, if you want to look at it that way. I can't sell them peace-and-love hippie fashion accessories, and besides, I don't *do* barter anymore. This is a cash business."

"Please," Belinda said. "My little girl's been kidnapped." In a few jumbled sentences, she babbled out the story of Starshine's disappearance. "So you see, I need the gun to get her back."

"That's tragic," the horned man said blandly. "But if I sold below cost every time a customer told me a sob story, I'd be broke in no time." He looked her up and down. For a second, the tip of his tongue slipped out of the corner of his mouth. "However, since it's an emergency, maybe I *could* make an exception to the no-barter policy. But, sweetheart, I really don't have any use for your jewelry."

"Then what do you want?"

The merchant leered. "You know. Do it well, and you can even keep your money." The arrowhead tip purple and throbbing, a drop of clear fluid glistening on the very end, his tail undulated into the air like a cobra rising from a snake charmer's basket. "Come around behind the counter."

Belinda felt revulsion and anger, but most of all, despair. No one cared that Starshine was missing. Everyone she asked for help—Rudy, Valentine, Governor Gayoso, and now this man—either turned her away or tried to exploit her desperation. For the first time in thirty years, the Underworld seemed the hell that many wraiths considered it to be.

And she supposed it was ridiculous to be squeamish in hell. You had to expect your share of degradation. Her eyes aching as if they could still shed tears, she started around the side of the booth.

Something touched her on the hip. Startled, she yelped, jumped, and looked down.

Frowning, Valentine peered back up at her. The dwarf had exchanged his motley for gray slacks, a white shirt, a navy blazer, and a provincial soldier's emerald sash with its black hourglass emblem. "What are you doing?" he asked.

The weapon merchant leaned over the counter, presumably so he could see who she was talking to. "She was about to pay for a purchase," the horned man said.

"Uh huh," said Valentine. "I'll pay for what she wants. With cash."

Belinda glared at him. "And then you'll want me to pay you back with what I was going to give him. Well, maybe I'd rather give it to him than you. *He* never promised to help me and then stabbed me in the back."

Valentine winced. "Just calm down, all right? You don't have to give me anything." He turned back to the vendor. "How much?"

The merchant grimaced. Evidently he would rather have had the sex. "Eight oboli." Valentine dug the coins form his pocket, and the other man handed the flintlock to him.

"Bullets?" said the dwarf.

The vendor smiled slyly. "Not included in the price."

Valentine touched his sash. "I'm a quartermaster up at the Citadel. I could steer plenty of business your way, if I thought you gave your customers a fair shake."

"All right," said the horned man. "You're killing me, but as a gesture of good will." He reached under the counter and brought out half a dozen lead balls. "Will these be enough?"

"Lantern and scythe, let's hope so," Valentine said wryly. He accepted the bullets, then offered them and the gun to Belinda.

She hesitated, then accepted them, sticking the flintlock through her belt and the bullets in her pocket. "Now I guess you think I ought to be grateful. Well, I'm not."

The dwarf's mouth twisted. "I've been hunting all over Under-the-Hill for you. Could we just take a walk and talk for a while? Please?"

"Well…I guess." They set off walking toward the block where slaves were displayed for auction. The current offering was a triumph of the flesh sculptor's art, a wraith with an anguished human face but the perfectly rendered body of a beautiful black stallion. The bidding was spirited.

"Were you really going to have sex with that creep?" Valentine asked. "Right here in the market, just for an old pistol?"

Belinda felt a pang of shame. "For a second, it felt like I didn't have a choice, or like it didn't matter." Her face twisted, and she choked back a sob. "What am I supposed to do? I *know* Starshine is probably dead. I know I'm probably never going to find the man who took her, not all by myself. I doubt I could destroy him if I did, even with this stupid gun. But I feel like if I give up the search, I'll go insane."

Valentine nodded. "I know how you feel."

"The hell you do," Belinda snapped. "You quit *your* search like a shot when the Governor offered you a little incentive."

"I guess I did," said the dwarf somberly. "Look, my life was short and nasty. My mother died giving birth to me—you wouldn't think such a little baby could rip her up so badly inside, would you? My dad was an addict who liked to beat the crap out of me, and had the good sense to spend what little money we had on drugs instead of extravagances like groceries and rent. From the time I was five, we lived on the street, and when I was eight, he just disappeared one night. I don't know if he got sick of looking after his freak son and ran away, or what. Anyway, after that, things got even worse for me. With him gone, there was nobody to protect me from all the *other* thugs and crazies who wanted to steal what little I managed to scrounge, rape me, or just kick me around for fun. And I was way too little and weak to protect myself. Somehow I survived till I was twenty-five, and then, one rainy January night, I caught pneumonia. I hadn't eaten for a while, so I couldn't drag my ass to the hospital, and none of the other bums could be bothered to take me. I died four days later."

Belinda remembered the gun seller's indifference to her own tale of woe. "Tragic," she said sardonically.

"I don't expect you to feel sorry for me," Valentine said as they skirted the crowd shouting bids on the man-horse. "I know you've got problems of your own. I just want you to understand. When I entered the Underworld, everything seemed so bleak that I thought I was in for an even more awful version of the life I'd lived in the Skinlands. I didn't think I could face it. I felt Oblivion eating me away from the inside, and even though it terrified me, I also wished it would hurry up and finish me off.

"Then I ran into Gayoso. He was out inspecting a portion of the Necropolis, playing high-and-mighty lord of the manor, and I caught his eye. He thought it would be fun to have a dwarf jester, like an honest-to-God king from the Middle Ages, and offered me the job."

"And you took it."

"Yeah," Valentine said. They reached the edge of the market and headed up a narrow, shadowy street. Somewhere far ahead, blades clanged together. "Are you kidding? I jumped at it. For the first time, I had a place in the world where I could be safe and comfortable. Even though my job was basically pretty humiliating, and when he was in a bad mood, Gayoso liked to make it more so, I would have done anything to keep it. And I guess that's more or less how things turned out. Montrose the Stygian gave me his friendship. He was one of the few who ever did. But when the Governor ordered me to help bring him down, I didn't think twice."

"Then you must have been *really* thrilled when your lord and master offered you a better job."

The little man nodded. "Sure. It meant security *and* respect. I'd dreamed of that, but never dared to think it could actually happen. But the catch is, now that I've got it, I'm *still* not happy. I *hate* it that I helped to ruin Montrose. I don't want to be a bad friend to you and Daphne, too. Besides, something isn't right."

"What do you mean?"

"Why would Gayoso turn so nice to me all of a sudden?" Valentine replied. "I've been with him for decades, and he never showed any signs of it before. In fact, lately he's been meaner than ever."

"I suppose he could have warmed to you because you did help him destroy Montrose, but that's not what you think, is it? You suspect he tried to make you forget about Daphne because he doesn't want anyone finding out the truth."

"I don't *exactly* think that," Valentine said, "because I can't imagine what he could possibly have to hide. *He's* not the mur—the kidnapper. I'd bet money on that. After all these years in his service, I know about his personal life, and he doesn't have any kind of sick interest in children. And even if he did, as the most powerful official in the province, he could arrange to satisfy it safely. He wouldn't have to endanger himself by running around Under-the-Hill in disguise, grabbing kids off the street."

Belinda sighed. "Then what is going on?"

"Beats me. Everything in the whole province has been strange lately; Fate knows how it all fits together. But I *am* going to help you keep looking. If I'm lucky, Gayoso won't find out about it. If he does, well"—the little man swallowed—"I'll just have to deal with it. The trouble is, we still need help. I don't know how to go about finding the man in the blue mask any more than you do."

The two ghosts stepped off the curb, swinging around a furtive Quick teenage boy in a black denim jacket, who was spray-painting the words GENERATION LAST on a crumbling brick wall. The sharp scent of the pigment mingled with the smell of sweat and marijuana which wafted from his body. When the message was complete, the kid opened a switchblade, jabbed the palm of his hand, and flicked drops of blood onto the letters. Tiny, hissing Nihils popped open in the brick, like mouths opening to drink.

"I don't think you give yourself enough credit," said Belinda. "You were resourceful enough to handle Rudy."

The dwarf grimaced. "Trust me, that was only because he was a moron."

"I don't know about that. But at any rate, I agree that we could *use* more than the token help Gayoso offered. Can you get in to see the other two Governors?"

"No. I mean, I probably could, but I don't think they'd listen to me. They're too cautious and suspicious. They know I'm Gayoso's flunky, and I wouldn't be surprised if they've even guessed I helped him get rid of Montrose. They'd think I was trying to set them up for something, so he could overthrow them, too. Besides, word could easily get back to him, and if we can avoid that, let's."

"Then who do we turn to?" she asked.

"Mike Fink. He doesn't have much use for me, but he doesn't like Gayoso, either. And Montrose clued him in to his suspicions that there are too many mysteries in Natchez, too many weird things going on behind the scenes. If we tell him there's a pervert preying on wraith children, and Gayoso doesn't seem to give a damn, I think he might get curious enough to hunt the man in the blue mask down. And what *he* hunts, he catches. Just ask all those Heretics chained up in the slave market."

"Then let's go talk to him." She stepped in front of Valentine and dropped to her knees. "And thank you for coming to find me. I have some hope now. Hope that at least we can find out what happened to Starshine, and punish the man who took her."

She put her arms around him. The little man stiffened, then relaxed into her embrace.

TWENTY

Montrose looked Louise up and down. Her black, begemmed layers of robe only hinted at the curves of the slender figure beneath, just as her golden mask concealed all of her features except her bright eyes, generous mouth, and chin. He made a minute adjustment to her scalloped stand-up collar.

"Now I know why Stygian civilization is so demented," she murmured, a hint of tension underlying the humor in her tone. "Your formal wear would drive anybody crazy."

He forced a smile. "It's not so bad once you get used to it."

"They used to say that about the rack and the boot, too. Are we ready?"

"As we're likely to be, I suppose." He gave her his arm, and, their garments whispering, they climbed the final flight of stairs and stepped out onto the flat roof of the lofty spire known as the Pinnacle of Lamentations.

The view was spectacular. From this vantage point, one could see almost the entire Onyx Tower complex, and the more plebeian precincts of the City of Dark Echoes falling away below, tier after tier of immense stone structures lit by the light of countless barrow-flame torches and lanterns. Scarlet and ochre sheet lightning flickered in the thunderheads which domed the island like a bell jar.

But Montrose was scarcely conscious of the panorama. He was too intent on the surviving Deathlords, each standing motionless on his appointed pedestal near Charon's empty throne, like grotesque chessmen. The Smiling Lord's steel visor lay atop what had been his dais. The eye holes seemed to glare at the Scot in accusation.

Montrose bowed low, and Louise followed suit. "Sister," quavered the Ashen Lady in the voice of a frail old woman, tones which utterly belied the power at her command. Montrose felt it nonetheless; it radiated from her like heat from a furnace. "Lord Montrose."

The lovers straightened up. The Council stared at them, and Montrose bore the weight of their regard as best he could. A frigid breeze began to blow, first from one quarter and then another, a herald of the impending storm. He found he was grateful for the way the wind plucked at the Deathlords' garments, lending them at least the illusion of animation.

Finally, so suddenly that Montrose jumped, the Emerald Lord hurled his crimson dice, which tumbled along and eventually came to rest on a vertical plane in midair. The Cavalier just had time to observe that he'd thrown a five. Then the Prince of Happenstance held out his hand, and the cubes shot back into it.

"Louise, Princes of Bohemia, Sister of Athena," intoned the Emerald Lord, the lightning glinting on his crown of thorns and wheel-of-fortune amulet, "you stand accused of defying the sentence of execution which an Anacreon of the Legions lawfully imposed on you, of slaying numerous loyal Hierarchs during and following your escape, and of assassinating the Smiling Lord himself."

"To keep him from slaughtering the rest of you," said the Heretic nun. "That ought to count for something."

"James Graham," said the Skeletal Lord. The silver rat on his shoulder twitched its wire whiskers as if its master had just switched it on. "Marquess of Montrose. Onetime Anacreon of the Order of the Unlidded Eye. You stand accused of defying the sentence of execution imposed on you by your liege, of killing numerous loyal Hierarchs during and following your escape, of helping an avowed Heretic to trespass in the capital of the Empire, and of assassinating your own master."

Montrose wondered if he should unmask, as court etiquette had mandated in his previous hearing. He decided that if the Seven—or was it the Six now?—hadn't demanded that he comport himself like an accused traitor, there was little point in doing it spontaneously. "Like my companion, I trust you'll agree that there were extenuating circumstances."

The Princess of Madness emitted an earsplitting screech of laughter. Her harlequin marionette, its crazy-quilt garments as garish as those of its controller, doubled over as if convulsed by its own mirth. "Tell your tale," the Laughing Lady said. "Tell your tale, and we will judge."

Montrose laid the whole tangled skein out in as orderly a manner as he could. Louise chimed in occasionally to describe something she'd experienced alone, such as her first encounter with one of the scaly, double-faced Spectres. The Deathlords listened without interruption, motionless as graven images once more.

"And then, when I thought the Final Death was going to claim me at last," the Scot concluded, "the Emerald Lord and the Skeletal Lord arrived and healed me. For which, once again, I thank you."

"Obviously, we did kill people escaping the Artificers' pit," said Louise, "and again as we made our way through the city and into the Onyx Tower. I'm truly sorry for that. But you see how it was. There was no other way to reach the six of you in time to derail Demetrius's plan."

By your own testimony," said the Beggar Lord, leaning on his crutch, his saffron tatters fluttering in the unquiet air, "when you set out to escape the Artificers' pit, you were unaware that the Imperium was in dire danger. That realization only came afterward. Therefore, clearly, when you struck down the smiths, you had no nobler objective than saving your own skins. Despite any subsequent benefit to the realm, that fact defines your behavior as illegal."

"And all must honor the law," said the Ashen Lady. The Quiet Lord, garbed in his murky red robe and mouthless silver mask, his empty sack of marvels and horrors dangling limply from his hand, nodded ever so slightly.

"And so you're going to punish us?" demanded Louise. "Then the so-called justice of Stygia is even more cruel and corrupt than any Renegade ever imagined."

"Have a care how you speak to us," said the Emerald Lord.

"Dread Lords and Ladies," said Montrose, "you are Charon's chosen, possessed of powers and insights I can scarcely imagine. Generally speaking, I would never presume to suggest that I could know your unspoken thoughts. But in this instance, I believe I do. All this talk of legalities and selfish motives is merely a blind. Now that you've had a chance to mull it over, what's truly vexing you is that you needed the help of two lowly fugitives such as ourselves to save your own illustrious hides. And that we were able to defeat a member of your own elite, madman and traitor though he was."

The Deathlords silently stared. Montrose fancied he felt a charge of sorcery building in the air, as if one of the princes were preparing to strike down him and Louise for his presumption. He itched to take Louise in his arms and fly, but it was inconceivable that they could actually get away.

After what seemed an eternity, the Laughing Lady howled her mirth. "Impertinent, impious words, Anacreon. But methinks they carry a certain ring of truth."

Encouraged that she'd casually restored his rank, Montrose said, "For what it's worth, Dread Lady, we couldn't slay any of you, even if we aspired to do so. We only prevailed against Prince Mars because Demetrius had so thoroughly addled him, and even then, we needed a gargantuan portion of luck."

"How comforting," said the Skeletal Lord dryly. "Nonetheless, it would be detrimental to the Hierarchy if word got out that a pair of ordinary wraiths destroyed any member of this Council, under any circumstances."

Was that the whole point of holding a sham trial? Montrose wondered. *To intimidate us into holding our tongues?* "I assure you, no one will learn of the matter from us."

The Emerald Lord pivoted suddenly toward Louise. Even though Montrose wasn't the target of the demigod's regard, he could feel the power that now infused it. The Sister of Athena gasped and flinched back a step.

"What of you, Heretic?" the Prince of Ill Fortune intoned. "Do you give your pledge as well?"

Despite the stress of the Emerald Lord's scrutiny, Louise smiled crookedly. "The story would make for wonderful rebel propaganda, wouldn't it? I can see why you're concerned. But when I promised to help James complete his mission, I made his cause, which was also yours, my own. It would be dishonorable to take anything that's happened since and use it against you."

The angel in green stared at her for several more seconds, then said, "We believe you."

"Sadly," said the Beggar Lord through his bronze mask, cast to resemble a leprous, eyeless face, "your reticence, though useful, will not prevent a crisis of confidence in our regime. An earthquake wracked the island. Malfeans hovered above it. Any number of our vassals know that we Seven actually took up arms against one another. By now, someone has whispered the sorry tale to a friend or lover, and before long, everyone will know it."

"I said we should destroy every warrior who accompanied us into the Onyx Tower," the Ashen Lady whined. Shadows twisted up and down her gnarled cane like serpents.

The Laughing Lady cackled. "And in the wake of our little misunderstanding, which of us trusted the others enough to be the first to divest himself of his bodyguards? I didn't hear you volunteering, Mistress of Senescence. And the Beggar Lord is right: It's too late now."

"It wouldn't be quite so bad if the entire Council had come back out of the Tower," said the Skeletal Lord. "But since the Smiling Lord has disappeared, many people will surmise he perished in the battle, though they'll imagine he met his end at the hands of his peers. The effect on the morale of the Legions could be disastrous. To some degree, every Hierarch warrior, even those who swore their vows to other princes of the Council, looked to the Lord of War for leadership."

"Can't you appoint a new Mars?" Louise asked. The demigods turned to stare at her. Once again, Montrose was all but certain he felt a charge of sorcery building in the air. "Look, forgive me if it's supposed to be a deep, dark secret, but it's rumored that there have been replacement Deathlords before. You aren't all the same souls whom Charon proclaimed senators back before the birth of Christ."

"Do not speculate about who we were, or when we ascended," the Ashen Lady said, anger in her high, wavering voice. The taut, vibrant feeling in the atmosphere intensified. "Do not invoke your Heretic gods in the very heart of our power."

"Please, excuse me," said Louise. "It wasn't my intention to pry, or to give offense."

"Assuredly not," said Montrose. "Louise is a stranger here, ignorant of the finer points of court etiquette." To his relief, the ambient tension abated. "And in any case, she raised a point worth considering. Whether the Emperor ever replaced a Deathlord or not, it seems Stygia needs a new one now. Why don't you select someone? When he shows himself to the populace, it ought to soothe them considerably."

"We have, of course, considered that," said the Skeletal Lord. Its ruby eyes gleaming, the silver rat picked its way daintily down his forearm. "But there are difficulties."

"No one knows what magick Charon used to wed the Smiling Lord to his mask," the Beggar Lord said. "It's possible that if we told one another how he elevated each of us, we could figure it out. But—"

"But we might also give one another insights into the nature and limitations of our powers," said the Laughing Lady, her tangled black tresses stirring in the wind. "Once again, who wishes to go first?"

"I was going to say," the angel in the yellow rags continued, "that even if we could work out what the Emperor did, there's no guarantee that we could do it, too."

"There's also the vexing question of *whom* to elevate," the Princess of Madness said. The marionette bobbed its head in solemn agreement. "I don't care to see any of my colleague's trusted protégés assume yon visor, and they'd be equally reluctant to have it go to one of my aides."

"And so you see," said the Emerald Lord, "our problems are many. But thanks to you, Anacreon and Sister, at least we and the Isle of Sorrows survive to confront them. And though no one else is *ever* to know of your achievement, it will be rewarded nonetheless. Lord Montrose, we will find a high place for you. Louise of Bohemia, we invite you to join the Hierarchy. We will make you a great lady of our Court. Or, if you will not, go in peace, laden with treasure. We ask only that you refrain from using it to arm rebel troops."

Montrose bowed. "Thank you, Dread Lords and Ladies." The angels gazed silently at him, and he realized that they now expected him and Louise to take their leave. "Forgive me, but do I understand that we're dismissed?"

"As we've explained," quavered the Ashen Lady, "we have grave matters to discuss."

"I understand," said Montrose. "With your permission, we'd like to discuss them with you."

After a pause, the Quiet Lord inclined his head.

"Thank you," said the Scot. "You've spoken of the difficulty you'll have quelling the anxieties of the your subjects, and replacing the Avatar of Violence. I *haven't* heard you say anything about the Spectres."

"You told us you killed this Demetrius," said the Emerald Lord, "and smashed the mirror which might have afforded his fellow doomshades passage from Charon's cavern into your master's Seat."

"That's true," said Montrose. "I also told you that Demetrius said that he and his fellows had devised a two-pronged strategy. The other part is unfolding along the Mississippi even as we speak. I want to lead an army back there to deal with it."

"And which of us, I wonder, will weaken himself by proffering a portion of his personal forces?" said the Laughing Lady.

"This is incredible," said Louise. "You Deathlords are supposed to be so *wise*, yet you didn't learn anything from the way Demetrius exploited your mutual distrust, did you?"

"To the contrary," said the Princess of Insanity. "We confirmed just how deeply and bitterly divided we truly are."

"None of you has to give me troops from his own Legions," said Montrose. "I can take some of the Smiling Lord's men. Or recruit from one of the forces sworn to the Hierarchy as a whole. The Grim Riders, the Sacred Band, or, if you'll grant me my preference, the Fifth Legion." He reflected fleetingly that it would feel good to don the regalia of a Black Hawk commander once again.

"No," said the Emerald Lord.

Montrose frowned. "May I ask why not?"

"In a time of turmoil, when our enemies may well perceive us as weak and vulnerable, we prefer to keep all available forces close at hand, to guard the capital against invasion and unrest."

"Exactly the result Demetrius hoped to achieve," the Cavalier replied, "and thus, good reason to do the opposite. The Isle of Sorrows is as near impregnable as any bastion could be. Surely you can risk the diversion of a fraction of your forces."

"Please," said Louise. "Thousands of wraiths are in jeopardy, and quite possibly many of the Quick as well."

"You don't know that," said the Ashen Lady. "You don't know what the Spectres are planning, or even precisely who they are."

"No," said Montrose, "we don't. That piece of the puzzle is still missing. All we know is that they feel they're avenging some ancient wrong. But consider the disaster they nearly wrought here, merely as a feint. Do you truly doubt that their attack against the Shadowlands could prove equally devastating?"

"I suppose not," the Laughing Lady said. "But in the final analysis, any one of our Earthly provinces is expendable. So long as we maintain an outpost somewhere in the Shadowlands, we can weather any number of defeats and calamities there. The capital, conversely, *must* endure, or the Imperium will perish with it."

Louise spread her hands, in supplication or helpless incredulity. "Why should anyone care if it perishes, if it won't even defend its own subjects?"

"When possible," said the Beggar Lord, "we do. But sometimes one must sacrifice a limb to ensure the health of the body as a whole."

"I think," said the Sister of Athena, "that the only health you're concerned about is yo—"

"Dread Lords and Ladies," said Montrose, raising her voice to cut her off, "I respectfully disagree with your decision, but needless to say, I accept it. Louise and I will travel to Natchez alone, and work with the Hierarchs there to defeat the Spectres. All I ask of you is a writ absolving me of all charges and restoring my authority."

"Are you certain you wish to do this?" asked the Emerald Lord. "The Tempest seems particularly unstable of late. One can sense there's already another Maelstrom brewing. The realm of chaos will be especially hazardous, the more so for two spirits traveling alone."

"You've played a hero's part already," said the Ashen Lady. "Faced a thousand perils and ordeals. No one will blame you if you now lay down your sword and enjoy the bounty your courage has won you."

Montrose felt the teasing caress of temptation. It *would* be considerably more pleasant to stay in the Onyx Tower. What's more, the demigoddess in gray was absolutely correct. If he hadn't earned the right, who had?

But how could he sit idly by while the doomshades menaced countless souls, some of them his own irregulars? How could he abandon his war against the Spectres when the monsters had forced him to slay the very lord he'd once vowed to protect?

Besides, he knew what Louise would opt to do, with him or without, so he really had no choice.

"I'm afraid we have a duty to go," he said.

"As you wish," said the Emerald Lord. "I will prepare your writ."

TWENTY-ONE

Against his better judgment, Dunn took another deep breath. St. Mary's Children's Hospital smelled of cleanser and antiseptic. That was all a human would smell. But the werewolf also caught the rich scents of blood, raw wounds, and pus. Saliva flooded his mouth, and his stomach growled. His skin tingled, trying to sprout fur.

Dr. Quitman gave him a smile. The hospital administrator was a dapper little man with soft, manicured hands, a blue silk tie, and a matching handkerchief peeking from the breast pocket of his expensive pearl-gray suit. The guy struck Dunn as a born pencil pusher, who probably hadn't treated a patient in years. "Hungry?" the human asked.

Dunn most certainly was. He should have known better than to expose himself to the scent of gore on an empty stomach. But he'd been running around like a ferret on speed since coming to Natchez, helping the ghosts get ready for D-Day, hoping he wouldn't run into any of his fellow agents from the FBI branch office. Now that he'd gone AWOL, that would be a complication he didn't need.

"I'm fine," the Black Spiral Dancer said.

"Sure?" Quitman asked. "I know what people say about institutional food, but the hospital cafeteria really isn't bad."

"Thanks, but I had lunch before I came." Down the corridor, in one of the playrooms, a little boy made machine-gun, explosion, and ray-gun noises. Dunn, who'd seen the plump, blond seven-year-old during the course of his tour, imagined himself sinking his fangs into the child's throat. After a moment, the boy blurred into Frank Bellamy. Shivering, Dunn thrust the fantasy aside. "And I think I've seen everything I need to see."

Quitman pouted. "You haven't seen the MRI. It's state of the art. We don't have to shut the children up in one of those cramped little cylinders...." He sighed. "But of course, that's not why you're here. I'm so used to showing reporters, visiting health care professionals, and potential philanthropists around the place that I have trouble shifting gears. Are you ready to give me your recommendations?"

"Yeah."

"Then let's go back to my office."

It was quite a luxurious office, where diplomas, certificates, and medical books shared space with plaques, ribbons, and photographs celebrating Quitman's achievements as a dressage rider, whatever that was. Through the window, Dunn could see the Natchez Eola Hotel, with a carriage full of tourists at the curb. The driver flicked the reins, and his blinkered chestnut gelding pulled the vehicle out toward the center of Pearl Street.

When he'd been in the room before, Dunn hadn't noticed the blood scent, but it was floating here now. Once a hunter registered such an enticing odor, it was all but impossible to screen it out, even when it was a distraction and a torment. He supposed he'd just have to bear it as best he could.

"Well," said Quitman, leaning forward across his desk, "what do you think? Is our security adequate?"

"I'm afraid not," said Dunn. He wondered if the taste of a cigarette would block out the blood smell, not that it mattered. The hospital was a no-smoking building, and though he didn't ordinarily worry about such nonsense, it would be stupid to alienate Quitman when he wanted to enlist the human's cooperation. "If a clever, determined psychopath from the outside wanted to hurt the kids, he could get onto the wards without a lot of trouble. And if somebody on the *inside* goes berserk, your problem's even worse."

"Good lord," said Quitman, "do you honestly think we need to worry about *that?*"

"Do you follow the news at all, Doctor?"

Quitman grimaced. "Of course. I realize the kind of things that have been happening, even in other medical facilities. But I *know* my staff. I trust them."

"And they probably deserve it," said the werewolf. "On the other hand, everybody trusted the killers, too, right up until the moment they snapped."

"The government must have *some* theory about what's happening."

"I'm just a Federal cop, not a scientist. But from what I hear, they have a million theories. Just no evidence to back any of them up."

"They haven't even identified any symptoms, any warning signs that someone is about to lose his mind?"

"No," said Dunn, enjoying the human's increasing agitation. This sort of bewildered desperation was precisely what the Atheist conspiracy had set out to achieve. "The experts at Quantico can't get a handle on it. They've collected tons of data on mass murderers and serial killers over the years, but none of it's relevant to the current situation."

"Well, it's just awful," Quitman said glumly. "You know, my wife thinks we should drop everything and move away. Not just to another part of the country, but to Australia. She thinks the phenomenon is going to spread." His lip curled. "Expert epidemiologist that she is. Amazing what people learn majoring in Art History these days, isn't it?"

"You can't blame her for being scared," said Dunn. "I've thought about resigning from the Bureau and clearing out of Mississippi myself. Because whatever's happening, how do I know it isn't going to happen to me? Or to the Fed standing behind me with a loaded gun ready to hand in his holster? But I guess cops and doctors are alike. We take an oath to serve the public. Which means we have to stick it out and cope."

Quitman nodded. "Exactly. I wish I could make her see that. But I shouldn't be wasting your valuable time moaning about how my better half doesn't understand me. What is it the hospital needs?"

"Better locks," said Dunn, drinking in the blood scent. His teeth and jaw ached with the urge to change form. "Security cameras watching every door and corridor. Twice as many guards on every shift, partly because they should also be keeping an eye on one another."

"Good grief," said Quitman, "do you know how much that's going to cost? There's no money in the budget."

"That's what everybody else told me at all my previous stops. Obviously, it's your decision what to do. It could be that nobody will ever give you any trouble. On the other hand..."

"Can't the police provide security?"

"We wish. They're stretched paper-thin as it is. What with everybody's nerves scraped raw, they're getting three times as many calls as they're set up to handle. And no call is simple anymore. Whenever an officer approaches the public, he sort of has to convince them that he's not going to flip out and start gunning them down before he can deal with the issue at hand."

Quitman sighed. "All right. We'll do as much as we can."

"I think that's smart. We need to talk about something else, too. An evacuation plan."

The doctor cocked his head. "I beg your pardon?"

"I told you that the scientists don't know what to make of what's happening in this part of the South. But they do know how to chart trends, and make projections. If we keep having more and more murders, and the public keeps getting edgier and edgier in response, it's *possible* that Natchez could have itself a full-scale disaster. Scores, maybe hundreds of crazy guys going on the rampage all at once. Or mobs of hysterical citizens rioting. Or both things happening at once. If that happens, the only way to protect all the people who need it most—like your patients—will be to bring them all to one secure location. Otherwise the police won't have enough manpower."

"You can't actually believe it will come to that!"

"I'm not a scientist, Doc, so I wouldn't venture to guess. I just know somebody made a contingency plan in case it does, and I'm supposed to bring you up to speed on it. If Natchez blows up, and the hospital is in imminent danger, a bunch of vans and ambulances will turn up at your door. Your staff will need to help the drivers load the kids into them as fast as possible, along with their records."

"And where will you take them?"

"Sorry, but for the time being, that's on a need-to-know basis. The fewer people we tell, the less likely it is that we'll give the information to somebody who will eventually go nuts. But it's a safe place, and it's got medical facilities."

"That's all very well, but some of these children shouldn't *be* moved."

"We won't do it unless we're pretty damn sure they'll be slaughtered in their beds if we don't."

Quitman grimaced. "All right, I understand. Our staff will need to accompany the children, of course."

"Our doctors and nurses will be glad to have the reinforcements," Dunn replied. "But I suspect that at least some of your team will decide they need to get home to their own kids and families."

"Possibly so," said Quitman. "I'll brief everyone on the plan, and ask for volunteers to stick with the patients for the duration. And pray to God that things never get so bad that they actually have to do it."

"I'll second that," said Dunn, rising from his chair. "And now, unless you've got more questions, I've got other places to visit."

When he exited Quitman's office, the aroma of blood assailed him again. It seemed even richer and more enticing than before. His head swimming, swallowing repeatedly, he strode down the hallway toward the elevator.

He tried not to look into the rooms on either side of the corridor, but a particularly sweet strand of the blood scent wafted through a doorway and tugged at him. From the corner of his eye, he glimpsed a tiny black girl with plaited hair lying asleep in a private room. Her mouth hung open, revealing the gaps where two of her baby teeth had fallen out. A Raggedy Ann doll lay beside her atop the quilt. The werewolf halted.

Why not, he thought, his shoulders beginning to swell inside his clothes, when it would be so easy? Just slip inside the room, close the door, snap the kid's neck, and eat his fill. It would be just one more mysterious atrocity, which shouldn't be a problem considering that he and his fellow conspirators were in the mysterious atrocity business.

But unfortunately, it would be. When the Natchez cops came to investigate, Quitman would no doubt tell them about the FBI agent who might still have been hanging around the hospital at the time of the murder. He'd probably allude to the government's grand and glorious evacuation plan, whereupon the local law would inform him that as far as they knew, there was no such thing. Which would spoil the con job Dunn had given him.

Forcing himself into motion, the Black Spiral Dancer told himself that he'd soon find some unfortunate human alone on the street. With luck, he could be chowing down in under fifteen minutes.

TWENTY-TWO

Mike Fink stalked down the line of stripped and manacled Heretic prisoners. Most of the captives trembled, cringed, and refused to meet the eyes of the man who, since Montrose's arrest, had commanded the Inquisition in the field. Others held themselves still and expressionless. A few dared to glower at him, and one woman, a rather pretty one with big brown eyes, a pale, buxom body and curly black hair, snarled, "Jehovah will punish you for your sins, Hierarch."

Fink jammed the muzzle of his Mag-10 Roadblocker shotgun under her chin, lifting her up onto tiptoe. He leered into her face, watching defiance wilt into fear, and then pulled the trigger. The darksteel shot blew her head into wisps of ectoplasm. Her body melted away in a cascade of black light before she could even topple to the ground.

Fink's irregulars laughed raucously. Some of the other prisoners screamed and wailed.

The former keelboat master frowned, a little puzzled by his own behavior. It wasn't that he regretted what he'd done, exactly. Even when he'd been alive a century and a half ago, he'd amused his drinking companions by shooting a tin cup off his woman's head, and if anything, he'd grown less squeamish about his entertainments since. On occasion he liked to ram an iron hook through a slave's body, shove him through a Nihil, and fish for Spectres. Or chain up a Thrall behind a barrier, with just a portion of his head peeking over the top, and have himself the ghostly equivalent of a turkey shoot.

But ordinarily, when he endangered, hurt, or killed somebody outside of combat, there was some sport or joke to it. This time, there hadn't been, even though a number of the men *had* laughed. He'd simply acted on impulse, and the result was the waste of a woman who would have been a lot more fun to screw than to kill, and who would have fetched a handsome price from the slavers.

Maybe Mother Prudence was right. Maybe the stress of spearheading the campaign against the god-lovers was wearing on him, at least to some degree. Much as he disliked consulting the Pardoner, partly because he sometimes had trouble remembering precisely what they'd said and done afterwards, perhaps he ought to call on her tonight.

He realized his troops were watching him expectantly, uncertainly, and felt a surge of anger. "What are you bastards standing around for?" he roared. "You know what to do. Figure out exactly what prisoners and other plunder we've got. Pick your shares—Johnny, you choose one for me—and deliver the rest to the Citadel. I'm going up there now."

He put a fresh shell in the shotgun and shoved the weapon into the scabbard on his back, where it hung beside his ax. Then he turned and tramped away from the Inquisition's motley fleet of boats, now moored at the dilapidated docks, his guerrillas, and their captives. Some sentry upriver had evidently watched the victorious crusaders sail by, then alerted the Governors to expect them, because a flunky—the wraith of a lanky young man with a buzz cut, whose tank-top showed off the bald eagle tattooed on his left shoulder—had fetched Fink's white, scarlet-eyed spirit horse down to the water.

Actually, the keelboatman still thought of Alexander as Montrose's steed, but he supposed his friend and erstwhile commander wouldn't begrudge him the use of the Phantasy. A wraith whom the Deathlords had no doubt executed in some excruciating fashion couldn't begrudge anyone much of anything. Scowling at the melancholy thought, he reached into the pocket of his jeans for an obolus to tip the hostler.

Alexander shied, nearly pulling the reins free from the unwary servant's hand.

Fink didn't know what to make of it. As far as he could judge, his movements hadn't been particularly abrupt, or otherwise alarming. "Take it easy, boy," he murmured, holding out his hand. "You know me."

The stallion backed away again. The hostler grabbed the beast by the bridle, but even so, couldn't control him. Tossing his luminous white head, Alexander merely dragged the wraith along.

Fink's muscles clenched in anger. He couldn't imagine what ailed the horse—he'd ridden him at least twenty times before—but by hell, he knew how to teach the rebellious creature who was master. He called on his Haunter Arcanos. Instantly the power rose inside him, like a vicious dog about to be unleashed on helpless prey.

Sneering, the guerrilla captain raised his arm, and his hair stood on end. The air hummed, and smelled of ozone. Alexander struggled to escape the hostler. The servant shot Fink an anguished, imploring look. Clearly he had some notion of what was to come, and realized the electrical discharge would fry him, too. But he was too frightened of the notorious former outlaw to release the spirit horse and scramble away without permission.

"Wait!" someone cried.

Startled, Fink turned. Valentine, looking to the river man's eye absurd and somehow offensive in his new green sash and contemporary clothes, came trotting out of a shadowy side street. Behind him skulked a small, sharp-featured woman decked out in hippie regalia, with a flintlock pistol tucked in her tie-dyed sash.

"I think I can calm him down," said the dwarf. "He knows me."

"Mind your own damn business," Fink growled.

"Think," pleaded Valentine, still advancing on the animal. "He's valuable, and if you zap him, you could destroy him."

Much as Fink disliked the former jester, he had to admit he had a point. Alexander would be worth a fortune even in Stygia, where, according to Montrose, captured Phantasies were somewhat more common. Here in the desolate Shadowlands, the stallion was damn near priceless. And the Inquisitor even liked the beast, when he wasn't acting crazy.

"All right," said Fink, "take a shot." If Valentine failed to quiet the horse, he could barbecue the two of them together.

Valentine eased toward Alexander, crooning endearments and reassurances. The stallion stopped trying to wrench himself away from the hostler and watched the little man approach. Eventually Alexander stopped trembling and lowered his head. Valentine petted him on the nose.

The dwarf turned toward Fink. "Whatever was making him skittish, I think he's all right now."

Fink felt an urge to cut loose with his magick anyway, just for the hell of it. Stifling the impulse, permitting his charge of mystical energy to dissipate, he walked toward Alexander. The Phantasy watched him placidly. For a moment, he had the odd fancy that Alexander had detected a difference in him, a difference that had vanished now, or crawled back into its hole, but then dismissed the notion with a scowl. Horses were notoriously stupid and erratic. That was one reason he'd always preferred boats.

He took hold of Alexander's reins. The hostler, still looking frightened enough to wet himself, had the Restless been capable of that particular bodily function, bowed and scurried away.

Fink sneered at Valentine. "You're stupider than I thought, getting in the line of fire when I've got a mad on and my Haunter powers all revved up."

"I just didn't want to see Alexander hurt." Valentine reached up with one of his stubby hands and stroked the spirit horse's shining leg. "Montrose really cared about him."

"And you were *such* a good buddy to Montrose." Fink still didn't *know* that Valentine had stolen the Stygian's treasonous journal to help Gayoso bring him down, but the dwarf's recent promotion had done nothing to allay his suspicions.

Valentine's face twisted, whether in annoyance or guilt, the river man couldn't tell. "I guess I also stepped in because I wanted to get on your good side. So I could ask you for a favor."

"Now that's a lot funnier than any of the lame jokes you used to tell when you were dancing around in your little clown suit."

"Please," said Valentine, "just hear me out. This is Belinda Talley."

The hippie edged forward, looking as wary and nervous as people often looked when meeting Fink for the first time. Still, she offered him her hand. "Hi," she said.

"Evening," Fink said, taking her hand and leering. "I know that most of the real men in these parts are away most of the time, fighting the Heretics. But even so, you can do a lot better than the runt here. Hell, I could spare you an hour or two myself."

"We do want some of your time," said Belinda, tugging her fingers from his grasp. "We need your help. Do you know about Valentine's friend Daphne?"

Fink rolled his eyes. "Not this again. You aren't going to tell me that you were in love with the little whore too?"

The hippie's mouth tightened. "No, Captain. I never even met her. But my little girl, who entered the Underworld when I did, is missing, too."

"Other Restless children have vanished, also," Valentine said. "And we think we know why." Speaking rapidly, excitedly, he tried to tie each disappearance to a silent man in a blue mask and a long coat, whom he suspected of being a serial killer.

Despite Fink's dislike for the little man, the story engaged his interest. It really did sound as if Valentine and Belinda might have stumbled onto something. And if some maniac was slaughtering children, that was rather a shame. There weren't all that many kid ghosts to begin with, and without them the realm of the Restless would seem even deader, even more like a thin shadow of the world of the living.

Still, it was none of his concern, and he said as much. "My job is running the crusade, not policing the city. Tell Gayoso your story. He can order the regular Legionnaires to chase your man in the blue mask. Fate knows, the gutless bastards aren't good for anything else."

"We did talk to the Governor," Valentine replied. "He said he'd look into it, as far as he was able, but it was pretty obvious he doesn't really plan on doing anything meaningful." He hesitated as if reluctant to confide something embarrassing. "And then he gave me my new job. It was like he was doing it to distract me from asking any more questions."

Fink frowned. "That's funny. Not that Gayoso, Shellabarger, and old lady Duquesne have ever given much of a damn about people getting themselves kidnapped and murdered in Under-the-Hill, but still, you'd think the spic son of a bitch would want to take action this time, if only to keep himself from looking like an asshole. He must know there's something about the notion of a child murderer that really punches people's buttons. And even if Gayoso doesn't care about his reputation, why would he want to stop you two fools from asking questions?"

"We don't know," Valentine said. "We don't know how to find the answers, either. But you do. If you can catch Heretics all over the province, then surely you can flush out one maniac hiding right under our noses here in Natchez."

"Of course I could," said Fink. "But like I told you, I've already got a job."

"Don't you care about the children?" Belinda asked.

Fink shrugged. "Not all that much. I've killed a few kids myself over the years. Never just for fun, but the notion of somebody else doing it isn't likely to ruin my evening. Hell, these are *ghost* children we're talking about. Most of them have been kicking around the Shadowlands for years and years. Some have adult minds, like Daphne, and maybe the ones who can't grow up aren't fit to survive."

Belinda goggled at him, clearly horrified at his attitude. Her dismay amused him, but, to his surprise, it also brought a fleeting twinge of discomfort.

"You could be right," Valentine said. "But I thought you didn't like Gayoso. We don't know what he's hiding. Maybe nothing, maybe we're reading him all wrong. But if he is covering something up, wouldn't it be fun to expose it?"

"I have to admit," said the hulking keelboatman, "that's a more persuasive argument." He shot Belinda a grin. "I wouldn't mind screwing him over. Hell, if we made him look really bad, maybe he'd get himself arrested like Montrose did, or at least be dumped from command of the Inquisition. Not that I particularly want to answer to Shellabarger or Mrs. Duquesne, either, but it might be a step up. They might be a little more sensible in terms of how much they expect of me and my boys, and how much support they give us."

"You'd also be carrying on Montrose's work," said Valentine. "You know he thought Natchez was facing some hidden threat. Something to do with a series of murders in the Skinlands, false Pardoners—"

The mention of Pardoners made Fink visualize Mother Prudence's round, placid face, and then, as if she'd whispered a warning to him, he suddenly realized what Valentine was up to. The insight brought a pang of anger. "You miserable little freak."

Valentine gaped up at him. "Excuse me?"

"You thought you could con me into going against Gayoso," said Fink. Alexander squealed and tried to pull away from him, and, intent on Valentine, he let go of the reins. He could catch and punish the rebellious animal later. "Then you warn him I'm plotting treason, I get arrested like Montrose, and you get *another* promotion."

"I swear by the Scythe and the Lantern," said Valentine, "that wasn't the idea at all. We just want you to help us look for the kids and the man in the blue hood. Nobody could call that treason in and of itself. I was just saying, if all the mysteries are tied together, then maybe by solving one—"

"You thought you could trick me," said Fink. Roused by his anger, his Arcanos power stirred, and he allowed it to express itself as it pleased. The air grew suddenly cold, and tendrils of frost crept along the cracked, filthy pavement and the derelict buildings on either side. "*Me*, Mike Fink, the king of the Mississipp! Damn your impudence!"

Valentine backpedaled. Fink decided to give him a few steps, just enough to make him hope he might actually get away, and then pounce.

"Please," said Belinda, lifting her hands in supplication, "you've got it all wrong."

Fink sneered at her. "The next time I look over at you, Missy, you'd better be naked." He lunged, grabbed Valentine, and hoisted him into the air.

Haunters drew their power from chaos itself. Thus, the effects could be somewhat unpredictable, even for an adept of the Arcanos. On this occasion, Fink was delighted to realize that the chill his magick had evoked had suffused his own flesh. When he shifted his grip on the writhing Valentine, he tore away clothing and skin which had frozen to his hands. He wondered if the same thing would happen every time he pulled back after thrusting himself into the hippie.

He sank his fingers deep into Valentine's flesh. The dwarf squirmed even more frantically, but of course, puny thing that he was, he had no chance whatsoever of breaking free of the strongest man on the river. In seconds, his lips turned blue, and the first sluggish wave of shadow rippled under his dead-white skin. "Freeze, you little rat," the mercenary said. Belinda stood and stared, her features a mask of anguish.

Rapid hoof beats clopped across the pavement.

By the time Fink whirled, Alexander was already rearing, towering over even a huge man like himself. The spirit horse's scarlet eyes burned like bonfires. His front hooves were poised to batter his master to pulp. Fink fleetingly recalled how clever he'd felt, the day he'd decided to have the beast shod with darksteel.

He lifted Valentine higher, using the dwarf as a shield. Alexander's hooves hammered down. One struck the little man in the chest, but the other hurtled past to smash into Fink's right shoulder.

Fink reeled backward and fell, losing his grip on Valentine in the process, though scraps of cloth and steaming, evaporating ectoplasmic skin still adhered to his fingers. Moving with a precise grace that was almost dainty, the white stallion closed in on him again.

Fink tried to draw his shotgun, but his arm didn't work. Struggling to focus past the shock of his injury, to maintain his control of his magick, he lashed out at Alexander with that.

Arcs of dazzling, crackling electricity leaped from the pavement and transfixed the spirit horse's body. The Phantasy shuddered, and the stench of burning flesh and hair filled the air. When the discharge stopped, Alexander collapsed.

Panting reflexively, Fink grinned. "That'll teach you, you bastard." And he meant to finish teaching Valentine as well. He willed a pulse of psychic energy into his shoulder—the wound throbbed fiercely, but began to heal—and peered about to see where the dwarf had gone.

As it turned out, he hadn't gone far. Half flayed and chilled to the core, he hadn't even managed to stand up. Instead, he was crawling spastically in the paralyzed Belinda's general direction, like some blind, soft creature one might find beneath a rock.

Fink flexed his right arm, then clenched his fist. The movements hurt, but everything was working again. He scrambled after Valentine and grabbed him by the ankle.

As he did, he realized his touch wasn't cold anymore. He'd expended the last of his charge of magick blasting Alexander. But it would be just as satisfying to destroy Valentine with pure brute force. He pulled the little man close, bit off the top half of an ear, and then started slamming his skull against the ground.

"Let him go!" Belinda wailed.

Fink ignored her.

"I mean it!"

The keelboatman stiffened his thumb to gouge Valentine's eye. Then a gun barked, and pain lanced through the side of his neck.

He looked up at Belinda. Eyes squinched shut, she was clutching her flintlock pistol with both hands. After another moment, when she finally dared to look and see what she'd done, her mouth fell open, and she trembled.

"Didn't think you had the nerve," said Fink, releasing Valentine and dragging himself to his feet. "And you're going to wish I was right." He pulled the ax off his back and started forward.

Valentine croaked, "Run!"

But the hippie stood and gaped at Fink's approach, her finger repeatedly, probably unconsciously squeezing the trigger of her empty single-shot pistol. The big man whirled the ax above his head.

A fresh surge of pain from his wounds washed away his strength and his balance together, and he fell heavily. The ax slipped from his fingers and clattered on the pavement.

"Move!" cried Valentine. "Help me!"

This time, Belinda heeded him. She stuffed the flintlock back into her rainbow-colored sash, dashed to the dwarf, picked him up, and clutched him against her chest like a baby. Staggering under the weight of her burden, she fled up the street.

"No!" snarled Fink. They were *not* going to escape. He hauled himself to his knees and fumbled out the Mag-10.

When he tried to sight down the barrel, he could have screamed in frustration, because his eyes played tricks on him. One moment, he saw two women stumbling away. The next, the whole shadowy, moonlit street melted into a gray blur.

"Come on," he whispered, "come on!" As if in response to his entreaty, his vision began to clear. Murkily he saw Alexander roll to his feet and limp toward Belinda. The stallion had burned black patches on his shining white hide, and one eye was a duller red than the other, as if the lightning had charred it blind.

Grunting, the hippie lifted Valentine onto Alexander's back, where he clutched at the Phantasy's mane. Then she tried to scramble up behind him, a task rendered difficult by her small stature.

Still, frantic as she was, she was going to make it onto the horse any second. Fink couldn't wait for his eyes to focus completely, or for the throbbing in his wounds to go away. He aimed at Alexander's withers—with luck, the expanding cloud of shot would hit the stallion and both his would-be passengers, too—and squeezed the trigger.

When the Roadblocker roared, his targets jerked. Valentine nearly tumbled off the spirit horse's back. But nobody went down. To Fink's disgust, he'd missed them altogether.

He fired the second of his three rounds. Missed again. Belinda finally managed to jump onto Alexander's back. Instantly, the wounded stallion lurched into motion, galloping at only a fraction of his normal speed, but running nonetheless.

Forcing himself to take his time, Fink sighted in on the moving target. He *had* it, was leading it just by a hair, squeezed the trigger. And at that precise instant, Alexander plunged into the mouth of an alley and disappeared. The Mag-10 boomed and kicked Fink's shoulder, uselessly.

A number of his irregulars ran up to him. He wondered why they'd held back until now, then realized they'd probably started toward him the moment the trouble began. It was just that the whole fight had taken less than a minute.

"Are you all right, Captain?" a mercenary in the back of the crowd asked hesitantly.

"Course I am," Fink snarled, struggling to his feet. Someone tried to help him and he shoved the fool away.

For an instant he contemplated telling Gayoso about Valentine's lies and treachery, but discarded the notion at once. It was common for Hierarchs to plot against one another as they competed for power and advancement. Rumor had it that each of the three Governors and even the Deathlords themselves aspired to depose their fellows. Thus, Gayoso might not consider that the jester had done anything wrong.

And even if he would, Fink had his reputation to consider. He couldn't see telling anyone that the Salt River Roarer himself, the walking, talking legend who bragged that he could out-wrestle, out-shoot, out-lie, out-magick, out-sail, and out-fuck any ghost on the Mississipp, had had trouble disposing of a dwarf, a hippie girl, and a horse. It was bad enough that some of his troops had witnessed the fiasco.

No, Fink decided, he'd handle Valentine himself, first time it was convenient. It would be more fun that way anyhow.

TWENTY-THREE

Valentine bolted upright. The brassy allegro music sounded like mocking laughter, and now, suddenly, something was wrapped around his hands. He desperately fumbled them free of it, clutched blindly at the air before him, but failed to grab a single one of the Indian clubs. In an instant, they'd clatter on the stage.

Something touched him on the shoulder. He screamed.

Belinda jerked her hand back. "It's all right! It's only me! We got away."

Valentine peered about. He wasn't in the Citadel after all. He was lying on a pallet in a grubby, sparsely furnished little room, dimly illuminated by the moonlight leaking past the window shade. The binding that had constrained his hands was a fringed buckskin vest that Belinda had evidently tossed over him. The music was rising through the floor.

There was a second pallet across the room, this one surrounded by a rag doll, a rubber ball and jacks, and an Etch-a-Sketch. Starshine's toys, most likely.

"You were hurt pretty bad," Belinda said. "You passed out on Alexander's back, and Slumbered."

"Yeah," Valentine said. He realized he had the usual jangly feeling in his head to prove it. "I had a nightmare. I was a jester again, performing for Gayoso and Fink. And on the left side of the stage were the man in the blue mask, and Daphne. He had her strapped to a torture rack.

"I can't juggle in real life, and I couldn't in the dream, either. Every time I dropped something, Gayoso made me pay a penalty. Either Fink would cut off one of my fingers, or the man in the blue hood would stick a darksteel dagger in Daphne. I had to choose which."

The dwarf grimaced. "If Daphne got stabbed too many times, it would destroy her. But the more fingers I lost, the worse I was going to juggle. Until we got to a point where I couldn't do it at all, and had nothing left to slice off, and then that would be the end of her, too. I had to try to balance things out, and the nightmare went on and on. Or it felt like it, anyway."

Belinda covered his hand with hers. "It must have been awful. But at least it's over now."

"That's one way of looking at it. Or maybe I should think of it as a warm-up for the terrible things that probably really are going to happen to me. Where are we?"

"My room upstairs in the Nightlight Theater. They let me keep it, even though I haven't worked on a show since Starshine disappeared." Her mouth twisted. "I think the owner wants to get into my pants."

"You mean you haven't let him? You didn't think twice about putting out for a gun, so why not for a place to crash?"

Belinda simply looked at him for a moment, then said, "I'm sorry you got hurt. But *I* didn't do it."

Valentine's guts twisted. "I know. It's just that what Fink did to me was bad. Worse than anything anybody ever did before, before my death or since." He gingerly fingered his bitten ear, and found that the missing part had grown back. "Maybe we should get out of here. It's your own home, for Christ's sake. Fink wouldn't have any trouble finding us."

Her eyes widened. "You're right. I was so rattled, I never thought."

"How long was I out?"

"I don't know. Several hours. It's nearly dawn."

"Then don't panic. If he was hot on our trail, he would have gotten here by now. Maybe he's waiting for his own wounds to heal. Where's Alexander?"

"In an empty garage across the street. He's going to be okay, too."

"Good. We can ride him out of town."

Belinda frowned. "What are you talking about?"

"We pissed off Mike Fink. We have to run away." Which meant giving up both the security of a berth in the Citadel and the dignity of his new rank. For a moment, he hated her for luring him down this road.

"Are you worried he'll tell Governor Gayoso that you tried to draw him into a treasonous plot? You didn't, not really, and in any case, it's our word against his. And you said that Gayoso *hates* Fink, from the days when he was a criminal and the Hierarchs couldn't catch him."

"Still, it would be the word of a petty clerk and a vagrant from Under-the-Hill against that of the most valuable military leader in the province. However Gayoso feels inside, we couldn't count on him to come down on our side if it would mean an open break with a soldier who's important to the success of the crusade.

"To tell you the truth, though, I'm not worried about Fink complaining to Gayoso. That's not his style. Most likely, he'll just come gunning for us himself. Although..."

"What?" Belinda asked.

Valentine shook his head. "Just that maybe I shouldn't try to guess what he'll do. I *thought* I knew the guy. I've heard all the stories. I've spent Fate knows how many nights in the Green Head, watching him party. But I'd never seen the man who jumped me tonight.

"The difference wasn't that he was violent. Fink will slug or even shoot somebody at the drop of the hat. But he doesn't go berserk without *some* kind of a reason, and that's what happened down by the docks. One second we were talking, and the next, he just flipped out on us."

"So you're saying that he might leave us alone?"

The dwarf snorted. "Hell, no. I'm saying that whatever crazy thing is happening in Natchez, maybe it's finally got a hold on him. It's time to get out before, one way or another, it swallows us up, too."

"What about Daphne and Starshine?"

"Gone to the Void. Even if you won't admit it, you know it as well as I do." He gestured to the toys by the other pallet. "Your kid'll never play with that crap ever again."

"You may be right," said Belinda flatly. "In that case, don't you want revenge?"

"Give me a break. We *tried*, okay? Now it's time to look out for ourselves."

"I thought you wanted to make amends for hurting your friend Montrose. To be loyal to Daphne."

Valentine's eyes throbbed as if they could still shed tears. He twisted, averting his face from her. "That sounded pretty good, didn't it? The problem is that I'm not up to the job. When things turned nasty, *you* shot Fink. The fucking horse *trampled* him. All the *dwarf* could do was take whatever punishment was dished out, and then be carried off to safety like a piece of luggage."

"If Fink had grabbed me first, I would have been helpless, too. What's that got to do with anything? We don't need a fighter—"

"Don't be stupid. Obviously, if people are going to try to kill us, we *do*."

"No, we need somebody smart—"

"That's not me, either. My only ideas were to talk to Gayoso and then Fink, and look how great that worked out."

"Somebody who knows his way around Natchez," Belinda continued doggedly, "and that's you. If you're going to run out on me, tell me what you'd do if you stayed. Then maybe I can do it in your place."

"You need to get out of here yourself."

"Just tell me, damn it!"

"If I was reckless enough, I guess I could try to find a way to go through Gayoso's stuff like I did Montrose's," he said grudgingly. "Or spy on him in other ways."

Belinda grimaced. "That plan won't work for me. I don't have the run of the Citadel. What else would you try?"

"Hm." He frowned, mulling it over, until an idea popped into his head. But it was too dangerous, and thus, not worth sharing.

"What?" Belinda asked. He guessed that some flicker of expression had alerted her that he'd thought of something.

He sighed. "It's crazy. It would get us destroyed for sure. But I was just thinking that if we don't know how to find the man in the blue hood, maybe we could make him find us. With bait. Buy a kid from the slave market, have him wander around Under-the-Hill, and shadow him."

Belinda frowned. "I don't know if I could *own* a child, let alone put one in danger, even to trap Starshine's kidnapper."

"Well, I don't know if we could afford one anyway, prices being what they are. But we could hire a Masquer to make one of us look like a kid."

The hippie's eyes widened. "That's pretty clever. Why do you say it would get us destroyed?"

"Why do you think? Because we can't handle ourselves in a dangerous situation. We proved that tonight."

"I think we proved the opposite. I *shot* someone. Deep down, I never thought I could, but I did."

"Right. First you froze up for God knows how long, then you jerked off a lucky shot with your eyes closed, and after that, you froze again. You were like Dillinger in drag."

She glared at him. "The point is, we're not helpless, and we shouldn't give in to fear."

"You just haven't got a clue, have you? Pack up your stuff. We'll ride out after the sun comes up, and most people have gone indoors."

"You go," she said. "I like your idea, and I'm going to try it."

"It would be too risky even if somebody backed you up. You can't possibly pull it off alone."

"We'll see," Belinda.

I just killed her, Valentine thought, *as sure as if I'd cut her head off. If the murderer doesn't get her, Fink or somebody else will. Why couldn't I keep my big mouth shut?* In essence, it had been yet another betrayal, and he loathed her for drawing it out of him.

"Fine," he said. "You do what you like. I'm out of here." He rose, crossed the room, and stepped through the surface of the door, feeling the pressure of her gaze between his shoulder blades.

TWENTY-FOUR

The cabin cruiser cut through the dark water with a bobbing motion that made Astarte feel clumsy and unbalanced whenever she stood up. Off to the right—or to starboard, as Marilyn's pilot would put it—several oil tankers sat at anchor, their forms vague in the night. Above them on the riverbank loomed an oil refinery, fouling the air with a nasty smell.

Seated beside Astarte on the foredeck, Marilyn gave a grunt of pain or effort, and then muttered, "Damn."

"Are you hurting?" Astarte asked.

"Absolutely," said the occultist, "but that's not why I'm sputtering curses. I was trying to accelerate my healing with magick, but nothing happened. You'd think that if I could revitalize a ghost queen, I could do as much for myself, wouldn't you?"

"You gave Marie strength she didn't have before. It makes sense that if a person pulls energy out of himself and then puts it back, he doesn't gain anything."

"That's very insightful," said Marilyn sourly, "but there ought to be a way around the problem. It's infinitely frustrating, knowing this newfound talent of mine could work miracles, reliably, every time, if only I understood the underlying principles. Since I joined the Arcanum, I've read Lord knows how many magickal texts, and some of what they teach turns out to be valid, but it's obvious they merely scratch the surface."

"At least you got to be part of the supernatural world," Astarte said, hating the resentful, whiny note in her voice but unable to hold her tongue. "Despite everything we've been through, I'm still stuck on the outside looking in."

"You have a ghost for a lover. If that isn't intimacy with the supernatural, what is?"

"It would feel a lot more intimate if we were on the same boat." She glowered at the expanse of water ahead. All she could see was a long, low barge floating downriver, but assumed that the *Twisted Mirror* was still steaming along in front of them.

"Agent Bellamy comes aboard whenever he's ready to materialize," Marilyn said reasonably. "You can't expect him to spend all his time here, even when he's trapped in the Underworld. I imagine it's painful for him to hover around you when you can't see or hear him."

"I guess," Astarte said. "But then he should let Titus bring me into his dimension again."

"I'm sure he'd like to, but he's trying to protect you."

"I don't want to be protected! I want to be with him, and to have what the rest of you have. To be back in the middle of the action. I don't want to know that magick and miracles are real, but just outside my reach."

"I sympathize," the Arcanist said. "I spent years feeling exactly the same way. But as you say, I finally found my way into the heart of the mysteries, even if the path wasn't one I would have chosen. With patience and perseverance, perhaps you will, too."

Astarte grimaced. "I'm not good at patience. Sometimes, when I'm hungry to touch Frank but can't stand the cold, or feel him dissolve out of my arms and back across the Shroud, I think, why the hell don't I just—" She realized she was saying more than she'd intended, and closed her mouth.

"Why don't you what?" Marilyn asked.

"Nothing," Astarte said. She resisted an impulse to put her hand on the Browning automatic under her black leather jacket, as if to keep Marilyn from taking it away from her.

The Arcanist's eyes narrowed. She seemed about to speak, then lurched around on her deck chair. "Something's happening in the spirit world," she said.

Astarte looked where her friend was peering. Saw nothing but the flat black expanse of the river.

Her blanket sliding off her legs, Marilyn grabbed her crutches and clambered up. Her long coat flapped in the breeze. Unsteadily, looking as if the rocking of the boat might pitch her off her feet at any instant, she hobbled toward the rail. "Tell the pilot to get us closer to the steamboat."

"How's he supposed to do that?" asked Astarte, jumping up from her own seat. "He can't see it. He doesn't even know it exists."

"You help him," Marilyn said. "I know you can't see it either, but estimate."

"Are you going to be all right up here?"

Marilyn dropped her crutches, swayed, and clutched at the rail. "Yes! Go!"

Astarte turned and scrambled down the companionway. She knew she shouldn't resent Marilyn barking orders at her, not when there was obviously an emergency going on. But she couldn't even tell what it was, and despite the alarm speeding her heart and drying her mouth, that blindness made her feel more shut out of Bellamy's world than ever.

TWENTY-FIVE

Lounging on the uppermost deck aft of the wheelhouse, Bellamy turned to look back at the cabin cruiser humming along in the *Twisted Mirror*'s insubstantial wake. With his inhumanly keen vision, he could make out Astarte plainly, even in the darkness. Her pale face, with its black makeup and piercings, wore its usual sullen scowl. The sight brought an intense pang of longing.

Titus laid a final milk-white stroke of color on his right profile, wiped his finger with a handkerchief, opened a second jar of pigment, and began painting the left side of his face blue. The resinous scent of the makeup stung Bellamy's nose, for a moment blocking out the reek of the refinery to starboard. "Does she like you better, now that I've made you white again?" the shaman asked.

"She didn't seem to care about that one way or the other," Bellamy replied. "She just wants to jump back across the Shroud, as often as you'll let her."

Titus grimaced. "Perhaps, on occasion, after things settle down."

"Are they ever going to settle down enough that there won't be Spectres lurking on the other side of the Nihils, and Shadows slithering around inside of each of us *abambo*, plotting to take control?"

"Sadly, no."

"Then I don't want her here. Particularly not if she's going to float around all wide-eyed and giddy like a kid at the circus. Until we think of a better answer, I'm just going to have to keep building up my Proctor powers, so I can spend more time with her in the land of the living."

"And you think that will satisfy her."

"I hope so," Bellamy said. "I'm assuming that if I build them up enough, my body won't feel cold to her anymore."

"Anyone can see that Astarte truly does love you," the old man said. "But I think you should remember that she didn't involve herself in the affairs of the *abambo because* of that. She journeyed to New Orleans because mundane existence doesn't satisfy her. Because she's thirsty for transcendent beauties and spiritual transformation, and, may the Orishas have mercy on her, hopes to find them among creatures like ourselves."

"Are you saying that I should keep bringing her into the Underworld?"

"Not necessarily," said Titus. He closed his left eye to paint the lid. "I'm saying that she'll never be content to let you be merely the lover who visits her every day to savor the pleasures of ordinary mortal existence. She'll never stop pressuring you to lead her into the heart of the supernatural."

"You may be right," Bellamy sighed. "We'll just have to work it out somehow, after we deal with the Atheist conspiracy. I wonder—"

A long, low shape scuttled up the companionway.

Bellamy turned to greet Antoine, then nearly flinched back a step. Because the alligator seemed indefinably different. Almost menacing. He stared up at the human wraiths for a moment, then growled, "I know I'm not the hotshot sorcerer of the team, Titus. But have you looked upriver lately?"

Titus and Bellamy peered out over the bow. At first the FBI agent couldn't see any cause for alarm. Then he noticed tendrils of a deeper blackness coiling through the dark air and water ahead. A wind began to gust, first from one direction, then another, rocking the *Twisted Mirror* but not disturbing the surface of the river. A hot, gritty feeling crawled on his skin.

"*Another* Maelstrom?" he said incredulously.

"So it appears," Titus said. "Forgive me for not sensing it forming, but I'm all but certain there was nothing *to* sense five minutes ago."

"You're just useless without your war paint," Antoine said. "What's the plan? Do we put in to shore?"

"I suppose we'd better," the old man said.

"I'm on it," Antoine said. He scrambled toward the wheelhouse to inform the pilot.

Bellamy gazed after the reptile *ibambo* for a moment. Antoine seemed his usual sardonic self. He supposed it was only his nerves that had made him think he perceived something amiss.

Lord knew, he had plenty to be edgy about, and the frequent storms weren't helping. He wondered if Astarte would be so eager to play tourist in the Shadowlands if she'd ever had to endure a Maelstrom, and glumly decided, yes, she probably would. She'd probably dance gleefully through the heart of it like Gene Kelly performing "Singing in the Rain."

The black riverboat with its macabre gingerbread shivered as it changed course, making for the nearer shore. Visible one second and gone the next among the refinery's storage tanks, shimmered the translucent form of a white plantation house, made up of a central structure with two long *garçonnieres*. The architecture was fundamentally Greek, but with a high-peaked, West Indian-style roof.

Bellamy had experienced more than his share of unexpected phenomena since entering the Underworld, but this was the first time he'd encountered the ghost of a *building*. He pivoted to ask Titus how such a thing could exist, and then the steamboat lurched, knocking both men off their feet.

As Bellamy lifted his head, the shadow storm unleashed its full fury. The wind howled, and stung his skin. It felt as if it were full of tiny razors, blades that could fray his flesh to tatters. Shielding his face with his upraised arm, he rose and staggered to the rail.

Glittering black Nihils now dotted the surface of the river like whirlpools. They couldn't swallow the water—they were on the wrong side of the Shroud for that—but a few yawned large enough to damage the boat or even devour it whole.

And the *Twisted Mirror* seemed to be drifting with the current and the wind. If unable to move under its own power, it *would* hit one of the rifts in space sooner or later. Stumbling on down the deck, clutching the rail to keep his balance, Bellamy peered down at one of the imposing paddle wheels. Given the angle, and the fact that the top of the device was hooded with a wooden cowl, it was hard to make out what, if anything, was wrong. But after a few moments he managed to discern that the wheel was turning, but sluggishly. A dark mass of *something* surrounded it below the waterline, and was evidently hindering its motion.

He turned. Titus was clinging to the rail on the other side. "We've got trouble!" Bellamy bellowed, making sure the shaman would hear him over the roar of the gale.

"I know!" Titus shouted. "Sinkinda interfering with the wheels!" He raised one hand and traced a complex pattern in the air. Sparks of emerald light winked on his fingertips. Meanwhile Antoine charged back into view and under the railing. His long body plunged into the black water like an arrow.

Bellamy drew his Browning and raced down the companionway. He wished he were carrying the automatic rifle stowed in his cabin, but was unwilling to take the time to detour and grab it. If he didn't reach the lowermost deck—from which he could shoot at the Spectres and have at least some chance of hitting them—immediately, he was likely to be too late.

When he staggered onto the middle deck, a shape hurtled out of the darkness. Startled, Bellamy lost his balance and sat down hard on the steps. The shape cackled madly and raised a dagger to stab him. Bellamy shot it in the chest.

His attacker collapsed, bands of black fire rippling through his body. At first, his attention drawn to the eroding body's hyena-like muzzle and long, mottled tongue, Bellamy assumed that the thing had been a Spectre which had clambered onboard from the river. Then he noticed the short, zebra-striped cape, and the thin silver bracelet, cast in the form of a coiling snake, encircling the left biceps. The creature had been a member of his own expedition until the power of the Maelstrom energized its shadowself and so twisted it into a servant of the Void.

Sickened, Bellamy lurched and made his way to the bottom deck, where several warriors had already gathered fore and aft of the paddle wheel to shoot bullets and crossbow bolts at the writhing black tangle under the water. He assumed that other soldiers had mounted a similar defense on the other side of the boat. Bolts of jagged green light—Titus's doing, no doubt—sizzled down from overhead, triggering muffled explosions beneath the surface.

Marilyn's cabin cruiser veered crazily back and forth, nearly passing through the *Twisted Mirror*'s stern at one point, then racing on upriver. Though the mortals' craft was impervious to the force of the storm attacking the sidewheeler, the sudden turns seemed likely to capsize it or run it into another boat anyway. Bellamy heard Astarte yell, "Left! Come back around! No, not that far!" The bewildered, frustrated pilot snarled an obscenity.

The blind leading the blind. In other circumstances, it might have been funny, but not now, particularly with Marilyn herself swaying on the bow, clinging to the steel rail for dear life, fresh spots of blood blooming on her bandages. Chanting in Latin to absolutely no effect, then crumpling onto the edge of the deck, where the next random motion of her vessel could easily tumble her into the water. Astarte cried out and scrambled topside.

Much as he sympathized with Marilyn's plight, Bellamy knew he could do nothing to help her. Astarte would have to handle that. He could only influence events on his own boat. Tearing his eyes away from the cabin cruiser, he took up a position in front of the paddle wheel, leaned out over the rail, and pointed his gun at the tangle of Spectres in the water.

As he did so, he realized he couldn't pick out Antoine from the mass of foes he was presumably attacking. Praying that he wouldn't hit the alligator, he fired.

Over the course of the next minute, wounded horrors floated to the surface, rotting away to nothingness even as they appeared. Occasionally a Sinkinda scrambled out of the water and on board the steamboat, laying about with fang and claw until the frantic defenders managed to cut or gun it down. But most of the doomshades stayed below the surface and continued to tamper with the wheel.

The wraith fighting alongside Bellamy screamed as the Maelstrom ripped his body into streamers of vapor. His crossbow fell overboard. A few seconds after that, the FBI agent fired the last bullet in his last clip, and peered wildly about for more ammo or a replacement gun.

"Whirlpool!" someone cried.

Bellamy looked down river. As he'd feared would happen eventually, the *Twisted Mirror* was drifting straight toward a swirling, seething Nihil big enough to engulf it. But a moment later, the paddle wheel began to turn a bit more rapidly. It was obvious that it and its mate were still fouled to some degree, but even so, vibrating with the strain, the black riverboat began to inch along against the current.

The surviving *abambo* cheered, and attacked the doomshades with renewed energy. Bellamy peered at the river, willing Antoine to surface. Surely the gator could see that the *Twisted Mirror* had resumed moving under its own power. If he didn't hurry back aboard, he'd be left behind amid the surviving Sinkinda.

But the reptile *ibambo* didn't reappear, which could only mean he was in trouble. Repressing a surge of fear at what he was about to attempt, Bellamy drew his darksteel shortsword, clenched the blade between his teeth, and clambered onto the rail.

Some well-meaning ally grabbed him by the arm. He wrenched himself free and dived into the water.

Like the air in the world above, the water existed to some degree on both sides of the Shroud. He found that with an effort, he could stroke and kick against it. But paradoxically, he could also feel the cold, liquid weight of it sliding unimpeded through his substance, a sensation so unpleasant that he shuddered in revulsion.

Spears and arrows plunged down around him. A crooked lance of green lightning blew a Spectre's head apart. Hoping to get clear of his comrades' attacks, Bellamy swam deeper, rolled over onto his back, and peered upward at the broad, flat bottom of the steamboat.

Even for wraith eyes, it was difficult to see through the benighted, murky water. However, aided by Titus's flashes, he could just make out the manner in which the Spectres were seizing, clinging to, and weighing down the paddle wheels. Jamming their own grotesque bodies into the works, allowing themselves to be torn apart or ground to nothingness, whereupon their fellows took their place. They plainly had no qualms about throwing their existences away, as long as they could harm someone else in the process.

Bellamy turned this way and that, looking for Antoine. Finally he saw the gator streak through the water, seize a Sinkinda resembling a huge, skeletal eel in his jaws, and roll over and over with the thing. The doomshade broke apart into a cloud of bones. Two other Spectres swam toward Antoine, and he whirled to meet them.

The *ibambo*'s scaly hide was nearly as mottled with punctures and slashes as it had been after the battle on Barracks Street. But he was clearly far from incapacitated. Bellamy could only assume that for some reason Antoine hadn't noticed the *Twisted Mirror* pulling out of its uncontrolled drift. It was up to his human friend to alert him. Holding his breath, even though he realized intellectually that he didn't need to, Bellamy swam toward the surface.

A Spectre resembling a jellyfish with an anguished human face on its side darted to intercept him, its translucent body pulsing. Its tentacles flicked out. Snatching the sword from between his teeth, hampered by the resistance of the water, Bellamy hacked at the creature's arms. More by luck than otherwise, he nicked the needle-like stinger at the tip of one limb. Even though he'd only touched it with his blade, the contact spiked pain through his hand and up his forearm. But the doomshade flinched back.

Intent on getting close enough to attack the monster's body, Bellamy kicked closer to it. Another tentacle flicked at his head, and he grabbed it behind the stinger.

That hurt, too. It burned like holding a piece of red-hot metal. He hated to think what an actual sting would feel like. Snarling against the pain, he yanked the jellyfish nearer and thrust his point into the center of its writhing face.

The Sinkinda popped like a balloon. Bellamy peered about, locating Antoine anew, and swam higher, the pain in his hands fading rapidly. As he drew nearer to the gator, he felt the churning, the suction, of the nearer paddle wheel. Another seeming impossibility, considering that the contraption didn't actually displace the water through which it rotated, but real nonetheless.

Tail lashing, strands of darkness oozing beneath his hide, Antoine surged up to the wheel itself, yanked a Spectre off one of the paddles, and dragged the monster down, his terrible jaws snapping open and shut. When he'd torn that foe to rags, he gazed upward, evidently choosing another.

And at that point, Bellamy reached him and touched him on the tail. With an agility no human swimmer could match, Antoine executed a sort of twisting somersault, spinning himself around toward the man who'd startled him. Even in the dark water, his eyes seemed to blaze, and his jaws gaped wide.

Bellamy's instincts screamed. He had to fight the impulse to lash out with his sword. Instead he simply raised his empty hand, signaling Antoine to halt, praying that his friend would recognize him before it was too late.

The human saw Antoine's jaws surge toward his shoulder. He imagined the gator wrenching his arm off, heard his shadowself laugh in the depths of his mind. Then Antoine faltered, and pulled back. He peered at Bellamy as if not quite certain he really did know him.

Bellamy wondered if Antoine was dazed from a concussion or something comparable. Wishing they could speak underwater, he pointed at the riverboat, creeping upriver toward the refinery once more.

Antoine followed the gesture, gazed at the *Twisted Mirror* for a moment, then turned and swam toward yet another Spectre.

Bellamy kicked after him. By the time he caught up with Antoine, the gator had bitten a doomshade resembling a man-sized, leprous monkey in two, and picked up a fresh set of gouges on his snout and neck for his trouble. The FBI agent thumped Antoine on the flank, demanding his attention, then pointed at the steamboat even more emphatically than before. The reptile glanced in that direction, glared sullenly at his companion, then propelled himself upward. But Bellamy could tell from his trajectory that he was intent on tearing another Spectre off a paddle wheel, not boarding.

Well, thought Bellamy grimly, at least Antoine getting closer to the *Twisted Mirror* was a start. He started after him, then glimpsed a flicker of motion from the corner of his eye.

He floundered around. The largest Sinkinda he'd seen tonight, a monster easily the size of a bus, was rising toward him from the riverbed. The thing looked a bit like a crude mud sculpture of a bear that was presently melting in the stream, with blobs and ribbons of slime breaking away from its body. Despite its ungainly appearance, it was approaching fast as a flying arrow.

Bellamy frantically pointed his blade at it. The world blazed green, and then turned black.

When he came to, he couldn't recall where he was or how he'd gotten there. He only knew he was drifting underwater. Drowning! Panicking, he tried to stroke toward the lesser darkness overhead, but his numb limbs barely stirred.

A flash of green illuminated the Spectres swirling around him, and the cloud of muck below, and memory came flooding back, including the grimly reassuring truth that ghosts didn't ordinarily need to breathe. Evidently Titus had blown the mud-bear to smithereens. Unfortunately, Bellamy had been so close to the blast that it had stunned him as well.

The *Twisted Mirror* accelerated, receding from him, its paddle wheels turning more rapidly. He tried to swim after it, but his muscles were still numb and unresponsive, altogether unequal to the challenge.

Though they must have recognized that the effort had already failed, the majority of the remaining Sinkinda continued their assault on the steamboat. But a couple—one resembling the rotting corpses of a pair of Siamese twins, the other a gaunt, bug-eyed, sexless thing wearing a harness of spiked leather straps—oriented on Bellamy.

Unlike some of their fellows, the creatures didn't look as if Oblivion had specifically shaped them for aquatic existence, and they stroked toward him clumsily. But not so clumsily that they couldn't catch him, half paralyzed as he was. He raised his sword hand, only then perceiving that the weapon was gone. He must have dropped it when Titus's thunderbolt knocked him senseless.

He wondered if he was strong enough to avoid the Spectres by shifting across the Shroud. Even if he did jump to the mortal world, taking on the vulnerabilities of the Quick, he might well drown before reaching the surface, but he didn't know what else to try. He struggled to rouse his Arcanos, and then jaws closed on his forearm.

Startled, he thrashed, and his assailant's teeth tore his skin. The creature gave him a brutal shake. In his enervated state, it was enough to stop him struggling, and when he did, he saw that it was Antoine who had taken hold of him.

Swinging around the Sinkinda, Antoine carried him in rapid pursuit of the riverboat. In a few seconds they came alongside the vessel, and surfaced. Hands reached out over the water to help them aboard.

TWENTY-SIX

Bellamy lay on the deck for a moment, savoring the fact of his survival. A pins-and-needles prickling down the length of his body roused him from his lethargy. He clambered awkwardly to his knees, and one of Marie's soldiers hauled him the rest of the way up.

Gripping the rail, he peered out over the flat black expanse of the Mississippi. The howling wind had died, and the Nihils which had opened on the surface were gone again. Evidently it had been a mere squall of a Maelstrom, ending as abruptly as it began.

His companions had stopped shooting into the water, and Titus was no longer hurling bolts of magick from on high. Either the Spectres had voluntarily broken off the attack when the storm ended, or the *Twisted Mirror* had outdistanced them.

Some distance down river, Marilyn's cabin cruiser drifted. Much to Bellamy's relief, the Arcanist still lay on the foredeck with Astarte and the pilot now crouching over her, a first-aid kit ready to hand. Astarte kept looking wildly out across the water, trying to glean some hint of what had happened to the wraiths, an effort that could only succeed if one of the *abambo* gave her a sign.

Bellamy couldn't shift himself into the realm of the living. The sidewheeler would cease to exist for him, and he'd fall back into the river. But he could project his image and voice across the Shroud. Invoking his Arcanos, he felt the barrier between the dimensions attenuate.

"Astarte!" he cried. Though he was shouting as loud as he could, he knew that if she heard his voice at all, it would be as an eerie whisper, just as she would see him as an insubstantial phantasm hovering above the water.

Marilyn's pilot—a fat, enormously phlegmatic man who'd seen more than his share of peculiar phenomena ferrying Arcanists along the Mississippi and into the bayous as they poked their noses into one enigma or another—nevertheless gave a violent start. Astarte peered madly about until she spotted the wraith. "Is everything all right?" she yelled, too agitated to remember that he could have heard her even had she spoken softly.

"It is over here," the FBI agent replied. "How's Marilyn?"

The mage lifted her head. "Fine," she groaned. "Poor, foolish Marilyn has simply been overdoing, that's all, straining too hard to master her new talents. A few hours' sleep and a smidgen of morphine, and she'll be good as new."

The pilot frowned at her. "Mr. Sebastian"—evidently he'd usually seen the transsexual in masculine clothing, and was accustomed to thinking of her as a man—"I know I'm just some guy you hire to run the boat and keep his mouth shut. And as usual, I don't have a clue what's going on. But it's obvious that you checked out of the hospital too early. You're bleeding."

Marilyn put her hand on his forearm and gave it a feeble squeeze. "I appreciate your concern, Jacques. I wish that I could have told you what my colleagues and I were up to on those moonlight excursions. It wasn't that I didn't trust you. I'd taken a vow of silence."

"As long as you paid me," said Jacques, "I didn't care what you were doing. I don't care now. I just don't want you dying on me."

"I'll certainly do my utmost to oblige you," Marilyn said. "But I can't go to a hospital—that is to say, back to a hospital—until I take care of my errand in Natchez. Be a dear and help me to my bunk, will you?"

The pilot and Astarte hauled Marilyn to her feet. The girl with the spiky, magenta-streaked hair gave Bellamy a look that was almost a glare. It was clearly driving her crazy that the crisis had come and gone without her being able to help resolve it, that she still didn't even know what it had *been*. "Can you come onto our boat for a while?" she asked.

"Yes," Bellamy said. Even if he hadn't wanted to be with her, he would have gone. Until Marilyn woke, Jacques would need his guidance to stay reasonably close to the wraith vessel. "But give me a few minutes. I have to take care of something over here first."

"All right," Astarte called. She and the pilot helped Marilyn below decks.

Noting with satisfaction that the tingling in his body had subsided, and his muscles seemed to be working normally once again, Bellamy peered about. His wounds beginning to close, Antoine was lumbering away toward the stern.

The FBI agent hurried after him. "Wait up, partner. I haven't thanked you for dragging me back to the *Mirror*."

The gator bobbed his wedge-shaped head in his approximation of a shrug. "Seems like we keep saving each other's asses, warmblood. No point making a big deal out of it. Look, I'm chewed up enough that I think I should go Slumber."

"That sounds like a smart idea," Bellamy said. "I'll tag along with you until you find a good place to bed down. Then I'll get Titus to take a look at you." They walked on past the paddle wheel. Water hissed and gurgled beneath the hull.

"You don't have to watch over me," Antoine growled. "I'm not wounded bad enough to fall into the Void."

"Thank God for that," Bellamy said. "But I want to know what else is wrong."

Antoine's saurian eye blinked. "Nothing I know of. I mean, except for Aztec Sinkinda and werewolves plotting to trigger some terrible disaster, and the nastiest string of shadow storms hereabouts since Hiroshima."

"I meant, what else is wrong with *you*. I jumped into the river because I figured that you must have noticed that the boat had started moving under its own power again, and if you weren't rushing to climb back aboard, you must be in trouble."

"I just needed to rip some more Spectres off the paddles, to make sure the *Mirror* really would get away. Maybe you didn't realize, but you two-leggers were hardly putting a dent in the bastards, shooting down from the deck."

Bellamy shook his head. "There was more to it than that. When I found you, you were confused. You acted as if you barely remembered who I was, and then, when I gestured at the boat, you didn't seem to understand what I was trying to tell you."

Antoine heaved a sigh. "Okay, I'll lay it out for you." He shot a baleful glance at one of the warriors loitering on the deck. "But not until we're alone. This is just between you and me."

"Okay," Bellamy said.

For most of the length of the steamboat, the walkways were relatively narrow, but at the front and back, the deck immediately above the waterline widened out into platforms suitable for carrying cargo. When Bellamy and Antoine reached the stern, the latter crawled to a heap of sacks secured by coarse hemp netting—gifts from Marie to the Governors of Natchez. Cocking his head, the gator briefly studied the pile, then said, "This'll do. Nobody'll pester me if I sleep under here."

Bellamy wondered fleetingly why Antoine didn't commandeer a stateroom. Maybe he felt more comfortable in the open air. The human glanced about, and saw that no one was nearby. "We're alone," he said, squatting to put himself nearer to eye level with the other wraith. "Talk to me."

"All right," said Antoine, his rough voice low. "Actually, I already told you the basics, but I don't blame you if it slipped your mind. We've been through more than our share of shit since then. What it comes down to is that the atmosphere, the *reality* in New Orleans makes it possible for there to be smart, talking animal ghosts. The reality in Stygian territory doesn't."

Bellamy stared at him. "My god, Antoine."

"Now, don't panic. I've gone north before, for a day or so, with raiding parties, and it didn't hurt me. I hardly noticed any difference. The problem this time is these damn Maelstroms. They get inside my brain, like static, and screw up my thinking.

"Down in the river, I lost it for a while. Became more like an ordinary stupid reptile. I knew I was supposed to get the Sinkinda off the paddle wheels, but I couldn't have told you why. And when you tapped me on the tail, it did take me a couple seconds to remember who you were."

"I remember how you hesitated before asking Marie if you could come along. You suspected you might have this problem."

"I also figured I could handle it, which so far, I am. And I was pretty damn sure you were going to need me, which, as we just proved, you do. What's the matter, are you afraid I'm going to turn completely wild, go Mla Watu, and chow down on you?"

"Of course not. You're about the only thing in the Shadowlands I'm *not* afraid of. But I am worried about your health."

Antoine snorted. "We're dead, remember? We can't expect a whole lot of health."

Bellamy grimaced. "Your well-being, then. Your sanity. Your safety. You know what I mean."

"'Course I do. But we're friends, aren't we? I wasn't planning on it, but somehow, after we rescued Titus, it just turned out that way."

Bellamy nodded. "I guess it did."

"Then I *need* to help you, warmblood. 'Case you haven't noticed, the Underworld's a cold, dark, empty place. Feelings—particularly the ones we can be proud of—are about all we have to keep us going. If you wimp out on them, you're giving yourself to Oblivion. So don't give me any crap about this, okay?"

"Fair enough," Bellamy said. He noticed that Antoine's zebra-striped bandanna had come loose, and retied the knot.

TWENTY-SEVEN

On the other side of the rise, something clicked. Montrose fleetingly considered taking to the air or veiling himself in shadow to scout ahead. But if he started invoking his Harbinger abilities every time he suspected some danger *might* be lying in wait, he'd likely exhaust his reserves of psychic energy long before he and Louise reached the next Legion way station. And so he merely readied his CAR-15. Then, his voluminous sable Inquisitor's mantle billowing behind him and the Lantern of Truth secured to his saddle nudging his thigh, he walked his paint spirit horse on up the road. Louise drew her own assault rifle from its boot, then followed. Her mount, a chimerical Tempest creature with the body of a roan mare and the head of a hawk, gave a short, harsh avian cry. The beast's hooves clopped on the worn, hexagonal paving stones.

Reaching the crest of the low hill, the Scot studied the landscape stretched out before him. The highway ran on through what appeared to be a wasteland of uneven ground, rocky outcroppings, and scrub growth. The faux vegetation was either slate gray or white as ivory. Near the point where the road faded into the gloom stood a weathered granite marker, a stela carved with a scythe and a bear at the top, and writing below. For once, the wind had died. Nothing stirred but the churning, flickering thunderheads occluding the sky, where a colossal six-fingered hand was forming amid the roiling vapor.

"I heard the noise, too," said Louise. "But I don't see anything poised to pounce on us."

"Nor do I," said Montrose, kicking his steed into motion. For a moment, the air had a sweet, floral smell, evidently emitted by the ashen, blighted-looking bushes to the left. "Perhaps it was only leaves shivering in a breeze. Or if it was a creature, we may have frightened it away. So far, so good, eh? The Great Bear Road has always been considered one of the less perilous Byways."

"I'm surprised you didn't take it on your previous journey to America," the Sister of Athena replied.

"At that point in time, most Harbingers felt it safer to travel by sea than by land. My instincts said the same. They might have proved correct, too, if Demetrius—or whoever he truly was—hadn't rigged the game against me by revealing my itinerary to his Soul Pirate friends."

"What do your instincts tell you now?"

"That it's a bad time to travel the Tempest at all, by any route. But we'll make it."

"I know we will. What can the Spectres throw at us that's worse than what we've faced already?"

They rode in silence for a time. Suddenly something buzzed, loudly enough to hurt Montrose's ears, and a swarm of winged creatures vaguely resembling horseflies swirled up from behind a bluff. There were several score of them, each the size of a wolfhound, and each flying toward the road. The Cavalier leveled the CAR-15, but intuition told him to hold his fire. Louise evidently sensed his hesitation and did likewise. Ignoring the wayfarers, the huge insects soared across the highway and on into the darkness. In a moment, nothing remained of them but the fading echo of their wings.

Montrose smiled crookedly. "For a moment, my love, I wondered if Fate had seen fit to vouchsafe you the answer to your question."

"About what worse could happen? No. Take it from a Heretic missionary, the Bright Powers don't operate that way."

"You sound so certain. And yet you've told me that in all your wanderings through the Shadowlands, you haven't found one particular deity or one particular creed in which you can believe."

"I believe we can Transcend," said Louise. "That there's a better place than the Underworld for us to go. I'm just a trifle hazy on the details."

"I remember possessing that same sort of faith," said Montrose, a little wistfully. Although as near as he could ascertain his mount didn't eat, the Phantasy had the annoying habit of halting to investigate grasses and bushes just as if it could. The paint stallion stopped and lowered his head, and he urged him onward. "It landed me in more than my share of trouble, but I confess that it also bolstered my spirits in times of adversity."

"You sound like a man losing whatever trust he reposed in the Deathlords," said Louise, brushing back a strand of her honey-blond hair. "If so, I can't say I blame you."

Montrose hesitated, not quite willing to acknowledge that she'd read him correctly. "I'm not altogether disenchanted. I do understand why the Seven declined to give us any soldiers."

"Because they're afraid of one another."

"When expressed in those words, it sounds craven and selfish, doesn't it? Still, it's vital to the stability of the Empire that there be no further strife among them. And considering what's happened of late, that's an appropriate matter for concern."

"I agree. And yet we both know they made the wrong decision."

"We do indeed," Montrose said. "If I learned anything as a soldier, before my death or after, it's that one has to take risks to accomplish anything."

"And it came as a shock to find that they aren't as wise or as bold as you."

Montrose grinned. "I wouldn't put it quite like that, but thank you for the compliment."

She smiled back. Her steed ruffled the gleaming bronze-colored feathers on its neck, then laid them flat again. "Don't feel too flattered," said Louise. "I'm a rebel. My opinion of the Deathlords was never that high to begin with."

"Well, cocky fellow that I am, I'll take it as an accolade nonetheless. You know, it's not that I never before considered the Deathlords to be acting unwisely. But I was never entirely certain I was right, and they, mistaken. Because they were, after all, demigods. Aloof, potent, and enigmatic. Even the Smiling Lord, who numbered me among his household."

"Well, they certainly seemed godlike to me," said Louise, "even though I'd resolved beforehand not to be awed by anything they said or did."

"Oh, they reek of power and strangeness, without a doubt. But I suspect now that it's simply an attribute of their office. A mantle the Emperor wrapped around them, and not something intrinsic to themselves. I feel that you and I have been afforded a glimpse behind the facade. And armored in all that magick and secrecy are souls not fundamentally different than ourselves."

"Like the Wizard of Oz," said Louise.

"In a sense. Except that our six wizards are nowhere near as kindly."

"So what does this insight mean to you?"

Montrose shrugged. "I don't honestly know. Perhaps nothing. Neither Charles Stuart nor his son was a perfect king, but I served them nonetheless, because I believed in the principle they represented."

"Stygia represents tyranny, slavery, and the transmutation of living souls into coins and jewelry. You don't believe in that."

"No," he said, "I suppose not, not anymore, certainly not merely for the sake of providing luxuries to the grandees. But I still believe in keeping down the Spectres, and the Legions are better equipped to do it than any other force in the Underworld."

She heaved a theatrical sigh. "Woe is me! For a few moments there I thought you'd experienced an epiphany, and so resolved the problem of where to spend the rest of our existences."

"I'm afraid not." He felt a sudden despondency, a fresh surge of doubt that they truly had a future together, and masked the emotion with a grin. "Perhaps we could winter on the Isle of Sorrows and summer with your rebel friends."

She chuckled. "Oh, brilliant, milord! Everyone on both sides would shun and mistrust us."

"Which would afford us plenty of time alone together," Montrose replied. "It *is* brill—" Abruptly he perceived the fabric of space kinking and fracturing across the desolate landscape. The paint stallion shied. As a creature native to the Tempest, perhaps the spirit horse also had some awareness of what was coming.

"What's wrong?" asked Louise.

"There's a Maelstrom brewing," Montrose replied. A cold, stinging wind began to moan, lashing the grasses and bushes this way and that. Thunder cracked, and a dazzling flash of lightning split the sky. When the glare faded, the wasteland seemed darker than it had been before. Strands of a deeper blackness writhed through the murk like tentacles questing for prey.

"What do we do?" asked Louise, her voice steady.

Montrose peered about, seeking shelter, or a spatial rift leading to another part of the Tempest, where the storm might not be occurring. There was nothing, not along this portion of the road. But as every veteran Legionnaire knew, stelae like the one ahead often marked the site of a portal between dimensions. "For the time being, we press on," he said. He freed the rope hanging from his saddle, knotted one end to his saddle horn, and tossed her the other. Her steed squawked and ruffled its feathers. "Attach this to your saddle. It will help us stay together."

Louise tied off the line. "Done."

Groping in a saddlebag, the Scot found his glossy black ceramic mask. It ought to provide at least a bit of protection against the wind. He pressed it to his face, then kicked the paint into motion.

The storm wailed and tried to rip his Inquisitor's cloak from his back. His eyes soon felt as if they'd been scraped raw. Squinting and blinking, he kept looking for traversible fractures in space, a cave, or even a large indentation in one of the hillsides. Still nothing.

His Shadow had been relatively quiet since his experience in the Crimson Gallery, as if his visionary confrontation with his old enemies had broken its power. Now, however, nourished by the Maelstrom, the parasite bestirred itself to whisper that his Harbinger powers were inadequate to cope with the present danger. His ineptitude was going to destroy him, and Louise with him.

Scowling, he strove to block the taunts from his conscious mind, assuring himself that he and Louise *were* going to survive. Honed by the demands he'd placed on it during the course of his recent adventures, his Arcanos was stronger than ever, and even in the old days, it had seen him through fouler storms than this. At least so far there weren't even any Spectres springing from the darkness. The Legions had evidently done a good job of keeping the area clear.

He twisted back and forth. Everywhere he looked, space kinked and bubbled in a continual ferment, but none of the fractures endured long enough for him to exploit it. He glanced back to check on Louise. Now wearing her own golden mask, her shoulders hunched against the gale, she gave him a nod to show him she was all right. But her mount wasn't faring as well. The wind had torn away most of its plumage and gouged raw white lesions across much of its body.

Montrose faced forward again. He mustn't stray from the road. Some ancient Harbinger far more adept than himself had determined its course and laid powerful enchantments on the paving stones. It was almost certainly safer than the ground to either side.

With a clatter, a nearby stand of plants resembling white bamboo stalks with long, serrated leaves transformed. Grew taller. Sprouted mandibles, multi-jointed legs, antennae, and triangular sets of bulbous faceted eyes. Montrose's stallion whinnied and reared. Struggling to control the animal, the Cavalier simultaneously pointed the CAR-15.

But he didn't need it. The creatures' metamorphosis from plant to insect was incomplete and unsuccessful. Still rooted in the earth, evidently trying to free themselves, they writhed frantically, spastically, and in a matter of seconds their exertions tore their spindly bodies to pieces.

Montrose and Louise rode on. A jagged bolt of lightning flared, glinting on a small, squat form ahead. For an instant, he could have sworn it was Valentine, then saw it was actually only a vaguely human-shaped rock.

A split second later, images cascaded through his mind, flickering by so rapidly he could only barely make them out for what they were. Valentine snooping in Montrose's quarters in the Citadel at Natchez, crowing with delight when he found the traitorous journal. The dwarf, now clad in conventional modern attire rather than motley, accepting a green sash from Gayoso. Mike Fink mauling the little man.

Montrose knew the Tempest was conducive to portents and revelations, and now it was evidently telling him that Valentine *had* betrayed him, and been well rewarded for his efforts. And that the jester had eventually run afoul of Mike—or was destined to. Perhaps he was plotting to ruin Montrose's lieutenant as well. His master Gayoso might well relish the former outlaw's downfall.

Montrose's muscles clenched with hatred. He'd offered Valentine an honorable way to advance himself, and the wretch had turned him down. Evidently his nature was so corrupt that he simply preferred skulking and double-dealing. He wondered if Mike had already destroyed the dwarf, and rather hoped not. He could derive a great deal of satisfaction from doing the job himself.

Something touched him on the arm. Startled, he jerked and peered wildly about. Louise had ridden close enough to put her hand on him. Because, preoccupied with his loathing for Valentine, he'd ridden off the road and dragged her after him. She'd probably shouted, but if so, her voice had gotten lost in the screeching of the wind.

His Shadow's laughter echoed through his mind.

"Thank you!" he shouted. Louise nodded. They turned their mounts in the direction of the Great Bear Road, and then the loudest peal of thunder yet reverberated around them.

Except that as it boomed and rumbled on and on, and the ground began to shudder, he realized it wasn't thunder after all, but the opening spasm of an earthquake. An instant later, a fissure yawned directly in front of the paint's hooves. The Phantasy reared.

Though reluctant to abandon the mounts, Montrose doubted their ability to make it back to the highway under these conditions. He snatched out his knife and severed the rope binding them, so that if one stumbled into a chasm, he wouldn't drag the other down as well. Then he seized the Lantern of Truth, hung it over his arm, invoked his Harbinger Arcanos, and levitated out of the saddle.

Something about this particular Maelstrom made flight more arduous than it should have been. Now that he'd severed all contact with the heaving earth, the wind seemed to claw at him twice as fiercely as before. He could feel his energy level dropping at an alarming rate. Ignoring the sensations as best he could, he lifted Louise off her steed, and, still holding on to her rifle, she wrapped her other arm around him.

As he soared toward the road, fighting the gale which had evidently abandoned its erratic ways to blow steadily in opposition to his progress, a patch of land directly beneath him crumbled. The pieces tumbled down and down into darkness, as if the landscape was only a shell suspended over a bottomless abyss.

Another piece of ground shattered and fell in on itself, and then another. By the time he touched down on the highway, the shuddering landscape was riddled with craters.

The road was shaking also, though not quite as hard as the ground around it. Louise set her feet on the paving stones, then immediately had to shift them to keep the earthquake from throwing her down. "I hate to sound lazy," she said, "but can't you keep flying?"

"I need to conserve my strength." He clipped the lantern to his belt with his rapier, knife, and Bren Ten automatic pistol. "That is, if you can walk at all."

She took a few cautious steps across the bucking surface of the roadway, her martial-arts training evident as she gracefully swayed and shifted to maintain her balance. "I can do it," she said.

"Then keep making for the stela. With any luck, it will provide an exit out of here."

They staggered on. To either side, the wasteland continued to disintegrate, until the highway became a bridge spanning a lightless gulf. When they were about fifty yards away from the marker, a portion of the road itself collapsed, cutting the path to their objective.

"*Now* we fly," said Montrose. Turning, he extended his hand to Louise. Her eyes widened, her mouth opened, and then something slammed into his back. Dropping the CAR-15, he staggered forward. Off the road and into space.

Snarling words in a sibilant tongue Montrose didn't recognize, the creature clinging to him clapped one cold, scaly member across his eyes, wrapped two limbs tightly around him, and clawed at his ribs. Struggling to reach his knife, Montrose wondered fleetingly where the Spectre had come from, and then an impact jolted pain through his body.

Half stunned, he realized he must have hit the side of the spine of rock supporting the highway. If he didn't arrest his fall, he might well keep striking it until he dashed himself to pieces. Doing his best to ignore the creature ripping at him, he called on his Arcanos, and felt the power rise inside him. His eyes still covered, trusting his Harbinger's intuition to lead him in the right direction, he tried to fly upward and away from the wall.

Evidently his instincts were functioning adequately, because he didn't crash into the stone. Jabbing backward with his elbow, he managed to connect with what, if the Spectre's anatomy was remotely like an Earthly creature's, should have been its midsection. The doomshade grunted, and its grip loosened just enough for the Scot to grab his knife and stab at its arms.

The member clinging to his face jerked away. He saw that he'd blindly flown some distance away from the ridge, and realized now that that was just as well. The whole thing was collapsing in sections now, masses of rock and earth tumbling into the pit. The remaining segments looked like pillars. From his vantage point, it was impossible to tell if Louise was still atop one of them or not.

Montrose went on stabbing savagely and pummeling his attacker with his elbow until the Spectre's hold loosened further. Gripping one of its cold, rubbery limbs for leverage, the Cavalier managed to wrench himself around to face it.

The doomshade had a round, pulpy, featureless head, like a piece of rotten fruit. Montrose rammed his knife deep into its belly, then shoved it hard. The five-armed thing fell away from him, into the pit.

Montrose flew upward through the stinging gale as fast as he could. Still, it seemed to take forever. Another pillar disintegrated before he rose above the level of the road.

As he'd expected, the stela still stood. Blessed with special enchantments, that section of highway would be the last to fall. And to his relief, Louise was kneeling atop another swaying shaft of rock. An assailant had gouged claw marks in the soft gold of her visor, but she seemed to be uninjured. All Montrose had to do was pick her up before her perch collapsed.

He swooped toward her. The icy wind screeched, tearing at him, and the world went momentarily black. When the flickering light from the thunderheads returned, there were four Louises stretching their arms out to him, each seemingly unaware of the others. Evidently the illusion was for his eyes alone.

It shouldn't have hindered him. He'd been heading directly for the true Louise, and so should still know which one she was. But somehow, suddenly, he didn't.

He hovered above the foursome, and the pillar roared and lurched. The paving stones cracked and ground together. Montrose realized he had no time to think.

He'd simply have to trust his instincts.

The shaft fell, and the women fell with it. Terrified that he'd made the wrong choice, Montrose dove. Snatching for his target's wrist, his fingers closed on solid flesh. The illusory Louises vanished.

Montrose flew to the stela. As he landed, the column supporting it began to crumble. With his Harbinger senses, he readily discerned the dimensional portal immediately to the right of the marker. Unfortunately, it was rippling, dilating, and contracting as dangerously as the distortions he'd noticed back down the road.

But unlike those, at least this one was large enough to work with. As the pillar shook more violently, he focused his power on the gate, willing it to stabilize. When he discerned that it had, if only for a moment, he grabbed Louise and carried her through.

He smelled the musky scent of mortal sex, then felt a sensation across his skin which was neither pleasant nor painful, neither pressure, heat, nor cold, but something altogether alien to normal human experience. An instant later he and Louise were standing beside another stela, this one carved with Charon's mask and a stylized fountain of flame. The portal through which they'd traveled blinked out of existence.

Montrose took a wary look around, up and down this new highway and at the blighted forest of twisted, leafless trees through which it ran. Nothing stirred. After the scream of the Maelstrom and the roar of the disintegrating landscape, the quiet here seemed almost preternatural.

Satisfied that they were out of danger, Montrose drew Louise into a long embrace. The pressure of her arms hurt the gashes above his ribs, but he didn't care. "I thought I'd lost you," he murmured.

"I knew you could catch me," she said.

"Yes, but which you?" He explained the illusion with which the storm—or his Shadow—had bedeviled him. "I don't know how I picked you out among the doubles. It wasn't my Harbinger's perceptions. They didn't help."

"It was your lover's perceptions," she said smugly.

"I imagine that's as good an explanation as any." They kissed.

After a time she said, "Quiet as it seems at the moment, I don't suppose this is truly the safest place to make love. Perhaps we should press on and continue this at the next outpost."

He sighed. "Probably so. That particular Maelstrom just razed a length of the Great Bear Road, a Byway that's endured since the time of Tuberous Caesar. A storm that strong could conceivably bleed down into this level of the Tempest. If it does, I'd rather it found us ensconced in a secure refuge. Assuming that such a place truly exists."

Hand in hand, they started down the road.

TWENTY-EIGHT

A hot, greasy feeling hung in the air, searing Valentine's skin. A breeze whispered—he had the unpleasant feeling that if he strained, he'd be able to make out words in the mournful sound—but failed to stir the sparse grass growing beside the two-lane asphalt road. Unless he missed his guess, another Maelstrom was on its way. Alexander tossed his luminous head as if he sensed the same thing.

It would be safer to ride out the storm indoors. Actually, it would be best to seek shelter in a genuine Haunt, with the fellowship of other Restless to anchor him and keep the gale from snuffing him out. But since fleeing Natchez, he'd been deliberately avoiding the other Necropoli of Mississippi.

Partly that was because he was afraid that Fink or even Gayoso had posted a reward for the apprehension of a runaway dwarf. Partly it was because he was afraid someone would steal Alexander. But he knew he had a deeper reason as well. He was ashamed to face his fellow wraiths, even though no stranger on the outskirts of Lorman could possibly know that he'd abandoned a grieving mother to lay a trap for her daughter's murderer by herself.

Scowling, he struggled to quash his guilt. He was doing the only sensible thing, and he'd tried his best to convince Belinda to do the same. If she still insisted on committing suicide, it was out of his hands. Legs aching, perched precariously on Alexander's saddle—he hadn't been able to shorten the stirrups enough to fit him—he peered about, looking for shelter.

Behind him stood the forest of longleaf pine from which he'd emerged twenty minutes before. Ahead and to either side were rolling cotton and soybean fields enclosed by fences. To his eyes, the fences looked rotten and dilapidated in the extreme, but maybe that was a trick of the Shroud. A few miles down the road, the lights of Lorman, shining behind a rise, stained a patch of the night sky gray.

He didn't like to ride Alexander at any speed faster than a walk. He was too afraid of falling off. That being the case, it seemed unlikely that he could reach the town in advance of the Maelstrom. But maybe he could hole up in some farmer's barn. He rode on, peering from side to side. The wind grew hotter and gusted harder, its voice swelling from a murmur to a snarl.

Finally he came upon a row of faded, nearly illegible signs tacked to the fence on his left. FRESH PLUMS. PEACHES. SWEET CORN. PAPERSHELL PECANS. Behind a gate secured with a padlock and a rusty loop of chain stood the tumbledown remains of what had been a produce stand. Spider webs of hairline Nihil cracks seethed in the walls.

Not exactly the Ritz, but it would keep out the worst of the wind, and hide him from any Spectres prowling the countryside. He tugged on the reins to turn Alexander in the proper direction. The Phantasy snorted, possibly an expression of contempt for his clumsy horsemanship, and headed for the shack, flowing through the substance of the fence as easily as water running through a sieve.

Up close, the stand smelled faintly of rotting fruit and vegetables. Crates and bushel baskets, some with a layer of filth in the bottom, sat on the ground before the door. Valentine nudged Alexander with his heels, urging him on into the interior. The stallion seemed to hesitate, then glided through the wall.

Inside the shack, the sweetish smell of decay was stronger. Beams of moonlight leaked through the grimy windows and the chinks in the roof. Against the far wall was a counter with a cigar box on it, perhaps the container the proprietor had used to hold his profits. More baskets and boxes rested atop long tables. Valentine was glad to see the furniture. He could use it to climb off and onto Alexander.

He guided the spirit horse up beside a table, then, clinging to the saddlehorn, his legs and lower back throbbing, dismounted. Intending to make himself as comfortable as possible, he felt badly that he couldn't do the same for the animal. He was sure Alexander would rest more easily if he took off his saddle and bridle. But he was worried that he wouldn't be able to put them back on again.

He gave the stallion an apologetic pat on the neck, then hopped down onto the grimy floor. A faint shuffling sound came from behind the counter. Startled, Valentine whirled. "Is someone here?" he asked.

No one answered.

It was probably mice, or some other animal. There were round black droppings the size of peas on the floor. Still, caution demanded that Valentine find out for sure. As he crept toward the counter, he shivered, his mouth grew dry, and he hated himself for his cowardice.

He peeked around the barrier.

At first it appeared there was nothing there at all. Then Valentine seemed to glimpse a complex pattern of shadows or stains on the floor and walls in the far corner. Finally, like an image on a movie screen coming into focus, the dark blotches turned into a gaunt figure, which shrieked, scrambled up from its crouch, and charged him with arms outstretched.

The dwarf backpedaled frantically. Crimson eyes shining, hooves clopping, Alexander interposed himself between the two ghosts and reared. The motion carried the stallion's head through the shack's relatively low ceiling.

Peering between Alexander's hind legs, Valentine saw his would-be assailant squawk and recoil. Huddling back down in his corner, shuddering, the tenant of this shabby, one-wraith Haunt began to whimper. Evidently sensing that the fight had gone out of the stranger, the spirit horse settled back on all fours without lashing out.

Valentine edged closer for a better look at the other ghost, then grunted in surprise. He'd seen countless bizarre deformities among the Restless, but never one like this. The stranger seemed to be made up of spirals of skin with nothing at all inside, like a mummy with both the actual preserved corpse and half the bandages missing. With no muscles or mass to his frame, he might well have proved unable to harm Valentine even if Alexander hadn't intervened.

"Take it easy," said the dwarf. "I don't want to hurt you. I just came in here to get out of the Maelstrom."

The empty man made a mewling sound.

"Come on," said Valentine, "check me out. Three feet tall and no weapons. Do I look like some kind of ruthless outlaw?" He eased closer to the stranger.

The other wraith gasped and pressed himself back against the wall. Through the gaps in what passed for his body, Valentine glimpsed a white shape behind him. An object he was evidently trying to conceal and protect.

The dwarf hastily raised his hands and stepped backward. "Don't panic. If you don't want me to come any closer, that's cool." Outside, the wind screeched, and even shielded by the walls, Valentine's skin prickled. "But I can't go away until the storm ends."

The empty man eyed him. It was difficult to read his expression when strips of his face were missing, but Valentine thought he looked a little less frightened.

"I'm Valentine," the small man said. "What's your name?"

The other ghost didn't answer.

"Can you talk?" Valentine asked.

The empty man made a whining sound.

Valentine sighed. Evidently his unwilling host was a Drone, a spirit whose mind had crumbled. Not exactly stimulating company, nor the ideal companion for riding out a Maelstrom.

"It's okay," said the dwarf. "You don't have to talk. I just hope you don't mind listening. If I run my mouth, I'll feel more real, and the storm won't take me. I'll bet this was your fruit stand when you were breathing...."

As he chattered on, the empty man turned his back, picked up his treasure, and studied it with single-minded intensity. Valentine saw that it was a piece of ruled, three-ring notebook paper, conceivably a letter from a loved one which the Drone had carried with him into death. Meanwhile the wind howled louder, and the Nihils in the structure around him seethed and glittered. One crack in the floor abruptly yawned wide enough to admit a Spectre, and the jester held his breath until it closed again. Several minutes later, he heard the thunderous tread of something huge enough to shake the earth, but the colossus passed on by without investigating the shack.

"Thank Fate *that's* gone," said Valentine. "Man-sized doomshades are bad enough. We don't need King Kong knocking on the door. A giant like that, you'd almost think it was a Malfean."

A band of shadow oozed through the tatters making up the Drone's back. He whined, and, shoulders hunching, lifted his paper closer to his eyes and stared at it even more fiercely than before.

The storm wailed, and the note began to steam. First the ink dissolved into wisps of blue, and then the paper itself melted into curls of white vapor.

The empty man clutched the letter to his lips, kissed it repeatedly, frantically, and then tried to stuff it in his mouth. But by that time, the last of it was gone.

Hands upraised, the Drone threw back his head and gabbled out his grief. Bands of black fire rippled through him, more rapidly now, eroding him.

Valentine scrambled to the Drone and wrapped his arms around him. His embrace squashed the loops of skin inward. "Don't let go!" he said. "Don't let the Void take you!"

Seemingly oblivious to his presence, the empty man wailed on. The shadow washing through his form alternately seared and chilled Valentine's flesh, but the dwarf forced himself to hold on.

"The paper doesn't matter," Valentine said. "It was only a souvenir. What matters is what it stood for. You were alive. Somebody loved you. Try to remember."

The empty man sobbed. Waves of shadow washed away his left hand.

Valentine was all but certain the Drone was a goner, but his heart refused to accept what his brain had determined. At that moment, he wanted to save the stranger as much as he'd ever wanted anything in the world. Which was ridiculous, considering that the other wraith was not only a stranger but barely sentient. But knowing the impulse was crazy didn't weaken it.

He squirmed between the stranger and the wall, took the Drone's head between his hands, and pulled it lower, forcing the stranger to look him in the face. Motes of shadow swarmed across the empty man's eyes.

"If you can't remember who you were," Valentine said, "then just pay attention to me. I *see* you. I'm talking to you. You may be dead, but you're alive, too."

The empty man whimpered and gave his head a tiny shake. Darkness surged upward from his toes to his head, erasing him. The power of the Void burned Valentine's hands like barrow-fire, withering them in an instant. Gasping, he lurched back against the wall. The tiny Nihils in the rotting planks nibbled at him like lovers. Crying out in revulsion, he staggered away and slumped down on the floor. Alexander watched him, his red eyes gleaming in the gloom. The wind howled. Gradually the pain in the dwarf's hands faded, and his fingers straightened.

Mulling it over, he couldn't imagine how he could have saved the Drone. Dwelling here in isolation, his mind rotting, the stranger had allowed his universe to dwindle down to one pathetic keepsake. And when it vanished, he lost his only reason for existing.

And Valentine felt a terrible kinship with him. After all, he was alone, too. He'd given up Montrose, Daphne, Belinda, his place in the Hierarchy of Natchez, and everyone and everything else that meant anything to him. He'd had good reasons, but the empty man had probably had his reasons for winding up in this miserable shack, also.

"No!" the jester snarled. "That's stupid. I'm not anything like the son of a bitch, and I'm *not* going to end up like he did."

Alexander cocked his head. The storm laughed.

TWENTY-NINE

On the march from the docks to the Citadel, Bellamy had noticed a number of differences between the ghosts of New Orleans and those of Natchez. The latter seemed to keep many more slaves, and to possess a greater abundance of material goods, no doubt due at least in part to the labors of the Artificers and their infamous Soulforges.

But some things remained constant. Like their neighbors downriver, the *abambo* in this city tended to make their homes in ruinous structures alive with the memory of ancient misery. The Citadel itself was a case in point, a cluster of massive brick buildings atop a hill, their shadowy, rat-infested corridors all but shrieking of misery and despair. It seemed likely that at one time, hapless Quick workers had toiled here in appalling conditions.

Antoine sucked in a deep breath, as if the emotional energy were something he had to inhale. "Tasty," he rasped. "My compliments to the chef."

"I can feel the power," said Marilyn. Despite Bellamy's advice, she'd decided not to use her wheelchair. Smelling of blood, fever sweat, and disinfectant, bundled up in her long coat, her sparkling aura predominantly violet and gray, she limped heavily along with the aid of a silver-headed malacca cane. "But I can't drink it in the way you three can. I wonder if I could learn."

They rounded a turn. Ahead was a pair of double doors. A sentry in a green sash stood to either side, a rifle in hand and a gaunt, hairless creature—a hideous blend of man and dog—crouching at his feet. Barrow-flame lanterns radiated greenish light and chill.

One of the envoys' escorts, a Legionnaire Centurion whose mouth had been sculpted into a fixed, exaggerated grin, said, "Are the Anacreons ready to see Queen Marie's people?"

The guard to the left of the door nodded. "Yeah, Sarge. You can take them straight in."

Antoine snorted. "They fuckin' *better* not keep us waiting."

His aged features jade on the left and crimson on the right, Titus scowled at the alligator. "Mind your attitude. Whatever you think of the Stygians, we came here to make them our allies."

Antoine rolled his eyes. "I know that, old man. I'll make nice."

"This way, please," said the Centurion. Gliding through the substance of the doors, he ushered his charges into the room beyond.

The audience hall was a large, high-ceilinged chamber illuminated by hissing torches. Unlike the hallway outside, the place was relatively clean. Some wraiths who could exert power on the warm side of the Shroud had evidently made an effort to clear away the worst of the cobwebs, dust, and grime. Banners emblazoned with a bewildering array of symbols—a black bird of prey, a fountain of fire, a hand dropping coins into a bowl, a question mark, a stylized roulette wheel, an eye, and the hourglass emblem from the soldiers' sashes among them—hung from the steel beams crisscrossing the ceiling. Patterns of small round holes in the floor revealed where lines of workbenches or something comparable had once been bolted in place.

The assembled Hierarchs fell silent and gaped, reminding Bellamy yet again of what an odd quartet he and his companions made. A wizened shaman with a two-tone face, a talking animal in a neckerchief, a maimed Quick transsexual with the telltale sparkles of a sorcerer flashing in his halo, and a white man who evidently had the confidence of the monarch of New Orleans.

The three dignitaries enthroned on the dais at the far end of the room regarded the ambassadors more impassively. On the left sat a small man in a contemporary gray suit and maroon tie, his head concealed by a green hood: Nathan Shellabarger, the Emerald Lord's agent. In the middle was a swarthy, beak-nosed guy in conquistador armor and a steel domino: Manuel Gayoso de Lemos, the Smiling Lord's follower. And on the right was a thin old woman with a bowl full of the Stygian coins called oboli and a large black hourglass—presumably the model for the images on all the sashes and flags—reposing in her narrow lap. She wore a long, dark, schoolmarm-ish dress, her gray hair was pulled back in a severe bun, and round, steel-rimmed spectacles perched precariously and somewhat comically atop her glazed white mask of Tragedy. Mrs. Duquesne, whose service was pledged to the Beggar Lord.

Titus bowed, and the other envoys followed suit. Marilyn grunted and froze doubled over. Bellamy prepared to leap across the Shroud and help her, but slowly, trembling and clutching her cane in a white-knuckled grip, she managed to stand upright once again.

"Good evening, Lord Titus," said Gayoso.

"Thank you, my lords and lady," Titus replied. "Allow me to present my companions. Antoine, I believe you already know."

"For a pirate," murmured someone in the crowd.

"This," continued Titus, nodding toward Marilyn, "is Marilyn Sebastian. A mage, as you probably noticed from her aura. And this"—he waved a hand in Bellamy's direction—"is Frank Bellamy. When breathing, he was an FBI agent. More recently he helped my sovereign defeat a plot to usurp her throne. All four of us speak with Her Majesty's voice."

"To be candid," said Gayoso, "your visit could have been better timed. At the moment, we're striving to purge every trace of Heresy from the province. Without intending any disrespect, I must tell you that the last thing we desire is emissaries of the Dark Kingdom of Ivory importing their own brand of false dogma into our midst. Particularly when they also flout law and custom by revealing our stronghold to a mortal."

"Please excuse a poor, ignorant foreigner for having the impertinence to interpret your own rules to you," Titus replied. "But if I'm not mistaken, Charon's Code would forbid me to show your Haunt to Miss Sebastian only if she had no previous knowledge of our world. Plainly, that's not the case. She can perceive us as easily as she can her fellow mortals."

"That's true, milord Anacreon," Marilyn said. "For instance, I can see that you're dressed like Cortez, but with a modern pistol holstered on your right hip."

"The mage sees clearly enough to suit me," said Mrs. Duquesne dryly. "And whether you wanted Marie's envoys to come upriver or not, Lord Gayoso, they *have* come, and I for one am curious to hear why. Why don't you stop grumbling at them and let them tell us?"

The Spaniard's mouth tightened. "As you wish."

"We've come to ask for your help against a common threat," Titus said. "A menace that could devastate your own territory if you don't take measures to stop it. It was Mr. Bellamy who first warned my queen about it, and I'd like him to tell you about it now."

As an FBI agent, Bellamy had grown accustomed to reporting to colleagues and superiors on the progress of an investigation. Still, gazing up at the masked faces of the Anacreons, he felt a bit self-conscious. Ignoring the sensation as best he could, he told them the story of the Atheist conspiracy. Of Milo Waxman's death, his own murder at Dunn's hands, and most of what had happened since. The one thing he edited out was Astarte. He hadn't been able to persuade her to stay away from Natchez, but he didn't have to let these Stygians, who were, after all, Titus and Antoine's enemies, know about her existence. Not yet, anyway.

When he finished, the three Governors stared down at him in silence for several moments. Finally Shellabarger said, "How much of this can you prove?"

"The Atheist murders are a matter of public record," Bellamy said. "So is the hysteria they've inspired."

Gayoso grimaced. "I very much doubt that a few Quick maniacs running amok could create problems on our side of the Shroud."

"And yet throughout history it's happened over and over," Titus said. "Disasters in the mortal world echo in ours. The fall of Rome coincided with the first great Maelstrom. The Black Death and the bombing of Hiroshima triggered others equally destructive."

"You can't compare gigantic calamities like those with the murders of a handful of people," the Spaniard replied.

"I believe it's the climate of terror and despair that truly matters," Titus said, "not the circumstances which inspire it. Surely you agree that shadow storms have become unusually frequent?"

Gayoso shrugged. "I can remember other seasons when we had to suffer through the same thing. But we didn't imagine diabolical conspiracies of Aztec Spectres and werewolves to account for it. We chalked it up to random variation. Surely *you* can't deny that there's nothing more random than the Tempest."

"But don't you detect a taint of corruption poisoning the minds of your people?" Marilyn asked. "We've heard rumors of an abnormal number of rapes, petty disagreements erupting into duels—"

"Nonsense," Gayoso replied. "If the people have been a little, shall we say, boisterous of late, it's because they're jubilant over the destruction of the Heretics. And because I've permitted a rough element from Under-the-Hill to rejoin the mainstream of society in exchange for their services to the Inquisition."

"We've also heard that quite a few of your citizens are losing the struggle with their shadowselves and dropping into the Void."

"You always lose a few souls when the Maelstroms blow. If you belonged in our world, you'd know that."

"I don't believe this," Antoine growled. "We came here to help you clowns—"

Bellamy stepped on the gator's tail. Antoine shot him a resentful glance, but fell silent.

"I apologize for my friend's rudeness," said Bellamy. "But I have to admit I share his surprise. We *did* come here to help you, asking nothing in return. Why are you being so skeptical?"

"As I said," Gayoso replied. "We're purging the Heretics from our midst. Perhaps that dismays you. Perhaps you'd like to divert us from our purpose by sending us on a wild-goose chase to ferret out an imaginary threat."

"Give me a break," said Antoine. "What do we care if you persecute your own subjects?"

"Some of the Heretics no doubt worship your own false gods," Gayoso said. "In any case, it can't please you to see a Hierarch army winning victory after victory against religionists of any stripe. Perhaps you're worried that once we've purified our own lands, we'll march south."

Titus cocked his head. "I hope that wasn't a declaration of war, milord Anacreon."

"No," said Mrs. Duquesne firmly, "it most assuredly was not." Her spectacles began to slip off. "Drat this thing." She removed the gleaming white mask of Tragedy, revealing a thin, austere, intelligent face, then replaced her glasses. "Lord Titus, it would help us take your story more seriously if you could tell us when, where, and how your Aztecs and wolfmen propose to strike."

"Unfortunately, we've told you everything we know," Bellamy said. "But if we look, we'll find the answers we need."

"What a confident young man you are." She turned to Gayoso. "Do you know, my lord, for once I can't fault your logic. Queen Marie might indeed wish to see the crusade fail. The whole notion of Aztec doomshades rising from the Tempest after five centuries to reconquer America does, on first hearing, seem unlikely. Yet the Empire has often found itself under attack by enemies even more ancient than that.

And perhaps the very outlandishness of our guests' story argues in its favor. Titus is sharp enough to concoct a more plausible lie."

The shaman sketched a shallow bow. "Thank you, milady," he said, with only a hint of irony in his voice.

Gayoso twisted toward Shellabarger. "And what's your opinion, milord?"

The small man in the sack-like hood hesitated. "I think our visitors gave us a very weird story that was pretty short on details, the details that we in Natchez need to know, anyway. But obviously, we don't want to run even a small risk of some enemy taking us by surprise. So I suppose it wouldn't do any harm to check into it."

"But it will," Gayoso said. "It will take time and resources which we ought to expend on the crusade. A campaign we're fighting at the behest of the Council of Seven themselves."

Mrs. Duquesne smiled scornfully, like a cruel teacher catching a pupil in a wrong answer. "A moment ago, my dear colleague, you were crowing that your, excuse me, *our* little jihad was on the brink of total victory. Now you seem to be implying it's so hard-pressed that it can't spare even a few Legionnaires to attend to another matter. Which is it?"

Gayoso opened his mouth, shut it again, and finally said, "All right. If you both want to assign some men to scour the countryside for Spectres and werewolves, then we will. Since I currently command more Legionnaires than either of you, I'll give some of my own Black Hawks the task. Will that satisfy you?"

"It's a start," said Mrs. Duquesne.

"Then it's decided," said Gayoso briskly. He turned back toward the four *abambo* gathered before the dais. "Thank you for your warning. We'll take precautions. I trust that nothing we said offended you. It's simply that our two lands have a long history of strife, and it was necessary to speak candidly."

"To the contrary," Titus said blandly. "We appreciate your honesty."

"I hope you'll spend some additional time here," said the Spaniard, "to refresh yourselves for the voyage home. You can sail tomorrow at dusk."

"What?" Antoine exclaimed. "What the hell—"

"My lords and lady," said Titus, raising his voice to cut the gator off, "apparently we didn't make ourselves clear. We didn't come *just* to warn you. We would like to stay and help put an end to the threat. And we *can* help. Mr. Bellamy is a skilled detective. Antoine has his own special knack for tracking people down. Miss Sebastian and I possess sorceries different than your own."

Gayoso scowled. "*Now* we see the true purpose of this farce. To plant spies, saboteurs, and perhaps even assassins in our midst."

"I give you my word," Titus said, "you're mistaken."

"Am I? Don't you have a detachment of armed soldiers on that black steamboat of yours?"

"Considering all the shadow storms we ran into en route," Bellamy said, "we couldn't have made it here without them."

"Titus and Antoine have perpetrated countless crimes against the Hierarchy," Gayoso said. "And according to your own story, this newly awakened mage of yours is also a Chancellor of the Arcanum. Do we Restless have a more ruthless enemy than that particular fraternity? How many ghosts have you imprisoned in your machines and pentacles, Miss Sebastian? How many have you dissected like laboratory mice to probe our secrets?"

"None," said Marilyn. She grimaced and shifted her shoulders as if trying to ease a pain. "I can't swear that no Arcanist ever did, but I haven't. And even if I had, it wouldn't be relevant to the issue at hand. Which, in case we've all forgotten, is defeating the Spectres."

"If there are any," the Spaniard replied, "I daresay we can handle them without you. Please set sail for your own country before midnight tomorrow."

"My lord Anacreon," said Mrs. Duquesne, "you forget yourself. The Smiling Lord placed you in primary command of the Inquisition, but in other matters, you, Lord Shellabarger, and I still govern this province as a triumvirate of equals, do we not?"

Gayoso glared at her. "Of course we do. I assumed I was expressing our common will. Surely you don't want to see a band of our ancient enemies ensconced within the capital."

Mrs. Duquesne gave him a wintry smile. "Never assume, dear. Or you'll inevitably embarrass yourself sooner or later."

"Excellent advice," Gayoso snarled. "Allow me to offer some to you. Don't cut off your nose to spite your face. Don't compromise the security of the entire province just to aggravate me."

"You're making assumptions again, this time about my motives. I truly do think Lord Titus and his companions may prove useful, just as I doubt both the desire and the capacity of such a small band to do us any irreparable harm."

Gayoso twisted around toward Shellabarger. "It seems that Mrs. Duquesne and I are deadlocked, milord Governor. You'll have to break the tie."

The man in the green hood hesitated. Bellamy suspected that Gayoso and Mrs. Duquesne were the more dynamic personalities, and that over the years Shellabarger had retained his office by playing one of his rivals off against the other, making sure that the balance of power never shifted too far in favor of either. "Let them stay," said the Emerald Lord's lieutenant at last. "Until they give us a real reason to think they mean us harm, or until we're sure that the threat they warned us of is never going to appear."

"I'll find our honored guests quarters in my part of the Citadel," said Mrs. Duquesne. "That way, if anyone is to be the victim of sabotage and assassination, it will most likely be me, and you, Lord Gayoso, may rest easy."

Titus inclined his head. "We thank you, noble lady, for your hospitality."

Thirty

This time, Cankerheart's potion had given Dunn a throbbing headache, and the noise emanating from the ongoing construction work in the center of the cavernous warehouse was making it worse. He wished he had a drink to kill the pain, but for the time being, the best he could manage was a smoke to mask the foul aftertaste in his mouth. He poured a line of pungent brown tobacco on the paper, rolled it up, licked it, and sealed it.

Cankerheart himself, who didn't need the repulsive drug to see dead guys, looked comfortable enough. The Black Spiral Dancer shaman sat hunched on a stool with the mangled remains of a calico cat in his lap. Repeatedly, he plunged his black-nailed fingers into the carcass, tore out a hunk of flesh, and gobbled it down. His hands, mouth, and yellow, pointed teeth were smeared with the stray animal's coppery-smelling blood.

Abruptly Gayoso strode through the substance of the front door and on toward his werewolf allies. One look at his scowl told Dunn that the wraith was the bearer of bad news. Mother Prudence, a fat woman with a round, pleasant face, waddled along beside him, seemingly struggling to keep up. If not for her tent-like purple robe sewn with religious symbols and the murky stains on her fingers, the phony Pardoner would have looked like some kid's doting aunt, the kind that was always baking cookies and cakes.

"What's up?" asked Dunn, lighting his cigarette.

"The enemies you failed to destroy in New Orleans have arrived in Natchez," said Gayoso bitterly. For a moment, his image faded, and then Dunn could see him clearly once more.

Dunn repressed a surge of anger at the ghost's bitchy attitude. "I assume you mean Bellamy and his pals."

"Of course I do." Gayoso glared at Prudence. "You said they'd never get here."

"I said they *might* not get here," the Pardoner replied, "considering that we weren't sure they even realized that Natchez is ground zero. And that they'd have to travel through several Maelstroms to do it. You know very well that I didn't make you any guarantees." She lowered herself onto a metal folding chair too narrow for her butt, then took Gayoso's hand and drew him onto another. "Now calm down and we'll decide how best to deal with the problem."

"Exactly which of our enemies are here, and what have they done so far?" asked Cankerheart through a mouthful of gory intestines.

"Bellamy, Titus, Antoine, Sebastian, and perhaps twenty-five retainers. They steamed into the harbor on a riverboat flying a flag of truce, then did exactly what you'd expect. They came to the Citadel, blabbed everything they knew about the conspiracy to the other Governors and me, and said they wanted to help us deal with the threat. I tried to discredit them and expel them from the province, but Shellabarger and Mrs. Duquesne insisted on allowing them to stay."

Across the room, one of the possessed workers dropped a metal tool onto the concrete floor. The sharp, echoing clang jabbed pain through Dunn's skull. Gayoso jumped as if someone had stuck a pin in him.

"As I see it," said Prudence, "we're not in horrendous trouble. I was surprised by how much Agent Bellamy and his friends have discovered." She gave Cankerheart the sort of mildly reproachful look a mother might bestow upon a wayward child. "Thanks to your misplaced diary, they know my people are Aztecs. But they don't know what's due to happen next."

"At first they didn't know what was happening in New Orleans, either," Gayoso replied. He sprang up from his chair and started prowling around the seats of his companions. "But they found out."

"Because it was pretty damn obvious Geffard was behind Queen Marie's problems," said Dunn. He inhaled smoke, savored the pleasant heat in his throat and lungs, and let the blue vapor out again. "Bellamy knew where to start looking for answers. Here in Natchez, he's got squat. He doesn't know that one of the Governors has joined the conspiracy, that Pru and her confessors are all Spectres, or that Cank and I are in town."

"And therefore," said Prudence, "long before he figures any of that out, we will have won. Any night now, the river will burn black. I can feel it."

"In other words, everything's under control," said Dunn to Gayoso. "So why are you panicking?"

"Because I'm risking everything," the rogue Stygian snapped, "and it disturbs me when it looks as if somebody might be on the verge of figuring out what we're up to. A few nights ago I had that miserable dwarf and his hippie whore whining at me, then they dropped out of sight, and now we've got this FBI agent and his cronies sticking their noses into our affairs."

Prudence reached out, caught his hand, and caressed it with her plump, black-stained fingertips. Gayoso's face softened. Evidently he found the gesture soothing, although to Dunn's eye, there was something subtly proprietary or even predatory about it. "But you heard about Valentine's quarrel with Captain Fink," the Pardoner said. "And you know that the dwarf is fundamentally a coward. He and his new lady friend must have run away for fear that Mike would kill them. They can't possibly threaten you now."

"What the hell are you talking about?" asked Dunn. "What have a dwarf and a hippie got to do with anything, and how come Cank and I are only hearing about it now?"

Gayoso and Prudence exchanged glances. "Nothing," the man in the cuirass and morion said. "That is to say, Valentine, my pet dwarf, was prying into a personal matter. Nothing directly related to our business, but it would have been awkward had it become common knowledge."

"No kidding," said Dunn. Gayoso reminded him of a pervert or a junkie trying to talk around the subject of his habit. Since the Governor was supposedly a baby Spectre now, and theoretically immune to guilt, Dunn guessed he must be covering up because he'd been doing something stupid, something that could have jeopardized their plans in one way or another. Whatever his secret vice was, maybe Gayoso craved a fresh fix even now. That would explain why he was so jumpy. "You want to tell us a little more about it?"

"No," replied Gayoso flatly. "As I said, it isn't relevant."

Dunn decided to let it go. The Wyrm knew, many Black Spiral Dancers had their secret appetites, compulsions, and madnesses also. If he started trying to sort out all of his associates' private depravities, he'd never finish. "Okay, we'll take your word for that. Let's get back to the main issue. What are we going to do about Bellamy and the others?"

"Manuel very deftly made sure it would be his own soldiers hunting for werewolves and doomshades," Prudence said. "Which is to say, men we've already turned. Given that the search is already crippled, and the culmination of all our work is at hand, perhaps we don't have to do anything."

"No," said Dunn, "I think we should get rid of them. I agree with you, I don't think that even a hotshot G-man like Bellamy would stumble onto anything in what little time is left, either. But you never know."

"Besides," said Cankerheart, leering, "you have a score to settle with him. He's slipped from beneath your claws too often, and he destroyed your *dear* friend Chester."

Dunn grimaced. "Of course I'm looking forward to having some fun with him. That doesn't change the fact that it'll be safer to dispose of these people now."

"Easier said than done," said Gayoso. "Mrs. Duquesne is sheltering them in her part of the Citadel."

"If they want to hunt for the conspiracy," said Dunn, "they've got to come out some time. Then we nail them."

Prudence frowned. "Aren't you worried that if they start disappearing, Mrs. Duquesne and Mr. Shellabarger will decide there really must be something to their story after all?"

"Not soon enough, not if Gayoso here keeps pushing other explanations. If Bellamy's gone, maybe he went undercover or out of town to follow up on a lead. Or maybe he's an enemy of the Hierarchy after all, and is off conspiring with the rebels."

The Governor nodded. "I suppose I can do that. Now, *how* will we get them?"

"One sniper armed with a good rifle can accomplish wonderful things," said Dunn, grinning. "Just ask the Warren Commission. But considering that these guys have proved they're tough and reasonably smart to boot, maybe we should try something a little more elaborate."

"Like what?" asked Cankerheart.

"Get the girl."

Gayoso cocked his head. "You mean Sebastian?"

Dunn snorted. "If that's your idea of a girl, you've got low standards. No, I mean Bellamy's little honey."

"But she's not here."

How did this moron ever get to be a Hierarch nobleman? wondered Dunn. "Just because they didn't schlep her up to the Citadel for the big palaver—which she wouldn't have been able to see or hear anyway—that doesn't mean she isn't in town. She followed Bellamy all over New Orleans, into our Dancer haven and the big showdown with Geffard, too. Why wouldn't she follow him upriver?"

"Well," said Gayoso, "my people did say that Sebastian arrived in her own boat. When you think about it, she'd have to, wouldn't she? Perhaps Bellamy's woman was aboard, also."

"Or maybe she came to Natchez some other way," said Dunn. "It's not important. What does matter is that she's just an ordinary live human. The weak link in the chain."

Cankerheart tossed the cat carcass to the floor, wiped his mouth on the back of his hand, and brushed at the flesh, fur, and gore clinging to his pants. "I'm getting a sense of déjà vu," he said. "As I recall, you hunted for this monkey all over New Orleans, and it took you forever to find her."

"But this time," said Dunn, "we know where Bellamy and Sebastian are. They'll lead us to the girl, and we'll proceed from there." He blew a smoke ring. "Trust me, it will work."

Thirty-One

Astarte crept down the dark, twisting alley, groping her way along the high stone wall on her right. The cold drizzle had soaked her to the skin. At her back, her mother called, whining for her to come home.

Astarte was tempted to obey. Go back to the ratty little apartment and her boring little job. It would drive her crazy, but it might be better than this endless seeking, chilled, alone, and miserable, through the shadows.

But whenever she was on the brink of turning back, an iridescent glow shone around the next corner, and a strange, skirling piping sounded, teasing her onward. Unfortunately, the light and music always died just as she was about to round the bend, as if the source had retreated farther into the maze-like tangle of enclosed lanes.

The alley terminated in a T intersection. She pivoted to the left, and saw one dead end just a few feet down. She turned in the opposite direction and saw another.

This was it, then. She couldn't follow the glow and the piping any farther. She'd have to go back to her empty, pathetic life after all. Bitterly disappointed, she struggled not to sob, and then someone touched her on the shoulder.

She jerked around. Behind her stood a lean, serious-looking guy maybe a few years older than herself, with a conservative haircut and a suit and tie to match. She knew him and didn't know him at the same time. But she was drawn to him, and when he smiled and opened his arms, she flung herself into his embrace.

When they kissed, her memory awoke. He was her own beloved Frank, and now that he'd shown up, she sensed that things were going to work out after all.

Sure enough, he turned and rapped on the blank gray wall, and a door rippled into existence. A little sliding panel opened at eye level, as if they were asking to enter an old-time speakeasy. Frank leaned close to it and whispered something she couldn't hear.

The door opened. On the other side was a plump, pink-faced, smiling little man in a powder-blue sports coat and a narrow-brimmed straw hat. Once again, for a moment Astarte knew she knew him, but couldn't call his identity to mind. Then she realized he was Vulture—R. J. He'd been dead—she thought—but now he was alive again.

She was about to hug him and tell him how glad she was to see him when the glow shone and the piping sounded behind him, beckoning her irresistibly onward. Grinning, R. J. bowed and waved her and Frank on down a short hallway.

Emerging from the passage, they found themselves in a large, high-ceilinged chamber with galleries running up the walls. A luminous, faceted orb, rather like a disco ball, floated unsupported near the ceiling.

Seen straight on, the light was even more wonderful than Astarte had imagined. Gazing into it, she glimpsed the answers to every question that had ever bothered her, and other secrets so far removed from mundane experience that no philosopher had ever even puzzled over them. Even better, the glow woke her senses and emotions to full, vibrant life. It was as if she'd been crippled and numb from birth, and had only now become whole and fully aware.

She stared at the orb for a long time. Indeed, she might never have taken her eyes off it if she hadn't sensed that, now that she'd found it, it would always be there for her. But since it would, curiosity finally prompted her to look at the other occupants of the room.

As before, she recognized each of them immediately, but needed another second to call their names to mind. The vampire Mr. Daimler, his single eye, pig-like snout, and twisted form as beautiful as she'd once thought they might be if she could cleanse the deficiencies of ordinary human vision from her eyes. Antoine, strong and majestic as a dragon. Titus, his wizened, painted face full of patience and wisdom. Stern Queen Marie, smiling at last. All of them had a shimmer about them, as if the light overhead had kindled a similar glow inside them.

Marilyn was there, too, unhurt, a fact which delighted Astarte, though she couldn't quite recall why she should have expected anything different. At first the Arcanist lacked the radiance her companions possessed, but then the sheen blossomed. Laughing and weeping with joy, Marilyn raised her hands, and sweet-smelling yellow roses fell from the air.

Frank gasped. Astarte turned. He was glowing too. Smiling, he touched her left hand, and an engagement ring set with a huge diamond appeared on her finger. The metal was so cold it burned, but the gift made her so happy that the discomfort didn't matter.

The orb pulsed, and she shivered with rapture. The light was transmuting and refining her essence as well. Her companions looked on, beaming, waiting to see what sort of miracle she'd perform to celebrate her metamorphosis.

She wondered what she should do. It would be nice to give Frank a gift in return. Maybe a Harley. A bike would loosen him up, and it would be exhilarating to streak down the highway with the wind in her hair and her arms around his waist. She raised her hands. Then the orb dimmed, and the blissful feeling inside her withered.

"What's wrong?" she asked, her voice breaking. "Why is it going out?"

Frank and the others gazed stupidly back at her through the gathering murk. Astarte realized from their bewilderment that the glow wasn't fading for them. Rather, she was going blind.

"Help me!" she cried as the room went black. She snatched for Frank, but even though he'd been scant inches away an instant before, touched nothing.

She blundered through the darkness, wheeling this way and that, calling his name. She thought someone answered, but couldn't be sure. If so, the cry was so distant and faint that it got lost in the echoes of her own voice.

After a time, a smudge of bluish light appeared to her left. She gasped and lurched toward it, then faltered. The glow emanated from her mom's portable TV on its wheeled stand. On the screen, two of the characters from *Melrose Place* were rolling around in bed. In front of the set was the stained, lumpy sofa, with three Budweiser cans, a dirty ashtray, and a half-eaten sub on a plate resting precariously on one of the cushions.

"No!" Astarte snarled. She wouldn't go back. She wheeled and ran away from the tableau, back into the darkness. The television and couch popped into existence ahead of her. She pivoted to the right, and the furniture shifted to block her path once more.

"Frank!" she screamed. Then she sensed him beside her, reaching out to save her. She floundered around, thrust out her arms, and his hands closed on hers.

Like the ring had been, his flesh was icy cold. The shock and the pain of it made her recoil. Only for an instant, but that was enough. When she fumbled for Frank again, he was gone. Her mother's entire apartment oozed from the blackness, closing around her like a trap.

She sobbed, and the darkness came back. Suddenly she wasn't standing any longer, but thrashing in a tangle of blankets. The AC hummed, and from down the hall came the clattering sound of someone filling an ice bucket from the machine.

A nightmare, she thought, her heart pounding, it had just been a stupid nightmare. She hadn't been magically transported back to Ohio. She was still in her hotel room in Natchez.

But though the nightmare hadn't been real, it reflected a terrible truth. She'd found the love of her life, like in some sappy old song or movie. She'd made her way into the heart of the supernatural, just as she'd always wanted. But now it was all slipping away.

She knew that Frank didn't mean to shut her out. He said he'd put her to work as soon as he found a job she could do. But meanwhile, she was stuck on the sidelines while her companions hunted for Spectres on the dead side of the Shroud. She hadn't even gotten to attend the conference with the Governors in the Citadel. Mistrusting the Stygians, Titus hadn't wanted to expend the magick power necessary to allow her to participate in the discussion.

I am going to lose everything, she thought. *Eventually Frank's going to decide that us being together just doesn't make any sense. Unless I do something about it.*

She doubted she could go back to sleep. She sat up to get a look at the clock on the night stand, then smelled cigarette smoke. "Hello," said Dunn's deep, lazy, amiable voice. He looked like a shadow in the darkness. "You okay? It seemed like you were having a bad dream."

Her pistol, loaded with silver bullets, was on the night stand, too. She snatched for it, and Dunn grabbed her wrist. "Take it easy," he said.

She raked at his face with the nails of her free hand. He caught her other wrist. She sucked in a breath to scream.

Something crackled. Her body burned and bucked uncontrollably. She realized he was shocking her like an electric eel, just as he had Frank.

Unlike the FBI agent, she didn't die from it, but when the current stopped flowing, and the werewolf dropped her back onto the bed, her muscles wouldn't obey her anymore. Dunn pressed a piece of tape over her mouth, handcuffed her hands behind her back, and then switched on the lamp.

He smiled down at her. "There. Now we can get down to business."

Though her body was still jerking and twitching, she thought she might now be able to call for help. She tried to scream through her gag, but the garbled sound that emerged was too weak to be heard outside the room.

"Are you scared?" Dunn asked. "For what it's worth, I'm not going to kill you yet. I'm not even going to rape or torture you, not seriously. I admit I'm tempted, but I'd rather get out of this dump while we're still young." He pulled off his suede jacket, and unbuttoned his shirt. "But we want to leave a clear trail for your friends to follow, and that means we want the smell of your blood and terror and my werewolf funk. So unfortunately, I do have to hurt you a little." His shoulders widened, and his eyes shone.

THIRTY-TWO

A trio of Legionnaires sauntered into view. Valentine had to struggle against the impulse to duck out of sight, even though, on the basis of several previous uneventful encounters with wandering soldiers, he'd decided that he evidently wasn't a wanted fugitive. Ordinarily, desertion was a capital offense, but apparently Gayoso valued his new quartermaster so little that he hadn't cared that he'd run off. Or maybe, just maybe, he hadn't wanted to draw attention to the dwarf and his tale of a murderer in a blue hood by issuing a warrant for his arrest. Either way, it seemed that Valentine was free to walk the shadowy, narrow streets of Under-the-Hill.

Yeah, right. Free until he ran into Mike Fink. With much regret, the jester had sold Alexander and used the money to buy a stiletto and a Glock 17 automatic pistol. But even armed, he had no confidence whatsoever that he could survive another encounter with the keelboatman.

He still couldn't believe he'd come back to Natchez, still didn't know precisely *why* he'd returned. He only felt that somehow Montrose, Daphne, Belinda, and the nameless Drone in the abandoned produce stand had ganged up on him to pressure him into it. And at the moment, jumping at every noise, his bowels watery, he hated them for it.

Nevertheless, here he was, prowling through the district, looking for Belinda. What made the task problematic was that—assuming she'd already found a Masquer willing to give her the form of a child—he might not recognize her when he found her.

A rapid thumping sounded from the mouth of an alley just ahead. Peeking warily down the passage, Valentine saw a boy, his face mottled with smallpox pustules, and a little girl with long pigtails tied with green ribbons. Both kids wore clothing appropriate to the early nineteenth century, but they were playing a modern game of one-on-one basketball, shooting at a rusty, netless hoop.

"Belinda?" Valentine asked.

The child ghosts turned and peered at him. "What?" asked the boy.

"I'm looking for a little girl named Belinda," Valentine said. "I thought you might be her."

The girl shook her head.

"Then sorry I bothered you." Valentine hesitated. "I don't know if you know it, but kids like you have been disappearing lately. Maybe you shouldn't play out here alone."

The boy reached into his hip pocket and brought out a straight razor. "Fuck off, midget."

Valentine cringed. *Fine*, he thought. *I hope the killer does get you*. Loathing himself for his cowardice—even a kid, someone his own size, armed with a blade when he had a gun, could intimidate him—he hurried on down the street.

The evening dragged on. On two occasions, passersby accosted him, demanding bribes. Otherwise, they'd tell Fink they'd seen him. Valentine had plenty of money left from the sale of Alexander, so he paid. But the second time, the tough who'd shaken him down, evidently smelling the possibility of a bigger score, began to tail him. Valentine ducked inside a dilapidated wooden building. With his long-legged pursuer's footsteps pounding behind him, growing steadily closer, the dwarf made a zigzag dash through several walls, then dove into the knee hole of a desk. There he cowered, trembling, until the would-be robber gave up the search, and, swearing, went outside again. Valentine waited another twenty minutes, then cautiously, peering this way and that, made his own exit in the opposite direction.

Once satisfied that the coast was clear, he reluctantly decided to proceed back toward the Green Head and the street of whorehouses behind it. He dreaded the thought of going anywhere near the tavern. Despite his newfound importance as an Inquisitor, Fink still liked to hang out there. But Valentine couldn't very well look for Belinda without checking that particular area. It seemed quite possible that the hippie would stake out the same vicinity from which Daphne had disappeared.

As he neared the river with its reek of silt, dead fish, and pollution, he heard the mercenary leader bellowing out one of his preposterous brags. He yearned to turn back, but instead contented himself with making a wide detour around the Green Head itself, so as to come out on the street of brothels halfway down. He had to quash a ridiculous urge to tiptoe.

The flickering lamps on the crumbling walls shed scarlet light and chill. Succubi and movie stars called from doorways and windows. Approaching the end of the double line of whorehouses, Valentine spotted two shadows, one the size of a full-grown man, the other no larger than himself, standing in the gloom ahead.

Reflexively holding his breath, he crept closer. The small figure was a little girl. With her skinny frame, sharp nose, and brown hair, she might well be the transformed Belinda, but he wasn't sure. Her male companion, however, wore not a blue hood with silver trim but a lacquered chartreuse wooden mask with a curly white beard that looked as if it might have been carved for some long-ago Mardi Gras. And he hadn't dressed in a long leather coat but the layered green cape and high boots of an officer of the Emerald Legion.

Valentine sighed, relieved to have his momentary quandary solved. Since the adult wraith wasn't the murderer, it would do no harm simply to step out into the open and ask the kid if she was Belinda. He opened his mouth to hail her, then realized that nothing would be easier, or smarter, probably, than for the killer to change his disguise. What's more, the man before him was the same height and build as the silent figure who'd lured Daphne away.

Scythe and Lamp, thought the dwarf, appalled by the mistake he'd nearly made, *I don't have the instincts for this*. He wished poor Montrose were here to help him. The Stygian would know what to do.

The man in green offered the girl his hand, and she took it. They strolled to the end of the block, then on into the blackness beyond the crimson lamplight. Taking care not to get too close, Valentine skulked after them.

They led him into the same empty section of the city where he'd met Belinda originally. The Quick had largely abandoned these few blocks of decrepit buildings some decades before. Even the majority of the homeless preferred to spend their time elsewhere, maybe because here there was no one to panhandle and no dumpsters full of discarded food to raid. Nor had many of the Restless settled in the area. Valentine had heard people say that, decrepit and Nihil-infested as many of the local structures looked, few of them buzzed with the echo of ancient pain. A ghost who chose to dwell in one might starve and fall into the Void.

A predator with intentions so vile that even the residents of Under-the-Hill would take exception to them might well bring a victim here, to molest her undisturbed.

If that is Belinda, Valentine wondered, *why does she just keep walking along with this guy? Why doesn't she whip out that stupid flintlock?* Probably because she wasn't yet sure that her companion was really the killer. She was waiting for him to give himself away.

The pair stopped outside the peeling wooden door of a derelict office building. The man in green waved his arm, inviting her to enter, but she didn't. Instead, they stood there talking. Valentine crept a little closer, but despite his preternatural hearing, still couldn't quite make out what they were saying. He assumed that the girl had suddenly decided it might not be such a bright idea to visit her companion's Haunt.

The girl had the high, breathy voice of a child, but even so, something about the tone and cadence reinforced Valentine's feeling that she was Belinda. To his surprise, there was something familiar about the low-pitched voice of the man in green as well. Perhaps if he sneaked just a few feet closer, near enough to actually hear what the masked ghost was saying, he'd recognize it.

He started to do precisely that, but then the man in green pounced on the little girl, so suddenly that, even if she did have a gun concealed in her clothing, she never even had a chance to make a grab for it. Startled, Valentine froze. The masked ghost punched the kid twice in the face, and her knees buckled. He picked her up and melted through the door.

Valentine gaped at the spot from which the pair had disappeared. He knew he should go after them, but what if he screwed up? What if it turned out that he was as helpless to rescue the girl as he'd been to save Daphne, or the Drone? As he had been throughout his whole miserable existence? Maybe it would be better to run back to the Necropolis and get some soldiers.

No. By the time he found someone willing to listen to him, Belinda—or whoever the child really was—might well have been destroyed. Valentine fumbled the Glock 17 out of its shoulder holster. For a moment he blanked on the weapon merchant's instructions, and couldn't remember how to release the safety and chamber a cartridge, but then the procedure came back to him. His hands trembling, he readied the compact 9mm pistol—which was still heavy and clumsy in *his* grasp—and ran to the office building.

Cautiously he stuck his face through the door. The foyer inside was empty. There were several doors along the walls, and a narrow flight of stairs leading upward.

Valentine strained, listening. *Thought* he heard a whisper of sound seeping through the ceiling. His mouth dry, he skulked up the steps, through darkness and the acidic stink of cockroaches. Though he knew it was impossible, he imagined he felt a heart pounding in his chest.

By the time he reached the second-floor landing, he was certain the noise was real, a mixture of gleeful chuckling and ugly words in a language he didn't recognize, but which made the hairs on the back of his neck stand on end. It was murmuring through the door on the left.

Please, Valentine prayed, for all that he didn't believe in God, *don't let me mess this up*. He resolved to catch the man in green completely by surprise, the way Montrose had supposedly surprised the Heretic Sandmen and Chanteurs at the battle of Grand Gulf. Trying to steady himself, he drew a deep breath, let it out slowly, then lunged through the door.

Beyond it was a room illuminated by the wavering greenish light of several barrow-fire candles, and dominated by the seething, glittering Nihil, a pit radiating twisting fissures like the arms of an octopus, gaping in the middle of the floor. A collection of painted symbols decorated the walls. Valentine had no clue what they signified, but, like the incomprehensible phrases he'd heard a moment before, they made his skin crawl.

The girl lay on a long table with a rubber-ball gag jammed in her mouth and an assortment of darksteel daggers, one as massive as a Bowie knife, others delicate as scalpels, surrounding her. This close, Valentine could tell that she was indeed Belinda. His back to the dwarf, the bearded mask discarded on the floor, the man in green crouched over her, about to snap a manacle around her left wrist.

Valentine meant to shoot the killer before the bastard even realized he was there. But in the moment it took him to aim the Glock 17, the other wraith sensed his presence, and whirled. The dwarf froze in shock.

Because the murderer was Gayoso.

Thirty-Three

Astarte lay hog-tied on the floor of the empty bedroom, suffering. Her throat was parched, her cuts and bruises stung and itched, and her limbs were cramped from being immobilized behind her back. Whenever she tried to shift them, the noose around her neck pulled tight and choked her, Dunn's way of making absolutely sure she couldn't wriggle free of her bonds.

The physical pain, however, was nothing compared to her mental anguish. The anguish of knowing what was to come.

She'd realized Dunn meant her to serve as bait in a trap. When he'd forced her into the derelict house, she'd peered this way and that, trying to see what kind of opponents her friends would have to contend with when they came to rescue her. But the building appeared to be empty.

"Looking for bushwhackers?" Dunn had asked. She hadn't replied, but her pitiful attempt at defiance only made him grin. "Naturally, if they were wraiths, you wouldn't see 'em. Even if they were Dancers, you probably wouldn't unless they wanted you to. But actually, we're alone. Sure, I *could* attack Bellamy and company with spooks, Banes, werewolves, and the whole Creature Feature. But your team has a nasty habit of escaping to poke their noses into my business another day. So in the interests of getting this crap over with once and for all, I decided to try another approach, something I hope old Frank won't suspect. See, critters like him and me sometimes get so preoccupied with supernatural dangers that we forget all the nasty gadgets you monkeys have invented. My gang and I are going to keep this charming mansion under surveillance. When your buddies go inside, we'll set off two bombs, one on either side of the Shroud. Sorry you have to check out along with everyone else, but at least it ought to be fast and painless."

She'd screamed and struggled anew, uselessly. He'd merely paralyzed her with another shock, carried her upstairs, bound her, gagged her, and left her.

That had been just before sunrise. As she could see through the grimy, cobweb-shrouded bay window, it was dark again. Surely Frank or Marilyn had discovered her abduction by now. They could show up looking for her at any moment.

First R. J. had died because of her. Then Marilyn had gotten herself ripped to shreds. Now Frank and all her other friends were going to perish. Unless, despite her gag and bonds, she found a way to warn them off.

She'd been desperately mulling the problem over all day, and had only come up with one solution. But to her surprise and self-disgust, even though she'd been already been contemplating something similar for days, she'd hesitated to try it.

Something creaked. She twitched, and heart hammered. She strained to listen until she was reasonably certain that the noise had simply been the old house settling, and not a footstep.

I've got to do it now, she thought, *while there's still time. Once I'm a ghost, I'll be free. I can warn Frank to stay the hell out of here. And then we'll be together, both part of the supernatural world forever.*

She flexed her arms and legs. The noose began to strangle her.

Thirty-Four

Around the last corner, on Union Street, the antebellum Greek Revival houses with their red brick and brownstone facades and white Corinthian columns were tourist attractions, perfectly maintained. But on this block, they were falling into decrepitude. Roofs were missing shingles, shutters hung askew, and lawns were overgrown. Some of the homes were even boarded up. To Bellamy, the area looked like a prime location for a collection of Haunts, but except for his own companions, he didn't see any other *abambo* around. Maybe they were all in hiding. If he'd spotted a Quick mage and a gang of twenty-some armed wraiths marching into his neighborhood, he might be inclined to duck for cover himself.

He inhaled deeply, but for the moment couldn't catch the mingled scent of blood, sweat, and werewolf musk they'd followed from the hotel. A thrill of near-panic jangled along his nerves.

He turned to Marilyn, Titus, and Antoine, who were marching—or in the fledgling sorcerer's case, hobbling—along with him at the head of the column. "Does somebody still have the trail?" Bellamy asked.

Leaning heavily on her cane for support, smelling of raw wounds and fever sweat, Marilyn bowed her head, concentrating. After a moment she said, "I'm sorry. My new perceptions aren't working as well as they have sometimes. To be honest, I can't even see you as clearly as I should."

Then what good are you? Bellamy wondered nastily, realizing even as he framed the thought that he wasn't really angry at her, but at himself. From the day he'd met Astarte, he'd been afraid that if she remained involved with the investigation, she'd come to grief, and yet he'd never managed to remove her from the situation. It was his fault that Dunn had finally caught her.

Titus waved his hand in a mystic pass, then touched his eyes and the tip of his nose as if investing those organs with extra magick. "With luck, I'll be able to pick up the trail in a moment."

Antoine snorted. "Don't strain yourself, old man. I've got it covered."

"You're sure?" Bellamy asked.

"'Course I'm sure! Remem…" The gator faltered, as if the words he intended to speak had gotten jumbled in his mind. "Remember when we tracked down Titus and the demons? I didn't steer you wrong then, did I? Your wolfman buddy dragged Astarte into that last house on the right."

Bellamy studied the structure, an abandoned, three-story octagonal house topped with a dome. The place was dark. Nothing stirred behind the windows, or beneath the pines in the yard.

"I don't see any signs of an ambush," Titus said.

"That doesn't mean it's not there," Antoine rasped.

"I agree," said Bellamy. "Sure, Dunn left us that note." *You all run home to New Orleans*, it had read, *or you'll never see the girl again*. "But my guess is that maybe he was just trying to make us think there *wouldn't* be a trap set for us. Considering what's at stake, I doubt he'd believe we'd just give up on our investigation to save any one individual, even Astarte. Besides, he knows I've seen what werewolves do with their captives." He tried unsuccessfully not to visualize the Black Spiral Dancer lair he'd visited, with the rotting, half-devoured corpses heaped about.

"So what's the plan?" Antoine asked.

"Whoever's waiting for us," Bellamy said, "let's be optimistic and assume they haven't spotted us yet. If we sneak up through the insides of the neighboring houses, maybe we can get right on top of them before they do."

Her change of expression half obscured by her mask of bandages, Marilyn frowned. "Remember, I can't walk through walls the way the rest of you can."

Bellamy thought sourly that if her magick wasn't working anyway, she might as well hang back, but he didn't quite have the heart to say so. "Then you use the houses for cover, and sneak up carefully. Keep your pistol ready. Anyway, assuming we can get next door to where we're going without all hell breaking loose, I'll go on in alone for some reconnaissance."

Antoine shook his wedge-shaped head. "No way, warmblood."

"It's just possible that one man can slip Astarte out unnoticed. Then we won't have to fight the perps on their own terms. And even if I can't manage that, wouldn't you like to know what we're facing before you go rushing in there?"

"I suppose so," said Titus. "But *I* should be the scout. I can do things you can't, such as veil myself in darkness."

"I know you can work miracles," Bellamy said. "That's what makes you too valuable to risk as point man. Look, I'll be okay. If anything tries to hurt me, I'll shoot it. You'll hear the noise and come running. I can hold out for the couple seconds it'll take you to reach me."

Titus grimaced. "I still don't like it, but all right."

"Then let's do it," Antoine growled. The column turned and slunk to the house on their immediate right. The wraiths climbed on up the portico steps and melted through the door. Wheezing, her sparkling halo gray and crimson with pain and determination, Marilyn crept on through the pool of shadow beside the porch.

The *abambo* skulked on through a succession of desolate rooms, exterior walls, and the weed-infested strips of ground between them. Many of the parlors and dining rooms were altogether bare, stripped of everything of value, but occasionally some forlorn bit of ornamentation hinted at the luxurious lives of the planters and entrepreneurs who had once inhabited them. A parquet floor, warped by water damage. Faded golden French Zuber wallpaper, hanging in tatters. An elaborately carved, high-backed throne of an armchair, with one leg snapped off.

After what seemed an eternity, the ghosts reached the house adjacent to their objective. Peeking through a broken window, Bellamy still didn't see any signs of occupancy next door. He jumped through the opening and the frame surrounding it. For a split second, the jagged shards of glass seemed to snag his flesh, although the sensation didn't hurt, merely tugged. Once on the ground, he dashed to the octagonal house and slipped his face through the side of it.

Since there was a crawlspace beneath the building, he found himself peering into an empty room from a vantage point about three feet above the floor. He listened and heard nothing but the hissing of Nihils and the faint skittering of vermin in the walls. But despite the ambient stink of wood rot and rat droppings, he caught the scents of Astarte's sweat and blood and Dunn's rank, bestial odor once more.

Bellamy laid his assault rifle on the floor, and then, planting his hands beside it, hoisted himself through the wall and up into the room. The weapon at the ready, constantly turning, he stalked on through the first level of the house.

All he found was filth and a marble fireplace, which, by the looks of things, someone had once tried to extract from the wall before abandoning the effort as too much trouble. It was beginning to look as if there were no Spectres or wolfmen lurking about after all. And yet the house *felt* dangerous. Something about the atmosphere gave him the creeps, or maybe it was just his apprehensions for Astarte jangling his nerves. Please, God, let her be alive.

As he started up the free-standing spiral staircase, he caught another whiff of her scent, stronger than before. Insanely reckless though it would have been, he had to struggle to resist the urge to call her name.

On the second floor he found deep, parallel gouges marring one of the walls. A werewolf had sharpened his claws here, but there was no sign of the monster now.

Still skulking, gun leveled, Bellamy climbed to the landing of the third floor, where a draft blew through the broken stained-glass skylight at the apex of the high, concave ceiling. Behind a doorway on the left, Astarte lay hog-tied on the floor. At first glance, all her cuts and bruises appeared superficial.

Bellamy felt a surge of joy, which instantly curdled into horror. Because Astarte wasn't moving, and her face was blue. A loop of rope constricted her neck, and despite his hypersensitive hearing, he couldn't hear her heartbeat. Nor did she have a visible aura.

He threw himself down beside her, simultaneously projecting himself across the Shroud. He used his darksteel shortsword to cut away the noose, nicking her neck in the process, then administered CPR, alternately breathing air into her mouth and pumping her chest. Now it was *her* lips and skin which seemed hideously cold.

Maybe Titus or Marilyn could revive her. He grabbed his rifle and fired a burst, then returned to his own efforts.

Perhaps fifteen seconds later, Astarte rasped in a breath, coughed convulsively, then breathed again. Her halo flickered into view. Bellamy sobbed with relief, and her eyes fluttered open.

"It's all right," he said. "Dunn tied you up in such a way that you'd slowly strangle to death, but I got to you in time."

She gaped at him blankly. It was obvious she was still dazed. Considering that her brain had been deprived of oxygen, it was no wonder. "No," she croaked. "Choked…myself."

"Trying to get free."

She weakly shook her head. "No…suicide."

He stared at her, unwilling to believe she meant what she seemed to mean. "I don't understand."

"To be with you. To be magick. But I never…left my body. Everything just went black." Her eyes widened as if she'd suddenly remembered some crucial fact. "I did it to warn you!" She coughed convulsively.

"To warn us of what?" Titus asked, crossing the Shroud and materializing beside them. No doubt all the *abambo* had entered the house by now.

She kept coughing and struggling to speak. At last she forced the words out. "Dunn hid bombs," she gasped. "Radio-controlled. Here and in the ghost world, too." A chill flowed up Bellamy's spine.

"Are you sure?" Titus asked. "Why hasn't he set them off already?"

"He's trying to make sure that our entire team is in the house," Bellamy surmised. "Since most of us are *abambo*, and we made a stealthy approach, that isn't easy."

"Then perhaps we can slip out again before he is certain," the shaman said.

"I doubt it," Bellamy said. "The three of us are framed in a big bay window." Titus's head began to swivel. "*Don't look.* I don't know where Dunn is, but I'll bet he can see us. As soon we move to leave this room, or give any sign we're trying to escape, he'll trigger the explosions. Before long, he'll do it regardless."

"Then what do we do?" asked Titus, calmly but with an undertone of stress in his voice. "All the Queen's warriors are in the house, too, searching the place. We have to warn them."

"I'll call them," Bellamy said, "too softly for even a werewolf to catch it from outside. But our men are *abambo*, so they'll hear me." He prayed that was true. "Attention, everyone. There are bombs in the house. Get out immediately."

"Now what?" Astarte asked.

"I'm going to count to three," Bellamy said, "and then you and I are going to jump up and throw ourselves through the window. Titus, you get yourself out however seems best to you."

"Understood," the old man said. "Good luck."

"Here goes," the FBI agent said. "One, two, *three!*"

Titus vanished back into the Underworld. Bellamy and Astarte scrambled to their feet and sprinted at the filthy window. Reaching it a half stride ahead of her, the FBI agent raised his arm to protect his face and crashed through the glass. They started to fall, and then the darkness blazed orange and roared.

Time seemed to slow down. Tumbling in mid-air, Bellamy saw the entire house flying apart around an enormous, expanding fireball. He realized that a blast of this magnitude was unquestionably going to destroy him and Astarte, and that if the explosion on the cold side of the Shroud was comparable, all his fellow *abambo* were doomed as well.

Then space stretched, also, as it had in the corridor in the police station, where Dunn had set his first trap for Astarte and Marilyn. Bellamy knew he was still plummeting right beside the disintegrating mansion. Chunks of brick and burning wood were hurtling all around him. Yet simultaneously, the explosion somehow looked far away, far enough to protect him from the force and the flames.

Which only left the fall to worry about. He slammed down hard, on one foot. His ankle snapped in a flare of pain, dumping him on the ground. He wrenched himself around, looking for Astarte. She was kneeling in the grass a couple of feet away.

"Are you okay?" he asked.

"Yeah," she said. "Look there."

Bellamy turned his head. Marilyn stood beneath one of the now-shattered, burning pines with her silver-headed cane raised in both hands. The FBI agent guessed that, limping painfully along outside, she'd never quite made it inside the octagonal house. And when the bombs went off, she'd managed to use her magick to shield herself and her friends from the blast.

She gave Bellamy and Astarte a glassy-eyed smile. "Not *entirely* useless after all," she said. Then she pitched forward onto a heap of fiery rubble.

Thirty-Five

Dunn wanted to watch the fireworks. But he also knew just how much plastique he'd planted in the octagonal house, so he thought it wiser to turn his back. Sure enough, the window through which he'd been peering shattered into a barrage of splinters, some of which landed in his hair and on his shoulders.

Brushing them away, he turned back to the opening and looked across the street. The explosion had not only virtually annihilated the domed, octagonal mansion but smashed half of the derelict home beside it. Yet, impossible as it seemed, Bellamy and his girlfriend were hunkered down more or less intact in the front yard.

After a moment, Dunn saw the problem: Marilyn Sebastian, striking some kind of Siegfried and Roy pose under a burning tree. She must have tossed off a spell of protection.

Dunn turned to the little stone statue he'd set on the shelf. He'd been told the thing was supposed to be a jaguar, although if that was really what the Aztecs had thought a big cat looked like, they should have devoted less time to building pyramids and playing football with severed heads and more to inventing optometry. "Tell me we at least nailed the spooks from New Orleans."

For an instant, nothing happened. His Spectre companion had probably been peeking out the window himself, and needed a second to reinstall himself in the artifact. A gleam came into the carved, bulging eyes. "At least some of the ghosts made it through intact, also," the image said in its dry, hollow voice. "Titus is floating in the air. The alligator and a number of the wraith soldiers are in the yard."

"Jumping Jesus on a pogo stick!" the werewolf snarled. "And Cank thinks that rookie sorcerer doesn't have any juice. Well, we're going to bag *somebody* for our trouble. Bellamy and Sebastian, anyway." He set down the radio detonator and picked up the sniping rifle he'd dragged along for the occasion. As he sighted in on Sebastian, the transsexual collapsed. Now the remains of the pine hid most of her body.

"Don't be a fool!" the jaguar statue said. "There are too many of them, and in a moment, they'll start looking for us. We've got to get out of here right away."

Dunn knew his companion was making sense, but the thought of letting his enemies escape *again* was just too much to bear. "You do what you want," he said. He tried to sight in on one of Sebastian's vital organs, but couldn't quite manage it.

"The mage is probably dead already," the Spectre said. "The way you mangled him, his body couldn't take the strain of the conjuration."

"Then I'll pop Bellamy," Dunn said. He shifted his aim to his fellow FBI agent, who was crawling frantically toward Sebastian as if something were wrong with his legs. *This one's for you, Chester, not that you weren't a goddamn pain in the ass.*

"You can't be sure of killing Bellamy," the stone figure said. "If he doesn't perish instantly, on your first shot, he can just fade back across the Shroud and heal—Wait! Do you feel it?"

"What are you talking about?" Dunn asked, beginning to squeeze the trigger. Then he sensed it, too. An indefinable foulness, a silent but somehow dissonant vibration, hanging in the air. It might have sickened a human, assuming he was capable of registering it at all, but to a Black Spiral Dancer, it was exhilarating. "Son of a bitch. Is it show time at last?"

"Yes!" said the Spectre. "And we'll be needed. Don't throw your life away for a beggarly portion of revenge. In a few hours you'll be free to punish your enemies however you want, for however long it amuses you."

"You've got a point," said Dunn. "Let's get the hell out of Dodge." He picked up the statue, and, invoking his Ragabash powers of stealth, skulked for the door and the stairs beyond.

Thirty-Six

Ignoring the jabs of pain from his injured ankle, Bellamy scrambled toward Marilyn. Astarte darted past him, grabbed the unconscious Arcanist, and rolled her off the fiery debris.

The lovers beat frantically at the flames dancing on Marilyn's coat and bandages. When the flames went out, Bellamy placed his hand under the transsexual's nostrils, and then touched her carotid artery. She was breathing, and had a pulse. He told Astarte as much, and she slumped with relief.

Titus materialized beside them. "Poor, brave soul," she said. "I can see from her halo that that took all the strength she had."

"She shielded you, too?" Astarte asked.

The wizened *ibambo* nodded. "All of us, apparently, on both sides of the Shroud at once. We only lost three warriors. It's a miracle."

Astarte hesitated. "Is she going to die?"

"I hope not," Titus said. "I'll try to revitalize her as I did before."

"Dunn," Bellamy said grimly. "He's still around here somewhere, most likely in that house directly opposite us. I'm going to slip back into the Underworld and fix my ankle, and then I'm going to find him."

He allowed death to pull him back into the Shadowlands. Antoine and Queen Marie's other soldiers popped into view. In the country of the dead, a second, greenish fire danced and crackled, superimposed on the one consuming the remains of the octagonal house. To Bellamy's surprise, the freezing chill of the one didn't cancel out the fierce heat of the other. Rather, he felt both simultaneously, a sensation so peculiar that it took him a moment to interpret it.

He sent a current of psychic energy flowing into his ankle. It throbbed once, and then the bone knit. Meanwhile, Titus gently took Marilyn's face between his hands.

His scaly hide mottled with pale burns, Antoine rushed up to Bellamy. "Tripwire?" he asked. "Or was somebody waiting and watching with a remote control?"

"Remote control," Bellamy said. "Let's go get him." He rose and pointed at a cluster of Queen Marie's soldiers in their zebra-striped capes. "You men, come with us. The rest, stay here and look after Astarte, Titus, and Marilyn." Wishing he hadn't left his rifle behind when he made his desperate dive through the window, he pulled his Browning from its holster and trotted toward the derelict home across the street. His squad followed.

As soon as he flowed through the door into the foyer, he caught Dunn's scent. Antoine turned his head this way and that, then oriented on the stairs. "Up there," the gator whispered.

"I figured as much," Bellamy said. "If you wanted to keep an eye on the room where he stashed Astarte, that would give you the best vantage point." He led his companions skulking up the stairs.

But when they reached the site from which Dunn had kept watch, they found that the werewolf and his accomplices, if any, had already departed. Bellamy felt his shadowself squirming in the depths of his mind, mocking his frustration. He had to fight an urge to scream and kick the wall.

He turned to Antoine. "Can you track him?"

The reptile led Bellamy and the human warriors back downstairs, then crawled around the ground floor for a while. "Sorry," he rasped at last. "I guess the Big Bad Wolf's got a talent for covering a trail that offsets my knack for following one."

Bellamy's muscles clenched in frustration. How was he supposed to derail the coming disaster when *none* of his allies was competent? An instant later, he realized just how unfair and ungrateful that thought was, and his impatience gave way to shame. What was wrong with him, anyway? Granted, fear for the kidnapped Astarte and the events of the last few minutes had rubbed his nerves raw, but even that wouldn't ordinarily make him disparage his friends. Something else had awakened his Shadow, and now the psychic parasite was slipping garbage into his mind.

Abruptly he noticed the hot, slimy feeling clotting in the air. "There's another Maelstrom coming." He hesitated. The warning sensation was indefinably, disquietingly different this time, albeit Titus had told him that no two shadow storms were exactly alike. "At least I think there is."

"Peachy," Antoine said. "That'll make the evening just about perfect. What do you want to do now?"

"Rejoin the others. Marilyn and Astarte need to get away from here before the police show up. And we *abambo* should move to a safe place to ride out the storm."

The companions they'd left behind had moved down the street, putting distance between themselves and the fires. Jaw clenched, Astarte strained to support Marilyn's weight. The Arcanist looked, at best, semiconscious. Evidently Titus had done everything he could for her, because he'd allowed himself to slip back to the dark side of the Shroud.

"No luck?" the shaman asked.

Bellamy shook his head. "Dunn pushed the button and ran. Let's get out of here." He projected himself into the Skinlands, and the other ghosts disappeared. Startled, Astarte jumped and nearly lost her hold on Marilyn.

"Here," he said, "let me take her." He lifted the mage in his arms. "We're moving out." He headed back toward Union Street. A raw ligature mark still striping her neck, Astarte fell into step beside him.

"Are we taking Marilyn to a hospital?" she asked, raspingly.

"She wouldn't want that," Bellamy said, "any more than you or I want to answer questions about what happened to her. On the other hand, we can't let her die. Let's see how she does over the course of the next few minutes."

"I hurt her *again*," Astarte said somberly.

"No," he said. "This is Dunn's fault, not yours."

Titus shimmered into view in front of them as she started to reply.

"What is it?" Bellamy asked.

"I'm afraid that our mission has run out of time," the old man said grimly. "Something is happening in the Shadowlands, something that leads me to believe that the Spectres are beginning their ritual. You'd better slip back across the Shroud and take a look."

THIRTY-SEVEN

When Gayoso turned, he saw Valentine standing just inside the door aiming a small pistol at him. He considered simply rushing the gun, but the sacrificial table was in the way, and even a pathetic little freak like Valentine might conceivably get off a lucky shot before the Anacreon reached him. He snatched up one of the larger darksteel knives and poised it over the unconscious child's chest.

"Stop!" Valentine yelped.

"No, *you* stop," Gayoso replied. "Have you ever even fired a pistol before, Valentine? Hitting the mark isn't easy, particularly if the weapon's too large and heavy for you to handle comfortably. I sincerely doubt that you could stop me from destroying the girl. But I promise that if you'll lay the gun down and step away from it, I won't harm either one of you."

"No way."

The Doppelgänger sighed. "Then I suppose we have a standoff." Valentine crept a step closer, no doubt to improve his chances of hitting his target. "*No!* Stay right where you are. Otherwise I'll gut her this instant."

His homely face twisted with anguish, Valentine froze. The automatic quivered in his hands. Now fairly certain that the dwarf would hold his fire for the time being, Gayoso began sending a silent call for help into the gaping Nihil in the center of the floor. Prudence had only barely commenced teaching him how to exploit the psychic bond that all doomshades supposedly shared, but with luck, *something* would respond to his summons eventually. Meanwhile, he merely needed to stall for time.

"Tell me about Daphne," said Valentine.

"I have her in a sort of makeshift oubliette. She's uncomfortable, but essentially unharmed. If we can come to an understanding, I'll give her back to you."

Valentine bared his teeth like a wild animal. "You're lying! You destroyed her! You destroyed all of them! I could tell you were hiding *something*, but I thought I knew you. I never dreamed…*this!*" He aimed the gun anew.

Gayoso could tell that the little man was on the verge of going berserk. In a moment he was likely to start blasting away, the threat to the girl on the table notwithstanding. And as best the Anacreon could judge, peeking from the corner of his eye, there was still nothing rising from the seething depths of the Nihil.

"There's so much you never dreamed," Gayoso said. "My personal fall from grace is the least of it. And if you shoot me, you never will know."

Valentine's eyes narrowed. "What are you saying?"

"Isn't it obvious? Our late friend Montrose suspected that a sinister conspiracy was plotting against everyone else in the province, loyal Hierarchs, Heretics, and even mortals alike. It turns out he was absolutely correct. If you'll promise to let me go free, I'll tell you all about it. Imagine what a hero you'll be when you run and tattle to Shellabarger and Mrs. Duquesne."

The dwarf hesitated. "How do I know you'll tell me the truth?"

Because I *know you'll never have a chance to tell anyone else*, Gayoso thought. *If help doesn't arrive soon, I'll go ahead and pounce on you myself.* Meanwhile, it might actually be fun to share the secret with someone besides his allies, to savor the look of growing dismay on Valentine's lumpish face.

"You can trust your instincts. You didn't have any trouble recognizing that I was lying about sweet little Daphne."

Valentine's mouth tightened, and the pistol quivered. For a moment, Gayoso thought it had been a critical mistake to mention the child whore again. Then the jester said, "Okay. Talk." His voice had roughened, as if he was imitating a tough detective in a TV show.

Repressing a sneer, Gayoso began to explain how the coming of the Aztec Spectres dovetailed with his desire to establish his own kingdom. As he neared the end, he finally sensed something approaching the other side of the Nihil. The hissing of the dimensional rift grew marginally louder, and a faint odor like the smell of hot wires tinged the air. He hoped Valentine was too wrapped up in the story to notice.

"It will never work," the little man said, sounding as if he was trying to reassure himself.

"On the contrary, it's quite feasible," Gayoso said. "Thanks to the pollution of the spiritual atmosphere, a very special Maelstrom should erupt from the Tempest within the next few days. Prudence and the other false Pardoners will tap its power to cast a spell which will complete our domination of the troops under my command, along with the many other Legionnaires who have seen fit to seek absolution.

Together, they'll launch a preemptive strike against my fellow Anacreons. The storm will also furnish the energy for the confessors to conjure up their own special citadel. It's a *wonderful* scheme, if I do say so myself. Even those busybodies from New Orleans wouldn't have been able to stop it."

"Who?"

"Oh, that's right, they steamed into town after you dropped out of sight. Some of Queen Marie's officers stumbled onto a smattering of information about the conspiracy, and came to help the good people of Natchez defend themselves. Alas, they arrived too late to be of any real use.

"Ah, but you didn't, did you, Señor Jester? Such a beautiful, intricate scheme, and now one meddlesome little homunculus is going to wreck the entire thing. It really is a pity."

Valentine glared. "You're damn right I'm going to wreck it. Okay, you kept your part of the deal, and now I'll keep mine. Move away from the girl, and I'll let you walk out of here."

"Never mind about that," Gayoso said.

The dwarf cocked his head. "What?"

"I've decided I'm not in a hurry to leave after all. You know how it is when you fail to satisfy a craving. If I don't stay and offer the child to the Malfeans, I'll be nervous and irritable all night."

"You're out of your mind," Valentine said, "and that's fine by me. I gave you your chance, and I'm glad you didn't take it."

Clearly, the dwarf was about to shoot. Gayoso poised himself to dodge, and then another Spectre finally reared up from the Nihil.

The servant of the Void had such a jumbled, chaotic shape that for an instant Gayoso couldn't quite discern what it was. Then he made out the scores of thrashing arms—small as the limbs of newborn infants—projecting from a central cylindrical mass about seven feet tall. At the top of the thing, an organ resembling a tattered, rotting orchid drooled yellow slime.

Sensing the doomshade, Valentine whirled. A dozen of the puny-looking arms attacked him, some grabbing, others snagging and tearing his skin with curved, delicate, feline claws. The dwarf tried to hurl himself backward, but failed to break free.

"Oh, dear," drawled Gayoso. "Suddenly it appears that you won't be confounding my wicked designs after all. Certainly not if I stab you in the back while my friend has you immobilized." Valentine fired three shots at the many-armed doomshade, and then it knocked the pistol from his hand. Gayoso started around the makeshift altar.

Something pierced his abdomen. For a split second, the sensation was one of simple pressure, and then agony ripped through him. As he doubled over, the sacrifice jerked her weapon out of his belly for another thrust. Obviously she'd regained consciousness some time ago, but had bided her time, playing possum. She'd even managed to take possession of one of the ritual daggers.

If only Valentine had burst into the room a moment later, Gayoso would have had the little bitch shackled. The unfairness of the situation enraged him as much as his pain.

He slashed with his own knife. The girl recoiled to avoid the attack, and tumbled off the far side of the table. Doubled over, he hobbled after her. He felt the black fires of Oblivion seething through him, rippling outward from his belly, maddening him further. Not that he feared the ecstatic consummation of annihilation in the Void. But it was intolerable that his enemies should survive him.

To his astonishment, the sacrifice dropped her knife and fumbled a flintlock pistol out from inside her shirt. Given another moment, Gayoso would have discovered that, too. She pulled the hammer back, involuntarily squinched her eyes shut, and pulled the trigger. The Anacreon sidestepped. The gun barked, and the ball sang past his head.

He lunged at the girl, stabbing, and she cringed backward. A second advance should have carried his blade to the target, but when he stepped, a fresh burst of pain made him falter. She scrambled on backward into the corner where he'd stowed his regular clothing, armor, and weapons.

The child backed right into his cuirass, overturning it with a clatter. She looked around wildly, spotted his automatic, yanked it from its holster, and pointed it at him.

But unfortunately for her, she'd neither chambered a round nor released the safety. Gayoso grinned, and, in no hurry now, stalked on toward her.

The gun clicked. Her brown eyes wide and her face white as milk, the child threw it.

The desperation tactic took Gayoso by surprise. The pistol hit him in the stomach, squarely on top of the dagger wound. He yelped in pain and fury and staggered forward, off balance, stabbing madly. The black blade gashed the child's scalp and sheared away a lock of hair, which dissolved instantly.

But it wasn't a mortal or even a crippling stroke, and as he raised the knife to attack again, the child somehow squirmed past him, out of the corner. When he blundered back around, he saw that she'd carried his rapier with her.

The long, straight sword was still in its scabbard. Small as the sacrifice was, she'd have an awkward time trying to get it out. Determined to deny her the opportunity, he lunged at her.

She swung the rapier like a club, cracking him on the knee. He gasped at the jolt of pain, stumbled, and she struck at him again. Reflexively he caught hold of her weapon and tried to wrest it away from her. She clung to the hilt, and the rapier hissed from the scabbard, leaving him with a useless leather tube and the girl with a naked blade.

Still gripping the sword with both hands, she ran at him. He tried to step backward and parry the point with his dagger, but he was an instant too slow. The thin, black blade punched into his belly just to the right of the knife wound.

Gayoso passed out for a second. When he came to, he was on his knees, and, her face contorted with glee, the sacrifice was aiming the rapier for another thrust. He tried to raise the knife into a guard position, but his arm rose slowly, shaking, too weak and spastic to be of any real use.

He was both a king in the making and the vessel of the only true power in the universe, and yet, through sheer luck, these two tiny, meaningless phantasms of the vast lie called Creation were about to vanquish him. He hated them, hated them, hated them!

Valentine screamed.

The sacrifice jerked around. Still all but paralyzed by the punctures in his belly, Gayoso couldn't take advantage of her distraction. He perforce contented himself with looking where she was looking.

The thing from the Nihil was gripping Valentine with at least twenty of its hands. The dwarf squirmed helplessly. The Spectre had bent its upper body into a curve like the crook of a walking stick, and now the tattered orchid vomited slime onto Valentine's head. His skin steamed, blistered, and charred.

The skinny, brown-haired child pivoted back toward Gayoso. Her sharp-nosed face still wore a snarl, and for an instant he was certain she wanted to slay him so badly that she was willing to let Valentine perish to do it. Then she wheeled and ran toward the many-armed doomshade.

When Gayoso had first occupied this room, it had contained no psychic residue. Since then, however, his own sacrifices and satanic rituals had charged it with the memory of agony, terror, cruelty, and hate. He reached out for the energy. It wouldn't heal darksteel wounds completely, not very quickly, anyway. But if the Nihil monster would only keep his enemies for half a minute or so, the infusion of power ought to suffice to put him back on his feet.

The sacrifice stabbed the cylindrical Spectre in the side. An expanding ring of shadow washed outward from the puncture. Still clutching Valentine, the flesh at its base bulging and rippling and its little arms pawing, the monster surged at the child.

It nearly caught her, too. Perhaps she hadn't expected a creature with no feet to cover ground so quickly. But she backpedaled just in time, then jabbed it again.

Gayoso managed to draw himself to one knee.

The little girl retreated around the room, wounding her pursuer with a series of stop thrusts. The monster began a high-pitched keening, then faltered and rocked unsteadily back and forth. Had it possessed legs, one might have said it was staggering. The girl stalked toward it. Suddenly as agile as before, the doomshade bent and thrust its crown of petals at her. Slime sprayed out and splashed her in the face.

Shaking, clutching the sacrificial table for support, Gayoso dragged himself to his feet.

Reeling back against the wall, the girl dropped the rapier to claw at the corrosive goo clinging to her face. The monster scuttled toward her. "Seize her, but don't slay her!" Gayoso said. He still wanted to attend to that particular chore himself. Indeed, considering the indignities she'd inflicted on him, he meant to make her suffer as none of his victims before her.

His skin crisscrossed with fine white gashes, Valentine wrenched himself free. Apparently the Spectre's wounds had weakened its grip, or else it had simply been unable to focus on the girl and the dwarf at the same time. Valentine scurried across the floor, grabbed the pistol he'd dropped, spun around, and started firing at the creature.

As Gayoso had predicted, the little man was no marksman, particularly in his current state of agitation. Most of the shots flew wild. But at least one didn't, and suddenly the monster dissolved into streamers of shadow.

Infuriated anew, Gayoso felt himself changing as a new facet of his Spectre nature asserted itself. The bones of his skull swelled and shifted into some brutish configuration. Tumors swelled and weeping sores opened on his face and neck. Ignoring the pain still burning in his abdomen, he managed to stoop and recover his own pistol.

Valentine tried to shoot him and scurry to the child at the same time, a maneuver which impaired his marksmanship still further. None of the shots struck home. Gayoso readied his gun.

The sacrifice dropped her hands from her blistered face. Evidently she'd rubbed away the worst of the slime. Valentine snapped off another shot, and grazed Gayoso's arm. Exhilarated with the lust for retribution, the Anacreon barely felt it. Grinning, savoring the moment, he drew a bead on the bridge of the dwarf's nose.

Valentine grabbed the child by the forearm and dragged her through the wall.

Fast as his wounds would permit, Gayoso scrambled after them. They couldn't outdistance him, not with such short legs!

And yet, when he glided into the abandoned suite of cubicles beyond the wall, the two wraiths were nowhere in sight.

Senses straining, he stalked from one partitioned work space to the next. With no result. After a minute, he was suddenly certain that Valentine and the girl had slipped from the area when his back was turned, then tiptoed down the stairs to the street. He ran down the steps himself, sprang out onto the stoop, pivoted this way and that, and saw no one.

Well, then, he'd just have to track them down. If he listened to its voice, Oblivion would show him the way. He stepped onto the sidewalk, then felt the dirty wind, hot one moment and the cold the next, wailing down the empty street.

A Maelstrom was beginning. He turned toward the west. A wall of darkness, blacker than the night, was rising above the rooftops.

The final storm, the disturbance his allies had worked so hard to create, had finally come. Gayoso was still so intent on hunting down Valentine and the sacrifice that, for another moment, even the arrival of his hour of triumph scarcely seemed to matter. But then sanity—or what corresponded to it in the mind of a Doppelgänger—reasserted itself.

He had to return to the Citadel at once, to orchestrate his *coup d'état.* He could catch the dwarf and the child later, when he was the absolute master of the province, and give them an infinity of pain. His anger subsiding, his features reverting to their former shape, he hurried back inside to don his customary attire.

Thirty-Eight

Peeking through a window across the street from Gayoso's lair, Valentine was amazed to see the Spaniard melt back through the door. He would never have expected his pursuer to give up so easily. He took Belinda's hand and they skulked in the opposite direction, through the abandoned luncheonette with its counter and stools, out the rear wall of the building, and into a narrow alley choked with litter decades old.

It was only then that he dared to speak, even in a whisper. "Are you all right? Are your eyes okay?"

"Yeah," Belinda said, tendrils of new skin creeping across her raw white burns, "now. I blinked when that thing spat at me, and that kept out the worst of the gunk." She suddenly scowled. "God damn you!"

"What?"

"You didn't kill him! You had a gun, too, and I'd already hurt him. You could've gotten him. But instead we ran away!"

Valentine grimaced. "You're welcome."

Her brown eyes narrowed. "What?"

"Skip it," sighed the dwarf. "Look, you and I were both hurt ourselves, you so bad that you were a sitting duck. Gayoso knows how to shoot, I don't, and I don't think I had but one or two bullets left. Besides which, did you see how his face changed?"

The hippie hesitated. "No," she said sullenly. "Everything was blurry."

"Well, he turned pretty damn ugly. As soon as I saw that room and you on the altar, I knew his Shadow had taken him over, but I didn't know he'd turned into a full-fledged Spectre, if you get what I mean. But he has! The way he looked right then, I'm not sure a *thousand* bullets would have stopped him."

"Well, since you chickened out, I guess we'll never know, will—"

Her sneer abruptly melted into a look of remorse. "My god, listen to me. You came back to help me, and all I can do is bitch at you. It's just that I know for sure now. Starshine really *was* tortured and murdered. There was nothing left for me but revenge, and we didn't even get that!"

"I know," Valentine said, awkwardly patting her shoulder. "I feel the same way. But we *will* get the perverted son of a bitch."

"How?"

"Well, it *seems* like all we have to do is get to Shellabarger and Mrs. Duquesne and tell them what we know. That's what Gayoso said himself. So I'm still trying to figure out why he didn't keep chasing us." A hot, gritty wind scraped his cheek, as if to get his attention. He turned and saw the curtain of blackness rising above the rooftops to the west. "Oh, shit."

"What is it?" Belinda asked. "Another Maelstrom?"

"I think it's more than that. I don't know exactly when you woke up, how much you heard, but I think this is the storm that's going to rev up the Spectres' big magick ritual and give them the power to take over the province. Gayoso stopped chasing us because he figures we don't matter anymore."

With a sharp snap, a jagged Nihil crack opened in the pavement at their feet. Off to the north, in the Quick section of Natchez, guns banged, and someone screamed. The Maelstrom was making its presence felt on both sides of the Shroud.

"If the bad guys are making their move," Belinda said, "then we have to warn the Governors right away."

Valentine shook his head. "How are we going to get to them when we don't know who to trust? Apparently a bunch of the Emerald Legion and Pauper Legion soldiers are going to throw in with the Spectres, too."

"Then what do you want to do? Just run away again?"

Valentine opened his mouth to tell her yes, then realized that *wasn't* what he wanted. It was only what he'd *expected* himself to want. "Uh, no. We have to do something. I just don't know—" He frowned as a thought hit him. "Maybe I do."

"What?"

"When Gayoso was filling me in, stalling until that *thing* popped out of its hole"—he shuddered at the memory of countless tiny hands scratching him, gripping him all over and holding him fast, and sticky, burning jelly gurgling down on his head—"he mentioned something about 'busybodies' from New Orleans, who came to stop the Spectres. Since they're new in town, they haven't had a chance to fall under the phony Pardoners' spell. And they must be tough, or Queen Marie wouldn't have sent them. If we hook up with them, maybe we *can* push our way into the Citadel."

To the east, sirens howled.

"Where are these people?" Belinda asked.

"That's the problem, I don't know! Except...Gayoso said they '*steamed*' into town. Don't you think that sounds like they came by boat?"

"Maybe, but it doesn't mean they're there now."

"It—the river front—is still a place to start looking."

She nodded grimly. Her expression of adult resolution looked peculiar on the face of a little girl. "Okay. Let's do it."

They trotted back toward Under-the-Hill. As the wind howled with increasing force, and Nihils yawned, Valentine realized that, considering that he and Belinda were moving toward the looming wall of darkness, they were probably heading into the worst of the Maelstrom, too. Once again, he looked inside himself, expecting to discover the urge to turn back, but it wasn't there. He wondered if he was miraculously turning brave, or, more likely, had just gone crazy.

Thirty-Nine

The wind wailed, chilling Montrose to the bone. He stared at the air in front of him, willing the kink in space to open. Louise stood watch, her curved Chinese sword with the red tassel dangling from the pommel in one hand and Montrose's Bren Ten in the other. She'd lost both her own guns along the way.

The soft, salmon-colored soil heaved, thrusting up a mound of earth. In the blink of an eye, the dirt became a creature somewhat like a panther, but with abnormally long forelegs, and a bare skull for a head. Louise didn't give it the chance to orient itself. She sprang at it instantly, bellowing a *kiai* and swinging her saber at its neck. The knob of bone flew from its shoulders, and its body crumbled into clods of clay.

From the darkness cloaking this desolate tableland came oozing, sucking sounds. The ground was giving birth to additional horrors. "Any luck?" asked Louise.

"No," Montrose replied, his head beginning to throb. "I'm afraid it isn't an especially cooperative rift."

But for better or worse, it was still the best opportunity they'd come upon. In their trek across the Tempest, they'd repeatedly run into storms and hordes of Spectres, perils which had cut the Byways and compelled the wraiths to change course. Had Montrose been given to grandiosity, he might almost have suspected that the Void itself was striving to keep him from reaching his destination.

But now, at last, he sensed not merely the Shadowlands but Natchez itself beckoning on the other side of this particular fault, if only he could rip the wretched thing open!

"Take as much time as you need," said Louise with the barest hint of irony in her tone. "I'll handle the dirt creatures."

Two more of the horrors—one somewhat resembling a disemboweled gorilla, with coils of dangling entrails dragging between its legs, the other a mantis the size of a wolfhound—loped out of the gloom. The Sister of Athena shot them, then wheeled to confront another beast that was skulking up behind her.

As if he'd finally managed to take hold of something tiny and slippery, Montrose felt his Arcanos lock onto the rift. Teeth clenched, straining, he pried the edges of it apart. A luminous blue hole appeared in the air.

He sensed the portal wasn't stable, but there was no more time to work with it. Clay monstrosities were slinking in from every side. "Time to go," he said. "Hold on to me." She stuffed the pistol in her belt, then grabbed his hand. They scrambled through the doorway.

Dazzling colors flashed before his eyes, and the searing taste of bile flooded his mouth. Something bashed him, hard but painlessly, again and again, tumbling him and Louise about like a marble in a pinball machine. Pits and fissures gaped in the whorled, twisting nothingness around him. In a matter of moments, the turbulence would flip the travelers through one of the gaps.

Gripping Louise's hand with all his strength, he peered desperately about with his Harbinger senses, looking for the one rift that would take them where they wished to go. After what seemed an eternity, he spotted it. It looked like an L-shaped crevasse perhaps fifty feet below him, although in this chaotic nowhere, neither distance nor concepts such as up and down had a great deal of meaning. He willed himself and his companion toward it.

Another smash hurled them sideways, toward a ragged scarlet gap like a bloody wound, which seemed to reach to swallow them. Then his Arcanos carried them swooping away and into the L-shaped gap.

A prickling danced across his skin. He felt a pang of excruciating sorrow, which nevertheless made him guffaw. The next instant, he and Louise were standing on a narrow asphalt street with a large Nihil hissing and glittering in the crumbling brick wall behind them.

The night was as dark and the wind as harsh as those they'd left behind on the plateau. Had Montrose not recognized this site, he might have supposed that that his sense of direction had failed him, and he'd simply transported himself and his companion to another section of the Tempest. But he did recognize it. He was on the outskirts of Under-the-Hill, which only seemed like a part of the infinite storm because a Maelstrom was blowing.

Jubilant that they'd reached America at last, he turned to take Louise in his arms. She was staring, her dismay manifest despite her scarred golden mask. His elation withering, he pivoted to see what had so unsettled her.

The street overlooked a stretch of the Mississippi. A curtain of roiling darkness hung above the river, blotting out the stars. Even more disquietingly, except for a narrow strip by the shore, the surface of the water was an inky, glittering black for as far as he could see in either direction. It looked as if the watercourse had turned into one stupendous Nihil.

Despite the shriek of the wind, he now caught the sounds of havoc ringing through the night. Gunfire. Shrieks. Crashes. Car alarms. Sirens. The Quick citizens of Natchez couldn't perceive the disruption in the natural order of things, but it was driving them mad anyway. He suspected the same thing was happening all along the lower Mississippi, in every community where the Aztec Spectres had sown the seeds of terror and despair.

For a moment, he felt sick. He and Louise had fought so hard to make their way here, and now… In a spasm of self-disgust, he thrust defeatism out of his mind and gave the Heretic nun his best confident-general grin. "From the looks of the river, our enemies have already begun the final stage of their offensive. If it were anyone but our valiant, ingenious selves popping out on this road to save the day, I'd be inclined to suspect we'd arrived too late."

Beneath the golden visor, Louise's generous lips curved into a wry smile. "Yes, how fortunate that you and I can work miracles. How shall we set about performing this one?"

"Transformed like that, the river is a power source, just like the vortex in Charon's vault. I suspect the doomshades are closeted together somewhere working high sorcery. We have to find the rite and stop it before it does whatever it's supposed to accomplish. That will require troops. Let's make for the Green Head. With luck, some of my irregulars and perhaps even Mike himself will be there. We'll collect them, then move on to the Citadel."

She gestured with the Bren Ten. "Lead on, milord." He drew his rapier, and they headed up the street.

Forty

Two men blundered into the path of the onrushing van. One turned toward the vehicle, goggled comically, then leaped back out of the headlights' glow. But the other—whose youth, short hair, white shirt, and thin dark tie reminded Quitman of a Mormon missionary—stood his ground, waving a claw hammer and shouting.

The doctor peered frantically about. He couldn't quite make out the nature of the disturbance through which the convoy was passing, couldn't discern if the people running this way and that were trying to harm anyone or merely looting the stores. But one thing was obvious. There were too many of them in the street.

Quitman pivoted toward the driver. "There's no way to go around that man!"

The driver was a chubby black man of indeterminate age, with hands so hairy they almost seemed to have fur. "Not a problem," he said, accelerating.

At the last moment, the young man with the hammer tried to jump out of the way. The van smashed him to the pavement and then rolled over him. One of the children in the back cried out at the jolts. An RN babbled, "Oh shit oh shit oh shit!"

Quitman gaped at the driver. "You hit him!"

"I've got my orders," his companion replied calmly. "Don't trust anybody, don't stop for anything. Deliver your cargo, no matter what. You want the kids to get to safety, don't you, Doctor?"

"Yes," Quitman said.

"Well, they will, but I can't help it if things get a little gritty along the way."

Quitman struggled to put the collision out of his mind. God knew, terrible as it was, it was only one small disaster on a night when a person could see chaos and carnage everywhere he looked.

He'd been working late, trying to finish his quarterly report for St. Mary's Board of Directors, wishing he were working his beautiful Tennessee walking horse Reba instead, when the call to evacuate came in. At first he'd thought there must be some mistake. Surely if Natchez had suddenly become unsafe, someone in the hospital would already have heard about it on television or the radio. But just a minute later, emergency bulletins began to flood the airwaves. Warnings of riots, arson, lynch mobs, mass murderers running amok, and heaven only knew what else. Not just in his own city—although they seemed to be getting worst of it—but up and down the lower Mississippi.

When Agent Dunn's fleet of vans and ambulances had arrived, and patients and staff had abandoned the hospital together, he'd seen firsthand what had the TV news anchors and radio announcers sounding so distraught. Buildings sheathed in crackling yellow flame. A cluster of people stomping a pair of police officers. A headless woman sprawled on the curb, a shotgun cradled against her body and the big toe of her bare right foot jammed through the trigger guard.

Hands trembling, Quitman hit the redial button on his cell phone. Rosalyn didn't answer. He'd felt immensely impatient with her the past few weeks. The way she kept whining that they needed to get out of the state before some maniac slaughtered them in their bed, he couldn't help it. But what if her fears had been one hundred percent justified? What if somebody had broken into the house tonight and—

No! he told himself fiercely. He wouldn't think that thought, wouldn't imagine that gruesome scene. His wife was fine. What he had to do was focus on was taking care of the children.

The van had reached another quiet area. He cranked down the window, stuck his head out, and looked backward, the slipstream fluttering his tie. Other pairs of headlights still shone in the darkness behind his own vehicle. It looked as if the entire convoy had made it through the last disturbance intact.

As he settled back in his seat, the driver took a hard right and sped up a narrow, unlit road. Judging from the ugly brick and cinder-block buildings streaking by on either side, they'd entered some sort of rundown industrial park. "Are you sure you're going the right way?" the physician asked.

The driver smiled. "The whole place looks deserted, doesn't it? Well, it's supposed to. We won't attract the psychos if they don't know we're here."

He made another right, then pulled up in front of a huge warehouse. There were no lights burning, but Quitman glimpsed a couple of shadowy figures standing near the door.

"We're here," the driver said. "I need you to get your people hustling, so we can unload as fast as possible. My buddies and I have a bunch more pickups to make."

"Certainly," Quitman said. For the next few minutes, he moved from one vehicle to the next, explaining the need for haste. Trying to calm frightened, bewildered children and the occasional half-hysterical member of his own team as well. Assisting in the work of gently shifting fragile young bodies. Making sure none of St. Mary's charts or medical supplies were left behind.

He realized that the work was making him calmer, perhaps because with something useful to do he didn't feel quite so helpless against the catastrophe engulfing the city. At any rate, when the last of the gurneys and handcarts rolled toward the warehouse door and the vans pulled away, he almost felt regretful.

"Nice going," said a deep, pleasant voice. His heart jolting, Quitman lurched around. Dunn stood just behind him, a hand-rolled cigarette smoldering in his mouth. "Sorry, Doc. Didn't mean to sneak up on you."

The physician took a ragged breath. "That's all right. I'm just feeling a little rattled."

"You and all the other sane people. Smoke? I can roll it for you."

"No, thank you. How…how bad is this, really?"

Dunn grinned. "It's not the end of the world, but you can see it from here. Seriously, Natchez is a war zone right now. I'm really glad your patients made it here in one piece. And you deserve a big hunk of the credit for that. Malcolm—your driver—told me that you had everybody and everything ready to go by the time he pulled up. And I saw how well you managed your people just now."

The unexpected compliment made Quitman feel a little flustered. "Well…thank you."

Tires squealing, a hatchback sedan rounded the turn and braked in front of the warehouse. Its headlights were on high-beam, and Quitman squinted and raised his arm against the glare, though it didn't seem to bother Dunn. A short, pudgy man in coveralls, a woman perhaps three inches taller and forty pounds heavier, and two little boys scrambled out of the car. The man and the boys looked dazed, the woman outraged, as if the anarchy consuming Natchez were a personal insult.

"Is this—" the pudgy man began.

"We're the Schotts," the woman said harshly, cutting him off. "Reverend Harper said that this was where to come." She gave the pudgy man a glare. "Assuming this fool read the map right."

"This is the shelter," said Dunn. "It'll help us out if you don't leave your car right in front of the door."

"I'll move it," sighed Mr. Schott.

"Bring the luggage, too," the woman told him. "I'm going to get the boys inside." When she looked at the children, her scowl gave way to a look of tender concern. She herded them toward the door, and Mr. Schott trudged back around the nose of the hatchback.

Quitman frowned up at Dunn. "I thought this was a shelter for patients with special medical needs. Those people look healthy enough to me."

Dunn shrugged. "I didn't hand out all the invitations, Doc, so I don't know the story on that particular happy family. Just that they really are supposed to be here, or they wouldn't have known to come. But I guarantee you, your patients will be taken care of."

"I'm sure they will," Quitman said. "I didn't mean to imply anything different. It just seemed strange, and—" He grimaced. "Listen to me, I'm babbling."

"Considering the pressure you've been under, it's no wonder. Let's get you inside, so you can sit down and take a breather."

The doctor shook his head. "I'm all right. But actually, I *should* go in, to help my team get their section of the ward set up."

"Whatever you say," the FBI agent replied. He took a final drag from his cigarette, then tossed it away. It hit the pavement with a scatter of orange embers. "After you."

Beyond the entrance was a hallway constructed of bare planks, sheets of plywood, and egg-carton-style soundproofing, which made a right-angle turn several yards down. Between the door and that point, two bare bulbs dangled from the ceiling. The passage had the look and the fresh sawdust smell of something that had just been slapped together.

"Why did you people build this thing?" Quitman asked.

"We were afraid that not everybody would make it to the shelter uninjured," Dunn replied, "and we didn't want kids looking in the door, seeing blood, and hearing screams. They might have been scared to come inside."

They rounded the turn. A door stood a few feet ahead. Despite the soundproofing, Quitman now caught a muffled jumble of noise, indecipherable yet somehow disturbing, just as he smelled a hint of blood and a rank, zoo-cage odor.

When he opened the door, the sound resolved itself into shrieking and an oddly cadenced chanting. He stepped into a high-ceilinged, cavernous space. In the foreground, huge, wolfish things, prowling for the most part on their hind legs, were separating children from their caretakers with savage efficiency. His own staff lay in gory pieces on the floor along with a number of other adult corpses. Mrs. Schott screamed, a monster swung its taloned arm in a backhand blow, and her head flew from her meaty shoulders.

An inhumanly large and powerful hand grabbed Quitman by the forearm. He looked up into the amber-eyed countenance of a beast-thing, its muzzle pitted with sores and its breath foul as a sewer. The doctor felt a scream catch in his throat. As easily as his prisoner might have picked up a doll, the ogre hoisted him toward its stained, jagged fangs.

"It's okay, Woundraper," said Dunn from behind him. "I'll look after the doc."

Grunting, the monster dropped Quitman, who found that his legs were too weak and rubbery to support him. Dunn grabbed him and held him up. The beast-thing stalked away.

"Did you take a good look at this?" Dunn asked. Shifting Quitman almost as effortlessly as the towering Woundraper had, he directed his captive's gaze toward the center of the room. Now Quitman perceived what happened to the children after the lupine monsters tore them from their dying caretakers' arms. "Pretty efficient, isn't it? Like a damn assembly line."

Quitman told himself he was having a nightmare, but knew it wasn't so. Somehow, this obscenity *was* happening. And since the physician had arranged the exodus from St. Mary's, he was to blame.

"If it makes you feel any better," said Dunn, "you're not going up there. For some weird-ass sorcery reason, the spooks can only use kids. Although I admit that something else kind of nasty *is* going to happen to you."

It vaguely occurred to Quitman that he ought to try to wrench himself away from Dunn. But terror, guilt, and sheer bewilderment still had him paralyzed. "What?" he whimpered.

Dunn gave him a slightly sheepish smile. "The thing is, this little dog-and-pony show has kept me hopping all day. I haven't had anything to eat."

FORTY-ONE

A once-dapper fellow in a cravat, gleaming red satin vest, and cutaway coat reeled down the street, hands outstretched, his face frayed to rags from his hairline to his handlebar mustache. The Maelstrom shrieked and gusted, and his left arm shredded into tatters of ectoplasm also.

It looked to Montrose as if the blinded wraith was done for, and with a twinge of regret, he started to pass him by. But Louise took the poor, unraveling creature by the shoulder, and, shouting over the wailing of the wind, cried, "Your Haunt! Is it nearby?"

The eyeless ghost gave a jerky nod. "Old boarding house," he croaked. "Blue door."

Montrose peered about. Even for wraith eyes, it was difficult to make out colors in the swirling murk of the storm. But after a second he saw a derelict three-story wooden building with flakes of pale blue pigment still clinging to its door. "This way," he said.

As Louise guided the blind wraith forward, a round Nihil dilated in front of her. A pale, plump worm of a Spectre, its twin heads whispering maledictions, writhed from the opening. Montrose drove his rapier into the creature at the point where its body forked, and it melted in ripples of black.

Louise led her charge up the boarding house steps. "Here you are," she said, and pushed him through the substance of the door. If he could ride out the Maelstrom anywhere, it would be in the shelter of his own abode.

Montrose and Louise trotted back up the street. The wind scraped at the Scot's skin, even through his porcelain mask and his voluminous, tattered Inquisitor's mantle. His Shadow writhed inside him.

The two ghosts negotiated a twist in the road. Half a block farther on, beside the inky Mississippi and the rampart of murk extending above it, was the Green Head. Several of his irregulars were just emerging from the dilapidated shack.

To the Scot's surprise, the mercenaries wore the same emerald sashes as the Governors' Legionnaires. During his time as their commander, they'd scorned such regimentation. Evidently something had altered their perspective.

But whatever it was, it wasn't important now. He shouted, "Hey!" None of the ruffians turned. Evidently they hadn't heard him over the cry of the Maelstrom. Striding forward, Louise hurrying along at his side, he unlatched the cowling on his Lantern of Truth. Perhaps the eerie blue light would capture the men's attention.

"Stop!" cried a familiar voice.

Montrose whirled to see Valentine, now clad in ragged but conventional modern clothing rather than motley, scurrying from an alley with a thin, brown-haired little girl at his heels. Both the dwarf and his companion were marked with white, half-healed cuts and scrapes.

The vision Montrose had seen in the Tempest, the confirmation of Valentine's betrayal, replayed itself before his inner eye, and he shivered with the lust for vengeance. In the final analysis, of course, his mission was what truly mattered now, but surely he had time for both. He could destroy the jester in a matter of moments and still catch up with the soldiers.

He raised the darksteel blade and dashed forward. Louise, who had heard his tale of Valentine's treachery, ran after him. The jester recoiled but the Cavalier knew there was no way his ungainly, short-legged quarry could outdistance him.

Valentine never even came close to it. After two steps, he caught his heel on an uneven spot in the brick pavement, and fell backward onto his butt. Grinning, Montrose aimed his blade for a thrust at the little man's chest.

As his arm began to straighten, the little girl threw herself in front of his point. He only barely managed to avoid spitting her. "Stand aside," he said, his voice thick with malice.

"No!" the girl replied. "Don't hurt him! He's trying to help you!" She had the high, breathy voice one might have expected, but with the subtle differences characteristic of child ghosts whose personalities had continued to mature after death.

"I doubt that," Montrose said, maneuvering around her.

"Please!" Valentine cried. "I admit, I did steal your journal—"

"Yes," said the Scot, "for easy money and advancement, after I offered you an honorable path to the same benefits."

"No!" Valentine said. "Only because I was afraid that otherwise Gayoso would toss me out in the cold." He grimaced. "But that doesn't matter now anyway. What does is that you can't hook up with those soldiers."

"Oh, yes, I can. Despite your best efforts to see me executed for treason, the Deathlords have reinstated me. The soldiers of Natchez are mine to command."

"Not those soldiers! Their Shadows are in the driver's seat. They'd kill you in a heartbeat. Will you just listen for a minute? The conspiracy of Spectres that you were worried about is real. They turned Gayoso into a doomshade, too. He brought fake Pardoners into the Citadel, and forced his own troops—even your mercenaries—to start visiting them. A lot of Shellabarger and Mrs. Duquesne's troops went to confess to them, too. As a result, all those people came under their influence, and now the Spectres are working magick to control them completely. Gayoso is going to use them to overthrow the other Anacreons."

"How do *you* know all this?" Montrose asked.

"Belinda—my friend here—and I stumbled onto the secret, that's all. You don't want me to take the time to tell you the whole story, do you?"

"No," said the Cavalier. "If you're lying to isolate me from the army and Gayoso, you'd just concoct an additional falsehood." He glanced at Louise. "What do you think?"

She shook her head. "I don't know. This man doesn't seem terribly wicked to me, but then, *I* don't know him. You'll have to decide."

Frowning, Montrose pondered the situation. By his own admission, Valentine had already betrayed him once. The Stygian's vision had seemed to indicate that the little man had done it willingly, for profit. It was certainly plausible that, anticipating a handsome reward from the Atheist conspiracy, he intended further treachery now.

And yet…

Much as Montrose hated Valentine, Louise was correct. The jester seemed sincere. Visions and prophecies were notoriously prone to misinterpretation, and actually, the little man's claims jibed with everything Montrose had discovered on his previous sojourn in the Shadowlands, and all that Demetrius had mockingly revealed in Charon's vault.

Mask and Scythe, should he believe the dwarf or not? He knew he had to decide quickly. He had a ghastly sense of onrushing disaster, of his last chance to avert it dwindling with every passing moment.

Abruptly it occurred to him that it was the *old* Montrose, the embittered cynic who'd schemed his way up the Hierarchy to a high office in the Seat of Burning Waters, who invariably expected others to betray him. And Fate knew, many had: young Charles, VanLengen, and all the rest of their miserable ilk. But others *had* kept faith with him, Gordon, Airlie, and the other staunch friends whose arms decorated the stained-glass window above his sarcophagus in Edinburgh. Even in the bleak, Shadow-haunted afterlife, he'd eventually found true comrades—Mike, Artie, the other prisoners from the Artificers' pit, and especially Louise.

There was no way to be certain whether Valentine was telling the truth or not, but Montrose did know that he didn't want to revert to the man he'd been before. Indeed, the notion revolted him. Lowering his rapier, he said, "I guarantee that if you're playing me false, you won't survive to collect your thirty pieces of silver."

Valentine shuddered as tension flowed out of his muscles.

"If we can't trust the soldiers," said Louise, "then I suppose we'll have to make our way into the Governors' Citadel, warn Shellabarger and Mrs. Duquesne, and break up the Spectres' ritual all by ourselves." She smiled crookedly. "Compared to invading the Isle of Sorrows and the Onyx Tower, it should be child's play."

"We weren't quite so pressed for time then," Montrose replied, his auburn lovelocks and the folds of his voluminous black cloak fluttering in the wind. "Nor were we traveling through a Maelstrom. This particular operation would require a precocious child at the very least. Still, it would appear to be our only strategy."

"Maybe we don't have to do it alone," Valentine said. "Supposedly some Les Invisibles types came up the river from New Orleans to help the Governors get rid of the Spectres. They haven't been to the phony Pardoners, so they shouldn't be under anybody's spell. Belinda and I didn't come down here to find you, milord Anacreon. We had no way to know you'd made it back from Stygia. We were hunting for those other guys. We thought they might be hanging around their boat."

Still acutely conscious of the seconds ticking by, Montrose felt an urge to press on to the Citadel without further delay. Yet there seemed little question that a larger band would have a better chance of reaching and destroying the Spectres. Moreover, he and his companions were still near the Mississippi. It wouldn't require much time to at least glance at the docks.

"Let's see if we can locate them," he said.

Forty-Two

As the four companions neared the water, the gale, blowing blistering hot one moment and freezing cold the next, grew even more abrasive than before. The wall of boiling darkness above the water appeared to stretch to the top of the sky. Occasionally Montrose thought he glimpsed unidentifiable but hideous shapes forming and dissolving in the murk, like the monstrous phantasms that appeared in the mass of thunderheads in the Tempest.

Someone had beached a keelboat on the shore. The Maelstrom gusted, and the shallow-draft vessel came to life. Cracking and crunching, the timbers ripped themselves apart, writhed about, and pressed themselves back together, creating the form of a troll-like figure which crouched on all fours.

Swords upraised, intent on dispatching the monster before it could complete its transformation, Louise and Montrose ran at it. A round Nihil opened in front of the Scot, and a horned, skeletal doomshade popped up like a jack-in-the-box, brandishing a tomahawk in either hand.

Montrose barely managed to arrest his forward momentum in time to keep the skeleton's first swing from cleaving his head. Dropping into a squat to duck beneath the doomshade's second blow, he counterattacked. His point chipped then grated along a rib. A hint of black fire oozed outward from the damage.

Undeterred, the Spectre scrambled forward, hatchets whirling like the components of a machine. Retreating, Montrose kept himself out of range when possible, parried when the skeleton scuttled into striking distance, and waited for the right opening. Off to his right, gunfire banged and wood creaked and groaned. He assumed the latter noise was the sound of the boat-troll moving, but didn't dare glance away from his own opponent to confirm his guess.

When the Spectre gave him the chance, he stepped forward with a stop thrust. His point caught the child of the Void squarely in the spinal column, just below the jaw. Its horned skull flew off its shoulders.

Though suddenly awash in ripples of darkness, the skeleton continued forward, swinging. Montrose leaped aside and, now too close to use his sword easily, gave the Spectre a savate kick to the knee. It sprawled forward onto the ground, and he stabbed it until it dissolved.

The Anacreon whirled. Crudely made and faceless, the wooden monster was about twenty feet tall. It lurched this way and that, swinging its simian arms at Louise. She danced about its feet, dodging the blows, chipping away at its lower legs with her saber. Bands of darkness flowed outward from the gashes. Periodically a splintery length of plank seemed to wrench itself free of the giant's body. The Sister of Athena was using her telekinesis against it, also.

Valentine stood a few yards back, plinking away at the boat-troll with a Glock 17. Montrose could tell that the dwarf was a novice at shooting, but his target was so big that some of the bullets struck it anyway. Belinda hovered at his side, her face a mask of anxiety.

Montrose charged the giant and helped Louise attack its legs. Its fists—tangled, fingerless masses—swooshed past him like wrecking balls. After a few seconds, the creature stumbled, swayed drunkenly, and disintegrated. The two wraiths scrambled frantically backward to avoid the resulting clattering avalanche of timbers.

"Are you all right?" asked the Scot.

Louise nodded. "It never even touched me."

"Good." He turned to Valentine. "Why didn't you draw that pistol before, when I rushed you with blade in hand?"

Valentine blinked. "It never crossed my mind. I wanted to team up with you, not hurt you." He hesitated. "I feel like I don't have any right to say this, considering what I did to you, but, man, was I glad to see you. It was like the answer to a prayer."

To his surprise, Montrose felt the weight of his animosity melt away. "Why don't we forget about what you did to me?"

The dwarf cocked his head. "Are you serious?" he asked warily.

"Yes. I did write the wretched journal, or at least my Shadow did, which on one level amounts to the same thing. And the plans it contained were treasonous. Perhaps you were justified in turning it over to Gayoso. In any case, if you hadn't arranged my recall to Stygia, my existence would have been much the poorer." He gave Louise a smile, which she returned.

"I'm glad something good came from it," said Valentine somberly, "but I still feel shitty."

"Well, if you have a need to atone, rest assured, an introduction to your African friends will do nicely." They hiked on toward the river.

The Restless of Natchez had long ago appropriated a dilapidated set of docks, discouraging all attempts by the living to refurbish the facilities for their own use. The rotting docks looked too rickety to provide secure mooring for any Skinlands craft, but in relation to the phantom vessels of the Underworld, they were solid as bedrock.

The Maelstrom wrenched broadhorns, keelboats, skiffs, pirogues, and launches this way and that, bashing and grinding them against the docks. One barge had broken the lines securing it and was drifting away downstream. At the far end of the area floated a magnificent black sidewheeler covered with bizarre carvings, including an immense skull face suspended between the twin smokestacks.

"I don't recall ever seeing the paddle boat," Montrose said.

"Me either," Valentine said. "And Gayoso told me the guys from New Orleans '*steamed*' into town."

The four wraiths broke into a run. Out in the glittering black water, something huge momentarily reared above the surface, then submerged once more.

As he neared the sidewheeler, Montrose felt a pang of disappointment. There were no lamps burning, nor anyone in view. Still, his companions at his heels, he trotted up the dock and over the gangplank, and boarded her. "Hello!" he shouted. "Is anyone here?"

No one replied.

The Scot threw open the door to the central cabin, an opulent salon with some sort of elaborate altar at one end of it. He called again, with the same lack of response.

"Damn it!" Valentine said. "This was a fucking wild goose chase! I'm sorry! God, I screw everything up!"

"Don't be silly," Montrose replied. "I can feel that the boat is a Haunt in its own right. It was quite reasonable to infer that Queen Marie's people might ride out the storm here. Perhaps they're ensconced in the Citadel instead. In any event, it seems we're on our own after all."

The wraiths hurried back out into the punishing wind. "Look!" exclaimed Louise, pointing to the south.

Montrose pivoted. Downriver, barely visible through the billowing murk, was a marina that did belong to the Quick. A number of black wraiths in short, zebra-striped capes were milling around in the vicinity of a cabin cruiser. On board the vessel glowed the auras of two or three of the Quick.

"That's them!" Valentine said. "It has to be. But what the hell are they doing down there?"

"Let's find out," Louise said.

As they approached, the African ghosts readied their weapons. Montrose sheathed his rapier and continued forward, displaying his empty hands. "We're friends," he said. "We're trying to defeat the Spectres, also."

A lean, somewhat haggard-looking young man with close-cropped hair stepped between two of the caped warriors. Somewhat to Montrose's surprise, he was white. "Do you know where they are," he asked, "and what they're doing?"

"Yes," Montrose said, "we believe we do."

The other wraith's eyes widened as if the Cavalier's answer had surprised him. Whirling, he shouted, "Titus, Antoine, come quick!"

Two more ghosts hurried up, one, an old fellow whose wizened face was painted crimson on one side and black on the other, and the other, a large alligator wearing a zebra-striped neckerchief, whose scaly tail swished along the ground. Montrose eyed the latter curiously. He'd heard of the animal wraiths of the African Underworld, but had never encountered one before. The reptile's scaly hide had a raw, worn look, as if the Maelstrom was taking its toll on him.

"Tell us what you know," the white African said.

As quickly as possible, oppressed once again by a sense of time slipping away, Montrose laid it out for them. "Will you march on the Citadel with us?" he concluded.

"Of course," said the old man with the painted face. He looked down at the alligator. "However, Antoine—"

The reptile emitted a menacing hiss. His human comrade faltered. "I'm going," Antoine said slowly, as if it was an effort to force the words out. "Don't hassle me about it."

The old man sighed. "Very well. The Orishas know, we can use every man."

"I'll come along as well," said a new voice, pitched in a register which made it difficult to decide whether it was male or female. And when the Scot caught sight of the speaker, he still wasn't sure. The shape of the slim, bandaged figure struggling to rise from the cabin cruiser's deck was essentially androgynous. Judging from the glittering motes in the mortal's gray and crimson aura, he—or she—was a mage, one whose body reeked of blood and fever sweat.

Two other mortals—a pretty young woman dressed all in black, with magenta streaks in her black hair and steel rings embedded in her face, and an obese man in a filthy undershirt—lifted the mage and more or less held their companion upright. "Thank you, my dears," the conjurer wheezed.

The white African frowned. "I don't suppose it's any use trying to convince you to stay behind, either."

"Certainly not," said the mage. "You mustn't worry about me, Frank. My veins are awash with wonderful, wonderful morphine. Trust me, I feel better than any of you."

The woman in black tried to look where the mage was looking, but didn't quite manage to point her face in the right direction. Evidently, unlike her companion, she couldn't see the wraiths. "If you're talking about leaving people behind," she said in a bratty voice, "don't even think about me. You're going to need somebody with a solid body to prop Marilyn up. Plus, I can shoot a few holes in Dunn."

Montrose wondered grimly just how much use Antoine, Marilyn, and the apparently quite normal Quick woman with the piercings were likely to be. But three and a half centuries ago, he'd led his frozen, starving, exhausted Highlanders to victory over the numerically superior Campbells at Inverlochy. Perhaps his new comrades had the same sort of grit.

He could only hope so, because there was no time left to worry about the welfare of any one member of the expedition. Only the objective mattered now. "Are you people ready to march?" he asked.

Forty-Three

As Gayoso approached Mrs. Duquesne's office, his mouth was dry, and he had to suppress a reflexive urge to pant. *Is this really going to work?* he wondered. *It is possible that I'm going to be rid of the supercilious old hag at last?*

As usual, a sentry and a barghest stood before the door to Mrs. Duquesne's office. The Legionnaire came to attention. The bloodhound glared, amber eyes shining inside its mask of gray iron strips.

"I need to see Mrs. Duquesne immediately," Gayoso said.

The guard knocked on the door, waited a moment, then repeated the Spaniard's request. The door—a Shadowlands artifact hung by Artificer's magick in a Skinlands frame—swung open. The Legionnaire stepped aside. The barghest gave a faint, disgusted grunt, as if disappointed that it hadn't been commanded to attack the newcomer.

Nets of gray iron chain covered the walls, floor, and ceiling of the office, to keep unwanted visitors from flitting through. The metal links rattled beneath Gayoso's boots. Mrs. Duquesne sat primly upright, two tidy stacks of paper, her mask, her bowl of oboli, and the black hourglass of Natchez on the desktop before her. Another pair of Pauper guards stood in the shadows behind her. Prior to Gayoso's assuming command of the Inquisition, and the resultant shift in the balance of power, she hadn't been quite so concerned with her personal security.

"Good evening, my lord Anacreon," she said, her tone dry and composed as ever.

Masking a fresh pang of loathing, Gayoso inclined his head. "My lady Governor. Have you heard about the violence?" Two of the false Pardoners had been set to work sneaking about the Citadel, attacking wraiths they discovered alone.

Mrs. Duquesne's thin-lipped mouth tightened at what she evidently considered a stupid question. "Of course. I suppose a Spectre or two has slipped into the complex, or some poor soul has fallen under the sway of his Shadow. Unfortunate, but such things happen during a Maelstrom. The watch will deal with it."

"This storm is different," Gayoso said. "Do you know about the curtain of darkness hanging over the Mississippi?"

"Yes," said the old woman, her condescending attitude slipping just a hair. "That *is* odd. The extent of the unrest among the Quick is similarly disturbing."

"In addition, we have agents of a hostile power abroad in the city, doing Fate only knows what. And, if we can believe them, a cabal of doomshades and werewolves plotting against us as well."

Mrs. Duquesne smiled contemptuously. "Let's try to be logical, shall we, milord? Either Titus and his associates are our enemies, or the conspiracy they warned us of actually exists. It's unlikely that both things are true. Still, I concede your central point. We have ample reason for wariness this evening. And therefore you recommend—what?"

"That we turn out *all* the troops to search the Citadel from top to bottom, and then patrol the Necropolis in force."

"Send the men forth to wander the storm? That's hazardous duty."

"That's why I think we ought to command them personally. All three of us. At the very least, the sight of us out and about will inspire confidence in the citizenry, and with the Maelstrom grinding away at their essences, confidence is precisely what they need."

"And here I was thinking you no longer desired my involvement in any of your military endeavors, my lord Inquisitor."

"If you see your role as purely administrative," Gayoso said, "I understand. But if so, then I think it only reasonable that you surrender the hourglass to someone who *is* willing to carry it into battle."

"That won't be necessary," the Beggar Lord's minion said, rising. She removed her steel-rimmed spectacles, donned her glazed white mask of Tragedy, and replaced the glasses precariously on top of it. Then she picked up the ancient timepiece and the bowl of coins. "Let's go muster the men."

"I've already made a start," Gayoso said, thrilled that, her sharp intellect and wary nature notwithstanding, she seemed to have taken all that he'd said at face value. She expected that for the duration of the storm, they were going to forget their rivalry and stand together as good little Hierarchs should.

Despite her two bodyguards trailing along behind them, he was tempted to fall on her as soon as they exited her office with its wards of protection. Why not? He was a child of the Void, with all the power that implied, and he'd be catching them all by surprise. It required an effort to compel himself to abide by the plan.

They glided through a door onto a rusty fire escape. The icy, howling wind kissed the exposed skin beneath Gayoso's steel domino. Two stories below, Legionnaires and irregulars had assembled on the parade ground, the former drawn up in formation, the latter milling restlessly about. The phosphorescent battle flags and standards of Natchez, the three Deathlords who theoretically controlled it, and the Order of the Unlidded Eye rose above the soldiers' heads. Masked as usual in his baggy green hood, his right hand in his hip pocket, Nathan Shellabarger, whom Gayoso had roused previously, stood talking to one of his Emerald Legion Marshals.

Mrs. Duquesne paused to peer downward. Holding his breath, Gayoso told himself she couldn't possibly suspect what was going to happen next. It was only her habitual caution that had prompted her to make sure that a reasonable number of her own Paupers were present before descending. And after a moment, she headed down the steps.

Shellabarger met his fellow commanders at the foot of the staircase. "We should have done this indoors," he said.

"We'll all be out in the storm quite a bit tonight," Mrs. Shellabarger replied. "We might as well start getting used to it." The three Anacreons strode on toward the reviewing stand on the far side of the ground. Their course took them between a phalanx of Grim Riders and a motley band of desperadoes from Under-the-Hill.

Gayoso burst out laughing.

The other Governors turned toward him. "Yes?" said Mrs. Duquesne.

Struggling to control himself, Gayoso shook his head. "Nothing. Just…" Half choking, he forced out the grating syllables Prudence had bade him memorize.

Shellabarger twitched. "What is that?" he asked. "It almost sounds like a Spectre language."

"Yes," said Mrs. Duquesne, hefting the hourglass, "indeed it does. What are you playing at, my lord?"

Gayoso glanced about, at the soldiers peering curiously back at him. Why the devil was nothing happening? He groped for a serviceable lie. "I…that is to say—"

Soldiers screamed and bellowed. Some sprouted hideous deformities as their dark natures claimed them utterly and warped them into Spectres. A few simply dissolved in flares of black fire. Many others glared with insane fury as their Shadows became dominant. As one, the possessed mercenaries and Grim Riders hurled themselves at Mrs. Duquesne and Shellabarger. Farther away, soldiers attempted to rush to the Governors' defense, only to find themselves hindered when traitors in their own ranks lashed out at them.

Shellabarger snatched his hand from his pants pocket. In his grip was what appeared to be the dainty, bladeless silver hilt of a knife. He swung it in Gayoso's direction, and the Spaniard dropped beneath the plane defined by the sweep of the other Anacreon's arm. Behind him, one of Fink's ruffians fell apart, his body cleanly bisected at the breast bone, dissolving into nothingness before it struck the ground.

Mrs. Duquesne inverted the hourglass. Sand trickled from the upper chamber into the lower, and Gayoso registered a sort of silent *boom!* as magick exploded across the parade ground. The attackers closest to the old woman suddenly appeared to be moving in slow motion. Some shriveled into apparent senescence, or shrank into infancy, then vanished. A few feet out from the hourglass, the time distortion began to diminish, until, at the edges of the field, the combatants seemed to be moving at normal speed.

As was Gayoso. Like his fellow Governors, he was *too* close to the magic's point of origin for it to enchant him. Feeling his features swell and twist, he whipped out his pistol. Meanwhile, Shellabarger cocked his arm for another attack.

Gayoso fired. The darksteel bullets caught the hooded man in the chest and slammed him backward, out of the bubble of normal time and into the midst of the possessed men. Still creeping, those who were able attempted to swarm over him, and he defended himself with equal sluggishness.

Mrs. Duquesne tossed her begging bowl like a cook flipping flapjacks in a skillet. Oboli flew out at the men who were trying to strike her down. Slow as they were, they had no chance whatsoever to dodge. The coins penetrated their flesh like bullets, and they went down.

Gayoso fired at her, and, despite the short range, missed. Some sorcery must have deflected the shots in flight. The thin lips beneath her lugubrious mask gave him the familiar, hateful, superior smile. With a shimmer, new coins appeared in the bowl, and she tossed them at him.

The hurtling money buried itself deep in his flesh. The pain was intense, but he could feel he wasn't crippled, and that was all that mattered. Grinning, he scrambled up from his crouch.

"Alms," she said in a whining, servile voice altogether unlike her normal tone.

Dragging streams of ectoplasm behind them, the coins erupted from Gayoso's body and leaped back into the bowl. His substance continued to flow even after the oboli came to rest, vanishing into the smooth brown wood without a trace. The pain he'd experienced before was as nothing compared to the agony wracking him now. The automatic slipped from his fingers, and his knees buckled.

"Alms," she repeated, and the pain grew even more intense. Waves of Oblivion licked the interior of his body.

No. It mustn't end this way. He shrieked a silent, wordless prayer to the Malfeans, begged for a measure of the limitless power of the Void. He attempted to hurl himself at his tormentor.

His legs felt so rubbery that for an instant he was certain he was going to fall on his face. Then he plowed into Mrs. Duquesne.

He rebounded as if he'd slammed into a pillar of granite. Some magick had both armored her gaunt, frail-looking body and rooted it to the earth. But even so, she rocked backward, her spectacles fell off, and Gayoso's essence stopped draining away, through strands of flesh still connected his body to the bowl.

He knew he mustn't give her a chance to start the process up again. He whipped out his rapier and drove it into her chest.

Rings of shadow exploded outward from the wound. "Alms," she croaked, and his flesh began to bleed away anew. He tried to pull the sword back for another thrust. She dropped the hourglass and grabbed the blade. Fighting for control of the weapon, they lurched back and forth.

For one final desperate moment, Gayoso had no idea which of them would destroy the other first. Perhaps they'd plummet into the Void together. Then, at last, several possessed soldiers penetrated the near edge of the time dilation. Suddenly charging at full speed, they surged over Mrs. Duquesne like a wave breaking on a shore. They howled and snarled like beasts as they dragged her down.

The old woman lost her grip on the bowl. The cords of ectoplasm, and Gayoso's pain and weakness, vanished. Giggling, he danced about the knot of struggling figures, driving his rapier into the tangle, not caring if he stabbed his own minions as long as he hurt Mrs. Duquesne as well.

A few seconds later, she melted away.

Gayoso peered about. Shellabarger was nowhere in sight. Presumably he'd perished. Across the parade ground, the corrupted soldiers were prevailing against their former comrades. Many of the loyal Hierarchs had fallen. Others were attempting a fighting withdrawal from the field.

He'd done it. He was the King of Natchez. Sword held high, exulting, he whirled around and around. With a noiseless *crackle*, the magick of the hourglass ended. Suddenly every combatant was moving at normal speed.

Reminded of the precious weapon's existence, the Spaniard pivoted this way and that, scanning the ground. "Looking for this?" asked a merry female voice.

He turned and saw Prudence in her purple gown decorated with its motley collection of religious symbols. Smiling, the plump, freckle-faced woman clasped the hourglass in one black-stained hand.

"I thought you'd be with the others, weaving the magick," he said.

"Are you worried that your troops will revert to their normal selves? Rest assured, they won't. To the contrary, they'll all be full-fledged Spectres in another hour or two. The spell is well and truly cast, and it doesn't require all of us to maintain it. So I thought I'd toddle down and see how you were getting along."

He grinned. "I'm getting along very well indeed. I destroyed Shellabarger and Mrs. Duquesne. Their few surviving soldiers are falling back in disarray. The province—excuse me, the *kingdom*—is mine! But I suppose it isn't quite time to celebrate yet. I need to secure the Citadel, and then the entire Necropolis. May I?" He held out his hand for the hourglass.

Her dimples deepening, Prudence held onto the weapon, as if she meant to tease him. "I know precisely how to secure them, Your Majesty. We'll simply have these splendid warriors of ours slaughter everyone they meet."

Gayoso wondered if she was joking. "That's a tempting notion. But I can't be a king without subjects."

"Alas, my sweet, foolish Manuel, I'm afraid that you aren't going to be a king at all."

A chill oozed up his spine. "What are you talking about?"

She sighed as if disappointed by his lack of perception. "Did you honestly believe that my martyred, vengeful people would be willing to share their land with the very race that cast them down? If so, think again. This brave new realm is going to be the domain of Spectres and Spectres alone."

"But we made a compact, and *I'm* a Spectre now, too. You called me your brother in darkness."

"And so you are. But in life, you served the King of Spain, whose army crushed the Quick Aztec nation, and so paved the way for your Heretics to annihilate the Dark Kingdom of Obsidian. You still proudly sport the armor of a conquistador. Did you never wonder why we'd agree to make *you* a monarch, you of all people?" She shrugged. "Apparently not, just as it never struck you as a curious coincidence that we worship the god of the Smoking Mirror, and you found your damnation in a looking glass."

Gayoso pivoted toward a mass of possessed soldiers, who, their eyes mad and feral, stood watching the exchange. "Slay this woman!" he cried.

They leered at him.

Stammering slightly, he rattled off the incantation that had initially bound them to his will. "Destroy her!"

"Did you really think we'd program them in such a way that you could turn them against us?" Prudence asked. "That would have been very sloppy planning on our part."

In the blink of an eye, the fat woman became a hulking, black-scaled thing with two crocodilian faces mounted on a single deformed head. Hissing, she raised her sword, a length of wood lined with bits of razor-sharp obsidian, and started forward. Lifting his own blade, coming en garde, the King of Natchez retreated a step. Then guns barked and crossbows twanged as a dozen soldiers shot him in the back.

Forty-Four

The city bus swerved this way and that, veering around disturbances when possible, plowing right through them when not. Montrose wondered if any of the people they were passing even noticed that no one was in the driver's seat. He suspected not. The ones who'd gone mad were too busy wreaking havoc, and the rest were too busy running for their lives.

The Scot and his companions were lucky to have found the vehicle sitting abandoned, one fender crumpled from a collision with a telephone pole, but still serviceable. Now that Titus had fused himself with it, it should carry them to the Citadel considerably faster than they could make it on foot, and its body blunted the force of the abrasive wind.

But at the speed the passengers were traveling, they were bombarded with a nonstop barrage of grisly scene, flashing past the windows at a dizzying pace. Six barghests, escaped from their handlers, melting a woman with the terrible power of their baying. Other wraiths perishing at the hands of roving Spectres, or evaporating into wisps of vapor. A mob of black mortals spiking an elderly Asian shopkeeper to the wall of his grocery. A teenager setting a tenement on fire, then pouring gasoline over his own head and walking into the blaze. Revolted but perversely fascinated, Montrose finally managed to wrench his gaze away from the carnage.

"Ugly, isn't it?" said Bellamy.

"To say the least," the Cavalier replied.

Bellamy looked at Astarte, who was seated one row up. Her pretty face grim and drawn, she was dividing her attention between her own window and Marilyn Sebastian, who appeared to be nodding off beside her.

"You're worried about her, aren't you?" said Louise, maskless for the moment, her scarred golden visor resting in her lap.

Bellamy hesitated—Montrose had the impression that the FBI agent was the sort of man who preferred to hide his emotions—and then said, "Yeah. We ghosts are getting rattled watching what's happening on the street, but at least each of us can also see that he has twenty friends here on the bus with him. From Astarte's viewpoint, she's alone except for Marilyn, who's half delirious. Sure, intellectually, she knows we're here, but I wish I could appear to her and give her moral support."

"Perhaps you should," said Louise.

Grimacing, Bellamy shook his head. "I'm not that good a Proctor yet. I need to conserve my power for later, when I might absolutely *have* to jump the Shroud. Don't get me wrong, Astarte's tough, she won't fall apart. But I know it's hard on her to be shut off from us, and I'd spare her that if I could."

"Because you love her," said Louise.

Bellamy smiled wryly, almost boyishly, affording Montrose a glimpse of the pleasant young man he'd been before his death and the desperate quest to foil the Atheist conspiracy had become the dominant facts of his existence. "Is it that obvious?"

Louise took Montrose's hand and gave it a squeeze. "It is to me. I'm attuned to that sort of thing right now."

The Scot felt a glow of happiness, or at least a relaxation of the apprehension clawing at his nerves. Then, above his head, something hissed, and he sensed space fragmenting.

He looked up. Black, glittering Nihils were swelling across the roof of the bus, including one directly above Louise and himself. "Watch out!" he shouted, scrambling up from the seat. He grabbed for the Sister of Athena to haul her out from under the rift.

Segmented tentacles like insect antennae erupted from the Nihil, snaking around Louise's head and forearms. Montrose discovered he wasn't strong enough to drag her free. Then, shrieking *kiais*, she battered her assailant's limbs with the edges of her hands. The arms loosened their grip, and he yanked her clear.

Gunfire and cries of alarm rang out as other Spectres attacked. The bus began to swerve crazily. Montrose realized that Titus must be in considerable distress. While he was inhabiting the vehicle, it was his body, and the Maelstrom had just stabbed multiple holes in it.

A pair of doomshades leaped down onto the seat he and Louise had just vacated. The creature with the tentacles was a spiderish thing with the severed, crimson-eyed head of an infant for a body. Cooing like any ordinary baby, it lashed its arms at Louise. Its companion, a raw, bloody thing like a flayed wildcat, pounced at Montrose's face.

He jerked up his hands, caught it, and flung it away. It landed lightly a few feet down the aisle and instantly charged him again. Hindered by the close quarters and rocked by the swerving of the bus, he only barely managed to snatch out his rapier in time for a stop thrust to the Spectre's head.

The monster dissolved in waves of black fire. Montrose spun just in time to see Louise dispatch the spider-baby with her saber. Her bandaged features taut with concentration, Marilyn made mystic gestures at other doomshades. As far as the Scot could discern, they weren't having any effect. Blind to the frenzied combat raging all around her, her face a study in frustration, Astarte peered this way and that.

A twisted figure whose body seemed to be covered with one continuous scab leaped into the bus. It was carrying a flame-thrower. Desperate to slay it before it could start spraying barrow-fire around, Montrose and Bellamy sprang at it.

The Scot stabbed it in the throat, and Bellamy's shortsword split its skull. The corpse dissolved instantly. Montrose looked around once more.

His side had won. The other Spectres were gone, the Nihils in the roof were shrinking, and the bus had stopped swerving. The Cavalier counted the survivors and found that they'd only lost two men. Not bad, considering. Though the drugged, wounded mage seemed to be as useless as he'd feared, the Restless from New Orleans were clearly seasoned fighters. Perhaps they were even formidable enough to cope with what lay ahead.

Bellamy projected his voice across the Shroud, whispering a few words of love and reassurance to Astarte. The girl with the piercings seemed about to grimace and say something unpleasant, but then she smiled and answered in kind instead.

The FBI agent dropped back onto his seat. "The fun never stops, does it?" he said glumly.

"Not during a Maelstrom," Montrose replied.

"You know, it seems like I've been chasing the Atheist for a hundred years. When I was alive and closing in on some criminal, I used to get excited. I wish I could feel that way now, but I'm too stressed out. Too worried. You people know a lot more about the Underworld than I do. Do *you* think we can still stop the conspiracy?"

"Katrina the Ferryman told James that it was his destiny to oppose the Spectres," said Louise, "as well as foreseeing that he and I would meet again. Marilyn said Katrina also appeared to her, to encourage her to remain in the struggle. You dreamed of the destruction of the Isle of Sorrows, the disaster James and I prevented. That suggests that your fate is linked to this menace, also. We're all meant to fight this fight together."

Bellamy gave her a skeptical smile. "Are you saying we're God's hand-picked team? That we can't lose?"

"Unfortunately, no," said the Heretic. "I have no doubt we can lose. But I do think it means we have a chance."

The wraiths had agreed they'd be less conspicuous approaching the Citadel on foot. Thus, the bus rolled to a stop at the base of the hill on which the fortress sat. The doors opened to permit Astarte and Marilyn to exit. Most of the ghosts simply glided through the sides of the carriage and hopped to the ground.

Titus flowed from beneath the bus's hood. His hide looking more raw than ever, Antoine scuttled up to him. "You...okay?" he rasped.

The shaman grimaced. "I'll have to be, won't I? Valentine?"

The dwarf crept from the darkness with Belinda following close behind. Montrose had made the working assumption that the false Pardoners were weaving their sorcery in the same sanctum where they'd been laboring to corrupt the Hierarch soldiers all along. Since Valentine was the only member of the expedition who knew where that place was, it was his job to guide his comrades there. He swallowed, then said, "I'm here."

"Then lead on," Titus said.

They started up the hill. Louise and Montrose made a point of sticking close to Valentine, to bolster his courage. Belinda clutched the jester's hand. Bellamy stalked along beside Astarte and the dazed, limping Marilyn, while Antoine crawled next to him. Some subtle difference in the way the alligator moved made him seem less like a rational, sentient being than a loyal hound guarding its master.

No one was on the street, though when the wailing of the searing, stinging wind momentarily abated, Montrose could hear whimpering, demented cackling, and stealthy footfalls in the dilapidated buildings to either side. The merchants' open-air stalls stood abandoned and in some cases vandalized, the bounty which the crusade against the Heretics had brought to Natchez lying trampled on the ground. Nihils seethed, swelled, and extended jagged new cracks through the surfaces around them. From the Citadel itself echoed screams, gunfire, and the clash of blades.

Halfway up the hill, one of the zebra-caped warriors sobbed and shredded into ribbons of ectoplasm. Louise murmured a prayer that the poor fellow's soul would somehow escape Oblivion and Transcend. Montrose picked up his AK-47.

The ring of flesh-sculpted, hideously elongated human torches still burned around the perimeter of the fortress complex. Montrose had imagined that when he reached this point, he might detect some indication of coherent military activity. Some sign that a decisive battle was even now occurring, or else that either Gayoso or his rivals had already gained the upper hand and were moving systematically to establish control of the Citadel. But from the sound of things, countless small skirmishes were being fought and incidental atrocities being committed all around the complex. He glanced at Louise, who shrugged to indicate that she didn't understand it, either.

"Keep moving?" Valentine whispered. Montrose nodded. They stalked on through the circle of torches. The frigid greenish flames lashed wildly about in the gale.

The dwarf led them down the narrow alley between two massive buildings with boarded windows. A tattered set of fringed buckskin clothing, rippling in the wind, marked the spot where someone had hacked the wearer to pieces. A few feet farther on, the passage debouched into what had once been a brickyard. Fragments of fired red clay lay among the weeds.

Valentine pointed to the structure on the other side of the yard. Below the roof line shone stylized representations of a smiling face and a fountain of fire, rendered in a luminous paint which ordinary mortals couldn't see. "The confessors work on the second floor. If you go straight across the yard, through the wall, and on out into the hall, there's a stairway on your right."

Bellamy turned to Marilyn. "Did you catch that?" he asked.

"Yes," panted the mage, leaning heavily on her malacca walking stick. "I can still see and hear you perfectly well. It's just all the rest of my magick that's falling apart. But don't worry, I'll get myself back on track." She turned her head to inform Astarte of their destination.

"Well, this would appear to be it," said Montrose to the company at large. "I'm going to fly in on the Spectres, and, with a modicum of luck, surprise and distract them. Anyone else who can fly should accompany me. The rest of you, charge to the battleground as quickly as you can."

"The same tactics you used against me at Grand Gulf," said Louise wryly.

"Let's hope they work as well in a better cause."

She put her arm around him. "I trust you won't mind carrying a passenger."

"I believe I can manage." He turned to his other companions. "You know what's at stake, lads. Show the enemy what the fighting men of New Orleans are made of. We'll go on three. One, two, *three!*"

Clasping Louise, he soared toward the spot Valentine had indicated, and Titus flew up beside him. Beneath them, the other ghosts raced across the brickyard, with the swaying, stumbling Marilyn, supported by Astarte, instantly falling behind. Montrose suspected that the battle would be over before the two mortals even found a way into the building.

He and Louise plunged into the crumbling brownstone wall. For a split second, he felt a jolt of the repulsive yet invigorating echo of misery resonating through the structure. Then the two wraiths hurtled out into a large room reeking of bitter incense.

The bluish glow of several barrow-fire lamps illuminated a pair of confessional booths, a couch, a desk on which reposed a stack of Rorschach cards, a whipping post and a cat-o'-nine-tails, and various other appurtenances of the Pardoner's trade.

Someone had shifted all such items into the far corner to make room for the ritual unfolding in the center of the floor. There the false confessors, a dozen in all, inky stains mottling their fingers, stood swaying and chanting around a spherical cage whose bars were made of darkness. Inside the orb floated hundreds of points of light, like a star field. Additional strands of blackness coiled among them, dimming their light and occasionally snuffing one out altogether. Montrose inferred that this was the sorcerous construct which had enslaved the soldiers of Natchez, and that whenever a star guttered out, it signified that some poor soul's Shadow had extinguished his better nature altogether. A number of guards, the majority members of the Scot's own irregulars, loitered about the chamber.

Montrose set Louise down, then they both opened fire on the Spectres. Titus melted through a grimy window, his Tommy gun clattering.

Three of the Pardoners dissolved into waves of murk. Montrose had hoped the black cage would wink out of existence as soon as one of its conjurers perished, but it didn't. Their guns blazing, the possessed soldiers charged the attackers.

Montrose didn't want to hurt them, but he knew that for the moment at least, he had no choice but to fight back. Shooting at the onrushing men, he simultaneously dodged to his left and on through a wall, then veiled himself in darkness. As cool shadow oozed across his skin, he slipped back into the Spectres' chamber. With luck, the irregulars would have trouble targeting an invisible foe, and therefore he wouldn't have to defend himself so fiercely against them.

Instinctively, he looked for Louise, and felt a pang of profound relief when he saw she was thus far unscathed. She was still shooting, but was clearly focused primarily on using her Spook Arcanos. Pieces of furniture flew, tumbled, and skated across the room, slamming the irregulars backward and creating cover for her as well.

His withered hands weaving patterns in the air, Titus had dropped the submachine gun to concentrate exclusively on magick. Crossbow bolts thunked to a halt and hung in the air six inches from his body, as if they'd plunged into an invisible sheet of wood. With a boom and a flare, a mercenary burst into flame.

Since the Heretic nun and the shaman were keeping the guards occupied, Montrose decided to devote his efforts to the Pardoners themselves. Unfortunately, with the combatants darting back and forth, and Louise's chairs, tables, and confessionals leaping about, he didn't have a clear shot at them. He levitated to the ceiling, above the fray, where, presumably, only a stray bullet or quarrel could find him, then flew on toward the doomshades.

In a moment, he was close enough to hit them easily. He aimed at the one on his far right, a small man with a three-piece suit, a watch chain and a gray goatee, who bore a distinct resemblance to Sigmund Freud. A gun roared, and pain ripped through Montrose's lower legs.

Startled, his hold on his magick shaken, he felt his cloak of darkness dissolve as he slammed down on the floor. Grinning, Mike Fink aimed his combat shotgun again. "I could only just barely see you before," he said. "But this time I'll hit you square."

Montrose fired the AK-47 and flung himself to the side. The Mag-10 boomed, and a second cloud of pellets crashed into the floor just inches from his head. Scrambling to one knee, he squeezed the trigger again. Fink staggered, and the shotgun bellowed.

Two of the pellets punched into Montrose's shoulder, and he gasped at the pain. But the rest missed, and he knew the Roadblocker only held three rounds. "Surrender," he gasped.

Fink sneered as if oblivious to the expanding rings of darkness washing outward from the bullet holes in his arms and torso. He dropped the shotgun and reached for the ax on his back.

Wounded himself, albeit less seriously, Montrose knew he should gun the outlaw down, but couldn't bring himself to do it. He leaped to his feet and charged, swinging the assault rifle back to bludgeon Fink into submission.

His thoughts collapsed into confusion, and suddenly he had no idea where he was or what he was doing. The huge man in front of him slammed an uppercut into his jaw, stunning him, knocking him down, and he still couldn't comprehend what was happening. It was only as the giant raised his ax that his mind unlocked. This was combat! Fink had used his Haunter powers to befuddle him, and now was about to destroy him.

Montrose snapped a kick into the keelboatman's crotch. Fink grunted and doubled over. The Cavalier scrambled up from beneath his adversary and pounded the big man's skull with the butt of his rifle. After the fourth blow, Fink collapsed on his face.

Montrose whirled. More possessed soldiers were charging him. It looked as if Louise and Titus were similarly hard pressed. Some of the false Pardoners shimmered from human form into the sort of hulking, reptilian, double-faced things he'd seen in Charon's vault. Hissing, obsidian swords lifted, they advanced to join the battle.

But then Montrose's allies burst through the far wall.

Antoine was in the lead. The alligator seized a lanky fellow in a Sandman's coat of garish multicolored patches, tore his legs off with a single wrench of his wedge-shaped head, spat him out, and scuttled on to his next victim. Just behind him, Bellamy shot a guard, then, pivoting, narrowly ducked the sweep of a cutlass. He fired again and hit the swordsman in the forehead. Valentine halted with only his face and shooting arm protruding from the wall, and then, looking sick with fright, twisted this way and that, trying to line up a shot.

Smiling savagely, Montrose turned and shot the first of the onrushing Spectres, exhausting the AK-47's ammunition. He drew his rapier and sprang at the next doomshade, feinted, deceived the creature's attempt to parry, and drove his point into its breast. The monster tried to swing its wood-and-stone sword over its head for a return stroke, but disintegrated before it could.

As the Scot charged the next Spectre, several lanky Africans fell into line beside him, assegais leveled, short, striped capes flapping. Together the wraiths stabbed and hacked their way through the remaining doomshades.

All but one. At the periphery of the struggle stood a confessor who still clung to human form, a fat, freckled, friendly-looking woman in a purple gown. From Valentine's description, Montrose recognized her as Mother Prudence, the leader. She was surveying the carnage with a bemused, indulgent smile, like a parent watching her children play a boisterous, meaningless game.

Montrose stalked toward her. She puckered her lips in a kiss, then, her bulk seemingly compressing to nothing, spun into a hairline Nihil crack in the floor like water swirling down a drain.

With her departure, the black sphere and the floating lights within it vanished. The possessed soldiers, those who'd survived, collapsed as one. One of the Africans let out a cheer.

Montrose didn't share his joy. Rather, he scowled at the Nihil in puzzled frustration. His Shadow's mocking laughter resounded through his mind, while outside, the Maelstrom howled on.

Forty-Five

Bellamy trotted up to Montrose. The FBI agent's left sleeve was torn from wrist to elbow, and a bloodless white gash showed through the rent. "Something's wrong," he said. "This was way too easy. Where are Dunn and the wolfmen? Where's the demon-god that Marie told us to expect?"

Montrose's respect for the other wraith's intelligence rose another notch. "Exactly. And where's Gayoso, for that matter?"

A coarse bass voice growled out a string of obscenities. Montrose turned to see Fink rubbing his battered head, then dragging himself off the floor. The Scot stood en garde.

Fink stared Montrose up and down. "You look like shit," he said at last.

Reassured that his friend had returned to normal, Montrose smiled. "I probably looked better before you shot me." He drank in a measure of the emotional energy humming through the old building, then willed his wounds to heal. His flesh throbbed as it ejected the shotgun pellets, which clattered to the floor. "How are you?"

"I've been better," the river man said. "It was like those Pardoner bastards locked me in a torture cell inside my own head, and something was cutting me up and feeding the pieces to my Shadow."

"This would be the same Shadow you once claimed didn't exist?"

"Fine, rub it in." Fink hesitated. "I'm, uh, glad you showed up when you did."

"You can thank Valentine for that. Without him, the rest of us wouldn't have known what was occurring."

Fink's eyes widened. "The midget? Are you kidding? Damn, and here I thought the night couldn't get any weirder." Behind him, Marilyn and Astarte finally rushed through the door. The mage peered wildly about, then slumped, letting her cane and her companion support much of her weight when she saw that the fight was over.

"Do you know what happened to Dunn and Gayoso?" Bellamy asked.

"I don't know any Dunn," said the burly mercenary, "but I heard Prudence say she destroyed the spic after he knocked off the other Governors. He thought she was going to make him the king of the province, but she double-crossed him."

"After which," said Montrose, "rather than deploying the possessed men to take control of the Citadel and the Necropolis, she simply directed them to prowl about and murder any wraith they met."

"That's right," said Fink. The rest of Montrose's comrades began to gather around to listen to the conversation.

"Because they never intended to conquer Natchez by mere force of arms,"

Montrose said. "They have something else in mind. They corrupted Gayoso and the local troops for the same reason they sowed chaos in Stygia itself. Essentially, as a diversion. To keep their foes occupied until it was too late to parry their genuine thrust."

Bellamy frowned. "That doesn't make sense. We know there aren't a huge number of Aztecs. How could they possibly hope to control the province, except by maintaining their hold on the possessed men and exploiting them to best advantage? But you're right, Montrose. If that actually was the heart of the plan, then why didn't every one of them, and every one of the werewolves, for that matter, defend the ritual?"

Marilyn was murmuring to Astarte, giving her a running synopsis of the discussion. The Quick girl grimaced. "If we don't figure out the rest of the Spectres' plan real fast, we're screwed, aren't we?"

"I fear she's right," Montrose said. "It occurs to me that none of us understands what's happening to the Mississippi. Perhaps if I fly up and take another look at it, I can glean some fresh insight into the enemy's strategy. Meanwhile, the rest of you, recover your strength and heal yourselves. Titus, you help those who need it."

The shaman nodded. "Be careful," said Louise. Montrose gave her a smile, then levitated through the ceiling and out into the night.

The wind, blistering hot at the moment, gusted even more strongly than before, nearly stripping the tattered black mantle from his back. The gale howled from the north, then the southwest, and then, for an instant, from directly overhead, nearly smashing him back down onto the roof. A doomshade resembling a huge, headless butterfly, the sickly yellow markings on its tattered crimson wings in constant flux, swooped close, seemingly investigating him, but then flew on in search of other prey.

The invisible grit in the air pinged and grated against his glossy black ceramic mask. He kept one arm raised to shield his eyes, until, fighting the storm every inch of the way, he finally rose high enough to get a good look at the river. Then he stared, transfixed with horror.

At first glance, it looked as if the Mississippi were in flood, but in reality, the water wasn't overflowing its banks. Rather, the monstrous black Nihil on the surface was expanding to engulf the shore, while the curtain of murk advanced with it, twisting and splintering space as it came.

All along, Montrose had wondered how the Spectres could consider the destruction of at least some of the Deathlords and the devastation of the Isle of Sorrows itself the lesser part of their plans. It hadn't seemed possible that any Earthly conquest, no matter how ambitious, could constitute as grievous an injury to their foes. But now at last he understood.

He dove toward the Citadel. It appeared to him that the rampart of darkness had been moving slowly, with a dreadful stateliness, but now, abruptly, it was only a few feet away.

When it swept over him, space knotted and stretched around him, threatening to tear him apart. His Shadow leaped up from the depths of his mind and tried to wrest control of his body away from him. Assailed from without and within, he battled the rift and his dark half at the same time.

It took him several seconds to master them both. Dazed, gasping reflexively, he realized he was now in free fall. Straining, he pulled up just in time to keep from crashing to the ground.

Flying under his own power again, he slipped back through the wall of the Pardoner's lair, noticing as he did that all the Nihils in the room had disappeared. Each of his companions, even the mortals, looked shaken. "What just happened?" Belinda wailed. "What *was* that?"

"We fell into the Tempest," Montrose said.

"Explain," Bellamy said.

"That immense Nihil on the river has expanded to swallow the land. On both the east and west banks, I assume. It's like a cancer, eating away mile after mile of the Shadowlands, the stratum of reality, that lies between the local Skinlands and the Tempest. That's why the Aztecs aren't worried about having enough troops to control the province. The Tempest is crawling with Spectres who will rally to their banner, and moreover, they know that ordinary wraiths can't survive in this dimension anyway, not for long. Mortals won't be able to live in direct proximity to it either, at least not happily or sanely. You've seen how they fall apart during a Maelstrom, and this will be like a storm that never ends."

Titus shook his head. "You...you must be mistaken. You're talking about a change in the basic structure of the universe."

"The universe does change on occasion," Montrose said. "Once upon a time, there were no Maelstroms and no Shroud, or so I'm told. You can step outside and investigate for yourself if you like. I'd very much like to be proven wrong, but unfortunately, I'm not. I'm a Harbinger. I recognize the Tempest when it opens its jaws and swallows me."

The old man sighed. "As do I, of course. It's just that it's hard to admit such a thing. This is a greater disaster that I could ever have imagined."

Marilyn whispered to Astarte. "Hey!" snarled the girl in black. "It sounds like you pussies are giving up!"

"She's right," said Louise, "but we're not, are we? Not after traveling so far, and overcoming so many obstacles. Not with so many souls, Restless and Quick alike, hanging in the balance."

Montrose drew himself up straight. "No," he said, "we're not. From my rudimentary knowledge of the greater mysteries, I assume that after one conjures an effect of this magnitude, one must labor for a while longer to stabilize it if it's to become permanent." He turned to Titus. "But you'd know better than I. Do you concur?"

The shaman gave a jerky nod. "That's likely."

"Then we have to find the rest of the Spectres and break up the *important* ceremony," Bellamy said.

"But how?" asked one of the African warriors. "We could be pretty sure that the bogus Pardoners were hypnotizing the Legionnaires from right here in the Citadel. But this other ritual could be happening anywhere."

"After Mother Prudence vanished down the Nihil, she presumably made her way to the Spectre stronghold," Montrose said. "Harbingers learn to track other spirits through the Tempest. Unfortunately, the structure of the place altered radically when it engulfed the city. That could have the effect of obscuring her trail, but I hope Titus and I will still be able to follow it."

"I suspect you've spent far more time in the Ocean and are far more accomplished at this art than I am," the shaman said, "but I'll help you all I can."

"Me too," Antoine rasped.

Montrose looked down at him. For a moment, he thought he could see the grimy floorboards through the alligator's body.

"Maybe you should stay here in the Haunt," Bellamy said.

"Stick it up your...thing. You *need* me, warmblood, and I'll be damned if I'll let those double-faced bastards win." His toothy grin seemed to stretch wider. "With those scaly hides, they could give us reptiles a bad name."

"I'm coming too," Marilyn said. "My perceptions still work, even if the rest of my sorcery seems to be on the blink."

"Forget it," growled Fink. "You'll slow us down."

The scent of her wounds and her drug-laden, feverish sweat wafting from her body, the mage smiled. "How fast do you think the rest of you will be moving, groping for a trail with the storm battering you? If I fail to keep up, you can leave me behind."

"Everyone can come," Montrose said. "God knows, we're likely to need every hand. As a matter of fact, we'll enlist every able-bodied Legionnaire and irregular we encounter on the way out. Considering the madness and betrayal they've just experienced, I doubt they'll be much inclined to trust us, but perhaps I can impress them with the Lantern of Truth."

"Let's do it," Bellamy said.

Montrose stared at the patch of floor where Prudence had disappeared, trying to sense a direction. Titus and Antoine stepped up to do the same.

Forty-Six

The dark, narrow street inverted itself, Bellamy's senses screaming that he was dangling upside down, about to plummet into the endless abyss of the sky. At that instant, the gaunt, rotting things with the hyena faces and the six-inch claws surged out of the shadows.

One of the creatures pounced at Bellamy. Still frozen with shock and vertigo, he failed to dodge the Sinkinda's first attack. Luckily, its aim was off, and its talons merely grazed his chest.

The flash of pain jolted him out of his paralysis. Desperately, he shoved the creature backward. Instantly it charged again. Fighting the instinct that insisted than the tiniest move could break the fragile adhesion holding him to the ground, he clumsily lurched aside and fired a burst from the assault rifle he'd picked up in the Citadel. The black soulfire crystals set in the front of the folding metal stock glittered with the discharge.

The Spectre dissolved. Bellamy pivoted, seeking another target, and saw that his comrades had already disposed of the other monsters. The world flipped right side up again. The sudden termination of the sensory distortion, if that was the right word for it, was nearly as disorienting as its onset had been. Nausea squirmed in his stomach, and he staggered to regain his balance.

The skirmish concluded, Montrose, Titus, Marilyn, and Antoine formed a circle to confer, as they'd done at least twenty times since departing the fortress. Scowling, Astarte hovered at the mage's side, ready to catch her if her legs gave way. Antoine had stopped speaking about fifteen minutes ago, but was apparently still focused on the task at hand, communicating with grunts and thrusts of his wedge-shaped head. Meanwhile, the other *abambo* stood keeping watch for the next doomshade attack, huddling against the cold, stinging wind and trying to tune out the vile suggestions and feelings their shadowselves were putting in their heads.

The landscape itself was changing. The Nihils were gone—once Bellamy thought about it, it made sense that you wouldn't run across entrances to the Tempest when you were already inside it—but other rifts, more varied in appearance, opalescent ripples in the air and fleshy, quivering fissures in walls, had appeared in their place. According to Montrose, nearly all led to other levels of the Tempest, though a few might open somewhere in the Shadowlands or even the Far Shores. A clump of slickly gleaming globules like enormous insect eggs clung to the side of a tenement, and a black fungus that smelled like vomit encrusted a lamp post. Vile, inhuman faces and creatures coalesced and melted away again in the clouds.

Unless Bellamy missed his guess, the changes meant that the reality of the Tempest was locking down, claiming Natchez for all time. He seethed with impatience. His Shadow cackled and danced.

At last, his wizened, painted face as weary-looking as Bellamy had ever seen it, Titus pointed to the north. "That way."

Montrose frowned. "Perhaps."

Antoine hissed and jabbed his snout toward an alley that snaked off to the east. Titus turned toward Marilyn.

"I'm sorry," the Arcanist said. "I can't tell one way or the other."

"Nor can I, really," Montrose said. "Prudence's psychic footprints were clear to me a hundred yards back, but here—"

The gator seized the hem of the Stygian's ink-black cloak in his jaws and dragged him toward the alley.

"All right, Antoine," said Titus. "If you're that certain, we'll go your way."

But should we? Bellamy wondered. Antoine hadn't been able to track Dunn away from the site of the bombing, and that had been before the gator's brain had started turning to mush. Yet he couldn't bring himself to express his doubts. Not when Antoine was his only true friend among the dead, and was risking everything to help. Frowning, he stalked on into the narrow passage with his allies.

A pair of skull-faced harpies swooped out of the darkness, keening. Their cry flooded Bellamy's mind with an irrational panic, but, shaking, he managed to stand his ground and shoot one anyway, while one of Marie's warriors put a crossbow bolt through the other. A minute later, the gale gusted, and the lean, long-legged body of another African began to disperse as if it were made of smoke. He dropped his assegai, bellowed a war cry, and clutched at the raised, ritual scars decorating his face. His form solidified again.

After three blocks, Titus moved to Montrose's side. Bellamy hurried close enough to eavesdrop on their exchange. "I'm still not picking her up," the old man murmured.

"Nor am I," the Anacreon replied. "How certain were you that we ought to go the other way?"

Titus grimaced. "Not sure at all."

"Antoine is sure. Let's give him a few more yards, and then I'll fly up for another look around. Perhaps eventually I'll spot something significant from the air."

Perhaps? Eventually? Furious, certain they were going the wrong way, Bellamy opened his mouth to demand that they backtrack immediately. At that moment, a long, ululating howl echoed from the darkness ahead. Though the shrieking of the wind nearly masked it, it was still recognizably a wolfman's chilling cry. Bellamy's shadowself writhed in disappointment.

The FBI agent strode to the head of the column. "That's them," he said.

"I've never encountered a werewolf myself," Montrose answered, "but I assumed as much." He checked his AK-47 and loosened his rapier and dagger in their scabbards. "All right, everyone. Let's advance silently for as long as we possibly can."

They skulked on to the point where the alley opened onto the next street. On the other side, a road led into what appeared to be a dilapidated industrial park, a warren of ugly, hulking, brick and cement-block buildings. Antoine poked his nose at the entrance. Montrose nodded, indicating that he'd picked up the trail again as well.

As the expedition glided between the gateposts, Bellamy glimpsed motion from the corner of his eye. He turned, and a two-headed Spectre charged him, clawed hands raised, crocodilian jaws gaping. Mindful that he and his allies were supposed to proceed silently, he raised his gleaming black shortsword, but never got a chance to use it. A stone whizzed up from the ground, struck the Sinkinda in the head, and shot on through. But the split second of contact had been enough to stagger the Spectre, and Louise sprang in and decapitated it with a sweep of her saber.

Bellamy turned. His companions were battling other sentries, and holding their own by the looks of it. But beyond the periphery of the struggle, a two-headed doomshade sprinted away into the gloom.

The FBI agent had no doubt that the creature was running to warn its fellows. He gave chase, and Louise hurtled after him. In a matter of seconds, they had left their allies behind.

Two more doomshades surged from the shadows, obsidian-studded swords whirling in their taloned hands. Louise whirled to face them, her feet settling into a cat stance and the saber swinging into a high guard. "Keep going!" she said.

Bellamy hesitated for an instant, then ran on. Ahead of him his quarry, evidently deciding it couldn't outdistance him, turned and wove its hands in a mystic pattern. Its claws struck sparks of bluish phosphorescence from the night.

The industrial buildings vanished. In their place was the parking lot of a seedy motel. Next door, a pink neon woman on the roof of a topless bar winked over and over again. Car exhaust stung Bellamy's eyes.

He felt a heart thumping in his chest, and the warmth of life glowing in his flesh. It looked as if he'd just emerged from one of the motel rooms with fat, drunken, frightened Milo Waxman in tow.

To all appearances, he'd traveled back in time and space to his rendezvous with the psychic in East St. Louis. To the moment that had set him on the road to his own death.

He told himself it could only be an illusion. Still, he began to shudder, because he knew that Dunn, in his wolfman form, was about to rise from behind the rented Camry. And the Quick Frank Bellamy had never seen such a werewolf before, had never had a chance to get over the overwhelming terror the monsters inspired in ordinary people.

A huge, black shape reared up from behind the car. Waxman gaped at it, whimpered, clutched at his chest, and collapsed. Bellamy felt his mind crumbling as it had before.

Dropping his shortsword, he fumbled the Ruger up to his shoulder, and remembered that that wasn't right. He'd only had his Browning before. Somehow that one bit of reality, bleeding into the nightmare, blunted the edge of his panic.

It isn't real, he told himself. *Charge the Spectre. It's right in front of you, even if you can't see it.*

Dunn bounded lightly over the Camry. His lantern eyes shone, and a viscous strand of saliva oozed from his jaws. Bellamy smelled the werewolf's characteristic scent, a foul, zoo-cage stench mingled with the odor of tobacco.

What if it wasn't *all* an illusion? What if the wolfman was really there, gliding toward his prey this instant?

Bellamy insisted to himself that it didn't matter. Dunn had already stolen his life. He was a ghost now, a dweller on the dark side of the Shroud, and as long as he stayed there, the wolfman couldn't hurt him anymore.

Sobbing, he drove himself forward.

Dunn sidestepped, placing himself directly in his path. The huge, clawed, black-furred hands shot out to snatch him up. Bellamy involuntarily shut his eyes.

Dunn's claws ripped into his shoulders. But only for a split second, and then the sensation disappeared. Nor did the *abambo* plow into the towering creature's body.

Bellamy opened his eyes. The landscape had shifted back to its original form, and the Aztec doomshade stood a few yards in front of him. Evidently, by refusing to behave as he had the first time, he'd shattered the phantasm conjured from his memory.

Still dry-mouthed and shaky with the residue of his terror, he lifted the rifle to club his tormentor. Then something slammed into his ribs.

The blow threw him off his feet and sent the Ruger flying from his hands. The creature which had blindsided him resembled a faceless statue assembled from chunks of stone, then covered with gleaming brown leather. Judging from its appearance, it wasn't an Aztec, but one of the other horrors of the Tempest which had begun to rally to their banner. Still dazed from the illusion, Bellamy had missed seeing it rush in from the side.

Spasming with shock and pain, he tried to scramble after his gun. The leather-and-rock creature threw itself on top of him and pinned him. Its four eyes blazing, the Aztec doomshade dropped to its knees beside the other wraiths, fangs bared and talons raised.

Bellamy struggled desperately, but couldn't break free. He tried to project himself to safety across the Shroud, but his Proctor powers responded sluggishly—too sluggishly to keep the Spectre from ripping him apart.

A long, low form raced out of the darkness.

For an instant, Antoine faded and became translucent, as he had in the Governor's

Citadel, but he seemed solid enough when he seized the two-headed Sinkinda from behind. His jaws nearly snapped the monster in two, yet it didn't perish. It turned and starting rending its attacker. Intertwined, the two combatants thrashed about on the ground.

Bellamy's captor turned its eyeless head toward the fight. His strength returning, the FBI agent took advantage of its distraction and wrenched one arm free of its grasp. He flung out his hand and managed to grab the Ruger.

The creature drew its massive fist back for a punch that could doubtless crush his head. If he wanted to survive, Bellamy couldn't avoid the noise of gunfire anymore. He frantically whipped the automatic rifle around, got his finger on the trigger, and sprayed darksteel bullets into his assailant's head and chest. The monster dissolved in a rippling curtain of black fire.

Staggering to his feet, Bellamy tried to aim the Ruger at the other doomshade, but found that he didn't dare shoot. The way the Aztec and Antoine were locked together, he might just as easily hit the gator.

Suddenly Antoine heaved and broke the Spectre's hold on him. With a crunch, his jaws bit down on both the creature's heads, and then he bucked and wrenched them off. The Sinkinda dissolved.

Antoine crumpled to the ground. His scaly hide hung in tatters, and ripples of shadow washed through his body, which repeatedly faded in and out of view.

"Are you going to be all right?" Bellamy asked.

The gator seemed to grin. "Stupid question, warmblood," he croaked, and then shadowy flames burned him away. Only his zebra-striped kerchief remained.

Bellamy's eyes throbbed as if they could still shed tears. Haltingly, he stooped, picked up the scarf, and then stood staring at it until Louise ran out of the darkness a few moments later.

The Sister of Athena's jeans were torn, but she seemed unharmed. "I heard shooting," she said. "Did you stop the other Spectre?"

"Antoine did," Bellamy said. "But..." He showed her the neckerchief.

Beneath her battered golden mask, the blond woman's mouth softened with compassion. "I'm sorry. I only just met you both, but I could tell you were friends."

"We were, but tonight, I doubted him. I was afraid the storm had turned him into some stupid animal. I didn't even try to talk to him as we were hiking along. I wish..." He shrugged.

"For what it's worth," Louise said gently, "I don't believe he could perish fighting to protect Creation, and to help a friend, and then fall into Oblivion. I think he Transcended, He's in a better place now."

Bellamy tried to derive some comfort from the idea, but he couldn't. It was too abstract, and too much at odds with the bleak, cold realities of the afterlife as he'd experienced it.

But gradually, something else ameliorated his grief. He pictured Waxman's fatal heart attack, and his own electrocution. R. J. Keene's death at the hands of the animated statue. The possessed man killing the Arcanists in their Chapter House. Marilyn's mutilation. The dangers which had repeatedly threatened Astarte.

He thought of the Atheist murders and the other massacres the conspiracy had engineered. The innumerable atrocities occurring up and down the river even now.

And his sorrow gave way to a rage like cold iron.

"Come on," he said, moving to pick up his sword. "Let's rejoin the others, and finish this."

Forty-Seven

Senses straining, spying for signs of an ambush, Montrose led his companions skulking forward. As far as he knew, none of the Spectre guards had escaped to warn their fellow doomshades. And he hoped that the Aztecs hadn't taken alarm at the single burst from Bellamy's rifle. Even if the enemy had heard it, people were discharging guns all over Natchez tonight. Still, it was wise to be wary.

He peeked around a corner. The lane running off to the side contained a number of parked cars. With his wraith senses, he could feel that some of their engines were still warm, just as he could hear the metal ticking.

As the column prowled on, deeper into the complex, they found many more vehicles, including a number of vans and ambulances. "Scythe and lamp," whispered one of the Black Hawks who'd joined the expedition at the Citadel, "if the Spectres used all these cars to gather together, we haven't got near enough men to take them out."

Montrose wheeled to face his companions. "Yes, we do, Legionnaire. We simply have to hit hard. You can see that our comrades from New Orleans aren't afraid to go forward, nor are the Grim Riders. Are the men of the Fifth any less brave?"

The Black Hawk swallowed. "No, sir. We're with you."

Montrose smiled. "Good. I was sure you would be. I wore the black bird myself, for centuries, and the Fifth never turned tail in my day. Forward, then. The Hierarchy and the Restless of New Orleans—and Creation itself, for that matter—are all depending on us. Let's win them a victory that the world will remember until the end of time."

The column prowled on. Bellamy made his way to Montrose's side. "I'm worried that the cars *don't* all belong to Sinkinda and wolfmen," he murmured grimly.

The Scot cocked his head. "What do you mean?"

"All along, their scheme has involved murdering the Quick. Maybe the grand finale requires the biggest massacre of all."

Montrose nodded somberly. "That's not a bad inference. It grieves me that, given the circumstances, I have no choice but to hope you're correct."

Another howl quavered through the night. Employing his Harbinger senses, Montrose made sure the company was still on Mother Prudence's trail, then pressed on. The scent of blood floated on the hot, stinging wind.

A huge, dark warehouse emerged from the gloom ahead. A hint of sound leaked through its walls. Two living figures stood by the doorway. Their auras were murky clouds of red, purple, brown, and black, the streaks of color rippling and swirling hypnotically. Montrose assumed they were werewolves in human form. In any case, it was obvious from the patterns of light that they were both violent and insane.

The Scot gestured for Louise, Bellamy, and Titus to accompany him, and signaled the rest of his allies to remain where they were. The four wraiths crept forward.

When they were four yards away from the doorkeepers, the one on the left suddenly hunched forward, peering. "Ghosts!" he said. "I mean, *enemy* ghosts! I *see* them!"

Titus gestured. The doorkeeper doubled over as if someone had punched him in the stomach. Bellamy leaped across the Shroud and darted in to stab him. The werewolf straightened up, his hands now twice their former size, covered with charcoal-colored fur and sporting hooked yellow claws. He lashed out at the FBI agent's face. Bellamy ducked the stroke and rammed his shortsword into his opponent's abdomen.

Meanwhile, the other shapeshifter reached inside his nylon windbreaker and drew a deep breath to shout. His throat indented as Louise seized it in a crushing telekinetic grip, locking the cry inside him. He fumbled out his revolver, but Montrose projected himself into the Skinlands, then drove his rapier into the werewolf's heart before the creature could fire a warning shot.

The doorkeepers collapsed, and Montrose and Bellamy allowed death to draw them back into the Underworld. The Scot beckoned to the rest of his troops, and they trotted up to join him.

Louise stared intently at the door, and it opened a hair. Montrose realized she was making sure that Marilyn and Astarte would be able to pass through without difficulty.

The Scot, Bellamy, and Titus led the company inside. Despite the excruciating tension of the moment, Montrose fleetingly noticed just how good it felt to escape the punishing gale.

Beyond the entrance was a makeshift corridor constructed of planks, sheets of plywood, and soundproofing, which dulled and jumbled the noises coming from the far end. The stink of blood was stronger, and mingled with the aroma of sawdust and a rank, bestial odor.

Bellamy looked sick. "It's a chute," he whispered. "Like in a slaughterhouse. Something to keep the victims from seeing what's waiting for them until it's too late to run."

They came to a right-angle turn. Montrose saw little point in proceeding on to the door at the end of the passage. Instead, he simply slipped his face through the wall in front of him.

Bloody corpses littered the floor. All bore the mark of enormous claws and fangs, and many lay in several pieces. Werewolves, some in human form, others, towering beast-men, and still others, entirely lupine, prowled among the carnage, feasting, their mouths encrusted with gore and their bellies distended.

It was a ghastly spectacle, but the cavernous room held worse. The werewolves were only killing and devouring adults.

In the center of the warehouse rose a stepped pyramid of black stone. At the base of it stood a number of mortals clad in loincloths, headdresses fashioned from feathers or the bones, teeth, and pelts of animals, and streaks of paint. In their auras writhed veins of black, and in many cases, their hands were torn and raw. Evidently they were possessed, and, heedless of injuries to their borrowed bodies, the Spectres had driven them hard to construct their temple.

With a brutal efficiency that nonetheless had the cadenced, repetitive quality of ritual, the doomshades were binding, stripping, and painting the bodies of the screaming, struggling children they'd somehow drawn to their lair. Then, one by one, they were dragging the youngsters to the top of the pyramid, where another trio of possessed mortals wearing far more elaborate regalia awaited them. An infant lay on the altar even now. A priest in a jaguar-skin cape and cowl brandished a gleaming obsidian dagger, then ripped open the baby's torso.

"Enough of this shit," growled Fink. Startled, Montrose turned, and saw that his friend had moved up to find out what the wraiths in the front rank were gawking at. Shotgun at the ready, the keelboatman strode boldly through the wall. Glaring arcs of electricity crackled and danced across the floor. Caught in the effect, two werewolves—one wearing the form of a true beast, with wormy sores covering much of its left flank, the other a lopsided, bipedal thing with the tusks and snout of a boar—shuddered and jerked, their flesh frying.

Montrose shouted, "Attack!" He and the rest of the company surged through the wall. He lifted his AK-47 to fire at the trio on the pyramid, then, from the corner of his eye, glimpsed a wolfman with the eight faceted eyes and serrated mandibles of a spider pouncing at him. He whirled and shot it instead.

The darksteel bullets punched holes in the monster's breast. It staggered, but didn't go down. Its fist, a misshapen thing with barbed spurs of bone projecting from the knuckles, streaked at him. Montrose sidestepped and shot the werewolf again. It reeled forward and fell on its face.

Montrose somehow sensed another threat, directly overhead. Looking up, he met the amber eyes of a werewolf that was somehow clinging to the ceiling high above. The Black Spiral Dancer snarled, released its hold, and dropped, rolling over in midair to land on the Scot feet-first.

Montrose barely managed to scramble out of the way. By the time he disposed of that werewolf, another was attacking him, and another after that. All told, he had to fight for another minute before gaining a respite to survey the battle as a whole.

To his profound relief, it seemed to be going very well. There actually weren't *that* many Spectres and werewolves present, and his force had caught them by surprise. Relatively few of his men were Proctors, but many—Spooks, Chanteurs, Haunters, and the like—possessed powers which allowed them to strike across the Shroud, often with devastating effect. Nearby, a wolfman spun madly around, clawing at his own face, while severed arms flew through the air, battering other monsters.

Astarte and Marilyn had elected to hang back in the relative safety of the doorway. Crouching, gripping her pistol with both hands, her pretty face grim and intent, the girl in black was firing at the werewolves. Clutching the wall for support, spots of blood mottling the bandages obscuring her face, the novice mage whispered incantations, but as far as Montrose could see, to no effect.

It was unfortunate that her sorcery was misfiring again, but with luck, they wouldn't need it. If she stayed in the rear, she might even survive.

Some of the possessed mortals preparing the children for sacrifice abruptly collapsed. Montrose allowed himself to slip back into the Underworld, just in time to see the scaly, double-faced doomshades emerging from the bodies of their hosts. Hissing and shrieking war cries in some cacophonous Spectre tongue, they charged the wraiths who were currently wreaking havoc on their werewolf allies.

Moving as if they'd spent countless hours drilling together, the motley assortment of Africans, Legionnaires, and irregulars who lacked the ability to reach across the Shroud raced forward to protect their comrades. Firing wildly, tiny among the other spirits and the huge werewolves lurching about the chamber, Valentine and Belinda gunned down an Aztec who was rushing Louise.

A few of the possessed mortals were still hauling children up the pyramid, and at its apex the priests continued to chant and rip the youngsters apart. Their actions were as calm and measured as before, as if it were their foes rather than their allies rapidly perishing on the floor below.

Well, thought Montrose, he'd have to see what he could do to shake their composure. "Charge the pyramid!" he shouted. "Break up the ceremony!"

The Aztec in the jaguar regalia lifted another small, wet, crimson heart in his bloody hands. Magick silently roared and crackled through the air.

Forty-Eight

Everyone sensed it, Quick humans, werewolves, and spirits alike. Some of the surviving doomshades roared in triumph, and in that instant, several things changed at once.

The pyramid seemed to grow taller and steeper even as the walls and ceiling of the warehouse melted away. The swirling clouds of the Tempest, with monstrosities and scenes of hideous torment forming and dissolving inside them, covered most of the sky. But in the east, Montrose could see the rim of the sun, slipping above the horizon. To his eyes, the orb was black, a source of absolute darkness rather than light, and his intuition suggested that as soon as it was fully risen, the change the doomshades had wrought in the structure of reality would be irrevocable.

The air above the altar rippled and shone, and space fractured around it. The rift became a silvery oval with plumes of gray vapor billowing straight upward from it in defiance of the frigid, howling wind. A figure appeared in the center of the smoke. Somehow it seemed immense, ten times larger than the dimensional distortion which framed it. For a moment, it was a man in a ragged gray cloak, carrying his severed head in his hand. Then the lightning-eyed voudoun god which had forsaken Geffard in his hour of need. Then a shape so convoluted and alien that Montrose couldn't decipher it before it transformed again. The priests abased themselves before it.

The storm shrieked, and a tornado of whirling murk enveloped the pyramid. A Grim Rider and an equally reckless mercenary, still acting on Montrose's order to charge, plunged into the vortex and disintegrated. Three Spectres who were retreating toward the monument perished just as quickly. Clearly the cyclone was a Maelstrom wind of such terrible force that *no* naked spirit could endure it.

Fink shook his fist at the funnel of darkness. Lighting blazed on its surface, though no doubt the effect had been intended to blast the figures atop the pyramid instead. Using her Spook powers, Louise hurled a stray hospital gurney at the same targets, but the cart fell from her psychokinetic grip as soon as it entered the vortex. Evidently, Arcanos magick couldn't reach through it. Bellamy fired his Ruger into it, with the same lack of effect.

Montrose had no idea how much the remaining possessed men and the few surviving werewolves could see of all this. But they obviously perceived some aspect of it, because they began to fall back to the pyramid. Armored in mortal flesh, they passed through the murky tornado easily.

Could a Proctor do the same, if he projected himself to the warm side of the Shroud? Montrose supposed he was about to find out. He drew himself up straight, brandished his AK-47, and shouted, "All of you who can, jump to the Skinlands and follow me!"

He projected himself into the mortal world, and the warehouse popped back into view. But an inky stain at the base of the east wall betrayed the presence of the malignant dawn, the pyramid still looked impossibly tall, and the cyclone was visible as a vague, swirling smudge. He could see the God of the Smoking Mirror as clearly as before, as if the deity existed in both worlds simultaneously.

Most of his Proctors had stayed in the Skinlands since the beginning of the battle, and thus hadn't heard his previous order. "Charge the pyramid!" he shouted. "And if you value your existences, don't lose your grip on the mortal world once you're inside that cloudy area."

"Understood," said Bellamy. Titus winked into view, and then the others. The wraiths dashed forward, and Marilyn, leaning on Astarte, hobbled along behind.

As he ran, Montrose faintly heard the cyclone wail. For a moment he was certain they were all going to perish. If bullets and crossbow bolts couldn't penetrate the barrier, why would his materialized body fare any better? Granted, the surviving werewolves and possessed men had passed through, but they must know the trick of it. He didn't.

He scowled away the craven thought and kept charging.

The wind tore into him as savagely as any storm he'd ever encountered. Oblivion seethed inside him like a cancer, eating him away. Beside him, other ghosts blinked out of existence.

Then the pain of imminent dissolution subsided to a faint stinging. A werewolf plunged down the side of the pyramid at him, and he shot it. The monster's rushing advance became a helpless plummet, and it landed in a bloody heap at his feet.

Other wraiths emerged from the vortex. Together, they started to battle their way up the pyramid, with the enemy resisting savagely every inch of the way.

At close quarters, no longer harried by phantoms striking with impunity from the cold side of the Shroud, the surviving werewolves and possessed men abruptly became a match for Montrose's party, the ferocity of the wolfmen offsetting the wraiths' superior weapons. Titus pivoted back and forth, hurling sizzling bolts of power, striving to tilt the balance in the attackers' favor.

Montrose shot a possessed woman. She fell, creating a momentary hole in the enemy ranks, affording him the chance to charge higher, if he dared. Certain that everything depended on reaching the top of the pyramid and somehow disposing of the entity that waited there, he sprinted up the steps, leaving his comrades behind.

A werewolf with yellowish fur and mismatched crimson eyes sprang at him. He fired a burst into its chest, blood splashed, and it went down, writhing. Hoping that one of his allies would finish it off before it healed, he clambered on.

He dispatched another Black Spiral Dancer, and then the AK-47 was empty. As he reached into his mantle for another clip, two possessed mortals, a fat old man and a youthful black one, sprang at him.

Sidestepping, he avoided the young one altogether, kicked him in the knee, and sent him tumbling. But the old man pawed at him, trying to grapple, and somehow knocked the assault rifle from his hand. The gun bounced clattering down the rough stone steps.

The Scot punched the old man in the jaw. Bone snapped, and he went down. Montrose drew his rapier, resumed the ascent, and then, startled, blinked.

He was suddenly at the top. Like many of the towers of Stygia, the pyramid wasn't as high as it looked. The trio of priests hurtled down at him. He wondered fleetingly if one of them was Mother Prudence, now cloaked in the body of a hapless mortal.

The Spectre in the lead was a chubby, middle-aged woman with a cloak of eagle feathers, and bone skewers transfixing her pendulous breasts. She lifted an ornately carved club to brain him, and he killed her with a stop thrust to the heart.

By that time, the second priest—a lanky, amiable-looking young man who, for some reason, still wore a small silver cross in addition to his Aztec regalia—was pouncing at him, hands outstretched to shove him out into space. Montrose dropped low, pressing his body to the steps in a *passata sotto* backward lunge. The doomshade flew over him and tumbled down the face of the monument.

The high priest was a tall, thin man in his thirties. Beneath his jaguar-hide cowl were a widow's peak of chestnut hair, a long nose, and eyes inky black with the energies of Oblivion. He clenched his fist, and pain ripped through Montrose's chest as if he were having a heart attack. The Cavalier lurched back a step, desperately holding his sword out to keep the doomshade at bay.

Grinning, the priest cocked his arm to strike his sacrificial knife against the rapier. The obsidian blade seemed to hiss and crackle through the air, and Montrose had no doubt that it would break his sword on contact. He struggled to block out the agony in his breast. To be ready.

The gleaming black dagger flashed into motion. Montrose dipped his point, avoiding the beat, and then, heedless of the precarious footing, hurled himself forward in a flèche.

The all-out running attack caught the priest by surprise, and Montrose's point punched into his throat. Blood spurted, and, dropping the dagger, he fell. The pain in the Stygian's chest vanished. He snatched up the knife, then turned to confront Tezcatlipoca.

For the moment, the God of the Smoking Mirror was a headless man in a ratty gray mantle again. Up close, he seemed to be about the size of one of his werewolf minions, yet somehow, simultaneously, so colossal that by comparison Montrose felt as minuscule as an ant.

And judging from the amused expression of the face of the severed head, the deity had been watching the battle with the unconcern of a man viewing a struggle between colonies of ants. "Congratulations," he said. His mocking voice seemed to issue from his dead gray lips, but also from everywhere at once. "You reached me. But do you truly believe you can slay a Malfean?"

For a moment, Montrose faltered, but then his fear fell away from him. "Why not?" he replied. "I slew a Deathlord. En garde!"

Forty-Nine

With her mage perception, Marilyn could see the murky vortex almost as clearly as if she were on the other side of the Shroud. She wanted to cringe from it, but drove herself forward anyway. And when she hobbled into it, clutching her malacca stick with one hand and clinging to Astarte with the other, she felt nothing at all.

By the time they reached the foot of the pyramid, the battle was in full swing. Astarte released her, hesitated an instant to make sure she could stand up by herself, then started firing her pistol at the enemy. Marilyn drew a deep breath, let it out slowly, and invoked her power.

The magick stirred inside her, but vaguely, weakly, not the bright surge of energy she'd felt when she held back Dunn, healed Queen Marie, and shielded her allies from the bombs. Praying she could achieve something useful with it anyway, she stared at one of the possessed mortals—a brawny, big-bellied possessed man who was currently aiming a rifle at a black-uniformed Grim Rider in a silver mask—and willed him to burst into flame.

One sweaty brown curl of her target's hair began to burn, but he didn't even notice the tiny fire. The rifle barked, and the Grim Rider fell. Death snatched him back into its kingdom, and his form vanished in ripples of shadow.

Partway up the pyramid, fire flared from Titus's hands, and a werewolf toppled. And though Marilyn wanted her comrade to destroy the servants of Oblivion, she felt a pang of bitter envy.

Perhaps part of her problem was range. If she got closer to the possessed men and the Black Spiral Dancers, maybe her sorcery could do some damage. Worried that Astarte would try to hold her back, she glanced around, only to discover that, reckless as ever, her friend was already climbing the pyramid herself. Wheezing and trembling, Marilyn hobbled onto the steps. Her body ached, but the drugs in her system made the pain seem remote and unimportant.

Once she was several tiers up, she stared at the same Spectre she'd targeted before. The flame in his hair having long since died without causing him any distress, he was fighting hand-to-hand against one of Marie's caped warriors, the barrel of his gun clashing against the African's long-bladed spear.

Marilyn tried to make sure the Aztec's blows would fall short by warping the space around his gun. Surely *that* would work. Distorting distance was the first piece of true magick she'd ever performed, and a trick she'd managed brilliantly only hours before.

Her power crawled feebly up her chakras, dying before even exiting her body. The possessed man slammed his rifle into his opponent's ribs. The African stumbled backward and fell to one knee.

Marilyn nearly sobbed in frustration. But she mustn't give way to self-pity, not when countless lives and souls were at stake. At least, like Astarte, she could still fire a gun. She shifted her cane to her left hand, then fumbled her revolver out of her overcoat pocket.

Above her, something rumbled. The rhythmic sound was a bestial snarl, but also recognizably a laugh.

Marilyn lifted her eyes. Several tiers up loomed a gaunt, gray wolfman. The creature's smoldering orange eyes had diamond-shaped pupils, and a knot of pulsing, worm-like tumors disfigured its chest.

The Arcanist pointed the wheelgun at it. The werewolf growled, a complex sound which might have been a word in the creature's own inhuman tongue. The Model 12 fell apart into its component pieces.

Disarmed, certain that the Black Spiral Dancer was about to pounce on her, Marilyn groped inside herself to unleash her magick, once again to no effect. Meanwhile, the beast-man surprised her by shrinking into its human form, a stooped, freakish gnome with jagged yellow teeth, pointed ears, and black nails. The same monstrous eyes burned in his sockets, and the same tangle of swellings writhed beneath the dirty white skin on his chest.

"Surely you don't need a gun anyway," said the gnome, sneering. "Not a mighty *human* mage like you. Not to crush a puny Dancer Theurge like Cankerheart."

Marilyn commanded the werewolf's fiery eyes to burst. Nothing happened. Cankerheart twitched a finger. The malacca stick snapped into three pieces. Thrown off balance, the Arcanist fell heavily onto the steps.

"Come on," Cankerheart said, his voice dripping mock encouragement, "just speak a word of power and blast me. Your allies *need* your magick, just as the Ferryman warned you. The great slut Gaia herself cries out to you, begging for deliverance. Titus can't turn the tide all by himself." Invisible hands grasped Marilyn gently, then set her back tottering precariously on her feet.

The mage looked from side to side. All her comrades were hard pressed, unable to come to her aid. She rattled off an incantation in Persian, a curse devise to shatter the recipient's bones.

Cankerheart's shoulder heaved. His arm flopped, then hung at an odd angle, as if it had popped out of its socket. But even if the dislocation pained him, his gleeful smirk never wavered. "That's a little better. At least I felt it. But it isn't anywhere near good enough."

An unseen hand slapped Marilyn on one cheek and then the other. In her weakened condition, the stinging blows were more than sufficient to deprive her of her balance. She fell back onto the rough black stone. The edge of a step cut into her ribs.

"Take a deep breath," Cankerheart advised. "Compose that magnificent wizardly mind of yours. And then I recommend you take your very best shot."

Marilyn realized that, insane, sadistic, and evidently harboring some sort of grudge against mages, Cankerheart hadn't been able to resist the temptation to taunt and humiliate her. But even he wasn't demented enough to draw the process out for long, not in the middle of a battle. If she couldn't invoke some truly potent magick in the next few seconds, her adversary was going to kill her.

She frantically reviewed the times when her powers had done her bidding. More often than not, she'd been frightened, in pain, or both. When her magick first awoke, she'd been certain Dunn was about to butcher her and Astarte, too. When she'd reflexively blunted the force of the bombs, she'd been similarly afraid and suffering from her wounds as well.

Could terror and pain spark her arcane talents? The notion made a twisted kind of sense. When she made love, it often took the sting of a whip and the cold, hard clasp of a set of shackles, the shivery thought that the top could do anything he pleased to her, to set her spirit soaring.

The problem with the theory was that her wounds were as raw and the danger to her friends and herself as great as before. She was frightened and suffering *now*, wasn't she?

Perhaps not. Not with the drugs in her system, or at least, not enough. In any case, she knew a way to raise the ante.

Cankerheart's magick grasped her to stand her up. She thrust her hands inside her garments, tore through her bandages, and clawed at the sutured gashes beneath.

A pang of excruciating pain stabbed through the buffer of the morphine. Blood gushed, soaking her chest and thighs in a matter of seconds. If the battle didn't end soon, allowing someone to give her first aid, she would unquestionably bleed to death.

And as Cankerheart's spell set her on her feet, her magick spiraled up and up inside her, without her even having to call it. Power pulsed in her eyes, her tongue, her lips, her fingers, her mangled genitals. Still breathless with pain, she laughed nonetheless, while the werewolf gaped in dismay.

Fifty

Bellamy fired a burst at the smoke-shrouded, shape-shifting god atop the ziggurat. Screaming words in a language the ghost didn't recognize, a buxom young blond woman charged down the steps at him, a revolver blazing in either hand. He could tell she'd been pretty once, before the spirit possessing her had forced her to mutilate her face and breasts.

The Ruger shivering in his hands, spewing spent cartridges, he cut her down. A pistol banged, and to his left, something grunted.

He whirled. A gaunt, gray werewolf with patches of writhing tendrils where its eyes belonged had been sneaking up on him, an enormous silver knife poised in its hand. In another instant it would have stabbed him, if the steaming, bloody hole in its flank hadn't made it falter.

Grinning fiercely, Astarte put another silver bullet into it. Bellamy fired, and his assault rifle punched a line of wounds from the monster's crotch to its sternum. The wolfman collapsed, the silver knife slipping from its grasp.

The weapon was as big as Bellamy's darksteel shortsword, and he assumed that against a Black Spiral Dancer, it would do more damage. He snatched it up and rammed it into the eyeless wolfman's throat. Blood spurted. The creature thrashed and then slumped motionless.

He turned to Astarte, quashed the usual futile urge to tell her to get to safety, and said, "Thanks." Side by side, they fought their way upward.

A wild crossbow bolt, shot by one of their own allies, whizzed between their heads. Bellamy dropped a possessed man who'd rushed him with a clanking nail gun. From somewhere behind him, Titus jabbered an incantation, and another Sinkinda's stolen body simply exploded, spattering the FBI agent with gore. The ambient smells of gunsmoke, wolfman fetor, and blood were almost enough to choke him.

From farther up the pyramid sounded a ghastly howl, a cry of rage and challenge.

A towering, black-furred figure with pointed bat-like ears and luminous eyes bounded down the tiers. The .44 Magnum looked like a toy in the werewolf's hand. Its finger scarcely fit through the trigger guard.

It was Dunn. Bellamy felt a surge of hatred. He opened fire, and Astarte did the same.

Dunn threw himself sideways, rolling. Nothing so huge should have been able to dodge with such agility. Even as he tumbled, the werewolf emptied his own pistol. One shot smacked into Astarte and spun her off her feet.

There was no time to check on her. Bellamy kept firing until the Ruger's magazine was empty. Dunn instantly snapped to his feet and charged. Here and there, blood gleamed on his black fur. A few bullets had found their mark, but the wounds weren't even slowing the werewolf down.

Dropping the assault rifle, Bellamy backpedaled frantically. He snatched his Browning from its holster and fired it.

Advancing almost as rapidly as before, Dunn ducked and sidestepped. The pistol clicked empty, and the Black Spiral Dancer pounced.

Bellamy threw himself down. Dunn passed right over him, the claws of one foot grazing his back.

The wraith knew he didn't have time to reload. Dunn would land lightly, on balance, and spring back up at him immediately. Wrenching himself around toward his opponent, he thrust out the silver blade.

Dunn was bounding up the ziggurat so fast that the knife should have plunged deep into his groin, but somehow he stopped himself in time. His eyes blazed, and his fanged grin stretched wider. For the first time, Bellamy perceived that his murderer returned his hatred in full measure. Even at this desperate moment, the realization gave him a pang of vicious satisfaction.

Abruptly the smell of ozone tinged the air, and Bellamy felt a prickling on his skin. He just had time to comprehend that Dunn had charged his body with electricity, and then the werewolf clawed at him.

Bellamy could neither counterattack nor block, for fear that any contact would transmit a lethal blast of electricity to his own flesh. He jumped backward, and Dunn's talons missed him by a hair. The monster kept coming.

Still dodging, horribly aware that Dunn would surely tag him any second, Bellamy retreated toward Astarte. If God or the Orishas or Destiny truly was backing his cause, there might be some silver ammo left in her gun.

She was sprawled a little closer than he realized. He caught his heel on her outflung leg and nearly fell over her. At that instant, Dunn lunged.

Bellamy had no choice but to jump backward, leaving Astarte's pistol in her hand. Dunn looked down at the unconscious girl, laughed a snarling, bestial laugh, and kicked her. Electricity crackled, and sparks flew. Astarte tumbled down the ziggurat to the warehouse floor. Her body spasmed, and then lay still.

Bellamy screamed and ran at the wolfman. Dunn whipped up an arm to block the silver blade. The point grazed a shallow gash above his wrist, but at the same instant, his other hand lashed out at his attacker.

Had the blow landed squarely, it might have ripped Bellamy's head off, but reflex twisted him aside. Dunn's talons merely nicked his chest and convulsed him with a relatively mild shock. Evidently the Black Spiral Dancer had expended most of his charge on Astarte.

Still, the jolt was enough to lock up Bellamy's muscles momentarily. He sensed more than saw Dunn lifting his hands for a follow-up blow, knew he wouldn't be able to dodge backward nearly as fast as he had before, and made the only other move he could think of. He dove between the towering monster's legs.

The desperation tactic must have caught Dunn by surprise, because the werewolf's claws missed. Bellamy slammed down on the stone, forced himself to scramble up and around, and fumbled his darksteel shortsword from its scabbard, providing himself with a blade in either hand. Dunn whirled to face him.

For the next half minute, the two combatants danced back and forth, striking, parrying, and dodging. Bellamy tried repeatedly, unsuccessfully, to cut the werewolf's enormous hands when they flew at him, and to spring in close enough to stab him in some vital spot. His shoulder throbbed and his breath rasped in his throat, as, subject to the limitations of mortal flesh on this side of the Shroud, his strength began to fail. Meanwhile, Dunn, seemingly tireless, lunged and clawed as agilely as ever.

He's better than you, Bellamy's shadowself whispered. *Stronger. Faster. Longer reach. He's going to destroy you again, just like he did in New Orleans.*

Bellamy struggled to block out the gloating voice. There had to be a way! He wasn't the same as he'd been the first time he battled Dunn. He was an *abambo* now, a supernatural creature himself. That should count for something.

Unfortunately, his only ghostly power was the ability to skip back and forth across the Shroud. And according to Montrose, if he crossed back into the Underworld while he was on the pyramid, the forces at play on the other side would destroy him.

Would they? Granted, they must be incredibly powerful, or he wouldn't be able to sense them from here in the Skinlands. But they didn't feel as strong here on the monument as they had at the edge of the cloud. Maybe he could bear them, just for a moment. It was worth a try.

He reeled backward, allowing his arms to droop as if his weapons had grown too heavy, a pretense which was nearly the truth. He let the black shortsword slip from his hand and clank on the stone. Dunn danced in, long claws reaching, foaming jaws opening wide, breath reeking of slaughter and tobacco.

Bellamy waited until the talons actually touched him, then released his hold on the world of the living.

The Underworld was a chaos of swirling darkness. He couldn't see Dunn, the pyramid, or anything else in the Visible anymore. A blistering wind flayed streamers of ectoplasm from his body. Oblivion churned inside him, alternately numbing and wracking him. His memories of the last few minutes and his very sense of self began to bubble away.

He pictured Astarte lying crumpled at the foot of the ziggurat. Somehow the image arrested the decay of his mind, if not the erosion of his body. Remembering that he needed to take a couple steps to wind up behind Dunn, he floundered forward.

The gale howled and smashed him in the face, as if trying to hold him back. When he judged that he had staggered far enough, he turned and tried to project himself back into the world of the Quick.

His shadowself rose from the depths of his mind, fighting savagely to wrest control of his body and powers away from him. The storm seemed to seize him with iron claws, anchoring him in place, while his form and his mind alike boiled away.

The torment seemed to last for hours. Finally, when he'd all but abandoned hope, all but forgotten why he was even struggling, the Arcanos magick rose inside him, opened a rift between the dimensions, and thrust him through.

As his thoughts snapped back into focus, he saw Dunn directly in front of him, facing in the opposite direction. In reality, he'd only spent a second or two in the Tempest. Evidently sensing his return, the wolfman began to pivot. Bellamy lunged and thrust the silver blade into the small of his opponent's back.

The wound crackled and smoked, and Dunn crumpled. Bellamy yanked the dagger free and rammed it in again. And again. For a few seconds, the werewolf clawed at him spastically, but failed to connect. Then a rattle issued from his throat, and the light in his demon eyes went out.

In his darker moments, Bellamy had imagined himself rejoicing over his killer's corpse. But now that the moment had arrived, he felt only fear. Heedless of the battle still raging around him, he raced down the pyramid and flung himself down beside Astarte. She wasn't breathing. He frantically rolled her onto her back, pressed his mouth to hers, and blew air into her lungs.

Fifty-One

Montrose sprang at the headless ogre, thrusting his rapier at the dark god's breast. A plume of the smoke billowing up around the Malfean became solid for an instant and parried the attack. Tezcatlipoca swung a huge gray hand at the Cavalier's head.

Montrose ducked beneath the blow and stabbed the obsidian dagger into Smoking Mirror's wrist. The razor-sharp volcanic glass cut deep.

Tezcatlipoca yelped, snatched his arm back, and then laughed. "Nicely done, little soul. No wonder my slaves were wary of you." A huge sword of bone, the edges lined with honed chips of obsidian, appeared in his hand, and he swung it up for a head cut.

Montrose raised his own weapons in a high guard—poised himself to dodge—and was caught by surprise when, abruptly, the giant changed into a jaguar the size of a small automobile.

Amber eyes blazing, the huge cat clawed at its prey. Montrose leaped back, but the hooked nails grazed down his torso anyway, ripping his raven Inquisitor's garments and the flesh beneath. For a moment, Oblivion gnawed at him.

Tezcatlipoca hissed and struck at him again. Extending his rapier, Montrose caught the Malfean's paw with a stop thrust. The jaguar jerked its limb back, and the wound puckered instantly, nearly stanching the flow of blood. The puncture from the sacrificial knife, on the other hand, was still bleeding freely, perhaps because the dark god had infused the weapon with a measure of his own power.

The trick, Montrose thought grimly, would be getting in close enough to strike a mortal blow with the shorter weapon. It was too bad he couldn't take to the air, or cloak himself in darkness, but unlike certain other Arcanoi, his Harbinger talents were useless on the warm side of the Shroud. If he was to prevail, it would have to be through sheer martial prowess alone.

Smoking Mirror became a towering bipedal figure once more. This time, his priapic body was painted black, and he wore bells around his ankles. He had a bear's face, striped yellow and black, with shining yellow eyes.

Montrose advanced, and the god's eyes blazed as brightly as the sun. The Scot flinched from the glare.

Half blinded as he was, his sight swimming with afterimages, it was instinct more than vision that warned him of the figure slinking silently in from the side. Pivoting, he thrust his sword at his assailant's breast, only noticing after the attack reached his target that he'd stabbed a masked, auburn-haired caricature of himself, imperfectly formed from coils of smoke.

The phantom dissolved. Montrose sensed something hurtling through the air at him. He threw himself flat, and Tezcatlipoca swooped over his head. In the second it had taken the Cavalier to dispatch his vaporous twin, the Malfean had assumed the form of a shadow, essentially amorphous save for its great, bat-like wings.

Smoking Mirror wheeled, flew over the bloody altar, and then split into two pieces. The larger became the decapitated ogre, and the smaller became the corpse-like creature's head. The latter shot at Montrose like a cannonball.

He dodged, struck at the head with the sacrificial knife, and missed. His attacker whirled dizzyingly around him, sometimes trying to ram him, sometimes snapping at him, its teeth clashing together. He stabbed and slashed at it repeatedly, but it moved so quickly that he only managed to nick it.

Montrose assumed that the head was trying to divert him while the body crept in to dispatch him with its sword. Keeping watch from the corner of his eye, he tried to look as if the desiccated thing whizzing around him had his complete attention. Indeed, the head was attacking him so furiously that that, of necessity, was nearly the case.

The huge gray body skulked forward. Bellowing a battle cry, Montrose spun and rushed it, the obsidian dagger extended to pierce its chest.

Tezcatlipoca wrenched himself aside. The knife skated along his ribs, leaving a long cut, but not the lethal wound Montrose had intended. Pivoting frantically, the Scot raised his rapier to guard against the Malfean's return stroke.

Smoking Mirror swept his weapon down in a two-handed blow. The force of it hammered Montrose to his knees. Then pain blazed in his wrist, and waves of heat and cold pulsed up his arm. The rapier slipped from his spasming fingers.

The severed head had flown after him, bitten his wrist, and was clinging to it now. The power of the Void flowed from its stained, broken teeth like venom, and its jaws seemed powerful enough to cut through bone and shear off his hand altogether.

But at least the head had stopped hurtling about. Perhaps Montrose could finally hit it square. Praying that Smoking Mirror's brain reposed inside the stinking, withered thing, he thrust the knife at one of its cloudy yellow eyes.

The head winked out of existence a split second before his point could make contact. Now Tezcatlipoca was the intricate, unfathomable creature he'd glimpsed previously, a slimy, heaving mass of entwined tentacles and alien organs. Gasping and shaking with pain, the blood of his materialized body pattering onto the ebon stone, Montrose struggled to rise and throw himself at his attacker. Then the god opened a thousand eyes.

Every orb was black as despair, and each was fixed on Montrose. Their terrible scrutiny froze him like a statue, and he felt himself crumbling away from the inside.

He strove with all his might to stand, and then to throw the dagger. To no avail.

He realized he'd never had a chance of defeating a god in single combat. It was a miracle he'd lasted as long as he had. Perhaps, like the Smiling Lord, Tezcatlipoca had invested a portion of his strength in his ritual, and had been reluctant to draw any of it back merely to annihilate one puny, impudent challenger.

Montrose wished he could turn his head and see Louise one last time, but it was impossible. His flesh and spirit unknit, speeding toward their ultimate dissolution.

An automatic weapon chattered. Bullets hammered Tezcatlipoca's writhing convolutions. Bloody now, teeth bared in rage or loathing, Bellamy stalked past Montrose to shoot the dark god at point-blank range. Evidently, while the Cavalier had kept Smoking Mirror occupied, the battle on the pyramid had gone well enough for at least one ally to come to his aid.

Some of Tezcatlipoca's myriad dead-black eyes shifted their gaze to Bellamy. The FBI agent gasped and collapsed, but the pace of Montrose's disintegration slowed.

From somewhere behind him, Titus cried an incantation. A small section of the Malfean burst into flame, the flesh melting like wax. But only for a moment. Then the god fixed the attacker in his gaze, whereupon the shaman's voice and the fire he'd conjured died together.

Hoarse with pain or exhaustion, Marilyn chanted in Latin. Her magick had no visible effect, but it must have done something, because Tezcatlipoca stared at her as well. Her plainsong ended in a yowl.

The dark god's anger rose, and power rose with it. Montrose could feel the magick building like a cloud of poison vapor thickening in the air. In a moment, the magick would erupt into some irresistible counterstroke that would sweep each and every assailant away.

Unless Montrose managed to move and slay him first.

It *must* be possible. Only a fourth of Tezcatlipoca's unspeakable eyes were peering at him now. He strained to scramble forward.

For one terrible moment, during which he felt Smoking Mirror's power poising itself like an adder preparing to strike, nothing happened. It was as if some injury had severed his spinal cord. Then, abruptly, he lurched to his feet.

Smoking Mirror's countless eyes seemed to bulge in almost comical surprise. Montrose felt the energy the god had amassed re-aiming itself at his own head. Flinging himself forward, unable to pick out a vital organ amid his adversary's bewildering mass of whorls and knots, he buried the obsidian knife in a spiral of squirming, fleshy petals.

The Malfean's conjuration discharged itself in deafening explosions of black energy, like an infernal fireworks display. But harmlessly, across the ceiling, without ever finding a target. Roaring and babbling in a hundred silent voices, Tezcatlipoca collapsed in on himself, or perhaps fell away from the mortal world along some vector normally perceptible only to Harbinger senses. In an instant, the hideous thing was gone, and the smoking oval rift snapped shut behind him.

Montrose staggered around to survey the scene below. The tell-tale stain on the east wall was gone, along with the stinging in the air. The surviving werewolves were trying to fight their way clear of the warehouse, but it didn't look as if any were going to make it. Possessed mortals fell unconscious as their doomshade masters abandoned them.

Wishing to view the Spectres themselves, Montrose allowed death to draw him back across the Shroud. On the other side, he found not the Tempest but the Shadowlands, with the totality of the warehouse back in place. Even the Maelstrom seemed to be subsiding.

When the world reverted to normal, Nihils had reappeared, and each of the scaly, double-faced Spectres was scrambling toward whatever opening was nearest. But it didn't look as if any of them were going to escape, either. Some were spontaneously rotting into ripples of shadow, as if the knife which had pierced their deity had slain them as well, while Legionnaires, irregulars, and Queen Marie's warriors maneuvered to intercept the rest.

Montrose's mangled wrist throbbed, and a sudden wave of weakness and dizziness nearly dumped him back onto the stone. He peered about for another moment, until he finally spotted Louise standing unharmed. Then he sat down, opened himself to the currents of pain, horror, and rage shrieking through the cavernous room, and willed himself to heal.

Fifty-Two

By the time Bellamy recovered the strength to stumble back down the pyramid, the battle was over. Most of his fellow Proctors having already returned to the Underworld, the gloomy, cavernous chamber appeared nearly empty, except, of course, for the corpses scattered about. Astarte was trying to comfort some of the surviving children who were huddling together in a corner, applying pressure to the exit and entry wounds in her upper arm, her black-painted lips curved in the sweet smile they wore so rarely.

Bellamy had breathed for her and pumped her chest until her first gasp and first thudding heartbeat, then rushed back into the fight. It was the hardest thing he'd ever done. For all he knew, her body would stop working again as soon as he stepped away. But he couldn't sit out the rest of the combat, knowing what was at stake. He guessed he was a cop through and through.

When she saw him coming, she gave a little girl clutching a stuffed Winnie the Pooh a hug, patted a hairless, emaciated boy in green hospital pajamas on the shoulder, and then rushed into his arms.

For a while, they simply clung to one another. Finally she said, "I don't know what to say or do for these kids. They're pretty much in shock."

"You could go into shock yourself," Bellamy said. "You shouldn't be on your feet. Don't you know I've had to resuscitate you twice in the last ten hours?"

She grimaced. "Stop scolding me. I'm okay. Titus put a spell on me. It stopped the bleeding and made me feel better. So why don't you just shut up and kiss me?"

He did. For a few moments, it was sheer joy. Then she shuddered involuntarily, chilled by the touch of his flesh.

It struck him that he and his allies had finally beaten the bad guys. If this were a movie, all the remaining obstacles dividing the two lovers would magically melt away. Yet the gulf between the dead and the living remained, vast as ever.

"What's wrong?" Astarte asked. "All of a sudden, you look so sad."

"It's just that you're right," he answered, reluctant to share the depressing insight. "These poor kids. I don't suppose they'll ever get over this night. The survivors of the possession probably won't, either." It wasn't a lie. He did pity them. It simply wasn't the whole truth.

A soft, cool touch settled on his shoulder. Turning, he saw Titus, his body slightly translucent, resting one hand on him and the other on Astarte. Behind the shaman, other shadowy-looking *abambo* were moving about. Evidently the old man had worked a bit of magick to permit his comrades to peer across the Shroud.

Titus looked utterly weary, and small wonder. After fighting as fiercely as anyone, he'd no doubt scurried about the warehouse ministering to each and every one of the wounded. "Most of the Quick will forget what happened here," he said, "and that's for the best. It will help their spirits mend."

"I hope so," Bellamy said.

Titus eyed him keenly. "But you still aren't rejoicing in our victory."

"I wanted to stop the killing," the FBI agent said.

"We did," Astarte said.

"Yeah, but not until a lot more innocent victims died. Heck, we gunned down some of them, the poor possessed people, ourselves. *God*, I wish we hadn't had to do that."

"So do I," panted Marilyn. She limped from the shadows, using a gore-stained assegai as a makeshift crutch. From the amount of blood encrusting the front of her garments, it was a miracle she wasn't dead. Bellamy assumed Titus had cast healing magick on her as well. "But we saved countless others, on both sides of the Shroud."

"She's right," Titus said. "You can't imagine how terrible things would be if the Tempest had come to Earth to stay. As it is, the madness will stop now. Indeed, you can already hear it subsiding."

Bellamy tried, and found that the African was right. Out in the city, the shrieks, sirens, and rattle of gunfire, like the wailing of the Maelstrom, were dwindling with the coming of the dawn. "I do hear it," he admitted.

"So cheer up!" boomed Fink. Unlike the majority of his comrades, the hulking mercenary seemed to have emerged from the battle completely unscathed. "You gloomy son of a bitch."

"All right," Bellamy said, pretending to shake his somber mood. "I guess that as soon as everyone's ready to travel, we can get out of here. And call the authorities to come and look after these mortals. Lord only knows what the government will make of the werewolf bodies." He smiled crookedly. "Maybe Dunn will wind up on the SAD dissection table."

Power suddenly, silently boomed and sizzled through the room. Someone gasped.

Fifty-Three

Louise met Montrose halfway down the pyramid, and they kissed. The fierce embrace made his torn wrist throb—his wounds wouldn't heal completely until he Slumbered—but in his bliss, he scarcely noticed. He kissed her thrice more, and then, avid to behold her lovely features, removed her scarred golden visor, cast it aside, and then did the same with his own.

Suddenly he sensed space contorting, and magick pulsing through the warehouse. Startled, he looked around.

In the center of the floor below loomed six masked figures in bizarre regalia, standing motionless on stone pedestals. A man in green, with a crown of thorns and a wheel-of-fortune amulet, holding a pair of crimson dice in his ivory-gloved hand. A woman with black, snaky tresses and garish patchwork garments, manipulating a harlequin marionette. A one-legged, beggar-like fellow in saffron tatters, equipped with a crutch and a begging bowl. A thin man costumed as a skeleton, with a mechanical rat perched on his narrow shoulder. A stooped, hag-like figure leaning on a gnarled cane, and a figure in a murky red robe and a mouthless silver visor. Each of the newcomers towered as tall as a werewolf, far bigger than they'd been when Montrose had last seen them on the Pinnacle of Lamentations, and each, at certain moments, appeared subtly translucent.

The Grim Riders, Black Hawks, and other Legionnaires froze in shock for a moment, then came to attention. The Africans and even Fink's mercenaries, who were more accustomed to thinking of the Deathlords as bogeymen than revered patrons, hovered uncertainly. Many looked as if they'd bolt if they only dared.

Montrose shared his comrades' awe, but beneath it ran a rivulet of scorn. "*Now* they appear," he whispered, "when the danger's past."

"And even so, they haven't come in the flesh," Louise replied. "This is some sort of projection. Well, I suppose we'd better go hear what they have to say."

They descended the ziggurat, approached the demigods, and bowed. After a moment, the Ashen Lady quavered, "Rise, Sister, and my lord Anacreon. Soldiers, stand at ease."

Montrose and Louise straightened up. After another unnerving silence, the Skeletal Lord said, his voice sepulchral as ever, "Lord Montrose, your judgment was correct. You were needed here. You and your allies have averted a calamity, and we of the Council thank you all." For an instant, the Cavalier glimpsed a few of the black spires of Stygia behind the archangel's back.

Titus cleared his throat, and as one, the Deathlords turned to look at him. If the shaman found their icy regard unnerving, he didn't betray the fact. Perhaps, now that he'd endured Smoking Mirror's terrible gaze, it truly didn't faze him. His left hand resting on Bellamy's shoulder and his right on Astarte's, he said, "If you'd like to show your appreciation to those of us who come from New Orleans, Dread Ladies and Lords, you can make a lasting peace with our country."

"If Queen Marie will respect the border," said the Beggar Lord, "then so will we."

Louise took a step forward. "If you're dispensing boons, then I ask that you halt your persecution of the Heretics along the Mississippi."

Another pause. Evidently the Deathlords were conferring telepathically. At length the Ashen Lady said, "The Hierarchy cannot tolerate Heresy anywhere in its dominions. However, the Spectres' scheme has done extensive damage to this province. For a season at least, it will be advisable for the Legions to concentrate on rebuilding and warding against external threats, as opposed to pursuing the Inquisition."

"Does anyone else want to beg a favor?" asked the Laughing Lady, her tone so poisonously sweet that Montrose would have been flabbergasted if anyone had dared. "No? Then perhaps we of the Seven can proceed with *our* business. As my worthy sister has observed, the territory is in disarray, with all its Anacreons slain. Thus, the first step in its restoration must be to appoint a new Governor. Valentine, the Spectres would have prevailed if not for you, and you've abided in the area long enough to know it well. We choose you."

"I discern from your deathmarks that you died of disease," said the Skeletal Lord, a hint of smugness in his hollow voice. "Therefore, you will swear your primary fealty to me."

The dwarf gaped at them. "I…I don't think I can do it," he stammered. "I mean, who would take orders from me?"

"Anybody, if *I* back you up," boomed Fink. Leering, he looked about as at ease in the presence of the Deathlords as it was possible for any lesser being to be. "Which I will, as long as you treat me and the boys right. Or at least until we get bored with being good little Hierarch soldiers."

"Maybe I can help you, too," said Belinda, "if you want me to. It would give me something to do now that Starshine's gone."

"If you want the office, take it," Montrose said. "You earned it, and I think you'll perform it well."

Valentine swallowed. "All right," he mumbled. "I guess. I mean, I'll try."

"A far higher position, the office of the Smiling Lord himself, also stands vacant," said the Beggar Lord. "If the Imperium as a whole is to flourish, we must anoint a successor, and after much study, we believe we now know how to invest him with the powers his role requires. Lord Montrose, in recognition of your services to Stygia, and because you are already thoroughly conversant with the affairs of the Seat of Burning Waters, we select you."

"We will permit the Sister of Athena to remember your former identity and to abide with you as your consort," said the Ashen Lady. Her manner was that of an empress granting an unparalleled concession, as, indeed, she was. Charon might well have destroyed the lot of them for proposing such a thing. "Provided she renounces any intent to overthrow the State."

Montrose felt as stunned as Valentine had appeared a moment before. In all the years he'd spent working and scheming his way up the ladder of the Hierarchy, he'd never dreamed he might reach the very top and become a god. Yet he knew with utter certainty that he didn't want the office unless Louise *was* willing to stay with him.

He turned to her, and she smiled at him. "Yes," she said softly, "if it's what you want. We said that it might not be so bad to be Stygians if we had the power to improve the system, and this way, you would."

Her words should have elated him, but instead, for some reason, they gave him pause. *Could* he change the Hierarchy, or, once his mind was wedded to the inhuman intelligence dwelling in the Smiling Lord's visor, and he was enmeshed once again in the labyrinthine intrigues of the Onyx Tower, would it beat him into its own decadent image?

He thought of the debauched, amoral cynic he'd been before his master ordered him to Natchez, and felt a pang of loathing. He'd rather perish than become that wretch again, or one of these aloof, ruthless, paranoid creatures posed on their ridiculous daises, either. Finally comprehending all that he most truly desired, seeing his path clearly, he faced them.

"I'm sorry," he said, "but I decline. I don't care to hide my face for eternity, nor do I any longer have the stomach to govern a realm of Soulforges and barracoons. In fact, I hereby resign from the Grim Riders. After four centuries of vassalage, it's time I discovered how it feels to be my own man." He unclipped the Lantern of Truth from his belt and set it on the floor, then removed his black Inquisitor's mantle with its Unlidded Eye medallion and laid them there as well. Louise took his hand and squeezed it.

This time, the silence dragged on for half a minute. Montrose wondered whether the angels were debating whether to annihilate him for his insolence. At last the Emerald Lord said, "We regret that your elevation does not please you, milord Anacreon. But we did not say you could decline it, let alone that you could forsake our service altogether." The red dice glittered in his fingers.

"Loath as I am to trumpet my own accomplishments," Montrose replied, "if any Legionnaire has ever earned the right to retire, it's myself. However, if you don't agree, perhaps I can buy my way clear." He proffered the sacrificial knife. "This weapon may have destroyed a Malfean, although in all candor, I suspect not. But at the very least, it wounded the beast badly enough to make it flee back to its lair. Surely the Council can find a use for such a potent weapon."

"Since you are our servant, the dagger is ours already," said the angel in green. "Why shouldn't we simply confiscate it, and give nothing in return?"

"Because you claimed you were grateful," Montrose said. "What does that concept mean to you? In addition to the blade, I offer my promise that I won't share Hierarch secrets with the rebels." He smiled. "Even if I favored their cause, I've had my fill of war. I intend to relax, teach Louise the delights of golf, and possibly even compose a verse or two."

Another pause. Finally the Laughing Lady shrieked with mirth, and the Quiet Lord inclined his head.

"So be it," said the Emerald Lord. "Send us the knife and we will grant you your freedom, Lord Montrose, though it leaves our Council incomplete."

His expression grim, Bellamy stepped forward. "I'll take the job," he said, "if you'll have me."

Fifty-Four

Bellamy had spoken on impulse, and was now surprised at his own audacity. And yet, why shouldn't he volunteer? Though he liked Titus, Montrose, and the others, Antoine had been his only real friend among the *abambo*, and Antoine was gone. No ties bound the FBI agent to Shadowlands New Orleans, Natchez, or anywhere else. He needed to make some sort of place for himself, find some useful role that he could play.

Fink roared with laughter. "And I thought I had big *cojones*! You just put in to be one of the lord high muckety-muck bosses of the whole Underworld. Shit, Frank, you're just a Lemure, and not even a Hierarch at that."

"And yet," said the Emerald Lord slowly, "the idea is not without a certain logic."

"Like Lord Montrose," said the Beggar Lord, "he opposed the Spectres with valor and wit."

"From one perspective, it's good that he's newly dead, and no Legionnaire," quavered the Ashen Lady. "If we anoint him, we can each be certain—well, relatively certain—that he isn't secretly the puppet of one of our peers."

"In any case, we need *someone*," the Laughing Lady said. "If we set up a new Prince Ares quickly, there may yet be time to discredit the rumor that a lowly pair of assassins"—to Bellamy's astonishment, she gave Montrose and Louise a wink—"managed to slay one of the Seven. I say, let's give the detective a try. If he doesn't survive the investiture, or crumbles under the weight of his office, we can always elevate another candidate later."

The Deathlords fell silent and motionless as idols. Bellamy assumed they were somehow palavering among themselves.

Frowning, Montrose said, "Agent Bellamy, you're being reckless to say the least. Do you understand that hitherto, it was always Charon who created Deathlords? The members of the Council may find themselves unable to duplicate the magick, and if so, their botched experiment could destroy you."

Bellamy shrugged. "I've been taking chances ever since I ran away from my desk at the Bureau to meet poor R. J. No point in stopping now."

"Even if you do succeed in becoming the Smiling Lord, you might not like it. I don't think you comprehend the isolation, the terrible choices you'll have to make, the countless atrocities that your servants will commit in your name."

"If anybody starts committing atrocities in my name, I'll tell him to stop. Look, you're right, of course. I have no real idea of what it means to be a Deathlord. But basically, it's all about holding the Sinkinda back, isn't it?"

"I suppose so," Montrose said. "Or at least, it should be."

"Then it sounds like an appropriate job for a cop."

The Scot smiled wryly. "Perhaps it is at that."

"We have reached a decision," intoned the Skeletal Lord. Startled, Bellamy jerked around. "Frank Bellamy, we will accept you into our company."

"But he gets the same deal Montrose was going to get," said Astarte. "Right? He gets to bring his girlfriend along."

His chest suddenly aching, Bellamy turned to face her. "I think that for that to happen," he said, "you'd have to die."

"No problem," she said. "I'll bet the Seven know how to kill me in a way that'll guarantee that I become a wraith."

"Even if that's true, I don't want you to lose your life. Life is precious. Most of the Restless would give everything they have for another shot at it."

"Then becoming a Deathlord is your way of *dumping me?*" she demanded. "Of running away from the whole Earth, just to make sure I can never, ever see you again?"

"I hoped we could work things out and be together. You'll never know how much. But I see now that it's impossible. The Restless and the Quick are allowed to keep on loving each other, but they're supposed to let go of one another, too. If I keep dragging you into my world, if I keep reaching out to you, death is going to reach out for you, also. Look how many times you've nearly died already."

"I'm willing to risk it!" she snarled. "Your world is the only one I ever cared about!"

"I wish you'd take another crack at finding the beauty in normal life. It *is* there, and you don't have to fight off doomshades, werewolves, your shadowself, and the Lord only knows what else to enjoy it. But I guess that's up to me."

"You son of a bitch, don't *do* this to me! Don't make my decisions for me! Don't treat me like a child!"

"I love you. Good-bye." He allowed death to whisk him back into the Shadowlands, then gave Titus a commanding stare. Grimacing, the shaman reluctantly removed his hand from Astarte's shoulder. She peered frantically about, looking for all the wraiths who had abruptly vanished from her sight.

Fifty-Five

Marilyn awoke to throbbing pains up and down her body. She groaned, and Astarte lurched up from her chair in the corner. Even in the darkened room, the Arcanist could see that her companion's face was still a mess, with dried streaks of her awful black mascara running down her cheeks.

"Are you all right?" Astarte asked. "Should I ring for the nurse? I don't think it's time for another pain shot."

"Don't be silly," said Marilyn. "What would be the point of a rich person checking into a private hospital if she couldn't get all the narcotics she wanted? By all means, call her. In a moment. I'm glad you finally stopped crying."

"Yeah, finally. When I fell asleep. I've never been like this before, except for when we saw the cops carry his body out of the cemetery on TV. I feel like such a wuss."

Marilyn reached out and took her hand. Weak as she was, it took a surprising amount of effort.

"I wish I could at least remember everything that happened," the girl in black continued fretfully. "I know the Deathlords appeared and made Valentine a Governor. I know Frank decided a ghost and a live person shouldn't be together, and said he was going far, far away. But there was more, and if I remembered what, I'd know *where* he's going."

"I think the Deathlords cast a spell to jumble everyone's memory," Marilyn replied. "I feel as if I should be able to figure out why, but somehow, I quite can't put the pieces together either. I imagine that that's a part of the magick as well."

"God damn him!" Astarte exploded. "He treated me like dirt! Why do I even care about him anymore?"

Marilyn sighed. "One of the eternal questions. Love's just like that, I suppose, like a scab you can't stop picking at. Have you thought about what you want to do now that our little adventure is over? Are you going to take Frank's advice and try to discover the simple joys of mundane existence?"

The girl with the piercings glared at her. "Get real. I was born to be a part of the supernatural; for a while I was; and one way or another, I'm going to be again. It *isn't* all some horrible forbidden thing that no one should ever see, no matter what that asshole thinks. It's strange and dangerous, but if you have the guts to explore it, you can find wonderful things."

"That's what I've always believed," Marilyn said.

The girl in black hesitated. "I know that from here on out, you're going to spend your time studying to be a better mage. Do you think maybe I could stay with you? Be your apprentice or whatever? Maybe I can learn to cast spells, too. Even if I don't, at least I'll be where I want to be."

The Arcanist smiled. "I'd like that."

Astarte grinned. "And maybe we can get our memories unscrambled. Maybe I can find Frank again, and figure out the way for us to be together. Right after I kick his ass for ditching me!" Fresh tears sliding down her face, she squeezed Marilyn's hand in both of hers.

Richard Lee Byers holds a BA and an MA in Psychology. He worked for over a decade in an emergency psychiatric facility, then left the mental health field to become a writer. A resident of the Tampa Bay area, the setting for much of his fiction, he is the author of the novels *On A Darkling Plain*, *Netherworld*, *Caravan of Shadows*, *Dark Fortune*, *Dead Time*, *The Vampire's Apprentice*, *Fright Line*, and *Deathward*, as well as the Young Adult books *Joy Ride*, *Warlock Games*, *Party Till You Drop*, and *The Tale of the Terrible Toys*. His next book, *X-Men: Soul Killer*, will appear in March, 1999. His short fiction can be found in numerous anthologies, including *Confederacy of the Dead*, *Dark Destiny*, *Fear Itself*, *Grails: Visitations of the Night*, *Freak Show*, *Blood Muse*, *Diagnosis: Terminal*, *Dante's Disciples*, *Sword of Ice and Other Tales of Valdemar*, *Superheroes*, *The Ultimate Spider-Man*, *Realms of Mystery*, and *Tales from the Eternal Archives: Legends*. He spends much of his leisure time fencing foil, epée, and sabre, and frequently competes in local tournaments.